Alice Borchardt shared a childhood of storytelling with her sister, Anne Rice, in New Orleans. A professional nurse, she has also nurtured a profound interest in little-known periods of history. She is the author of *Devoted, Beguiled, The Silver Wolf, Night of the Wolf, The Wolf King* and the first book in the Tales of Guinevere, *The Dragon Queen*.

Praise for *The Dragon Queen*:

'The version of the Arthurian cycle rendered in *The Dragon Queen* is a completely revisionist one . . . Borchardt uses her materials, some traditional but many of them original, to create a fully fledged work of the fantastic that is wildly imaginative and astonishingly exhilarating . . . filled with fresh and unanticipated marvels' *Interzone*

'Slowly draws you into its mythological world . . . intriguing and promising, with an unusual perspective on the Arthurian tales. Borchardt weaves in threads begging to be followed up' *Starburst*

'A fabulous and fantastical rendering of the familiar legend of Arthur and Guinevere. As well as some spellbinding scenes of magical confrontations and pagan rites there is also a keen sense of history that gives the story a firm grounding in reality. This is a rich tapestry of a novel' *Historical Novels Review*

'A vivid portrait . . . Bold, courageous, prophetic and possessed of powers that enable her to communicate with dragons and wolves . . . this Guinevere enchants and engages the reader immediately . . . Borchardt further stakes her claim as a writer of breathtaking eloquence' *Publishers Weekly*

'Magnificent . . . Borchardt is a powerful storyteller with a passionate voice . . . Her richly textured narrative is a highly charged emotional read, blending her imagination and legend into a vivid backdrop where her characters live' *Romantic Times*

'A writer with the vision and scope to conjure up her own thrilling mythos and the craftsmanship to render it in breathtaking shimmering prose' Anne Rice

By Alice Borchardt

Devoted
Beguiled
The Silver Wolf
Night of the Wolf
The Wolf King
The Dragon Queen
The Raven Warrior

THE
RAVEN
WARRIOR

ALICE
BORCHARDT

BANTAM BOOKS

LONDON • NEW YORK • TORONTO • SYDNEY • AUCKLAND

THE RAVEN WARRIOR
A BANTAM BOOK : 978-0-553-82491-9

Originally published in Great Britain by Bantam Press,
a division of Transworld Publishers

PRINTING HISTORY
Bantam Press edition published 2003
Bantam edition published 2004

1 3 5 7 9 10 8 6 4 2

Copyright © Alice Borchardt 2003
First published in the United States by The Ballantine
Publishing Group, a division of The Random House Group Inc.

The right of Alice Borchardt to be identified as the author
of this work has been asserted in accordance with sections 77
and 78 of the Copyright Designs and Patents Act 1988.

Set in 10/12pt Sabon by
Falcon Oast Graphic Art Ltd.

Bantam Books are published by Transworld Publishers,
61–63 Uxbridge Road, London W5 5SA,

Addresses for companies within The Random House Group Limited can be four
www.randomhouse.co.uk/offices.htm

The Random House Group Limited supports The Forest Stewardship
Council (FSC®), the leading international forest certification organisation.
Our books carrying the FSC label are printed on FSC® certified paper.
FSC is the only forest certification scheme endorsed by the leading
environmental organisations, including Greenpeace. Our
paper procurement policy can be found at
www.randomhouse.co.uk/environment

MIX
Paper from
responsible sources
FSC® C018072

Printed and bound in Great Britain by Clays Ltd, St Ives PLC

THE RAVEN WARRIOR

PART ONE

PART ONE

CHAPTER ONE

AS I SUSPECTED, STEALING FROM professional thieves takes some skill and a lot of hard work. We took shifts at the oars once we were out of the territory of the Painted People and didn't, as was more usual among peaceful mariners, go ashore to sleep.

She – the ship – was decked only lightly, boards nailed over her ribs and hide bottom. We were drenched by squalls and frozen by the icy spring seas breaking over our bows. But, Lord, she was fast! Small and light, propelled by ten at the oars by day and six by night. We all took rowing duty, as I said, the ones not pulling at the sweeps eating, then sleeping on the narrow deck between the rowing benches. Or we slept when we could.

At times we would row into an icy rain squall. Then the sleepers had to rouse themselves and bail like mad, not to keep her from sinking but so as not to slow those of us plying the oars. She wouldn't sink, but if her forward progress were slowed, heavy seas might break her up. Whereas, more or less empty of water, she was able to ride the combers like a floating cork, and in calmer waters, skim along as might a bird.

We had no sail, since we wished to announce neither our passage nor arrival to any watching coastal people.

And watch they do, being as they are used to trouble coming by sea.

I don't like to remember the start of our voyage or our first few days aboard. We were all seasick and none too sure of ourselves at the oars. But Dugald, who is my Druid, gave me medicine for seasickness. True, it tasted like the floor of a town midden pit and stank worse than a herd of goats, but withal – it worked. And most of us recovered well enough to devote ourselves to the oars within a day or two.

I'm not sure Dugald considers himself my Druid. Once he was my guardian, then my teacher. But when I became a woman and a queen, I felt he should be my Druid. He couldn't agree less. He says I'm a child and only an honorary ruler, and not to be so presumptuous as to drape a mantle of authority over my shoulders.

I wished I had something to drape over my shoulders. Gods above and below, it was cold in that boat. But I knew if I could pull this off, I would be rich and a real queen. So I must make the attempt, no matter how great the hardships involved.

Four days out of port, I understood I had good companions. Our flotilla – there were three small ships – held seventeen men each. 'Men' not always being actual men; some were women. But there was a man at the tiller of each boat; Maeniel, my foster father, on one; Gray, an oath man of mine, on another; and aboard this one, Ure, a relative of Gray's, an experienced man of the sea.

Ours was the lead ship; the rest followed us. Ure knew the coast and its hazards: rocks, reefs, sand spits – though with our shallow-draft, those weren't a problem – currents, and, last but not least, pirate nests. He told us he would undertake to keep us clear of them all.

In return, we didn't ask him how he knew so much and promised to devote ourselves to the work of the oars. When I asked him if we shouldn't have some dry land practice first, he fixed me with an eye cold and green as a breaking winter sea and said, 'One learns best by doing. And when you do a thing day to day on a regular basis, you will eventually learn all there is to know about it. Sometimes more than you want to know.'

He was right; by now, eight days into our voyage, I knew a lot more about rowing than I ever wanted to. About blisters that broke and bled, scabbed over, then broke open again the next day and bled. About excruciating pain in the arms, back, and neck. About the discomfort of perpetually wet clothing that chafed and itched, or sleeping on a hard, wet, stinking plank among the wet, stinking bodies of fellow crew members. Of huddling together with them to try to coax a little warmth from one another. Not to mention the joys of hanging off the stern up to your waist in the icy sea as the small craft you are clinging to battles fifteen-foot waves while you try to take care of necessities, since there is no room aboard for such nonsense as chamber pots.

See, the water ran to the back of the craft because she was lighter at the bows, so the steersman bailed with one hand while he clung to the tiller with the other. Guess what he used to do the bailing?

When I was much younger, I used to think the sea was romantic.

Despite our many struggles, we moved with almost unbelievable swiftness toward the south and the forts of the Saxon shore. On the tenth day, we arrived at the mouth of the river that flowed through the Fenlands. Ten days of rowing in the heaving, pitching sea. We were all glad to pull the narrow craft into the tall reeds and sedges, rest, and wait for dawn.

It came without a sunrise, a gray illumination of ridged storm clouds. I was sleeping, my head on the gunwales, when I awakened to see Maeniel, as wolf, slip

11

over the bow of the boat next to ours and vanish into the water. I had slept hard and drooled; it dried on the side of my face and left a damp spot on the wood near where my lips rested.

There was no color in anything, and the sedges, reeds, and cattails were a dark frieze reflected in the silvered water. Everyone else was asleep except Ure. He was sitting in the bow and his eyes met mine, green as slag glass and twice as hard. I opened my mouth to ask him where Maeniel was going. His hard gaze edged into contempt.

I reflected that I knew exactly where the Gray Watcher was headed. And Ure had no use at all for what he called senseless blather.

No sense waking half the boat to ask a question when I knew the answer already. I put my head back down on the gunwale. I didn't think I could, but I drifted off to sleep.

When I awakened again, Maeniel was climbing back into the boat. He was dripping wet and wrapping one of Gray's mantles around himself. I rose; pulling up my stiffened body was a painful effort. But I stepped to the deck and tiptoed around the sodden sleepers between the rowing benches until I reached the three standing in the bow, Gray, Maeniel, and Ure.

'What?' I whispered.

'Nothing good,' Maeniel said. 'The smartest thing might be to turn around and go back.'

Ure grunted.

Gray whispered, 'Say on, Lord Maeniel.'

'I didn't think their strong point would be this strong. The pirates have refitted an abandoned Roman fortress about ten miles upstream. There are seventy to a hundred men there, all mature, able-bodied warriors. Twice our force and more. Better armed, tried and tested in battle.'

'Ships?' Ure asked.

'I counted twenty careened and upside down on land. A few more in the water,' Maeniel said.

'We have what?' Gray said. 'Forty boys, three men, and eight women.' He shook his head. 'We should look for easier pickings.'

I felt my failure, and, yes, the failure was mine. Though I sat on the Dragon Throne and it was acknowledged I had the right to be there, the subchiefs hadn't fallen in with my plans to carry war to the Saxon raiders who harried our highland coasts and Out Islands. When I visited the villages recruiting among the war bands and coast watch, none were willing to chance such a hazardous endeavor as striking at the Saxons in their home ports.

Yes, they had hailed me wildly at my accession to the Dragon Throne, but in the cold light of morning, they had second thoughts. What did a woman, a child, as yet, know of warfare? I got the useless, the outcast, the weak, the orphaned, the despised among the boys.

And as for girls, the ugly. One had a strawberry birthmark that covered one cheek and part of her mouth. Another was taken captive and left for dead by the same Saxon raiders. Another hid her harelip. The others, drudges, broken by hard labor before they were in their teens, without friends or kin, bearing the load of endless work by day and the weight of their owners' bodies by night. Leading lives so filled with misery that they had come to believe any chance of freedom was better than their day-to-day existence. If they should fail and fall into death, why then . . . so be it. Nothing beyond death could be worse. 'At least I can sleep,' one called Albe told me.

'At least we could burn their ships,' I said bitterly.

'As I said, there are some in the water,' Maeniel told me. 'We would probably be run down in the open sea.

The pirate craft are oared and also light and very fast. Not to mention much better manned.'

'Suicide!' Ure said.

'Over the wall by night and take them in their beds?' I suggested.

'Full of ideas!' Ure commented. 'No! These are children, not blooded. I'm a corrupt old devil, but even I won't be a party to the slaughter of innocents. For such tricks you need a group of experienced men.'

'Any others?' he asked.

I hunkered down and looked up at the three men. 'Yes,' I said.

Ure made a beckoning gesture. 'Say!' he said.

'What's inside that fortress? Is it stone or wood?' I asked.

'Wood,' Maeniel said. 'But on that scale . . . you can't.'

'I can,' I said between my teeth. 'I can.'

Then I reached over the side and fished out a floating branch, narrow, maybe a foot long. Very waterlogged. I clamped my right hand around it. With a whistling hiss, steam erupted around it, erupted the way steam does when water is poured into a hot metal pot. Then from the top to the bottom, the dry stick burst into flame and was ash before it had time to heat my fingers.

'I'll go over the wall while you and the rest strike at the gates and burn them out.'

Maeniel studied me. 'The reason the Romans abandoned the fortress was the damp began to undermine the walls. Like as not, what's in the fortress that isn't wet is at least damp.'

'There's that,' Ure said.

I rose from my heels and stood looking the three of them in the face. 'Bet your life, bet your patrimony, bet your hope of heirs, when I put my hand on something, it will burn.' I raised my scarred right hand and held it up before them.

14

'Yes,' Ure said, looking at Gray. 'It's a plum, this place, and well worth the risk.'

Gray looked uncertain.

Maeniel studied me sadly. 'Very well,' he said at length.

'Nothing is sure, ever,' Ure said to Gray. 'Nothing.'

When I turned, I saw the youngsters in the boats were awake, sitting up and staring at the four of us. *Outcasts,* I thought. Maybe this is the advantage of being in the company of the last and least. None of them looked afraid and most seemed ready for anything.

The Brotherhood of the Bagudae.

Black Leg was already lonely. He moved away from the forest near Tintigal, where he'd left them. He missed his family, blood family or not. Even that terrible-tempered old Dugald, though these days all he did was scold or lick his chops about how 'she' was progressing into a real noblewoman.

But, of course, he missed her most of all. He wished sometimes they were still children. When they were young, before the pirates came, the two of them used to snuggle together against Mother's warm belly. He would turn human just so she could cradle him in her arms. Most times he had no use for the shape, except when climbing around in the rocks to get birds' eggs or going up trees after fruit. And from time to time attempting to understand some of Dugald's stranger ideas.

Like those choirs of angels. He had put up a fight when Dugald tried to get him to memorize them, thrones, denominations, principalities, powers, and so on. He'd told Dugald in no uncertain terms that he had no interest in the classification of impossible, nonexistent beings. Dugald told him a lot of people would believe he, Black Leg, was a nonexistent being. Black Leg replied that he was here now and no one could deny his existence. If Dugald could produce an angel, he, Black Leg, would learn how to place it in proper ranking order with no further complaint.

'She,' the fair one, thought it was hilarious. Magetsky, up in the rafters, waxed loud, filling the room with raucous laughter. Dugald lost his temper. Magetsky, the raven, abruptly left, pursued by a small, dark thunderbolt. Kyra discovered she wanted to visit Etta, Gray's wife. Maeniel went hunting, and he, Black Leg, and Guinevere went and slept in the woods.

That was the last time, though. Not long after, Kyra separated them, saying it wasn't seemly any longer for them to share a bed. People might talk.

'About what?' he asked indignantly.

No one offered a straight answer, not even his father, Maeniel.

He didn't think about it much after that, because then Mother died. Somehow he had known in his heart that a time of innocence and joy was ended. When Mother's pyre was ashes and she was gone, he told his father that he wanted to learn to be a man.

Maeniel had given him a long, thoughtful look. A speaking one. But wolves do not lightly try to interfere with one another's freedom or give advice, even when requested to do so.

But he did say one thing. 'Don't get involved in their struggles. They are endless and usually futile. Wolves settled things between themselves before the beginning of time, but these creatures have never come to an accommodation with God's creation or with each other. Still, I suppose you must let them break your heart once. Then perhaps you will learn.'

He had wondered at the time what his father meant. Now he was sure he knew. He remembered her with great bitterness and more than a little sorrow.

The lands he moved through were rugged, wild, and unsettled. He remained wolf as he traveled. There were two or three packs about; they hunted the stony defiles between the hills even as the occasional big cat still ruled the heights. But Mother taught him to be an efficient, able wolf long before he ever thought about turning to his human side. So he had no problem avoiding them.

It was spring and there were females in heat that drew him, but he wasn't ready, not really mature enough to fight for the father right. In any of the packs, poaching on the territories of the leaders would sooner or later lead to an attack, possibly by the whole pack. Wolf law said you presented yourself openly, took your place in the hierarchy, then challenged the leader. The treacherous interloper would meet the bared fangs of the leader and his inner circle, all yearning to shed his blood.

Farmsteads were scattered on fertile patches of soil throughout the forest, but they were, without exception, surrounded by high, earthen banks surmounted by palisade fences. The resident war dogs that protected the livestock were nothing a lone wolf wanted to mess around with. So he moved secretly and silently through the countryside until one morning, just before first light, he came to a valley with a lake.

He should have known.

From the first moment, it raised the hackles on the back of his neck. A wolf would have left. But with him, there was that human component.

So he trotted downhill into the fog that filled the bowl of the valley.

No humans. That in itself should have made him suspicious. But he was far too inexperienced to have his anxieties roused by the absence of something.

Light was spreading from the east into the silent forest at the lake's margin, illuminating the haze that hung between the trees with long shafts that were almost as

17

discrete from each other as a handful of sticks. Nothing. No wolves, no humans, and in a place as beautiful as morning in paradise. He couldn't believe his good fortune. Indeed, he shouldn't have.

He sensed the water was very close. Then he smelled it and found he was trotting along through a very shallow marsh. Ahead even through the fog he saw a stretch of open water and a dim shape that might have been an island. The light striking down from above was losing its grayness and turning slowly to gold, trees to green, and the water to a multicolored gem as it cast back the reflection of the surrounding forest.

He bent his head and drank, troubling the absolutely smooth surface with his tongue. When he raised his head, he found the fatigue of the long night's trip weighed heavy on him. He was not used to traveling so far so fast as a wolf.

And then he reflected that, while lonely, he was at least now free of the thousand constraints that had beset him as a human being. He could return to the forest, seek a warm nest in bracken and dried leaves, and enjoy the luxury of sleeping as long as he liked.

He stretched as languorously as a cat, stiffening each of his hind legs in turn, yawned, and just about then . . .

He felt the weight of a big, heavy hand on his neck . . . and every hair on his body stood straight up at the sound of a triumphant crow of savage, evil laughter.

Igrane knew from the slightly withdrawn, preoccupied look in his eyes that he was up to something. They had, after all, been lovers now for over thirty years. But since he was far older and smarter than she was, she was unable to guess what.

She hoped the bright lechery she saw in his gaze would prevail over any magical experiments he wanted to undertake. Hoped that he would dismiss the servants, throw her on the floor, and possess her violently.

Sometimes he did it that way. At others he played with her, tormenting them both for hours, until they both reached a frenzy of desire before he allowed her fulfillment and release. Both memories were erotic in the extreme. But they were shadowed by other, darker occasions when his desire to cause her pain and punish her for (as he saw it) ensnaring him into an erotic commitment he despised over-rode all other considerations in his mind.

The strongest part of his being was his desire to dominate political events. Women – even boys from time to time, he took both – were mere amusements. But she drained his powerful magical abilities like a leech. She clung to him, she pleasured him as no other ever had. And in return, he kept her young and beautiful.

But sometimes . . . sometimes he forced her to con-tribute the unguessable. . . .

When they were both stuporous with food and wine, he said, 'I have a gift for you.'

It was growing cold on the terrace above Tintigal. Her women were gone and his menservants had rather thank-fully melted away into the dusk. They, too, felt the tension between the two adepts at the table.

Over the sea the cloud spires were lifted into flame by the sun's last rays. They burned over the dark water like the towers of a city in flame.

She shivered. 'Let's go in. You can give me the present as we recline before the hearth. Come, my love.' She reached for his hand.

Suddenly he wasn't empty-handed any longer. A cup was in his left. The stem and footing were of gold, which girdled the coiled spiral of a shell, a white shell glowing inside and out with mother-of-pearl.

'It's beautiful,' she said, but her heart was hammering and she could barely breathe.

19

'Yes. Now take it in both your hands and drink.'

'Wine,' she whispered. 'I'd rather not. I've had . . .'

'Drink!'

The word had the force of command. At the same moment, she felt his right hand encircle her neck, her long, regal neck. He stroked the hollow at the base of her throat with his thumb. She'd seen him kill men that way, crushing the ridged cartilage of the larynx with his thumb, leaving them to kick and gasp their lives away while he watched with evident enjoyment.

She seized the cup with both hands and brought it to her lips. Its contents filled her mouth and nose both, so she couldn't even scream when she was drawn into the spiral coil of the vessel.

She seemed to move down a glowing white, curve-walled corridor filled with pale, diffused light. The inner shell was not transparent but translucent. She fled along a rough pathway like one following an ever-narrowing spiral staircase down and down to some unguessable destination, unable to halt or go back because the walls and floor weren't sufficiently bumpy to allow her to stop or crawl back.

Panic struck as she reached a passage so narrow that she could no longer walk or, at last, even crawl. She screamed, and at her first scream, she debouched free of the shell, rolling across a carpet on the floor of Merlin's stronghold.

The place both awed and terrified her. It was part of the sea. A sea on some world she was sure the rest of mankind did not share.

The room was luxurious. Soft rugs, jeweled with many colors, lay like pools of brightness on stone floors. Velvet-covered couches were scattered around haphazard flowers blooming in a dark shadowed mezzanine. The whole front wall of the room was glass, some kind of glass that overlooked the sea. And when the tide was in, as it was now, the blue and green waves crashed against the glass, towering over her as she lay on a soft, scarlet rug on the floor.

The glass-not-glass allowed sound and air to pass through its permeable surface and the room was scoured by the sea wind. She screamed again as a gigantic wave towered over her and broke, foaming against the glass wall before her, and the wind tore at her hair.

She scrambled toward the back of the room, where a gigantic double-walled Roman fireplace formed the back of the long sea-view room.

'That's it. Incinerate yourself,' he said contemptuously.

She sat up, shivering. 'You know I hate this place,' she whimpered.

'Too bad,' he said. 'But whatever you feel, stop squalling or I'll have you gagged. Or maybe I'll just have one of my servants cut out your tongue.'

She knew he was capable of doing either one as easily as the other, so she was silent.

He waved his hand and it seemed the glass between them and the raging sea grew denser. The noise of pounding waves lessened and the wind dropped. She realized it was near night in this place, as it was at Tintigal, and some of the brightness in the room was from the fire at the back, fanned by the wind.

The glow faded and the room grew darker. Beyond the windows, the sea churned higher, the waves now breaking on the roof above the window wall. The trees were scattered around the room in pots, some in leaf, others laden with fruit, and some in flower. Peaches, plums, apricots, apples, and quince. They yielded to his power, dormant flowering, fruiting at his will.

As she watched, he picked a pale white plum, dewy ripe, from one of the harvest trees. He reached down and put it in her mouth, where it dissolved, honey-sweet within, tart and biting at the skin.

21

'Spit the pit into my hand,' he said.

She held back, keeping the fissured seed in her mouth. But then he caught her hair in one hand and shook her. 'Don't you dare! I will tear out your tongue!'

She spat the pit into his hand. He snapped his fingers, and two of his golems appeared. She knew this was going to be worse than anything she'd anticipated, maybe worse than anything that had ever gone before.

The golems always frightened her. They were dead men still inhabiting their bodies. Unlike others he raised, they were not zombies suited only for simple tasks. They retained intelligence and volition, even though they were clearly corpses. Gutted, cooked to render away fat, then soaked, tanned the way a hide is tanned, then sewn back on withered muscle and cartilaginous bone. The faces were tight, dry masks, the eyes lifeless, hard, opaque, and pale, but with a dark ring where the pupil had once been and a spark of light at the center.

'Your clothes,' he said, 'or shall I have them strip you?'

She shuddered. 'No!' she whispered. 'No!'

She rose to her knees and was naked in a few seconds. She had been prepared for him, wearing nothing under her gown and shift.

Merlin pointed at a dark stair leading down into another, larger room that she could see only dimly below. She hurried to keep ahead of the two golems, running down the shallow steps into the large room.

Even though night was falling outside, it was filled with light. The roof was a glass dome of fitted pieces, as were the windows of the first room she had been in. Above the dome, the sea crashed and boiled frighteningly.

Once the domed room had been a small bay, carved from the cliffs above by wave action. But someone, something, had enclosed the bay in glass, smoothed the floor – it was polished gray basalt – and pushed out the encroaching sea. Now it thundered and roared as if in mad frustration at this usurpation of its powers.

Yes, this was a place of awesome power; she recognized that. Not sea, not land, and she stood there at the moment of not day, not night, not darkness, not light.

Igrane whimpered with terror.

Merlin wasn't interested. He whispered an incantation and a symbol flared into life on the mottled gray floor. It was a Saint Andrew's cross, an X. It was set in the floor among the remains of sea creatures that lived long ago and left their images pressed into the rock caught in stone. Not dead completely, yet not alive, either.

'Hurry,' Merlin snapped. 'The light is fading! Tie her.'

She screamed when the golems seized her. They hustled her to the glowing cross-shaped marking in the center of the floor, then tied her arms, fastening them at the wrists to two lines that vanished into the shadows above. Then one of them kicked her legs apart and placed her feet on the glowing X she stood on, so that her body formed another X above that on the floor.

She tugged and found she couldn't move her feet. They adhered to the glowing lines beneath.

She screamed again.

Behind her, she heard Merlin test the whip. It cracked across the chamber with the sound of snapping wood. Light filled the room and Igrane looked up and around into what seemed a thousand mirrors, all reflecting both of them.

He was standing behind her, whip in hand. Oddly, she felt relieved. She had been afraid he was going to kill her. But a whipping wouldn't do that. He had whipped her before and seldom lasted beyond two lashes. By then his desire to see her suffer was at war with his overwhelming need to possess her, and the need to possess her won.

She felt the surge of power from the symbol she stood

on; erotic need consumed her. She was almost ready to beg for the lash.

She saw in the thousand mirrors around her the movement, snakelike and savage, of the thing in his hand. A second later, it coiled at her loins.

Her response was a shriek of uncontrolled pain. God, it had never felt like this before.

She saw a weal leap up a finger's breadth and width across her buttocks and down to her thigh, the tender part just between her legs. Then, as the agony faded into a more tolerable ache, the wound began to leak blood from its center.

'No!' she screamed as the next one came coiling around her body above the buttocks at her waist. The tip flicked her nipple and split it like a ripe cherry.

She watched transfixed with horror as blood from her breast flowed down her belly and thigh, and dripped down on the floor. She didn't scream again, but fought the ropes that tied her wrists and whatever power that caused her feet to cling to the floor like a madwoman.

Then she went limp with almost unspeakable relief as she realized he was walking toward her ... he'd had enough ... oh, God! A few seconds later, she felt his arms around her waist and his lips on her neck.

'That was worse,' she whimpered. 'Worse than all the other times. Please, please cut me down.'

'My poor dear,' he whispered in mock sympathy. 'Hold yourself in readiness. It's going to get worse still.'

But he did release the ropes holding her arms and forced her to the floor, positioning her on top of the X-shaped symbol. The light in the room died, and, above through the glass, she saw the green and churning sea. It was almost nightfall outside, and she knew he must be in a hurry to complete the spell before darkness wrapped this coast in gloom, because she saw him glance uneasily upward.

Abruptly, light blossomed all around her and the mirrors returned to the glass dome above her. She saw herself reflected everywhere. She glowed with beauty in the flow of brightness from beneath the floor, naked, her sex shaved clean, skin tawny, her hair a flood of black silk cradling her pale, fair face. Helpless, because she found the X-shaped medallion held her tightly to the floor.

Desire grew and she saw her labia part slightly to reveal the swollen, hot passage that seemed the center of her being. Her image darkened as he covered her with his body, and she found she looked up not at the mirrored ceiling but at his face, teeth bared, a mask of desire.

She groaned with both outrage and pleasure as he entered her body.

'Oh. Oh, my sweet, hot, tight, soft. My darling, my rich course of all joy. I am enfolded in moist, red velvet.'

Not a good sign, the last clear-thinking corner of her brain informed her. He never spoke tenderly to her, no matter how hotly he desired her.

But the light from the cross-shaped symbol blazed around both of them and her whole body exploded into orgasm. But then, what seemed a tidal wave of pleasure burned away into incredible pain. She threw back her head, almost blinded by its intensity. Even childbirth, the worst pain she could remember, hadn't hurt so much.

The first sight she had as she lay gasping as the pain at last ebbed away was his face grinning down at her, and the first sound his triumphant laughter. Their bodies were separated, but something like a steel rod parted her female portions. He was trying to enter her again.

'No! No! No!' she screamed.

He laughed again. 'I wonder how many times you will be able to survive it. The best, the very best I ever had, only lasted through five thrusts. He was a strong man – most women only make three. Come now, my sweet, my

25

angel, my beauty. Be nice. Let me in again. You will, you know. In the end you will. They all do. Best get it over quickly. Struggling only prolongs my pleasure and your suffering.'

His next thrust was like being battered by a stone phallus, but somehow, even though her body was glued to the floor like iron filings to a magnet, she managed to twist away.

She had often wondered but never wanted to know how he came by his vast powers. Now she knew. He was able to use this room, this place, to call them up from the earth, call them up into his body and spirit by using those he desired as a sort of intermediary. He took the strength they pulled from this wonder she lay on, but they experienced the concomitant price of such a transfer of power: the pain.

In the thousand mirrors above, she could see him kneeling between her legs, but she was beginning to glow with the excitement of the building fire beneath her. He reached around, palms cupping buttocks, fingers reaching then catching the soft lips of the innermost portal, drawing it open to his rigid member. She threw her head back, trying to knock herself out against the stone floor. Her vision splintered into a thousand lights, but even so, she could feel him entering her again.

When her eyes cleared, she found she couldn't see the mirrors above. She couldn't tell if she was half unconscious or if indeed something was happening above him. It was as though she looked up through the meshes of a net, the only difference being these meshes writhed. They moved closer, further down, toward him.

A moment of crystal clarity followed while she weighed her choices.

She could warn him.

No. Never.

It might kill her, too.

Better to die that way than this. Even if, as she saw now, the meshes of this net were snakes, white ones with black eyes and tongues and a faint green line down their slender backs.

An instant later, they enfolded him. She felt the hard, muscular strength of the narrow bones as they wrapped themselves around him. They moved like no snakes she had ever seen, in a completely coordinated fashion.

It was his turn to scream and scream as he rolled away from her prone body across the floor. Then he was silent as he concentrated his entire intellect and will on the struggle.

He tried to kick free, and for a few moments, it looked as though he might succeed. But they wrapped themselves around his legs, immobilizing him from ankle to hip.

He pulled one arm free, but when he tried to claw the other loose, a half dozen coils lapped around the free arm, pinning it to his body.

The struggle ended when one coiled around his throat and deprived him of breath whenever he tried to move. At length, he lay still.

The voice came out of nowhere. 'Dung fly maggot. Filthy pile of stinking carrion. I've been waiting to corner you for some time now. Such vicious games as you play leave you vulnerable, you crawling louse.

'You told me the boy Arthur was harmless. You told me he would never learn to elude the watcher I set over him. You lied about both matters, and now she is gone. They are all gone. All those caught in the antechamber. Those whose souls I trapped for companionship in an eternity of loneliness. She escaped me. She whom I loved, she who was my only consolation – has set out across the sea of eternity alone without me.'

Then the voice slipped into another language, one Igrane didn't understand. But it must have been an

27

incantation, because the snakes began to strike. They buried their fangs in his chest and throat, and – she smiled to see it – his groin, just at the spot where the penis joins the body.

His back arched, his mouth opened, but she could hear nothing. The snakes were now lines of light and they sucked his substance away into their bodies, and then very simply, without leaving a trace behind, they were gone.

We picked up the boats and carried them into the marsh. We didn't want to leave a trail. Or at least, that's what Ure said, telling the rest of us that a trail by land in a swamp left far less disturbance.

And, oddly enough, I found he was right. The track was muddy or grass-covered; the mud oozed back to fill in footprints and they simply didn't take on the damp turf. Had we forced our way through the rushes and cat-tails, we would have left clear evidence of our passage.

It took me a little time to realize I was walking along a road. It wound in and out among trees, past ponds thick with water weed, cress, and lily pads. Or along the edge of more open water, filled with fish. We moved quietly and I saw the fish rise, making circles on the water as they took insects on the surface.

Twice, tree trunks were visible, laid in parallel rows to bridge low spots where we waded up to our ankles.

'Is this a road?' I said to Ure.

'Yes.'

'There are people living here?' I asked.

'No,' he said. 'Not now.'

Knowing his lack of affection for chatter, I forbore to question him anymore.

What I most remember about the marsh was its silence. I was brought up on a seacoast, where the sound of wind and wave was a constant background to all human activities. Even in the barley fields, we heard the sea's roar and the wind swept the heading crops into a bowing, rippling mass, which gleamed in the sun just as the sea waves did before its unending breath.

But here was true silence, broken only by the flop, pop of a leaping frog or fish, or the distant cries of ducks and geese as they fed among the long grasses and sedges that bordered this strange and, I think, ancient, winding road.

'Snakes,' someone else, I think Albe, said nervously.

'Too cold yet,' Ure answered. 'Later, when it grows warmer, I would fear to walk here without a stout stick, but we are safe enough now.'

After that, we trudged on quietly, the silence seeming to enter us the way water is poured into a bowl and lies motionless, forming a mirror of sorts for anything above it.

Maeniel, Gray, Ure, and I took the lead; the rest followed behind. Those who had been sleeping took up the boats, automatically leaving the rowers to walk unencumbered. But none of us were really what you would call fresh, not after ten days at sea. And I wondered how much strength any of us would have to call upon when we faced battle.

I was frightened. I might not have the strength in my right hand to make the buildings in the fortress burn, even if I poured my strength, my life, my whole soul into the task. Would it be enough?

About then the wind changed, and we smelled them.

Gray stopped. 'Christ! What's that?'

Ure laughed very softly. 'The Saxons,' he said.

'Uncle?' Gray said. 'Do you never explain?'

'No,' Ure said, and he continued on. But Gray balked mutinously.

Maeniel sighed. What we were smelling now he had probably been aware of for some time. But the wind early in the morning had been at our backs. Now, as the road however tortuously moved inland, we were catching a land breeze, and it reeked, the stench so strong it made your eyes tear.

Ure, seeing the rest of us frozen where we stood, paused again.

'The Saxons,' Maeniel said quietly, 'devote every tenth captive to their gods.'

'Especially the weak, the old, the sickly, and the rebellious,' Ure said.

We rounded the next bend in the road and saw them dangling in the trees. Even before the road had been built there must have been a considerable island of dry land, because there were many trees, even those that won't grow on flooded land. They were festooned with the dead in all stages of decomposition.

To the right of the forested island, I saw a thicket of pilings projecting from the water where a village must once have stood. The pilings were half rotted by damp, but the tops were charred and blackened by fire.

We stood stock-still where we were as the rest came up behind us and looked over our shoulders at the terrible sight. Someone began to cry. I don't know if it was a boy or girl. I only know Ure's eyes swept the whole group of us with a look of icy contempt and the weeping was silenced.

'Well, now you know,' he said. 'Make your choice. Run or fight. Which is it?'

Gray was on his knees vomiting at the side of the road. Maeniel wore his wolf look – the gaze he turns on the yearling cubs when it comes time to loose them toward their first kill. I stood paralyzed, feeling both my knees and my guts turning to water.

'Must we pass this way?' I asked.

'No,' he answered. 'But I thought it was as well you did. These are not deer you hunt, but men, killers of other men.'

I looked around at the others. Everyone was silent. The girls were bunched behind me, but the equally pale and frightened faces of the boys were indistinguishable from theirs.

Next to me, Albe's eyes were empty. 'I will not go living into their hands again,' she said.

Next to her, Wic, the girl with the ugly birthmark distorting her features, shrugged and said, 'No worse than my village when it was filled with carrion crows after the attack.'

One of the boys whispered, 'My master beat me every day. Think on it. None but the queen has anything to go back to.'

'The queen,' I said, 'is not going back. We will abide the dead.'

To this day, I don't know how I did it. Part of it was pride, I'm sure. I couldn't let this band of outcasts show more courage than the descendent of the Iceni queen. But the other part was, I knew how important our little voyage was.

The Painted People and the kingdoms of the Out Isles were hard-pressed by the Saxon pirates. Hand in glove with their brethren that guarded the coast, they formed a pincer movement that, in the end, threatened the independence of the rest of the free people of Alba. Uther would soon be hard-pressed to maintain his position in Wales, and the Painted People deprived of their alliance with the Veneti. And without control over the North Sea fisheries and the resources of the Out Islands, they would fall like ripe plums into the hands of the southern Saxon conquerors, led by Merlin.

If no one did anything to stop these raids, the command of the seas would fall to the Saxons. And, make no mistake, whoever rules the sea here also controls the land.

I danced the dance, stretched out my hands, and took

31

the power offered by my seat on the Dragon Throne. Maeniel warned me the night before the dance there would be no going back, and there wasn't. So I did as a chief should do; I took the first step forward. The rest, without further question, followed. Even Ure.

The view of the small forest on the island didn't improve as we drew closer. But we continued on. The crows were at them, and at first we thought we frightened the birds, because, with a cry and a rush of black wings, they flew up and away from the things in the trees.

'I didn't think we were close enough to startle them away from their dinner,' Ure said.

But then we heard voices.

Igrane felt the power fade and withdraw from her body. No longer attached to the symbol on the floor, she rolled to her side, then crawled away, whimpering with relief. He had been going to kill her; she knew it. This time he had really been going to kill her.

She had always been sure he hated her power over him, and this time he had intended to be rid of her. To burn her away as a sacrifice to whatever earthly, demonic power resided in this strange place.

She had been to his dwelling before, but never here to this part. Above, the sea roared and the room with its high, domed ceiling grew darker and darker as the light faded from the symbol on the floor. Fearfully, she thought about his two servants. God! She didn't want to meet them.

She came to her knees. Her eyes searched the room in the growing gloom. She saw what remained of them.

Whatever powers took Merlin, it had dealt with them first. All that remained of them were bags of human hide, full of shattered, dark bone. It looked as though they had simply been crumpled as a bit of discarded paper might be by the fist of a giant hand.

She gave a gasp. Whatever took him must have awesome power. Merlin was the strongest being she had ever met; the creature that could destroy him didn't bear thinking about.

The light was very dim now, the big room deeply shadowed. She found herself shivering with cold. Something, a robe of sorts, was draped over a sofa nearby. She seized it and wrapped it around her body. It was silk, heavy, raw silk.

It must be his, she thought. He had prepared it so that he could relax when he was finished destroying her. He would have been replete, sated with food, sex, and bloated with the staggeringly rich draft he sucked from her loins, while she lay spent, twisted, and dead on the white symbol below.

The robe hung over her shoulders. It moved of its own volition and wrapped itself around her. Sleeves lifted over her arms and a hood covered her head, then the two halves closed in front of her.

She staggered with fear. Clothing that dressed her, the fabric wrapping itself around her as though driven by a command, was another new and terrifying experience. But the gown was warm and caressed her skin with a thousand gentle fingers.

She was standing near the sofa from which she had taken the robe. It seemed her knees didn't want to hold her up any longer. They folded. She sat, then drew up her feet and slid to her side and lay down.

Darkness rolled over her like a wave.

'A wolf!' a voice screeched. 'A wolf! They promised me a wolf!'

Black Leg found himself lifted and gripped in the

embrace of a pair of powerful arms. Almost paralyzed by terror, Black Leg gave vent to a most unwolflike screech.

'*Yiiiieee!*' It ended on a high note, and he turned human, the better to grapple with his attacker.

When the owner of the formidable pair of arms realized he was clutching another human male, he backed away, hunched down, and began weeping.

'No. No. No,' it moaned. 'You are not he – they promised me a companion wolf, but you are no wolf but a man.'

For the first time, Black Leg got a good look at his attacker. Got a good whiff of him, too. He seemed old and was filthy. His hair, nails, and beard looked as though they hadn't been cut in months, maybe years. The dirt under his nails was black, his hair a tangled mass that hung down on either side of his face. And the beard was long, filled with dead leaves, twigs, and bits of whatever the creature had been eating, substances Black Leg didn't care to speculate about. It was hunkered down on its heels, sobbing, nose running in two mucous streams down the uncombed mustache into its beard.

'No, no, no! I will despair and die. You cannot be the one,' it sobbed. 'The voices said nothing about such powers. Where? Where is the wolf? My wolf, my friend, the promised protector?'

Black Leg was shaken, filled with a mixture of pity and fear. He had never seen a human being in so wretched a condition.

The thing began to crawl away through the shallows, toward the boggy shore. Its mouth opened and Black Leg saw that its teeth were those of a young man, white, even, with strong, pink gums.

Black Leg shuddered, looked down at his own nude body, and realized he had been smeared with filth by the thing's arms and hands. He waded deeper into the lake to clean himself. He was afraid to turn wolf again, lest he

34

bring on another assault by the fearful being. He sighed with pleasure when he was out far enough to be in up to his neck. True, the water was cold, but only briskly so. Only cold enough to bring up the reflex that heats the blood in the young and can make a swim even in icy water a profound pleasure.

In the first light of morning, the water was murky and he felt the long fronds of waterweeds stroke his calves, knees, and thighs. He was walking on a velvet carpet of vegetation a few feet below the surface. A floor soft and yielding but at the same time crisp and somehow protective of his feet.

Nice. Nice, he thought. But then he noticed the weeds seemed to have a lot of prurient curiosity. He was being fondled and caressed by something that felt finned, scaly, and yet almost slimy like a fresh-caught fish. The touch explored him so gently that at first he was disarmed by an intense rush of pleasure. Then he realized he was being felt up by a . . . fish!

'Yeeeee!' He wasn't proud of the screech he gave while setting a record back to land. It sounded a bit feminine, at least to his ears.

But when he reached solid ground, he was nervous enough to become wolf again without thinking about his first encounter. But he was reminded immediately.

'Thank God. Thank whatever gods may be. He has returned. Let me embrace you!'

Black Leg became human again. 'No!' he shouted. 'You stay away from me!'

The old man on the shore began weeping. And something else reared up out of the water. It was heavily draped in waterweed, but Black Leg could see enough to note that it had fins, scales, and hands with webbed fingers.

'Holy Christ!' he yelled.

'What's the matter?' the thing in the water said. 'You didn't like it?'

The old man on the shore drew himself up, pointed one long-nailed, grimy finger and thundered, 'It is the Lorelei. Begone, for being you wolf and man, flee ere she begins her seductive song and calls you to your doom!'

'You old fool!' the thing in the water shouted back at him. 'That's saltwater . . . I'm fresh. At least get your evil supernatural beings straight. You have been sorcerer. And while you're at it, get away from my lake.'

The old man on the shore flung a sphere of fire at the fishy-looking thing. But a waterspout leaped up in front of it and put the fire out.

The old man on the shore sank down, moaning, his head in his hands. 'Weak, I'm so weak. Hunger and cold have sapped my strength. I am no longer fit for battle. Soon, soon, if the wolf, my guardian and protector, doesn't come, I will die.'

Black Leg felt a sharp pang of guilt. 'Maybe . . . I am the wolf,' he said quietly. 'I don't know. I started off thinking there was something I had to do . . . and . . .'

'You half-wit,' the thing in the water snapped. 'You turn me down and you're gonna pick him up? What's with you? You don't like girls, I can see that. But taking up with this rickety old wreck. What is in your empty head?'

'You don't look like any girl I ever saw,' Black Leg snapped.

'Oh, shit! I forgot!' she said, then sank back into the water, vanishing without a ripple. A second later, she reemerged.

Black Leg goggled at her. She was beautiful in a very strange sort of way. Tall, slender, blond, with deep-blue eyes, long arms and probably legs. He couldn't tell because she was dressed in a gown that seemed made of small green and burgundy lily pads dotted with tiny white flowers. They fitted her, forming a drape over one shoulder and clinging to breast, hip, and thigh. She radiated a delicate beauty; her straight nose and curving, sensuous lips were parted in a half smile and the rising sun made a golden aureole of her fine, fair hair.

'What do you think,' she said, turning sideways to give him a sultry glance and a good look at her jutting, pointed breasts.

'I'm a shape-strong, too,' she said, batting her eyelashes at him.

'So I see,' he said. He began wading out into the water toward her.

'No! No!' the old man moaned. 'Don't be fooled . . . don't be drawn. See her pale face, white skin, her clinging dress, part of the lake itself? She cannot hide her true nature. Her grace is that of the swimming serpent. See the length of arms, legs, waist . . . a serpent is what she is and she will lap you in her coils, crush your bones in her embrace, empty the air from your lungs with her lethal caress, and carry you away to drown.'

Black Leg studied her carefully. 'You do look sort of snakeish. . . .'

'Snakeish! You – shitass – snakeish – I'll give you snakeish!'

The glob of mud, slime, and any other unpleasant things she could find on such short notice landed – plop – in the middle of Black Leg's face. Another double handful of filth landed on the old man's head. He promptly ran screaming into the forest.

Black Leg backed away, clearing his eyes, and was relieved when he looked out over the still, misty water and realized she was gone. He went wolf, found a clean, shallow stream, and washed.

Kyra had been strict about washing when he was a cub, so he tended to be even more hygienic than the average human. True, he had rebelled often, but Maeniel (who, by the way, took a bath only when he wanted to) gave him scant sympathy and even held him down for

Kyra to complete a scrubbing. Mother ignored his discomfort and said, 'Kyra is pack. When you share a life with someone, you had best humor their crotchets.'

And after a time, Black Leg became resigned to cleanliness, and though he would never have admitted it, even began to like it.

When he was finished, he shook himself dry and went hunting. He got a young hare and, putting aside his own hunger, went to find the old man. He located him sleeping on a bed of bracken in a hollow near the stream.

Black Leg dropped the hare near his hand and went to look for a stick he could use as a fire drill. When he returned, he found the old man had awakened, eaten the hare – raw – and then gone back to sleep.

Black Leg sighed, settled down, and managed with a great deal of effort to get a fire going. He wanted fire, because truth to tell, he was frightened of whatever was living in that lake. Then he went wolf again, curled up, nose covered by his tail, and went to sleep.

Something woke him, a wolf sense, not part of his humanity. The stars told him it was late, the night sliding into the deep trough of silence when all things sleep – even the predators replete with full bellies or resigned to hunger as he was. A few days on short rations are nothing to a wolf.

What? He didn't move and no observer would have noticed anything different about him. The old man was very still on his bed of fern.

Well breathed, Black Leg thought. His snores were soft buzzes. He curled on his side, and the new uncoiling fronds moved slightly with each inhalation and exhalation of his breath.

No! Not him.

Black Leg's eyes searched the stream bank, then he saw her. The Lady of the Lake. She was seated on a mossy

38

stone. She was silvered by moonlight and was dabbling her feet in the cold, clear water.

We went to ground without the slightest need of a signal from anyone. Both sides of the road we marched along were hemmed in by brushy cattails, reeds, small and large, and thick growths of sedge stretching far out into the shallows. Yes! They, the people of the burned village, would have made sure that the materials for matting baskets and even house walls were growing close by. It provided a lot of cover, much of it snagged and tangled among the osier willows that bordered the path.

Albe and the girl named Wic lay next to me, and across the weed-grown track, I saw Ure looking at me between the reed stems. The voices grew louder, and a few moments later, we saw two armed men emerge from the corpse-laden grove of trees. They were pointing and laughing at the things hanging there. I knew they must be from the pirate camp further up along the river.

We lay silent; no one made a sound. We were deep in the marsh, and the spaces around the island and the road were filled by open water. The sun came and went, now sparkling on the mirrorlike waters, now plunging it into steely gloom as the dark clouds flew past above. The wind blew not at our backs or faces, but from the sea at our sides, carrying the stench of decay away from us, toward and also away from the two sightseers on the island.

They approached the corpses in the trees more closely. And I could hear their words, though since they were spoken in another language, I couldn't understand most of them. I spoke enough Frankish and Saxon, for those were the languages they were using, to comprehend the gist of their conversation. They were speaking about the dead, how they died, not the method but how they behaved when they knew they were to be sacrificed. Who fought, who pleaded and begged, and from time to time, they spoke in praise of those who went courageously steadfast to their doom.

The sacrifices had been performed in a variety of ways. Some hanged, a few hung by their feet, head in the water to drown. And I knew from disturbed earth in places that some had probably been buried alive. The worst, I think, were those impaled on trimmed saplings. They had been driven onto the stakes up through the genitals, and from the expressions frozen on the faces of some and the twisted rigor in the bodies of others, it must have taken some of them quite a while to die.

This was what awaited us if we failed. The cold in the earth I lay on seemed to seep up and fill the marrow of my bones. It was as though I could feel the others, feel their fear, the need to run and not stop until they were far away, where they could breathe clean air again.

Tonight, I thought. *We will wait here until nightfall, then load the boats and slink away.*

With that resolution, I felt an instant and tremendous relief of tension. Run! Yes! Run! I was a fool to think I could carry this off. A fool.

Maybe I would have run. Maybe that night, when darkness fell, I would have given the command and we would have fled toward the sea and home. Then what would my life have been? Better, more peaceful, or ugly and short? Who knows? You choose, as I did that day on the shore, when I went with Gray to meet the pirates.

And here I chose again.

The closest of the sacrifices to us were a man and, I thought, a woman. They had been impaled. The man was dead, that was clear. Part of his face was the slick red of raw meat, the rest a writhing mass of maggots. She was almost intact, though withered, her head thrown back, long hair dangling, floating from time to time in the breeze from the sea.

When they reached her body, one of the two Saxon sightseers picked up a stick and prodded her body. Her hands moved. And I realized with sick horror that she wasn't dead.

The one with the stick laughed and made a remark I understood most of. He said, 'I wonder what she would think of her lover now, if she could see him. But so sad—' He laughed again. 'The crows have taken her eyes.'

And I saw they had. She looked up at the sky with red, empty sockets.

Next to me I felt Albe stir, and I realized she was up on one knee, sling in her hand, lead shot in the other. She looked down, our eyes met. They had left her for dead, the pirates. In her face was the weariness of permanent hate, hate that no longer creates rage or even anger in the person who bears it. Hate so ingrained and permanent it yields to nothing, not love, compassion, or even justice. Hate that burdens its possessor forever. Hate that makes you glad we die and are relieved of our obsession with murder and extirpation of its object forever.

Her empty eyes asked me a question, and I . . . I nodded yes.

The one holding the stick died first. I doubt he knew what hit him. One side of his face caved in.

The other turned toward us, hand on his sword hilt, eyes panicked.

I was on my feet, knife in hand, ready to close with an underhand thrust, when his forehead caved in. Last to die was the impaled woman; the lead shot shattered her skull and blood and brain dripped into the still water.

When I turned to look, our whole force was in the road, weapons in hand, ready to attack. But Ure was up out of the reeds and giving commands. 'Get down, you fools, or I'll unman every one of you!'

41

Everyone was a bit afraid of him. They dropped.

'Idiots!' he snarled in a low voice. 'How do you know there's not more of them beyond the trees?'

Gray stood up. 'My lady . . . what have . . . ?'

That was as far as he got. Ure pivoted as smoothly and quickly as an angry cat and punched him hard in the stomach. With a gasp, Gray doubled over and fell to his knees.

'You shut up, you fool!' Ure whispered. 'Tell me, lack wit, will all your jawing bring them back?'

Still gasping, Gray shook his head. 'No.'

'Good. Then shut up and make yourself useful.' He was still whispering. 'Take this swift little slinger here—' He indicated Albe. '—and see if there are any more of them.'

Gray glanced at the crowd of corpses dangling from the trees. Ure laughed an ugly, grating laugh. 'Boy, the dead are the least of our worries.'

Albe looked at him, her face white, the scars on her cheeks standing out in jagged red lines. 'My kill,' she said, pointing to the two bodies.

Ure smiled; a muscle in his cheek jerked. 'Fear not. I'll see you have the stripping of them.'

So it was. She did. And they were a rich pair. A torque, four finger rings, two good swords, three knives, plus metal-studded belts and clothing they had worn. No helmets or armor, but they were alone and had come in a boat and brought food and drink – a lot of drink – aboard. That and what food we had left over from the voyage we parceled out among ourselves.

The island ended in a little hill made of earth dragged up from the marshes by those people who built the village and whose bodies I suspected were the first hung by the Saxons in the grove. The hill looked like it had been one of those fortified watchtowers the Romans built. They probably used it to signal the fortress in the distance if boats were seen entering the river, because when Gray, Ure, and I reached the top, we found worked stone there. But we surmised that it had been abandoned long ago, both it and the fortress, when the marsh began to undermine the walls, and the defenses moved inland.

The Saxon troops that the Romans had left to defend the shore against their brothers on the Continent now allowed them to use the ruin in the distance to launch raids against the Painted People in the north. Saxons fighting Saxons; it raises the eyebrows. But both Dugald and Maeniel taught me that the Romans were more than happy to hire one set of barbarians to cut another set of barbarians' throats. Or at least that had been the Roman plan at first. But now the Romans were gone and we were left to deal with the results of their miscalculations.

The troops in the fortress knew better than to raid along the Saxon shore, but anyone else was fair game. I must tell you, this went on everywhere, and Dugald and Maeniel attributed the rot that spread on the Continent in the scattered remnants of the old Roman Empire to the custom. The Frankish King Clovis lent money to the Saxons, and every year they doubled his money by raiding the coast of Britain and the Out Islands. As Clovis saw it, what happened to us was no skin off his nose.

He similarly paid the Huns to attack the Burgundians and let them keep whatever they captured from said Burgundians. They all did it, even the pope, or so Maeniel and Dugald told me, who was more than happy to employ them to fight his enemies on Italian soil.

This sort of treachery pervaded all of society. Most local lords were happy to allow brigands to use their lands as a base of operations, provided they raided only his enemies. The emperors in Constantinople paid off barbarians who threatened them, sending these tribes to attack the kingdoms of the west.

And everywhere the ordinary men, the people of the

cities, the small farmers in the countryside, suffered the tortures of the damned. The Roman lords extracted taxes from them until they were forced to sell their children into slavery to pay off the tax gatherers. Then, when the barbarians took over – and in the end, they usually did – they collected taxes in kind, cloth, food, draft animals, and such, until the impoverished small artisans and tillers of the soil died of starvation in large numbers.

In the end, many ordinary people took matters into their own hands and formed the Brotherhood of the Bagudae and tried to wrest control of their fate from the hands of their overlords, barbarian and Roman. Maeniel saw the Bagudae as the last hope of what had been the Ancient Imperium. Dugald did not agree, and their arguments filled my mind from the time I can remember anything at all. The pair of them, for better or worse, brought me up to see the larger picture, and one day, to rule.

And that was why I was here sitting on the cold grass at the foot of the muddy hill, eating bread and cheese and swigging really nasty-tasting wine to wash it down.

'I can't tell this from vinegar,' I told Ure. 'Why must I finish this?'

'It's food,' he said, 'and your strength is important. You, your actions, are the key to our plans.'

I looked up and around the circle of faces surrounding me. They were pale, pinch-faced, cold, and gobbling their food just as I was, but every eye was fixed on me.

I had to climb the walls of that fortress and set the defenses and dwellings within on fire, and force the defenders out. We had only five or six good swords among us, about two dozen knives, but everyone without exception carried a sling. And they were all nearly as fast and accurate as Albe was. We carried ten sacks of lead shot, and everyone had pebbles and small stones tucked into their belts.

I had to force the men in that fort out through the gates and into a hail of missiles. If I did, we would win. If I failed, we would lose and die.

I felt a little dizzy.

When I was finished eating, I hunkered down with the rest and we sat huddled together for warmth – and we listened to Ure.

He produced a shears. 'I want your hair, all of it, boys and girls.'

'Why?' I asked.

'You know why,' he said.

'Yes, but I don't think all the others do. You need to explain.'

He nodded. 'The men running out of that fortress will be better armed than you are, and the first thing they will do is grab your hair and slice your head off. If you don't give them a convenient handle, they can't do that.'

He snapped the shear blades together. 'Your hair! All of it.'

He got it. We slicked down what was left of it with mud.

'Next thing you need to know is what to do after "he"—' Ure grinned. There was no mirth in it. '—finds he can't get a grip on you.'

We waited.

'You save your last shot, rock or lead, it doesn't matter. Put it in the sling and swing it toward his . . .' He paused. 'What?' he asked.

'Head,' someone said.

'No.' He bared his teeth again. 'You swing it toward his what?' he asked Albe.

'Balls,' she said.

'Yes! There's a good girl,' he said. 'Now, I want everyone to repeat what I just told you back to me.'

The troops looked dismayed.

'You can use your own words, but I want it all.'

The first was mistaken. Ure clouted him so hard he got a nosebleed and began to cry. But Ure made him repeat himself until he got it right.

Ure didn't speak further to me, so I rose because I had an idea. Gray and Maeniel were standing aside, watching. I walked over to them.

'God! He's good,' Gray said. 'If they stand a chance at all, it will be because of him.'

Maeniel nodded.

I looked up at them. 'I'm going back to the village.'

'You mean to the house posts standing in the water,' Gray said. 'Why?'

I shifted my gaze to the Gray Watcher. 'They were our people,' I said. 'They understood we are one people, the dead, the living, the yet unborn.'

'They are gone,' Gray said.

'No,' I said, looking away over the marsh, over the still waters that reflected the sky. 'They are not gone, but still there. At least, some of them, waiting. Waiting for me.'

He uncurled himself, became human, and studied her. 'What are you doing here?'

She snorted. 'I decided not to cut off my nose to spite my face. You're the best-looking thing I've seen in about a thousand years.'

'What do you want?' Black Leg asked.

'God!' she said, raising her fist to the sky. 'I sure can pick them. Do you hear? This idiot wants to know what I want. Hear that? He wants to know what I want! Well, Mister Hung-Like-a-Horse, what the hell do you think I want?'

Black Leg felt himself turning red all over. 'You sure that's all you want?' he mumbled.

'I'm sure,' she said grimly.

'You're not going to drown me?'

She answered slowly, as if speaking to a child or one somewhat intellectually impaired. 'No! Why the hell would I want to drown you?'

'To . . . so . . . you could eat me,' Black Leg answered.

'Why the hell would I want to eat you? I know your kind are sometimes not too bright and logic certainly isn't one of your strong points. But trust me, even I couldn't figure out a good enough reason to want to kill and eat you. No, the longer you live, the better I like it.

'I know you might not believe this, but from time to time some moron does fall into the water in one of the lakes and springs I frequent. And then, if I'm not around to yank him out and chase him back on shore, the bone-head does drown. Trust me, eating those things is not my first impulse. *Yeech!* It's not even my last. The sons of bitches stink! And I usually get the unhappy task of dragging the remains to shore and dumping them so their people can find and dispose of them.

'Trust me, fool, you wouldn't want to hang around a drowned corpse too long, much less eat one. After even a day or two in the water, bloating . . . but Christ, why am I explaining this nonsense? What I want to do is get it on.'

Black Leg stood up and glanced down at the sleeping old man. 'Who . . . ?'

She rose and glided toward him. 'How the hell should I know?' she answered.

'Why . . . ?' Black Leg asked.

'The shit is a sorcerer, who probably got crossways with another powerful sorcerer. That's what those big-time magical practitioners spend half their time doing, getting one up on each other. You'd think they could find better things to do.'

She was not as tall as she'd looked standing in the water, but she was a comfortable size for kissing. Black

Leg wasn't used to kissing, but after a few minutes, he got into it.

But when he came up for air, she said, 'Damn! Hot damn! You are going to be good. I'm glad I didn't stay in my palace and sulk. You and that old fool pissed me off.'

But Black Leg was preoccupied. 'Sorry,' he said absently. But at the moment he was searching for her breast with his mouth.

She was wearing a dark dress of shiny, greenish purple lily pads. They were shaped like arrowheads and they clung to her, draping themselves over one shoulder. Three blue flowers belonging to the water lily glowed in beams of moonlight that seemed twined in her hair. She was fragrant and smelled like crystal water that somehow harbored the scent of flowers.

He pushed aside one or two of the tiny lily pads with his tongue and found a nipple. He suckled gently.

'Ummmm,' she said. 'My, my, aren't we a darling. Do that again.'

'I'd love to,' Black Leg said. 'But this dress gets in the way.'

'Yes. Well, she likes you, too . . .'

'What?' Black Leg asked.

'The water lily. I'm wearing her.'

'He is an offering to love.' The voice was soft, it seemed only a breath, and Black Leg couldn't be sure he heard it. 'Thank you for letting me share him.'

'Not at all, dear,' she said, stripping off the dress gently. It came away like a gossamer veil, roots, stems, leaves, and the last of the flowers clinging to her hair. Then she dropped it into the stream, where it floated away, pads and flowers on the surface, roots and stems dangling in their element, water.

'Are you here?' Black Leg asked, because now, with the dress gone, it almost seemed he could see the moonlight shining through her.

'Oh, yes. Sometimes I'm translucent, sometimes even transparent. But as long as you see my outline, I'm here. Close your eyes and just use touch.'

Black Leg's hand slid down over her stomach, down to between her legs. He had some education about what was expected of a male at this type of encounter, and he and his foster sister spent some months one summer spying on lovers. Everything he felt seemed to be in . . . order. Nothing unusual. . . .

He probed delicately. 'Is this where it goes?'

'Yes. You're a good boy,' she replied in a throaty whisper.

'My,' she said, reaching down and exploring his body. 'Um . . . you're not only a good boy, you're a big boy,' she cooed. 'I like that. You're even bigger than I thought you'd be.'

'Will it fit?' he asked apprehensively.

'Be quiet,' she said as she covered his mouth with hers.

She stretched out a hand toward the old sorcerer. A faint dark haze hovered over him.

'Don't hurt him,' Black Leg said.

'No. I'm just giving him a little deeper sleep, so he won't bother us.' She spoke as she drew Black Leg toward a thick, soft patch of fern.

When she sank down into the ferns, Black Leg again had the odd sensation that he could see through her body, see the fern fronds form themselves into a bed for her and clasp her legs, hips, breast, and face as she sank down among them.

'Ah,' she whispered as she lifted one hand and drew him down toward her.

'They seemed to know you,' Black Leg said as he knelt between her legs. 'The ferns, I mean.'

'They do, dear, they do. Now, let's try it out and see if it will fit.'

'It's tight,' he said.

'That's the idea,' she told him. 'I'm ready. Hell, you don't know how damn long I've been ready.'

'This feels wonderful,' he whispered. 'Wonderful. I don't think I ever felt anything this good before . . . ever. It is all right to move?'

'Oh, yes. Move all you want. Take your time. We have all night.'

Then they stopped thinking and talking, because both seemed irrelevant to what their bodies were doing for each other, and sank together into bliss.

Later – some time later – she managed to talk him into a midnight swim. She was pleased to find out he was a good swimmer and enjoyed the water.

'My father taught me,' he told her.

'You father? He like you?' she asked.

'Wolf and back? Yes,' Black Leg said. 'Maeniel.'

'I know him!' she said.

'He never mentioned you,' Black Leg said.

'No, I don't mean know him personally,' she said. 'But by reputation. He's got a good reputation. Last I heard, he was shacking with a she-wolf up by the Roman wall.'

'Shacking!' Black Leg said.

'Handfast, jumped over the broom with, keeping company, in tight with. No criticism implied, a secular marriage. Damn few of us go ask the priest to bless us, though it has happened.'

'Won't a blessing mess you up?' Black Leg asked.

'Shit, no! Doesn't bother us. Probably would seem unnecessary to a she-wolf, though. But like as not, it wouldn't bother her either. She might think it a nice touch. Maybe.'

A cloud drifted over the moon and a few drops of rain sprinkled the water. In the sudden darkness, Black Leg heard someone singing a faint but ravishing music that seemed carried on the breeze from some far-off place.

'What?' Black Leg asked.

'She's . . . she's singing. Just enjoy it.'

He did, resting on his back, floating in the lake until the song seemed to dwindle away into the vast silence of night and the stars.

'Who?' he asked.

'The blue water lily,' she said. 'This is the night of her nights. She spends all year preparing for this – these – nights when her flower glows receptive under the moon. Last year it rained like a son of a bitch, flat poured for five days straight nonstop. She didn't get anything done, but likely in the next few nights her favorite moth will find its way out over the lake and . . . she will be able to carry on her line.'

Black Leg was slightly shocked. 'I didn't think flowers . . .'

'What the hell did you think flowers are for, you bonehead?'

'Oh . . .'

'She's dreaming about love, and while she dreams, she sings. And when she sings, I listen. Not too many like her left. She came from another world, one before this one. Being one of a last few is a tremendous responsibility, and she takes it seriously. But they just aren't well adapted to this place. Believe me, it's a lot more rough-and-tumble than it used to be. God! What is that awful noise?'

'I'm sorry,' Black Leg said. 'It's my stomach growling. I'm hungry.'

'Cripe, why didn't you say so? Come on.' She rolled over and dove.

He didn't follow, and a few minutes later, she surfaced again.

'What's the matter with you?' She studied his face for a second, then said, 'Oh, no! Oh, shit! Are you going to start that stupid stuff about me drowning people again?'

'Well . . .' he said.

51

'Listen, nitwit. Why do you think you're floating so nice?'

'I . . .' Black Leg began, then realized he had been floating very easily. The lake held him up rather the way a soft bed might have. 'I . . . don't . . .'

'Yeah, you sure don't,' she said. 'Think at all. The water's holding you because I'm asking it to. That's what I meant about those stupid mopes drowning when I wasn't around. If I had been, I would have dragged them off to shore and told them to pick some less unpleasant way to . . . shuffle off this mortal coil. All I'm doing is inviting you home for dinner.'

'Whose dinner?' he asked.

'Jesus!' Her eyes rolled toward heaven. 'Trust me, you jerk-off. I can do better than raw human any day. I got a lot of friends. We water spirits always do. Now, come on!'

This time he followed. She moved in her own light. Then he realized they were in a tunnel. It seemed made of black rock with letters set into the stone. The letters glowed gold, sunlight gold, metallic gold, the soft textured gold of flowers. Some were green, now grass green, verdant green, emerald, the cloudy shadow of the gemstone, orange, scarlet, purple, amethyst-red fire and roses. After a time, he ran out of comparisons for all the colors he saw.

The passage wasn't filled with water, either. He could surface and take a breath if he wanted to. The first time he did, he found himself floating in a tranquil river under a clear, star-filled sky. In the distance, he could see the firefly lights of a city or a large town.

She surfaced next to him. 'Don't do that,' she said.

He shrugged. 'Why not?'

'That tunnel is – ' She broke off. 'How the hell do I explain? You know what you are?'

They were both up to their necks in the river,

dog-paddling, and the water was cold. At least, to him it was.

'No! What?' he snapped back.

'A damn primitive savage!' she yelled.

'A what?' he shouted, outraged. 'Hey, lady, you invited me along – '

That was as far as he got. She dove, grabbed his legs, and pulled him down. He went under with a yell of fury that nearly drowned him, because his mouth was still open when he went under.

He tore free of her arms, kicked out to keep her off, and found himself bobbing up like a cork. When he next surfaced, he found himself in yet another place. It was broad daylight, and he was in a high-sided canyon of red stone. The river was high, and the current a millrace. The water was being beaten to a froth of white by the action of the current pounding rocks that seemed to sprout like fangs from the riverbed. His body slammed into one hard on his left side, and his left arm went limp.

The water was cold and very clear. He saw the bone leap through the skin as his upper arm broke.

Then she was beside him. 'You goddamn stubborn fool! You unlimited asshole! You . . .'

A tall, thin spire of rock appeared just ahead. She threw her arm around him, pulling him to her breast. The pain hadn't hit yet, but Black Leg knew it would in a second and the arterial blood, red from his arm, was a long streamer in the roaring water.

A second later, her other arm was around the pylon of rock that lifted from the water. He was facing her and saw her eyes dilate with fear. He looked around and saw the falls directly ahead.

CHAPTER TWO

UTHER RODE TOWARD LONDON. HE began the journey from Morgana's stronghold when he heard the Saxons at the fortress along the coast held the horse fights this year. That meant they would have chosen a war leader, and he knew he'd best move against them before they could feel for a vulnerable spot and jump him.

He was in trouble without his son. More and more in the last three years Uther had associated his son with him in ruling. More and more the youngster had been picking up the slack.

Merlin had well known what he was doing when he exiled the boy. Aside from the drastic emotional blow it dealt him, Arthur's absence made the king's job twice as hard.

The High Kingship was the nexus of forces that in the nature of things were diametrically opposed to each other. The system he headed worked well and had done so time out of mind. And in the process made Alba one of the most prosperous places outside of the east where irrigation produced almost unimaginable wealth for some and unspeakable misery for others.

But Alba, the White Isle, had escaped the cruelty of becoming too stratified a society, with a few literally drowning in wealth, the many either broken by the burden of finding shelter, clothing, and enough food to keep body and soul together, the lowest classes serving their masters as domestics, household labor, beasts of burden, shepherds, field hands, and manual laborers, or having to offer up their bodies to gain the right to at least temporary existence as whores or gladiators.

Alba and her people had for a long time escaped this fate. Tradition said the Painted People had created this system and – never conquerors – had been able to peacefully persuade the rest to accept it.

It was vested in their women. Women like Morgana, who could speak for the land goddess and could create a king either by birth or the acceptance of him in sacred marriage.

For this is where we all come from, the dark, moist passage between a woman's legs. And if the woman will not open her body to us in love or squat down and bring us forth in blood and torment, then we cannot live. And if we cannot warm the earth with a plow or send out beasts to feed on her green mantle, then we would wander over the land that rejects us – and die.

But a woman can be forced and the earth ruined, and both happened when the Romans came. The prosperity of Alba and Gaul drew them like vicious wasps, and they, not ever understanding the great achievements of his people, destroyed it without ever understanding that there was anything to destroy.

Against stupidity, the gods themselves contend in vain. And the same might be said for greed, also. The conquering, militaristic Romans had an ample supply of both in their nature.

Before the Romans disrupted this magnificent and ancient system, the high king presided over a balanced realm. The fair south, ruled by its cattle lords, produced a vast quantity of food, more than enough even in the worst years to banish famine forever from the White Isle. His people, the Silures, ruled themselves in accord with the warrior societies. The democracy of the war band drew them together to resist outsiders even as they in the end successfully held off the Romans. They paid a high price for their freedom, but it had been worth the cost. His people were rich in timber, amber, gold and silver, hides, and iron.

The king was usually chosen from among them because he was able to win the support of the powerful war bands. But he in turn usually chose his tanist and successor from among the rich, southern farmers. And that ruler in turn chose his tanist from the Painted People.

So the High Kingship moved from one power base to another. The deep forests of Wales, the southern ring-forts such as Maden Castle or Cadbury, to the high fastness of the oak wood overlooking the North Sea dominated by the Pictish queens – the Dragon People, as they were called.

The Veneti helped tie them together. They were in the beginning a subtribe of the Painted People, but in time they became a sailing and trading society. They helped the Painted People exploit the rich fisheries of the cold, gray sea, where whale, ling, cod, and walrus abounded. But they also sailed south into the blue Aegean, the lands of honey, oil, and wine. They traded with the Egyptians at the Nile Delta, the Minoans at Crete, and the distant city-states on the plain of Sumer at the Tigris and Euphrates Rivers, and were represented at Sidon and Tyre in the cities of the Phoenician Coast.

Then the Romans came.

They smashed the prosperous southern kingdoms, depriving the high king of his most important power base. After Bodiccia's revolt, they made war on the people themselves, exterminating without mercy the best farmers in the kingdom and selling the few surviving women and children as slaves.

But the land was still there, and the land was good and rich. Others moved in to fill the vacancy left by the murdered tribesmen, displaced farmers from Italy, legionary veterans too old or crippled for the endless wars the Roman state engendered. Landowners from Gaul, fleeing the chaos created by the brawls among Roman aristocrats, fighting for the now dwindling spoils of conquest, endless brutality, and bottomless greed remaining from the great thieving conquerors of the past.

Then, last but not least, the weary Roman authorities who feared and distrusted the peoples of Alba hired the Saxons to defend the fortifications and estates that controlled the Humber, Wash, and Themis, and were the key to dominating the island's rich heart. This was an assault on its freedom – a stake through that same heart.

These Saxons were the natural allies of the landowners of the south when, to their boundless horror, they were abandoned by the once seemingly all-powerful Romans. They were fearful of the Picts to the north and the tribal people to the west and the Saxon seafarers trying to dominate the sea lanes.

To their credit, the high kings who had led the long resistance to the Roman Imperium in Wales and the highlands now were willing to include the southern landowners in their kingdom and offer them the protection the Romans had failed to accord them.

But the south felt it had the right to rule the west. Their allies, the Saxons and the archdruid Merlin, were treacherous to the bone. Merlin's power play led to the murder of High King Vortigen. In the ensuing power struggle, the disparate parts of the kingdom had a lot more strength than Merlin and the Saxons gave them credit for. And after seven years of savage warfare, the Roman-British landlords to the south realized they must yield and allow the High Kingship to be revived if they hoped for even a semblance of peace.

A semblance, that's what it was. A counterfeit of what had been a fairly smoothly functioning alliance. Brushfire wars flared on the borders of Wales, Saxon pirates harried the coast, and the endless diplomatic meddling of the dying imperium created friction where none was warranted, all of this making the high king's attempts to keep the peace difficult, and at times, next to impossible.

But the game was not over yet.

Uther had given his life to it and Arthur might successfully return the High Kingship to its primal power and influence. That was why he had been born and trained to rule since he first drew breath. And why Merlin and his bitch paramour had tried to destroy him. Uther shuddered at the memory of the day he had . . .

'My Lord King.'

Uther gave a start. Morgana was riding at his knee.

'Mind your pace, my lord. We are killing the horses,' she told him.

Uther drew rein and slowed his mount to an amble. Then, hearing the beast blowing, to a walk. He looked back and saw his force strung out behind him, not a good formation in potentially hostile country.

'I was . . . preoccupied,' he said.

'Yes,' she answered. 'But we left the forest some time ago.'

Uther knew that in the open his force might easily draw an attack. Probably not a serious one, not this early in the game. No, the early stages would likely be a feeling-out contest. To give his opponent – whoever the Saxon lords had chosen as a war leader – an early victory would be a dangerous mistake.

The Saxon lords would still have their doubts about

their new leader. If he carried off even a small-scale assault successfully, it would go far to remove those doubts.

Uther could still see the traces his people left on the land. In the distance, the low hummocks of a plowed-down ring-fort, no more than a half-ruined stone circle, and the groves, the sacred groves still planted along the watercourses and around springs. Or in areas where the ground was too broken to yield to the plow. The Romans made up lurid stories about what went on in these groves, not having the slightest understanding of why they existed.

The road went past one ahead. The trees, oak and beech, looked as though they might offer welcome shade and forage for both horses and men. It was a large one, a small forest in reality, and likely included a spring or two, where they could water the horses and replenish their own supplies.

Normally he would give it a wide berth in open country like this. Such woodlots could conceal an ambush, also.

He nodded toward Morgana and pointed. 'Get some of the boys.'

She raised one arm and signaled with her fingers. Six young men dashed forward and paced the king. They were drenched with perspiration, as were their lathered horses, but the horses pranced without the encouragement of whip or spur, and the boys looked delighted to be noticed by their king and chief priestess.

'Secure the grove ahead,' Uther directed. 'We will rest there, and I don't want to ride into an ambush.'

The youngsters tore out whooping and yelling, horses racing over the ground toward the trees.

'My God,' Uther whispered. 'To be young and foolish again.'

Morgana laughed, but sobered immediately. 'Foolish it

is,' she said. 'If anyone is waiting there, they will certainly draw their fire.'

'That's the idea,' Uther answered.

One of the dark priestesses reached Uther's side. She wore the skin of a panther over her helmet, the curved fangs pressed against her forehead, the paws hanging over her shoulders, claws dangling. She was slim, her long, dark hair braided in seven plaits that dangled at her shoulders. Her arms were tattooed and her face bore blue-stained scars like the rake of a cat's claws.

She grunted her approval of the boys' tactics, then set off, followed by a dozen older warriors, moving more slowly. Uther knew at least a hundred more of the Cat Society waited in the background to follow up if an ambush should occur.

He really didn't expect one, but it was safest to check.

Morgana raised her arm again and moved her fingers in a complex pattern. And Uther knew that, should an ambush occur, without his ever giving a command, the remaining warrior societies would encircle the grove and slaughter the attacking troops.

This far out into the hinterlands, they would probably be poorly armed, slingers, archers, and spearmen at best, while his men were heavy cavalry, riding the Celtic saddle that molded itself to the horses' backs and whose horns bent under weight of a rider and supported his thighs, maintaining him firmly astride his horse. Moreover, they all had boiled leather armor sewn with metal plates, carried good swords and bull hide shields that could deflect the swiftest arrow, the most viciously slung sling missile, and even an iron-headed spear.

'Good exercise for them,' Morgana said. 'But no one is going to bother us here. If they're waiting, it will be further down the road toward London, likely at a river ford. Or in the city itself.'

'Then they will be disappointed,' Uther muttered.

'Because I'm not going to London. At least, not as king. When we depart the grove this evening, I will ride to London with a few of my most trusted men. You and the dark ladies will turn and invest Cadbury.'

'Cadbury. The place is a ruin,' Morgana said.

'Doesn't matter. It can be held even by a small, poorly armed force. And I want you to take and defend any other hill-forts you can.'

'God!' she whispered. 'I see your strategy. But the risk. If the Saxons should be in the city already? You could be killed.'

'I know,' he said. 'But if I'm not, I will know who is loyal and who isn't. Move into the hill-forts and consolidate your position. If I am killed – and you will hear of it if I am – attack the city. Show no mercy. Wipe out the Saxon garrison there, disperse the inhabitants, burn it to the ground. It is the dwelling place of the most powerful families in the Themis valley. Then scorch the earth from Cadbury to the wash. Burn every farm and villa from the meanest to the mightiest. Trample the green wheat, girdle the orchards, drive off the livestock, spoil what the army cannot consume. Ignore the cities. They will wither and die without the countryside to sustain them.'

'My lord,' Morgana whispered. 'That would be a costly campaign, not only in terms of our own army. But many of those still loyal to the high king will turn their backs on us and go their own way. Besides, think of the horror and devastation. We will strangle our own blood. Not since the Iceni revolt have any dared to strike so murderously at our own realm.'

'Yes,' Uther said. 'But once the campaign is completed, the south will be no further trouble to the rest of us for a generation or two, and it will give us time to reinvent the High Kingship and rebuild our ancient alliances. When I took the road with the greater part of our warriors, it was my intention to do this. But I can't bring myself to be the cause of the destruction of so many innocent lives. So much that remains good in our realm. Morgana, I can't. I must try to find some other solution.'

'It would be a . . . solution. Of sorts,' she said.

'A solution, a savage crime. A nightmare from which our people might never recover,' Uther said. 'If we move now, the big estates, the Saxons guarding the shores, will never be able to muster an opposing force. And make no mistake. If I die, I die the last high king of the Britons. There will likely never be another. So, Morgana, if I fall, carry out my orders. I have spent my life as you have, building this army. Use it to do as I ask.'

Morgana sat on her horse, feeling the chill in her bones. In her heart she knew Uther was right. Her people would never be able to muster an army like this again.

While she watched, the young men came straggling back, laughing, from the grove. Someone had surprised a sleeping deer. She and her fawn were slung over the saddle of the priestess, while the woman walked, leading her mount.

She grinned at Morgana. 'We have a good start on supper,' she said, poking the empty-eyed doe.

An arrow protruded from the neck of the doe. She'd been field-dressed and was still dripping blood on the ground.

Morgana bowed her head down to her horse's mane and clenched her fist in the long, coarse hair.

'Are you ill, my lady?' the war priestess asked.

Morgana pulled herself upright. 'No. No. Merely tired. It's been a hard ride.'

'Well,' the priestess said. 'We can camp here safely. I got the deer and saw the tracks of wild cattle. But no trace of humans, though there is a ruin there.' The woman made a sign against the evil eye. 'It's near the spring. Someone worshiped there . . . once. There is a pillar and a tree with a face in the wood. But nothing more.'

Then she continued on, leaving Morgana and Uther standing there.

The rest of the army was catching up. Some were exploring the grove, others preparing to light cooking fires. A few shouts and whoops in the distance suggested the soldiers had located the wild cattle.

The two leaders sat side by side. Morgana was working out the logistics.

Invest the hill-forts. She could easily take them by surprise. Few, if any, were adequately defended.

Then she could use them as a base to raid the farms and villas all summer. No, she couldn't take the fortified places, but she could lay waste the countryside. Like Bodiccia, she would run wild for a few months.

But then! Retreat back into the heavily wooded countryside of Wales and Dumnonia. Uther was right; it would take years for the south to recover. If she were sufficiently remorseless, two generations or more.

She shivered. To accomplish that, she would have to do as the Romans had done after the Iceni revolt: slaughter the men, sell the women and children into slavery. There would be buyers aplenty; the slave trade was booming.

'I want you to give me your word that you will do as I ask,' Uther said.

Morgana swallowed. She really had no choice; he was her king and she was sworn to obey him to the death.

'I'm not sure I can,' she whispered.

'Your word, Morgana,' he demanded. 'I want your word, as you are my chief consular. Promise me you will do as I ask. Harden your heart and do as I command.'

All around them the army swirled, lighting fires, unsaddling horses, setting up pickets for the pack animals, a cheerful babble of noise as they laid out their encampment. The two still sat alone together, mounted, speaking in low voices.

'Very well. I promise. But in return, I want your promise you will take Gwain and Cai with you when you ride to London. They are the best of the best. You can have no nobler companions.'

Uther nodded. 'I will. Send them to me at sunset.'

'So soon?' Morgana said.

'The quicker the better. If anything is to be done, I must get to the powers that be in London before their minds are made up. Your promise, my lady.'

Morgana said, 'Yes, I give you my word. Not even grass will grow where this army passes when the war horns blow retreat.'

What I was doing, or rather going to do, was dangerous. I didn't know how dangerous. But even if I had clearly grasped the perils of calling up the dead, I don't think I would have been turned aside by the risk. Because it was nothing to the physical risk we were running. All of us. If I couldn't burn that fortress, we would likely die, if not in battle, then in that grove with the rest of the unfortunates the Saxon pirates devoted to their gods.

Those spirits weren't loving, merciful, or compassionate. The Saxons primarily asked them for luck, and they drove a hard bargain. If the pirates got it, the spirits expected to claim their share of the spoils. And that included the prisoners and slaves.

Now the things crouching in the grove were glutted with blood and cries of terror and pain, and pale maggots crusted rotting flesh. So perhaps they would sleep while I worked my wiles. I hoped they would deem the two – no, three – we killed as simply another offering.

When I reached the village, or rather the posts that once held houses, I tried not to look to my right where the things hung in the trees. It gave me chills to think that

64

my summoning the dead might make one of the bodies swinging from a rotted rope break free and try to seize me. But when I turned toward the house posts, I found the wind was to my face. I couldn't smell them, and I could feel only an emptiness where they were.

And I understood whatever might happen, their spirits were free and gone up among the stars to follow what paths they would. Yes, even the woman Albe slew out of mercy for her plight.

Death by murderous sacrifice had sent them into the winds of heaven. I felt the peace, a strange peace that is the end of pain. A sense of absolute release.

But not on the side of the road by the village. Both water and air were unnaturally still, and I was sure some lingered.

Life is a fire. We all burn. That is the meaning of my fire hand.

But we burn slowly. You can feel the heat rising from the young newborns in their cradles, toddlers at their mothers' breasts. How and why we burn I don't know. And I wonder if our kind will ever know. But we do. And even in the old – the very old – you can see the darkening coals still glowing in the ashes.

I knelt facing the house posts. They were carven and some of the carvings survived even the fire that destroyed the houses. They twisted with things belonging to the marshland, serpents, serpentine long-necked water-birds, sedges, cattails, pickerelweed, and wild water lilies, eels and fish, frogs, toads. And crowning the posts where the tops remained, the sea eagles, hooked beaks agape, talons clenched in birds, fish, frogs, or snakes, rearing proudly to cry defiance at the sky.

The birds are Her creatures and the priestesses who gather the clean bones of the dead wear bird masks. And the sea eagle is the most ancient guardian of the dead.

I put my hands, both hands, palms up, into the water

and looked out over the still, silent mire beyond where the houses once stood. Not even a breath of breeze ruffled the perfectly calm surface. It mirrored the sky, scattered sprinkles of sunlight that touched the water. But the clouds were more like soot now and it looked to rain before nightfall, so the sparkles came and went. And I looked beyond time into eternity.

The first face that formed between the palms of my hands was a child's. He – for it was a boy – looked up at me with the beautiful incomprehension that is absolute innocence.

He died, but didn't know how or why and didn't even resent that he had. All he knew was that one moment he had been warm, sleeping snugly between his parents with his brothers and sisters. And the next, a confused impression of shouts, the stench of thick smoke, and then the knowledge that he was part of the dark, cloudy water and would be for some indefinite time.

I drew my mind back and let him go. I had a brief impression of dark hair and eyes looking up into mine, then the eyes faded to hollows in a small skull. Then it also vanished away and again I was looking down into my own reflection.

Then she came. Finger bones clutched my right hand. I could see them glowing whiter than flesh, wrapped around my hand. The nails bit into my skin, I think drawing blood.

Rage was all that remained of her. She didn't think or know who or what she was. She knew she had been murdered, drowned not in water but mud, after she had been used by the attackers. Used in a variety of painful and ugly ways.

She wanted her man and her children, but couldn't find them. She rode the sea tides daily, tumbled along the bottom in the green gloom. Boundless rage and despair soaked into my mind the way water sinks into dry earth, seeming to vanish but changing the nature of the soil as it saturates it.

I felt weak and ill, and I wanted to vomit. I was full of that vile wine that Gray, Maeniel, and Ure practically forced down my throat. It clouded my mind and weakened me.

So I didn't pull my hand out quickly enough. But let's be fair. Even had I been capable of considered reflection and clear thinking, I might have welcomed him, because I needed help desperately and I wasn't sure what it might take to burn that fortress and the men inside of it. If you are going to do evil, you can't cry off just because the means to your end turns your stomach.

But I did vomit when the snake coiled around my wrist. When my stomach emptied itself, I tried to be careful not to let the spasms alarm the reptile. I saw the triangular head through the water and knew if it cared to strike, I was doomed, because it was one of the poisonous ones.

The musculature of a snake is wonderful, tight, hard, and almost infinitely flexible, yet cold and menacing at the same time.

I go back and forth about whether he ever was completely human. I have never been able to really decide. But on balance, I think he was.

I do know how he died, though. The rite is an ancient one, but once so widespread that even the Romans knew about it, though their favorite way of propitiating the gods directly is burial alive. When victims were intended to be placed in the divine presence intact, not used for entertainment the way condemned criminals are, fed to beasts or forced to fight as gladiators do, the Romans buried them alive and left them to suffocate in stone chambers underground.

But we preferred to shoot them to death with arrows. The man – and it is always a man – is hung up, then the

67

archers fire arrows into his body, taking care not to kill him because the longer the offering lasts, the better the oracle is and the more the dark powers are pleased.

He died this way twice, when the people who built the village came to settle here, his blood running into the water as a life stream hallowed their efforts. And at the end, when the Saxons stormed and burned the houses, they gave him to their gods.

But I don't think they could take him. He was too much part of the fens. I felt them in him, the deep channels where the water is clouded and green and silt drifts along the bottom pulled back and forth by the tide. Not water, not land, a shadowed ooze that nurtures the creatures of both land and sea. Fish, shrimp, crab, and crayfish, a hundred kinds of ducks and geese fed on the abundant crustacean life and pale-green waterweed that filled the pools, canals, ponds, and ditches. Bog plants flourished, purple-flowered spikes of pickerelweed, broad green leaves lifting from the water to spread cooling shade in the shallows. Abundant yellow-flowered cress choked the freshwater canals, and fed the geese that settled like pale clouds on the water and nested among the hard stems of horsetail and reed.

He had power, the thing that flowed up my arm from the coiled serpent. Power bought and paid for in pain, blood, sorrow, and death. The way all real power is bought. They had been his people, and at dawn he climbed the house posts, using the carvings as a serpent ladder, and coiled on the matting at first light, near the fire. And awaited his offerings of live mice, milk, and honey.

And always he received them.

The serpent fell away from my wrist toward the dark depths, though I could tell it was loath to leave, for their kind burns lower than ours do and they love our fire. He obeyed the command of his 'possessor.' And I understood more of hate, love, anger, and revenge than I had wanted to. My mind was drenched with all four, and I knew I could burn that fortress down.

Black Leg wasn't prepared for the sick fear that gripped him when he saw the blood in the water. He had never experienced a major life-threatening injury before. But thanks to a fairly large number of minor ones, he knew what to do.

The worst being when he and Guinevere had been detected by a pair of lovers they were sneaking up on. A rock thrown by the strong arm of an adult male can cause a fearsome injury. The first stone clipped her over the ear. He didn't feel the second crack into the back of his head. They both were already in full flight, running away as fast as they could.

When they slowed and came to a stop about two miles away, she told him, 'You have blood running down your neck, staining your collar.'

He reached back, felt the warm, sticky trickle, tasted it to be sure . . . then plunged into the wolf. He was a boy again before he hit the ground, still wearing his clothes but rolling on the turf, the injury healed. When he got his footing, he saw she'd been hurt, too, and the blood was pouring down over and around her left ear.

'No!' he said, then realized she couldn't do the same thing he had.

She gave him a strange look, the sort of look she had given him when she sent him away. Only then he hadn't understood what it meant. Not then. But later, after she told him they could never be lovers, that look became clear to him.

His blood was staining the rapids red. Black Leg knew he had to chance the falls.

He went wolf.

He heard the water spirit scream, 'No!'

Then he shot into space.

'Fall. . . .' He heard his father speaking. 'Curl your body in on itself.'

Black Leg did, pulling his tail up between his hind legs, arching his neck to push his head down between his forelegs. Beauty, terror, detachment; all lived in his mind simultaneously.

Beauty because the falls was a breathtaking thing of beauty, the water a wavering, golden curtain in the afternoon sun, limned with rainbows as the light struck down into the mist. Above, he saw the water spirit come down. At the ledge, she elongated, dissolved, becoming one with water, light, and mist.

Then something like a horse kick hit his back. That was terror, because his whole body went numb and he thought his spine had snapped and he didn't know if even the change could heal that.

Then, at last, detachment, because he was sure he was going to die and rather belatedly understood that he would be dead before he could worry about it or even feel any pain. He saw his own muzzle with bubbles rising up from his mouth, forepaws drifting beside the dark nose.

Then the Weyvern appeared in the blue gloom, the giant dragon jaws picketed with teeth like spearheads. Reflex thrust him into the change, and he almost laughed. What the hell was wolf or man going to do against a thing like that?

A split second later, the claws on one foreleg closed around him like a cage, four claws around his back, one thumb claw across his chest. Up, up, up they flew. The Weyvern broached like a porpoise or a leaping whale, coming almost a full body length out of the water.

Black Leg vomited, then screamed.

A second later, he was free and the monster dove

down, vanishing into the dark, hazy blueness at the foot of the roaring, storming falls.

Black Leg may have walked on water. He was never afterward sure how he got out of the river. The only thing, or things, he remembered about the next minute were the sight of a nearby shore made up of fallen slabs of stone tilted helter-skelter against one another and a seemingly unpleasantly long time span before he reached it.

Then a second later, he was standing well away from the water on one of the more horizontal rocks, looking down and watching 'her,' the water spirit, rising from the depths with languid grace, swimming up toward the light. Every hair on Black Leg's back, neck, and head stood straight up. She broke the surface and swam toward him.

'That was you!' he screeched. 'You! What – do – you – really – look – like?'

She ducked under the water to protect her ears as echoes boomed out from all over the canyon.

'Jesus Christ! Son of God – Savior,' she added hurriedly. 'Stop screeching. As for what I look like, you stupid asshole, what the hell do *you* look like? Wolf, human, human wolf? Holy and eternal God, I don't know what to grab. I damn near killed you. I was just hoping you wouldn't change again, you pinhead, while I was getting you up to air, and manage – in spite of my most earnest efforts – to drown yourself.'

'Why that thing?'

She looked deeply annoyed. Deeply annoyed.

'Bend an ear in my direction and listen . . . quietly.' She was speaking in a rather low tone of voice, but Black Leg backed up a few paces anyway.

'That thing – those things, I should say, once there were a lot of them – swims tremendously well. Once upon a time there was no river they couldn't negotiate, though most of the time they lived in the sea. But they are long gone now, yet the shape is still encoded into my ... my ... God, you're ignorant as dirt. Life substance, and I can be one, if the need arises. As – it – just – did. Satisfied?'

'I don't think I want any more to do with you,' Black Leg said stiffly.

'Yeah, fine. How are you going to get home? Because I have a horrible feeling we're both stranded.'

'Stranded?' he heard himself say dimly.

'Yeah! Stranded!' she said as she hauled herself out of the water onto another nearby flat rock.

Black Leg noticed she'd found herself another dress. It was a mass of round, green, succulent leaves, dotted with small, red flowers, blazing scarlet flowers, in fact. It fit rather like a loincloth on the bottom, but was more of a bustier at the top, surrounding and supporting her small but well-shaped breasts.

'New friend?' he asked, gesturing at it.

She nodded. 'Grows on the rocks around the falls. It has problems, or maybe I should say *he* has problems. It's a he. Well established vegetatively, but hasn't seen a female in a long time. Believes there must be some downstream, though, because there's a small bird thing comes around for nectar and will make deliveries if asked.'

'Dugald didn't teach me about these things,' Black Leg complained.

'Probably thinks they're beneath his notice,' she said.

'Why are we stranded?' he asked.

She pointed down to the water. 'Remember the passage?'

Black Leg nodded.

'I can't get back to it,' she said.

Black Leg had been squatting down on the rock. He stood and took stock of the situation.

To his left, the falls plunged down from what seemed

72

an incredible height. On all sides, the canyon walls rose ever further up toward a blue sky. The pool he was looking at formed the widest spot in the canyon; ahead, the rock slide ran along one side of the river, forming a jumble of boulders at the foot of the wall.

'Where are we?' he whispered.

She looked morosely out over the blue pool and said, 'I don't know.'

'How can you not know?' he snapped. 'You know what's along the passage. I swam into it with you.'

'Yeah, and you'd have been just fine if you had done what I told you. But no, you had to go exploring on your own. The opening in the passage is above the falls, and unless you can figure out a way to fly, we're cut off until I can find another gateway back into it.'

'You can't fly?' he asked rather weakly.

'No. It's among the few things I can't do. Mind you, I'm one of the most powerful supernatural beings you will ever meet – but flying is not one of my many accomplishments.'

'We're in trouble,' Black Leg said.

'The boy is a genius. He finally figured something out.'

'I'm sick of you telling me how dumb I am,' Black Leg flared up at her.

'Then try using your head for something better than to hold your ears up,' she snapped back.

'What are we going to do?' He heard a sort of quiver in his own voice that frightened him.

Then he became a wolf. He found the shape consoling, and at the moment, he needed a little consolation.

He didn't get it. The wolf informed him that he was hungry and that it was high time Black Leg did something about their mutual problem.

He returned to his human shape.

'We're hungry,' he told her sullenly.

'Yeah – I forgot. When they're not horny, they're

hungry. And they always turn to the nearest woman and expect her to do something about it. If not one, then it's the other.'

'Why do you work at being nasty?' he snapped.

Her eyes closed. She put one finger at the top of her nose between the eyes, and food arrived.

The rock she was standing on was more or less level. A cloth appeared and covered part of it, the tail end hanging down toward the river. A platter of sliced meat, followed quickly by a bowl of gravy. A plate filled with fruit appeared, then a big loaf of bread, along with two wine jugs.

'Come on. Let's eat,' she said. 'I was hoping to serve this at home, but since we're lost . . .'

'How . . .' Black Leg began.

'No!' It was a rather resounding *no*. 'Shut up and eat. Start with the questions, we get into a fight . . . next thing you know, the food is cold, it's sundown, and we're still hungry. Eat! Questions later.'

Black Leg hopped across a bunch of slabs to the flat rock where she stood, and they fell on the food as though they were both starving. When they finished, both leaned back against the sun-warmed stone and tried to get a little glow on from the wine.

By now the sun had moved and the canyon was growing darker. The constant wind that flowed along the river was a little chilly on Black Leg's bare skin. But he didn't want to turn wolf; the slight buzz he was feeling would disappear. He knew this from a rather unpleasant experience when he'd gone drinking with Bain, the chief's son, and some of his friends in the war band.

They hadn't believed him about his wolf side – or they pretended not to believe him in order to get him to perform. He had been drunk enough to do so. He leaped into the air and made an idiot out of himself by getting tangled in his clothing and rolling all over the shingle beach, trying to free himself.

He hadn't known his father was nearby until he saw his eyes glow behind Bain and his friends.

Maeniel launched himself at them with a roar so loud that several of the drunker ones nearly drowned in the incoming tide trying to escape him. Then – they were both still wolf – his father got him by the scruff of the neck and shook him until his teeth rattled and Black Leg yowled for mercy.

He ended up stone-cold sober, being dragged home by the ear by a very vile-tempered Maeniel. Wolf or human, Black Leg's ear was tender and remained in the same place. His father was furious and had a good grip.

Maeniel wasn't one to lecture, but his comments on the way home about drunken foolishness and the abuse of protective powers sank in and made a strong impression on Black Leg's mind. And being sobered so quickly was rather like a hard kick in the stomach.

So Black Leg relaxed and concentrated on maintaining his mild level of intoxication.

'Nice, isn't it?' she said, looking up at the falls and the shadowed river.

From time to time the eternal wind brought mist drifting down from the falls to further refresh them and please the little vine she was wearing. Or maybe almost wearing, because those beautiful smooth, creamy breasts remained bare, even though those brilliant red flowers and leaves surrounded and supported them.

'What are you thinking about?' she asked.

'I'll bet,' he said, 'I'm thinking about the same thing you are.'

She chuckled. 'Men only think about two things, and the other one is food.'

'Seriously,' he said. 'How do we get out of here?'

'Seriously,' she answered, 'I don't know. Are you anxious to leave?'

He had one hand on her leg. As with the water lily, the red-flowered vine made music. It didn't sing, but in the distance, Black Leg could hear a stringed instrument being plucked one note at a time as it rippled through a melody that managed to be alien and yet hauntingly familiar at the same time. His hand moved up and his fingers brushed the dark smooth leaves and the satin-soft flower petals at her groin.

'Gentle friend!' she whispered.

Black Leg felt it withdraw and saw from the corner of his eye that it had taken residence among the fissures of the stone around them. She was warm and the rock they lay on still held the sun's heat. Then he remembered the Weyvern.

'Not that it matters,' he said, 'but what do you really look like?'

She laughed a little and he felt her lips on his. 'I don't really look like anything. I'm mostly water.' She snorted softly. 'So are you. Didn't that Druid who brought you up teach you anything?'

She blew into his ear softly, very softly, and chewed gently on his earlobe with her teeth.

'Yeah!' Black Leg said as the small love bite took full effect.

'God, but you're easy,' she said. 'Want to see if it still fits?'

'Oh, yes!' This was fervent.

'*Mummmoo. Ah,*' she said. 'It does. Fancy that. Oh, yes, you're a big boy. A very big boy. I could forgive you for anything.'

He thought that was nice to know. But for a short time, they were very busy and he forgot what she'd said.

When they finished, he lay for a time with his head pillowed on her arm, studying her profile silhouetted against the warm orange rock walls on the other side of the canyon.

'Where did you get the food?' he asked. 'And what was that meat? It was good.'

'In the shape we were in, anything would taste good,' she said. 'But . . . the meat was probably horse and the food was an offering. So since it was offered, I control it. I brought it here so we could snack. He's a good cook and his people are old friends of mine.'

'He?' Black Leg asked.

'Cregan,' she supplied the name. 'He's probably the best warrior in the world.'

'You know about things like this?'

She nodded. 'I get around and I hear things.'

'Think he would take a . . . pupil?' Black Leg asked.

She sighed deeply. 'Damn! You have aspirations in that direction?'

'Yes!'

She cuddled him a little with her arm. He kissed the curve of her breast above the nipple.

'Nice. Nice. Why don't you just stay with me?'

Black Leg immediately pulled away. She sighed again.

'I forgot,' she said. 'You're young. Got to get it out of your system. Am I right?'

'Probably,' he answered. 'Besides . . .' His voice trailed off. He didn't want to offend her and was also a little afraid of her. She had shown a rather casual use of what were probably immense powers.

'I know. I know. You don't love me,' she finished the sentence for him. 'I'm good for a tumble in the hay – maybe a lot more than just one tumble – but your heart belongs to that bitchy blonde who dumped you for some jackass she saw all of three times in her life. Oh! But – he's a king!'

Black Leg went wolf and tried to jump up. But with casual ease, she got him by the scruff of the neck and pulled him back down.

'Quit it! And listen.'

Black Leg decided it might be the better part of valor to do so. He lay quietly, head against her arm, human again. The ability she'd just demonstrated to change him back from wolf to man was far beyond his comprehension.

'Are you a . . . are you "Her"?'

She began laughing. 'No, I'm not a goddess. I'm mortal, just like you. And like the Faun your little blond friend killed.'

'How do you know about that?' he asked.

'How do I know? The whole world rang with the pity and terror of it.'

Suddenly he was afraid for Guinevere. 'She . . . didn't . . .'

'I know, I know.'

His head was still resting on her left shoulder. She waved her right hand in a dismissive gesture.

'She – the Child of Light, because that's what her name means – she did what she was told. The great goddess had condemned him to death. The little one just carried out the sentence. But we mortals are entitled to our opinions. He, the Faun, was of my kind. There are very few of us left. The Fauns ruled the forests; we the waters; the dragons the seas.

'Since he was one of my kind, I find myself even more devastated by his death than I thought I would be. Though he was guilty of great evil, it was hard to see him slip away. Though he forgave your friend when she set him free.

'Warrior. You want to be a warrior?'

The abrupt change of subject disconcerted Black Leg. He sat up on the edge of the slab and dangled his feet over the river. It was still warm, but the sun was withdrawing more and more. In the canyon, the shadows lengthened. The wind was beginning to grow cold. Black Leg felt uneasy.

'Soon it's going to be dark,' he said. 'If we can't get back, I don't think it will matter much about what I want to do with my life. I want to have one to play around with.'

She laughed. 'Hell, I've been down lots of roads along the tunnel. Got stranded a few times. I always got out all right. So will you. You're long-lived, like me. The power to change does that – gives you long life.'

'That's why she turned me down,' he said.

'Yeah. And I can't say I blame her. We're best with our own kind. But still, I think she could have given it a little tiny bit more thought than she did. But the only bigger screwballs than human men are women.'

'How so?' Black Leg bridled.

'Simple. She knows you well. Hell, she knows you almost as well as she knows herself. You're good-looking, good-natured – that's important – smart, and she gets her arms around you long enough to know you're probably good in bed. But nooooo . . . she can't wait to go running after . . .'

Black Leg waited a minute, then prompted, 'What?'

'I don't know,' she said. 'He used to come to my well in the mountains with his kin. They made offerings and didn't pollute the water. They knew the rules and taught him how to behave himself. But in my life, I've met maybe four – no, five – mortal men who frightened me. He's one of them.'

'Fine!' Black Leg commented. 'Just fine.'

She nodded uh-huh. 'Just fine. And I've had a long life. But this kid scares the shit out of me.'

'How long?' Black Leg asked.

'Full of questions,' she said.

'You cause me to want to ask a lot of questions. You are one peculiar being.'

By now she was up and seated beside him.

'I suppose I am . . . to you. But believe me, I'm

79

completely predictable. Part of the logic of the universe.'

'The logic of the universe?' Black Leg repeated.

'Yes,' she said.

'Well, I wish you would logic us out of here. It's getting cold, and I'm getting scared.'

'Turn wolf,' she said. 'Your fur . . .'

'No,' he told her. 'I'm about half drunk on the wine. If I turn wolf, I'll lose my buzz. I won't be cold, but I'll be even more scared than I am now.

'You must be getting cold, too,' he said. 'Your friend's not back.'

'The vine,' she said. 'I know. And I'm sort of bothered by that. It's scared and I'm not sure about what.'

'It can't tell you?'

'No. The water lily's more verbal, but it's been alone a long time. There's no gardener here to look out for it. And its music . . . is . . .'

Black Leg heard the trill of notes again. A distant harp.

'It won't come out, and acts like it expects me to know why. But I don't comprehend the language it speaks well and—'

Just then the bird landed on a spearhead of rock near Black Leg's arm. He was astounded, thinking at first that it was Magetsky.

'What's she . . . ?' he began.

Then the bird gave a cry like a single, ringing note of a silver bell, and he knew it wasn't Magetsky, couldn't be.

Black Leg found he was afraid of it. His hackles rose and he felt the wolf slide over him like a cloud covers the sun and creates not darkness but shadow change. And he knew something more than the wolf was summoned. He drew on reserves he didn't know he had.

The bird gave another cry and the ravens swept like a black wave down the canyon from caves above the waterfall.

The bird went for Black Leg's eye with its sharp, onyx beak . . . and got it.

There wasn't time for Black Leg's brain to register the shock of absolute pain that losing an eye creates. Instead, it comprehended something infinitely worse, willed by the thing that inhabited the bird.

'I cripple . . . I destroy your life, wolf. When I am done with you, wolf, you will be bereft of sight, hearing, your mortal body punctured with a thousand wounds that will by suppuration cause you untold agony. You will have life of a sort for a time. But you will not desire to continue your existence in such a guise. And so you will pass from hence into a sea of madness, then all unknowing into oblivion. I am from the dead and the change is useless against my power.'

Even as the bird took his eye, Black Leg's jaws closed on it. The thing powdered the way a chunk of wood turned to charcoal by a roaring blaze retains its shape even though its remaining substance is ash.

Then the powdered ash was turned into a horde of dark, hard insects, all burrowing into his coat toward his skin.

He changed – for only a split second was human. And he realized the bird's threat was made fact. He retained only one eye and was being eaten alive by the shimmering coating of insects covering his body.

In that split second, he tried to see where she had gone. Where she had been sitting, the Weyvern clung to the rock. It seemed made of stone, mottled green stone flecked and veined with red. A dragon seemingly hammered out of the rock composing the riverbank.

Black Leg screamed. The Weyvern's mouth opened and he was bathed in flame.

Arthur slept in the tower he received from the Queen of

the Dead. He sat between two waterfalls with the ancient vessel at his feet. Even in his dreams he was still a king and he sensed he must have been a king even when he floated in his mother's womb and kicked at her belly.

He had been a king and known it even as a child when he had been tormented by his mother, Igrane, and her lover, Merlin. He had known they wished to quench the strength in his heart. But they failed, thanks to Uther, and he stood on the threshold of his inheritance. His own man, one who would rule in his own way, and never allow his power to be usurped by another.

A king is a sacred being, the high priest of his people, who may be offered to the gods if the circumstances should arise. That called for the most valuable thing they possessed. Arthur understood this, and it was bred into his very bones.

She had given the cup into his hands and allowed him to quench his thirst just before the final ordeal. Now it floated before him, glowing in the dark silence of sleep, and her voice commanded him, 'Drink.'

He caught the cup between his hands and drank. He received a mouthful of blood.

Because he was a king, he could in no wise refuse her, and he swallowed. He found himself in the dim, steel cavern where they first met. But the roof was gone, and he stood among ruins that lifted their structures against a cold, gray sky. Beyond the boiling clouds the sun still burned, but it was only a somewhat brighter spot among the ashen clouds.

He glanced around at the chairs of the rotunda that once held the remains of the nonhuman dead and saw that each was occupied by an icy blue fire. She spoke to him from the high seat. 'It is done. We are free. It is time for you, your people, to claim their inheritance.'

'What is this place?' he whispered, studying the desolation around him.

'The end is in the beginning,' she said. 'As the beginning is in the end. This is the place where our world ended and yours began. I have done my best, but I can offer no better explanation. For what it's worth, our thought is demonstrated by the tower. Oh, King, let its logic rule you. The greatest thinkers among your people wrote nothing down but taught by the example of their lives. Oh, King, immortal in name and fame but placed beyond all comprehension, fare you well.'

Then they were gone, shooting up to and through the clouds that darkened the midday sky almost unto night. He woke gazing into the beauty of the glowing cup on the floor. He rose and saw it was filled with rich, cool milk. He was hungry and weary. He lifted the cauldron and tasted the milk.

The topmost room of the tower revolved like a kaleidoscope around him. Reality is a guess made by the mind, based on the information imparted by the senses. Here the speculations of reason (not lightly put aside) were suspended. The how of such an accomplishment was incomprehensible to him, and he bowed to the master builders of the tower, acknowledging their skill and intellect.

The why was more clear: movement from location to location.

Beyond the waterfalls, on each side of the throne, he saw a glade, a glen filled with forest, birdsong, and falling water, very green grass, abundant tree growth, bushes laden with fruit and flowers. The pale mist of shallow cataracts hovered, cooling and dampening the emerald parkland shadowed by oak, elder, birch, apple, and sloe.

He lifted the cup and drank again. He saw the sea crashing against barren cliffs, an angry sea, seeming to want to tear out and uproot a palace composed of glass that crouched at the foot of the cliffs. The waves moved over it, pounding, caressing, thundering at the mosaic of windows that formed its roof. The cloud-shadowed sun came and went, illuminating both palace and surging sea. Green, clear, dark, almost black, ever changing, never resting, the waters moved over the transparent domes beneath.

Igrane is there, he thought. *No, her journey is her own now. I am no longer a part of it.*

Then he passed through a murk fire and darkness. Her blue eyes looked into his, a cruel torment in them. Hurriedly, he lifted the cup to his lips; he wanted to go to her.

You will be my queen, he thought.

But she was swept away. The room revolved more quickly than thought, to a place where he saw his people gathered in a meadow. This time he didn't think but spoke.

'A king is a high priest!'

The vast kaleidoscope was still. He walked toward them, the vessel between his hands. Balin gawped at him as Arthur strode out of the dawn mist on the river near the bridge.

Arthur saw that in the night the rest of the women had joined the men. The bone fires that sent the dead to rest smoldered, still sending up wisps of white smoke. They had been built along the river. The mist trapped the last evidence of the fire and shared mortality with grass bowed by the weight of dew.

Higher up the banks, some of the men had taken a scythe to the grass and cleared a comfortable campground. It was very near the thorn tree where the silver mask hung. The tree was now in full bloom, and the rose and snow flowers glowed soft as a cloud in the first light.

'You won!' Balin said.

Arthur smiled. 'I don't think she asked a victory of me.'

'What did she want then?' Eline asked.

'My soul,' Arthur answered. 'I yielded it up to her.'

No one said anything, but the question was in every eye and rested silent on every tongue. Arthur answered the unspoken words.

'She received it into her hands and did no evil thing to it, but returned it to me, cleansed and filled with peace. If this is a victory, it belongs to us both.'

'No! Then it is us she cursed,' Balin said.

'You have your cattle back,' Arthur said. 'How are you cursed?'

'The milk,' Balin said. 'The milk from the cows is tainted. Some of it smells of blood. Other cows yield a substance that looks like liquid dung. The rest of the beasts, those with weaned calves, are dry as dust, udders wrinkled and shrunken.'

'We can't make bread,' Eline said.

'I have some milk here.' Arthur spoke very softly. 'Try it.' He offered the vessel to Eline.

She accepted it and drank. When she was finished, she gave a deep sigh. Her eyes met Arthur's over the cup in her hands.

'Good! But is there enough to make bread for us all?'

'I think you will find it so,' Arthur answered.

Another woman approached with an earthenware bowl in her hand.

'Give me a bit, Eline,' she said. 'God knows I can cut it with water and have enough for my man and little ones.'

Eline nodded and filled her bowl. Another approached, then quickly behind her, more came forward. Preoccupied with her task, she filled a dozen before she realized the cup would not empty. In fact, the more bowls Eline filled for the women, the more quickly the milk poured. The gathered women glanced at one another, then Arthur.

'Shush,' he said, lifting his finger to his lips. 'The sun's edge has not touched the rim of the hill. Take your fill of the milk, for it is what she, the Queen of the Dead, intended. Between night and morning, between sunset and dark, are the moments we touch the other world. In a place that is and is not, we find both peril and mercy. Drink! And inherit your world. She yields it to you.'

'You will be our king,' Balin said.

'If you wish, for as long as you wish,' Arthur answered.

The cup made the rounds, the men drinking their fill, the women drinking also and taking enough to make bread for their children. Even Bax took a lap as Eline offered the cup to the dog for a moment as it was passed with unflurried haste from hand to hand.

There is evil in the world, disease, pain, death, terror. The loss of loved ones, intractable human problems that destroy individuals and whole families. Drunkenness and folly. There is evil in humankind, anger, baseless envy, hate, greed, and a shadowed streak of destructive cruelty that seeks out the means to give pain to others, and at times ourselves. To take an evil delight in wreaking havoc on the natural world simply to prove we are its masters.

But there are moments when we escape the burdens of our common humanity and transcend the evils the flesh is heir to. Arthur understood this was one of those moments when humans stand hand in hand before nature and form a circle of peace. We carry away from these rites the strength to live, to labor, to love. This was one of those moments, sent by the divine thought of the universe to sustain us. And Arthur knew he was king leader and high priest to these people. And if need be, their first and most important sacrifice.

He drank last, again from the cup, and as the new sun gilded the silver mask hanging from the high branch of the flowering tree, he drained the last of the milk and found the cup empty.

I don't remember getting back to the rest where they waited looking, gazing at the fortress across the water. But I did.

I sat with them on the grass beside the mound that once held the signal tower and we waited. The wind from the ocean continued to blow the stench of the dead away from us. There was still some wine left from the supply we had taken from the Saxons. Ure and Gray shared it out among the rest of us, though I declined.

They held me, the dead. I knew, because Ure asked me a question. He got an answer. One of them spoke to him. Yes, the voice issued from my mouth, tongue, and throat, but I didn't say the words, nor were they in a language I understood.

For a second he looked startled. Then he met my eyes with an expression of cold comprehension. And I knew he understood, somehow understood where I had been and what I had been doing. Then, features impassive, he strolled away behind me toward where Gray and the Wolf Lord, Maeniel, were standing. I didn't follow him with my eyes. They were still under my control.

The two spirits within me were still fixed on vengeance and their minds, such as they were, remained directed at the fortress, a shadow against a horizon of gray clouds. As night closed in, sometimes it rained passing spatters or even brief, drenching downpours. After sunset there were lights at the fortress and some on a beach nearby.

It must have been near midnight when Ure whispered, 'Everybody up and into the boats. 'Tis now or never.'

We rose as one. I couldn't tell if any of us felt fear or not. Maybe it didn't matter what we felt. Once a decision is made, the flow of events carries you on, the way a river in flood sweeps a fallen leaf onward toward an unguessable destination.

I had one consolation amidst the hatred and desolation that was battering my soul. I had summoned the most dangerous of the dead and could do no more.

The boats moved out over water invisible to our eyes. I am told that near cities it is easier to see at night because the light from the human dwellings reflects back from the clouds. But we were near no city or even any modest village or town. The marsh lay in utter Cimmerian blackness, relieved only by the brief apparitions of the quarter moon through occasional openings in the clouds. The water between ourselves and the fortress was a shallow, brackish lake dotted with islands of reeds and saw grass. Fireflies collected over the grassy hummocks, and we steered our boats between what looked like clusters of stars.

We knew we were close to the fortress when we felt the pull created by the river current as it flowed swiftly past the broken walls. We plied the oars with a will, crossed in spite of the current, and landed below the spot where the fortress stood. The Romans had located it on the highest ground for many miles, but even so, it was none too safe. The gates that once opened to face the river were gone, and the walls that once surrounded them were a high, unstable jumble of fallen masonry, fully as forbidding as the intact walls on the other three sides.

The hunger in my heart for vengeance pulled me hard, at a run. A run that began as soon as I left the boat.

Why not? I thought. Gray, Maeniel, and Ure would know where to mass our forces.

Long ago the Romans moved the gates to one side of the fortress, the one that faced upriver. They would go there and wait. Wait for me to play my part. That was crucial. I must burn the pirates out.

'She,' the one who was drowned in the mud . . . or had she been buried alive? I wasn't sure. 'She' took my hand. I felt her fleshless fingers twine with mine. 'She' played here as a child and under the water at the foot of the ruined wall was a quay where ships once docked. I could walk along its stones and reach the lowest point of the wall. True, the quay was now underwater, but even with the spring river in flood it wasn't so deep that an approach couldn't be made.

'She' tugged at my hand and I followed. Just then the moon shone briefly and I saw that where I felt the pull on my fingers there was nothing to be seen, even though the flesh on my hand crimped at her grip. A chill brushed me, and I knew it came from the cold water at the bottom of the channel that tumbled her bones. I felt a sickening sense of grief for her. She hadn't been very smart and had been a person of few attainments, but she had loved her own and she wanted to live. I have never known anyone who truly wanted to die – but instead of life, she received cruelty, pain, madness, and, finally, darkness.

So I followed her touch down into the fetid water. Fetid because those inside used the broken wall as a latrine and garbage dump. The stones of the drowned quay were slimy and the water was at best most of the time up above my knees. But she pulled me along with a power greater than that of the river current that battered me and tried to suck me away into deeper water until at length I reached a point where I could begin to scramble up a sloping pile of stone to the top. From there I could look down into the fortress.

It wasn't an easy climb, and the next day I found a myriad of cuts and bruises on my hands, feet, arms, and legs caused by the vile detritus I had crawled through. But just then I felt none of them, only a sense of unholy triumph that belonged not only to my two unseen companions but to me as well. I cannot say if they had infected me with their hate or if it arose from what I had seen these vicious expert predators do to my own Picts, the Painted People. There was a lot of wood in that fortress, and would it ever burn?

The Saxons had repaired the Roman walkways around the parapet. Beneath them were shacks where their loot, human and otherwise, was stored. The whole center of the fortress was taken up by a drinking hall, the all-purpose gathering place of the war band.

Then the moon returned, summoned, I think, when the eternal denizen of the marsh called out to his patroness. And in the cold light that flickered as the density of the moving clouds changed, I saw my path down from the wall top to where each post supporting the walkways was lodged. I smelled the stench created by the slaves crowded together in the squalid quarters beneath them, and my stomach cramped at the aroma of roast meat and spilled ale in the drinking hall.

Now something that was created by myself and my three companions, an utterly different entity than any one of the three of us, cried out, 'Burn it, Priestess! Burn it now!'

So I did.

I never remembered how I got down from that wall top. The next thing I can remember clearly is pressing my right hand against the first post. Fury raged in my brain – it wouldn't catch but hissed like a nest of serpents and sent out billows of scalding steam and thick, fire-damp smoke. Someone or something gave a yell of rage and fire raced away from my fingers up the post, streaking like an arrow to the top, where the planks that formed the walkway exploded into flame. I knew I could do it, that in fact it was as good as done, I thought as I raced to the next. They were the devil to ignite, those posts, but I knew the devil rode with me.

I went from one to the other as quickly as possible. I can't think I had a plan, but in the back of my mind I knew the posts supporting the installation at the parapet would be the most difficult to deal with. I had to get to them first and make it impossible for any surviving pirates to defend the fortress.

I was at the eighth post when the screams began. Above, the walkways were crumbling, raining down flaming embers and burning brands on the slaves inside. My whole soul thrilled with horror when I realized they were chained inside. I turned, stumbling back toward the first shed.

But 'they' stopped me, sending me down into the mud around the drinking hall. I fought them.

'No!' Ure said, jerking me to my feet with one long, powerful arm.

I gaped at him, wondering how he'd gotten inside and why he was here.

'There is no time!' he roared, spinning me around and slamming my body against the wattle-and-daub walls of the drinking hall. 'They are doomed. Burn the hall – now – or I'll kill you myself.'

The screams of terror, pain, and helplessness ringing in my ears, I slammed both arms palm down against the timbers and threw my whole life and soul into the effort. I created a . . . pyre.

Wattle and daub is wonderful stuff for burning. But this was beyond imagining. The structure went up with a roar, walls, roof, and timber supports all blazing. Smoke was burning my eyes and setting my nose and lungs on fire.

'The gate!' Ure shouted. 'Now! It's time! Burn the gate!'

'Where is the gate?' I shouted as I began retching. It was no longer possible for me to see. The inside of the fortress had become a sea of smoke illuminated by bursts of flame.

Ure was going down, gasping, suffocating. 'Close your eyes. "They" will show you.'

Then he was gone, because oil and wine had been stored in the hall and gouts of flame were spurting through the broken walls. I twisted, trying to get away from them, my clothes, such as they had been, gone. I could feel and see my faery armor glowing in a green network all over my flesh, holding back the fire but beginning to sear my flesh with its heat. Yet I did as Ure told me and closed my eyes.

Even through the roaring blaze around me I felt the chill of their presence. The gates were dead ahead. I fell to my knees, unable to bear the airless, smoke-laced heat, and crawled toward them.

When I escaped the inferno that had been the drinking hall, I was able to get to my feet again. But there were armed men between me and the tall wooden portals. They hesitated and indeed I must have been a figure of terror: naked, hairless, glowing with the gold-green of my armor. But one bolder than the rest appeared in front of me, sword in hand.

I was past thought, well into battle madness and still dangerous because I was not without weapons. I felt the sword crash into my left arm, numbing it. But I kept coming, knowing no way back. The palm of my fire hand slammed into his chest. It burned through his cuirass, steel plates sewn to a leather backing, through the quilted padding beneath. His flesh melted like soft butter in my fire and his bones burned. He had not even time to scream. His skeleton glowed ruby-red through skin that melted away like running wax or a ruined garment. He fell, jerking, charring, turning to powdered ash even as he died, almost before he died.

The rest fled. Even the blazing murk around them seemed less terrible than this.

My body crashed against the iron-bound oak doors. I

was fire and nothing but fire by then. It almost seemed the ancient black oak that had sealed the fortress time out of mind welcomed an end to its living death as an object of human use. The great doors vanished in a blast of light, heat, and powdered, blowing ash.

I fell, and from where I lay in the mud, I watched the surviving Saxon garrison charge right into our slingers. Even above the fire I could hear the dreadful squishing thuds as lead shot met flesh, blood, muscle, and bone and they died around my prone body like a breaking sea that thunders, rushes, and then is silent.

They had me – the two evil things I had invited into my soul. I had a second of consciousness, sight, and thought before they seized my mind, my twisting limbs, my consciousness, eyes, and tongue. And in that moment I saw Ure striding toward me, hair gone, skin blackened by burns and smoke, clothing in rags . . . his eyes yellow, glaring, pitiless as a striking eagle's.

Ure grabbed me by the neck. The things reacted first with astonishment, then rage that anything would dare challenge them. I had no power over my arms and legs, but I did see his face, blurred and distorted by my tearing eyes. His eyes were cloudy-green stone, his teeth bared. He laughed again, the laughter of one who raises a sword to strike his fallen enemy down forever.

On the field behind us, my untried boys and girls were meeting the disorganized and terrorized pirates and finding out how easy it was to kill. The fortress was a roaring pyre and the slaves chained were still screaming. Those screams were almost inhuman now. So terrible were they that they sounded like some force of nature, a storm wind from the sea, keening and wailing among broken rocks on a barren shore. But I heard it all only distantly and dimly as Ure seized me by the neck, twisted my clawing right hand behind my back, and dragged me into the water.

He shook me the way a wolf shakes a hare to snap its neck and end its struggles. Then he plunged my head beneath the surface.

God! I wake even now from nightmares remembering and thinking: *Is that what it's like to drown?* My lungs burned my throat as I sucked in water trying to breathe. It's a good thing you can't remember pain, because the agony of drowning was so all-encompassing.

I did not feel pain. I *was* pain as every part of my body spasmed at the icy rush of water filling my mouth, nose, throat, and lungs. Dirty water, too. It tasted of mud, slime, blood, and cold, dank death. So terrible was it that for a second I broke free of Ure. Up I rose, out into the air again. But I couldn't breathe. I was coughing and retching too badly.

Then Ure had me by the neck and was twisting my arm up, and the dark water, dancing with the orange highlights of the burning fortress, was rushing toward my face again. A second later, I was under it and I sensed my struggles were weakening.

This time I'd managed to get a little air, but when it was gone, Ure held me down and I knew in a few seconds I must suck in the evil, cold mixture of silt, slime, and water around me. Then I would drown. By then, between my horror at what I had done, the sick anguish of possession, and the raw pain in my body, I was almost ready to welcome the end.

It was too much for her. Too much like the death she died before. I felt her let go and drift away, back to her bones, rolling along a shallow channel of brackish water near the sea. For a timeless time, I was with her as the ebbing tide sucked at her bones, half-buried in the ooze at the bottom. Through the empty eye sockets of her skull, I could look up at the dazzling arch of stars blazing a bridge over the ocean. And I sensed that not only the tide tried to pull her free.

Go, I thought. *Go. You have your revenge – not that it matters.* He burned, and the terror of my hand, the hissing stench as it went through a living being and vaporized his heart, shook my mind.

Then she was spreading – that's the only way I can describe it – spreading the way light fills a room when a lamp is lit. At first there is only darkness, then a tiny spark when flint strikes steel, then light is everywhere. She seemed to fill the night and I could not follow. It was death and I was jerked back into my tormented flesh again, struggling in Ure's grip.

He jerked me upright just as my mouth opened to breathe in water. We stood knee-deep in the shallows while I retched and coughed violently, at the same time trying to empty both my stomach and my lungs of water. He shook me again because I had managed to reach back and claw at his face with my left hand.

The pain was terrible. Never let anyone tell you being shaken by a strong man doesn't hurt as muscles and tendons are torn free of bone. We were facing the land, and I could see the fortress clearly. It was a pyre, then there were no more screams and I knew nothing could live in the heart of that furnace. Our men and the Saxons were only black, struggling silhouettes against the raw brilliance of the flames.

By that light, I saw Maeniel at the water's edge, face set in the wolf's killing snarl, teeth bared, lips drawn back over fangs already seeming to drip blood in the glow from the burning fortress. He came lunging up for my throat.

Frantic with fear, I managed to twist away from Ure and heard Maeniel's jaws snap shut inches from my neck. But I was dead and knew it as I watched the wolf land and the water sheet up from his plunging body. Maeniel might miss once – twice, never!

He turned, water swirling from his fur as his body

turned even while he was in the air. His haunches dropped to catch a purchase in the mud, to brace him for his next jump at my throat.

I felt the serpent. It writhed in my body. My hips and breasts twisted, undulating like the long, legless, armless body. It was so mad with fear it had lost control and forgotten I was human and couldn't move the way it did.

I lost my footing and went down just as Maeniel completed his turn and went for my throat again. I felt it wrench at my flesh, tearing the way a fingernail rips free when it's caught in the bark of a piece of kindling when you split it with a knife. I have done that while collecting firewood, torn out one or two while wrenching the bark away from dry wood.

My body, my insides, seemed to tear as the serpent gathered my substance to form its own. I felt the smooth, scaled body first in my throat. It stopped my breath and slid over my tongue. My mouth must have gaped as wide as it would go, because it passed my lips and teeth like a smooth, hard breath and struck as hard as it could at Maeniel's rushing body.

I heard Ure give a yell of triumph. He was so fast, his hand snapped shut on its neck and he jerked it clear of my body just as Maeniel's front paws hit my chest and shoved me back toward the muddy bank. Ure was holding the horribly writhing, twisting thing at the neck and I saw it was trying to flip a coil around his arm and seize him. But he wouldn't let it. He turned and hurled it far out over the black water. I saw it twist, drawn between the lake and the stars, then it vanished away.

He dragged me out of the water, cursing my stupidity for allowing the evil things power over me. 'Don't you know better?' he roared.

'You're a sorcerer,' I managed to gasp out.

'Yes,' he said with another menacing grin, and a very evil one. 'Not at all like that timorous fool Dugald you set such store by. Fear not. I'll teach you better. I'll teach you how to control them – make them your slaves and get them to do your bidding at will.'

I understood. He had persuaded my evil companions to leave by convincing them he was going to kill me. And he nearly had. Maeniel helped him. And I was free.

The pirates were almost all dead, and we watched from the water's edge as our men – and they were men now – cut the throats of the few living wounded and began to strip the corpses of their kills.

There was not time, only everlasting repeating cycles: spring, summer, autumn, winter. Then spring again.

Nothing changed, not really. Babies were born, the elders died. The dead weren't gone but an absent part of the community, temporarily absent because their spirits, freed by the bone fire, would wander for some little time and then return, seeking a womb. And when they found a couple in the throes of desire, they entered her body and breathed life into the couple's mixed blood, and so came to live again.

Our memory of paradise, Uther thought when he rode into the grove behind Morgana. He was decided and his plans were made. Or so he thought. He would leave tonight and ride with Cai and Gwain toward London.

The more Uther saw of the little forest, the happier he was with it as a place to camp. The trees were centered in open country. The priestess leaders of the warrior societies had set sentries, and any attacking force would be visible for miles. The food spitted over the open fires was beginning to cook and good smells brushed the king's awareness. Nearby his oath men had set up what was almost a pavilion for him, a hide-and-cloth tent painted with his house's ancient symbol of the dragon, white, blue, and gold. His standard, the same dragon, billowed on a pole in front of the tent. It, like the tent, was made of hide and cloth. Hollow, the head faced into the wind, and with every strong gust the wind flowed through it and the dragon cried out, the dark, sad music of war ringing in its voice.

How long, he wondered, had it been summoning men and women both. Commanding them to emerge from lives of happiness and peace to step forward, stand, and die, its noise and the trumpeting belling of the war horns speaking the challenge of stag, bull, boar, and wolf. The dark male statement of desire. I am strongest, I am best. She-beast, with valor and slaughter will I win your love, the immortality burning between your thighs? When, oh when did we begin this folly?

Morgana jerked him out of his reverie.

'My lord, we have duties here.'

'Yes,' Uther answered, brushing his hand before his eyes as if to banish some dreadful vision.

'If,' she continued, 'this was a holy place as Shela, who first looked at it, suggests, it is our duty to sacrifice to its inhabitants. Not to show respect for them is to invite terrible ill luck. A king is the high priest of this people. It is your duty to placate them, lest they take it into their minds to do us some injury.'

Uther nodded. He wanted his supper badly, and he had a long ride ahead of him this night. So he was in a hurry to be done with what, after all, was only a social gesture, albeit a supernatural one.

'Collect something for the offerings,' he told her, 'and follow me.'

'Honey, wine, oil, mead,' she suggested.

He shrugged. 'Any or all of them, but not too much. It doesn't do for a king to appear stingy, but we will need all our supplies before this . . .' He hesitated over the word, then finished strongly, '. . . before this war ends.'

He strode into the forest, leaving her to follow. Once

past the screen of brush at the edge, the woodlot opened up. The trees were almost exclusively oaks, small, dense, and dark stands of holm oak scattered among ancient giants. In fact, Uther couldn't remember ever seeing so many old trees in one place. None of the trunks could be spanned by the arms of one man, and many were so wide it would take at least a half dozen to make a chain around them. In some places there had been faces set into the wood in low relief, but the bark had grown back over the dedicated tree and even his practiced eye could no longer discern the spirits that once must have inhabited them.

As he strode deeper and deeper into the woods, he left the noise of the campground behind and silence walked with him. Because the trees were so old, the forest canopy was open and the westering sun shone down into it. He walked through a sort of parkland of dappled sunlight, soft shade with none of the deep darkness that hovered under the smaller groves of holm oaks.

His neck prickled when he realized the small, dense groves were thick with mistletoe, and he found himself avoiding them. The grass was short and almost, it seemed, as if some large animals must have been recently pastured here. Water collected in stumps at low places and he saw the tracks not of cattle but cloven hooves. But what sheep or goat could leave tracks so large?

He found what he sought at the edge of the wood, the entrance gazing out over the open plain. He wondered that the priestess hadn't realized what it was, then decided she must not have been intended to see. But he was king and priest – he knew.

But for fire, all the world was dark then. The lamps they had were trembling, tiny flames that did little to dispel the encroaching night. They sat and watched the stars rise. Moon and sun came and went, but the stars remained ever-lasting and eternal, circling the pole forever.

This was what they wanted, the end of time. Life is good, but how could a life be so fair that one would want it to continue the same forever?

The barrow was wedge shaped, like others of its kind he had seen. The tomb chamber was at the high end and had a direct line of sight across the plain. The newly dead were placed just inside the entrance, where they could watch the stars rise. They yielded their flesh to the earth, melting down to become one with it. But the stars came lifting from the horizon to carry away their souls.

Time stops for the stars. They achieved in their barrows its end. How bitterly he envied them. He and his people were carried along in time's rush as a fallen branch is by a wild river, to be battered, remolded, and changed forever by its flow.

Just then he heard movement in the woods behind him. He was alone! He had left Morgana and his oath men at the edge of the woods.

A second later he had his hand on his sword hilt and was turning to face his pursuer.

Morgana stepped out of the trees. She was carrying a string bag filled with leather containers holding the offerings to be made at the tomb. Uther let go a deep sigh of relief and noticed that his whole body was covered with perspiration.

Morgana paused, studying him. 'Did you think me an assassin?'

'Yes!' Uther answered. 'It is difficult to know how many among us the Saxon lords might have corrupted. Or perhaps it wouldn't even take a bribe. A king makes so many enemies that it could simply be some grudge-bearing underling cherishing cold malice in his heart who would choose his time to stick a knife in me. You have the Cat Sith, Cai the seal, but I would die at once.'

'To be shape-strong is an advantage,' Morgana said.

100

'But till now, I hadn't thought it to be so much of an advantage. I am not like that Maeniel you know. I can't do it whenever I wish simply by wishing. Neither can Cai – certain conditions have to be met. And I am not sure what all of them are.'

'I think they are about to be,' he said, and pointed at the barrow.

'Christ!' she whispered. 'They! Still here!'

'Christ,' he said, 'has nothing to do with it.'

'No?' she asked. 'The cross is a symbol of the four directions that bind the universe!'

'I hadn't thought of it that way.'

She gestured at the bag in her hand. 'I brought a lot. You are right, it doesn't do to be stingy.'

She led the way to the front of the barrow and it did look to the west across the open country.

'They watch for the stars,' Morgana said.

The door at the high end of the barrow was a triangle, formed by two tall stones resting against each other at the top. Beyond it were the two stone platforms where the watchers lay, one on either side, and beyond them, darkness. Morgana knelt in the long, soft grass that flowed away out across the plain like some vast green sea. Even though the barrow faced roughly west, it had been angled in such a way that the dying sun didn't break through the night clasped within it.

'I can feel their eyes,' Morgana said.

Uther looked out at the wind-stirred grass stretching out toward the horizon. It shimmered with the slanted rays of the setting sun.

'I wonder what life was like when kings trusted their people?' he asked.

'Like this,' Morgana answered. 'Serene, silent, without fear or woe. As we are here now. Brother and sister together under an afternoon sky. Have you eaten today, brother mine?'

101

He shook his head. 'I had no appetite. No stomach to break my fast on so evil a day of decision.'

'Then sit down. I cannot think the sleepers here would deny us a share in their feast.'

Uther pulled off his mantle and spread it on the grass. They both sat down and shared out of the provisions from the string bag: bread with sausage and onions, honey, butter, and wine.

'They were ever hospitable,' Morgana said, 'and taught that tradition to us. No meat, but for the sausage cooked into the bread,' she told him as she passed him a small, flat loaf.

He spread butter and honey on it and ate. 'How long were they here before . . . before we came?'

Morgana shrugged. 'When I studied with those who knew about them, I found there was no agreement. Except the belief that the barrows were built after the mounded tombs but by the same people. But all said they seemed to be the first ones here, even before the sea rose and this became an island. How long they ruled alone is unknown. Perhaps at least a thousand years, but more likely three or four.'

Uther made the sign of the cross. 'So long, so long. I cannot imagine it.'

Morgana filled a leather cup with wine and handed it to him. The sausage in the bread was salty. He drank deeply, feeling a strange peace entering his mind and body.

'Is the wine so strong?' he asked, looking out over the shimmering grass toward the sun approaching the haze at the horizon's rim.

'I cannot think it,' Morgana answered. 'Most likely it is the peace here. Whatever the builders of the tomb sought for their dead, they found it. This feast, the one we two share, is part of it. But we must wait until dark and make the offering to the first stars.'

He was finished eating.

'Stretch out and rest for a while,' Morgana said. 'I will keep watch. Have no fear, we can find the rest in the dark. I brought a torch so that if we were caught out at sunset we could find our way back.'

'Night ride. Yes, I have a long night ride ahead of me,' he said. Then he lay down, still dressed and armed, and went to sleep.

Morgana sat cross-legged next to him and watched the sun change the world around her as it moved through time, down toward the horizon. Moment to moment the changes in the light – its color, the shadow length – brought her deeper communion with the murmuring world around her. Life is not yes or no, but a continuum. Birth to death, youth to age, day to night, all move in sweeping arcs that cannot be fully comprehended unless contemplated in stillness.

The Cat Sith woke in Morgana, furred, lithe, strong, all-comprehending, as the last orange sunset glow faded into an opalescent blue twilight. And what had been Morgana lazed in the grass, a mass of rippling muscle covered by the velvet-spotted coat of leopard. Armed with fang and claw and an instinctive lethal bite, the most formidable killer known to man.

Cat love is tragic, because a cat was never meant to love. Most cats are fierce solitaries that mark no time and walk through the multiplicity of experience alone. A cat cannot earn love, nor will it yield to a social being's importunities and demands. Cats, even more than the human and canine tribe, cannot be enslaved. They can only be victims of human inconstancy and neglect.

To be the Cat Sith was to know these things, and what had been Morgana did. But she loved the man sleeping beside her. She rose to her feet. Even in sleep Uther's hand rested on his sword hilt. She licked the hand one swipe with a rough tongue.

Uther stirred, muttered and moaned in his sleep. All that was left of day was a blue ribbon on the horizon. The cat's eyes expanded, and Morgana, the cat, saw clearly the two figures standing at the entrance of the barrow tomb.

She knew, powerful as the Cat Sith was, she couldn't help him. At least, not yet. She was too much the solitary. Love was a burden, and if he failed, the Cat Sith's heart would break and she would die.

No, Morgana must surrender him to other guardians, and they waited at the door to the tomb. To the Cat Sith, there remained only the night.

The flames that enveloped Black Leg's body reduced his attackers – whatever they had been – to dust. And in addition, burned off a lot of his fur. He saw the Weyvern leap toward him. Her claws closed over his seared body, and they went down in the river below.

Half blind in the dark water, his wits dissolved into mad panic, Black Leg struggled to free himself from her. This was no refuge for him, his mind screamed at her. In less than a moment, he would breathe water and drown.

He was stunned when she screamed back at him; he heard her as clearly as if she had spoken.

'Damn you for a stubborn fool! Cooperate with me, idiot, or you'll drown!' The last word was a shriek.

Caught between her claws, the narrow scaled body wrapped around his and, sinking into the deepening gloom of the pool at the bottom of the falls, Black Leg cooperated. He yielded – let go. The horror of the fate the dark bird described to him rang in his mind. This quick silencing of his voice was infinitely better than the slow decay the bird promised.

For the first time he acutely felt his divided nature. The man rebelled, but the wolf opened his mouth, breathed water, and . . . did not drown! A few seconds later, both Weyverns landed among the rocks amidst the whirling currents generated by the cataract above.

Now – how in the hell did she do that? Black Leg thought.

True, he was a much smaller Weyvern than she was. But . . . he possessed a sinuous, muscular body, opened and closed powerful webbed claws, and erected a formidable array of dorsal spines.

Hey, this isn't half bad, was his thought. *I could get to like it.*

Quit muttering. The thought was directed at him. *If you want to talk this way, you have got to put together clear, declarative phrases.*

Black Leg did. 'What were those things?' The spines on his back rose and every scale on his body tightened.

'Hell if I know,' was the answer. She managed even as a Weyvern to look annoyed.

'Think I could learn to do this myself?' Black Leg found himself enunciating very clearly.

'Hell if I know that either,' was the aggrieved reply. Then she continued, 'At least I know why the little vine was afraid. Poor thing had good reason. And be careful of how you use oxygen. Gill breathers aren't very efficient – was one of the few weaknesses these creatures had. They were better off on the surface, but I don't think we should try to go up now.'

'Feel how cold it is,' Black Leg said. He saw emphatic agreement in the other Weyvern's expression.

'Snowmelt river,' came back to him. 'Like it or not, though, I think we should wait until dark.'

She must have seen the emphatic agreement in his expression, because she said no more.

The catch to this situation was that everything took effort: maintaining the Weyvern form, combating the cold, steadying their minds against the pull of Weyvern nature and the mortal terror the ravens inspired in them both.

He was dozing, claws clenched in the rocks, when he felt a pressure wave and knew she must be moving her tail. Black Leg understood that once these creatures must have used movement to draw attention to their wishes, because every other Weyvern in the area would know what certain movements meant. This one was a simple tap on the shoulder.

'Up now?' he asked.

'You're getting good at this,' was the reply.

Black Leg was so pleased by the compliment he would have blushed, had he been human. As it was, all the Weyvern could do was crack its knuckles modestly. She wasn't free with compliments, at least not about anything but his sexual prowess.

'Cold's going to finish us if we don't,' he said.

'All right. On three. One. Two. Up.'

They suited the action to the words. The river currents were warmer aloft. When they stuck their heads out of the water, they found the ravens gone and a vast, almost icy moon shining down on them. As one, they swam toward shore.

'I never saw a moon like that,' Black Leg said.

'Yeah, I know,' she answered. 'And it's one of the things that worries me about this place.'

They were human again and speaking normally. Neither of them wanted to go ashore, so they found a shallow grotto hollowed out by spring floods just above the water and crawled in. Black Leg went wolf and was relieved to find himself completely healed. She tucked herself into the curve of his furry body and they both dropped like rocks into a sleep of exhaustion.

He woke to the morning light and the knowledge that he was in the worst trouble of his life. He didn't move and didn't turn human because he didn't want to wake her. He studied her face in the colorless early dawn light

106

and decided she didn't look good. Her face seemed to have aged overnight; her skin was pale and she had dark circles under her eyes. But worst of all was the condition of one of her hands. The arm terminated in a hand-shaped puddle of water.

He found it frightening evidence that she was being reclaimed by her primal element. Then he was startled by her voice.

'You see that?' she asked.

'Yes. Can you?'

'No, but I can feel it. Let me concentrate.' She did and the water molded itself into a hand again. He lifted the hand to his lips and kissed it.

'I am an idiot,' he said.

'No recriminations,' she said. 'They're a waste of energy, and I don't have much.'

He nodded. 'What would help you?'

'I draw my life from the well of my native waters. Somehow we have to find a gate and get back.'

He looked up at the towering falls, a vast plume blown by the morning wind.

'No, I don't think so. You would have to climb the rocks beside the cataract and a fall might kill you if you couldn't change fast enough after you landed. Besides, even if you got to the top, where would you find a rope . . . and then those birds . . .'

'Yes, those birds,' he echoed as he gave a slight shiver. 'Look at me. Oh, yes, I'm going to become a mighty warrior and here I am with my guts turning to water when I think about them.'

'Don't borrow trouble. We're going to have to try our luck downriver.' She dove in and he followed.

At first the river began to widen out, and they were swept past sandbar banks on either side. But then a strange thing began to happen. The water level began inexplicably to drop and the canyon walls to close in until they were walking in a sunless, narrow gorge beside a trickle of water that had once been a raging torrent.

'This is bad,' he said. 'Have you got any idea what's happening?'

'Not even the beginning of one,' was the answer.

'What got the water?'

She replied with a truly hostile glare.

The walls of the canyon were so close together and so high that they let in very little light. The Weyverns trudged along through misty gloom, over a smooth road of waterworn stone.

'Strange,' she said. 'It's almost cold here.'

He wasn't cold, even if he was wearing only his skin. And he gave her a startled look – his skin crawled!

She was old.

The breasts he had so admired hung like empty bags. Her skin was dry and wrinkled. On her hands, the skin had drawn back from the nails, leaving them claws. Her face was wizened, deeply lined, eyes sunken and luster-less, lips slightly drawn back from her teeth the way a drying head leaves the teeth bared in a final, evil smile.

He turned his eyes away as quickly as possible.

'Yes,' she said. 'I'm dying.'

Black Leg felt as though someone had dug a fist hard into his stomach. They continued walking.

'How? Why?'

'How? I am cut off from the waters whence I draw my life. Why? At least in part because I used considerable of my remaining power to turn you into a Weyvern so we could escape the birds.'

'No "we" about it,' he said. 'You could have gotten away easily. But . . . I was . . . if you hadn't done your best trick, those ravens would be picking my bones now. This is my fault.'

'No!' The word was a whisper, as though it were an effort now for her to talk. 'I hate dying, but I hate worse that there are so many things I didn't live to teach you – one is that nothing is purely anybody's fault. Blaming is the most futile thing you humans do to each other.

'No, if anyone is culpable, I am. I should have warned you before we entered the tunnel. Told you to be careful. But I was so hot to take you to my place that I didn't think to warn you about the transit. And just what I didn't want to happen – did.'

'What is the tunnel?' he asked.

'No one knows, and I mean no one. Not even "Her." '

Black Leg made as if to stop.

'No,' she told him. 'Keep moving, whatever may happen to me, little wolf. You have to find shelter before dark.'

He obeyed.

She continued, 'The tunnel is . . . old. No one knows how old. But consider this. I've been around so long that your people don't even have the mathematical concepts to discuss my age.'

Black Leg remembered a conversation he'd had with his father about time. His father had no use for the current theories about the age of the earth, though he did say Dugald's people had a better grip on the idea than most Christians did.

'I'm sure that's true,' he replied.

'Very well. Then look at it this way. The tunnel was very old before I was born. And trust me on this. That's an awesome amount of time. There are supposed to be directions written into the walls about where to go, but no one knows how to read them any longer. I travel in it – when I do travel in it – by God and by guess.'

By then Black Leg was feeling a little cold. He glanced up at the towering walls on either side of him.

'We may never get back,' he whispered.

'That's a real possibility,' she answered. 'Now shut up, because it's taking everything I've got just to keep up.'

He didn't trust her and kept glancing back to make sure she was still following. He knew when she went down and didn't get up.

He didn't need anyone to tell him what to do then. He walked back, picked her up, threw her over his shoulders like a scarf, and went on walking.

He wondered as he did if he could eat any of the sparse vegetation growing on the canyon walls. Most of the stuff within reach was lichens and moss. Here and there some ferns clung in thick crevasses where dense clumps of moss flourished. They had big, crunchy fiddleheads. He broke them off and began eating them.

Not bad. Sort of a celery-cucumber taste. But when he tried to feed them to her, she simply turned her face away and wouldn't let him put them in her mouth. That movement was the only way he knew she was alive.

She seemed too weak to speak. She didn't even look old any longer, but was rather more like a plant cut off from its roots, slowly withering away in the sun. She was limp, very light and soft.

He heard the singing a long way off. It reminded him of the red-flowered vine she'd worn when they last made love. But this melody was much, much more complex.

As he moved along, it grew louder and louder. This puzzled him. He remembered her saying that the females of the red-flowered vine lived further downstream.

He knew not all plants sang. The ferns, for instance, did nothing at all when he snapped off a frond. The ones she favored were different.

There was a lot of dampness in the canyon. Black Leg knew about fog. Fog is what happens when cold, moist air hits heat. The water in the thin but steady stream in the center of the canyon was cold. By night, the hot, dry air above probably blew down into the canyon, meeting the cold, moist air at the bottom. Clouds of damp mist formed, drenching the canyon walls. And the narrow gorge became a cloud forest.

Ferns, mosses, and lichens lived at the bottom, where there was little light. But higher up, large flowering plants and even small trees flourished. Black Leg could see they created a balanced system. At the bottom, the plant life was thick because though there was less light, more moisture was present. Above, where the sun was brilliant, the light lovers were sparse because of the lack of moisture.

I can live here, he thought, breaking off a few more fern fronds.

He wondered if the music he heard went directly into his mind or if it actually resonated in his ears. Then, abruptly, his question was answered by a tone so piercing that it felt as though someone had driven a nail through his eardrum.

'Christ,' Black Leg whispered, and stopped walking.

The pain ebbed. But when he tried to take another step forward, the damning scream jolted his skull again.

He lifted her from around his neck and rested what was left of her body on the canyon floor. She no longer looked even remotely human, but rather reminded him of a boneless, ropy vine slowly shrinking to nothing. Indeed, it was possible now to see the rock whereon she lay through her fading body.

Black Leg endured a moment of dreadful despair as his mind conjured up a future here abandoned and alone, eking out a living on what scraps he could find in this bleak wilderness . . . without her.

The music began again, a sobbing motif, diminishing chords vanishing into nothingness. It seemed to echo his present, leaden despair.

He looked up and saw a pendant cluster of flowers clinging bare root to a ledge above, near the canyon's rim. The music returned and seemed to soar with delight.

Black Leg began to climb. The going was easy at first. All the years of erosion had softened and pitted the rocks near the bottom, and plant roots dug their way into the stone and offered handholds. As he got higher, though, he found the decreasing vegetation offered fewer places where he could get a good grip.

But centuries of heat and cold fractured the stone, shearing it away to create ledges that allowed him to find secure, if precarious, perches for his fingers and toes. However, the stone was sharp, and he lost a few fingernails and cut his toes badly.

No question of turning wolf to heal those cuts, and for the first time in his life, he endured persistent pain and understood more about human suffering than he ever had before.

He was experiencing a new humility when he heard the music loud in his ears, singing a paean of triumph. He was face-to-face with the flowers.

He knew they must be the female flowers belonging to those she'd worn when they made love near the waterfall. They were also red, with a scarlet lip shaped like a deep cup filled with honeydew. Other delicate spotted yellow petals arched above, protecting the sweet contents of the cup.

Frightened almost to paralysis by the thought of falling, Black Leg let go with his left hand and plucked two. Holding the stems between his teeth, he began to make his way down.

He found his path easily enough by tracking the darkening smears of his own blood that marked the means of his ascent. When he reached the bottom, trembling and gasping with desperate relief, he saw her hand outstretched to take the flowers.

They seemed to vanish into her flesh, and he watched as she returned to life, haggard, pale, and weak but as beautiful and graceful as ever.

'I need more,' was the first thing she said.

Black Leg gave a sigh of acquiescence, limped down to the river, drank deeply, and turned wolf to heal his injuries. Then he returned to human shape and climbed the canyon wall again. And again . . . and again.

She seemed fully restored, her long blond hair almost a garment, her eyes filled with light when she rested her hand on a weary wolf's neck. And told him the flowers informed her that there was what they called a 'garden' ahead and she and Black Leg might find food there.

Black Leg remained wolf, and in a very short time they found what the flowers called the garden. The canyon enclosing the river widened, opening up an area about a half mile across. The swift-flowing stream became a very shallow lake, rich with good things. Some of the plants Black Leg recognized; others were strange to him. Conventional water lilies filled the center of the lake; reeds, sedges, and feathery bog plants grew so thickly in the shallows, they almost obscured the water. Beyond the pool, patches of crop plants grew on terraces that rose tier on tier in a gentle slope up to the canyon walls.

They stepped out of the darkness and found themselves walking on an almost completely overgrown path that ran along the lake at the center. The terrace to one side of them was filled with massed, coiling vines that held what looked like melons. They were in all stages of growth from green balls up to yellow-orange giants beginning to blacken, rot, and scatter their seeds back into the rich, soft, dark earth.

She picked up one that looked perfectly ripe. Something rather like a panpipe hooted softly. Black Leg, still wolf, looked up at her inquiringly.

'I don't know,' she said. 'Sounded like a warning. Be careful.'

She dropped the melon on the path. It burst open, showing a yellow-green center, moist and filled with rod-shaped seeds. Black Leg was so hungry, his legs felt weak. He shoved his face into the melon.

A second later, he withdrew it, letting fly with as much of a scream as a wolf can give, and bolted hell for leather into the water. He dropped the wolf shape in the shallows and waded in, trying to wash his face, mouth, and eyes all at the same time.

She doubled over laughing and said, when she got herself under control, 'Hero you may be, but I think you will never learn caution.'

'Christ!' he shouted. 'I might just as well have tried to eat fire!'

Even as a human his face was red, his eyes swollen.

Something like the sound of a cluster of glass bells resounded through the garden. She smiled and cocked her head to one side, listening.

'They talking to you?' he asked.

'Trying to. I told you before it's been a long time since anyone like me came here. They have missed . . . us. Part of what makes it difficult is they're all speaking at the same time.'

Black Leg could hear the distant, mingled strains of what sounded like a massive fugue, the musical lines of which merged into a magnificent tapestry of sound. He knew about music; he'd had some education about it from Dugald and Maeniel, who knew the sacred and profane compositions of the Greeks and Romans. He also knew the songs of wild things, birds, wolves, whales, and dragons. He knew music as a high form of communication, sacred, dangerous, and beautiful, capable of inspiring listeners to deeds of valor and incredible self-sacrifice; and also on the darker side, to cruelty, heedless violence, and suicidal despair.

The Greeks sang when they marched into battle, as did the Romans and his people. The music of death bound an army together and took them forward, triumphant over fear, to look into the empty eyes of absolute annihilation.

'There are a lot of them here, aren't there? I mean, the kind you know,' he said, then asked, 'It bother the vine that we took the melon?'

'No more than cutting your fingernails or hair bothers you,' was her answer. 'Seems the melons aren't the part we want, though they were a condiment to the people who planted them. Try the flowers.'

She picked one. 'Delicious!'

They were, Black Leg thought after he'd eaten five or six and was beginning to feel better. They were big, yellow, soft, and moist, with a creamy taste. There were a lot of flowers on the terrace occupied by the vines.

They wandered on, tasting, touching, and listening to the manifold melodies and sensual delights offered by the hidden garden. There was a fig that sang and dripped purple, sweet fruit. Another fig that didn't sing, with greenish-yellow fruit. Twined among its branches was a vine that bore a spherical, black-red fruit with a rich, sweet acid and slightly salty taste.

They were both gorged and relaxed – Black Leg had discovered the greenish-yellow fig had the same effect as a mild alcoholic beverage – when they at last sat down to contemplate their new kingdom.

'If it wasn't for those birds,' Black Leg said, 'I'd think this was paradise.'

'If it wasn't for those birds,' she repeated, 'we wouldn't have to worry about finding shelter for the night.'

Black Leg glanced around uneasily. 'Your friends tell you what's up top, outside these canyon places?'

'No,' she answered. 'They don't want to talk about it. For some reason, they're really afraid.'

'Yeah, well, that bothers me,' Black Leg said. 'When the first little vine was frightened, we found out he had good reason. This garden ... or whatever ... was created. It didn't just happen accidentally. Someone – or maybe some things – built it. What happens when they come to harvest their crop?'

'No!' she said, her voice dreamy. 'No, they are gone . . . long gone . . .'

She rose, seeming almost in a trance state, and waded out into the lake at the center of the garden. She was only ankle-deep when she dissolved into droplets, which fell into the still water like a small rain shower and vanished.

Black Leg found he was queasy and cold. He wouldn't admit to himself how frightened he was. This strange, sometimes terrible, place had come close to killing them both. He looked up again at the blue, sun-suffused sky above and saw that it was growing late. Those birds, if birds they were, had come at dusk. When they'd entered the garden, the lake waters had danced with golden light. Now they were dark, the water plants green shadows against an inky tarn.

The canyon must run due south, and the sun must be close to completing its journey into the west. Where, oh where to hide?

He went wolf. The wolf could see better in the gathering dusk, and besides, the chill rising from the glacier meltwater was beginning to fill the air. The dying sun reddened the east canyon wall, and the wolf's eyes, more attuned to the gradations of light and shadow than any human's ever could be, picked up the darker slits in the rose-colored stone. They reminded him of the slits made for archers in the fortifications of Hadrian's Wall. Then there were what looked like holes at the back of the top terraces.

Black Leg sensed night moving swiftly toward them. He remembered that the dark birds had appeared when the sun ceased to shine into the canyon at all. Now the last golden light was moving up the stone as the sun sank deeper and deeper into the west.

He discarded the wolf shape for a moment and ran

down to the lake, waded in, and slapped the water, hard, two or three times with his open hand. She rose from the lake like a Venus formed by the waves. The sight of her nearly stopped the breath in his throat, she was so lovely.

This time some sort of water fern was knotted at her hips like a skirt that swept down into dozens of curved-wand ornaments with tiny but vivid lilac flowers. Other finely cut, lacy fronds supported but didn't conceal her breasts.

'Damn, you're beautiful!' he said as his eyes devoured the long-limbed, graceful body.

'I won't be so beautiful long, if I can't persuade these waters to support my life,' she said. 'That was what . . . I was trying to do. I think if I could stay all night . . .'

He glanced back at the narrowing band of golden light nearing the canyon walls.

'The sun is going to set in a few minutes. I don't think I can do the Weyvern shape again, not without draining your powers. And we used up most of the flowers on that vine, the one that restored you. But I think I might have found us a hiding place up near the canyon wall. I think it's hollow in places.'

'Goddamn it! I thought I was getting close . . . but . . . come on, let's try your way. At least take a look. I believe we can probably make it back to the river if we can't hide. Then, if it has to be, you can turn Weyvern again.'

'Let's go!'

They both ran up, he dropping into wolf shape on the first stride. They climbed, wolf and woman, up the terraces as though climbing a flight of giant steps to the top near the canyon wall. She peered in through one of the narrow, vertical slits.

'Yes,' she said. 'There's some sort of opening behind these windows.'

The light was visibly fading now. Black Leg ran along the base of the canyon wall, nose down, looking for an entrance. He found one, a hole only big enough to offer entrance for a wolf and a slender woman. He dove through and they found themselves inside a rocky chamber that seemed to run along the base of the canyon wall.

The roof of the chamber wasn't high enough to allow them to stand. But he, as wolf, and she, kneeling, could look out through the narrow embrasures into the valley below.

'I don't know if this is a perfect hiding place,' she whispered.

'Yes,' Black Leg said. 'How do we block the door?'

She touched the embrasure opening and said, 'It's covered by glass or something close to it. Then there must be a way to close the door.'

The wolf obligingly trotted to the door. Nothing. Only a small, arched hole that opened out onto the highest terrace at the top of the canyon.

He stuck his head out and glanced up at the ribbon of light at the top of the canyon wall. It had narrowed visibly. He looked down at the terrace. This highest terrace, which overlooked the whole valley, was covered with coiling vines.

The wolf slid out and turned human. 'Maybe I can block the opening with dirt,' he said.

He grabbed one of the large vines at the root, thinking to pull it up and back the soil beneath it into the opening. The scream that began at the lowest range of wolf hearing, then rose past the highest ultrasonic, seemed to pierce his eardrums like nails, worse, far worse than the attention cry of the dangling flowers at the canyon's rim.

Black Leg was paralyzed by pain, and the vine coiled around him like a giant serpent and brought him down.

It took us some time to realize we had taken the fortress and destroyed its garrison. Utterly destroyed them.

118

Maeniel was at my side; Ure and Gray stood holding their swords.

The dead were scattered in front of the gates, as were a few of our people. There was still plenty of light, though the catwalks along the walls were only blackened timbers and glowing coals. Around the courtyard, the drinking hall was a seething bonfire at the center. No longer recognizable as a building, it seemed only a pile of burning logs.

There is no more to be said.

I sat wrapped in a salvaged mantle, shivering, while the rest picked the place clean. The cloth stank of smoke and wet mud, but I didn't care. I couldn't find it in my heart to care much about anything.

Farry and his people bought all we could bring them, and we banked the gold and silver with the Veneti.

We hit two more places, both smaller than the first but almost as rich. And when we turned our boats back toward home, we slept on sacks lumpy with loot. When we landed at Ure's steading hidden in an estuary to the north, I was a real queen and we were all rich.

Ure piloted the boats to land. His people had a hall near the sea, high enough up to escape the tides but not so far as to be in among the trees.

'They are sacred, these big, dark pines,' Ure told me. 'And proprietary rites must be made before we can cut one.'

An age agone, a river cut through the mountains and down, opening a path where none had been before and emptying into a lake that mingled at last with the sea. The path the river cut through the trees was densely overgrown by the gigantic pines, and they had fallen or been cut to form a screen over the rushing white water beneath.

'The salmon come here,' Ure said. 'Wonderful fish fighting their way up the savage rapids to the top. Many die, but those who live taste of the wild, pure water, the clean pine, and the wind that rushes through the river cut to the sea. We are theirs, these dauntless creatures, and they are ours when we two are sundered. And some day we will be, if I read aright. They and we will both die.'

A long speech for him.

I was wearing in my soul the dullness and sorrow of the battles I fought and won.

'You are older now,' Ure said, 'than when you set out.'

'Yes,' I said as I climbed out of the boat and walked up the beach toward the hall. 'I have touched the dead and they left their mark on me. No, I am not as young as I was.'

Ure laughed.

'Where do your people live?' I asked.

The hall stood alone in the narrow, dry land strip between sea and forest. That forest was something remarkable. Dense, the trees giants that let in only a little light, and with a carpet of needles so thick I was sure that every step was cushioned by them. There was very little light beneath those trees except in those odd places where a lightning-burned tree had fallen, leaving an opening in the entwined branches of the canopy.

I looked at Ure sideways and repeated my question. 'Where do your people live?'

I had trusted him when we started out. But then we had nothing worth stealing. Now we were dripping gold, and Ure was no candidate for sainthood.

Maeniel and Gray were at my side, but as always it was Maeniel's word I sought. He considered Ure as one wolf does another. Ure didn't flinch.

Gray looked offended. 'My uncle's hospitality is sacr—' He broke off because Ure laughed again.

'My Lord Maeniel, have you ever gone for a walk in a large city after dark, with a full purse at your belt?'

'Yes,' Maeniel answered. 'When I wanted to introduce some variety into my diet.'

'In that instance I was stranded in Constantinople without money to pay my passage back. And a purse may be weighted with lead, as well as gold.'

'True,' Maeniel answered. 'Where is this leading?'

'Not to treachery,' Ure said. 'Sometimes the biter is . . . bitten. I wouldn't chance it.'

The boys were disembarking from the boats now and wading into shore. Only they weren't boys any longer. Nor were they only armed with slings. They each carried a sword, most had helmets, all had shields. Assorted knives, axes, and a variety of maces completed their equipment.

We wore a variety of clothing, some of it still reeking of blood spilled when the original owners took their death wounds. In my case I had the woolen mantle Ure found for me after we destroyed the first pirate nest. And yes, despite airing it out, it still stank of smoke – nice – and carried the sharp, bitter taint of burned meat – not so nice. Under it I wore a white silk dress, part of a curtain or bedsheet – who knows? I threw it over one shoulder. Albe had whipped a seam up on the side that passed under my arm. I drew it in at the waist with a belt, gold knot-work adorned by pearls and clouded emeralds.

In addition, three torques were at my neck, two gold and one silver, a half dozen bracelets, several anklets. Golden scroll bracelets clung to my upper arms. All proclaimed my leader status and my success against the pirates.

I wore no weapons; I needed none. My right hand had been baptized by blood as it burned its way through a warrior's body. The complex metal knot-work that is my people's vision of the universe clustered so thickly there that it was almost impossible to see the skin, or at least it did when I felt frightened or angry. At other times I was as I had always been: pale, fair but with a light tan.

121

My hair was coming in again, red-gold curls all over my head as yet too short to dress.

No, I could see why even so tough an old pirate as Ure might not care to try robbing us now.

'But you know,' Ure continued, 'my people will feast you and expect presents in return ... and then late tonight, after the feast, we will want some of your ...' He grinned, one bushy brow lifted. 'Yes, they will want some of your ... luck.'

As he spoke, I saw the girls all rigged out in their best finery, strolling down to greet the men.

An hour or so later, we sat in the great hall. I had the high seat with Maeniel, Ure, and Gray. The hall was shaped like an overturned ship. The fire pit ran down the center. It was a long one, and a whole deer, two boars, and a wild bull were turning on spits over the coals. The air was heavy with the scent of roasting meat, mead, beer, and blood.

Yes, there had been a quarrel over the champion's portion – but Maeniel didn't let it come to a killing. Albe was hell bent on proving herself as dangerous a warrior as any of the men, and she had. Seems she was mistress of the art of unarmed combat. Some of the Pictish women were deadly in that respect.

This is, you see, the salmon leap. The scarlet-bellied fish carries no sword, but it can climb the most treacherous rapids and waterfalls by simply using the coiled power of its muscles. As did Albe. Confronted by her adversary, she dropped her weapon and, pushing off from the table, somersaulted over his head, landed behind him, and whacked him in the head with a lead-lined glove she just happened to be wearing.

He awakened eventually, somewhat the worse for wear, and forgot the quarrel. Soon he was hanging on Albe's neck, swearing he would love her forever.

'Yes,' Maeniel said. 'If she keeps his brains addled enough, he probably will.'

I ate well enough. Wild boar is a wonderful meat and these had fattened on pine nuts and bracken. The flavor of the ribs was delicate, yet rich. The beer was deeply malted, dark, and sweet. And the mead. Ah, what can be said of that. This was a mountain brew, and in summer on the high slopes beyond the forest, before the sheep arrived at their summer pasture, the heather blooms, joined by the gorse. The pimpernel twines among the lupines, white, yellow, deep blue, and daisies grow everywhere, black, orange banded with red and yellow. The bees stagger drunkenly from flower to flower, maddened by the springtime.

A drought bespeaks the splendor of summer's return and seeps into a young woman's blood, bones, and hot loins. Makes her feel a goddess, and she dreams of love but feels the rise of lust the way a proud tree feels the sap racing up to fill the buds on the branches with flowers.

So did I think, sitting in Ure's hall.

As it grew later, the feast became more rowdy. The boys had their fill of battle, but many – most perhaps – knew nothing of love. They were, as I said, the weak, the poor, the outcasts, the despised. The ones the young girls mocked, knowing no reason to want to make a match with them. Now they were blooded! Men! Wealthy warriors, who had dared the proving touch of battle and the sea.

Most would be sought after now. Some would want to return, parade their success, and strut in front of the girls who had ignored or made fun of them, thinking now their families would sing another tune. And given the massive amount of loot in our hollow ships, almost certainly they would find their popularity quite gratifying.

But of others, I wondered. For some the cruelty had been so unrelenting, the wounds inflicted so deep, the pain and loneliness so devastating to their minds and spirits that they would seek other harbors rather than endure what to them was a farrago of hypocrisy. Turn their backs on the communities that sometimes only allowed them to survive, and seek other, more welcoming steadings.

I thought this might be true of Albe and Wic. They and the other girls sat near me and watched with cynical eyes the rather graceful and all-too-willing seduction of their male companions.

'Be some sore heads in the morning,' Wic commented.

Albe chuckled in reply. 'What I want to see is who's wearing what in the morning. The jewelry, I mean.'

'The girls will get a lot of it. I'm resigned to that. I should have gotten Gray and Maeniel to . . .'

'No,' Albe said. 'It was only to be expected. You're their queen, not a wet nurse.'

'Do you have to sit here?' Wic asked. 'I know the kings do, but my back teeth are floating . . . all that damn beer . . .'

'Let's go visit the bushes before . . .'

Just then one of the boys got up, wove toward the fire pit, pulled down his trousers. His organ lifted nicely, and unaided, shot an arcing stream into the flames. He was cheered on raucously by the assembled company.

'He's proud of it,' Albe said. 'Look, no hands!'

Wic grunted and tossed the contents of a wine cup into the fire. It roared up, and the exhibitionist let out a wild yell and fled, pulling his trousers up as he did. He turned, glared at Wic, and called her a couple of interesting things. She answered in the same vein, and two of her more descriptive epithets were new to me and imaginative enough to raise my eyebrows.

Dugald, I thought, would be horrified.

'I don't think my royal highness has to sit through this nonsense,' I said. 'Let's go check the boats. Most of the wealth we've . . . stolen . . . captured . . . is there.'

We eased out into the clean night. Together the three of us walked toward the beach, where the ships were pulled up on the one finger of sand running along the rocky shingle. This close to the sea, it was cold, and drifting billows of mist flowed around us from time to time, moving steadily inland into the pine forests clothing the mountainside.

No human has a nose like a wolf, but what I have was trained by association with my family, and I am conscious of odors others overlook or ignore. When we got close to the beached boats, I smelled Maeniel, wolf, wood smoke, human male perspiration. Wolf is not dog, but a sharper scent of wild with a tinge of blood. It reminded me of Mother. Hers was almost sweet, not so bloody, rather like milk.

I was surprised. I hadn't seen him leave the hall. But then, knowing Maeniel, I knew I shouldn't be surprised.

I didn't speak, but began to rummage in the boat for the shoes Talorcan, the Boar, had given me. I was lacing them on when Maeniel broke cover and joined us.

'Ure left a message for you. He told me to tell you come to his . . . lair, he called it. He has something he wants to discuss with you.'

It's not an easy place to go, his lair, as he puts it. More fog surged past us, pushed by the sea wind. I could taste it on my lips. I would say, the road to his dwelling is a test in itself.

'The river flows down the mountainside steeply here.' Maeniel pointed up the slope at the end of the inlet, where white water emerged from slopes covered with giant pines into the brackish lake at the head of the fiord.

'The trees have been felled to form a sort of ladder over the river. I don't know how they did it, because the pines are yet living trees. But each is canted over the rapids from one side or the other, and you must climb from trunk to trunk to get to the top. A dangerous journey.'

'Sounds like something Ure would do,' I said.

Maeniel chuckled. 'He is a strange one.'

'He is a sorcerer,' I said.

Maeniel studied my face for a second. 'No doubt,' he answered. 'For he smells of the trees, even on the sea or after the battle. Filthy, burned, muddy, bloody, he still reeked of rosin and needles, damp bark and mist. Yes, the mist there eddies on the shore and into the forest by night. He is strange. Cold, but not evil, I think. Yes, go climb the mountain, and as you take each step, leave grief behind in your journey to the top.'

'I would I could do that,' Albe said.

'My grief is on my face,' Wic said, speaking of the ugly birthmark that disfigured her. 'I can never leave it behind.'

'Why don't you try?' Albe told her.

She shrugged, but when I walked into the forest, she followed.

It wasn't an easy climb, but then, I wore the shoes Talorcan gave me. They gave my feet strong purchase on the broad tree trunks that were stretched over the river. It ran through a shallow, steep ravine, down toward the beach. The water was whipped to a froth by the jagged rocks that rose up from the riverbed like so many fangs.

I found the mead I had taken burned out of my body, and the difficulty of climbing from one tree trunk to another held all my attention. Between the spray from the pale rapids and the eddying mist, it was wet on the tree ladder, and I suppose it was cold. But the effort it took to gain each upward step soon had all three of us gasping and sweating.

This was no ladder to be climbed step by step. As we gained each tree trunk, we must walk along the damp, sometimes slippery moss-covered trunk to find the safest spot to cross to the one above it. Below, the river hissed, gushed, and sometimes roared beneath us.

'Would we be killed, I wonder, if we fell?' Albe asked.

I looked down and considered the mess of rock and white-water spume. Yes, there were places where it looked as though the drop wasn't that great or the grade the water flowed over not that steep.

'I don't know,' I said. 'Depends where you happen to land. But I see areas where the water pools clear of rocks and debris. Yes, the current's swift, but you could get your footing in the shallows.'

But as we climbed higher and higher, the journey grew more perilous. There was further to fall.

There was no moon and the absolute stillness of a pine forest crept into your soul. The climb required concentration, the way chess does, and it freed the mind, focused consciousness on immediate problems, and slowly silenced the mild undercurrent of worry and self-criticism that forms a background to human consciousness most of the time.

To allow the mind to drift was dangerous. Wic first noticed this and told us of it. The trunk of one tree was angled up higher than the rest, and we must climb it like squirrels to reach the trunk belonging to the next tree in the series. Wic was ahead of Albe and me when the limb she was using to pull herself forward and up snapped with a loud crack, pitching her back toward the two of us.

She slipped or twisted herself to one side; we never knew which. But Albe got her by the seat of the pants. I dropped down and straddled the log so quickly I hurt my tailbone. But I got my arms around Albe's waist and jerked her back into a seated position on the log.

Wic twisted, threw one leg over the log, got a grip on a branch stub, and sat up, which left them sitting in line, gasping for breath. We all relaxed and just rested for a few moments.

I managed a 'What!'

'The old man has a powerful geis,' Wic answered. 'You do not reach his aerie without submitting to it.'

'And what is it?' Albe asked.

'To get to the top, you must . . . *must,*' she repeated the word for emphasis, 'yield up your greatest sorrow. I was rebellious and yielded to the woe of my ruined face. I brooded too long on it as I climbed, and the geis struck at me. As I fell, I knew how precious life is and saw my bones broken on the rocks below, my blood draining away into the water. And I knew I did not care so much about it.'

'The time of thought is nothing,' Albe said.

Then we got to our feet and continued on, reaching our next step in what seemed now a ladder to the sky. The river was far below, but here it broke into big pools that swirled and glowed like the pearly inside of a shell in the starlight. I welcomed being drawn back into the problems of the climb rather than think about what I had done at the first fortress.

The second and third assaults left few traces on my consciousness, though they had both been bloody enough. I think in all three we made a clean sweep of the pirates. To be brief, we killed them all.

Even now I cannot confess to sorrow. That was the way of it then. Mercy for the vanquished is the luxury of those with strength and the power to contemplate the morality of war. In the struggles we faced then, to lose was to die. And make no mistake, we made sure they did.

But innocents get in the way. Innocents always get in the way. And they, too, pay the price of the violence that explodes around them.

After the first battle, I took a walk into the fortress, on the path around the furnace I created in the Saxon drinking hall. As I told you, the slaves had been chained in sheds along the wall. Most still were fettered where they died.

The Saxons inside the hall left little trace, the calcimined bodies kicked and clubbed to pieces as their bodies were plundered and an exhaustive search made among the ruins for every scrap of weaponry, armor, gold, or silver that could be found. But the slaves had nothing and they were left undisturbed where they lay, bodies twisted in the ashes.

In every case I found the face and looked upon it. Yes, even the children, and there were a great many children, those over seven being a favored commodity of the traders. And in an hour I knew and saw every variation of pain.

Let the rest be silence.

But even in silence the mind's eye sees each one, and the portrait created and then burned into the memory never fades. And each picture intruded between my eye and the stars, the dark, towering pines, and the glowing river below.

So I, too, slipped before I reached the top.

The last steps up the forest ladder were a tangled mass of large trees and saplings. At one time the river must have undermined the slopes of the hill and brought about a massive collapse of the rocky escarpments near the top. At one time it must have plunged down toward those pools we could see below in the form of a waterfall. But after the boulders rolled, the tree roots tore and the earth shook. The river found a slanting bed, the largest trees died, and in the unaccustomed light, saplings flourished only to be uprooted as each spring flood tore more deeply into the riverbed.

But the other trees, stubborn organisms, did not die but formed a green and brown net walk, which led at last to the top. Wic, Albe, and I went forward with trepidation, knowing we stood the most to lose now. A fall from here probably would kill us, and each step we took changed the stress factors that held the pile in position.

The log I put my foot on rolled. My shoe slipped, and I fell over. Desperately I hooked one knee over a branch and hung swinging over the rocks and plunging water below.

The dead are always with me. With all of us. This is the virtue of my people's point of view. Life is a continuum of the living, the dead, and the yet unborn. Two I remembered especially: what must have been a woman and her child.

She had turned the small one around, placing her back to the blaze. The tiny corpse was cradled in her arms. The mother's back was burned through to the bone and the flaking ash bared the curved spinal column and the places where the bone became ribs. She must, I thought, have tried to give the child time to suffocate before the flames took her, since she interposed her own body between her, the child, and the final agony of the devouring flames.

I did this, I thought. *I burned this place.*

The faces I looked upon yesterday are hazy in my mind, but I can see those two clearly yet. And I will do so until I draw my last breath and beyond.

Where does the responsibility for such a horrible death lie? On the shoulders of the pirates who chained them there? On mine? I, who all-unknowing burned the fortress?

And had I known how many innocents would die there, should I have backed away? Abandoned my resolve to destroy those thieving Saxons who were raiding among my people? Crouched hiding among the mountains of my home and let the marauders work their evil will?

An old conundrum – old, old, old. Older perhaps than the world we stand on. But one that anyone who takes the road of action must face.

Evil is a mystery. One might plumb the depths of

knowledge, learn all there is to know of the universe – capture and wield godlike power – and yet not be able to answer the question of why this woman and her child died. I accepted my share of whatever blame might be. And I knew I could not place Ure's geis between myself and truth.

I gazed down into the ghostly, frothing water below. *Must I die?* I thought.

Then Wic had me by the hair and Albe by the belt. Together they pulled me up and rolled me onto the trunk of one of the nearly horizontal trees.

I hung there silent, stretched along the length of bark, my arms around the tree's comforting circumference, legs dangling down on either side.

'That was a near thing,' Albe said.

Pain lashed me, and I knew I must have nearly dislocated my hip. The pain climbed to a shrieking peak, then ebbed away as I clutched the tree trunk desperately.

'Can you climb again?' Albe asked. 'I don't think we have far to go. If not, stay there. I'll fetch a rope. That Ure . . . that devil . . . he must have a rope. I'll fetch one. Make a loop and lower you to the ground. Wic and I can do it. We're strong enough.'

'No. No.' I found I could speak. 'Let me rest for a few seconds. Flex my leg.'

I did. There was some pain, but the leg worked and my back wasn't wrenched. I managed to scramble to my feet, bracing myself against a branch sticking out at a right angle to the pine trunk, and found the pain not enough to keep me from walking or climbing.

Albe pointed up. 'Look!'

I did, and saw a walkway cutting through the trees, made of split pine planks with a rope rail on one side. It didn't take long for us to reach it. When we did, I saw we were at the top and I could look out over the trees below, down to the beach and the sea beyond.

Ure lived on a platform in the trees. The platform was broad, and at least a dozen pines grew up through it. I don't know how he lived where he did. The broad platform was bare but for two places where rock mountain spurs lifted through the planks. One was a cone that glowed with fire; the other, some distance away, held water. A spring bubbled up from the rocks, flowed into a basin, then down to the river.

Ure was sitting on a sewn leather cushion near the fire. All around us the mist moved ghostlike, trailing veils among the pines. They were wet, and water drops sprinkled the platform when the wind blew.

Something . . . a pinecone . . . dropped to the platform as a somewhat stronger gust of wind caused the trees to sigh more loudly. Otherwise, it was silent here. A living silence that encompassed the pines, the veiling mist, and the sweet smell of green, growing things.

I hailed Ure. He looked up at me and chuckled.

'Get a cup,' he said. 'Sit down and we will visit.'

'Cup?' I asked, and then saw three cups near the spring at the other side of the platform.

Amazed, Albe, Wic, and I walked toward the cups, gazing around in astonishment at the level floor of the platform and the tops of the giant pines. Their scent was thick in our nostrils, and the silence moved through our souls the way the wisps of fog drifted among the trees.

When we drew close to the cups, they lifted themselves and came to our hands. These cups were very strange. They were ceramic, the outside black-pitted and rough. But within the glaze was smooth and filled with red-gold rainbows.

I dipped my cup into the water and let it fill. But when I raised it to my lips, the clear water foamed, darkened, and became mead.

Albe gave a cry of delight as hers foamed also. But not into mead – beer.

Wic went last; milk appeared. She gave Ure a shy glance.

'Thank you,' she said. 'It's been so long since I had any fresh, sweet milk. I love the taste.'

He nodded, and I saw three more cushions were close to the fire.

'Impressive,' Albe said. 'You are a sorcerer.'

'Cheap tricks, that is not the heart of sorcery.'

'What is it then?' I asked.

He shrugged, but didn't answer. He looked out across the platform at the horizon and the stars sinking into the sea. We went over and sat on the cushions and joined him, near the fire.

Wic drank deeply, but when she set the cup down, it was full again. Albe did the same with her beer. I drained the mead, but when I felt a strange . . . 'push' is the only way I can describe it . . . I deflected the intent of the cup and it remained empty.

'I can't touch you, can I?' Ure said.

'No,' I answered. 'It's a sort of seduction I don't need. Or want.'

I glanced over at Wic and Albe. They each sat frozen, eyes open but unseeing.

'They aren't here?' I asked.

'No,' Ure answered, then voiced my unspoken thought. 'It's harmless. A brief spell. And it is we who have left them, not they us. I spoke to Kyra last night.'

I looked around. 'She's here?'

'No,' was the reply. Ure was still a man of few words. 'I am against this,' he said.

But then he pointed to a cluster of pines growing up through the platform. Slung from one of the low branches in a net bag was the head. Not Cymry's, but the Faun. The dark-brown eyes looked into mine, gentle life in them.

'You disapprove?' I asked.

133

'Yes!'

'Reasons?' His spare speech affected me.

'The omens,' he said. 'I cast them.'

'You saw ruin?' I asked.

'No! That's just it. I saw nothing.'

Nothing. I have heard of this, but it has never happened to me before. And I have asked questions of the powers time out of mind.

Ure spoke softly. 'When cities bloomed along the coasts of Italia, there was I born and sailed the wine-dark sea, bringing iron to Gaul. So were the first swords hammered out, forged, and tempered. Iron was born, and the golden age ended. Those spirits that ruled the earth then could not stand against cold iron.'

The mirror I questioned mocked me with a vision of my own face. The thrown sticks fell through the cracks between the planks on the platform, and he pointed toward the spring at the other end of the platform. A pine bough fell into the water, splashed it in my face, blinding me. I called the powers and I received only silence as a reply.

The mist thickened and I found I could barely see Ure and the fire. I could feel the moisture wet my face and the inside of my nose. Albe and Wic were gone. Ure, I, and the fire alone remained.

'You are the queen,' he said. 'Sovereignty lies between your legs, girl. That was why after the fight I had to free you or drown you, one or the other. There was no pretense in my assault. If those two demons hadn't fled, I would have killed you.'

My mouth was dry and I realized why I had been so afraid when he came at me. The fog was a pale haze around us. I couldn't see into it. I knew even now he was considering whether to kill me or not.

'Yes,' he answered my unspoken thought. And I knew he was the most powerful sorcerer I had ever met. By comparison to him, Dugald, Igrane, and Merlin were only children.

'You're now wondering if I can kill you.' He smiled and I saw the blunt, yellow teeth gleam. He picked up the cup that held the mead and threw it against the stone surrounding the flames. It shattered into dozens of pieces. They lay on the platform planks scattered, shimmering with their internal rainbows and matte black exterior.

I know I made a sound of distress. The cup had been so beautiful. He stared at it and as I watched, the pieces drew together. Then it moved to the position it had occupied before, and it sat near my hand, the dregs of the mead still in it.

'You are very powerful,' he said. 'Most mortal men and women would have seen nothing. My powers are probably not greater than yours, but I am older, more a cognoscente of evil, and much more experienced.'

'You mended a cup,' I said.

'No, I didn't,' he answered.

I was afraid then, because I understood what he really had done. So afraid my face felt numb and I wondered if I ought to take action. Now!

But those smoky green eyes of his held me, the way a snake's gaze holds a stricken bird. He grinned again and let me go.

'You made the cup never be broken at all,' I said.

'Good answer,' was his reply. 'And you know what? I can make you never exist at all.'

I slid off the cushion and sat on my heels. 'Then why don't you?' I asked.

He looked away from me and into the murk around us.

'The heart of sorcery,' he said, 'is the power to make the world into the sort of place you wish to live in. Accept my geis. The other two did.'

135

'No!' I said. 'I am no more yours than I am Arthur's, Merlin's, or Mondig's.'

As I answered I felt the morning breeze freshen, driving out the mist, and I realized it was that hour just before dawn when the light brightens and day enters the forest, the shore, and the sea. The tall pines were very still, the only sound the drip of water falling on the planks of Ure's platform. A faint perfume emanated from the living trees.

Ure sighed, a strange sound from so harsh a character as he was.

'It is time,' he said. 'Question the Faun before the sun rises.'

'Yes, I suppose it is,' I answered. 'I must find a way to fetch Arthur.'

Things, Black Leg thought, weren't going the way he thought they would.

'Stop wiggling! Goddamn it, stop!' she was saying. 'I'm trying to heal you. Heal you at least enough to stop the pain. And you're jumping around like a goddamn scared rabbit.'

Black Leg drew in a deep breath. His skin where the vine had embraced him felt like it had been burned, and a combination of itch-searing rawness and general soreness made him want to leap into wolf form to shed this horrible discomfort.

'Don't you dare!' she whispered. 'Don't you dare! They can tell . . . those birds . . . if you do. They're all over the place outside, and I don't know if the vines can keep them out of the door.'

Cold fear counseled Black Leg's instant obedience. Jesus, those birds. He was very still. Angry rebellion flared for a moment in his mind.

It's not fair, he thought. *Goddamn, it's downright*

humiliating. I wanted to be a warrior. Fight other men who came at me carrying swords and wearing armor so I can defeat them with my superior strength, skill, and cunning.

But between girls who jumped out of lakes and wanted lots of hot sex (actually, that hadn't been too bad), crazy old sorcerers running in and out of bushes, nasty vines, singing flowers, pepper-laced fruit, and birds whose malice chilled him to the bone, he wasn't getting many chances to shine as a warrior. This was not the way he'd envisioned his adventuring when he left home. He was smart enough to know he was getting a really superior education. But what he was being prepared for wasn't at all clear to him.

He opened his eyes a little. They felt swollen and he thought that he might be blind, but just for a second until he turned his gaze to the narrow windows looking out over the gorge they were in.

It was dusk. He could see her face near the window, looking out anxiously.

The birds. Those birds were there.

She glanced down at him. 'You with me?' she said.

Black Leg managed an '*Ua!*' and she nodded.

'Keep still. Christ, they're all over the place. But you pissed off that vine so bad – it's still wiggling around out there like a scalded snake – that they don't dare come near the door to this hole we're in. I'm almost glad we found something those buggers are afraid of. Even if it did cost you. I think they know we're around here somewhere, but they aren't sure where. And if you change, they might spot us and manage to force the door. Those vines are mean, but the goddamn birds are stronger than anything. I can feel it. And I don't know if I have the strength left to turn myself to stone like I did before.'

He moved slowly. His body screeched in agony when he did, and then there was a peculiar numbness about his

137

thighs and torso that frightened him more than pain would have. But he managed to sit up and look out also.

For a second he wondered where the ravens were, then saw that they were flying, wheeling in a flock down into the gorge. So far down their wing tips almost brushed the river. Then back up, up into the slanted rays of the dying sun, the shiny black of their feathers gleaming with golden fire as the light poured over them. Then turning into a curtain of darkness as they entered the shadowed gorge below.

'An awesome sight,' he whispered.

She agreed. 'Yes, awesome and chilling.'

'What are they?' he whispered.

'My powers fail me where they are concerned. I thought myself a being of sagacity and wide experience in both my world and many others. But they humble me. I cannot imagine what they are. Putting it succinctly, your guess is as good as mine. But I think the moon in this place banishes them for a time.'

'They are hunting us,' Black Leg whispered as she leaned into his arms. She was wet, fading again, he thought, dying.

He could feed her. He had today. But the water wouldn't answer her needs, only substances from the flowers that spoke in musical ways. There simply weren't enough here for her to live on.

The cool wetness of her wilting flesh felt good against the raw skin on his chest and abdomen. He looked down at himself and felt sick. He was burned red with raw, weeping patches from his chest to the tops of his thighs. And moreover, he was discovering the stimulant effect of certain types of pain.

Oh, no, he thought, because he knew he wanted this, but didn't. The triggers were so deep in his brain that he couldn't reach them to turn off the pain-pleasure junction.

In a haze of desire, he watched the company of birds rise into the dying sun, then fall like some magnificent living curtain into the growing dark until the sun no longer shone on their bodies and they turned. Flying low over the waters to escape the rising moon, they followed the river of water, a river of wings vanishing down the gorge into the darkness.

She was trembling. Or was he the one quivering with a vicious delight?

'I die,' she whispered as her nails bit into his back, his inflamed hot flesh making her clutch doubly painful.

'Don't you dare. You are ... killing me!' she whimpered.

'No! No! If you're so afraid, tell me you don't want it too.'

She moaned, clawed at his face. He felt the wetness but wasn't sure if it came from her dissolving flesh or from ribbons of blood that poured from his lacerated cheek.

'When you go, I'll be alone,' he whimpered. 'I'll never look into your eyes again. I want something.'

He was entering her body, her soft darkness, velvet darkness. His body cringed at the thought of what he was about to do, but he found his mind detached and rock solid.

He shuddered as his whole being seemed to pour like a waterfall into the point of exquisite fire between his legs.

'Take it! Take it all!'

The pleasure ceased, cut off at the instant of absolute gratification, and his genitals shriveled with absolute and utter pain. He rolled away from her, retching violently, the spasms of pain bending his body into an arch, locking his muscles and nervous system into convulsion. Again, and again and again.

Until after an eternity of suffering, he collapsed and all

his sphincters let go: piss from his penis, shit from his ass, drool from his mouth, tears from his eyes, and his stomach spasmed and emptied a cupful of bitter acid onto the stone floor.

He blinked his eyes to try to clear them. Did clear them and saw the she-wolf where her dissolving body had been, strong and healthy, gazing at him with wide, shocked, yellow eyes.

The two shadows stood in the wind-ruffled grass looking down at him as Uther awoke. He remembered his thoughts about time, its end at the barrow doors.

'They succeeded in their endeavor, didn't they?' he said.

'Yes,' one of the shadows answered. 'We are their achievement.'

Uther sat up. 'Where is Morgana?'

'Gone. She left a message for you.' One of the visitors spoke, pointing to the ground.

Uther saw the paw marks of the Cat Sith clearly delineated in the sandy soil.

'Ah,' he said.

'She knew we would accompany you on your travels.'

Uther wasn't sure he wanted a close look at the pair. His neck prickled with alarm. *They could not be living beings,* was his thought.

'I'm not sure I want your company on any journey I might make at present,' he said. 'Unless . . .'

'No! You are a living man,' one of them said. 'And so are we.'

Uther rose to his feet and faced them.

'The Brotherhood of the Bagudae greets you. But to join us, you must yield up your sword. But fear not, we have a replacement.'

They were only shadows still. Uther scratched at the

stubble on his cheek with his right hand. Where was Morgana? Even as Cat Sith she should not have abandoned him.

The Bagudae! He'd heard of them, the bane of the dying Roman Imperium. But they were in Gaul, Iberia, Italy, not here among the Britons. How could this be?

'Wherever the builders of the stone tombs went, we come.' One of the shadows made this statement. 'You called us. You came to our door. We will show you our paths, guide your footsteps into the Saxon camps. Come. They are still holding the horse fights, still choosing a king. There are many things for you to learn in London. Lew's City, it is still called. Yield up your sword.'

Uther was tired; that was all he could think. He had looked forward to dozing in the saddle on this journey under the stars. Now they wanted his sword. What were they planning to do? Lead him out on foot into the wilderness alone?

'Show me this replacement for my horse and sword. And you will no doubt mean for me to dispense with my mail helmet and shield.'

'Yes.' The answer was soft but firm. The shadow on the right unslung something he had on his back. He was carrying it much the way a long sword is carried, in a baldric that touched against his back in the same fashion as a large sword. He stretched out the bulky object to Uther and placed it in the king's arms.

This was no sword. Much more broad and thick, the only way to receive it was to enfold it into an embrace. Uther knew what it was as his arms closed around it. And he was glad for the darkness because he was ashamed of his tears.

Uther surrendered his weapons without a qualm or quibble. Sword, hauberk, and helmet went into some mysterious place in the barrow. He kept his mantle and sax – the sax Morgana gave him so long ago on the

141

day . . . the day he found he must be a man . . . the day his two brothers died in Gaul serving some pretender to the purple, the imperial throne of the Caesars. The day he last touched the harp. Only she had known he put the instrument away from him forever, afraid even to touch it lest it distract him from the single-minded pursuit of the High Kingship – his destined fate. Put it away lest the simple touch of his hand on the case rise up his arm and strike his heart with such pain that he would be unmanned.

He burned his need and his grief forever, leaving it hanging on the wall in the young man's hunting shelter – a place that he would never visit again, being now too important, preoccupied, busy, involved with a life devoted to the struggles of rank.

Uther slung the harp over his back, drew his mantle up over it and his shoulders, and set out with the two into the night.

For a time they followed the road, but then, steering a course by the stars, they left it and set out over the countryside. Roman villas were everywhere, but his companions threaded their way between them, keeping to the strips of meadow, forest, and waste that lay between the broad expanses of cultivated land. A few, it is true, had been abandoned in the upheavals that accompanied the end of Roman occupation. But good land was not something usually left uncultivated; and most times, though the central residence might be a burned-out ruin, the land was farmed by those who owed allegiance to owners who were safely ensconced in the walled towns that dotted the countryside. Owners who were not slow to collect their due at the point of a Saxon sword. Owners who were more than happy to burn any village that showed an unwillingness to pay the extortionate taxes that funded the Saxon mercenary forces who served as their enforcers. Owners who rounded up children every year to be sent to the east as slaves.

Uther and the two from the tomb threaded their way between the villas, silent and unseen through the darkness. They were good guides and seemed to know the country well. Their star knowledge was greater than his, though his was not inconsiderable.

Near dawn – he realized dawn was approaching by the setting of the Pleiades, and the dew was beginning to soak his leggings – he knew that they must have covered a great deal of ground. They slowed to hunt.

The rabbits were out feeding on the wild greens, cold, crisp, and dampened by the settling ground mist. His companions took them on the fly. A rabbit confronted by a predator freezes, then jumps left or right. A human has a fifty-fifty chance of nailing the rodent if he moves before the rabbit jumps.

Most of the rabbits died so quickly at the hands of his escorts that they never had a chance to scream. Uther was interested to see that out of ten, they got six. The seventh was a pregnant doe and had to be released.

When they paused at a stream to clean and gut their catch, Uther became aware he could see. For a moment, he had reservations about looking at them. What, after all, might have arisen from a tomb in the dead of night? But in the growing light, they seemed human enough. Both were dark, so weather-beaten they looked as though they might never have slept in a bed in their lives. They were of indeterminate age, not old but then not young, either, and leather-clad from head to foot. Identically dressed, soft leather boots, trousers and tunics of the most supple tanned hides he had ever seen.

Then he saw they must be twins by the shape of their rather fine features: identical eyes, mouths, noses, eye and skin coloring, the same dark, thick curly brown hair.

Two boys, he thought.

Then one pulled off his leather cap to wash his face in the stream and long hair drifted to her neck.

Oh! Uther thought, knowing in his gut what his head didn't want to accept. Brother-sister lovers. God, what must such a tie be like? Unbreakable, absolutely unacceptable, they must both be forever outcast.

She smiled at him, twisted her hair, tucked it up under her cap, and became a boy again.

'Who will I be without crown, horse, sword, or hauberk?'

'A great bard, a famous singer,' the man said.

His sister laughed. 'I know you will.'

'A disguise?' Uther asked.

'I was told to tell you no, a profound truth,' the woman said.

To his surprise, Uther felt tears in his eyes. 'It's been too long. The music will never return.'

'As to that, I . . . cannot answer. The plot was none of my devising,' she said.

Then the two hurried up the slope. The trees that shaded the streambed opened into a meadow. It was silvered with ground mist.

Uther followed them across the meadow until they came to a green mound only faintly visible in the drifting mist. They circled it until they reached a spot Uther thought must have once been the entrance. There, on a flat stone, sat a bowl of curd cheese mixed with honey.

'She did not forget us,' the man said, lifting it from the stone. 'Now, let us break our fast.'

They crossed another meadow and entered a grove of trees, mixed oak and beech. The ground was thick with acorns and mist. Boar sign was everywhere.

Uther was uneasy, but his companions moved forward confidently. 'They, the servants of Dis, never trouble us. No one can see us here. We will cook a stew, but first you must eat some of the honey and curds.'

Uther was so weary, he was happy to do so. He sank down on a thick drift of dead leaves and filled his stomach with the bowl's contents as he watched the two build a fire, gather greens and a few tubers, and place them together with the hares in a leather vessel suspended over an open fire.

He was uneasy about the fire.

'They can't see us,' the young man said.

'Why not?' Uther questioned. 'The wood is not that thick.'

'I don't know.' The girl appeared troubled for a moment, but then continued, 'They never do.'

Just then a hound broke cover, trotting into the small clearing. He turned his head and the dog met Uther's eyes.

The king went rigid with terror.

A man, rudely but well dressed in leather leggings, tunic, and a fine, woolen mantle, followed. By his clothes, he had to be a local lord or even a magistrate. Likely one of the villas they had passed in the night belonged to his family. And Uther knew he would be up so early checking his rabbit snares. How could he not see the three people here?

But he didn't. He seemed to see nothing unusual. He snapped his fingers at the straying hound, called on it to heel, and strolled on.

The girl laughed. The nobleman paused, looked back over his shoulder, seemed bewildered for a second. Then he shrugged, looked uneasy, and made the horn sign against the evil eye. He ordered the still straying hound back to heel and hurried on, vanishing in a moment into the pale mist.

'You see,' she said. 'They don't and they never do. See us, I mean.'

The fear Uther felt a moment before was nothing to the chill terror that filled his soul now.

'No!' he said. He had difficulty articulating the word; his mouth was dry, his lips and tongue would hardly move. 'No, they don't, do they?'

'Some places belong to us,' the young man said. 'This is one of them.'

They were Alex and Alexia, orphans of the Bagudae. Or so they introduced themselves.

'They leave us, you know, on temple steps – to die or be taken and brought up, later to be sold as slaves.'

'The Bagudae rescued us,' Alex said.

'She was a courtesan in Alexandria,' Alexia told him. 'We remember her . . . sort of, I think. We were too dark. She couldn't convince her lover we were his children. We were an investment that never paid off, and when her lover left her – or was killed . . . we don't know which . . .'

'Politics is a lethal preoccupation,' Uther said.

'Oh, definitely,' Alexia said.

Alex continued, 'She was loath to throw good money after bad and had her servants leave us on the porch at the Temple of Isis.' He added thoughtfully, 'A good woman of business, though a poor mother.'

'Yes,' Uther agreed. He felt slightly sickened but said nothing else.

'You sleep now,' Alexia said. 'The stew will be ready in a few hours. We will wake you when it is.'

He felt he had endured too many shocks today, far too many for a man his age. He unstrapped the harp and rested it safely against the drift of dead leaves beside him. Then he loosened the laces on the soft boots he wore, wrapped himself in this mantle, curled up on the same pile of leaves, and slept.

He found he lay knees drawn up on a mat in a tomb. A very simple lamp, with a thumb-depressed lip holding one wick, burned near the entrance. It illuminated a harp case leaning against the wall.

He became aware that he inhabited a newly buried corpse. Oh, yes, he knew – as in dreams we know things we cannot know in the real world – that all this happened a long time ago. His spirit returned briefly to his cold, stiff flesh to be sure the harp was there. And when the lamp burned out, it would depart for its distant destination.

Silence – the mind talks, never shuts up. Keeps up its constant commentary on the ever-changing flow supplied by the senses. It argues, analyzes, fears – is amused, discontented, blasphemes or laments. Silence – the tomb was silent, always would be silent, as its occupant lay in utter stillness, being transformed into dust.

The lamp guttered, flared one bright flame, and lifted from the clay lip before utter blackness descended. The king's mind ceased to speak as the flame dropped to a spark, glowed a spot of red in the darkness, then vanished.

The music returned. He drifted among the leaves of a forest as gray rain pattered among them. The sea surged, pounded, hissed, roared. The wind spoke to the forest, a roar, a hush, a hiss, a whisper. Boughs groaned in a storm, rain not a patter but a pouring rush, a river ragged between its banks thundering, gurgling, sucking, and sobbing. The limbs and knobs of branches clattered in the freezing winter blasts. Tree trunks snapped in the cold snow cascaded from roofs with wet thuds. Big snowflakes tinkled as they fell during a windless, frozen night.

Uther tossed in his sleep as a rabbit screamed its death cry in the jaws of a fox. A stag belled, crashing his antlers against the brushwood to clean them of velvet, and blared his challenge to the other males. Uther's people sang their prayers and in the music found more meaning than in the woods.

When he woke, he found the harp was already in his hands. He was tightening the pegs to tune the strings.

The next day, they stopped at an inn. Uther saw two things clearly. One was how easy it would be to fool people about his identity.

The night before, he'd shaved both beard and mustache. He looked a different man even to himself, and he reflected that his problem might be proving his identity to those nobles in London who knew him and had, he hoped, remained loyal. He had no mirror, but used a pool near the spring to study his face, and the transformation had been astonishing.

The second had been the power of his harp.

The inn was a poor enough place, part of a villa on the road to London. The wealthy who rode in mounted parties guarded by Saxon warriors were lodged at the villa, a wealth-fortified dwelling that overlooked the road from a nearby hill. The inn at the crossroads was much less of a secure place. A room with tables and benches, and barrels ranged against the walls were tapped for beer, wine, and mead. A fireplace at the north end of the room served for cooking, and indeed, when the king entered, several birds were turning over the flames, the spit driven by a blind, discouraged-looking turnspit dog walking in a cage near the fireplace.

'I think the beer is safest here,' Alexia whispered softly.

'Where do the guests sleep?' Uther asked, glancing around.

'There is a loft over the fireplace,' Alex answered. 'But were I you, I would wrap my mantle around myself and bed down on the floor.'

Alexia laughed. 'The loft has straw in it. They don't change it often, and it is . . . shall we say, "inhabited." ' '

Uther shivered. Not much choice. Outside, the wind was blowing in hard gusts. The sky was gray. Uther knew by dawn the skies would be clear but the dew would be frozen on the grass blades. Sleeping in the open without shelter would be miserable tonight. The inn offered the best chance of even a halfway comfortable night, even though Uther noticed that when the wind gusted hard outside an icy draft swirled around him and the toes in his boots were numbed by the sudden chill. His bones ached and he knew it would rain soon. So he resigned himself to a hard bed.

The woman who kept the taps approached him as he entered.

'Ale,' he said, 'for me and my friends.'

She eyed the pair askance. 'Can you pay with anything better than a song?'

Her eyes and nose were red. She seemed angry and sad. Then he reflected what her life must be in this wide spot on the road to London and pitied her.

He gave her three coppers from his scrip and got a look of respect in return. Then she directed them to a seat on the bench closest to the fire, not an unmixed blessing, since the firewood was green, wet, or both. When the wind gusted, it made his eyes tear.

Currency was catch as catch can, since most of the mints had stopped working when the Romans left. Copper was circulated until it wore away. Silver suffered from heavy clipping (the edges were shaved off and the shavings melted down by the money changers, attached now only to aristocratic households). The few who had gold hoarded it, so the woman probably never saw much.

The three coins vanished into her clothing and would probably suffice to buy the three of them food and lodging for the night.

The wretched dog on the turnspit wheel slowed to a stop. The woman smacked him with a strap, and the dog began to walk again and the spits to turn.

The king averted his eyes. The animal had once been

149

big, perhaps a mastiff used to run down wolves or other dangerous game. Why it had been mutilated and put to this work he couldn't imagine. But then, perhaps he should be grateful. The thing was only a dog. He had a time or two seen children treated the same way.

The king shivered, not completely from the cold, and tried to warm his hands at the inadequate blaze. Outside the rain began. He saw more people were entering the room, some travelers, others looked to be servants or tenants of the estates nearby, come to get out of the weather and have a drink. Their clothing steamed and the room began to stink.

He and his friends were served ale and bowls of stew. To his surprise, the food was good, though the stew was more vegetable than animal, mostly turnips and dried apple with some sort of sausage. The bread on the table was laced with onions and cheese, and as he ate, the woman pulled a bird off the spit and placed it on a bread trencher near his hand.

Alexia reached for the bird, a look of inquiry in her eyes. Uther nodded. She pulled off a leg and thigh for him and shared out the rest with her brother.

When he was finished eating and drinking, the woman returned and offered him a basin with warm water to wash and a clean cloth to dry his hands. Uther sighed. Three coppers, such service. This was probably the best this little inn had to offer.

'My lord.' The words were whispered behind him, then echoed, 'My lord, my lord, *domine,*' the old Latin form.

Uther hesitated, not sure this might not be a trick. Were itinerant singers called my lord?

He turned and saw that behind him the room was full. At least thirty pairs of eyes studied him, looking out of the darkness. Some were eating and drinking, but others simply sat, hands folded, watching him. These were the poorest, who probably had no way to pay the score.

'My lord,' the whisper came again, 'give us a song.'

Outside the rain was changing to sleet. He could hear the tinkle against the wattle-and-daub walls. He knew it would be beginning to freeze the water running in the thatch above.

His heart faltered. He could almost hear it miss a beat; perhaps it did. The terrible truth was he didn't know if he had a song to give them. He certainly hadn't one this morning. Tuning the harp had been easy, well and good. He had done that. But except for a few limited strains he somehow remembered even after all these years, it seemed he had forgotten most of what he knew.

He easily fell prey to discouragement, imagining that in the past he had only succumbed to vanity in believing he could ever join the company of bards; the great bards that chronicled his people's history, achievements, and, if the truth be known, their rich, ancient philosophy of life. He had been preparing to present himself for examination at the winter festival when Morgana had come to tell him his brothers died in Gaul. . . .

He had some silver in his scrip. Not much, but enough to buy drunken oblivion for everyone in the room. One silver coin would probably be sufficient. The woman who kept this place probably hadn't seen above seven or eight silver coins in her life.

Her voice broke in on his thoughts, sharp, shrewish, angry.

'What! Now I know why you're all here . . . and on a stinking cold night like this. Come to make fools of yourselves over a man with a dough cutter.'

Uther flushed at the crude term for any stringed instrument.

'Get out of here, you stupid pig fuckers! You mind your business, I'll mind mine. He's paid and paid enough not to be bothered with the likes of you!' She swung the

151

strap, the one she'd used on the dog, at a beggarly-looking man behind Uther.

Just then a strong gust of wind struck the building. The fire belched smoke into the room and everyone turned away, coughing, eyes tearing. Uther thought of his vision of the tomb. This is the fate of all living things, silence and darkness. Eternal silence? Eternal darkness?

Reason enough for music; reason enough to send his hands groping for the harp in its case at his side even as he spoke to the tavern mistress in gentle reproof.

'Madam! I will sing for a bit. It doesn't matter. Share a bit of drink with the thirsty and dry. I will pay the score.'

The woman looked about to be angry until Alex proffered a silver coin. She made the coin vanish so quickly, Uther almost wondered if he had seen it in the first place.

When his hand touched the harp, Uther heard the music twining, rising, falling, rippling in his mind. Dancing with the whispered sounds of sleet on the walls, the roof, the parchment-covered windows of the room.

Melodies he hadn't thought of in years filled his mind. Alexia produced a double flute, Alex a shawm. His fingers wandered on the strings, testing, listening to sounds he couldn't believe *he* was making. So beautiful they were even in their individual purity to his unaccustomed ears.

The fire on the logs before him hissed as the damp, wind-driven sleet blew into the grating above it. He began to play to the flames, blue, yellow, and then warm orange and even dull red as they ate into the green logs. Softy, he called them, summoned them to warm the room and the people crowded into it. The fire rose a bright yellow, glowing like a sun on water, flames in a silken presence fluttering above the logs in the joyous combustion, the glow of life itself.

The central log on the fire disintegrated, splitting in the center and drenching the other two logs that hadn't quite caught in glowing, dull-red embers and flaring white sparks. The wood hissed again. Steam rose and then was whisked away by rising flame.

Uther didn't hear the gasp of awe behind him or the tremble in the rippling, flooding notes of the flute Alexia played. He was gone, entering his music the way light transforms mist into columns of haze, turning a many-pillared forest into a cathedral of illusion.

The firelight filled the room, glowing on the rapt faces of his audience listening to a paean of delight, and swept them away with him into the contemplation of a universe fashioned, transfiguringly loved, and ordered by God.

When he was done, not finished but simply too weary to continue, the storm was past and the night sky blessed by uncountable stars, the air crisp and cold. The fire on the northern hearth was burned to ruby coals. The crowd took their leave quietly, the only sound the crunch of footsteps in the frozen grass. They had all had as much as they wished to eat and drink, and the hostess was enriched by not one but two silver coins. He was trembling with weariness when he and the others sought their beds on the floor.

The dog woke him, slobbering, whimpering, moaning. He opened his eyes. Alex was resting against his back, Alexia snuggled at his stomach. He had known a time when a warm female body would have filled him with a frenzy of desire. In the morning he would tell them to change places, but otherwise, he was only annoyed. And even so not very annoyed. Together they were warm as a blanket.

He looked toward the fire and saw a kind of silver haze over the coals. It triggered the memory of the last time he had seen his son. Arthur had come to him in the night, calling him to witness Merlin and Igrane working

153

black magic. Later, upon thinking of the fact that his son got into his room unchallenged, he had come to the conclusion that a subtle but powerful spell had been at work.

He had seen the same haze near the fire, but thought it only moonlight. But tonight there was no moon. He remembered the absolute dominion of the stars when he stood at the door to say farewell to his audience.

Magic, and tonight of all nights. The thought wearied him. He was a man of his hands – as it is said – be his hands on a harp or a sword.

His right hand closed on the hilt of the sax in his belt. The dog was silent now, but Uther heard paws scrabbling on the floor. The sound was frantic.

Uther thought of the miserable, mutilated animal. Perhaps it would be a good thing if he took the sax and struck the animal in the ribs on the left side where the heart thuds. A good deed, but what was using the dog to seek him?

'Yes, a good deed!'

The voice was a whisper that came from near where the dog lay. Uther knew the voice.

'Merlin!'

Laughter, audible laughter originating in the dog's throat.

'I am tormenting it, trying to get it to rise and rend you.' This voice was only in his mind. Then, 'I am lost. Lost, lost,' the dog moaned. 'In hell – in the dog – in the forest. In hell, in hell.'

'Merlin, what has got its claws in you?' Uther asked.

'The king, the king.'

'I am the king. I have done nothing to you,' Uther whispered.

'Bade. Bademagus!' Sobbing, cursing incoherence succeeded this statement. The sounds were separate. The voice in his mind, the struggles of the animal near the fire, were loud in the room.

'Stop,' Uther whispered. 'You will wake the rest. Is that what you want? The woman will take a strap to the dog and you will feel it. How long have you been in the dog?'

'A night, a day, a night. Until the tally was two weeks.'

The animal's mind is winning, Uther thought.

'It wanted respite for its suffering,' Merlin's voice continued. 'It got meeeeeeee.' The word trailed off in a wail of despair.

'You tried the magic of Dis. But hell is where you belong, sorcerer. You and your bitch, fuck, you tortured my son.' Uther was surprised at the grim satisfaction in his soft voice.

'You tried. You failed. You didn't save him. You didn't stop us in time.' There was a vicious spite in the answer.

'Be still!' Rage choked Uther. 'I'll kick the dog's ribs in – and enjoy it. I know the damage you and she did. I know. I see it sometimes in his eyes. But not, thank God, always. No, not always.'

The animal panted, whimpered.

'Come here!'

'No,' Uther answered. 'Ruined as that animal is, I'll not step within reach of its chain.'

The animal's teeth ground. 'Would you know what path to take to defeat the Saxons?'

The last thing Uther wanted was the advice of whatever was left of the sorcerer. It was obvious there had been a falling-out between the two villains. And Bade, Lord of the Summer Country, had gotten the better of the encounter. But from the first that devil Merlin had been the most politically astute of his advisors.

As a king, he had no right to turn away useful information, no matter how repellent or dangerous the source. He rose, pushing himself slowly and carefully to his feet. As he did, he drew the sax, smothering the blade in the folds of the mantle. It might take a second to deploy it, but that couldn't be helped. The dog was blind, but he didn't know if the sorcerer's spirit also was.

He took the few steps, which brought him to where the dog lay near the spit wheel. The panting breaths of the crippled beast were rapid and harsh.

'You will kill me.'

'Yes!'

'It and I long for death. I want your word.'

'You have it. Now tell me.'

'They come tomorrow.'

'Who?' Uther was bewildered.

'The horses and the sacrifices. What you must do is—'

Uther saw the dog's haunches twitch. That was all the warning he got. It had been a mastiff, a battle dog bigger and stronger than even he had realized. He didn't know the lunge had begun until he saw the rotten, blackened but still-long, ragged fangs rising toward his throat.

There was no time to get the sword into it. But he swung the pommel ball down toward the rising black skull. Steel, a war hammer in a pinch, the pommel split the dog's skull even as Uther was blinded by a brilliant flash of light.

CHAPTER THREE

LBE AND I TOOK ANOTHER PATH
back to the shore.

'A wondrous place,' she said, and turned
to look back to Ure's lair. Both awe and longing were in
her voice.

I seized her by the hair and jerked her head around. She
cried out in pain.

'Don't!' I snarled. 'Don't give him any more power
than he already has.'

She stood obedient next to me, looking down the path
across the rocks that led down next to the white-water
rapids beneath the forest road. My fingers slipped free of
the thick curls springing now from her scalp. He had
taken our hair before the battle, making no distinction
between boys and girls. And I thought that sacrificial rite
might also have added to this unlikely sorcerer's spells.
Though, God, he didn't need any additional ammu-
nition! His power still staggered me.

Wic had been hurt too much – too long – by the
treachery of those she looked to for love for her to resist
him. She became one of his acolytes, there to remain
mistress, lover, servant, follower, trusted companion,
friend, all and in a certain way none of these things. Until
. . . until . . . I didn't know how long. Time stopped at his

lair. We would never know. No life could be long enough.

I'm not sure Albe knew what we had turned away from. Not really comprehended it. I had a better idea, but my muscles knotted with fear as I remembered that the Faun told me I must return. For some reason, I must return.

'You cannot take the dragon,' the Faun had said. 'There is no sea. She will accompany you, be your companion.'

The sea, the ocean realm of dragons, had been a constant in my life since the day I was born. How could I go where there was no sea?

There were tears on Albe's face, and I saw I had hurt her. I think she is impervious to bodily pain, but to be treated roughly by one she adored . . . me . . . was such as to bring her grief.

'I'm sorry,' I said. 'I didn't mean it. I'm afraid.'

She glanced at me, pain in her eyes, but didn't reply. I stopped, sat down on a log, and watched the white water rush past us in the half dark. She paused and, still standing, turned her back to me, looking at the water.

I began to unlace the shoes Talorcan had given me when we trod the mage of Dis. I was going to do magic, and my feet must touch the ground. The Faun said so.

'Here, you wear them.' Holding them by the laces, I extended them to her.

She looked complimented and frightened at the same time.

'Here,' I repeated. 'You may need protection.'

She gave a brief laugh. 'Yes, from the real owner of these shoes.'

'I don't think he would object to . . .' But then I broke off. He might, and then God knows what the Death Pig might do.

But then, while I watched, they changed – developed a

bit of heel and ended looking a bit like the campaign sandals Roman officers commonly wore with a metal plate in the center and many small straps holding the sole to the plate. They were just her size.

My feet are big and were Kyra's despair. When I was young, some convention demanded ladies – great ladies – have small feet. The greater the lady, the smaller the feet. But there was no keeping me from running barefoot, so I ended with a firm foundation.

But though Albe's face was scarred and most of her looks gone, she still had a good figure, long, graceful legs, and small feet. She must have been a beautiful girl until the raid that destroyed her family and before she sacrificed her face in token grief.

'You see,' she had told me, 'I must not be a woman, for I am the only one left to avenge them. And vengeance must be taken, or their spirits can never rest.'

I shivered. That is one of the worst things about us – us and the Saxons. It is why we are so interested in law. Why we worry about justice and spend more time on trivial cases at law than the Romans ever thought of. These blood feuds. It would be too long and complex to explain here, but vengeance is not a matter of hot blood with us. It is a duty, and if Albe felt chained to the need for vengeance, then she would likely never have any life at all.

But then, perhaps after having been raped, then thrown into the sea to die – and that's what had happened to her – perhaps she had no wish for a conventional woman's life.

'Best put the shoes on then,' I told her. 'If you are going with me, I think you will need their protection.'

She sat down beside me. 'Where are you going?' she asked as she began doing up the laces.

'I don't know,' I told her. 'The Faun gave me directions. He said follow the coast till the sea is gone. Do this before dawn.'

Albe looked up. 'But how? If you are following the coast, how can the sea be gone? You can't follow the coast and escape the sea.'

I studied the water rushing past. 'I know,' I said. 'That's why I'm warning you to consider your hide before you follow me. You have money now. Your honor is restored. Marry, reestablish your family. It is said "a woman clad in gold is the most beautiful of all." '

'I'm not such a fool. Most men would despise me – as I am now. And would any who would take me for the wealth I bring to a match be worth having?'

'I cannot say.' I shrugged.

'Besides, I've a mind to see the world. And I must find out how one escapes the sea by running along the shore.'

She had finished with the shoes. 'So comfortable,' she said, standing and trying them out.

'By the stars,' I said, looking up through the lattice of pine branches above. 'It is near first light. We have not much time.'

I felt the damp rocks with my toes. The millrace river sent up enough spray to wet everything on its banks. I was wearing Maeniel's sword on my back. Her sword was shorter, more of a sax. A falchion, Eure called it. She found it somewhere in the ruins of the pirate fortress we had destroyed. The hilt was walrus ivory, cunningly carved with hollows for the fingers. Like a sax, the blade was sharp on both sides up to the middle, where it humped.

Albe was strong. Most men would have had difficulty using that blade, it was so heavy, but she wielded it like a child's toy. I watched her try it on a branch three inches thick once. On the downstroke, the weight of the blade sheared through the wood as though it were warm butter. I didn't like to think what it would do to a human being.

But I think her favorite weapon was still the sling. She

always wore it in her belt and constantly replenished the sack of smooth, round stones of the kind she favored most. It was always close to her hand and ready.

I settled the sword on my back, straightened my belt, and made sure my mantle was well wrapped around my shoulders.

'We run,' I said.

'How do you know?' she asked.

'I feel it,' I said.

We began to run, flying down the path beside the river. When Mother was alive, we ran often: she, myself, Black Leg as either wolf or boy. Starting out early, we ran downhill until we reached the beach, then flew along the shingle. Black Leg, when he was wolf, followed Mother. But two-legged, I must pick a path, thinking each time where my feet would land.

It was like playing chess. My mind emptied of all else. Whatever trouble was in my thoughts when I began to run, it was always wiped away by the concentration necessary to cover ground swiftly while climbing steep hills, racing across the treacherous slopes, dodging through the ravines. Or even simply dashing along in and out of the waves that sometimes foamed to my knees while keeping my footing on water-slick stone. Mother felt it was good exercise for any young animal to learn to pick a path and travel swiftly in any and all circumstances.

I forgot Albe. I forgot the battle. I forgot the dying and the destruction. I simply ran as the Faun told me. I felt a communion with the earth through my feet. The rocks that channeled and protected the river were measured strength, pine needles a drift of sweet-scented softness.

There were more pools, still places among the some-times savage rapids, than I had realized. We splashed through them as soft, broad-leafed plants, the whipping reeds, velvet moss, and clean mud touched and pleasured my feet and legs. I ran as Mother taught me, with absolute concentration on each spot my foot fell.

Yet I was also aware of the world around me. The sky was beginning to lighten before we reached the shore. I knew, because though there were many stars, I could now see the pine shapes as beautiful gray silhouettes against the bowl of heaven. When we reached the bottom of the road and headed across sand toward the shore, I saw light on the water. The tide was out, the sea quiet, the waves only gentle, curling forms that fanned out, then sank into the sand. Seen only from the corner of my eye, the drinking hall where we had dined last night was now dark and silent, as dawn, like an unannounced visitor, began to call at its doors.

I saw no one. We met no one. And indeed, I wondered if any were awake at this hour besides myself and Albe.

I sensed as much as saw the water reacting to the first touch of light, like glowing silver brightening imperceptibly as the sun approached the edge of the world. Albe and I turned at last, running in those shallow combers so soft, so smooth, yet not quite silent, whispering as though the great sea had some secret knowledge to impart to this place of boundaries between one world and another. This was the dream, I thought, remembering how Kyra long ago told me she knew Dugald had gone to the other world, but growing fearful, had turned back.

Was the Faun right? Was I journeying to another world?

No. I still felt the sea, saw it shimmering brighter and brighter as the world, like some great vessel, carried me and all living things toward sunrise. I saw the waters, silver, white, gray, gold, gleaming ahead and spreading out on my right side. In a moment the sun would rise and the water give back red, gold, purple, amethyst, blue, and sheer silver to the sky above.

For the first time I stumbled, and looking down, found I was running on stone. Puzzled for a moment, I slowed, and Albe crashed into me. We both staggered.

I laughed, but she gave a stifled shriek and said, 'Oh, God! God! Look!'

I stopped because she had and looked where her finger pointed, out to sea. Or where the sea had been, for it was as the Faun promised – gone!

Igrane woke and found it still dark in the chamber where she slept, though she realized the tide must be out, because she could see stars through the dome above her. The robe she was wearing seemed to want her to go back to sleep, because it moved gently, swathing her more tightly, and it seemed to warm her feet and hands. It had frightened her when she first put it on. Clothing that moved of its own volition was a rather terrifying experience. But now that she was used to the gentle clasp, the caressing touch, the silken velvet texture, the way it warmed her hands and feet, she was seduced by the luxury of the experience.

Until she saw the light approaching. It came from beyond the room, where Merlin had pulled her into this world. Moving at a walk, it crossed the upper room where he had forced her to eat the plum that rendered her helpless before his spells. Then it began to descend the stair that led to the temple (this was how she thought of it) where he'd placed her on the glowing symbol that nearly drained away her life.

That same symbol flared to red brightness as whatever being that carried the light reached the foot of the stair, paused, and moved toward her. The dark-red symbol pulsed as though keeping time to the beating of a human heart.

Igrane sat up. The living mantle accepted her change

163

of position submissively, draping her shoulders and lifting a fold over her head. Igrane became aware the room was very cold, and her breath steamed in the air. But she was warmed by fear and, most of all, by growing rage. He had very nearly destroyed her, and the sheer indignity of being rendered so helpless, and subjected to degradation so complete, woke a deep, visceral anger that shook her body. Whatever this was, if it made even the slightest threatening gesture toward her, she would kill it.

It came close enough to see that a cowled figure held a lamp. Or was it a lamp? It seemed a star trapped in the center of a crystal teardrop.

'So it is true. My dream is true. He is gone,' a voice whispered.

'For the present,' Igrane answered.

The reply was laughter, laughter that sounded like a stirring of dead leaves moved by a cold autumn wind.

'If he was taken in the way my dream informed me, he is not gone for the present, unless your idea of the present is a hundred or more years.'

'That long.' Igrane sighed.

'That and more. He treads the maze of Dis. Bade sent him there. He couldn't kill him. No, Merlin ... the Merlin, is too powerful.'

Igrane laughed, a silvery tinkle. 'That makes me very happy.'

'Then we share the same feelings about the fell necromancer. I see he tried to kill you the way he *did* kill me.'

Igrane glanced at the ruined bodies of the two golem undead servants who had tied her up, readying her for the whip.

'You are one of them. Don't come near me, and I don't want to see your face, either.' The hysteria in her voice astounded even Igrane herself.

Again the serpent laughter. 'Don't be so haughty, my fine lady. Once he was done with draining you dry, flaying your corpse, rendering muscles into gristle, changing your fat to tallow by boiling your bones, you too would have looked much like me. The smooth, warm, rounded curves of life beneath honeyed, soft skin, all would have departed. Those fine white teeth of yours would have grinned from between dried lips, as mine do, and the demon fires glow in your eye sockets.'

'Oh, Christ!' Igrane whimpered. 'It that . . . ? Oh, God!' Then she leaned over and vomited on the floor near her feet. 'I knew those servants of his frightened me, but he never described what . . .'

There was no more laughter, and this surprised Igrane.

'No, he wouldn't,' was the thoughtful, almost sad, reply. 'I remember he told me once we were almost the perfect servants. He need not worry about treachery, stupidity, or greed. When he was done with us, he dismissed us to our tombs, where we lay silent, imprisoned, sleeping. Sometimes dreaming, sometimes harboring nightmares, until we were summoned by him to serve again.'

Igrane pushed the mantle back from her head. The cold air felt good on her hot face.

'I've made a mess,' she said.

'No!' The cowled figure gestured. The stuff on the floor dried, fell to dust, and a puff of air blew it away.

'This place . . . those clothes . . . he created . . . it. How . . . ?'

A sniff from the cowled figure. 'He? Create this? No! My little dear, it created him. Whoever owns it is Merlin. The Merlin. He is gone, whoever he was – Emyrs some say. I cannot tell. I never knew his name. Otherwise, I would not be this dried trophy, testament to his sorcery. I would have bound that name in death ruins. I may yet.

'No, that – ' She pointed to the symbol. 'That is the

165

heart of this place.' It still throbbed, lightening, darkening, but still seeming to be illuminated by a scarlet glow. 'It summoned me, telling me there must be a new candidate for the position of Merlin.'

'Who?' Igrane asked, realizing it must be between the two of them.

The cowled sorceress answered, 'Need you ask?'

'You,' Igrane said.

'Foolish one. I'm dead. Yes, animated, but to all intents and purposes, dead. The person allowed to take the Merlin's seat must be living. Igrane, Queen of Cornwall, that person is – you.'

Black Leg woke in warm water. It felt so good, he kept his eyes closed, thinking it might be a good dream and not wanting it to go away. Afraid he might awaken and find reality too much to bear.

'Huh! Fine warrior I am. What am I going to do? Curl into a ball and hope to be without pain?'

He opened his eyes. She was bending over him.

'Thank God,' she said. 'I was afraid you might have damaged yourself too badly to recover.'

'Jesus!' he replied. 'Every time I wake up, I find out you came across another little green thingamajiggy that does something weird. What's this one?'

He was glancing around at the bath he was in. It was located in the back of the cave where they had been hiding, in a hollow fed by a spring trickling slowly from a crack in the rock wall at the rear of the cave. It was lined with greenish-gray, fuzzy, small plants he had only barely noticed when they crept in here to hide.

Then he felt something at his groin and anal area that felt decidedly . . . strange. Then he screamed, 'Oh, my God! It's eating me!!!'

He tried to sit up and scramble out of the hollow. She slapped him back down.

'My hero!' she snarled. 'It is not! Besides, you never seemed to object when I did it.'

'Holy God! I knew you'd get me killed sooner or later.'

'No, stop it! If it was going to eat you, it would have hours ago, when you started up. When . . . when you – ah – messed up the floor.'

'Hell. Now you're prudish!'

'Hell, no! I'm polite!' was the reply. 'But if you want, I can be explicit. You pissed and shit yourself, then vomited. And son of a bitch, you sure ate a lot, 'cause that was one of the worst messes I ever saw. It stank, too. I couldn't do anything. I just lay there on the floor and hoped those damned birds didn't get in. Because I couldn't mobilize the wolf body enough to even stand up. But you wet down all those little whatevers and they started taking care of you right away.

'The rock started dripping water, then the air temperature warmed. And those . . . I think they're some kind of lichen . . . began filling with moisture and they didn't seem to be doing you any harm, so I concentrated on learning the wolf body as fast as I could. By the time the moon came out and the birds left, I could walk. And I went out and gobbled down as much food as I could and brought back as much as I could carry. So shut the fuck up and lie there in the water while I feed you, 'cause if they haven't eaten you by now, they won't! Goddamn it! Got that?'

Black Leg did, and subsided, though he kept watching the water for blood. He didn't see any, and the sensation never got any worse than that of a scrubbing with a slightly rough sponge. In a short time, he decided she was right, and as his stomach filled up, he began to feel much better. That is, until he looked through the small opening in the rock where the spring originated.

He nearly bit off some of her fingers.

'You know,' she told him, sounding dangerous, 'I'm getting tired of you.' She was examining her hand.

'I didn't hurt you!' He was a little disgusted, because he sounded defensive.

'No?' she said.

'No! Besides, you didn't see what I just saw.'

She went wolf and bared her teeth – all of them.

'Look! Look! If you don't believe me, look!'

She leaned over him, got a good eyeful, then jerked back.

'They're . . . they're . . . dead!' She was woman again, her face pale. She had freckles now, and they stood out against her skin.

'Yeah,' Black Leg said. 'And did you see that one looking right at us?'

'I don't think I've ever been anywhere quite so full of nasty surprises.' She spoke thoughtfully.

He was feeling stronger and sat up, hips and legs still in the moss-filled hollow. 'You're sure they're dead?'

'No!' she answered in a dull voice. 'I'm not sure of anything anymore. Not after what you just did to me – not after all the things that have happened. What's wrong with me anyway? I feel so weak.'

'You're probably just tired,' he said.

'Tired! Tired! I'm not the sort of being who gets tired. Yes, I can sleep. It passes the time. But I never get tired. I told you, I'm not the sort of being who gets tired.'

'You are now,' he said rather grimly.

He got his arms around her and rested his head on her shoulder. She rested hers on his.

'I think I'm better now,' he told her. 'The food, the water. I feel stronger.'

'Is this what tired means? I feel worn out, but irritable and alert. God, you saved my life with what you did. And I've been acting like a complete bitch ever since.'

168

'Yeah, it's hard to take,' he said. 'It's changed you, and I can't help but think that, in the long run, you won't be happy with the changes.'

'No? Well, I'll learn to be happy with them. If you hadn't done whatever it was you did, I wouldn't be here for the long run at all.'

He was looking past her at the narrow window slits. 'The moon's out, if that is a moon.'

'I know. The birds won't come while the light comes into the valley at all. They can't seem to bear the light of either sun or moon.'

'We should get some rest,' he said. 'But I don't like sharing this hideout with whatever those things are in the other room.'

'They're dead,' she said flatly.

'We hope. We wish. I just don't want to find them in . . . say a few hours . . . creeping in here to join us. Like I said, one of them was looking right at me.'

'Quit it!' she snapped. 'You're messing me up. This isn't the place to gather round the fire and tell ghost stories. Besides, we got no fire.'

The room was dim. If either of them had been completely human, they probably wouldn't have been able to see at all. The strongest light came from the enormous moon outside, but the moss glowed a strange, clear shimmer that reminded Black Leg of massed stars. Because he was wolf and she used to finding her way in the depths of rivers and lakes, their vision was adequate. But neither wanted to confront what they had both seen through the opening in the rock.

She reached out, lifted a clump of the lichen that had warmed and cleaned the chamber. She blew on it and it glowed more brightly.

'Not great, but better than nothing,' he said. 'Sort of a corpse candle.'

'Are you working at annoying me?' she told him. 'If

you are, stop it! Things are tough enough without you sniping at me.'

They both shifted into wolf form and began to investigate the long, narrow room they were in. She carried the clump of glowing lichen in her mouth. The rock wall on the side opposite the windows appeared impenetrable.

Yes, there was a lot of the strange lichen on both walls and floors. Now that they knew what it could do, it was noticeable even in its dry, resting state. And yes, the crack that opened to trickle water appeared to have many counterparts. But he could see no door or any other opening wide enough to admit him to the room that must exist on the other side of the rock wall.

'Well, if we can't get in there to them, they certainly can't get in here to us.'

They were human again and knelt in each other's arms.

'You did save my life. I'm not sure how to react,' she said as she kissed him. 'Usually mortals don't give. They just take. At least in my experience that's all they do.'

'I never thought about it,' he said, kissing her back with obvious pleasure.

'That's one of the problems,' she answered grimly. 'You don't think about much.'

His hand was twined in her hair, and she was all heat, nipples erect, sinuous curves pressing against his – velvet, sinuous curves. They sank down toward the floor together.

'My lady,' he whispered before inserting his tongue into her mouth. 'As far as thinking is concerned, you are not guiltless in that respect. Let us not throw stones at each other.'

She said, 'Ahhhaaaa,' because they were each exploring each other's mouth with their tongues, and body with their hands.

'I hope you don't have anything radical in mind,' she

whispered when at length they both surfaced from the bliss.

'No. Only pleasure.'

'There is plenty of that,' she whispered.

There was.

The little clump of wet lichen dimmed as though offering them privacy. They fell asleep in each other's arms.

The arrival of the birds at first light woke them.

His eyes opened first. When he saw her eyelids rise, he laid his finger on his lips.

The birds remained longer this time. They began to devastate the garden. Screaming the raven call to arms, they attacked the trees, throwing down the fruit whether green or ripe, attacking the vines with a cold-blooded malice by cutting their stems. Attacking the earth around the masses of tender, sweet, bitter, and aromatic greens that filled every crack and cranny between food beds. The life of the valley endured the attack in stoic silence. He knew such attacks must have come before; they had learned to accept them.

She hadn't, though. The blue eyes closed and tears began to trickle from under her lids.

He watched the carnage helplessly until the sun came to the rescue. The ravens rose, a black, swirling mass. The flock churned like a whirlpool over the water, then flowed out of the canyon like a river toward wherever they roosted by day.

'We caused this, didn't we?' he asked quietly.

'They know we're here. That's a safe assumption,' she answered. 'The garden shelters us, so . . . they took out their frustrations on whatever hapless creatures they could punish.'

'Think they left us anything to eat?'

'Oh, yes. There's too much out there to be destroyed in a few minutes. That is all they had before the sun got to them.'

171

He nodded and they walked along, back to the entrance, side by side. Suddenly she stopped.

'Oh, hell. I know how.'

'How what?'

She didn't answer, but dropped down flat and peered under the solid wall.

'Oh,' he said, then lay down beside her.

The slit wasn't very big. Beyond, they could see the other room. It was filled with bones and there was way too much light.

'Do we have to?' he asked.

'Yes, I think so. There's an entrance in there somewhere. I can see sun on the walls. We're damn lucky we woke up at all. If those birds had gotten in with us . . . I'm going to try as a wolf.'

It worked. She had to lie on her belly and wiggle under, but she got in. He was bigger and lost a lot of hair and some skin, but was able to follow.

The bones weren't white but yellowed and black with age. He touched the femur of the nearest one with his nose and it fell to dust. She rose as a woman and began to explore the chamber, peering at the bony fragments, then at the obvious entrance where the birds must have gotten in. Like the other chamber, it was long and narrow; the opening was at one end. It wasn't large, about the size of a shield boss. Too small for a human but big enough for even a very large raven.

'How did they break through the stone wall?' she asked, mystified.

'Doesn't matter,' he answered. 'They did.'

'I don't know,' she questioned.

'I didn't believe you about those lichens but . . .' He paused and stood over a set of bony fragments that looked as though they had been ripped to pieces. The skull was lying in the rib cage; the bones of the leg and arms were jumbled finger bones, scattered everywhere as though something had fed on them. In other cases the torso was separated from the entire spine in fragments as though the individual had been disemboweled and the feeding had begun before it was entirely dead.

'I know . . . I know one thing,' he said fervently. 'I sure as hell don't ever want to meet those birds again. Let's get out of here!'

'No!' She glanced up from the pile of remains she had been inspecting. 'Think,' she said. 'What I accused you of last night is equally true of me. You were so kind as to point that out. Neither of us is thinking. All we've been doing is panicking and reacting to one threat after another.'

'And?' he asked.

'This chamber is the first really good clue to what happened here that caused this world to be the way it is. And it's another world, I'm sure of it. One I've never been to. If we hope to survive, we've got to work this out. Because if we don't, sooner or later those birds are going to get us. Last night we were just lucky. But we can't expect that to last.'

'No. No, you're right. In fact, you sound depressingly like my father and Dugald, and they're the smartest people I've ever known. Not the best – my mother was the best – but both of them are smart enough to take on that ugly old Greek. . . .'

'Socrates?' she asked.

'That's his name. Anyway, they could argue him to a standstill and leave him with a lot to think about. Let me go see if I can climb up and see out the hole. Find out if there's some way to block it.'

'Try not to disturb anything where you walk. I want to get a good look at them where they are.'

He nodded, then moved carefully toward the opening in the wall. When he reached it, Black Leg saw it was only a bit higher than his head. He reached up, and though the broken stone was sharp, he was able to find a smooth spot where he could get a grip. Then he settled his toes on a rough knob of rock above the floor and lifted himself high enough to see out.

He found himself looking down into water. A pothole? Then he realized it wasn't a natural feature but chiseled out of a shallow depression in the stone. Yes! The water that came in through the cracks in the rock had to be piped in from somewhere. This dwelling was much higher than the river.

But the thin rock wall between the reservoir and the cave had been the weak spot. He pulled himself in a little higher, so he could see down into the water. Yes, the boulders that broke the wall were in the bottom.

He dropped down to the floor and reported on what he had seen. She was standing near him, looking at the room toward the other wall.

'They came in here.' He gestured toward the opening. 'My guess is this was some sort of hospital. Reason I think so is the Romans had doctors who traveled with the army, and that was all they did, take care of the sick and wounded. There's lots of that lichen, the kind that took care of me last night, in here. The wounded were in these pools.'

She nodded yes. Except for those massed at the other end, the bone piles were scattered rather evenly, each either in or close to a depression in the floor, like the one he'd awakened in last night.

'The walking wounded, or maybe the attendants, tried to make a stand at the other end. That's why there is so much bone piled up there. But the birds were too much for them.'

'Think any of them got away?' he asked her.

She looked for a moment reluctant to answer. She had an unpleasant expression on her face.

'No,' she said. 'I don't. The reason is the skeletons at

the other end are pretty much intact, but the wounded were . . . helpless. The birds, when they finished off the defenders, came back and had some . . . fun. Maybe they stopped and ate.'

Yes, the skeletons occupying the depressions were jumbled almost beyond recognition. Sickeningly, Black Leg considered the fact that some arms, legs, fingers, and hands were still articulated, suggesting the wounded had been dismembered while still alive.

'Dismembered,' she said. 'Disemboweled and eaten alive.'

Black Leg, remembering the almost unbelievable malice in the first raven's voice when it spoke to him, decided she was probably right.

'They were shape-strong, too,' she said.

'Shape-strong? No!' Black Leg said.

'Ummmmm. Look at the bones, Doubting Thomas,' she said.

Black Leg began to walk along, studying the remains in each depression until he reached one that was more or less intact but horribly spread-eagled. The distinction was clear – the head and arms were catlike. Most of the torso was missing, but the hips, legs, and feet were definitely human.

'Didn't help them much,' he said at length.

'No, didn't help us much either. The only thing that did help was our ability to hide in the river.'

Then they both walked slowly toward the back of the cave where the last stand had taken place. A drift of black feathers covered the floor between the skeletons.

'Looks like they were able to put up a pretty good fight. Even accounted for a fair number of those birds,' he said as he reached down to pick up a feather.

'No!' She grabbed his wrist. 'Aren't you sick of sticking your hand down holes to see if there's snakes in them?'

He was about to get angry, but decided she was probably right. And, he reflected, he was a little sick of the ugly surprises he'd stumbled across exploring this world.

'Anything connected with those birds is probably dangerous,' she said.

'We should take a look,' he said.

She took a deep breath, closed her eyes. 'I can still turn to water if I want to. I believe . . . let me see.'

He waited.

'Yes,' she said, opening her eyes. 'I can.' Then she reached down and picked up one of the dark feathers.

The result was anticlimactic. Nothing happened.

'Looks like an ordinary feather,' he said.

'Feels like an ordinary feather,' she said, brushing the tip on the palm of her left hand. Then she lifted the feather into the sun to examine it in the bright light.

He had time to shout a warning as he saw the edge change, flow, then glitter like a razor. The feather twisted free of her fingers and slashed down at her face.

She got her arm up in time, but the feather opened a five-inch gash in her forearm, one so deep Black Leg briefly saw the white tendons that move the fingers. But then the feather fell out of the sunlight. She concentrated and the gash in her arm vanished as the feather – only a feather again – drifted harmlessly to the floor.

For a brief moment, Black Leg leaned on the wall. She stood, eyes closed, still clutching her arm.

'God Almighty!' she whispered. And Black Leg was sure it was no curse.

When he felt steady again, he said, 'Let's get out of this cursed place and find something to eat.'

He turned and began to walk along the wall, checking for a place to roll under and get out. He kicked something, looked down, and saw a skeletal arm. He realized that all the dark things scattered among the bones weren't feathers.

He crouched down and saw that the skull was the one he'd glimpsed through the wall crack last night, the sight that led to the discovery of this chamber. The dark shapes covering the bony arm looked as if they might have belonged to some sort of armor.

He glanced at the skull again. He found he couldn't imagine what sort of creature it had been. The bones of the arms, legs, and torso were human enough, but oddly those of the hands, feet, and skull weren't.

'They were caught,' Black Leg said, 'during the change. Not just the ones in the moss pools, but every one of them. How those birds couldn't catch us, we were both too fast for them.'

'It didn't help you much,' she said.

'No, but you were able to get away. I don't understand.'

'You don't understand. Let me tell you. Don't feel rained on. Nothing about this cursed place makes any—'

She broke off because he was reaching for one of the dark objects circling the skeleton's arm. She drew in a sharp, startled breath but didn't warn him.

'We have to try to find out,' he said as his hand closed around the object. The only thing that happened was that the bones powdered and fell immediately to dust. Black Leg started slightly, but then, seeing that he came to no harm, continued to collect the dark scraps until he held them all in his hands.

She bent over and took the largest one, cradling it in the palm of her hand. 'Doesn't seem dangerous,' she said, then called on her own particular spirits.

The palm of her hand filled with water, and the dark object suddenly took on a jellylike consistency. She dropped it to the floor, where it landed with a slight plop. Just at that moment a breeze blew through the opening in the wall at the far end of the room. Or at least it seemed a breeze. It swirled the dust left by the powdered bone into a mini-whirlwind and sucked it out through the opening in the broken wall into the light beyond.

Black Leg shivered.

She whispered, pointing down, 'Look.'

It lay on the stone floor where the jellied mess had fallen from her hand. It looked like a dark hole in the stone floor, except that across its surface, symbols played, changing slowly in a sliding flux the way they had on the walls of the tunnel that brought them both to this strange, dangerous place.

'What do they mean?' he asked her.

'I told you. I don't know,' she answered. 'I am, by your standards, incredibly old, but believe me, that tunnel was very old and long-abandoned by its makers when I was born.'

Black Leg reached down and touched the rag of blackness with one finger. And more quickly than thought, it flowed over his hand and formed a glove covering both hand and forearm.

His shout of terror was lost in the rush of wings.

Splitting the dog's skull killed it instantly, and Uther knew for a timeless moment that the tormented beast was free of its earthly shell. The rejoicing on the animal's part was simple, very pure joy. Inarticulate though the beast was, Uther sensed its gratitude.

The flash of light represented Merlin's fury as he reached out to try to destroy Uther and his power expended itself against a shield Uther hadn't even known he possessed. Then both presences were gone. The dog's dying shell convulsed at his feet, the broken skull spraying blood and brains all over the hearth. The banked fire hissed like a snake pit and a vile stench rose from the glowing ashes. The harp in its case thrummed a deep, rich chord and the flames leaped from the ashes, roaring, consuming the spattered flesh and blood.

The animal's carcass lay limp at Uther's feet. Impelled by who knew what impulse, Uther hurled it into the seething blaze. There it seemed to become involved in a dash of magic. The fire suddenly damped down almost to nothingness and the dead animal writhed as though filled with unnatural life, lifting its head, eyes red, glowing like coals, livid tongue protruding from the jaws as though trying to get its legs under it to leap again for the king's throat.

Uther stood sword in hand, feet braced apart, ready to confront the dead thing should it attack again. He laughed the powerful, free laughter of a king. A king who, in the final analysis, committed soul and body to stand between his people and evil.

That seemed a signal, and the fire blazed again, consuming the slain beast, the devilish instrument of darkness, Merlin's darkness. Uther turned from the blaze and saw everyone in the room was awake, and through the small parchment-covered windows, the sun was rising outside.

Bread, some fresh cheese, and oat porridge did for breakfast. Uther gave the lady of the house another silver coin to feed everyone still present. When the crowd departed (none thanked him), he helped the lady of the house clean and carry the trash to the midden heap.

Alex and Alexia were indoors, boiling water to wash down the stone floor. Uther didn't feel he owed her the labor, but in winter human dwellings were thick with smoke and stank of spoiled food, damp mold, and unwashed bodies. Uther simply wanted a breath of cool, clean, rain-washed air.

It had been freezing the night before, but now the sky was blue, the brilliant, hard blue of winter. The air was almost balmy and last night's sleet melted to puddles, reflecting the sky's brilliant blue from their places among the muddy brown road.

'I am Eme,' the lady of the house told Uther.

Uther stopped, startled, for he knew what the name meant.

'Do not use that name unless we are alone,' she continued in a dry voice. 'No one else knows it. Least of all . . .' She pointed away toward the buildings of the villa topping a hill nearby. 'Least of all the master of that stronghold.'

'No,' Uther said. 'No. I won't. I wouldn't, in any case.'

She nodded. Then she glanced away at the villa, her eyes flat, cold, and empty.

'I think he may suspect, but he doesn't know.' She paused for a second, then added, 'He calls himself Count Severius, but as far as I know, has no Roman blood.'

'Wants the best of both worlds, doesn't he?' Uther commented.

'Wants the best of all worlds,' she answered. 'He killed my son.'

Oddly, Uther felt the weight of the harp on his back. He said the conventional thing. 'I'm sorry.'

'It was over ten years ago,' she replied. 'There was no need. So many conquerors. Our family is buried deep. Even before the Romans, people from the Continent had defeated and pushed us aside. But we were among the priestly families and even the Romans deferred to us at least a little. Yet to take my son from me was cruel. A child – that is always cruel.'

Uther nodded.

'The boy played near the villa. The war dogs got him.' She laughed, a sharp cackle, snapping twigs. 'When I asked for justice—' She pointed at the villa again. '—he gave me one of the dogs.'

'An unworthy object for your cruelty.' Uther spoke sternly, but as if to an equal, because if the name were any indication, she might indeed be royal.

'I know that now,' she answered. 'But it is dead – and I didn't speak to justify myself, only out of concern for you. He will hear about your music. There is little faith in my lord count, so he won't believe all he hears. But he will believe enough to summon you to entertain his guests. Be warned. Hurry away now, if you wish to reach London, because those he summons cannot escape his hospitality until he gives them permission to depart.'

Uther felt his neck prickle. He glanced again at the complex of buildings in the distance.

'We will leave within the hour,' he said as he hurried toward the door.

But the harp halted him. It strummed itself softly and in the distance he heard music. Even Uther didn't remember the Romans. But sometimes, as with all ancient armies, they sang as they marched.

The music was not like those melodies he had been taught. It was deep and harsh, like the discipline of a Roman legion, martial and masculine. They favored the pipe, drum, and trumpet, like the paean that took warriors into battle and celebrated valor in victory or defeat, Uther felt it through the soles of his feet, through his skin, and it resonated in his bones.

He turned back toward the road.

They came.

Eme whispered, '*Ahhhhh* . . .'

'The horse fights,' Uther said. 'They will finish them here.'

'Yes,' Eme answered. 'It seems so.'

'He wants to be king, this count?' Uther asked. 'This count – would he be count of the Saxon shore?'

Eme nodded. 'Yes!'

The music was closer. Uther stood, his back to the wattle-and-daub wall of the inn. Those remaining inside

181

streamed out through the door, into the street, to watch the procession pass.

A group of Saxon mercenaries came first. They wore the remnants of Roman garb, an odd mix, muscle cuirasses with plumed helmets, tunics, but with added trousers and cross-gartered leggings. They carried not the Roman gladius-type sword, but long swords.

Uther didn't see any spears, and he saw only one or two saddles. His eyes narrowed. Not true cavalry, they probably dismounted and fought on foot. His boys would make chopped meat of them.

But fight they would, because the oval shields they carried were hacked and scraped, and each man was a scarred and tough-looking survivor. Each man was dripping with jewelry, the reward of victory. They were adorned with bracelets, arm rings, torques, and finger rings, and glittering baldrics held their swords. They looked down at the largely peasant crowd with contempt.

A mob as yet, Uther thought. Not an army, but dangerous, very dangerous.

Behind them streamed what Uther thought of as the hungry ones. Younger sons who could afford horses but no really good swords. They carried long saxes, the single-edged knife that gave the Saxons their name. A good many Roman swords were in evidence, the short gladius, and even the curved scimitar Roman cavalrymen carried as a backup weapon. Boiled leather armor was the best these could muster.

Last of all – trailing – the most dangerous of the gang were the rabble, in a way the most frightening ones of all, since they would, win or lose, stream onto the battlefield to cut the throats of the wounded for their valuables, or rob the dead. These were the men, and sometimes the women, who dreamed of battle and cared nothing of who won or lost. They would kneel on the floor beside the table of conquest and quarrel over the scraps that fell from the fingers of the powerful. It was a measure of the poverty in the three ancient kingdoms that there were so many.

The high kings had once been incredibly powerful; and tribute from the south made them so, until the Romans came and diverted the wealth in the south to their own uses. The high king had once been able to call on the wealth produced by eighteen royal villas. Then the Romans took them and the tributary lands surrounding these centers. They diverted the goods in gold, other metals, and food crops produced by the villas to their own use, impoverishing the high king. Romans gone, the Saxons now controlled these important centers and were rapidly turning them into power bases.

'This is the muster of how many of the southern villas?' Uther asked Eme.

'Only one,' she answered.

'Only one!' he repeated incredulously.

She nodded.

Gods above and below, Uther thought.

But then it made sense. The Saxon lords would be recruiting as hard and fast as they possibly could.

The Frankish king had things well in hand now on the Continent. Between the popes and the Lombards and the imperial government at Ravenna, Italy would be as quiet as it ever was. But in the north, beyond the Rhine coasts of Africa, and in those frozen lands deep in the North Sea that were only legends even to his people, they swarmed: Huns, Goths, Vandals, Visigoths, Alans, Franks, Burgundians, Frisians, Thuringians, Alemanni, Chastuari. And that list of names but scratched the surface of those pressing in at the gates, all dreaming of loot, women, and above all the rest, land. Land, and more land for themselves.

They came and they died by the thousands, but those who survived, like the ones riding in the forefront of this mob, would grow rich and powerful, garnering the leavings of the dying empire. The Romans opened the floodgate when they took barbarian troops into the legions, and now were being overwhelmed by this human tide of warriors. And, of course, he and his people must face and try to contain them also.

The music had not been played to announce the procession of warriors. The stallion was behind them. No one was taking any chances with the horse. He was led on a double lead by two groups of footmen, one on each side.

An awesome beast, Uther wondered where the Saxons could have obtained him. At least seventeen hands, he dwarfed the beasts ridden by most of the Saxon warriors. The legs seemed oddly slender for so large a horse, but Uther saw, as the animal plunged and struck out with a forehoof at one of his human handlers, that the powerful legs were in perfect proportion to the rest of the deep-chested, strong-haunched body.

There were three men on each lead rope. Three men on each side.

'Hold him! Goddamn you, all of you!' someone shouted. 'Hold him or I'll have the six of you on crosses before nightfall!'

'Speak of the devil,' Eme whispered.

The man riding alone behind the horse wore gold Roman armor that blazed in the new sun.

'Count Severius, I take it,' Uther whispered.

He was big, a man whose size matched the bulk of the stallion. He also would dwarf other men the way the horse showed up the small size of other horses. The similarity ended there. The stallion was a gray, dark as a storm cloud, with almost black nose, mane, legs, and tail. The man was blond and beautiful. Clad in the Roman armor, he seemed a young god, the reincarnation of an Alexander or an Augustus.

184

He rode a gray mare that might have been the female twin of the stallion being led along ahead of him. She was also magnificent and rather restive, Uther thought, as she chewed at the bit and danced sideways along the road.

He concluded that she was probably the reason the stallion was so unruly. In fact, the curb she wore was so strong that red foam was visible at the corners of her mouth, and her head tosses flung it on the spectators lining the muddy trace.

Uther was disgusted by the sight of so beautiful a creature as the mare being abused by a cruel curb. The disgust must have shown in his face, because the nobleman's blue eyes met his. Uther knew he had been a king too long, because their gazes locked and held, and the blue glance fell first.

The blond count checked the mare and guided her to where Uther stood, his back against the inn wall.

'Who are you?' the count asked. 'Who dares show your dislike for the evidence of my success and power?'

Uther suddenly realized he was very much alone. A moment ago, he had been standing among others, watching the procession. Now they had suddenly vanished, even Eme.

It wasn't in him to deny the challenge.

'A fair beauty,' Uther said, looking at the mare. 'Too fine a beast to be ridden with so cruel a curb. And, my lord, I am not one of your people and was unhappily unaware my approval was to be demanded or even desired.'

With difficulty, Uther kept himself from flinching, because he was sure a blow from the nobleman's whip or fist would end the matter right there.

But it didn't come.

Instead, the blond god laughed. The laughter didn't reach his eyes. They remained as cold as the enameled blue winter sky.

Then the man in the saddle leaned down close to him and spoke in a soft voice that included only the two of them.

'You aren't afraid of me, are you? Amazing! Almost everyone is afraid of me. Certainly all who know me are. Such ignorance, my friend, my very dear friend. You are in need of instruction. It will give me the greatest of pleasure to undertake that task. In fact, that is how I derive my greatest joy in life, from this process of instruction. It pleases me greatly to find I have acquired a new subject for my attentions. I think I will find you among the most gratifying of my acquaintances.'

Then he eased the mare back to the center of the road, speaking softly as he did to one of his men.

Uther felt a queasiness in his belly. How much of that was bluff? And how much was real? Most of it, was his own bleak reply. Men like this count had almost unlimited control over their dependents. The rickety structure of Roman law, and sometimes Christian teaching, had in the past served as some sort of check on the cruelty and ambition of men like this. But both were conspicuously absent now, and horrific stories circulated about the savage punishments decreed by the great landowning noblemen for even the slightest infractions. Most of them were drunk with power. But even among tyrants, this one seemed exceptionally bad.

Three Saxon mercenaries arrived, one on each side of Uther, one in front of him. None of them looked happy. None would meet Uther's eyes.

'My lord asked that we escort you to the villa,' the best-dressed and obviously the highest ranking of the three told the king.

'Indeed,' Uther said, striving to look amused. 'And suppose I decline to accompany you?'

'I wouldn't do that, sir,' the young man replied. He

was gazing at a spot somewhat to the right of Uther's left shoulder.

Uther nodded. 'Now?'

'Now!'

Uther nodded again, and without further comment, obeyed.

'Did you know?' Albe asked me somewhat accusingly.

'Yes,' I answered.

'How?'

'The Faun told me. I didn't believe him, or rather, I couldn't quite comprehend how it would be possible. But yes, I followed his orders.'

Albe blinked at me. I shifted the sword on my back into a more comfortable position and strode forward boldly, even as I explained myself – or tried to.

'He told me I must go to Arthur. But on no account could I allow myself to be captured by the King of the Summer Country, since I was one of the gates to power. I should die rather than allow myself to confer sovereignty on the wrong man. That's your job, to kill me rather than allow me to be used in such a way. That's why I took you with me.'

'No!' Albe cried.

'Yes!' I shouted even more loudly as I hurried along. 'Before the sun sets tonight, you must give me your word of honor that you will take my head and return it to the rulers' gathering place, in the north among the Picts.'

Albe didn't speak again.

The strangeness of this world grew in my mind. The road along which we were walking was made of hexagonal stones, blue-gray in color, and it undulated over what I knew must have once been a coastline. In and of themselves, the stones were odd. They seemed connected. Not human-made but as though a comb from some giant beehive had been unrolled on a seashore just above the dunes.

Those dunes were thickly overgrown with tall, feather-headed grasses, each clump of grass surrounded by low-crawling vines bearing heart-shaped leaves and a profusion of butter-yellow flowers. The blue-gray stones that comprised the road had been in place so long . . . I found I didn't care to think about it. In places they were half-buried by rocks falling from the barren slopes above us; in others, by windblown sand. But it seemed impossible to completely cover, because whatever shape the land took, they followed it. The piles from slides were slowly shoved aside as it tilted gently to remove, then climb over, them. Where mud and sand drifted, the surface was so smooth that as the mud dried, it and the sand would be blown away by the unending wind that blew swiftly still from the deep-gullied hills that sloped down. Hills that had once been covered by the sea.

'Why are you running, Guinevere?' Albe asked.

I realized I had been running, almost running, at least. So I slowed and let her catch up to me. The little road wasn't very wide, but it easily held two walking abreast. Indeed, it would have been wide enough for a wagon or a war chariot.

'Why are you running?' she asked me again.

'Because I'm frightened,' I told her. 'This is a very strange place, and I cannot imagine what my journey through here portends.'

Just as well I slowed, because we had come to a ravine. The hexagonal road pavers tilted themselves as they descended to form a shallow stair to the bottom. Here we were a bit sheltered from the wind, and I felt the flush a brisk wind raises in my exposed skin.

'What did the Faun tell you besides what you have said already?' Albe asked.

She didn't seem even a little bit disturbed by the fact

188

that I had in one morning led her into another world and then asked her to kill me. But then, we both knew the rules. As I had taken and enslaved Cymry, so could I be taken and enslaved; and before death, my body used to open the gates of power to another man besides Arthur. Albe was to see that didn't happen.

All the great queens and kings have a follower sworn to kill them, take the head to return it to their followers so the king's wisdom, power, and magic cannot be used against his or her own people. Because if the king is a priest, the lady who cradles him between her thighs is an even more sacred queen.

I had not bothered about it before, because Dugald, Ure, and the Gray Watcher knew well enough what I was, and so would have done their duty by me, had I fallen in battle. In truth, I thought that's what Ure was doing when the evil spirits overpowered me after we destroyed the pirates. It was a very near thing, but Ure had been able to bluff them out. So I was alive.

But defeat or rape were not events I should be allowed to survive. If no one else was there to ensure I died uncontrolled and unpolluted, I must see to matters myself. So I brought Albe. As I said, she knew these things as well as I did.

We stood for a moment looking down into the dead sea bottoms. The ravine had once been a river, and it had shaped a delta, an estuary that led down and down. Somewhere underground there must have been water flowing, for the long downward-leaning sandbank was fertile still. Scattered bushes, grass, and trees flourished on the slopes, each large clump of grass, bush, or small trees protected, surrounded on all sides by the omnipresent, thorn-covered vines. The air was cool and dry.

I was a little surprised at the dryness, but then, I thought, a world without oceans must perforce be dry.

'I kill easily,' Albe said.

'I know. I saw you kill the two Saxons when they emerged from the swamp. Then the eyeless woman impaled on a post.'

'I didn't once. I can barely remember. It hurts too much to remember how it was before . . . the pirates came.'

'Your face?' I asked. 'How . . . ?'

'We were huddled in the scuppers of the ship, the other girls and I. I twisted out of the ropes he had me tied with. I found a shard, piece of an oil flask broken long ago. I used it on my face. He wasn't bad to me. That was worse – he wasn't bad. I remember the shock of pain and pleasure. I should have had it on my wedding night. He took my wedding from me. That was worse. The life I should have had, he stole it.

'He said I was ewe lamb and I should be his comfort through the voyage. He would care for me, then sell me to a rich merchant, because being well-fed and only used by one man, I would keep my looks. The broken piece of clay wasn't sharp, so I broke it again. Then it had an edge. I used it on my face. That turd, that filthy turd, he had no profit of me.

'They threw me into the sea. That's the next thing I remember, almost the first thing I remember: the pain when the salt sea scoured the places where I had sliced my cheeks to the bone, because I have forgotten the rest. But yes, since that day, I kill easily.'

I stretched out my hand to her. She took it, then I clasped it with my other hand, so hers was between my palms. Her hand was warm.

'Shouldn't I kneel?' she asked.

'No. Why bother? You . . . your hands found that broken oil jug. If it hadn't been there, you would have used your nails. You meant it, then as now. That's all I ask.'

'I swear,' she said.

I tightened my grip, then let go.

'I have it on your oath.'

'My oath is to you and no other. I have no man, no child to hang on my sleeve.'

'Well and good. For that is where kings get their oath men, and queens must have them, too.'

Just at the moment, I saw something crossing the sky gleam. A flash in the sun.

'Did you see?' I asked.

'I cannot say,' Albe answered. 'I never saw anything like it before. A bird?'

'Do birds reflect the light?' I asked.

'Sometimes,' Albe said.

I wasn't convinced, but whatever it was, was far away and very high up. So we couldn't tell.

Below us, the river delta flowed away, a green snake down and down into a canyon so deep, the bottom was only a green shadow in the distance.

'How can people live here?' Albe asked.

I was mystified. 'I know no more about this place than you do,' I answered.

You see, we were both only too used to the lush green place where we were born. There was always something to eat there. The tidal flats teemed with life, shellfish of all kinds. The rivers were filled with fish, especially salmon, as was the sea. True, some years we had to subsist on acorns and hazelnuts, but we only occasionally went hungry. And even then, there were birds and bird eggs.

But here? I studied the ravine, thinking I should see animal tracks. But there were none, and no bird nested in the rocky cliffs along the sides of the ravine that stretched up and away from us into the rugged mountains that overlooked the shore.

'A barren place,' Albe said. 'Do you think we will starve?'

'There is a road, and where there is a road, there must be people. People eat.'

'I don't know.'

Albe frowned, looking at the road that snaked up and down, around rocks, and through low places on the river bottom where we stood. 'That road, those stones, are very old. They might have been here for a long time.'

I thought about the great wall that crosses the downs. I saw it once when Maeniel took Black Leg and me to hunt horses. There are a lot of them in certain places, especially where the wall runs through open country.

Maeniel says the Romans kept them to haul supplies. After the wall was abandoned, not long after the Romans left, they could be found running wild in great numbers. Maeniel took some to eat, and at times we rounded up others and sold them. Black Leg and I played on the wall and in the ditch that ran in front of it. He always got to be a Roman and tried throwing javelins at me. But I was a slinger. I'm not as good with the weapon as Albe. To be that good, you have to practice for most of your childhood. But I can use one credibly in a pinch.

Black Leg smacked me in the forehead with his spear as I came scrambling up from the ditch. He used the butt as the Romans sometimes did. For complex reasons, that made me angry. You see, no one uses the wrong end of a spear on a respected warrior.

I ran back from the wall, snatched up a stone, and gave him a black eye. Then he got mad, threw away the spear, went wolf, and dropped down into the ditch. I ran in again, toward the wall, and as he lunged up out of the ditch, I got the sling around his neck.

Maeniel and Kyra arrived about then and separated us. But after that, there were no more play tussles. Maeniel told us both, 'You're getting too dangerous.'

I thought about Black Leg, wondered how he was and what he was doing. And I hoped he would become the great warrior he wanted to be.

'Come back!' Albe said.

I turned and looked at her, surprised.

'Come back?' I repeated.

'From wherever you just went,' she said.

'I was thinking of a friend,' I answered. 'I wonder if I'll ever see him again.'

Albe glanced back at the road. 'There's no one back there I would think about with that look on my face.'

'What look?'

'A loving, regretful sort of look.'

I was intrigued. 'Really?'

'Really.' She nodded. 'Really, really. He must have been something.'

'My foster brother,' I said.

'Ha!' she answered, and looked skeptical.

I changed the subject, because she was right. I missed him and didn't realize how much he meant to me until he was gone.

'I was thinking about the Roman wall, too. And you're right. The people who built this road may have abandoned it long ago.'

'An uncomfortable thought,' she said.

'Yes,' I answered, then looked around. On one side, the mountains – barren mountains – towered. On the other, the empty sea bottom stretched away and down, only desolate, dry undulating hills leading into unguessable and quite possibly uninhabited deep canyons.

'The road it is – the road it must be,' I said.

We had a time climbing up the other side. It was higher than the one we had come down. Beyond the ravine that had once been a river, the going got harder. The strange stones were never level under our feet. The mountains here drew close to the shore, and steep slopes and high cliffs blocked our view ahead and behind. The sun rose higher in the sky.

'I'm not hungry yet,' Albe told me. 'But I'm beginning to feel some thirst.'

Ahead of us, the road topped a ridge that must once have been the talon of a mountain claw sunk in the seabed. In the dead river, there was green.

'Where there is green, there must be water,' I said. 'Beyond this ridge, there may be a low place.'

When we topped the ridge, we saw that another stream must have flowed out of the mountains at its foot, because a sandy wash with steep walls exited toward the barren sea bottom. Even from where we stood, Albe and I could tell it was covered by green plants.

One method of raising water in barren country is to dig a hole in a low spot and let it fill. I asked Albe about it.

'We can try,' she said.

But she was preoccupied, gazing off into the distance at the maze of canyons that had once been an ocean.

'I'm thirsty,' she told me, shading her eyes with her hand. 'But thirsty or not, this is a wondrous place. Look. You can tell a lot more about what's out there from our perch. We haven't been this high before.'

She was right. From here, I could look down into the bottom of the vast, broken lands below, and I saw many of the deepest rills were thickly clad in green. Not on the steep slopes leading down into them, but at the bottom. And in places, we looked down on clouds that gathered over the profoundest valleys and rained on the deepest gorges.

'How beautiful,' I whispered.

I saw the gleam of tears in Albe's eyes.

'I could leave my heart here,' she whispered. 'The light is so strange.'

'Yes. Yes, it is.'

As though high up, a haze cut off some of the sunlight and muted the harsh colors of sand and barren rock until they were washed out a bit. Rather like hanks of wool dyed but then thrown out into the sun to draw out the edged brightness in the colors. The colors in such wool mix well and seem to dissolve into one another, but above all, they wear well and are difficult to see against shifting shades of forest, field, sea, or shore. One wearing them seems to go, at times, almost invisible.

This place, and the air, were fragile. I thought I could stretch out a hand and tear the fabric of time and space, laying bare some reality beyond.

Albe drew in a deep breath and whispered, 'After the pirates, I dreamed of escape to some shadowed realm where I could wander untouched by memories that drove themselves into my soul like knives. Not the memories of bad things – we all must endure in one or another kind of suffering – but the good things, the loves, now forever lost to me. I believe I have found that place, the one I so longed for.'

'I hope you have,' I answered, wondering at the pain that drove such a heart's desire. 'But me, I'm homesick already for the sea and sand, rock and shallows. The dialogue with the seething water and the ringing shouts of quarreling gulls. I only wonder how I will ever find my way home.'

But then I thought: Mother would have nipped me on the rear for such meandering. 'Go get water,' she would say. 'You'll feel better.'

She could do that, you know. Give a sharp nip to a troublesome whelp – and one that stung but never left a mark except, as Black Leg said, on the memory.

So I added, 'Let's not think on it too much. God, my mouth is dry.'

The slope was fairly steep, but the stones dug themselves into the rocks and occasionally formed small switchbacks that helped along the steepest parts. It didn't take long for us to reach the bottom. Another ravine like the river bottom we had crossed before, but this one was very narrow and led away tortuously into the mountains.

The sandy bottom of the ravine was crowded with plants. Albe stepped in among them, looking for a clear spot to dig . . . and . . . screamed!

I think Talorcan's shoes saved her, because she didn't fall among them but stumbled as though pulled along by her shoes. Back in the road, she fell, writhing and moaning, clutching at her ankles and feet.

'Oh, God! Oh, God!' she sobbed.

I dropped to my knees beside her, mystified and worried at the same time. I didn't realize the low-growing weeds were the culprits until I felt the sting of attack on my wrist and arm. The plants were armed with thorns at the tip of each leaf and could strike out with them.

I slashed back with my suddenly armored hand, and the plants screamed and bled. I pulled Albe toward the center of the road, knelt next to her, and checked her ankles. I could see clearly that there were four red, swollen areas, two on each ankle and foot. She was no longer screaming, but shivering as though chilled, and curled on her side, watching the plants I'd damaged.

One died, stem broken, bleeding its substance into a scarlet puddle that turned hard and black, then dissolved into ash. The other, not so badly injured, the stem remaining unbroken, ceased keening as the damaged leaves curled tightly in on themselves, withered, and fell to the ground.

'What are they?' Albe whispered.

'I don't know and don't care to speculate,' I told her. 'Girl, you look like death.'

'I feel like it, too,' she answered. 'Something evil is in me.'

I was beside her. I crawled quickly to her feet and, kneeling, placed my left hand on the swelling above the ankle. I could feel the heat in my palm. This foot and leg were swelling fast, now almost twice their normal size.

I'd seen that happen with broken bones and sprains, and I found myself very frightened not just of what might happen to my new friend, but for myself should I be forced to face this strange new world alone. *Selfish*, I thought, *selfish*. And I looked into Mother's face. Her tongue lolled, and she laughed at me the way she often did when I was a young child.

'One is the other.'

This is a saying among wolves, the greeting one pack member gives another who has been absent. My heart felt filled with joy. Mother and I were alone in a cool mist, surrounded by the ever-blooming white roses of faery. The perfume drenched the air.

'Love,' I said.

'Love,' was her reply in the midst of wolf laughter. Then she was gone, and I was kneeling at Albe's feet.

'Ah, God,' she whispered. 'Your hands draw out the pain.'

I found I was holding both of her ankles; the swelling was leaving them even as I watched. But someone else was saying, 'The penalty for what you have just done is death!!!'

'God, I'm not surprised he tried to kill you,' Ustane told Igrane. 'Your whining is worse than a baby's.'

Igrane gave the corpse woman a look that should have ignited her clothing, but Ustane just laughed.

'My lady, save your energy,' Ustane said. 'The worst event that can befall a mortal has already happened to me. And if you don't pay heed to my warnings, and somehow that dangerous sorcerer breaks free of the Lord of Death, this is the first place to which he will return in his quest for vengeance. He will find you here, and doubtless, in his desire for power, make you his—'

'Stop! Stop! Goddamn you, stop!'

'Curse in vain.' Ustane laughed again at Igrane. 'He already has damned me.'

Then they were both distracted as a wave broke so hard against the rock platform supporting the bedroom that Igrane could feel the salt spray dampen her skin. They both remained there in Merlin's crystal, mounted fortress. Igrane remembered Ustane's words as she looked out at the lurid colors of the sunset blazing over the surging green water.

He did not create this place; it created him. And to rule it, she must stand on that symbol on the floor. The one that, with savage agony, almost drained the life from her body. Well, she couldn't. She wouldn't place herself in a position of such terrible risk. Ustane had been clear about the matter. Even Merlin couldn't draw power from the fiery heart of this magic place, not without suffering horribly, just as she had.

That was why he used an 'intermediary.' She had not been the first. Nor had Ustane. There had been others, many others. They occupied the vast vault where Ustane slept when she was not wanted, each resting under their own effigy.

Ustane had been beautiful. Igrane had felt an almost wild jealousy when she first saw her. But a glance at what remained of Ustane wiped that away. And she had gotten used to Ustane's help. Food, clothing, other amenities such as perfumed baths and books must be summoned from somewhere, and Ustane knew how to call them up.

Igrane stared out at the fiery sunset, feeling the sea breeze on her skin. The bedroom held only a bed and not much else. It stood on a platform in the center of the room. The coiled shell of ammonite, brilliant in opalescent mother-of-pearl and mounted in gold filigree, towered over Igrane. The bed was formed by the massive shell's last chamber, where the tentacled predator of the open ocean once lived. Sleeping on it was like lying on air. The massive, deep mattress and comforter were filled with fragrant down. The sheets and pillowcases were a rich, dark-blue silk.

But the room, as the other rooms in the crystal cave, seemed to have almost no walls, only a haze of magic, which could be as substantial as a sheet of glass when a storm thrashed the rocky coast. But then it could turn into a whisper of obstruction when she wished to enjoy the sweet sea breeze, drink in the salt air, and gaze at the magnificent bulwark of the rocky coast as it was kissed by the ocean.

'I will not touch that horror graven into the evil heart of his place. Never. Never again.'

Ustane sighed. 'What? Will you wait until he returns and leads you to it?'

'I can't think Merlin will escape the dreadful King of Bade so easily. You forget, I saw the serpent spell that took him. That king – oh, he is not a man – is master of serpent spells. That was how he conveyed Arthur to his lands. I saw the sea witch sleep at Bade's behest when Merlin cut off the serpent from her scalp and used it to send Arthur to the great sorcerer's prison.'

'Then you yourself must find an intermediary,' Ustane said.

'You mean, I can do the same thing Merlin did?' Igrane exclaimed with delight.

The living sparks that formed the eyes in Ustane's cadaver face glowed with an evil brightness.

'The idea intrigues you.' Ustane chuckled, a crackle of fine bones snapping. *Bird bones*, Igrane thought uneasily.

'Yes. How?' Igrane demanded. She pulled at the fur robe she was wearing. Obligingly, it lifted itself higher around her shoulders, raising a thick collar to protect her face and neck from the quickening night breeze.

Beyond the platform, out over the ocean, a distant storm was beginning to cast itself between the coast and the dying sun. The low-hanging clouds turned bloody, and the sweeping veils of rain burst forth into a thousand rainbows.

'See?' Ustane whispered. 'The ruling spirit of this place approves your choice.'

'Meaningless. A mere matter of sea, sun, and sky,' Igrane said.

'Come, come, woman. Those who built this place took pains to make sure they could contemplate the visionary beauty of the natural world in all its untouched splendor. Do you think they did not derive wisdom from it? Do you not feel power rise in your own heart when you sleep in that bed and the sound of waves lulls you to sleep and the stars in their millions form a canopy over your head? Are you so dead to the glories of heaven and earth, of life itself, that you can, in your selfishness, ignore the beauty around you?'

Igrane closed her eyes and began to cry. 'Here I am, uprooted from my royal past, my home, my women, my friends among the nobility. All the small comforts I took for granted. I would give anything to bathe in my own pool and give a state dinner in the hall of Tintigal.'

'Then return and do so,' Ustane snapped. 'An easy matter for you now. You are in possession of the fortress. The cup that Merlin used to fetch you here? Its magic is independent of that scaly sorcerer. It will in fact convey you wherever you wish to go. But remember, if you yield up the enchantment of this place, the food you eat, air you breathe, you will begin to age and die like all others.'

Igrane burst into a storm of weeping. Ustane began laughing.

'Leave me alone!' Igrane screamed. 'Much more and I will banish you to your tomb.'

Ustane only laughed louder, because two days ago,

Igrane had done just that – returned Ustane to her grave after she flew into a fury when Ustane told her the only way to achieve final control over Merlin's power was a painful visit to the symbol in the other room. But the rub was, Ustane wouldn't return when she was summoned by a lonely, frightened, and even somewhat penitent Igrane. Instead, she terrified Igrane into submission by absenting herself for a while day and night, leaving Igrane to struggle ineptly with awesome forces she could neither understand nor control.

'I didn't mean that,' Igrane said hurriedly.

'I know you didn't,' Ustane replied. She didn't tell Igrane that her deliberate absence had also cost her dearly. And it had. But she was determined to control and use this weak-willed creature, this nearly broken and discarded reed of Merlin's.

It was almost dark now. The sun was only a deep, salmon glow on the horizon. The wind, the silence, and the starlight, coupled with the eternal and omnipresent ebb and flow of the waves, reduced Igrane to profound desolation.

Ustane began, calculatingly, to comfort her. 'Hush now, my pretty. Don't sob so. You will spoil your looks with weeping.'

'What good are my looks to me in here?' Igrane whimpered.

'The intermediary,' Ustane said.

Igrane lifted her head. 'I had forgotten. But I'll wager it isn't easy. Otherwise, you would have mentioned it long ago.'

'It isn't,' Ustane replied. 'He or she – you can use either – must be a practitioner of the dark arts, and an able one. And then you must trick such an adept into assisting you. Not an easy task, nor a safe one. But a woman with your looks might ensnare even a very clever man against his better judgment. As indeed you ensnared Merlin.'

Being careful not to touch Igrane, Ustane handed her a napkin. Igrane dried her eyes and blew her nose.

'You must be hungry,' Ustane whispered as she gestured with one hand.

A table appeared, covered by a silken cloth, and the darkness was dispelled by one of those teardrop-shaped lamps such as Ustane carried with her. This time it arrived alone and hung in the air above the table at about the height of a candle, flame glowing.

'It's still very dark,' Igrane said.

Obligingly, the lamp brightened, filling the bedroom with light. A chair, comfortably cushioned, appeared at the table.

'Before you dine, my lady, I think it's time you had a look at your own face.'

'No!' Igrane cried out, and pulled up the fur robe to cover her face. 'No! No! No! Please!'

'My lady.' Ustane spoke firmly. 'Would you send a man into battle without allowing him to examine his own weapons? Would any ruler enter battle without knowing how well his forces could perform?'

'I haven't seen a mirror since I came here,' Igrane said.

'I will have your servants fetch one.'

'No!' Igrane said. 'Not another of those intimations of mortality. The sight of the last ones, bony fingers on the handles of a golden tray, almost destroyed my appetite for the day.'

Ustane laughed again. 'There are some better-looking ones. I'll send for them.'

A few moments later, four women glided into the room. They were all beautiful, all nude, and all carried cardrop-shaped, glowing lamps.

Fascinated, Igrane beckoned the first one closer to her. She came, and as she approached, it became clear to Igrane that these women were as dead as Ustane.

'How exquisite,' Igrane whispered.

And indeed, the girl was almost perfectly formed, with creamy skin, small, upright breasts, slender waist, ample hips and thighs, and long, graceful legs. Her skin was of an alabaster whiteness, too white. As she approached more closely, Igrane could see she was more or less bloodless, lips, eyelids, breast tips, and the ends of her fingers pale blue. Four narrow slices in her neck marked where she had been bled dry. Her wide blue stare was empty and fixed, and the lovely oval face void of expression. Before death, her nipples had been pierced, and a tassel of gold-black pearls and rubies hung from each one. Her pudenda had also been pierced, and longer tassels moved between her legs, enhancing, not concealing, her clean-shaven sex.

Igrane gave a gasp of mingled horror and delight.

'Merlin?' she asked.

'No,' Ustane said. 'I found them. They have been here a long, long time.'

All four women had been treated the same way. The second was golden-skinned, with brown hair. The jewels dangling from her body were silver and topaz. She had been bled out at the groin. The third was red-haired, with creamy skin and decked in emeralds and white pearls. She had been bled at the wrists. The fourth was almost transparently pale, more so than the blonde but with long, ink-black hair, and even drained as she was, her vivid deep-blue eyes glowed in her livid face. She had a wound between her ribs and it was apparent her heart had been pierced.

'Good God!' Igrane said. 'If not Merlin, then who?'

'Who, indeed?' Ustane replied. 'They endured a rather long and apparently loving preparation for their final state. But somehow, I doubt if they enjoyed it.'

'No,' Igrane whispered.

They reminded her of a comb jelly Merlin had once shown her. He had taken it in his net as an ingredient for some spell. It was still living in the jar in which he'd placed it. It also moved as gracefully through the water as these girls moved gracefully through the air. It also glowed from within, as they did, with a faint, phosphorescent light. When she tried to touch it, the jellyfish had the same amorphous feel as the blond one's hand, and the hand was as cold as that denizen of the deep ocean.

'They are of limited utility,' Ustane said. 'They aren't very strong and are rather slow, but they won't disgust you and are actually good hairdressers.'

Ustane clapped her hands. 'A mirror, my dears!'

Two of the ladies left and returned with a mirror. It was larger than a hand mirror, a square pier glass that showed Igrane her head and upper body. Sheer delight drove every other thought out of her mind.

'That can't be me, but it is. Oh, my God! It is!'

She was young again and at the height of her powers. Beautiful as Aphrodite or Helen when she bared her breast to Menelaus and the sword fell from his hand.

'I believe . . .' she said, turning her face this way and that, '. . . I believe I am more beautiful than I was at sixteen. My skin has a glow to it that it didn't have then. My lips are a bit fuller. The experience of life and love shows in my face but not in a bad way. I am innocence and seduction, both at once.'

Then her eyes closed and she waved her hand. 'Take it away. The vision of my own beauty is too much to be borne. What? Oh, what must I do to keep this? Is it real? Would it endure in the world I came from?'

One of the beautiful ghostly women cupped one of Igrane's breasts. She pushed her away and watched the woman's arm fall into transparent tatters, then re-form itself again and play with her nipple.

'Ustane!' Igrane spoke insistently.

'I am here.' Ustane's voice came from beyond the circle

204

of light where Igrane was seated. Only her eyes glowed, sparks in the darkness.

'Then answer me,' Igrane said impatiently.

'I can't,' Ustane said. 'I don't know the answers. I only know that Merlin's little contretemps left you in an incredibly strong position.'

The mirror was gone. Igrane leaned back in the cushioned chair and gave herself over to the ministrations of the four wraiths. One of them pulled her robe aside. She was nude under it.

'I've been so tense.' Igrane sighed.

Two of the creatures devoted themselves to her breasts, one to her neck and ears; the fourth knelt between her legs and parted her knees gently.

'This should relax you,' Ustane said.

'I would do anything . . . anything to keep this,' Igrane whispered. 'To keep this . . . power, this beauty, forever.'

'No one,' Ustane said insinuatingly, 'would recognize you now. Not even your husband or your son.'

'Uther forsake my bed years ago . . . and Arthur is beyond my reach.'

'Nothing is beyond your reach now. Nor would that old fool husband of yours recognize you. And I'll wager he wouldn't turn away, either.'

'Voluptuous.' Igrane spoke musingly as one of the shadowy attendants lifted a cup of wine to her lips. 'This is unalloyed pleasure. No fear, no guilt, no man to make demands. Trouble me with his importunities. And when I am done with these pretty things, I simply dismiss them and they return to the dark realms where they dwell.'

'Yes,' Ustane said.

Igrane's body shook with a spasm of pleasure as the one between her legs tongued her in a practiced manner.

'How long can they keep this up?' she asked, even as she moved trembling into another spasm.

'As long as you like, my dear. Just as long as you like,' Ustane told her.

Black Leg slapped at the birds with his armored hand, and it destroyed them. He was thinking that, in this manifestation, they weren't as strong as in the other. But as they died, the flying silver metal shards spattered into his skin. As if frightened by his ferocity, they drew back, and Black Leg felt the warm blood streaming down his chest and stomach.

The winged things weren't really birds any longer, but spots of the kind looking too long at something bright leaves as an afterimage in the eye. The sun was blazing through the opening at the end of the chamber. They leaped toward the light as a flock and jumped into the sun rays, then turned to pounce, glittering like a thousand razor-edged knives.

'No!' Black Leg heard his own panicked scream.

Slap! He felt another armored glove cover his left hand, then a third wrap moistly around his whole torso. But the hell birds didn't come straight in. They split into two groups. One went for his unprotected face, the other for his bare legs.

But Black Leg was a wolf, and when the bird knives arrived, his face wasn't there. The creatures were wiped away by two coordinated blows from his paws, battered into fragments so tiny, they drifted down like glowing dust toward the floor.

Abruptly, the sun went out and the chamber became utterly dark. He heard her give a yell of triumph and knew she must have pitched another piece of the same substance over the opening through which the sun's light streamed. Now man again, he hunkered down, hoping she was right: the birds couldn't function in complete darkness.

He could feel her close to him, and when her arms embraced him, he only found it a little strange that she should pick so dangerous a moment for love play. Then he felt the fear and knew whatever was embracing him, it wasn't her. Its pelt was short, silky, and fragrant. The lips were hot, the hint of teeth under them, fangs.

Then lichens began to glow and it vanished as though it had never been. He found her hand in the faint light, and they both crawled out under the wall.

The daylight was a shock to Black Leg's eyes. Outside the narrow windows, the garden was blooming and singing as though the long, bad night hadn't happened. There was still food piled against the wall. His legs were bothering him, and totally forgetting the armor, he went wolf to heal the lacerations. But when he landed all four feet on the stone floor, he found he was still wearing the armor, only now it was suited to a wolf, not a man.

She divested him of it very carefully, while he went to work on the food with a will. When they had both finished stuffing themselves, they sat and examined the armor. He was human again; the vegetable food suited a human better.

'It's the first thing we've found that works against them,' he said.

'I know, but do you recognize those symbols?' she asked.

'Like on the inside of the tunnel?'

'Yes. They are a sure sign that the makers of the tunnel made this, also.'

'What's bad about that? From what you tell me, they were pretty smart.'

'They were, and their weapons can be dangerous.'

'Didn't you ever try to figure out the symbols?'

He had softened the armor in water and made a glove out of it. It was joined, so his fingers and wrist could move freely. He took a rock and struck hard at the back of his hand. The symbols on the glove flared, but he felt nothing. It turned the edge of the rock with astonishing ease. He concentrated, studying the glove where it covered his fingers. When he thought of them, talons three inches long sprang out of the glove over his fingertips.

'You're damn right they're dangerous. But not to me,' he said.

He drew the talons through a melon rind lying on the floor of the cave, and the talons sectioned the melon rind like so many razors. Then he reached out toward the lichens on the wall.

'Leave them alone,' she said. 'They're doing their job, just like that vine out there that you were so foolish as to try to pull up.'

He opened and closed the glove. 'I'd like to see those vines try to attack me now.'

'One weapon,' she said, 'and already he's swaggering.'

'That's snide,' he said as he dove under the wall to collect a few more armor pieces.

There in the gloom Black Leg didn't feel so confident. The only light was the lichen glow, and the dead were ghostly amorphous shapes in the gloom. He shivered as he remembered the kiss.

But he collected the remnants of what the first corpse he'd seen had been wearing and slid back out quickly. He went to the pool where the lichens had cleaned him and placed them in the water, then methodically began to dress himself.

'Why dangerous? How dangerous?' he asked her.

She was dressing, too, wearing some of that really unpleasant vine.

She considered for a moment. The vine didn't make a bad garment. Yes, it left her breasts bare, as the other one had, but it supported them and twined attractively at her arms and legs. It had small, heart-shaped leaves and blue, flat flowers with long orange stamens and a black pistil.

'A sexy flower,' he said.

'That's what flowers are: sex. And yes, your attraction to me last night when you gave me your wolf self wasn't entirely an accident. It's an aphrodisiac.'

'I overdosed,' he said.

'That's putting it mildly.'

'I did that on purpose. I couldn't think of any way to persuade you to take it otherwise. And I was afraid you'd die. Besides, I want to hear about dangerous. And what about my tail?'

She rolled her eyes. 'A true nonlinear thinker. What the hell are you talking about?'

'The armor. Why dangerous? And how can I get it to cover my tail when I'm wolf?'

'Come on. Let's go down to the lake. The sun is out and it's a beautiful day.'

She talked as they walked. 'The armor is dangerous because the universe has logic.'

He sighed.

'It does it like a seed. You plant a seed, and after a while, you get a tree. An acorn, an oak; a hazelnut, a hazelnut bush.'

'This I know.'

'Yeah? Why?'

He was silent. 'This I don't know.'

'My. At last some modesty. The universe is the same. From small beginning it grew into what it is now. Sun, moon, stars, the celestial sphere. And it's big, very big, bigger than your people can ever possibly imagine. To put it simply, the people who built the tunnel and created the armor understood how the universe started and why it became the way it is. Their language reflects the logic of the universe, and you can't – and I can't – understand their language unless we comprehend that logic. That's why no one has ever been able to understand the tunnel, or read the symbols written in it. The universe is filled with all sorts of beings, and you wouldn't believe how many of them have tried.'

He stopped and looked out at the little lake. The sun was high in the sky, and he could look down into the center and see that it was deep and clear. A shape moved in the shadowed gloom of long, spiral waterweed at the bottom.

'Fish?' he asked.

'Something,' she replied. 'I'm not sure I want to find out. Every time I find out something new about this place, I get more upset. Thanks to you, I don't need the water any longer. I can feed like a human.'

They sat down on a flat rock and shared large, red, juicy fruit from a vine coiling over a bush covered with blue berries.

'So what harm do you think the armor could do to me?' he asked.

'I think if you put it all the way on, you might find out.'

'This is too big for me,' he said.

'I know,' she answered. 'And I'm sorry.'

'I'm still going to put it all the way on. I think it's our ticket out of here.'

'I know,' she said. 'That's the trouble. All I wanted was a tumble in the hay. Oh, boy, I said. I'll bet that cute thing is fun and games. What he doesn't know about the birds and the bees and the flowers and the trees, I can sure teach him. I brought back a hero. You are that thing, you know. When you gave me part of your own being to save my life, I knew it.'

The garden sang to them. The reeds piped; something sang a distant trill when the wind blew. A waterfall of notes wandered downstream toward them from trees that bent low over the water and trailed long, weeping branches into the stream, rather like willows do. But no willow ever had golden flowers that rained perfume into the slow eddies of the central pool.

'Are you missing anything? I mean, did human wolf-ness take anything away?' he asked.

'No. In fact, the tree is telling me about the fish. They're old and slow, even older than the plants. They have been here a long time. The tree says, "Don't catch them. There aren't any more where they came from. These fish are the last."'

'Look,' he whispered, and pointed to the canyon wall across from them. It had begun to weep, the water seemingly welling out of the porous rock, running down the walls into the plant beds below. They were built in an intricate maze, and as the water filled each one, the soil swelled and the plants turned greener. The guardian vines, like the one she was wearing, became a mound of green fuzz, dotted with white. Next to them, lilies bloomed, or at least that's what they looked like, blush pink and white, spotted with brown.

Then something low, gray-green, and furred burst into scarlet blossom. The music swelled as each group sang in thanksgiving for what they felt was rain. The beds were planted in the same shapes as the letters he had seen on the armor and on the walls of the tunnel. An eternal garden surrounded him, created to be a microcosm of the universe, its fragrances, its colors, its life sacred to the beings who shaped it to reflect the beauty of all life everywhere.

'The fish,' he said. 'The tree tells you they are very old. Maybe they can give you more information than the plants can. The trick you did before. The way you turned into rain. Can you still do it?'

'Trick,' she replied, 'is an unhappy description of that particular power of mine.'

Black Leg answered in the same vein. 'There is a certain poverty of description in the language for several of your activities. I do the best I can. No offense intended.'

She laughed, waded into the lake, and fell into droplets that ringed the calm surface of the water for a few seconds, then were gone.

He studied the layout of the garden. He felt he might stay here for a thousand years simply contemplating the exquisite care with which the garden had been fitted together. And, of course, that's what it was: a page like the carpet pages in an illuminated missal from one of the Christian monasteries. And in a flash of insight, he saw what many wiser minds had not seen, how this script must be read. He went back to where his armor lay, thinking about his father.

They had sat together beside a fire in the hills and discussed human wretchedness while they listened to a pack in the distance plan a hunt. It was cold and already there was a frost on the grass. A high, chill moon illuminated the ice-limned gorse and heather around them. His father quizzed him as to what the pack planned.

'The elk are moving down from the high pastures. The father and mother of the pack spotted three yearling fawns that look weak. They plan to ambush the bachelor herd about a mile away and take one.'

His father nodded approvingly. 'Very good. Want to join them? Supposed to be three, so we could join the hunt and take one for ourselves.'

'Why? We killed today, a mare in foal. We have as much meat as we can carry home. If we killed again, we'd have to waste most of it.'

'Spoken like a true wolf,' Maeniel said.

'How can you tell? It's been years since you were a full-time wolf. Do we change so little?'

'Not at all. Never. I remember things that happened thousands of years ago as though they occurred yesterday. Before – as Dugald tells it – the water rose and drowned the vast plains that were once dry and now are the North Sea. We hunted elk here, and in much the same way as this pack hunts them now. A stealthy tracking of the herd, then the tests to see which ones are strongest. We know each member by their own particular scent and can describe his appearance and behavior to one another.

'The wolves spoke of one called Blaze. He is strong, but slow, and if they can drive him into broken or boggy ground, they might get him. But then there is One Eye. Been diseased from his birth, but he is wary and very fast. If they can blindside him upwind, he won't stand a fight. Another has fallen into the habit of kneeling to eat, fishing under cedar breaks and hazel bushes for herbs still green in spite of frost. He's fat, but has callus pads on his knees. If they ambush him from above, the callus pads limit his agility.

'We have hunted them time out of mind. When they had a six-foot spread of antlers and hooves like war hammers, it was the same then as it is now, and we went about it in the same way and talked with each other about the same things.'

Black Leg shivered. He didn't believe the part about a six-foot spread of antlers. No, that simply wasn't possible. But he had his own memories. As yet he hadn't turned those pages in his mind and tested some of the things his father was telling him. He wasn't sure he wanted to. His father had been wild at birth, before his transformation. Black Leg had grown up among humans.

Maeniel grinned at his son across the fire. Black Leg felt guilty. It was as though his father knew what he was thinking. So he changed the subject.

'They change, don't they? The humans, I mean.'

'They don't do anything else,' Maeniel said. 'And have been ringing in changes since they came into existence. Who can say what they will one day be.'

'Dugald says—'

'Don't quote Dugald to me. Not if you value your hide.'

Black Leg gave his father a very nasty but very wolf look. It said as clearly as if he had spoken, 'You are my father and pack leader. Therefore, I respect you. But that's not a good reason to take advantage of another who has not yet reached the fullness of his strength.'

Maeniel looked away, somewhat abashed. Good manners were important in a wolf pack, and between senior and cub. He had been guilty of a breach of etiquette.

'Very well. Dugald says . . .' Maeniel stated.

Black Leg continued, 'That you hang around with humans because their strange ways fascinate you.'

'That's one reason. Yes.' Maeniel poked at the fire. 'This is another. No other creature can do this.'

'Make a fire?' Black Leg asked.

'Yes. And this.' Maeniel took a stick and began to write in the dirt: Alpha, Beta . . .'

'The alphabet.' Black Leg was astounded. 'But what's so special about that?'

Maeniel broke the stick and met Black Leg's eyes. 'You could teach a wolf the alphabet, my son, but you could never teach him to use it. Yet all of what they are flows from such things, especially that one. They are going somewhere, moving through time. Wolves are as the Stella Polaris pole star. We do not change.'

Black Leg felt cold, and not entirely from the mountain night. He didn't like it when his father talked this way. 'I would rather be a wolf and think about deer with stomach trouble or weak legs.'

Now he stood here in the midst of this beautiful garden, almost, but not quite, ready to call the change.

The garden was almost filled with water now, and it glowed around him like some huge, polished jewel. A symphony of color, light, and, yes, sound, because everything sang, even the things he hadn't heard sing before, a magnificent chorale that moved from entity to splendid entity. Each soloing, then sinking back into the symphonic whole as the baton of leadership passed to another being.

He had thought grass surrounded the lake in the center, but as he watched, the grass bloomed with a thousand mauve-tinted white flowers, then the petals fell, white and soft as snowdrifts among the long, green gorse stems. Scarlet berries succeeded the flowers.

Again she embraced him, the furred creature from the cave, and he felt her mold her hips against his. And for the first time since he entered this wild, wild place, he was conscious that he was naked as his erection throbbed almost painfully at his groin.

But in a breath, she was gone. Black Leg knelt, plucked a handful of the red berries burgeoning in the grass, and put them in his mouth. He didn't need to swallow; he felt the effect of whatever they contained fly though his veins, transforming his body into a vessel of pure light.

The noon sun was high above. He burned with its light, a light that was also pure knowledge. And he understood once and forever that damnation and salvation were one.

Death! I thought, and jumped to my feet. I was taken completely by surprise and every instinct in me screamed that this was a very dangerous moment.

I jumped back again. I was no stranger to the hero's salmon leap. I wanted distance between myself and a man who had said that the punishment for what I had just done was death, even though I wasn't clear on what I had done. Killing the plant; healing Albe?

She was lying in the road as though in shock from the pain and the injuries she had received. I had a brief chance to study the warrior who had just spoken. For warrior he was – armored in something that looked like bronze, a helmet of the old Greek type, one that covered his entire head and most of his face. It had a horizontal opening that allowed him to see, and a narrow slit for the nose and mouth. Otherwise, the visor and the long cheek pieces hid his features. The other three men – the fourth was a woman – wore more ornate but somehow cheaper-looking, formed waxed-leather armor, dyed green-brown and dark purple.

I didn't have time to notice any more about the three, because the bronze-clad leader gave me a look of lethal indifference and said, 'Kill her!!! Let the other one live for a time. She may offer some sport.'

He glanced at the brown-clad man and jerked his head in my direction.

My goodness. That *was* elaborate armor. My opponent wore leather pants with leg and thigh protection, inlaid with dull gold. A gold chain-mail shirt over an inner garment of fitted leather. A muscle cuirass, but it was not formed all of a piece like the Roman ones. Instead it was made of a mosaic of leather plates, each one outlined in the same dull gold. He looked not a man but like some exotic insect sheathed in magnificent, glowing chitin. He was a warrior work of art at the same time. His shield was as beautiful as the rest, leather with a golden boss and rim, inlaid with golden swirls of intricately patterned, fine lines.

Too bad, I thought. Because he had his sword out and was coming for me, hard and fast.

I knew I wouldn't be able to get my sword clear of the sheath before he would be on me. So I jumped aside and slammed my right hand into the leather shield. I felt the surge roaring up from my guts and knew I was putting almost too much into it. I might exhaust myself before the battle began.

The shield exploded into flame. The metal must have been gold; it has a low melting point, and the molten metal sprayed both of us.

My armor turned it, but he was hit by a droplet in one eye, and he hurled the flaming shield in a broad arc, out over the low-growing plants. It landed among them. He screamed in pain and clapped one mailed glove to his eye—

Then he saw where his quickly discarded shield had gone.

This time his scream was even worse. I was trying to free my sword, but the agony in the sound distracted me. His sword dropped from his hand, hitting the ground. With a ringing cry, he fell to his knees, then bent so far over, his forehead touched the stony road. He clutched at his head with both hands and began beating his forehead against the hexagonal pavers, sobbing with horror and despair.

Meantime, we had all underestimated Albe. She took out one warrior with a sweeping kick while still lying on the ground. He had been incautious enough to stand too close. His feet went flying from under him. He had no chance to break his fall, and his helmeted skull hit the stone road with a clang. He jerked once and lay still.

How she got the second with a sling stone, I'm not to this day sure. But she did. He was very well armored, but his mouth and lower jaw were exposed. And believe me, that's all Albe ever needs. He staggered back and went down, bleeding badly from the mouth and nose.

I've never been sure why I did what I did then. I turned, leaped across the road, and went after the shield blazing among what I was sure was an important crop. No one defends a weed patch the way this bunch defended this tiny hunk of dirt.

I felt the plants strike at my ankles, but my armor turned them. On my second step, the ground gave, and I thought my foot went into mud. But the stench took me; and even as I realized what my foot landed on, I snatched up the flaming shield rim and spun it out across the road, into the barren sea bottoms beyond.

Then I had to emulate a frightened rabbit and take some long hops – because I was finding out something else about those dangerous weeds: they compensated for resistance. The strikes against my legs were getting harder and harder, and the armor was beginning to give way.

The one whose shield I'd burned was kneeling upright in the road, gazing at me in rapt astonishment. As for myself, I couldn't wait. I tore off my sandals and tossed them into the sand, away from those loathsome plants, to clean them.

We all stood looking at one another.

'You may go,' the bronze-clad man spoke in a haughty manner. 'In the normal course of events, I would call up a team able to deal with you and finish you off. But what I have to do here is too important. . . .'

The one with the bleeding mouth and nose was on his feet. Albe slipped another stone into her sling.

'No,' he said. I was a bit astounded that he could talk. It appeared that, though she had certainly broken something, it wasn't his lower jaw, since he raised his head in a halt gesture and spoke.

'Peace. Peace. I yield myself beaten, your prisoner. Whatever you like will be yours.'

Albe still looked like she might want to finish the job, so I said, 'Hear him out. Only let fly if he makes a threatening move.'

Then he turned to the bronze-clad one. 'Amrun, are you mad? We can't let them go. Did you see how she got that shield and has come to no harm?'

'Brother, I saw everything. Keep your mouth shut. My lady, your powers are indeed remarkable. But whatever your business here, conclude it as swiftly as possible and leave. You must be from among the jungle kingdoms, and we need none of your evil practices, . . . your disgusting—'

'Oh, God!' The wounded man moaned. His face was obviously hurting, but I could tell he was also infuriated by his companion. 'Shut the fuck up! She can't be from the jungle.'

'I'm not,' I said. 'The only way I ever heard of a jungle, it was somewhere in Asia, up the Nile River.'

'What are you then?' the wounded man asked.

Albe and I looked at each other and shrugged. We weren't sure how to tell him.

'Picts,' I said.

'Your rank,' the bronze-clad Amrun snapped.

'I am the Dragon Queen,' I told him. 'My name is Guinevere. I'm a sacred woman.'

This seemed to calm both of them down and shut them up. I don't think they understood a word I said, but they did seem content in their belief that we probably did not come from the dreaded jungle kingdoms.

The one with the bleeding face sat down. Where his face wasn't smeared with blood, it looked greenish. He vomited blood and water at the roadside, but he continued talking. 'I don't understand any of that. But, Brother, I believe they are at least respectable and may be invited to the city.'

Albe had drawn closer to me. 'I'm not sure if I should be glad or sorry about that,' I whispered to her.

The other two were stirring around now. The one who had hit his head was sitting up, but he had a sort of lost look and I didn't think he'd be giving anybody any trouble soon. The one whose shield I'd burned had smacked both face and forehead against the road a little too hard. His face was bleeding, and while he didn't look lost, he was dazed. The one with the broken face hadn't gotten his color back, and he looked to be getting ready to throw up again. The girl was sitting down, a bleak expression on her face. I noticed her arms and legs were heavily padded. It didn't take a lot of brains to figure out what was going on here.

The one in brass armor spoke again. He motioned us to pass him, saying, 'Go forward and wait for us at the city gates. There are food vendors there, and you may purchase some. Doubtless the food sellers will want some of your jewelry in exchange for water and sustenance.'

'Doubtless,' I replied. 'However, we're not going anywhere till we find out what you're going to do with that girl.'

The one with the broken face gave me a sharp look. 'Brother, we have food and drink with us. We can share it with them – '

'I'm growing weary of this insolence. We have an important task to perform. Now, do as you are bid, or I will have our family cast you off.'

The girl stood for the first time. 'Please . . . Meth! Don't . . .'

'Be quiet,' the bronze-clad warrior snapped at her. 'You were chosen properly by honest lot, were you not? Silence becomes you.'

Meth staggered to his feet. 'Shut up, Amrun, and I mean it. Wounded I'm still a better fighter than you are, and if you don't close your mouth, I'll kill you now and take the consequences.'

Everyone looked a bit horrified, but Meth ignored them. 'You must . . . must . . . show me how you did that.'

I assented by nodding and walked toward the plants. I waved my arm near them. My armor leaped out on my skin, and I brought my hand closer. The vicious thing stabbed at me. The spine bounced off my armored hand.

Looking down at them, I saw the plants were beautiful, with broad, green leaves that overlapped one another in an almost mathematical rosette. The leaves were light green at the edges and darkening toward the center until they shaded from deep green to purple near the stem. The whole plant resembled a flower, while I suspected the flower itself was insignificant. It didn't surprise me. I had seen similar plants in my own world.

I moved my hand again and watched a heart-shaped leaf curl itself into a spike, the tip glittering with a sticky-looking honeydew I thought must be poison. Albe's reaction, the quick swelling, suggested the presence of poison to me.

'See if it has fruit on it.'

'You do it,' I said. 'You're armored.'

'Watch!' He peeled off one of his gloves. It was formed of metal plates on the outside and mail on the inside. It was a beautiful piece of work. He brushed one of the leaves with his glove. The spine went through it as though the glove were made of curd cheese.

He waved the empty glove at me. 'This will stop a sword cut, but not one of those thorns. Simple armor is not enough. But I can tell that what you have isn't simple armor.'

'A gift from my father,' I said.

Meth laughed. 'Who was he? One of the Tuatha de Danae?'

'Probably,' I said.

The laughter faded from his eyes. 'You aren't joking.'

'No.'

He rose to his feet. 'Cateyrin!' he called out to the girl. 'Fetch the boxes.' Then, to me, 'Please? Look for the fruit. They seem to be crystal buds.'

I crouched down. This one had three flowers. They

221

were small, vivid scarlet, and tightly closed. However, it had one fruit. It was oval and looked as though it were made of glass covered with swirls of ridged lines.

My armor surprised me, rising at my command. I stretched out my hand and, despite a few whacks from the long-spined leaves, plucked it.

I held it up to the light, then gasped as the colors changed. First it flashed like a clear crystal, and all the colors of the rainbow filled the surface. Then it became clear yellow, but only for a second. Suddenly, it was molten gold, followed by light green, emerald green, then blue-green. Azure blue was succeeded by the blue of a summer sea, then brown, red-brown, until it rested at garnet.

'Beautiful!' Albe said.

I glanced away from the gemlike seed and saw Meth kneeling at my feet. The look in his eyes was almost one of worship.

'Stop that!' I said. 'Get me some food and drink. Albe's hungry and thirsty, and so am I.'

He didn't move, so I rested the back of my left hand against his cheek. I didn't see Mother, but the rose scent filled the air. When I pulled my hand away, his face looked better. Some of the serious swelling that disfigured it was down.

He scrambled to his feet. Cateyrin was already returning with the food and boxes.

I pointed to the other three warriors. 'Go sit down on those rocks by the roadside where I can watch you. Now,' I asked Meth, 'how many of these things do you want?'

'Five boxes,' he said.

'Serve Albe,' I told Cateyrin. 'Give me the boxes and strip off that padding. You won't need it.'

It was the beginning of a rather long, weary afternoon. Meth and I placed the boxes in the shade of a rock, since he told me the jewels didn't need to be exposed to the sun as I collected them.

'Best that be done by whoever purchases them,' he told me.

I went looking for fruit. 'The damned place is a graveyard,' I snapped at him as I eased around the edges of the ravine where the plants grew.

'The price of five boxes is usually a human life,' he said as I handed him one.

'Why?' I asked.

'We have to have them.'

'Why?' I was looking down at a dozen or more plants growing up through a pelvis and rib cage. I plucked four from it quickly.

'It's all the city of Gorias has to sell.'

'Gorias?' I stood oblivious to a couple of really hard smacks from those spines. 'Gorias? Your city is named Gorias?'

'Yes.'

'Fire,' I said.

'Falias, Gorias, Findias, Murias. Those are all that remain but for the jungle lands, and the denizens of those swamps are as dangerous as the snakes they rule.'

The wind blew down the ravine toward the Dead Sea, clouding the air with a fetid stench. I moved toward the fresh corpse I had stepped on. There were paths among those plants; they weren't what I'd call safe. But following them meant the difference between three whacks by those spines and thirteen or even maybe thirty. I had already observed that they fruited best near the dead.

The corpse had indeed soaked into the soil. He . . . or was it she? I couldn't be sure. The thing was facedown and that was good, since I didn't want to look at its face. But it had padding a lot like Cateyrin had been wearing. I filled two boxes from the . . . he called the plants Gorias Purples. Then I made my way quickly back to the road.

'Seems to me,' I told Meth, 'you could spread the damage. Let the person rest up between times.'

'Doesn't usually work,' he replied. 'The poison seems to be cumulative beyond a certain point. Most die, and in agony, a few days after they are dedicated. No, usually after so many spikes drive into the skin, the hetrophant becomes euphoric. They are lifted out of themselves into a visionary state. If that happens, it's very productive for their guiding party, because they get a lot of fruit and the celebrant dies in ecstasy.'

'A doom rapture?'

'That's what they call it,' he said.

I rested for a second against a pile of rock. Albe approached me with a glass jug and a cup. She offered me wine. I was not expecting much, but it was wonderful. It wasn't wine, but some other beverage. Mead? I found it warmed and strengthened me.

I wasn't grateful. 'Maybe that doom rapture gets a little help?' I asked Meth.

He was a poor liar. His eyes widened and his face slipped into a look of innocence that wouldn't have fooled an eight-year-old.

'I can't imagine – ' he began.

'No? Well, I can,' I snapped.

He glanced furtively at the others, seated along the roadside.

'All right. All right. But the celebrant is going to die anyway. Some of them are brought back to their families, and I've never known one to survive. Those plants . . . the mariglobes . . . are truly venomous. Except that you seem to have some special powers and can withstand them.'

I couldn't, but he didn't realize that. My armor isn't perfect, and if I went on collecting those fruits long enough, I would die like the other celebrants, as he called them. My relative immunity was transient.

I went back to work, and in no time, we had filled the other boxes. In the meantime, Amrun and the other two warriors had their heads together.

Meth studied the five full boxes. 'I almost don't believe it. Usually it takes all day, because the celebrant gets slower and slower, then has to be coaxed, then bribed and drugged, sometimes threatened and even beaten. . . .'

'I don't need to know this,' I told him. 'And I would just as soon not.'

Meth took the boxes and walked toward Amrun, knelt at his feet, and, rather humbly, presented them to him. Something flickered at the edge of my vision. I moved my eyes to the left and saw Albe slipping a lead shot into her sling. I felt the skin on my face tighten, but I didn't want Amrun to see I was ready to fight.

Amrun had a kind, almost benevolent expression on his face.

'My lord, accept this as a token of my true submission to your will.' Meth intoned the words in a ceremonial fashion. 'And pardon my seeming opposition. Now Cateyrin may be preserved for another occasion. Forgive me, my lord.'

Amrun stretched out his hand to take the boxes. He must have palmed the knife, because I didn't see it until he used it to cut Meth's throat.

Blood sprayed everywhere. Meth went down screaming.

Cateyrin shouted, 'No!' and went for Amrun with a knife in her hand.

But he'd turned to run and looked to show us a clean pair of heels. He'd grabbed those precious boxes with his left hand even as he cut Meth's throat.

But then Albe had a lead shot in her sling. There was an opening between his helmet and the back plate on his armor. It couldn't have been more than an inch wide. Albe found it, though, or rather, her lead shot did.

Amrun had reached the top of a low rise just ahead, but when the lead stone severed his spine, he dropped where he was like a wet rag. The one in brown armor had his knife out, ready to gut Cateyrin, and I didn't see how she could do much against him. My sword was out before I knew I had my hand on the hilt. But I thought I would probably be too late.

Brown Armor took an underhanded slice at her torso. I didn't see the knife in her hand. It was small, and she did miss his throat with it.

The one in green armor had taken his helmet off, never a safe move around Albe. I don't know if he tried something or she just killed him on general principles. A little housekeeping chore – get him out of the way so he wouldn't involve himself in any mischief. But when I tore my eyes away from Cateyrin and Brown Armor, I saw he was already dead.

As I said, Cateyrin missed Brown Armor's throat, but he had a prominent Adam's apple and her knife had a hook on the end of it. He went spinning round and round, clutching his throat and trying to scream and breathe at the same time.

Cateyrin screamed and look horrified by what she'd done. Albe obviously didn't share either sentiment. She charged in and tripped Brown Armor, then kicked him into a thick stand of those horrific plants growing at the roadside.

I had a graphic lesson in how useless conventional armor was against the plants' defenses. It took Brown Armor about fifteen seconds to die, and I imagine it was a long fifteen seconds.

When Brown Armor stopped convulsing and twitching, I saw Cateyrin was on her knees beside Meth. She had a small case with a leather strap on it. She pulled out a bottle and poured it over Meth's throat, and I saw well enough that Amrun had made a hash of killing him. The cut in his neck wasn't deep, except on one side, and it had opened only one big vein. The stuff Cateyrin poured from the phial hardened when it hit the air, sealing the wound shut, and the bleeding from the jugular ceased instantly.

Meth lay quiet, looking pale and shocked. Then he rolled on his side and whimpered, 'Cateyrin, my sweet Cateyrin.'

When she saw that the damage from Amrun's knife was repaired, she jumped to her feet and kicked him hard in the stomach. His armor blocked a lot of the kick's force, but he felt some of it, because he curled up like a sick caterpillar and threw up whatever he had left in his stomach.

'Sweet Cateyrin! I'll give you sweet Cateyrin, you unmitigated son of a bitch!'

She drew back a foot to kick him again, and Albe said, 'Stop that! You can kill him if you want, but don't mess him up so he can't walk. We can't be bothered to carry him.'

Now, Cateyrin had just seen Albe kill three people. The anger vanished from her face, and she assented to Albe's request immediately, backing away from Meth as though he were on fire.

Albe strolled over to strip the corpses, beginning with bronze-armored Amrun.

'Maybe we ought to skip the city,' I said as I concentrated on helping Meth sit up.

'No! No, you can't!' Meth cried.

'He's right,' Cateyrin said. She was collecting the five boxes of crystal fruit. 'Things come up from the jungle at night to hunt. That's what Amrun meant when he said he would cast Meth off. That means he and his men would put Meth outside the city gates and abandon him to die. Meth's only a purple, and his fealty to Amrun was all he had. I'm even poorer than Meth. I'm only a gray, and a pretty dark one at that.'

'This color thing,' I asked. 'It's some sort of rank?'

'All civilized people know . . .' Meth began.

'If I were you, Meth, I'd shut up and let me do the talking,' Cateyrin said. 'So far, your decisions haven't been all that productive. And trusting Amrun to protect you when you knew what a stupid, mean-minded—'

'Enough!' I said. 'Both of you.'

Then Albe added, 'Suppose you do shut up and let her talk. She's the first person who's made any sense since we got here.'

'Yes, it does have to do with rank,' Cateyrin explained. 'The city is run by seven great families. The Fursa are one of them. Meth was brought up in their household, and so pledged his fealty to Amrun. I told you not to. I told you—'

'Do not go on about what you told him,' Albe interjected. 'Continue.'

'At any rate, when the time of choosing came, the lot fell on me.'

'You choose the person who picks these berries by lot?' I asked. 'Is the lot honest?'

'It's supposed to be,' Meth said.

'So!' Cateyrin rested her hands on her hips. 'How come they always choose a commoner?'

Meth looked a little uncomfortable, but persevered. 'The others are not entered in the lottery as often as commoners. In fact, the higher the rank you are, the less often they drop your ball into the cage.'

'I've heard tell some are never entered,' Cateyrin snapped. She was looking up at Meth defiantly.

'Wait!' I said. 'I can see there are a lot of differences of opinion here, but the sun is westering and if what you say is true, we will need to be at this city before nightfall. How far away is it?'

'About a half hour at the most,' Meth said.

'More like twice that,' Cateyrin argued. 'And besides,

when the sun goes behind the mountains, the streets aren't safe.'

'Usually nothing happens till dark.' Meth looked impatient. 'Besides, how do we get in? The Fursa high lord will be there with his guard, waiting. And when he finds out Amrun is dead, he's going to have his men slaughter the lot of us.'

'Is Amrun the only one he cares about?' Albe asked.

Both Cateyrin and Meth turned toward her. Cateyrin answered, 'Yes. Amrun is the only one he'd miss.'

Meth said, 'I don't—'

'Meth!' Cateyrin sounded infuriated. 'You and I both heard him tell the High Lord of Mochtac that no one of note was killed after a battle that took the lives of fifteen of his men. Your best friend, Kerwan, died in that fight, and he said "no one of note!"'

Albe laughed. 'Sounds like they are no better than some of ours. Fine,' she continued, 'you dress up in Amrun's armor, and we walk right through this gate and keep on going. Will that work?'

'It might,' Cateyrin said. 'In fact, I think if we move fast, it would. My mother will be glad to see me.'

'You hope!' Meth snarled. 'Besides, you know what the penalty for impersonating a ranker is. It's death.'

'So how many times can you die?' Cateyrin asked. 'Believe me, if he finds out you had anything to do with Amrun's death, he'll tie you to a griddle and roast you over a slow fire. You know that, don't you? Don't you!? If you don't believe that's what he'll do, tell me I'm wrong. If not, put on that armor right now.'

Albe had done a pretty fair job of stripping all three men, including the one who had fallen among the plants. She'd hauled him out by his heels.

Meth marched over and began stripping off his own trappings and putting Amrun's on. He grumbled a lot, but he did it.

'My lady?' Albe spoke to me courteously. 'Is this course of action agreeable with you?'

'Keep on,' I told her. 'You're doing just fine.'

We dumped the corpses among the plants, then set out along the road, walking in what Meth and Cateyrin told us was the direction of the city. As we walked, Cateyrin and Meth tried to explain how matters stood in the strange world we'd entered. They didn't agree on much, but between the two of them, we got some idea of what was going on.

The city was ruled by seven noble families that apparently, as far as I was able to figure out, quarreled about everything. They all wanted sole rule of the city, but none of them had, as far as anyone could remember or any historical account reported, ever been able to achieve primacy. The historical accounts weren't reliable, since each of the seven families had their own version of the past, and it differed considerably from all of the others. The commoners – who were, by the way, the majority of people in the city – were forced to ally themselves with one or another great family simply in order to survive. They were obsessed with the politics of the city.

When I inquired about the mariglobes, I couldn't get much information out of either of them. I don't think they knew what the things were for, only that the powerful in the city used them as a route to still more power, and that young commoners like Cateyrin were sacrificed to obtain more of them.

About then, we reached a steep ridge, and the road moved up by switchbacks toward the top. Cateyrin explained, 'This is why I said it was an hour or more back, because it's mostly downhill from the city to the mariglobe valleys. But it's uphill going the other way. But,' she added cheerfully, 'there's a wonderful view from the top of the ridge.'

'I'll just bet there is,' Albe said. Then she chuckled and grinned at me.

I let Cateyrin and Meth get a little ahead of us. 'I don't think her death was real to her,' I whispered to Albe.

'No. No, she's a child, and he's not much better. Had the Fursa view of things beaten into his head since he was a kid. Believes everything that bonehead Amrun told him.'

'Amrun's head wasn't hard enough. Neither were the other two's heads,' I said.

'What should I do? Carve my face again? Gather and burn their bones, my lady?' Albe asked.

'I wouldn't ask it of you.'

'They threatened you, my lady,' Albe said.

'Yes, and paid the forfeit. Did you find anything decent in the strippings?'

'Enough to be worth the trouble they gave me, which wasn't much. At this rate, I'll be a wealthy woman yet. Want a share?'

'No. I have plenty. You earned it. Take care when we reach the city. I get the feeling these people don't rest much from running blades into each other.'

'Well, we just have to be better at it than they are. So far . . .' Albe crossed her fingers '. . . we are.'

We stopped talking then, because the climb had become onerous, and we labored to reach the top of the ridge. When we did, we stopped and took a breather. And I forgot my sore muscles and cramping legs because we saw the city in all its splendor, illuminated by the rays of the slanting sun. The mountains beyond the city were even higher than the one that held the city. They towered snow-clad over the closest peak to the shore. A watercourse tumbled down this final high spire of rocks. Probably, I thought, fed by snowmelt from the heights.

The city was built along the river, both to contain and protect it. Its buildings lined the rift created by the river and spread out on either side of it.

'You didn't build that,' I said accusingly to Cateyrin as I pointed to the city.

'No. No.' She shook her head. 'We found it here when we came.'

The river tumbled down from the heights through successive waterfalls, each centered in a green mountain meadow, thick with trees and grass. The city's towers were set well back from the green meadows created by the rush of the falls, and the towers of the city looked to be grown from the rock itself. Near the bottom, they were almost black, sprung from the ancient dark rock that ribs the earth.

Then this dark rock shaded into an iron-rich red. The towers, as though conjured from the stone, were scarlet; but here and there, black, as though the ore in the red rock congealed under the hands of its builders and sprang up like the rusted heap of a smith's secret iron hoard. I had seen my friend Gray's hoard when a child, and the twisted rise of metal vines reminded me of the woven wire of a sword ready to be forged.

Above the towers was a honeycomb of folded sandstone filled with quartz, laced with geodes that flashed the fire of their multicolored contents with splotches of scarlet, violet, blue, purple, and fine-grained quartz. Above the layer of limestone, the mountain turned to granite, dull gray, then fractured into lighter-colored, grainless marble.

The river flowed through it, though, I thought, so high up the grass must be sparse, low, and frost-covered in the deep night's cold. But the meadows were green and glowed gold-green in the slanted sunlight.

The towers there, drawn from white, grainless marble, flashed in the sun as though coated with fine, tiny crystals, as indeed perhaps this fine, hard stone was. The whiteness, as much that of stone as frost, threw back the light so brightly into my eyes that at first I didn't realize someone – a small figure – toiled across a platform at the very top, which jutted out over the valley and the city.

The platform looked small from where we stood, but I realized it must have been very big, because it obscured the pinnacle of the mountain, and the human standing on it was dwarfed by its breadth and width. The human figure ceased moving and something glinted at his back.

Once when I was no more than eight or nine, Maeniel, Mother, Black Leg, and I went night fishing. It was spring, and at dawn I lay warmed by my wolf companions. At first light, I opened my eyes and saw a butterfly pupa on a grass stem nearby, and the crease-winged, drab insect emerged. I lay, too warm to stir, and watched it climb to the top of the long grass stem, and among the pearls of dew, watched the wings drop down, the stiffening veins harden as it became a thing of splendor, dressed in mottled brown, violet, purple, and, at last, gold. Then, opening and closing its wings in the new sun, it unrolled the long proboscis, drank from a pimpernel flower, and flew away into sunrise.

This is the closest I can get to telling you about what I saw then on the platform at the mountaintop. These wings were gold, and they spread out on either side of the figure I saw on the platform. Little by little, section by section, expanding on either side of the figure standing alone on the mountaintop. So bright was the reflection of the sun on those wings that I was near blinded. They were the color of molten gold, and before they were fully expanded, they were larger in proportion to the human figure than the butterfly's wings were in proportion to the insect.

And they glowed with such a dazzle that for moments they seemed to obscure the sun, to drink the very light itself. I found out later that, indeed, they did.

Then the human figure ran forward and leaped from

the end of the platform into space. My heart was hammering with fear as though I rode those wings myself as they glided down over the city, and it seemed the winged creature would come to a nasty end in the deserts of the sea bottom. But then, as a hawk when it drops from its cliff nest, the rising warm air currents lifted the broad wings higher and higher, until it circled the city below, then soared away toward the southwest over the lost, forsaken, empty sea.

I pressed my hand against my heart, which was hammering so hard beneath my left ribs that the thudding was almost pain, and asked, 'Meth, was that a human being with wings? A man or woman? And what magic could be used to grow such appendages?'

He laughed at me. 'No magic, but a sun cape. There aren't many left, and hellish dangerous things to use, they are. But only with sun capes can we reach the other cities. He will be setting out from the Fursa clan for Falas to bring them the mariglobes and receive the fire stones in return. We're going to need them this winter.'

'God,' I whispered. 'I wish I could ride one of those things.'

God, I prayed, *let me someday ride one of those things.* This prayer was silent and to myself. I will ride one of those things, because the need to spread those wings out on either side of me and fly is greater than my desire for my king, for power, or even for life itself. And one day I will have those wings or die in the attempt to get and use them.

I will march steadfast to whatever dark fate shadows me, but . . . oh, God! Let me fly.

CHAPTER FOUR

T HE UNSPEAKING SAXON GUARDS conveyed Uther to a cell somewhere deep within the confines of the villa. The villa was a gigantic place, much larger than the king had thought looking at it from the road. He completely lost track of where he was as he marched through one courtyard and into another, then along an impressive colonnade, down from there into a vast kitchen garden, and past a line of stables. Finally they reached what looked like it had been a storehouse for legumes and cereal crops but had now been turned into a very ugly prison.

The long corridor that ran down the center of the building was lined with doors to the cells. The one he was shown into – his guards may have been quiet but they were extremely courteous – was simply a stone room, obviously intended to keep sacks of wheat or dried beans from damp mold or the depredations of rodents. The only air and light in the room were furnished by a narrow slit window, high up on one wall, blocked by both bars and wire mesh. The door was solid oak, the planks in it mortised and tenoned to form a tight fit. It was held closed by an iron bar bolt on the outside.

He was left there. The door slammed shut and he

heard the clatter as the iron bolt shot into an opening in the stone wall. The room was cold, the chill icy. The bars and wire in the window above did nothing to block the north wind, and the king was glad of his heavy woolen mantle. But he wondered if its warmth would be sufficient come nightfall.

He also wondered if he should have been more obsequious in his dealings with the nobleman. Then he gave a soft snort of derision when he thought about the certainly ambitious and probably sadistic young man. The nasty peacock deserved that and probably much worse at someone's hands. Too bad he wouldn't be the one to mete out the punishment the 'count' had most likely already earned.

He'd once had to deal with a small group of deserters from one of his own war bands. They were not only deserters but also murderous thieves and rapists, who left a ten-mile-long path of grief and destruction behind them. The Viper Society priestess had chosen the punishment. The drunken young fools were bundled into pitch-soaked brush and faggots, then thrown onto the bone fire of their victims, one by one.

'It contents the dead,' Morgana told him. 'They are assured of vengeance.'

Oddly, once caught, bound, and sentenced, the culprits died like men. There were few screams from the pyre, and then only in the last extremity. This particular 'Count' of Dung would, in a similar situation, screech like a stuck hog.

A man bears his ills, deserved or not. His pride bought him this one. Bear it!

The king circled the room. Walls tight, Roman stonework. One couldn't insert a fingernail between one stone and another. The window was too high for a man his age to jump up to. That's all he'd need now, a sprained or broken ankle.

Some things are simple. The tomb had been simple. A few jars of wine, a platter of bread for the journey into the next world if the inhabitant cared to depart hence. A lamp left burning so that the spirit of the dead man could warm itself at a last light, and then eternal silence and darkness. But oh, yes, there was the harp leaning against the wall in the last flickering light of the last lamp he would ever see.

The king was very weary. He hadn't slept well between his efforts with the harp and his meeting with Merlin. He was exhausted. He lay down on the hard floor in what he felt was the least drafty corner of the chill cell. He pillowed his head on the harp case. It was boiled, waxed leather reinforced with wood, and the weight of his head could not damage the instrument within.

For a long time he slept without dreams, but when he woke, it was seemingly pitch-black in the cell. It reminded him too much of the tomb for a moment, then his hands found the harp case under his head.

That is music. It blooms against the darkness of death the way a flower blooms against a black backdrop or the misty dull green distance of a great city. Blooms and gathers the light into its shape and form, glows and infuses meaning into the darkness or the even more daunting jumble of the rain-drenched city caught in the shadows of growing gloom. Form in emptiness, light and color in darkness. Beauty glowing against the gloomy green darkness of the rain-swept cityscape. Sound in silence.

When he woke again, he knew it must be sometime in the day. There was more light in the room. He shifted his feet to drive the cold from his toes. The walls, floor, and what bit of the sky he could see from the window were gray. As gray as his mind, his hair, and even his soul.

I am old, he thought. *I am old.*

He knew this with an assurance he had never felt before.

His eyes closed. *It will not hurt to sleep a little now before I sleep forever,* he thought as he drifted off again.

Again, it was dark. But this time the sky was clear and the stars filled the window from edge to edge, and he was overjoyed by them because he had never quite realized how beautiful they were or how many.

When he slept again, he dreamed of his son, the Summer King. When he looked up at the boy standing over him, he was again filled with a very simple joy and felt the tears on his cheeks.

The boy seemed concerned about him and bent down. 'Father, you're cold in this place, and must be hungry and thirsty, too.'

The king smiled and lifted himself up on one elbow; and the boy Arthur, who seemed to walk in his own light, thrust a cup into his hand. Uther drank gratefully for what seemed a long time, until his thirst was completely quenched, but found he couldn't finish the cup. When he looked up to hand the cup back, the boy was gone. There was a plate on the floor with bread, butter, and bacon on it, warm as though it had just come from the fire.

He ate gratefully, then went to sleep again, warmed by water, milk, mead, and then wine, because the cup seemed to hold all three. And his stomach was filled by bread, butter, and bacon, on which he generally breakfasted of a morning. That was how he knew it must be a dream. Whoever heard of such?

When he awoke again, the cell was filled with pale morning light and the bolt of the cell door was being drawn. Count Severius entered the cell, accompanied by the young man who had captained the detachment of mercenaries who locked him in. The plate and cup were at Uther's elbow.

He sat up, rested his back against the wall, and spoke politely to the count. 'Your pardon, my lord. As you see, I am trying to rise to greet you, but you must allow me a moment to get to my feet, since I am old and more than a little bit stiff.'

The count caught sight of the plate and cup. His eyes widened in outrage.

'Who dared . . . who dared give him food and water? When?'

Uther climbed to his feet. The count's companion turned and strutted down the hall. In a few moments, the room was filled with soldiers.

'I gave strict orders he was to be locked up and left alone until I gave further orders to the contrary.' The rage in the nobleman's face and voice cracked like a whip over his people, and indeed they were on their knees, already crying for mercy.

The young officer stepped away from his lord and the groveling guards. He looked down at the harp case.

'My lord!' he said crisply. Silence fell. 'I cannot think you were disobeyed. None would have the temerity to flout your orders. He breakfasted at the inn and no doubt had the food with him when he was locked away.'

'Think so, Aife?' the count asked.

Uther felt the world lurch and come down in a different configuration. The handsome Saxon boy was indeed a woman, and a woman was the captain of his guard. Her beautiful blue eyes met the king's, a stony sort of contempt in them.

'His kind are as much about mystery as they are about music.'

'And what would you know of my kind?' Uther whispered.

Something quivered between them for a second, fragile as a cobweb's grip on the two trees that support it, but something Uther hadn't felt in years; something that can only exist between a man and woman. Then it vanished, invisible as a cobweb when the dew dries, but it remained.

239

She turned away. Her eyes swept the groveling men at arms.

'None would dare flout your orders, as I said, my lord. If any did, I would cut out his heart while he lived.'

'Out! All of you!' the count snapped.

They looked glad to leave.

'You didn't search him, my perfect one?'

'No, my exalted one,' she replied. 'You didn't order it. And while I never do less than you command, I never do more either.'

Severius turned to Uther. 'Strip.'

Uther removed his clothing, piece by piece, thinking as he did that he probably looked ridiculous. In fact, he didn't look at all bad. He was thickly furred, hair on his chest, arms, and stomach, and even his back. He had always been stocky. Now he had a bit of a paunch, but only a small one; and it, like the rest of him, was rock hard.

'Jesus!' Severius exclaimed. 'Look at his scars.'

Ah, yes, the scars. He had a lot of them, each with a story attached. But then he had more or less – mostly more – spent his life fighting.

When he got to his linen drawers, he paused. He was hoping they wouldn't make him pull them off, also.

Severius kicked the cup and plate aside. None of them noticed that, though they struck the wall with a satisfactory crash, neither of them broke or even so much as chipped.

The count bent down to pick up the harp case.

'I wouldn't do that, brother mine,' Aife admonished.

'Why not?' Severius jeered. Then, motioning toward Uther, asked, 'What can he do?'

'You're right,' Uther said. 'I'm only an old man, rather scantily clad at the moment. But things like that harp have a way of defending themselves.'

She took her knife and carefully raised the lid of the

harp case. A serpent lifted its head from among the strings. She snatched the blade back and let the lid fall.

'Christ!' Severius exclaimed.

'Get that thing out of there!' She drew her sword and pointed it at Uther's throat.

He moved the tip aside very carefully with one finger. Then he knelt next to the harp case and lifted the lid.

The harp rested in its velvet and brocade wrappings. He reached in and lifted it out carefully, and placed it gently on the floor. There was nothing about it that would conceal a snake. It had no sound box, but was made of one piece of oak. It bore a double set of strings.

Then he eased the scarlet brocade and velvet cloth out. He unfolded it and then shook it out. Nothing! He turned the case upside down. Shook it.

Both Severius and Aife examined the cloth and case. She was still holding her sword.

'Let him go,' she told the count. 'Send him on his way.'

'No! My God, no!' the count snapped. 'The stories the people told about him – those that heard him play in the tavern – they were simply amazing. I didn't believe them, but there must be a grain of truth there. Think, Aife. Think what he might be able to do for us.'

'Do for us? Do to us, you mean!'

'You. Old man, are you bribable?' the count continued. 'You can't love dressing in castoffs and tramping the roads.'

'Castoffs?' Uther said, glancing at the heap of clothing on the floor.

'Yes. Some patron or other of yours obviously treated you well once, but . . .' The count kicked at the warm but ragged-edged mantle and worn tunic and trousers. 'These have seen a lot of hard service since.'

'Yes,' Uther admitted. 'That's true.'

'And so have you. Christ and his saints! Look at the scars on you.'

'That's also true,' Uther admitted. 'My life has not been easy.'

'Well, if even a part of what my singularly superstitious tenants believe about you is at all possible, you are set for a soft life here for . . .' The count hesitated and smiled. 'As long as you live.'

Uther returned the smile with a suitably ironic one of his own. 'That being exactly as long as I honor your wishes as I would a god's and fulfill them.'

The smile vanished from the count's face and an ugly, blunt, cold look replaced it. And Uther knew, as when they first met on the road, he had laid bare an unpleasant dark place in the man's soul.

But then, to the king's astonishment, Alex and Alexia appeared at the door of the cell. Alexia was wearing a bright-red dress of some material so soft that when she moved, she might almost as well have been naked, so thin and clinging was the cloth. Alex wore skintight, very soft tanned leather. In the clear light of day, Uther realized how small and fragile his companions were. Compared to the hulking guards who accompanied them, they seemed children.

The count spun around and studied the pair.

'They came looking for him.' The guard pointed at Uther. 'He is called Simon the Singer.'

The count laughed. 'How diverting. Tumblers, unless I miss my guess.'

'Yes,' Alexia said. 'And very good ones.'

Alex back-flipped into a catching position and Alexia cartwheeled onto his shoulders. She stood, steadying herself with her fingertips against the ceiling.

The count laughed and clapped his hands. 'How wonderfully diverting. Can you do that naked?' he asked almost innocently.

Uther felt the heat in his face.

The count elbowed Aife, high laughter redoubled.

'Bathe them. Give them clean clothes, and prepare them and yourself for the feast tonight.'

Alex cupped his hands. Alexia came down, using his hand as a step. Severius strolled out, unconcerned, still laughing, but Aife studied Uther for a second.

'He should listen,' she said.

'Yes,' Uther answered, 'he should.'

Alex and Alexia gathered up the cup and dish that were still lying in the corner of the room. Aife watched the king don his clothing again. Then she led the three of them out into the clear blue day to the bathhouse. She didn't speak to him again; her face was stiff with disapproval.

Alex and Alexia went somewhere else. Uther avoided the cold plunge and scrubbed himself in the *tepidarium*. There were attendants, but he dismissed them and bathed alone. Standing on the drain in the floor, he scrubbed with the rough pumice-filled soap and dipped his own rinse water out of the central pool.

One feature of the *tepidarium* was three clear glass windows that looked out beyond the plow land and pasture toward the still, forested hills beyond. The room was very bright, there being high, clerestory windows in the domed roof also. When he was finished washing, he wrapped a linen towel around his waist and turned toward the door, hoping for a servant with fresh clothing.

She – Aife – was standing there with a bundle in her arms. He stood shocked, wondering how long she'd been there. She placed the bundle on a stool near the door. He could see even from where he stood the mantle, tunic, and trousers were fine cloth – expensive.

'Why do you do that?' she asked.

'What?' he asked, though he knew very well what.

'Blush,' she answered.

'I was wondering how long you had been there. I'm

not used to women looking at me when I'm naked. And the fact that you're a young, pretty woman makes it all that more embarrassing.'

'I'm not a woman,' she said.

'No?' he asked.

'No! I was interested. There is no place on your body without a scar.'

He smiled a little ironically. 'Well, one,' he said.

'No!'

And he realized she had no sense of irony or modesty, either, because she said, 'Even that place is marked.'

And he remembered she was right. He had nearly been parted from his left testicle by an assassin who went for his groin with a double-edged knife and missed.

'What's the worst wound you ever had?' she asked. 'That one?' And she pointed to a zigzag scar that crossed his abdomen, traveled up his ribs, and ended at his collarbone.

'No, though it gave me a lot of trouble. This was the worst.' He pointed to a small but ugly puckered scar on his left arm. 'The wound mortified. The arm swelled. I was among my men, and there were no women about.'

'They are much superior to men at leechcraft,' she agreed.

'I burned with fever and could hold nothing in my stomach. By the fifth night, I was dying, and – '

'Five nights? So long?' she asked.

'I am a strong man. Makes living easier, but dying harder.' He smiled grimly. 'On the fifth night, the bird-masked women came with their bright-eyed leader. I woke from a fever dream and saw them standing six on each side of my bed. She of the glowing eyes stood at the foot.'

'I know,' she said. 'I've seen them. The bright-eyed one told me . . . I couldn't be a woman. She barred my path.'

'My men were mourning me as dead. But she told the bird-masked women not to prepare the mercy cup for me. You cannot imagine the pain and fire consuming me. I wanted them to make an end. But in the absence of her permission, they wouldn't do it. So I accepted the suffering, knowing one way or another, it would end.'

'Do we dream her or is she real?' Aife asked.

'I can't say,' the king answered. 'My men didn't see her, but the bird-masked priestess said no matter how many times they cast the divinatory wands, she would in no wise answer yes. Then she, the bright-eyed one, caused a fire to be kindled and began to pack my swollen arm with hot cloths. Or was it my sister who came and did so? I have never known, never been sure. Sometimes when I look at my sister's face, I see those shining eyes.

'I screamed with the pain, but "she" would not relent, and by dawn the hot packs had drawn the poison from my arm. The fever broke and I slept. It took some time for me to recover, but I did.'

'She is a very bad thing,' Aife said. 'And she punished me for not wanting to be a woman. My father would have no wife, but only concubines, so he brought up my brother and I as sons. We rode and hunted with him, but you know, a girl may not play the boy forever. And when I was fourteen, he sent me home to my mother. She wasn't pleased.'

Uther had no problem with that. He could see the woman facing a slender hoyden she was supposed to tame and turn into a marriageable property.

'The price of my return was that the count must come and honor her bed.'

'And she conceived,' Uther said.

'Yes.'

Uther knew how the game was played. Desire was simply another counter on the board. The woman was furious about being neglected, and probably furious with the husband. Since she couldn't take the object of her wrath to task, she struck at the girl.

245

'I began to bleed the day I arrived, and she sent me to a hut near the forest, where unclean things reside.'

Uther knew. His people were given to such practices also. A girl's first passage into womanhood was fraught with peril, both for herself and any who came into contact with her. Nor were they easy on boys, either. He vividly remembered the stricken look in his son's eyes when he told his father he had gone to sleep a child and awakened as a man.

He and Morgana had done their best for him, but he must still retreat to a stone room in the mountains and, though the boy never spoke of it, the king knew something dreadful had happened there. Dea Arto had claimed him, and his son returned to join the fiercest, most cruel, most primitive of all the warrior societies. He became a bear. In his life, Uther could never remember a bear dying in bed, and he knew Arthur wouldn't yield up his life in that comfortable spot, either.

Uther rested his hand on her neck. There were tears in her eyes.

'Don't trouble yourself so,' he told her gently. 'The power to give life is a costly one. The powers of heaven don't bless the hours when we know we have left the peace of childhood behind.'

She bit her lip, slicing an incisor down into it until it bled. A thin red stream trickled down to her chin.

'The blood,' she whispered. 'I and the hut stank of it. It was only a lean-to, but there was a small house nearby where women were supposed to reside and give the alarm if the girl in the lean-to had problems. They . . . the ladies of the grove . . . sacrifice to drive off evil shadows that might creep in from the dark wilderness and strike at the girl undergoing her first passage.'

'Yes.' Uther nodded.

'When I came there, it didn't seem so bad. The ladies were kind and gave me a drink to ease the cramps. And in the hut was a warm, dry bed. I went to sleep. When I woke, it was dark and silent. Rain pattered on the roof of the hut. There was no light from the place where the priestesses of the grove slept.

'I rose. I was in pain. My back hurt. You know, women say sometimes those cramps hurt almost as much as childbirth. These did. But I managed to get to my feet and go to the house where the women resided. I was hoping they would give me another drink.

'But they were gone. The house was empty, and all the fires on the hearths inside ash. So, you see, I knew they had been gone a long time. And I knew. I knew my mother wanted to ruin me. There were stories about how she ruined other girls of whom she was jealous. Sometimes she scarred their faces; others she had beaten and crippled their bodies. But in my case, that wouldn't matter, because I was my father's daughter and men would marry me, crippled or not. She meant to have my honor. And I was in so much pain that the idea of a man putting his thing up there was . . . the most horrible thing I could think of.

'I hunkered down at the hearth. The stones were still warm from the fire. I saw a staff, a blackthorn staff, on the floor. I seized the staff, pushed the end into a crack between the floor stones, and leaned on it. The wood was so hard, I didn't think even with my slight weight on it that it would break. And in truth, it bent nearly double. But then, it broke at an angle, leaving me with a club and a spear. My father taught me how to do this. Break a stick at an angle when you need a spear quickly. I made for the door. I was going to hide in the forest in the deep coverts.

'But I was too slow. I saw the first man. He was standing in the doorway, between it and myself, outlined against the rolling storm clouds above. He seized my left arm while speaking to someone nearby. "Here she is," he said. "Come. We must hurry. Get this done before the daylight. Will you go first or shall I?"

'The spear was in my right hand. I drove it through his body. He let go of my arm and took a back step, then another. I don't think he quite knew what had happened. It was so dark. He couldn't see how badly he was wounded.

'His friend spoke then. "Hey, what's wrong? Why did you let . . . ?" But the first man fell against him, and he went to his knees. He shouted, "What's wrong? She's going to get away!"

'I had the clubbed end of the staff in my right hand. I don't remember how it got there, but it was. I hit him on the head with it hard, and kept on hitting him until he stopped moving. Then I did the same with the other, because when the first was still, he kept twisting around, trying to get the spear out. I knew I couldn't let him do that.

'The rain had stopped and the wind was blowing. I walked into the grove. But once I got past the trees at the edges, I saw the grove was gone, the big trees felled, and it was as though the ground was almost paved with the rotting stumps. And in between the stumps, saplings had sprung up, but they weren't healthy. Each one was crusted with lichen moss and overgrown with mistletoe. The grove was ruined and would make no more mast for the winter run pigs. This place was not blessed but cursed.

'I met her there. She held a cup in her hand and was accompanied by a one-eyed, crippled stag. I fell to my knees. Her eyes were as you said, filled with light. They glowed as though the cold winter moon was in them. The stag was no more a stag, but the Horned One, a man bearing the antlers of the rutting male. The one-eyed one with the tools to open a woman.

'She handed the cup to me. I drank, and the pain left

248

me. I felt nothing, even as he embraced me and bore me to the ground.'

'What happened to your mother?' Uther asked.

Aife shivered, then walked toward one of the windows in the bathhouse. 'She went into labor, was delivered of a stillborn boy. Then, near dawn, she died. The blood loss, I think.'

'Why are you telling me this?' Uther asked.

'Because you know. You've seen her. The others don't believe me. Not really. Not even my brother. I brought you good clothes. Tell me – you didn't have any food concealed in that harp case, did you?'

'No,' the king answered.

'I knew that,' she said.

Her back was to him. She was gazing out the window at the forest. He dropped the linen bath sheet and began hurriedly to dress.

'If I hadn't found a reason for the cup and plate to be there, he would have had your guards tortured. And probably you, also.'

'He's now count of the Saxon shore? He has money from the pirates?' Uther asked.

She nodded, her back still to him.

'Goes without saying he has larger ambitions,' Uther commented.

'He wants to be emperor and is collecting people he thinks can help him. You are one of them. So am I.'

Uther added up the political situation on the Continent. The Franks held Gaul, held it loosely. They fought among themselves constantly. Italy and what remained of Germania were ruled and protected by again loosely held barbarian principalities that, in theory, owed allegiance to the emperor no longer residing in Rome but in Ravenna.

Uther's blood ran cold. It was just possible that with the right mix of successful warfare, treachery, and murder, he might succeed. But so far as the king could tell, nothing the Imperial Pretenders gained lasted.

Truth to tell, all that survived in the chaos of the decaying empire was a shrinking fiscal structure, whose function was to secure land for the rich and collect taxes from the poor. The completely ephemeral structures of the various barbarian kingdoms lasted only as long as they could field armies to protect their fiscal domains. When these large landholdings that fed the polyglot mercenaries who preyed on them were either lost to another predatory force or ruined by endless warfare, the kingdoms of the Visigoths, Lombards, or Huns were swept away like sand castles overtaken by the sea.

Given sufficient ferocity, cruelty, and good luck, Severius might wear that purple one day, and in the meantime, he would strip southern England of what little stability and safety remained and further impoverish a peasantry already ground down almost to dust by taxation.

'No!' Uther whispered. 'No!'

'Yes.' Aife turned from the window.

He was dressed now, and indeed the clothing she had procured for him was luxurious. A mantle, wool on the outside, lined with scarlet silk. Fine linen shirt and trousers, cross-gartered leather leggings, boots, and a linen undershirt with embroidered sleeves that matched the embroidery on the short-sleeved tunic.

Alex and Alexia entered, and without further ado, Aife led them toward a magnificent basilican building that was at the heart of the villa complex. Uther knew there had been a forum in London, but this villa and its environs must once have been the heart of Roman power in Britain. The formal gardens were extensive and, at this season of the year, barren. But the tall spires of the Mediterranean cypress remained, as did the brushlike Lombardy poplar, which marked out the paths and flower beds. These and the façade of the basilica might almost fool an observer into believing he or she were looking at an impressive carryover from Roman times.

Uther, Alex, and Alexia followed Aife silently along an avenue lined with the tall Italian poplars. Uther was trying to pretend awe. He was not having to work hard at it. The setting impressed him in spite of himself.

They reached a set of broad, shallow steps that led to double bronze doors. Aife pushed open one door and entered.

The hall was arranged for dinner, with a table set on a dais at the end of the room and other tables on each side stretching as far as the door. Once it must have been the administrative center of the province and had a roof. It did now, but not the one the Romans gave it. At some time or another in the past hundred years, the basilica must have burned and the upper stories reduced to ruins. It had been reroofed with wood beams and lead plates after the manner of his people, but the symbols were not like any heretofore seen.

Dragons, cats, bull, and boar were present, and serpents. Yea, Gods, the things were everywhere, coiling among the other beasts. And there were representations of human beings, all dying impaled by the bulls' horns, torn by the boars' tusks, bitten by serpents, and struggling as the cats inflicted the death bite.

Uther shivered. There was nothing lifelike about these carvings, only a sense of the inescapable tenacity of death; and everywhere, gazing at him from around the ferocious beasts and tormented humans, the serpents' fixed smiles. He fancied he could smell the reptile reek and then realized he could.

Aife led them the length of the hall, toward a golden camp chair, the kind Roman leaders carried with them in the field. It was held together by a pivot at the center, so that it could be packed flat for transport.

'It is said to have belonged to the great first Caesar himself,' Aife boasted, pointing to the chair.

It was wood, but lavishly trimmed with purple velvet and gold inlay. The chair was raised on a dais at the end of the room under the remains of a dome set with clerestory windows that let in light to brighten the dais where the chair rested, and a pit lay directly in front of it. Uther knew now where the reptile reek was coming from.

They were white, pale, coiling, slowly moving shapes in the gloom of the pit. The dark stone set off the ivory glow of the writhing bodies at the bottom.

A snake pit.

He'd heard of them, of kings who kept them, but never seen one. There was a body in the pit. It looked male, but young. The light from the high windows in the dome illuminated that end of the pit. Uther could see only the head and face. He was seated in the corner, his cheek resting against one of the walls.

But for the corpse pallor, his face was in repose, and he would have seemed to a casual observer to be asleep. Until the observer noticed the gross swelling of arms and legs caused by the bites of venomous serpents. He was bound, hand and foot.

'Yes,' Aife said. 'My brother wouldn't want any of them to hurt his pets.'

Uther drew back.

'Ah, he is dead,' she said, studying the corpse. 'Last night he still breathed, so I left him.'

'What did he do?' Uther asked.

Aife laughed, a dry laugh. 'He married without my brother's permission.'

Yes, and Uther knew why he had been made an example of. These lords collected fees whenever their tenants – colony slaves, really – married. He had seen these southern lords sometimes, in order to squeeze every

252

last iota of labor out of their people, make men and women contribute free labor for years, simply to enjoy the privilege of being wed to the one they loved.

'The punishment seems excessive, considering the crime,' Uther said mildly.

'The punishment for crossing my brother is always death,' Aife answered.

'Ah, I see,' Uther said.

'Do you? I think not. To see, you must live with it day by day for seven years, as I have. He made the boy's wife watch. They say she is mad.'

Yes, Uther thought. *They would say so, if only to protect the girl.*

Aife shouted loudly. Three men ran up and joined them at the edge of the pit.

'Get it out. The hall has to be ready for dinner tonight.'

The white snakes moved in the gloom, a fearful rustling. The men looked frightened.

'Can't we just leave him there? After a while, the rats come and they . . .'

'No! My lord's friends will begin to arrive soon. They might be disgusted by the sight. Certainly, their women will be!'

Alexia laughed. 'Have you a rope and a hook?' She gestured toward the man in the pit. 'He's wearing a belt.'

Yes, Uther thought. The pit was shallow, no more than five feet. A tumbler could do it easily. The air and stone around were cold, the serpents torpid.

'How does he find so many white ones?' Alex asked.

'By offering a five-gold-piece bounty for each one delivered to him alive and unharmed,' Aife said. 'Not all of them are vipers, but there are more than enough that are. There are snake tubes in the walls. They shelter in them when it gets really cold. No one knows how the rats get in. And the flies – maggots – play some role in the disposal process. Well, they fly.'

Yes, Uther thought. Not all the white things were snakes. Some were bones, and a pair of reflective beady eyes peered out of the gloom.

What an end, he thought. *Bitten by vipers, gnawed by rats, food for maggots.*

Someone had returned with the rope and hook. They were no longer dependent on the feeble light of the windows. Another servant carried a lamp.

The lamp was let carefully down into the pit. The rats vanished, and the pale snakes moved to the edges of the pit.

Alexia, laughing, hurried away toward the door. She came running, reached the edge of the pit, dropped and back-flipped into it, landing at the feet of the corpse, facing the body. In a second she had tucked the hook under his leather belt.

Almost too late, Uther saw the slim, white shape of the serpent where it had been shadowed by the corpse's leg. Uther's mind caught the fleeting image of its swift, smooth strike at Alexia's ankle. Alex was faster than the reptile. He landed on top of it, foot pinning its head. He cupped his hand for Alexia. She leaped into it and, from there, to his shoulder and out. As she turned, Uther threw his arm around her body, steadying her while Alex caught her outstretched hand and pulled himself out of the pit.

The snake, unharmed, writhed, then struck at nothing.

By now they had acquired a gallery of interested spectators, and the three of them, Uther, Alex, and Alexia, were showered by a tumult of applause.

'I can see I missed something. What?' The voice belonged to Severius. He entered by way of a small door near the raised dais. He had a woman on his arm and a torchbearer beside him. But Uther knew no one was looking at him or attending to him at all. Every eye was fixed on the woman beside him.

She was simply the most beautiful woman they, any of them, had ever seen. She was wearing a many-layered dress of white, sheer Coan silk over a heavy, silk shift. The dress and shift were lavishly decorated with gold embroidery. Her jewels were purple amethysts set in a gold collar at her neck, a half dozen strands of pearls below the collar. Armlets, bracelets, and a diadem on hair the color of a midnight sky, and set off skin that glowed with the rich tints of cream and rose.

The face was that of a dreaming angel. The face, though. That face was very familiar.

Who? Uther thought. *Who?* Then recognition followed, brutal and shocking as a kick in the stomach.

Igrane!

When she rose from the pool and found him, Black Leg seemed to be sleeping. He was, she thought, as beautiful as a young god, lying on his side among the grass and flowers.

But she became alarmed when he wouldn't readily awaken. She tried one or two things she knew that worked, worked even with the dead. But her fear grew when she found nothing would penetrate the shields around his dreaming mind.

She lifted her head and studied the garden, and knew that somehow he had penetrated the knowledge she and so many of her kind had tried to learn for so many long years in the past. She felt a stab of envy, followed quickly by an even greater anxiety than she had ever felt before.

She lifted his upper body and cradled his head against her breast. He was animal and man combined, a touch of ancient beauty left to a world that had lost most of it. And from an incredibly long ago time, they were reaching out for him.

We learn more than one way. The flower of the

intellect is overvalued by mankind and even by demon-kind, because that was what she was. But there are other ways to learn, and they are mysterious, frightening at times, but perhaps far, far more important than what we do with our intellect.

He and his father learned to do some things quickly and fearsomely well. As a warrior, even she was aware of Maeniel's reputation for agility and skill. Humans and even such as she sacrifice speed and more than a little skill to get the formidable self-conscious intelligence that characterizes humanity. But chance and perhaps divine intervention had combined both in him. And the lost genus of the first of earth's great civilizations had required just that doubling of mind power. In him, the instructions that formed the garden on his lost world had found their chosen prey. And she surmised that even now he was reading his primer, an introduction to knowledge so vast that down through endless ages, it still dominated the earth.

Nothing is without cost, and she knew he could and must pay some dreadful price for his achievement; and the first installments would be in innocence lost and in sorrow for the world of peace and beauty he left behind him. So she cradled him in her arms as he, like a child hidden in the womb, absorbed the garden's mani-fold beauties, and his ears and deepest mind listened to the songs of life, a beauty ever ancient, ever new.

She felt the turning of the planet through the stone where she sat, the wheeling stars that pass down the con-stricted tunnel of time. Suns exploded, galaxies coalesced like sea foam, spinning in tide pools. The detritus of the dying stars spoke in the blackness between worlds of life's complex logic, expressed in the long chains of molecules that energize the shapes of living things.

The garden around them took up the theme, and in light, color, form, and a veritable symphony of sound, poured the beauties of this complex matrix into her ears and his mind. Night and day, sunrise and sunset, a roving rainbow of burning beauty, forever dying, forever renewed, for when the last sunset of the last day on the last planet of the last star is done, the vast energies of eternity would draw all that is or was possible back to begin again.

The sun passed its zenith and began to light only the high ledges of the canyon wall. The birds came flowing down the river in the twilight, a ribbon of shadow. She clutched him more tightly and prepared to slide into the river and call the Weyvern for both of them, because within the reach of the deep pool, she had fed on the spiral waterweed, on fish roe offered by her hosts, the jeweled fish hiding among the reeds. She was very strong, thanks to his contribution to her skills.

But the birds were no match for the burgeoning garden. She could feel their fear as the paean of song rose from the glowing flowers, catching the last shadowed dusk. And the flock floated by into the shadowed canyons beyond.

At length, the moon rose, a huge, glowing sentinel that drove away starlight and silvered water, trees, grass, and leaves, enhancing texture but drowning all but the most vivid violets, pinks, and purples with its light. She was still cradling him, drowsing in the moon glow, when he opened his eyes.

Her arms tightened. 'My love,' she said.

'I don't know,' he said. 'I've been somewhere. It's not enough. I'm not enough. I love you, I do. Time curves away from us, but in the end, I think you are the one.'

'Yes,' she answered, and kissed him. They dissolved into each other. Both were water. And they fell into the river like dense fog or rain, troubling the surface not at all.

He drifted down and the glowing jewel-like fish studied him with quiet eyes set high in their skull plates.

He understood how old those fish were, and his mind turned from a yawning gulf, a chasm of such vast proportions that his mind couldn't grasp it except as those first seas of earth. His brain sought sleep, antidote to madness. His mind slept as his body made the transition and he woke.

He lay beside her on a beach. The sand was snow-white, a white so pure it picked up the color of the sun rising out of a calm sea into a clear sky. The water was still; the waves eddied up the beach, not foaming, only spreading, glowing with the molten colors of the new sun. And when they reached their fullest spread, they sank, their glow vanishing into the sand.

'No. I don't want this,' he said. 'I never wanted this. I never imagined anything like this.'

'Love me,' she told him, resting one finger on his lips. 'Love me and forget all the rest.'

And her flesh was hot at the breast tips and groin, cool at the neck and belly, smooth as velvet, silk velvet. His body joined hers, hot at the groin, and she cradled him between her thighs, legs gripping his hips. Drawing him up, gliding like a sea foam that tops a breaking wave, and then plunging him down, down, down, into darkness where even in sleep knowledge – too much knowledge – was torment.

He woke in her bed, himself again, but knowing that from now on he would be intolerably burdened. The walls of the room were bare white and still, somehow calming. The only thing between him and the sky was a grating. Or was it a grating? Perhaps it was a plant, a very slow-growing plant with very hard, fernlike leaves and shining brown, braided stems.

He thought on her flowers and surmised she probably had tamed some exotic thing and used it to roof her bedroom, because the domed, marble ceiling was broken, the edges of the break smoothed by whole centuries of rain.

The bed had sheets over the tick and was flush with the floor. A rose vine clinging to the edges of the broken roof by long, pale roots with green tips dropped its petals on the bed and white marble floor, and the sheets. . . . Or were they sheets, because they moved out of the way of their own volition when he rose and walked toward the doorway.

Windows – or were they windows or just openings in the wall – looked out on the whitest sand beach he had ever seen. The noon sun shone on it so brightly that he found his eyes flooded with the purple glow that too much light rouses. Beyond the beach were the transparent green shallows of a sapphire sea. A steady yet not hard breeze blew through the windows, cooling the room.

For a few moments, he was uncomfortable because he couldn't find a place to relieve himself, the purity of the beach being such that he didn't wish to contaminate it. But then he found a shallow alcove in the next room. A flow of warm water ran through it, down into what looked like some sort of porous rock, where the water vanished from sight.

Beyond the alcove was another, dimmer room containing a large, round pool. Above, the broken, domed roof was covered by the same iron fern and harbored another rose clinging to the edges of the opening. The one in the bedroom had been pink; this was bloodred and its petals were scattered like ruby droplets over the water in the white marble pool.

He bathed and then, entering a small foyer, walked out onto what had been a colonnaded porch. But the columns were broken now, and it was roofed only by an overhang from the side of the house. Tables spread with food nested under the overhang: fruit of all kinds – peaches, pears, apples, table grapes, plums – and more hearty fare, milk, cold meat, cheese, wine, and bread, all fresh, all bursting with flavor.

He breakfasted on milk, cheese, peaches, and grapes, then waded out into the sunstruck shallow sea. Those earliest of living things – stromatolites, cushions of calcareous, green algae – clustered near the beach, sheltered by the rocky arms of the bay. They grew to enormous size, beautiful green-velvet hassocks in water so clear that his wolf's eye could almost count the grains of sand on the bottom.

Is this the first place or the last? he asked himself. The wind, the silence, the sea, and the sand.

'But,' she answered, 'I don't know and never cared to find out.'

'No!' he said. 'Really.' And he turned toward her, unsurprised.

'No! Really!' she repeated. 'This is the place I invited you to at first. This is my home insofar as I have one.'

He gazed out over the water. 'It's beautiful here, and very peaceful.'

'Yes,' she said, 'and beginning or ending of the world, it only stands to reason that those animals and plants that emerged first are probably tough enough to survive till the end.'

'Tell me your name?' he asked.

'No!' she replied.

'Haven't I earned it?'

'No. You have come closer than many mortals.'

'Closer than *any* mortal,' he countered.

'Yesssss,' was the reluctant, slow reply. 'But no! Love me?' she asked.

They returned to the beach and embraced, feet in the slow, shallow combers. In the distance near the horizon, a line of squall clouds appeared and, moving slowly toward land, began to darken the sky.

'Does it rain here?' he asked, stroking the curve of her back to bring her hips and thighs higher, over his penis.

'Yes, sometimes,' she whispered as she bit his lip and drew blood.

Desire was a thrill in his body. He felt himself a stone phallus, as though he could endure forever at the shattering crest of satisfaction. Her moan of pleasure was a sobbing cry of helplessness as they were swept together into what seemed an end to thought and perhaps even life itself. The throbbing pulse of fulfillment went on and on and on, until a cold wind from the summer sea pulled them into consciousness again, and the gray and white storm clouds began to extinguish the sun.

They rolled apart.

'God,' she whispered. 'All I wanted was a tumble, and now this.' She was a pale silk rag against the glowing sand.

He rose to his knees, and she watched as he drew a character in the damp sand just above the wave line. He was very careful of the curves and dips. He looked out into the oncoming storm, at the rainbows playing in the trailing veils of rain. He frowned, his fine brows almost touching each other. Then he surrounded the character he'd drawn with quantifiers, little hooks and twisting lines that balanced the curving character in a square, then made a circle around it.

Belatedly alarmed, she shouted, 'No! Those damn things are dangerous. No one knows how to control them. This whole place could . . . vanish, explode.'

'Too late,' he said, leaping to his feet. 'What I wanted to do is in process.'

The character he had first drawn was red-molten, glowing and seething the way sand in a glass oven glows as it softens and becomes flexible in the unspeakable heat of the forge. She jumped to her feet, backing away as the radiant heat scalded her body.

'No!' she screamed again as the fire spread into the

sand around it, all of it shifting, liquefying, glowing.

The rain squall hit, and she ran toward the broken porch of the ruined dwelling. Over the spot where he'd written the character, a whirlwind hung, drawing ferocious winds from the rain, steam pouring up and into the whirlwind, which vented it up into the boiling clouds above.

Then the rain became a blinding flood, and she found herself clinging to his almost iron-seeming body. Her nails lacerated his flesh, her face pressed against his chest, as she tried to escape the ice pellets and the rapidly dropping temperature as the storm sucked the raw heat from the land into violent updrafts, which carried the moisture so high it froze. Then it sent down a surge of hail over them, and the barren hills and mountains beyond.

As quickly as the storm had arisen, it was gone, and they stood together, looking out over the sea as the squall moved inland to freshen the coast.

It rested on the sand near the water, a crystal bowl not large but beautiful, with an endless play of rainbows in its substance. She let go of his arms and walked toward it as though hypnotized, and lifted it in her hands, holding it to the light, its unchanging yet ever-changing rainbows and kaleidoscopic beauty a splendor and a delight to the eye. So fragile was it that when the wind struck it, the glass sang, telling in a multiplicity of notes the strength of the wind and its direction.

My mind was still filled with the flight I had seen when we started down the trail to the city gates. I wasn't watching the road, until Albe spoke in my ear.

'I don't like this.'

She was right. The road dipped down the hillside and was a prime place for an ambush. The hexagonal blocks ran between high walls of broken rocks and through occasional ravines, washes, and pour-offs.

'Cat country,' Albe said.

'How would you know cat country?' I asked.

'My family had flocks of sheep. I brought them from the island to the mainland to graze in the winter when the islands are scoured by wind and rain. There were cats in the rocks among the sheltered valleys where there is grass no matter how bad the weather gets. Cat,' she said. 'Small cat, sometimes large cat.'

Meth was still leading the party, but armor isn't the most comfortable thing to walk in, and I caught up to him easily.

'Cat?' I asked.

He jumped. 'Oh, yes,' he said. 'Why do you think it isn't safe to go out at night? Can't you smell it?'

Then I found I could. When the sea – the Dead Sea wind – slowed (it never really stopped), the rocks around us reeked of male cat musk.

I drew my sword. He cringed at the blade cry when it slipped the sheath.

'I didn't do . . .'

'I know . . . I know,' I reassured him. 'I just want to take point.'

He dropped back gratefully, actually a little too far back. And I knew Meth's heroism wouldn't extend to trying to protect me against any type of attacker.

I tried to remember what Maeniel taught me about cats – big and little. They love broken country filled with rocky jumbles, cliffs, and mountain trails. They are elusive, seldom seen unless you come across their sign on sand or in low, muddy places.

Yes, there were yet a few big ones. The clouded leopard once roamed all of Europe, but they have become increasingly rare, since their pelts are much sought after; their depredations against livestock in the high summer pastures are even more serious than those of wolves. But there was something about them that had—

The weight hit my neck like a sack of sand, flattening me belly-down on the trail. My elbow hit a rock, numbing my hand to the wrist. I felt the fangs slide on my armor at the neck, and I remembered what I had forgotten – the cat's death bite. The most dangerous part of the cat's attack is its killing bite.

I did as Maeniel taught me: I snapped to my hands and knees and bucked like a horse. The claws on my breast and arm slid on the armor, and I tore free. I spun around, sword in hand to confront my enemy.

He was a white, marked with clouded semicircles. He stood his ground and screamed in fury. He was as large as a full-grown male wolf. The screech he gave echoed throughout the rocks around us.

'Nooooo! I had you! You have armor! You had no armor when I jumped! NO FAIR!'

'Fair enough for me, you sneaky young killer!'

'I'll have you yet!'

He lunged forward, inside my guard. I swung the sword hilt and my fist at his nose. He let out another eerie scream as the blow landed hard.

'Ouch! That hurt!'

I laughed and jumped back so I could get a clear swing at him with my sword. Another voice intruded into my consciousness.

'You young fool! Get out of there now! Can't you see you're overmatched! Run!'

But he didn't get a chance. Albe was there, and she had her sling. The lead shot landed with an audible thud at the base of the cat's skull where the neck joins it. He went down, a sprawl of furry limbs, deeply unconscious.

Meth and Cateyrin ran up. Meth drew his knife, and I knew he meant to cut the cat's throat.

'No,' I said. I had talked to the thing and I wasn't going to kill anything I could talk to. Not right away, at least.

'No!' Cateyrin shouted also. 'This is a young one. They can be enslaved. Some of the houses do it.'

'Even then they're dangerous,' Meth said. 'Besides, he may have friends about.'

'He does,' I answered.

Albe drew her sword and glanced around.

I shouted, 'You! Show yourself! What are you? His father?'

From a distance, I heard, 'Oh, Christ. No! A shapeling.' This was followed by a scrabbling in the rocks, then silence.

Then I realized Meth, Cateyrin, and Albe were all staring at me in astonishment.

'Albe?' I asked.

'You made a sound, just like the cat did,' she explained.

Yes, it was true. I did talk to Mother and the dragons as I had to the Faun.

'I want it,' I said, pointing to the cat. 'Tie it up, Albe.'

I never found her at a loss about anything. She managed to tie the cat up in such a way that I could throw its furry body over my shoulders like a big scarf. I had a few scratches, and a trickle of blood found its way down the cat's neck from the bruise at the base of its skull, but otherwise, both of us were uninjured.

Cateyrin and Meth began quarreling about the cat, one wanting to kill and skin it, the other castrate it, then sell the neutered male to one of the great families. I didn't feel any desire to do either. The impetuous half-grown male seemed to be a troublemaker, and I felt very likely he would try to ambush us again. But we soon walked out of ambush country and the rock walls towered over us above.

The rock walls and the city grew bigger and more impressive by the moment. The cat woke up. He began to struggle.

'I told you,' Meth said. 'Kill and skin him.'

The cat let out a yell of rage.

'You stop that,' I said.

'If you cut his balls off now,' Cateyrin said, drawing her knife, 'he won't . . .'

This time the cat let out a yowl of sheer terror, then a series of really lethal-sounding screeches and hisses.

Albe had made him a crude muzzle with a strip of rawhide. His head was hanging next to my neck. I brought my armor up and dropped him to the ground hard. Then I drew my sword.

The cat really began to wiggle and scream then.

'Moooooootherrrrr!'

'Mother?' Albe said.

This surprised me. 'Cateyrin said it is a young one,' I said.

Since cats don't talk the way humans do, the muzzle didn't keep him especially quiet.

'You can understand him?' I asked.

'Most times. I think it's the shoes. Talorcan's shoes.'

'Stop screeching for your mother,' she told the cat. 'She—' Albe indicated me – 'isn't going to harm you.'

'Mooootherrrr!' from the cat. He was damn near deafening.

'You keep that up,' Albe told him, 'I'll skin and gut you all right . . . then I'll kill you.'

'Oh!' Meth said.

'That sounds horrible,' Cateyrin said, sounding awed.

The cat was shocked silent.

'Good!' I said. 'Keep quiet and keep still while I cut you loose.'

Maeniel taught me the sword. I could have freed the cat even while he was in full writhe, but it was easier this

266

way. He sat up and began licking himself to put his fur in order. And between swipes, he glared murderously at Albe, Meth, and Cateyrin.

'Now,' I said. 'You've got your dignity and your freedom back. Go away and trouble us no more.'

He didn't leave. He threw another glare at the rest, then studied me with narrowed, green eyes.

'You are a Daughter of the Danae,' he said.

'A mortal Daughter of the Danae,' I corrected him.

'Nonetheless, a Daughter of the Danae.'

'I suppose so,' I answered. 'Why?'

'What an opportunity!' he said.

'What opportunity?' I asked. 'A minute ago, you were yelling for your mother. Get out of here.'

'Don't remind me.' Then he rose and began to pace back and forth, lashing his tail.

'Friend,' I said, pointing to the city towering above us with my sword, 'I have business at the city. And you are in my way. . . .'

'I would . . . I would . . .' He was still pacing. Then he stopped and faced me and got the rest out. 'Enter your service!'

'What?' I said. I was flabbergasted. 'You tried to – '

'I know. I know.' He continued pacing. 'I know all that stuff about your being mortal . . . but see, I know I'll never be as big as some of the rest. I probably won't get laid till I'm fifteen, if then,' he told me dourly. 'The male clans are very status conscious. And hell, I'm the runt of my litter. The girls beat up on me all the time. I need an edge. You could be it.'

'I don't know what you need,' I told him. 'I do know what you've got: nerve! You tried a kill-bite on me. Given any choice at all, I would have been your dinner. Now, get out of here!'

He laid his ears back. 'Hey, listen! I can do things for you. If you're traveling with one of us, we can usually

267

help keep the rest off. And we're the ones who make it so dangerous out here at night. Besides, why do you think they cut the nuts off the ones the city people catch? A big male is a high-status possession. People pay attention when one of us strolls by.

'Boy,' he continued, 'when I tell the male clans I was in service with one of the Danae—'

'I'm a mortal Daughter of the Danae,' I told him.

He laid his ears back again, his eyes slitted. 'I know that, but they don't have to. Besides, I don't know if it matters. Anything. Anything, babe, that has to do with the Danae is very high muck-a-muck. Believe me . . .'

'Why should I believe you about anything when you just told me you'd lie to your own people?'

He looked nonplussed, then indignant. 'I expect to take an oath. I haven't taken any oath not to string along the clans. Maybe just a little bit. So don't get so hoity-toity with me!'

'You're letting him talk too much,' Albe said. 'If you let him keep on talking, he'll convince you.'

'What do you think?' I asked her.

'He's so . . . motivated.'

'You bet!' the cat answered. 'What say?'

'Yes. And it's got to be a solid oath. And no biting.'

He jumped up and placed his paws on my shoulders, then butted his forehead between my breasts. 'I promise to obey orders, be faithful, and only bite dead food unless otherwise instructed. Want that more flowery? I'm up to a lyric, some blank verse, maybe.'

'No!' I said. 'But there is one thing I do want to know. Your name.'

He had dropped back down and was looking up at me. 'I don't know,' he temporized.

'I do. The name!' I repeated. 'Now!'

'Akeru,' he said.

'No!' I said. 'That's your people.'

'How do you know?'

'I'm not sure.' I wasn't. Knowing the right name when given is part of power. I hadn't realized before I had it, but I did.

'Tuau,' he said in a low voice. 'And don't spread it around.'

'Take point,' I said.

He hissed viciously.

'No arguments – point. Now!'

He lashed his tail and marched ahead of me down the narrow defile. It opened into a rather wide valley. It once must have been a lake that emptied into the sea. Now it was farmland or pastureland, irrigated by branches of the river that flowed through the city.

A city has to feed itself, and this was how this one did. Seven branches of the river were diverted into canals that irrigated the lake bed. It stretched away on either side as far as the eye could see until the edges were lost among the jagged tree-clad mountain slopes surrounding it. A fertile oasis in a barren land. A causeway ran along each canal to a separate city gate.

'I take it no other family would allow us to use their entrance to the city?'

'We'd be killed on the spot if we tried,' Meth said.

'I don't know,' Cateyrin said. 'We could try to bribe our way in using the mariglobes.'

'That's not a good idea,' Meth said. 'Once they had the jewels, none would feel any obligation to protect us.'

'Huh. How much obligation do you think the Fursa will feel toward us when he finds his ewe lamb among us dead and you wearing his armor?'

'Hush,' I said. The sun was westering, and the valley was filled with shadows and golden light. 'We will take the devils we know in place of the devils we don't.'

Tuau was beside Albe, rubbing his face on the laces of

269

Talorcan's sandals. '*Purrrrr . . . humm . . . purr.* You're gorgeous, you know that?' he told Albe.

She studied him cynically as she scratched his neck and ears.

'Oh, God.' He sighed. 'This is so good. Gooood.' Then he caught sight of the knife in her other hand. She must have palmed it. He froze.

'You thinking of *usssing* that?' he hissed.

'No,' Albe said. 'My lady approved you, but I'm not a trusting soul.'

'*Ummmmm.*' He rubbed some more against her hand. 'Oh, God, I'm such a sucker for that.' He went down on his back, wallowed, and let her scratch his stomach, while he emitted purrs of ecstasy. 'They told me your kind could be wonderful. Sensual to the most.' His eyes rolled back in his head.

'Hup!' Albe shouted.

He twisted in the air like a snake and came up with her left wrist in his mouth, fangs denting the skin. However, her knife point was just about an inch from his eye.

'We aren't going to hurt each other, are we?' Albe asked.

He released her wrist with an apologetic sound. 'Sometimes it just gets too intense. We lose control.' He hunkered down, crouched at her feet, and sighed.

'We'll get along,' Albe said reassuringly.

'Good,' I said. 'Because I need the two of you to back us up when we talk to the man Meth has to see to get past the gate. Soon as he knows Amrun is dead, the Fursa's going to order an attack. Meth said we're going to have to fight.'

'We can get past them if we take them by surprise,' Cateyrin insisted stubbornly.

'Let's hope,' Meth replied.

'The streets near the gates are a maze,' Cateyrin said. 'If we can slip past them and run in among the buildings, they won't dare follow.'

Rather ruefully, I wondered, *Why?* But I didn't ask. Cateyrin and Meth would only get into another quarrel and delay us still more. If the Akeru infested the valley after dark, it certainly wasn't safe here. He said he was a runt, but I had my doubts. He weighed about ninety pounds and carried a full complement of teeth and claws. I might be able to hole up and beat off an attack by his kind, but how could I protect the rest?

'Lead on,' I told Meth. 'I'll be right behind you.'

'That's not consoling,' Meth said.

'It wasn't meant to be. Albe, Tuau, you stay back. Cateyrin, take care of the contents of those boxes. You say they're valuable. We may need to pay bribes.'

'Let's give them to the Fursa,' Meth said. 'I feel we owe him something for . . .'

'Bullshit!' Albe said. 'Cateyrin, you hang onto those boxes. Hear me, girl. You, dreadcat, walk in front of me.'

'Dreadcat. I like that,' Tuau said.

'Now march!' I said.

We did.

The valley was as intensively cultivated as any place I've ever seen. As we walked along the causeway, I saw a lot of the lake remained. But it was covered with floating rafts that were made of poles and matting, then covered with dirt and intensively farmed. Many grew cereal crops, wheat, the low, hard wheat that makes such good dumplings and flat bread. But I saw others covered with rye, barley, and even oats.

Many had root crops with large arrowhead-shaped leaves wonderfully colored in red, gold, silver, and shiny dark green. Those were tethered at the center of the lake, where the sun was brightest, with canals between them that could be traveled by boat. But even the canals must have been a source of food, for they were choked with cattails, water lilies, and water hyacinths.

Tethered near the causeway were larger islands covered with trees: plum, peach, quince, medlar, and even fig, and others I didn't recognize. On both sides of us, the lake stretched out into the distance as far as the eye could see; blue, green, gold, russet, covered by the richly cropped, floating islands. Its very lushness was in contrast to the barren hills and even more ferociously bare mountain slopes that cradled it. Close to the edges of the lake, greenery flourished. But even a hundred or so feet beyond the water, the plants thinned out into occasional islands of vegetation that dotted the slopes on the hillsides all around.

A lean place, I thought. Leaner even than the sea-pounded, fissured shores where the Painted People struggled to get a living.

Just then, behind me, I heard a sound like thunder. The causeway was narrow, as I said.

'You women get in the mud.' He – the voice was male – spoke of the shallows and islands of farmland tethered beside the causeway.

I leaped out onto one covered with a low growth of barley. The rest followed, and the herd, in a double line tethered to each other neck to neck, thundered past.

The herd was led by a man running alongside the first two beasts. He was pulling a lead rope. The animals reminded me of antelope, but they were bigger, with long, twisting double horns, powerful bodies with thick chests and haunches. Bay animals with dark-brown coats, black legs, hooves, horns, and noses. They had fangs, something no hoofed beasts where I come from have ever had. Their mouths reminded me of a boar's, with the fangs – no, tusks – pointed downward and large, serviceable teeth fit for grinding down though vegetation or biting off a man's leg.

Another man was running beside the double column of animals. He also held a lead rope attached to two animals, and he kept them in line as they thundered along the causeway. Another man brought up the rear.

I flashed on the man at the rear. He was sun-browned and hard, wearing only the sort of loincloth that Roman gladiators once wore, ends tied at the waist, a long piece brought up between the legs and flapped over the front. Almost, it seemed he had a pelt of fine, light-brown hair that covered the tops of his arms, chest, back, neck, and bearded his chin. His stomach, inner arms, and hands were smooth and hairless, as were the backs of his legs.

The double column of animals must have slowed at the front, likely to pass the city gates, I thought. He threw his weight against the column rear and they slowed. The harnesses that bound the beasts together tightened.

The rearmost animal lashed out with one heel and caught the man holding the rope a hard blow to the thigh. He went down to one knee. Even as I watched, the purpling red mark leaped out on his skin. For a second, his weight was thrown against the double file of antelope and the column slowed and almost stopped.

Someone laughed. He glanced toward us and his eyes met Albe's.

I remember I was stunned by the lightness of his eyes. They were so clear, a crystalline gray, that the irises seemed almost not to exist but would have melted into the whites but for the fact that they had a dark, almost black, ring around them.

The look he gave Albe was a devouring one that said, 'I want you!' Stunning as a slap in the face.

Albe returned a frankly slow, salacious grin. This surprised me, and then I remembered her statement about taking pleasure even in rape. But then, she had not forgiven the one who had desired her, even to the destruction of her life. And the scars on her face were a

273

testament to the ugly fact that she had forgiven neither herself nor him.

Then the herdsman (I later found out that's what he was) writhed and clutched at his throat; and I saw he wore metal chain around his neck. In a second, he was on his feet, chasing the unruly animals toward the city and through its gate.

'How could you?' Cateyrin asked Albe.

'What?' Albe replied.

'Look at him as though he were a man.'

'Hell, he was, wasn't he? And a damn fine-looking one, too.'

'No!' Cateyrin snapped. 'He was Fir Blog.'

I was mystified, but didn't get a chance to pursue it because Meth said, 'Hurry! It's our good luck the square inside the gate will be a mess because the herdsmen don't stop for anything. Their drivers don't allow it. And likely, the household guard, led by the Fursa, won't be able to surround us. Maybe we can slip past.'

'Fine,' I said, jumping to the road. I started off at a jog, Meth running beside me.

He was right, but we were almost caught.

I had never seen a true city before. The plaza was filled with people. They all seemed to be cursing and running around, trying to put their sale stalls together again. That wasn't what caught my eye, but the towers that surrounded the plaza. They were not completely black, but blue-black. The sides of some were translucent, and I could see beautifully garbed men and women moving around in them. Some were standing on balconies, looking down at the free show below.

The shops, grouped at the foot of the towers, were in the late afternoon light a collection of jewels. The nearest shop to the gate was a cloth seller. It was stuffed with streaming bolts of silk, velvet, and brocade, seemingly in every color of the rainbow;

and a few, perhaps even the rainbow never knew.

The next shop, lit from above by a glass roof, was filled with bottles glowing with red, yellow, scarlet, blue, murky gold, orange, amber, brown, or black, the multiplicity of whose shapes almost defied description. Perfume? I wondered. Wine or something I did not know or had not yet encountered? The others, some sold raiment, some furniture. I saw beds, chairs, whatnots, who knows, all painted, polished, and inlaid with rich designs.

Intermingled with the more permanent shops were the food sellers' stalls, and they seemed to have been the ones most disturbed by the herd's passage. Chickens, ducks, and geese, and some animals that looked like rats, ran loose, getting under everyone's feet as their owners frantically tried to catch them. Fruit, cabbages, onions, garlic, berries had been spilled and lay heaped near the baskets that once held them.

A rack hung with joints of meat sprawled at my feet. Tuau rushed forward and snatched up a plump roast.

'Indeed, it is truly a wonder,' I heard Albe say. 'But don't let us stay to admire it. Move, Guinevere.'

I moved, leading our party in a serpentine path over the dead, black rock that floored the square. I recognized the Fursa, who wore even more elaborate armor than Meth. He stood among his people at the center of the square, a dozen or more men with him.

I glanced right and left. Albe was on my right, Cateyrin at my left.

'When we get past him, follow me,' Cateyrin said.

'Do it!' I shouted to the rest, and went head-on, directly toward the Fursa.

He was smart enough to know something was wrong. His sword was out. I elbowed Meth aside and caught his blade with my own. Maeniel taught me the trick.

I locked his blade at the hilt, spun around, my back

against his body, and jerked his right leg from under him with my right foot. He hit the stones, his armor making a very satisfactory crash.

Cateyrin was already making for a side street at a dead run. It was more like a tunnel than a street. The towers and the bridges between them darkened it into deep shadow.

'They know where we'll make for. Move!' Meth shouted.

We reached a stair, a narrow one that led up, curving away among the black towers. From a walkway that bridged the street, a man looked down at us with idle, indifferent curiosity. A woman peered down from a balcony; she wore gold and black brocade. Then there were no more bridges, and the narrow stair was walled by the towers. We had to move along one at a time.

Cateyrin slowed. 'I don't think they will try to follow us here. One determined person can hold the street.'

'An eerie place, this city,' I said, remembering the broad plaza at the gate, the glittering shops, the translucent towers. The ones the stair ran among were obsidian black, with such a high polish that they reflected the blue-gold clouds of the evening sky.

'Probably they won't bother with this street at all,' Meth said. 'They'll go around and try to catch you at your mother's house.'

'It's longer that way. It will take them time to—'

'No more arguments,' I ordered. 'We're committed to this route. Save your breath.'

We needed it. The stair wound up and up, until we came to a garden. Yes, a garden in the sky. The beds, like the rafts that floated on the lake, were made of wood and matting, and gigantic urns held trees.

Meth stopped dead still at the entrance to the garden.

'*Here,*' he hissed at Cateyrin. 'Here. You brought us *here*!'

'Yes. It's the only way I could think of,' Cateyrin said.

Meth moaned. 'Oh, no.'

'Oh, no, what?' I asked.

He didn't get a chance to answer. She appeared in front of me and roared.

Everybody ducked behind me. Tuau rumbled, 'Aunt Louise!'

'That,' I told the cat in front of me, 'is the best set of teeth I've ever seen.'

She was one of the Akeru, and a lot bigger than our young friend, Tuau.

'What are you doing here, runt?' she hissed at Tuau.

'She's Danae,' Tuau said. 'Don't mess with her.'

'Yes,' I said, trying to sound dangerous. 'I am.'

'Liar!' she spat. 'You and your friends get out of here!'

'How did they capture you, Aunt Louise?' Tuau said.

She gave vent to a vicious snarl. 'I'm working contract mercenary, runt. And I have my orders. Get out of here.'

'We don't want to harm the garden,' I said. 'Just pass through.'

'Aunt Louise, *pleeeeease*,' Tuau moaned.

'You tiresome brat! How come you get into everything?'

She paced back and forth in front of the archway where we stood. I think she probably outweighed me by twenty pounds, a pale, white-coated, rangy figure.

Maeniel told me about cheetahs. I admit, I didn't believe him, but he had given me close descriptions of cheetahs, lions, tigers, and leopards, wildcats and lynx. And yes, there were still some panther-sized cats roaming Europe. I had seen them at a distance.

Her face was oddly sensitive, with large, sad eyes. She ceased pacing, sat, and threw me a cold look.

'I get to eat the intruders I catch. I'll have one of you. The rest can pass me by. Let's see.' She eyed Meth. 'Too much armor. Be like eating a turtle. You, girl,' she told

Cateyrin. 'Scrawny, no meat on your bones. You.' She gazed at me. 'He says you're Danae, and while I don't believe it, I don't care for any surprises. That leaves you, Nephew.'

Tuau was leaning against my leg. I felt him trembling, and looking into Aunt Louise's green gaze, gold eyes, I could understand why.

'But,' she continued, 'it's against my principles to eat family, so I'll take the ugly one.'

'Oh, you will, will you?' Albe said.

Fine, I thought. I was still holding my sword, and I reversed the handle and brought it up hard under her chin.

'Go!' I shouted.

The blow lifted her forefeet off the ground as Cateyrin charged past me, closely followed by Meth, with Tuau bringing up the rear at first. But soon he pulled into the lead.

She was fast, Aunt Louise. I'll give her that. She was away from me, backing even though I was sure she wasn't fully conscious, and blood was foaming at her jaws. She gave a long, loud, wavering scream, and another of her kind charged out from among the flowers. He – and he was definitely he, balls dangling between his back legs – was even bigger than she was. He didn't hesitate for a second.

Behind me, I heard Albe laugh. I raised my sword as he bounded into a leap to fall on me and take me down. I raised the sword without much hope. He was so big, even if I got the sword into him, his teeth and claws might finish me in spite of my armor.

But at the last second, Albe jerked me clear. The cat missed, coming down on all fours beside me.

'*Yiiiiiiiiiieeeeeeeeee!!!!*'

It was without doubt the most ghastly scream I have ever heard an animal give, as the big male curled in on himself and began frantically to lick an important (to him) part of his anatomy.

Albe knew where to land that lead shot.

'Get out of my way, my lady,' Albe said. 'I'll finish them.'

The male decided discretion was the better part of valor. He fled without delay and without shame.

But Aunt Louise faced us down. 'Think you're good, don't you? You better not miss.'

'I never miss,' Albe said.

'No! We don't want this to be a killing fray. Back off and let us pass. Albe, watch out, there may be more of them.'

Aunt Louise didn't move, but she didn't advance, either. Behind us, a balustrade separated us from a drop into the lake below. I was shocked to see how high we were as we ran along it toward a narrow stair where the rest waited.

We passed a clean, red scatter of bones among the flower beds. The bones weren't recognizably human, but the two skulls that accompanied them were.

'Trespassers, I suppose,' Albe said.

We reached the other stair and found it led right up and out over nothingness. The treads were attached to the outside of a tower. *Attached* is a bad word; they flowed out of the ribbed stone of one of the black and red ones. They were at broadest about ten inches wide. That's not a lot when you're looking at a four-hundred-foot drop. It goes almost without saying that there was no sort of a rail.

Meth went first, followed by Cateyrin, me, Albe, and Tuau. He muttered under his breath, 'She always was a hard-assed bitch. Think of it. Wouldn't even cut one of the Danae a little slack. What's the world coming to when the old gods are not honored?'

'Oh, for heaven's sake, shut up,' I said. 'I don't need you distracting me.'

Albe laughed. We were making the best speed possible, edging our way along, backs to the tower behind us, taking the steps one by one, feeling for each next step and getting a solid stance before we went on.

'Look,' Albe said.

'Look at what?'

I was busy glancing back to see if Aunt Louise might be trying to follow and watching those ahead inching their way along to be sure they were safe. Silly, as I think about it now. What could I have done in either eventuality? Aunt Louise would be in the same precarious situation we were in. Worse, because she was a large animal that had to go on all fours, and this stair had been built to accommodate human feet.

And if one of us fell, what would the rest do? Catch him or her? Laughable. The rescuer would go down with the victim.

Yet Albe was holding my wrist.

'Don't,' I said.

She let go, being also a woman of common sense.

'Look,' she told me. 'Is it not beautiful?'

To be worried about beauty at a time like this! Yet she was right. All of one side of the valley could be seen from our perch. The sun, sinking into the misty horizon, burned a bright path over the water on the lake below and reflected in hues of copper, gold, and molten metal on the polished sides of the towers. The land below was posed in that green-gold shimmer that signals the approach of night.

'Yes,' I answered. 'Albe, it is. And dangerous, also. The sun is going down and the rocks will give back their heat into the winds.'

Already they were rising and gusts tugged at us.

Meth gave a low croon of distress. Armored, he was the most vulnerable of us all.

Cateyrin encouraged him, 'Keep going. It's not far. The

280

first time I came here, I was terrified, but after that, I came here every day. Well, almost every day. And it was easy. Believe me, you haven't far to go.'

But Meth was proceeding ever slower, until finally, he froze where he was. I looked back at Albe and Tuau. She was cool, her face calm as she looked out toward the sun, its light reflected by the shimmering walls of a distant gorge as it sank in the distance. The wind was growing wilder and wilder. It tugged at my body, whipped at my hair, and at times numbed my face with its force. Cateyrin was weeping openly, begging Meth to keep moving.

I edged toward her until I stood next to her, my body pressed against hers. I knew what I had to do. Coldly, I nudged her along until we were very close to Meth.

'Please! Please!' she cried. 'It's only a little way now. I promise . . .'

'Be quiet!' I said. 'Meth!' I didn't know I could sound like that. 'Meth!'

He turned a terror-filled face toward me. The wind hit again, and his eyes closed against its force. We felt dust and debris blown up and carried on it blind us for a second.

'Meth! Get moving!' I shouted. I still held the sword in my right hand. I had not sheathed it. 'Meth, if you stay there, I'm going to take my blade and drive it through your throat. If you freeze where you are, we will all die. Hear me! Get moving!'

I was looking at Meth across Cateyrin's face. Her eyes were closed, tears running silently down her cheeks.

The wind hit again. The glow was fading from the towers around us. I knew we had not much time, and I might perish along with Meth if swinging the sword overbalanced me. But I knew I had no choice. By the time night fell, the winds would be fierce, and standing on the narrow stair, we would never be able to withstand them. They, and the cold I suspected would go along with them. We would hang on for a time, but in the end, we would perish, one by one, falling into the dark lake below.

I readied myself for the stroke.

Arthur did the things a king did for his people in the Summer Land. It was reflex with him, and he now knew that even in his mother's womb he had been a king. While dreaming, he knew the burdens of leadership, because that's what a king was in his world: a man who chooses to confront the difficulties the small, segmented societies faced in their settlement of this corner of the planet.

There were no people who did not know the forms and the fulfillment of this template as it was applied to reality. The Greeks had kings; they became too overbearing, and so their political authority was withdrawn. The Romans were instructed about kings by the Etruscans, and for the same reasons had also dispensed with them. But when they founded their great city, Rome, it took a king to lay its boundaries.

The Saxons knew of kings, and law, and the earth queens who were needed to create kings, as had the Gauls and the Germans from beyond the Rhine. They all knew, and however they might flout the ancient code, they understood that in the end, it must prevail.

A king must be able to do three things: fight, enforce the law, and love to maintain the life of his people. Arthur had not loved, not yet known a woman. Only Dea Arto, who had summoned him to the Bear Society. She had come to him during the week after he woke a man. The pleasure had stolen upon him during that calm, silent interval between sleep and waking, and he spent it among the linen and fur that covered him in the place where he slept with the other boys in a stone chamber at Morgana's stronghold. He woke with a memory of pleasure so piercingly powerful that it engendered an almost instant guilt.

And after he came completely to his senses, he was ironically aware that fear and guilt both were the proper reaction, since he could no longer remain among the innocents who shared the chamber with him. He had, as best he could, hidden the evidence of his adulthood, and then rose and went to find his father.

The pleasure startled his body in the same secret, sudden way while he was sleeping in the loft of Balin's barn, and he yielded to its flood of exquisite joy before he had time to understand what was happening to him. He opened his eyes to the dank rafters stretching over his head and knew She had summoned him as She had when he was still a boy.

Dea Arto. She was honored with honey berries and wine, autumn fruits, yet it was spring in the Summer Country. He rose and came down the ladder to where the horses were stabled. They were awake in their stalls, heads up, ears pricked as though listening for something. One stamped a foot softly; the other backed and tugged hard at the rope that held his bridle.

The stalls had no doors. The only thing that kept the horses there was the tethers attached to the wall. Arthur's clothing was hung on a nail driven into the - center post of the barn.

Still watching the horses, he whispered, 'Presently,' and dressed as quickly as possible.

The horses were mare and stallion. The stallion backed so hard against the lead rope that Arthur slipped the makeshift rope bridle over his head. But unwilling to leave the mare, he stood stamping his feet and whickering a warning, softly, desperately.

Arthur ran to the mare and cut the bridle off. She and

283

the stallion tore out of the barn silently, terrified of . . . something. But there wasn't anything.

Arthur followed them cautiously. The night greeted him. There was a shadow glow on the horizon. Moonrise? The breeze fanned his face; insects churred in the grass.

The house where Balin slept with his wife and child was dark and silent, door and windows barred against the night and its perils. These were wild lands.

What? Arthur thought. *Cat? Bear?*

The lords of the mountains, the bears, her children, weren't the tamest of creatures. They had been known to break into stables after horse meat, smokehouses, and even the occasional human dwelling.

Yes, moonrise. The light on the high clouds was increasing even if he couldn't yet see the silver face. The two horses stood like statues in the center of the meadow that sloped down to the river, the faint silver light gleaming on their smooth coats, heads raised, looking toward the wild, toward the plateau where he first had been exiled to this strange, lovely land. Toward where the moon was rising. Their heads up, ears pricked as if listening . . . to what?

And then Arthur heard the distant cries, the wailing and sobbing, screaming and cursing.

It had hunted him before, and now somehow it had slipped past the wards on the plateau, its ancient prison, and was hunting him again.

The horses spun around and fled. Inside the house, Arthur heard the dog, Bax, his roaring alarm bark rousing the family. Arthur ran toward the house and even before he got there, the family was in the doorway, Balin in his nightclothes, Eline, his wife, wearing a dark caftan and holding the baby in her arms.

Bax leaped past them and ran to Arthur, sniffed him once, then looked in the direction of the rising moon and snarled.

'Oh, my God,' Eline said. 'A War Song!'

'Is that what you call it? I was imprisoned on the plateau with one,' Arthur said.

The muttering, sobbing, moaning, and screaming was growing louder and louder as was a sound made by the Thing's winds in the trees.

'The Thing on the plateau could only track me by day.'

'The king makes them special for his enemies. Usually enemies he thinks more of than us.' She gave Arthur a look of profound respect.

'I'm sensible of the honor, I'm sure,' Arthur said. 'But in a few minutes, the horrible Thing is going to charge out of the woods and join us. Any suggestions?'

'Run!' Eline said. 'That's the only thing I know. They don't move very fast. Since this is a night one, it can't hunt by day and . . .'

Bax gave a snarl that was almost a roar, . . . and it burst from the forest, trailing its sounds of grief, terror, and pain and spewing a cloud of leaves, bark, branches, and pieces of brush.

'I'll try to lead it away,' Arthur said. 'Up toward the plateau, into the wilderness.'

'Take Bax.' She pointed to Arthur. 'Bax! Protect! Obey!'

Dogs are smart, but Bax was the most intelligent dog Arthur had ever met. He shoved his nose into Arthur's hand, then ran down the meadow toward the river. Arthur gave his sword to Balin, kept his knife, then followed Bax.

They ran together along the edge of the wood, until they got close to the river. Then Arthur turned, Bax by his side. He watched as the dreadful being turned, swarming along the edge of the forest to follow him. As on the plateau, everything that could, fled. Things that couldn't – trees, shrubs, the woodpile for the smoke-house – exploded into flying, splintering debris when the

Thing's noxious substance touched them. The woodpile splintered into lethal shards, and Arthur began his run when he saw a wedge of oak driven a foot and a half into a pine tree.

Pine wood is soft, but not that soft, he thought, during his headlong flight under the trees. Bax led the way, and Arthur was surprised how expertly the dog picked a path. First along the river, willow, beech, water oak, then deeper into the glades of deciduous forest, ash, elm, and broad-branched black oak and here and there tall, fragrant linden, pale ash, and hickory. The ground was damp; his feet pounded along a soft carpet of loam, newly renewed each autumn by the falling leaves. The moonlight was bright now, and lay in pools of silver, brightness broken by dense black shadows. Shadows so dark it almost seemed to him that if he leaped into their velvet vortex, he might vanish and elude his dreadful pursuer forever.

He had been through so many strange things since his exile here, he half believed it might be possible.

He noticed Bax, running just ahead of him, kept to the light, so he followed the dog, being unwilling to try that strange exit. He had duties here to his people.

He was also glad they were not running toward the tower. It might shelter him from the fearful Thing he could hear grumbling, cursing, breathing behind him, but then he had never seen the tower do anything negative, harm any creature that entered it. Weeds and grasses grew unobstructed between its stones, flowered or fruited at will, and had their seeds borne away by the wind. Birds, butterflies, large, sometimes beautiful, sometimes drab (or were they simply more subtly beautiful?), moths moved through the dusty shadows as night approached.

The birds built their nests, made bird love, quick sharp, exciting bird love, raised their young, and were preyed on by nothing but the hawks and eagles, who made their nests among the rocks near the falls. And in this he could see no harm, but only the powerful continuity of an ancient pattern.

No, this terror might be able to destroy the tower or him. In some deep way he felt the tower's marvelous beauty was something he would willingly sacrifice his life to protect.

The ground was rising, and the slope growing steeper. More and more the trees he ran among were pines, and here and there clearings existed, where some forest giant had been felled by lightning in the storms that rolled down the mountains over the valley. The clearings were filled by crab apple, medlar, quince, wild plum, cherry, and blackthorn. It was spring; some were still in bloom and their flowers glowed like the vast drift of stars that arched above, visible faintly through the circle of moonlight. Their scent was thick in the air around him.

But then he was through the clearing and among the pines again. The slope grew steeper, though the footing was good. Too good. He didn't want to try to make a stand here. The big pines above him had shed needles that were three- to five-feet deep on the forest floor, and they would burn like tinder.

Once from the valley he'd stood with his people watching a storm sliding down from the snowcapped mountains beyond, across the green tree-covered slopes below. Lightning from above set the dry pine forest ablaze, and they and he watched from the common land where they grazed their cattle near the tower as the fire, moving ahead of the storm's updrafts, scorched the slopes above, tree after giant tree becoming a tower of flame. Coughing as the wind-driven smoke and ash settled into the hardwood forest near the river.

'Has it been known to reach the valley?' he had asked Balin.

Balin nodded, white-lipped. 'If the lowland woods catch . . . yes. They are dry right now. Ones who have been here longer than I tell of it. "We all had to run," one told me. Another man spoke up that "that year we lost half of our cattle, all our crops, and in the spring, so many were hungry the king simply sent his men to round up the survivors and drive them back to his stronghold." '

Eline had looked away from Balin. 'One of them was his father,' she explained.

And Arthur saw the tears were tracking down his cheeks.

'I was lucky,' he said. 'I was old enough to work, so they made me a field hand.' Balin hesitated. 'I never saw my parents again.'

Arthur said, 'There is no fear of such a thing happening now. I control the tower. It and the vessel within would sustain us however dire the famine.'

Arthur saw that the people around him looked heartened. Far less frightened, Eline smiled at the rest and said, 'We have a king!'

Arthur was uneasy, but a lifetime of training kept his face a mask of certainty. Yet he didn't know if he had been telling the truth or not. He'd never had to put the tower and vessel to the test.

The storm was moving at a run, the fire only at a walk. The rolling clouds overtook the blaze, the flame vanished into a haze of rain, and all that remained was a temporary dark spot, like a smudge against the green.

No, he didn't dare light a fire among the towering trees, even though exhaustion was tugging at him. He had been running uphill for a matter of fifteen miles and wasn't sure how much longer he could last, when Bax led him out of the forest. He hadn't known this place was here. From the valley, it couldn't be seen: a series of low, bowl-shaped mountain meadows that led down and around the peak he had been climbing, then down and around the slopes of the next peak, into a terrifyingly dark forest below.

True, he could run through the first of the chain of meadows and up the next slopes that climbed steeply, first to a tree line, then up barren rock and moss, toward a glacier that flowed between the high passes and frowned down on the tiny glens below. But there was no place of refuge beyond the meadows. On the open, exposed slopes, the thing would catch and destroy him.

No choice. He must make a stand here or nowhere.

He plunged forward, down to the meadow below. It was a place of unearthly beauty in the moonlight. A spring that probably originated in the glacier above dropped a thread of a waterfall into a rock basin at one end of the open space where it broke into dozens of streams, tumbling over dark, thick, moss-covered rocks into a string of pools all along the center of the meadow.

He ran downhill toward the water, through long, pale, shimmering grass that dampened his trousers and leggings. He had to rest – get some of the water before he could fight.

But he stopped, because Bax was not following him. Instead, the dog was standing stock-still, looking toward the multiple low falls and pools near the high end of the meadow.

Arthur straightened up and saw them. At first, he took 'them' for a pack of wolves, the largest pack he had ever seen. Then he knew they couldn't be real wolves, even though they had the slanted eyes, rangy build, and moon-polished coats of their living kin. No, these had to be something else. Why?

Yes! Real wolves' eyes would glow like polished fire, opal, in the moonlight this bright. These beings had only thick, black darkness behind their slanted openings where their eyes should be.

Thump!

Arthur spun around. Near Bax a stag leaped the ridge-line and ran down into the meadow. Silently the wolves gave chase.

Arthur drew back to let them pass. Tarnished silver shimmers flowed past him in mad pursuit of that massive-antlered being that floated over the rippling, long grass that for a moment mirrored a wind-driven sea.

Cold, Arthur thought. Cold the wind that seemed to spur the silver hunters and the dark prey.

For a second they vanished from sight. Then they reappeared in a lower meadow . . . and another, until they vanished into the awesomely dark forest beyond.

Bax joined them.

After the fire, Arthur had asked Eline why Balin's parents had returned to slavery so tamely. She told him that the longer they wandered this wild land, the more inexplicable and frightening the things they encountered. He had been dissatisfied with this explanation at the time; he was less so now.

He reached the water and scooped up some in his joined palms, but stopped when two of the symbols from within the cup flared in his palms and the water vanished. He was on his feet and backing away from the pool in less than an eye blink.

There was magic here, as there had been in the tower. Magic he couldn't understand.

In the distance, he heard the ugly mutter of the War Song. Bax woofed softly.

Arthur's mouth was dry, but he didn't try to drink again. The dog took out running toward the next meadow down. Suddenly Arthur was climbing through slippery moss-covered rocks and stumbling through water-filled pools, till he reached the grass below.

This meadow was bigger than the one above. He was

trapped here. The moon was right above him and the light bright as day.

There was nowhere else to go.

The meadow ended in a shallow lake, and beyond the lake stood the dark forest. He was sure it must be trackless. In fact, the moon shining down into it showed clearly how dense it was. Wilderness was part of his life, but only in dark midnight tales had he ever heard of such a place. But his blood remembered.

The branches were matted above, the trunks of the ancient oaks so close together that one must struggle through them. Men caught in the toils of a curse wandered here. By day the light was almost shut out by the hard evergreen leaves, and the direction for the sun could only be guessed at. By night, mist and moonlight strangled the fixed star guides. There was water enough only to torment, food enough to stave off death for a few months of horror and struggle over and around the knotted roots that covered every level place. A lethal, pathless waste. The fate of men lost in this wood was to at last yield up all hope, lie down, despair, and die.

A sheer cliff rose on one side of the meadow, and another fell away on the other. The wood beckoned him away to madness. He wondered how many men's bones moldered within it.

Behind him, the War Song blocked the road back.

'I would destroy you.' The voice was everywhere and nowhere.

'Don't waste either breath or energy on maledictions,' Arthur said. 'I know.'

PART TWO

CHAPTER FIVE

CREGAN WOKE BEFORE DAYBREAK. YES, this would be the first day of the full moon. He'd better fix up something for her and take it to the well.

He sighed. He could smell himself ... or was it the men's feasting hall? No women lived here. None were even supposed to approach it. Right now, *no one* would approach it at all, not from downwind at least.

He scratched the hair on his chest and studied the hawks standing on their perches in a ring around the outer edge of the circular structure. He knew that by spring the place usually got a little ripe. But last night's comments by the heads of the village in the valley were unkind, to say the least, and the statement of the seeress, Magda, that he burn the whole thing down and start over was a bit extreme. He didn't care for taking orders from the women, and he'd told her that.

Ha! was the reply. She went on to tell him that since he'd made a serious attempt to cut the throat of the last man to give him unwelcome advice, he'd best grow used to her opinions, since most men were since then wary of offending him. And someone must of necessity acquaint him with unpalatable truths.

The fact was that he was afraid of her. No one knew

all the things she could do, one of the least of which was to declare a man impotent and keep him that way for as long as she liked. This unpleasant reputation dated from the time of her first marriage. Her husband struck her, not an uncommon thing, but she took it amiss and told him if he raised his hand to her again, she would make his balls crawl back up in his body. He had (hit her). They did (crawl up in his body) and would not come down. Nor had they resumed their function when the poor man had a fatal encounter with the business end of a spear.

She had inherited all his property and pursued a comfortable state of widowhood ever since. And moreover, Cregan found no man, however courageous, was ever completely relaxed in her presence. He reluctantly included himself in that company.

He rose to his feet naked, stretched, and listened to the shouts in the distance. It was a cold morning, but the bathhouse was enjoying an unseasonable amount of popularity. He concluded that the impression made by her remarks yesterday might account for this.

'I'll probably have to burn it down,' he whispered, then went to join the warriors in the long, narrow sweathouse.

A little later, he sought out Magda. She had six sons. Before she took a fatal dislike to her husband, the man had done his duty by her. So her grandchildren and daughters-in-law did most of the household chores. She was weaving on a warp-weighted loom in her dooryard, keeping an eye on her hardworking kin. The men were in the fields or readying the flocks to begin the journey to the high pastures. Her daughters-in-law were toiling industriously, spinning, dying hanks of wool, grinding grain for the weekly bread making.

And indeed they had best work hard. Anyone in her household who didn't ran some rather strange risks, and two of her sons were veterans of rather acrimonious divorces occasioned by the young ladies' unwillingness to meet Magda's high standards. The rest kept their noses clean and obeyed her orders.

Cregan came up behind her, pausing to study the fabric on her loom. It was a textured miracle of silk, linen, and wool tapestry, showing the four worlds as seen from above. They looked like concentric circles, each sporting their proper colors, the outer and bottom circle, a mixture of brown, black, scarlet, orange, and sienna, a convocation of autumn. The first inner was green and brown, the greens of a midsummer forest tangled with brown, black, rock darkness, yet shimmering with touches of sun on water or on the leaves on the topmost trees in the forest. Pastels ruled the last two circles, and they were marked with brightness and the subtle shifts that rule the kingdom of light.

Cregan was about to clear his throat and announce his presence when Magda spoke.

'I know you're there, Cregan, so don't start making odd noises.'

'Yes, Magda.' Cregan tried to sound humble.

'Don't be so damn unctuous, you withered, vicious old snake. It's hypocritical and doesn't suit your character.'

'I suppose I was a bit drunk last night.'

'Stinking, piss in the corner, shit in the bed drunk,' she said. 'Burn your hall!'

'Magda—' he began.

'Shut up. Burn that vermin-infested, filth-encrusted pile of shit and do it within the week or I'll take a torch to the place myself.'

Cregan's jaw muscles worked. 'Magda—'

'But,' she continued inexorably, 'what you want is in that pot over by the fire. Two whole loins of wild boar, cooked with apples, carrots, and bacon. The sun hasn't touched the valley yet. She will be waiting. Honey and wine in the net bag beside the pot. Take those two. I personally cannot see what she sees in you, but I suppose even among the immortals flawed judgment is possible.'

Cregan thought on the loss of his balls, thought it might almost be worth it, but was discouraged when she said, 'No, it wouldn't. I'll think up something special just for you. And remember, before the week is out, burn it.'

He had to climb a ways before he reached the well. It was an unprepossessing pool in the shadow of a slab of black rock guarded by an olive tree. The changeable shimmer of the gray-green leaves greeted the wall stone; pines were a lacy silhouette against the brightening sky. Rowan trees were thick around the well; heavy flower heads cast their strange scent into the air and fallen petals stippled the water at his feet.

The footpath over dove-pearled moss to the water was very narrow. When he reached the edge of the water, Cregan paused and placed the food, honey, and wine at the edge of the pool. He'd unstoppered the wine jug and made ready to pour the contents into the pool when someone said, 'Just leave it. She will pick up the offerings when she gets ready.'

Cregan said, '*Yiiiiiii!*' and froze.

The youngster was standing on the other side of the well, next to the big, black rock that formed one side of the pool. Cregan was an old and deadly warrior. Most men found it impossible to get within thirty yards of him without his being aware of them. He was also reasonably sure he had been alone when he put the food down.

His next thought was that the youngster was a good-looking kid. He was rather simply dressed, wearing a mail shirt. Good quality, that shirt. Trousers, boots, and cross-gartered leather leggings. He had a black wool mantle edged with silver embroidery. Odd pattern – something about it made the hair on the back of Cregan's neck stir. It looked like the letters of some alphabet, closely spaced and so tightly configured that but for the eyelash-thin separations between them, they might have formed a single, solid band.

The hide helmet was strange, also. It fit tightly and came to a point at the forehead, rather like a bird's beak. The eyes, ruby-red, peered over the beak, and the body and wings formed the back and cheek pieces. They flared out to protect the sides of his face, and the first primaries curved around under the lad's eyes.

Cregan's skin crawled when the eyes, after studying him for a moment, closed and seemed to vanish into the helmet's stark blackness.

'Good day to you, sir,' the youngster said. 'She instructed me to present myself to you. I am Lolatia.'

'Are you now?' Cregan asked. He noticed a slight wheeze in his voice.

'Yes,' was the reply.

'I can't pronounce that name, and it has been whole centuries – even before the Romans – since that dialect was spoken. The only reason I know it at all is because some of the oldest prayers are written in it, and those prayers were already old when Hannibal crossed our land on his way to the Alps. He paid us to divine his fate and sacrifice among our trees for the welfare of himself and his men. 'Tis said near a thousand of our young men joined him – the Romans were making pests of themselves then. Besides, I reckon the pay was good. Only seven or eight of those who joined him ever returned. No one can or will say that name now. The language is dead. The closest I can come to it is Lancelot.'

'Very impressive. Lanzalet.'

'That's close enough.' Cregan sighed.

The boy went carefully to one knee, placed his hand on his heart, and asked, 'May I join your company?'

'Did She ask you to come see me?'

'Yes. And She says, "Don't dump the wine into the

pool. It's hell getting it separated from the water. Sometimes it ruins the taste." '

'We wouldn't want to do that, would we?' Cregan said, giving the pool an apprehensive glance. 'But doesn't She worry someone will steal it?'

'She has ways of dealing with that.'

'Yes,' Cregan said. 'I imagine She does. So, fair sir, rise and join my company.'

'Thank you.' Lancelot/Black Leg rose and followed Cregan into the valley.

On the way down, Cregan told him, 'They will want to test you. You don't ride with me unless you're tough. Are you tough?'

'I don't know,' Black Leg said.

'Modest, too,' Cregan commented, then sighed again.

'Will they all jump me at once?'

'No, that's not allowed.'

'Oh. Fine, then everything should be all right.'

'Boy, there are over forty men who are my companions.'

'Oh,' Black Leg said. 'How many at a time?'

'Only one. That's the rule. It doesn't matter if you're defeated eventually, just so you give a good account of yourself. No weapons allowed.'

'That's all right. I haven't any,' Black Leg told him. 'Phew! What's that?'

Cregan gave a long-suffering groan and muttered, 'I suppose our little drinking hall might be getting a bit overripe this spring.'

'I'll get used to it,' Black Leg said.

They arrived at the courtyard in front of the round-house door. It was big, with low stone walls surmounted by a steep, cone-shaped roof. Last summer's bread wheat had been grown on the roof, and the scraggy stalks made the thatch look as though it had hair on it.

The courtyard held a fire pit for cooking and was

floored by flat-sided, wooden cobbles. Cregan handed Black Leg a horn and said, 'Blow.'

Black Leg pulled off his mantle and threw it over Cregan's arm as he took the horn with his right hand. Cregan stretched out his other hand for Black Leg's helmet, but it took wing and flew into a tree.

Cregan's whole body jerked, and he muttered, 'Yes, you're a friend of Hers all right. I wish they'd seen that. They wouldn't be so eager. But let's have at it.'

Black Leg blew. The horn call echoed among the rocky hills. Birds flew up from the trees all around, and everywhere people began running toward the warrior's house. Some action was in the offing. Men began to stream out of the doors, some half-naked, some completely so, most rubbing their eyes and looking annoyed.

'What! Who is this child?' a big redhead yelled, gesturing at Black Leg. 'Fool that you are, Cregan, what cradle have you robbed? You, boy! Go home and grow another inch or two before you return.'

Black Leg was nervous. He had never faced anything like this before. He had wrestled Maeniel every day until his father could no longer pin him. None of the young men in the village had been able to give him an interesting fight with any weapon. Even barehanded he was deadly against a fully armed man. Maeniel had seen to that. But all that had been mere practice. This looked to be a real engagement. He was nervous, palms, armpits wet.

He dropped down and dusted his hands with ash from the fire pit, then rose, took his stance, feet slightly apart, hands at his sides. No one was near his back; his wolf senses would have informed him if even a cat moved behind him.

Yes, there were at least forty men standing outside the hall, and spectators from all the nearby dwellings were crowding in around the wooden block courtyard, more and more arriving every minute. God, he was frightened and wondering if he were going to embarrass himself.

'Gentlemen,' he said softly, 'I haven't broken my fast today, and I'm hungry. Would it be possible to expedite matters?'

They loved it.

'Expedite matters! Oh, my God,' the redhead roared. 'By all means, let's expedite matters.'

And he came flying toward Black Leg at a dead run.

Black Leg stood his ground to the last second while noting the redhead was going for a bear hug. Then he pivoted to one side so quickly that it had to be seen to be believed, and broke the redhead's arm.

Red landed on his back, clutching his broken arm at the wrist to support it. Then he rolled, rose, and backed away, a look of astonished respect in his eyes.

Bull, the next, was on the way. Black Leg positioned himself carefully. His boot toe slammed into this one's breadbasket, and as he doubled over, a second kick got him in the backside. It was downhill from the courtyard, and he could be heard crashing through the undergrowth for some distance.

Somehow, the third landed in a tree. No one was sure just what Black Leg did, but it seemed effective.

The fourth was naked. It may be stated here, no one tried that again. The fifth tried to butt him and was redirected into a tree.

The sixth (by then they were learning) circled him, trying to get Black Leg's back to a friend of his. Black Leg broke his jaw with a knee and as his opponent was falling, turned, knocked the friend's legs from under him with a sweeping kick, then got him by the arm and dislocated his shoulder.

Cregan stepped in, sword glittering like a new icicle.

'A foul ends it,' he said. 'If none can take him one-on-one, then he has bested you.'

Black Leg stood still. He was a bit mussed, but he wasn't even breathing hard.

'I am at your disposal for as long as you like,' Black Leg said in a very formal manner.

Cregan gave a nasty laugh, then slapped him on the back. 'I can't afford any more wounded. Come. Let's eat breakfast.'

They were a hellacious crew. But they showed Black Leg a lot of respect. Even Red, who it transpired had expected the very trick Black Leg/Lancelot worked, but even armed with foreknowledge hadn't been able to stop him. Black Leg had simply been too quick and too strong for him.

Breakfast was sausage, bacon, ham, porridge, and bread. Black Leg, having seen and smelled the men's house, had determined not to sleep in it. He didn't have to. That very night Cregan sent him out with Red (his arm in a sling) to learn the countryside and reconnoiter.

'They are going to burn it,' Red told him.

'Thank God,' Black Leg said fervently.

Red thought this hilariously funny, and laughed all the way down into a very wild valley dominated by a gorge. Black Leg looked back after they had covered a few miles and noted he could see nothing of the dwellings belonging to Cregan's people. Not even smoke troubled the sky near the mountains.

'Badugae? Is that what you are called?' Black Leg asked Red.

Red shrugged. 'So Cregan says. I don't know. Like so many of the rest, I'm a runaway *colonus* from the Champagne, a wide, fertile country near the Seine River. The Roman villas there belong to the Franks. Or rather, I should say those are the men my master paid taxes to. Barbarians who call themselves Franks. My master's daughter married one, a Frank, and now they don't collect so many taxes from my master.'

Black Leg felt uncomfortable. 'What was his name?'

Red grinned. 'My master? Or my ex-master, you mean?'

Black Leg blushed. He knew about slaves and the *coloni* bound to the land in the south of England, France, and all over Italy. But he had never met one before and wasn't sure how to ask him about his life.

'Yes,' Black Leg answered.

'I don't know, except that he was a great man and his Frankish and Hunnish guards did what they liked to any who offended him. So we feared them greatly. Him, too.'

'What happened that you came here?' Black Leg asked.

Red looked into the distance. They were traveling downhill through a mixed oak and scrub pine forest.

'We are coming to a low place. I have seen pig there.' He handed Black Leg his spear. 'If we startle one, I want to know what you can do with this.'

The spear was long, narrow at the tip with pronounced flanges that formed a deadly barb.

'Won't get it out easily,' Black Leg said.

Red laughed. 'That's the idea.'

'He will turn on you,' Black Leg said.

'Ah, and haven't I the greatest warrior in the world with me?' Red asked.

Black Leg knew of the pigs before they came to them. The wind was blowing his way. He knew how many: two boars and three sows, one with an almost grown litter. He stretched out his arm to stop Red, then put his finger to his lips. The wallow was just ahead.

He picked up an oak knot fallen from the tree above. He threw it in the direction of the wallow, where it landed with a satisfactory splat. Pigs exploded in every direction, and Black Leg's arm lofted the spear before he had time to choose. As it flew, Black Leg wondered if the heavy spear would fall before it struck the one (a young boar) he'd managed to pick.

It didn't, but broke at the precise moment the pig caught up with it, and drove itself through the animal's body, pinning it to the earth.

Red laughed again. 'Young one, you're a wonder.'

'No,' Black Leg said. 'I've done a lot of hunting. We'll eat a good supper tonight.'

The further down the mountain they walked, the more the forest thinned out. They crossed the remnants of a Roman road.

'It used to follow the river to a wooden bridge downstream,' Red explained. 'But last year a rock slide wiped out the lower end and the bridge. So it goes nowhere now. Just as well. The thing made Cregan nervous. Those roads, you know, boy, they were built so you could put a legion somewhere fast. Now this road is too broken to follow, even if there were any legions left to travel it.'

A few minutes later, they reached the river gorge and then stood surveying the countryside.

'Nobody knows how long Cregan's people have lived here. They fought Caesar and he didn't think it was worth the trouble to dig them out of their hills. Every spring they drive their flocks to the high meadow, and in autumn they come down, slaughter the surplus animals, and live on meat, milk, cheese, butter, and barley the women raise around the farms they cut out of the forest. We try to help our brothers. If they raise the standard of revolt against the Roman landowners and their barbarian troops, we go and fight beside them as long as we can, and we welcome those who have to flee the cruelty of tax gatherers. Or the slavers who buy up the surplus young men and women from the great Roman landlords and ship them to the slave markets in the east.

'There are a lot of us. No one knows how many. We make no promises and take no oath but to assist each other whenever we can and to hang on and outlast the great landowners. The Roman officials, the barbarian mercenaries who murder, enslave, and steal all that is worthwhile in life from the people of the earth. Yes, Bagudae we are, and if enough of us last long enough who remember freedom, we will remake the earth. We can but try. Now, see there are no humans nearby while I build a fire and cook the pig.'

Black Leg's head was spinning. *Too much, too quickly*, he thought. He left Red at the edge of the bluff over the river.

A few miles downstream, he saw a practical place to ford the river. He went wolf and left his weapons (such as they were) and his clothes in a tree. The river crossing turned out to be only a brief swim. But he had to cover a few more miles before he found a shallow place to climb the bluff.

Then he swung out in a wide circle to investigate the countryside. It was wild and beautiful, but being brought up among farmers, he concluded it wasn't terribly fertile and the very sedentary Romans hadn't tried very hard to hang on to it. Yes, these people perforce clung to their old way of life, one the Romans had difficulty profiting from. This had been, in his father's eyes, the reason for the failure of the empire in the west: the Roman inability to comprehend or assist any other way of life than that revolving around the military. You live by the sword, you die by the sword; and the Romans had remained relentlessly military until the very end.

The tax base had eroded. Barbarians poured in over the frontier; the limes, a chain of forts, that once guaranteed order decayed. Still the whole Roman focus remained on the legions, even if said legions were now composed of inefficient and rapacious barbarians who fought to the death over the empty title of emperor at least once, usually twice, every generation.

Black Leg found some evidence that a Roman villa of considerable size had existed here once. But it was long gone now. Farms belonging to its tenants were piles of weed-covered rubble, and their fields so long overgrown that their boundaries could no longer be traced. He found wolf, bear, boar, and cat sign, but no indication that humans inhabited these scrub forest lands at all.

He trotted out on a rock spur that allowed him a view of the entire countryside. Behind him were the foothills of a mountain range that towered blue-white and fragile-seeming in the distance. To his left, the river gorge flowed out of the mountains, the bluffs falling lower and lower until they were gone and it ran unobstructed along the plain. Ahead the forest thinned out also.

Black Leg sat, lifted one hind leg, and prepared to scratch behind one ear. Then he realized, when his hind foot claws met a hard surface, that he was still wearing his helmet. When he changed shape, it had also changed to conform to the shape of his head.

He uttered the low whine that translated into, 'Why?' in wolf.

'I serve you.' The voice sounded within his mind.

Wolflike, he cogitated and did not respond. When she told him her name, the bird had appeared. It wouldn't go away, despite all his efforts to banish it. And she told him it was part of his geis and he must accept the creature's service.

Black Leg had not been happy, and was even less happy when she explained some of the various problems inherent in the relationship of a mere mortal like himself and a superior being like herself. They made peace in the usual way, then set out across the beach to find dinner. There was a large, clawed being living in the shallows

307

that resembled a spiny lobster. He collected a half dozen. She somehow found fuel enough for a fire, and they steamed the crustaceans and ate them. The claws being the most desirable parts, the meat was sweet.

After that, they lay in each other's arms by the dying fire.

'Can't I persuade you to stay?' she asked. 'We lack nothing here. Most people would see our situation as paradise.'

He was looking up, and he noticed the sky held no familiar landmarks. He felt a long, slow chill creep over his body even as his foster sister had when she also had been taken from her own time. Only his disorientation was worse, because the differences between this sky and his were so profound.

'Where are we?' he whispered.

'At the end of time or its beginning. I have never cared to investigate,' was her answer. 'I told you before.'

'I didn't fully comprehend it.' He sounded awed.

Then he began to weep silently, open-eyed. She took his hand and held it while the stars began to fall, streaking out of the blackness, cutting their paths of fire across the still, silent panorama of the universe.

'You know what those are?' she asked.

'Yes.' He nodded. 'The garden told me. So many things I didn't know, so many things I still don't understand.'

'The days and nights pass here much the same way as the tide rises and then falls. From time to time, a storm lashes the coast, but it passes. Sometimes it's a big storm; sometimes a small one. But it doesn't matter any more than the rise and fall of the tides. Nothing changes here; everything remains the same. I put a piece of fruit on the table, a ripe peach, and when I return a hundred years later or even a thousand, it's still as fresh-ripe and sweet-smelling as it ever was. The same, always the same. I melt into the water and let it brush me against the sand. I melt into the sand and am taken up as vapor and carried high up to where the stars shine even by day, and am a wisp of ice cloud forming a ring around the moon by night, a whisper of brightness across the blue by day. And after I have drifted this way for eons, I return and everything is still the same. The fruit just as ripe, the sea just as blue, the breeze refreshing as it was before I left. Nothing has changed or will change forever. I love you.'

'I know,' he whispered through his tears. 'I know. But I can't stay. It's not in me. I would die to bring some change here. In the end, I would grow mad or find my way home.'

'Yes,' she answered, soothing him as she might a troubled child. 'Yes. Tomorrow I'll show you the way.'

And she had, but stipulated he must take the helmet with him.

A wolf doesn't cry, and for a moment he considered changing just to weep. But then he pushed the problem out of his mind. The countryside was beautiful as the declining sunlight brushed the foliage of the trees to a mirrored sheen and drenched the earth with ruddy light. A harsh place with pockets of poor soil that supported only scrub oak and rather tormented, hungry-looking pines. But he thought it might have been better country before the Romans tried to farm it. And beyond the lowland forest, the plain was fertile. There would be people settled beyond the forest.

But not here. There was no one here. No human, that is. The wind blowing at his face would have told him if there were.

He dropped down from the rock and made a wide circle through the tangled forest. He found nothing and was crossing the river when he stopped to watch the water become a miraculous mirror of the changing sunset sky. He paused and dropped his muzzle into the water, then the helmet took wing and settled itself as a bird on a rock surrounded by water – water that mirrored the purple, gold, and red flares that filled the sky.

Black Leg abandoned the wolf.

'It gives you power,' Black Leg told the bird.

'Beauty always does, my lord.'

'My lord,' Black Leg said. 'What is this respect?'

'Not respect,' the bird said. 'Gratitude. You killed me. Now I can sleep.' The bird's eyes glowed red against its dense, black plumage. 'I'm dead. There is nothing in me but carbon and iron. I return only to ask help for my friends.'

'No!' Black Leg said. 'And I can guess who you are. The first. You put out my eye.'

'That I did.' The reply was accompanied by a raucous raven laugh. 'But in return, you were kind enough to kill me.'

Black Leg remembered something like a coal powdering between his teeth. 'You left a bad taste in my mouth. You still do.'

'Wait. You will encounter a taste of something even more vile. Only . . . it will be in your mind.'

'To hell with you!' Black Leg said. 'Or rather, go back to what you were and, geis or not, leave me alone.'

'No geis. Say rather, fate,' were the bird's last words.

A second later, the helm was on his head and the last light was fading from the water. He could smell the pork cooking in the distance. He donned his clothing and returned to the encampment with Red.

The pig was cooking over a pit of hot stones. They uncovered it and shared out a jug of wine.

'See anyone?' Red asked.

'No,' Black Leg said. 'Should I have expected to?'

'Sometimes. Three out of five times, we do. They break down into three categories: brigands, refugees, and soldiers the landowners send up here to try to dig us out.'

'Um.' Black Leg was pulling pork off the carcass and wrapping it in flat bread they had brought along. 'And?' he asked.

'Brigands, we run off. Refugees, we accept, if they swear to obey our rules. A column set to dig us out. . . .' Red grinned. 'That's pure profit. Been asked to dinner by any of the girls yet?'

Black Leg took a long pull on the wine. 'Um . . . a . . . yes. Two. Does that mean something?'

Red grinned wolfishly. 'Who?'

'Well, one wasn't much. A little dark-haired thing. Mona, she said her name was.'

Red whistled. 'Ho, boy. Mona. She doesn't . . . I mean, that's the hottest thing on two legs. She can fuck like a . . . I mean, you better be this long.' He placed his hands about a foot apart. 'And good for eight hours on your knees and elbows.'

Black Leg turned brick-red and almost choked on a mouthful of pork. Red pounded him on the back until he got the pork down, then gave him another drink of wine.

'I thought . . .' Black Leg gasped. 'I thought . . . she was being hospitable.'

'Oh, she's hospitable all right. She can hump all night. Who was the other one?'

'She was only a child.' Black Leg sounded shrill even to himself. 'Her mother, or maybe it was her stepmother, invited me—'

'Ho!' Red yelled. 'Let me guess. Magda!'

'Yes. But she's a young girl.'

'You're off to a good start, my boy. In a month you'll have run through all the available women. One time I was hunting high in the rocks. I startled a lioness. My bad luck. She didn't run. So I took it upon myself to supply the discretion demanded by our mutual situation.'

311

'You ran,' Black Leg said.

'So fast you wouldn't believe. She was a hundred and eighty pounds of tawny muscle, with four-inch claws and six-inch teeth. But she treed me.'

'Bad,' Black Leg said.

'Yes. But I still had my spear, and as I kept aiming it at her eyes, she didn't care to climb up after me. So there I sat whilst she paced up and down beneath until . . .' Red raised his finger. Black Leg cleaned a rib.

'Until the male showed up and I found out why she'd seemed so cranky. Before God, boy, it was a humbling experience. He jumped on her back, seized her by the neck. She screeched at the top of her lungs and they began. The sun went down, the moon rose. Then, sometime later, the moon set, the stars shone brightly. I grew so cold I near froze. My ass did freeze one ball, and my fingers, toes, and upper lip grew numb. But, by God, the two of them never let up.

'Once or twice, the ground being steep there, they braced themselves against the tree and damn near shook me out of it. Up to then, I had believed myself a great man. But that she-cat left me in the dust. Then come dawn, the lion gave out and she raked her claws across his shoulder and bit his ear before he slunk away.

'Then she looked up at me a bit soulfully. I thought . . . my poor wits were close to wandering by then, and just as I was about to break into loud sobs and beg for mercy, I heard the voices of Cregan and his men come to rescue me. They had set out in search of me when they realized I hadn't returned at nightfall. They scared her off, and I thank God for it! If ever I saw rape in the eyes of creature, it shone in hers.

'A near thing, that. So near that when we got back I crawled under the covers of my bed and sucked my thumb like a three-year-old for four days, until Cregan

312

melted some snow in a pot and poured it over me, bringing me at last into my right senses.

'I only tell you this, my boy, by way of warning you off dangerous females. For there's some in our camp that could outdo that cat and three more like her. Magda, she has six daughter-in-laws and twelve granddaughters. I wonder which four or five she wants you for.'

Black Leg had cleaned six ribs and was starting on a seventh. 'You are the most amazing liar,' he said.

'True!' Red laughed. 'Only too true. But it does help pass the time pleasantly, doesn't it?'

Turned out Red hadn't described the half of it. At least about Mona, he hadn't. He'd forgotten to mention she screamed like a catamount every time she came, and that was frequently enough to keep the whole village awake until almost dawn. Black Leg gave it his best shot, or rather shots – he lost count after six. And his prowess at other things besides fighting was duly noted far and wide.

His dinner with the seeress Magda was interesting, to say the least. She gave him the beautiful mantle that she had woven, the mantle that mapped the four worlds.

A very fine meal concluded with a plateful of honey and raisin cakes. The men were away running sheep to the high pastureland. But for Magda's nodding grandfather, there were no men at the meal, only the ladies, the eldest, Magda, in her sixties, all the way down to the youngest granddaughter of sixteen.

Black Leg sighed and rather reluctantly passed on the last honey cake. But when he looked up, he saw twelve pairs of eyes giving him much the same sort of look that he had bestowed on the honey cakes.

He fled, murmuring incoherent excuses about having to go on patrol in the morning. Cregan and the rest thought his eager and completely voluntary willingness to undertake this duty absolutely hilarious.

And the next morning before daybreak, he found himself moving downhill, armed with a spear and a very old falchion, a vintage but very ugly single-edged sword. It was one no one else wanted because it was a brute of a thing to swing. But once in motion, it was capable of shearing off a man's head and shoulder with one not very hard whack, and Black Leg liked it.

He was much stronger than most humans, and had a lot more stamina. He could swing the falchion easily for a half hour and kill everything he touched. Besides, he planned to hide it with his clothes and spear near the river and proceed as a wolf.

He did, and he was wolf when he came upon the party of Huns.

Igrane recognized him immediately and smiled like a shark sensing blood in the water. His whole body chilled, and he felt the weakness of an oncoming fever. Her bright beauty drained the vitality of those around her. Uther knew he was in the presence of a powerful, evil magic.

Igrane had been twenty years older than himself when they were married. When they stood before the altar and he'd closed his hand around hers, he had known Merlin was her lover. But he took her because Cornwall came with her, and he knew the dark sorcerer's powers kept her young . . . young enough to bear him a child, Arthur.

She got what she wanted – permanent power. It was still a man's world and once firmly in possession of the High Kingship, he might have been able to discard her. But she gave him an heir, one he badly wanted. One he loved. His son, Arthur. So he tolerated her cruelties, her betrayals, her more than occasional treachery with her mentor, Merlin, until the day he found her and her paramour torturing his son.

Storms battered the coast that spring. He had come to Tintigal for an ancient rite. The chiefs of the tribal groupings in Cornwall would gather at that haunted fortress with its ancient spring, and swear fealty to the high king. There is a footprint at Tintigal, a footprint in stone, said to have been made by a god that marked the spot where the high king receives the homage of his chieftains, and through them, his people. They do not kneel, these men, and neither do their women, but beat their swords and spear shafts against their big, leather-covered shields and raise a mighty shout as the high king places his foot in the sacred hollow in the rock stamped out by the ancient, nameless god. Then the women scream in the voices of sea eagles.

Three times the shout is raised . . . three times the eagles scream. For as it is said, one shout for a warrior, two for a chief, and three for a king. The eagle's whistling cry presages the fate of the king's enemies and at last the king himself.

There were no exact dates when this was to happen, and the day after his arrival the savage weather and high tides flooding the causeway to the mainland forced a postponement of the rite. On the second day the storm passed, leaving the sky blue and a fresh-washed clean-ness to the air. The many visitors managed to reach the fortress and find quarters, but the strong tides kept the causeway flooded and prevented many of the notables from making their way to the rock.

Igrane and Merlin feasted in her chambers and left the king to the drinking hall, where he did his duty and entertained his important followers. The nasty pair thought the rite had been accomplished on the second day and Uther, who took care not to linger in their vicinity any longer than necessary, was believed by them to have departed.

He had not.

Being hailed and shouted at was only part of his duties on such occasions. They were looked on by his supporters as auspicious times to request favors and make complaints. So he spent his evening in the hall listening to long-winded discourses as he was subjected to reams of unsolicited advice, venomous backbiting (they all tried to undercut one another), lengthy bouts of whining and sullen discontent, occasional attempts at extortion, blackmail, and downright unabashed and unconcealed begging and pleading for favors he would not, could not, and occasionally dared not, grant. This was what he got from the men.

The women were worse. They had seduction on the brain. They were – even the most ancient – the most overpainted, overperfumed (his nose ran constantly), underdressed, and dangerously corseted mob he had ever seen. At the feasts, he felt as though he were being confronted by every other pair of breasts and buttocks in his entire realm.

His oath men enjoyed the show, sometimes to the point of drooling delight, or unashamedly scored where and when they could. The disgruntled ladies, having worked themselves into a fury of sexual aggressions, sometimes – a lot of times – said what the hell and made assignations freely. Late in the evening, those not blind drunk crept away to keep these appointments in the many nooks and crannies of the vast fortress.

These experiments in infelicitous infidelity led to altercations – altercations Uther had to settle. Specifically, fifteen fistfights, six knife fights, four sword fights, and a moderate amount of regrettable domestic abuse. Not all the ladies were able to evade discovery by their husbands, and two required the services of Uther's personal physician.

While both law and custom allowed husbands to discipline wayward wives, many of the ladies' families were not very tolerant of that behavior.

You did WHAT to my sister?!

And Uther was forced to intervene to prevent a serious blood feud between two very powerful families.

By the time he had contained all this aggression and the participants began to drift back to their homes, Uther was exhausted and somewhat resentful. Most of his oath men were wearing broad smiles, but he hadn't gotten any. The king decided to rest before beginning his progress to the next of the almost constant crises that demanded his attention, and so he delayed his departure for a day. It was time to fight, and he was old enough to be weary of the endless warfare that was the lot of rulers in his world. It was pirate time.

The Irish would sail toward one coast, the Saxons the other. Serious logistical problems would arise, and he was considering how to deal with them this year when the screaming began.

There is Magic. No one else in the room heard it. His oath men were nearby, many of them dallying with women who had more complacent husbands. The room was filled with talk and laughter.

Uther rose from the table and went outside to the stair. A dreadful foreboding filled his soul. He knew 'they,' the witch he'd married and her paramour, were torturing something.

He was wearing soft leather boots; his feet were silent on the stone stair. When he reached the top, he realized the thing they were torturing was his son.

He had very little recollection of the next few minutes. He did remember the pain in his fist when he struck Igrane. Some teeth flew out of her mouth, and he (in that corner of the mind that is rational when the rest of us is not) considered that he might have killed her. He found himself indifferent to the consequences, even though they might be very serious.

He remembered hitting Merlin, the sorcerer,

two-handed. The blow to the chin must have lifted him from his feet, because Uther remembered his face rising slightly above his own, distorting as the man's jaw shattered. Not broke, shattered under the force of that two-handed strike.

He pulled his mantle off to wrap the boy in it, because the child's clothing was soaked with the filth the complete loss of control of all body orifices creates. He also remembered telling his oath men to kill anyone or anything that barred their way out of the fortress, and he was dimly aware that in a few instances, they had.

Night found him far from Tintigal, riding through the scrub forests that covered the low mountains near the coast. He and his men camped in a valley close to an ancient well. He cleaned the boy up at a stream that he knew originated in the mountains above.

The child didn't even flinch at the cold water, and Uther took great care to show no anger in front of Arthur. It was clear that the youngster was frightened enough already.

The well where they camped had no known significance; no chief or king lived nearby. But it had a priestess. She had come here long ago. The Christians hereabout accepted her as a saint. The others, who weren't Christian, understood she filled an ancient office as the keeper of living waters.

He climbed until he saw her house. As it was round, part of the earth, he understood it must be hers. She sat quiet in its pebbled dooryard, watching the sunset turn to twilight. An old woman now, they would place her bones in the house and collapse the roof. It would become a shrine. She would have no successor. The local Christian clergy would make sure of that.

As he emerged from the forest, she gazed at him, and he saw the light glow in her eyes. The boy wasn't afraid of her. No one old had ever done him any harm.

The old woman in the forest had had none of the spurious youth about her that Igrane and Merlin possessed. Gazing at the impossibly young creature before him now, Uther thought of the honest mantle of time that lay over his shoulders and that of all humans. Somehow Igrane had shrugged it off. So had Merlin. But remembering the suffering of the thing in the dog, he wondered if it had been an unmixed blessing.

This impossible Igrane's eyes were fixed on his face, and her smile grew more predatory by the moment. He felt as he had the night when the evil sorcerer spoke to him, a sharp sense of imminent doom. It seemed time stood on one side of him and death on the other, both ready to lead him to the marriage bed of the devouring witch. She would suck the seed from his loins and like a drone bee confronted at his once and final wedding with that immortal queen, he would wither away into the shadows, dying both ravished and emasculated.

He had seen the queens land after mating flights, the male insect's gonads trailing from the tips of their bellies, and wondered what it must be like for the drone meeting her high in the sky. The triumphant she – being the whole object of his existence and her merciless love his doom. Genitals ripped away, the lust spasms of his ravaged body transferring this ultimate seminal flow into the future of the race. Glory and death . . .

Aife touched his hand and the illusion of death and desire shattered the way a still pool fragments when a gout of rain troubles the surface. The frightening mixture of love and death vanished, and he was engulfed by the rank, reptilian smell of the snakes and the charnel stench of the pit. Igrane's face twisted in a spasm of fury so brief that Uther was sure no one else saw it. Then she turned to Severius, smiled, and pointed to him.

But the crowd of hangers-on and well-wishers was growing by the moment, and they surrounded the glowing couple and pushed Aife and Uther away from the objects of their veneration. Aife stood quietly, holding Uther's hand as the pair moved away, taking the company with them.

'Can't you feel it?' Aife shivered. 'It's cold, so cold. She freezes my blood. My brother said he had been approached by a wealthy heiress from the north.'

'Did he tell you her name?' Uther asked.

'Saraid,' Aife said.

'Best,' Uther translated. 'It's hardly a name, but I suppose she is in some ways the best.'

Aife lifted his hand. 'Good,' she said. 'It's not cold any longer. When I saw her come in, it seemed the entire hall was pervaded with shadows and an icy chill. But look.' She pointed to the windows above. 'The sun is shining. The gray skies are gone.'

Uther hadn't realized the windows were glazed, so dark had the day been, but now those to the west sent down long shafts of dusty light into the gloom-struck dining hall, almost making it look pleasant. The snake pit was empty; the pale serpents' eyes were sensitive to bright light, and they had taken refuge in the snake tubes that surrounded the open part of the pit. Here and there a rat's mirrored eye flashed as stray rays of brighter light found their way into the darkness at the bottom.

'She will be his newest.' Aife glanced through the double doors of the hall to the formal gardens where her brother and his entourage drifted toward the large main reception hall.

'Newest?' Uther questioned.

'Yes. He dangles the prospect of marriage to his vast lands and his influence with the Franks in Gaul before the face of every propertied woman he meets. They give him expensive gifts, then find they haven't enough money to persuade him to part with his freedom. They're probably lucky. Within a few months of marriage, they'd be dead. That's the name of the game in Gaul. Boys are paired with aging women. The women seldom last long enough to enjoy their pretty little plums. Not unless they are served by clever physicians who keep watch on their food. Sweet twelve- and thirteen-year-old girls are bestowed on mumbling old men.'

'Ummm,' Uther said. 'In that case, I suppose it's sufficient to let nature take its course. With that type of incentive, I suppose most of them . . . overdo it.'

Aife shrugged. 'Come to my rooms. Play for me.'

'I have no songs for women,' Uther said.

This was true. The music of his time was built around war. That was why some of the Greek thinkers hated and feared it. The other problem was that music could not be fully grasped by reason but spoke directly to the emotions and from them was imparted to the soul.

Those very rational Greeks and Romans feared and hated anything that would not yield to their vaunted rational analysis: music, religion, and woman are all mysteries, so they were feared, excoriated, and avoided by the philosophers.

Aife dropped Uther's hand and looked toward the snake pit, her eyes closed, lashes sweeping down to rest against her cheeks. A ray of sunlight illuminated her hair and sparked on the fair, golden lashes. Then she turned her face toward him and opened her eyes. The sunlight glowed out of them as it had when he struggled in illness and raging fever, sure he would die of the infection in his arm and just wanting the endless pain and uncertainty to be over. That bright, compelling, terrible gaze held his and would not let him turn and wander away into the final dark.

'Yes,' she said. 'Music speaks to war and warriors use the paean to drive themselves into a frenzy. The war horn drowns out the cries of the dying when armies clash face-to-face. The praise song is for heroes – those who die are

321

always heroes – and they are seen in epic song to be immortal in the minds of other men. But that is not where music was born, not where it attained its fullest beauty and power. Music is a creature of unreason, but then, so are love and death. Music is the speech the soul of man has with God, or whatever can answer the question. Why anything? Why not nothing? Why should the anything that is you or me, or the birds beyond the high windows that fly between us and the cloud-scattered blue sky, exist? Be here now together, breathing the air of spring? Oh, yes, my love, my beloved. When we reach my bower, you will have music for me.'

Black Leg treated the Huns as a wolf would. They analyze any sort of prey.

There were twelve of them, and in spite of the oldest, most seasoned warriors being Hun, the leader was a Pict. Since Kyra taught him the tribal Pict markings, Black Leg knew this one must be from near the Irish seacoast. The Huns had campaigned in the south of France, and this Pict had probably taken service with them.

Eight, by their weapons and armor, were Hun. Furred caps, oval shields, squat ponies, and a somewhat Eastern cast to their features. The Pict rode a tall horse, dark, as the Pict horses usually were. He remembered Kyra telling him that even the Romans had gone out of the way to try to capture horses from the Painted People. Being mounted on such a beast alone marked the Pict as a senior man and a dangerous killer.

The remaining three warriors were so scruffy that he could only make a general guess at their origins. He suspected they didn't have an affiliation with any people – not in the sense the Huns or the Pict did. The Pict probably had a family and some children. He might share his wife with a couple of brothers. But they would honor him if he returned and mourn him if he didn't. The Huns – he knew little of their social arrangements, but the red markings that blazed from their shields were similar and they very well might be related to the great Hun chief Attila himself. He knew barbarian chiefly families could stretch out to the twelfth or thirteenth degree and include hundreds of people. Even the slightest connection to a successful warlord was cherished, nurtured, and, often as not, lied about and exaggerated.

No, the remaining trio were the last and least, the wretched residue of Roman conquest, *coloni*, slaves, serfs, bound to the land, doomed to wear out their lives in silent, unrewarded labor. Opportunists and runaways.

One man is no man, he remembered Kyra saying. These were not men. They would die easily. The rest were the problem, and they would be a serious one, since they were escorting a wagonload of loot.

The contents of the wagon were tightly wrapped in oiled leather, but Black Leg could smell perfume, iron, gold, and silver. Yes, they have odors, especially when they rub against each other and small molecules are free to drift on the afternoon breeze. Silk, linen, and wool are rank to the wolf's nose, and they formed part of the contents, too.

The party followed the bottom of the watercourse, down toward the lowlands. They would not be easy to take. By day as the ox-drawn wagon rolled along the stony, shallow riverbed, the Pict leader sent outriders to scout the path ahead and cover both sides of the riverbank to be sure no ambush was being prepared. He chose the spots where they camped well, the highest ground for miles. Or, failing an elevated position, he took a grotto or cave in the riverbank that could be fortified against attack.

Black Leg shadowed them for two days and saw they were close to reaching the lowlands where they would be beyond Cregan's reach. In another two days, the river they were following would be out of the wilderness and snaking through cultivated fields on the plain. Black Leg was just about ready to break off his reconnaissance when he received proof that the dark Pict who led the party had spotted him.

The party had broken camp just at first light and ridden off into the pale, cool dawn mist when Black Leg entered the clearing on the river bottom where they had spent the night. He had to admire the leader's disposition of his forces. He'd made a fire, unharnessed the oxen to graze but left the loot wagon near the fire, and strewn blanket-wrapped logs around it while he and his men took secure refuge in the broken rock formations that formed the high riverbanks. As neat a trap for a party of careless brigands as Black Leg had ever seen. They would ride in, attack the blanket-wrapped logs, and be slaughtered by the men hiding in the rocks.

The wolf sighed, then moved in, investigating the campsite with nose and ears. Fire, ashes wet, completely out, very good. No telltale traces of smoke left behind to call future foes.

His ears said the party was moving away at the expected speed in the expected direction. Blood, an attractive smell to a wolf, coming from near the food preparation area. Scraps of red meat, large ones. He was moving toward the pile of meat scraps with a view of wolfing them down when the man in him brought his body to a halt.

No! Why?

He was wearing the raven helm. Suddenly it was a bird and with a loud raven alarm cry, it vanished into an oak overhanging the riverbed. Black Leg stood quiet, studying the meat scraps. At least half a dozen, still red and oozing blood. Deer meat. They were small, all except for one. Black Leg walked toward it, then pawed it with one of his forefeet.

The thing came apart and revealed the sharpened and barbed end of a rib bone tied in a circle with a soft, rawhide strip. A trap adapted to the wolf's gulp-and-swallow way of eating.

Had he carelessly swallowed the meat, his digestive juices would have dissolved the rawhide, and the rib would have sprung open and pierced his intestinal tract. Fighting such an injury with the change would have been a fierce and painful battle. One he might well have lost. Had he been a real wolf, he would have faced certain death.

The camp had been placed on a broad sandbank near a shallow ford between two deeper pools. Black Leg turned quickly and ran for the ford, but before he reached the water, the Pict loomed up before him on horseback, shield up covering his left, a large spear in his right hand.

Instinctively, Black Leg moved away from the spear. He didn't see his mistake until the Pict turned his horse and, gripping one of the high saddle horns, leaned over and slammed the edge of his shield into Black Leg's neck and shoulder.

The wolf gave a yell of sheer agony and panic as he felt his right leg go numb and his left collapse. *Death is upon me*, Black Leg thought, and felt only astonishment.

In a few seconds, he'd gone from early morning lethargy to mortal peril. He knew a second where his whole life was in the balance and was aware he must pass this test or die, because the Pict was turning and, within a second or two, his lance would be in Black Leg's body, through his heart.

Black Leg tried to gather his legs under him and, while he couldn't feel them, his kinesthetic senses indicated that his body had righted itself and was moving forward. The lance – its iron head edges gleaming as though newly honed – darted down toward him.

There was really only one place to go, only one chance. He used his powerful wolf haunches to push off, leaping between the horse's forelegs at the saddle girth. It was padded leather, reinforced with twisted hemp cord. He tried and failed to sever it with his teeth.

His weight forced the horse back on its haunches, forelegs rising as it half reared. The Pict was confused. The wolf should be on one side or the other, making a break into the broad, shallow ford – an easy target for the Pict's spear. But instead, it seemed to have vanished.

Black Leg chewed saddle girth as he had never chewed before, his half-numbed body swinging from side to side, the human in him praying to God that the Pict hadn't figured out where he had gone. The horse knew, and spun wildly in a circle, trying to shake him off.

And the Pict figured out what had happened.

In a staggeringly fine bit of horsemanship, he brought his mount under control. In place of stirrups, the saddles of the time had four horns. When the rider bent left, the left horns folded over the thigh and held it in position. The right horns did the same at a right bend.

Black Leg felt the saddle shift in the girth and knew the Pict was reaching under with the spear.

Nooooooo . . . It wasn't even a thought any longer. He let go, crashing down limply into mud and water at the river's edge. One of the wildly dancing horse's fore-hooves slammed into his shoulder, nearly dislocating it, and driving the breath out of his lungs.

The Pict backed the horse, ready to drive his spear into the fallen wolf's body . . . when . . . the saddle girth finally . . . at last . . . parted, sending the rider flying over the horse's rump, into the shallow ford.

The wind tore at me again, and dust blinded me when my eyes cleared. I saw Meth was moving, albeit slowly and carefully, one step at a time around the tower. My body was pressed against Cateyrin's and I felt her long sigh of relief.

'Oh—' she began.

'Be quiet!' I told her. 'He's moving. Be content! Follow him!'

'Y-y-yes,' she whispered, and suited her actions to her words.

When we made it around the building's curve and could see the dark archway that was our goal, things became much easier. It seemed no time until we were clear of our precarious position and standing out of the wind in a courtyard, looking back at the stair we had just used to escape Aunt Louise's attentions.

Meth was leaning against one semitransparent wall. 'My heart was trying to leap out of my chest,' he said.

'Here.' He seized Cateyrin's hand and pressed it against his left ribs. 'I don't think I've ever been so afraid before in my life.'

'My poor dear.' Cateyrin wound her arms around him. 'My poor darling.'

'My poor stomach,' Albe whispered. 'This is nauseating. What a whiner. Did he think the rest of us enjoyed that? I'll be forced to cut his throat soon if he doesn't shut up.'

'Shush. She wants him. We're taking refuge with her mother. Let's try not to poison the wine before we drink it.'

Tuau hunkered down beside me and began to cough, a disturbing sound from a cat.

'What's wrong now?' Albe asked, sounding bored.

Tuau got his breath. 'Goddam dust . . . bitch!' Then immediately began coughing again.

'Damn! Cateyrin!' I called as Tuau went on coughing. 'Where can we find some water?'

'In the middle of the garden,' was her reply.

Yes, sure enough, there was a garden under a light well in this courtyard also. But I hadn't noticed it because the light was failing. It was very small, only a shallow bed surrounding a basin into which water trickled rather than flowed.

'Yes, and what happens when we try to take the water?' Albe asked. 'Does something jump out of the ground and try to kill us? They're everywhere, these gardens.'

'Yes, we have to – food is one of our biggest problems,' Cateyrin said. 'And no, nothing will try to eat you for taking a drink of water here. Just don't pick the plants.'

'Perish the thought,' I said.

Tuau let fly with another string of honking coughs. He sounded as though he might strangle to death. I hurried toward the basin. Sure enough, there was a dipper. I filled it and brought it to Tuau.

He slurped, not lapped.

'Christ!' Albe exclaimed.

'She' stepped out of the darkness inside the black tower.

'The towers are glass, tinted glass, but if you are close enough to the walls, inside you can be seen,' Cateyrin explained.

She was very beautiful: bejeweled, wearing a head-dress, necklace set with glittering violet stones, gold filigree cuffs, and anklets that formed a mass of golden chain dripping with tiny bells. She studied us 'women.' I could see her thinking as her eyes rested on Albe and myself. Cateyrin received the same treatment, as did Tuau. Then she saw Meth.

She smiled; it was a bewitching one.

He ogled her and grinned back stupidly.

She lifted her arms to show off pink-tipped, perfect breasts, then turned to one side and bent over. I couldn't see him, not completely. He was only a shadow through the curved glass. But we all watched, fascinated, as he came up behind her, entered her body, and used one hand to stimulate her and the other to guide her hips back and forth over his organ in such a way as to achieve maximum pleasure for himself.

She turned her head and again smiled at Meth. He moaned, and fell back against the wall behind him and closed his eyes.

Cateyrin spun around and slapped him as hard as she could. He let out a yell.

'What was that for? I didn't do anything.'

'You were thinking about it,' she said between her teeth.

I glanced away from Meth and back at the glass wall. 'She' was gone and her partner with her.

'The show's over,' I said. 'Let's get out of here.'

Indeed it was growing darker and darker. We had no torches or any form of light with us, and it might be difficult to negotiate the stair.

'Maybe if we give Tuau another drink of water . . .' Meth began.

Cateyrin slapped him again. This time he hit her back. She staggered away, reeling, her nose streaming blood.

I heard Albe's sword clear the sheath.

'No killing!' I shouted.

'My lady, you're making life difficult for me. I can't think which of them is worse: his instant lechery, her frantic jealousy.'

'I be nod aleous!' Cateyrin shouted. I considered the possibility that her nose was broken.

I could barely see now, but this courtyard looked to have only one exit. I pointed toward it.

'Cateyrin! Is this the way to your mother's house?'

'Yeth.' Cateyrin was blotting her bleeding nose on her shirt.

'Then get going now. March! Move!'

Meth shot a fearful look at Albe. She smiled back – it was not a pleasant one, containing as it did elements of both threat and derision. Then he and Cateyrin obeyed.

'Take point,' I told Tuau.

'Oh, hell. Why can't . . . ?'

'I'm going to cut the throat of the next person who starts an argument about anything,' Albe said in a quiet, conversational tone.

Tuau obeyed, albeit grumbling under his breath, though not loudly enough to be clearly heard.

The stair spiraled down, and down. At times we had to feel our way through almost pitch darkness. At others, light shone through the semitransparent walls and we could see well. Besides light, I heard talk and laughter and even fancied I heard a word or two I recognized. But we could see nothing clearly, and though I had a sense of being in a densely inhabited place, we encountered no one else during our passage down.

At the bottom, the stair began to widen out. We were all winded and tired. I gave the order to stop. The speed and alacrity with which I was obeyed demonstrated it was a good idea.

Cateyrin's nose was still bleeding, and Albe moistened a cloth pad.

'My lady,' she said. 'May I call on your healing skills?'

I touched Cateyrin's face. The air filled with the pepper scent of roses.

'Oh, my!' Albe exclaimed. She was sitting on a step a little above Cateyrin. I was bending over them. 'Roses. Cateyrin, the air is filled with them. Where did they come from?'

'She's Danae. Tuatha de Danae,' Tuau purred. He was stroking himself against Albe's bare legs on the other side.

'Sit,' Albe said.

With a sigh, he complied. 'Mean. Mean. All of you, just selfish.'

'You will get yourself overexcited and try to take a bite,' she explained. 'Cats are like that.'

'Can I rub my cheeks on you? Oh, please! Please?'

Meth said, 'God, she was beautiful.'

'You idiot!' Cateyrin started to stand up.

Albe pushed her back down. 'Stop it. You have no claim on him. What he does is his own business.'

'You don't understand,' she wailed.

My hand had done good work. The swelling around her nose was down.

'Cateyrin!' Meth shouted. 'You're being a jealous bitch. I don't believe a word of those stories. They're all made up by skinny little twats like you or old baggy hags like your mother and her . . .'

'You ingrate. Keep your mouth shut about my mother.'

I clapped my hands and brought the screeching to a halt. 'Stop!' I commanded. 'Cateyrin, what don't we understand? Take a deep breath and tell me. Slowly and clearly.'

She gave Meth a nasty glance. He returned a sulky glare.

'She's a Circe! A Fand!'

I knew the names, but wondered what they meant here. Circe turned men into pigs and Fand was . . . well, no one was quite sure what Fand was. She came in sleep to men who were going to be mighty warriors. But some families sacrificed to keep her away, because she sometimes ruined them for real women and they took such chances that they were not long lived. So she was both courted and dreaded.

'Tell me!'

'She makes slaves of the men who come to her as lovers,' Cateyrin continued. 'She's like a drug. They can never get enough of her and they can never escape.'

'Nonsense!' Meth shouted.

'One at a time,' I ordered. 'Let Cateyrin talk.'

And talk she did. Seems many, not all, but many, who fell under the spell of a Fand were willing to do anything to remain in her company. They voluntarily allowed some sort of device to be placed around their necks that controlled them, and most of the farmwork was done by the Fir Blog and similarly collared men. The Fand, who started out as a real woman, became stupendously rich, long lived, and beautiful.

There were dreadful stories about men who wore away their lives in a semidream state, toiling in the fields under the sun – lost to their wives, children, friends, and other family members simply to be allowed to sit at the Fand's feet and adore her and sometimes touch her hand.

'It doesn't work on everyone,' Meth snapped. 'A lot just walk away after a few tumbles.'

'And you believe you are one of those?' Albe asked.

'Yes . . . yes, I do. We could have found refuge with her better than at your mother's place. It would be the adventure of a lifetime to have a Fand.'

'Why didn't you warn us?' I asked Cateyrin.

'I didn't think she'd come out for a party made up mostly of women. She only showed herself once or twice to me when I was young.'

'You are such a grown-up now,' Albe said, laughing.

'Since today, I am.' She did her best to look grim, but with her lower lip sticking out, Cateyrin seemed about eight years old.

'God help us,' Albe whispered. Then she turned to Cateyrin. 'Girl, what can we expect when we come out of this stairwell. You and Meth already said the streets aren't safe at night.'

Meth and Cateyrin glanced at each other. 'Well,' she said slowly, 'there are the gangs. Every street has one. In fact . . .' She glanced up the dark stairwell we had just come down. 'I'm surprised we didn't meet one here. I was afraid we might.'

'What do they do?' Albe asked.

'Una . . .' Meth and Cateyrin looked at each other again.

'We're not sure,' Meth said. 'They seem to do whatever they want to. Depends on what they think they can get. We were good children and always home before dark. So I'm not sure.'

'Oh, fine!' Albe said. 'Great! Wonderful! Brigands!'

'Maeniel says all cities have them,' I told her.

'We have a lot,' Cateyrin said solemnly.

'Why do I believe you?' Albe rolled her eyes.

Sarcastically, Tuau commented, 'We are a well-armed party and you are protected by one of the Akeru.' He threw a defiant glance at Albe. 'I'm not to be sneered at.'

A slow grin spread over Albe's face. *Oh, no*, I thought. It doesn't do to break down a warrior's confidence.

So I interrupted, 'We have some food and drink left. Let's finish it here and get moving.'

When I got up, my legs were stiff, my ankles sore. *I'm tired*, I thought, surprised. You see, I wasn't used to fatigue, not this kind. *Too much*, I thought. My mind was dulled by unexpected and dangerous events. If packs of brigands were awaiting us, I must be alert.

I closed my eyes and summoned my armor. It came and covered me with a vivid intensity I had not heretofore experienced. I glowed, my fair skin pinked by excitement and patterned in the speaking images my people used to express the complexity of life. The knot work and intricate, vining spirals that speak to our souls.

Once we used them on everything. They were carven into leather, wood, and stone, woven into cloth and intricate, colorful braids. When we couldn't speak each other's languages, we used these symbols to communicate. Before the ogam alphabet or the Greek were conceived, the wise among the peoples of Europe from the Out Isles to beyond the Rhine could mark the turning of the years, rising and setting of the stars, and even calculate the hours and moments by the shadows cast by the sun as it traversed its long arc across the sky. They are our everlasting prayers to our gods, abstract statements of a belief in the community of life and that of the living, the dead, and the yet unborn. I wore them on my skin and called on them for protection.

I couldn't see myself except in the eyes of others, but they looked satisfactorily impressed. Tuau's pupils widened, turning his eyes from emerald to black.

'My, my. I'd only half believed you were Danae. But now . . .'

'Let's go,' I said.

The stairs widened as we dropped down to the black tunnels that seemed to form the base of the city. The air felt damp and a mist filled the air. The lower we got, the more it thickened, until we were traveling in a gray void.

'Fog, thank God,' Cateyrin whispered to me. 'I had hoped for it.'

'Why, girl?' Albe asked. 'It makes it easy to ambush us.'

'Hush,' I whispered. 'Move as silently as you can. If we can't see them, they can't see us, and won't be expecting an armed party.'

We were no longer single file, but had spread out a bit. About then, we left the stair behind and were traveling in a tight group down the center of a corridor whose roof and walls were lost in the thickening mist.

'Where is the light coming from?' I asked Cateyrin. I was uneasy about it. The fog was illuminated in silver-white, as though by bright moon glow. 'Is the moon out?'

She glanced at me as though I had taken leave of my senses. 'What's a moon?'

I placed that question aside. I'll deal with it later, I decided.

'The light?' I repeated.

'Starlight,' she said. 'The roof here catches starlight and makes it brighter. Look.'

She pointed to an opening in the fog above and I saw them. Thousands of tiny hexagonal cells. Like the eyes of an insect, each with another tiny hexagonal cell in the center. The roof was lumpy with them, and they were of all different sizes. The brightest stars had large ones, the dimmer stars small ones.

'There are all sorts of things here that make light,' Cateyrin continued. 'Some good, some very bad. This is only one of them.'

I was about to ask what happened by day . . . when a terrible scream sounded not far behind us. Albe and I stopped, turned, and looked back.

'No! No! No!' Cateyrin tugged at my hand. 'God, no! Don't stop! Keep moving!'

Tuau was pressed against Albe's leg. 'It's a kill,' the cat muttered. 'I can smell the blood and torn guts from here.'

Cateyrin pulled frantically at my hand and, though she was white with fear, she didn't speak above a whisper. I cut my eyes at Meth. He also looked terrified. Albe and I obeyed and hurried along. I found I was shivering. The corridor was dank and cold. It grew perceptibly darker. I looked up and saw the roof was broken here, a big hole above us.

They rushed us just then.

CHAPTER SIX

MAKING THESE THINGS MUST BE work, Arthur thought as he watched and listened to the War Song approach him. It was in the meadow lower down yet, and there might be time.

Arthur sprinted toward the broken rock that edged the long drop into the pine forest below. Bax, the dog, followed.

Bad footing, Arthur thought as he reached them.

Bright as moonlight is, it still doesn't dominate the way daylight does, and the black shadows concealed hollows where a running man might easily break a leg or an ankle. Death – that would be certain death because the War Song would rip his body asunder with the same ferocity it did the trees and brush it encountered crossing the me

en right. The grass near the edge of the cliff and dry. It would burn. The wind from battered the edges of the meadow, vegetation and keeping it bone-dry.

w and sinew since he first used he plateau where he'd been im- War Song, and he'd been had grown greatly skilled at kindling fire. He crouched down among the shattered boulders and stony rubble. Bax howled a warning.

The screaming, wailing, and sobbing intensified as he saw the War Song had reached the slope that led down into his meadow of last refuge. Maliciously, it paused and, digging itself into the slope, hurled shards of broken rock in every direction. Bax yipped and crouched beside Arthur as one slashed his shoulder.

Arthur gritted his teeth and bowed his head to protect his eyes. He felt as though ice touched him on the cheek five or six times, on the arms once, along his ribs, and at his stomach.

'No!' He fought the desire to run. Now or never. This was the best spot, filled with tinder-dry, broken brush and wiry, dead grass. And he could tell why the wind from the glaciers above battered him. It also threatened to blow him and his fire-making materials into the valley below.

'Shush. Be still,' he begged that wind even as one missile bigger than the rest cracked against his forehead and skidded across his scalp. Blood dripped down into his right eye, blinding him as fire blossomed under his hands.

He looked up. The moonlight wavered as the thing came between his eyes and the silver orb. The screaming was deafening. For a moment, the wind did still, giving the grass all around the tiny pile of kindling time to catch, then leap with a roar into thick branches belonging to a winter-killed blackberry vine. They turned to ribbons of fire, carrying flame to the tinder-dry grass all along the edge of the meadow.

Bax fled toward the lake at the far end of the meadow. The War Song made a perfectly hideous sound that pierced Arthur's brain like a driven nail. The sheer agony in it staggered him. Then the War Song fled toward the thick green grass in the center of the meadow.

Arthur shook off the pain the dreadful yell caused him.

He had nothing now. The flames had burned away a lot of his shirt, and when he fled the valley below, he'd brought no weapons with him except a knife. That and his fire-making materials and his sling were lost in the blaze he'd kindled.

But he reached down and snatched up a clod of earth crowned by a swatch of flaming grass and hurled it at the War Song. A slender column of flame propagated along the outer edge of the whirling mass of debris, flying shadows and darkness that formed the center of the War Song. Arthur ran out of the flames toward the lake at the edge of the dark forest.

Then the flames died and the War Song pursued him again. It had no more rocks to suck up into his whirling, screaming substance, but it battered his body with clods of mud, whipping grass stems, shattered small branches, and stinging pebbles. He threw up his arm to protect his eyes and ran back into the fire. It was hotter now, the flames taking the grass roots filling in damp spots that hadn't caught at first and igniting the wood of the larger saplings that sprinkled the edge of the cliff. He snatched up another clod of earth, this one bigger than the first, and hurled it at his adversary.

Again, it backed. Again he was battered by the scream. His shirt was gone, his leggings smoldering. A stunted birch sapling near him was a tree of flame.

Ignoring the pain it cost him, he snapped the trunk with his hands and, swinging it two-handed like a club, ran toward the War Song. The flaming grass had done its work. A dozen small fires burned on the thing's surface, delineating the slender shape reaching up toward the stars.

Not enough! Still not enough!

He was so close he could feel the flailing and battering of the terrible winds it used to wreak its destruction on everything before it. He felt the bare skin of his arms and chest being flayed by their power as he slammed the blazing birch into the shadow thing outlined by the fires.

Perhaps the only thing that saved him was it tried to back up. It did, and then it roared up toward the stars in a screaming, almost infinite column of flame. The blast flung Arthur back and he landed with Bax in the shallow lake at the end of the meadow. *Whump!*

He staggered to his feet and realized the whole meadow had gone up. The radiant heat of the fire was scorching his face. He lifted an arm to shield his eyes and saw the hairs curl crisp and vanish.

He and the dog struggled into deeper water, toward the dark wood.

Deep, he thought. *But not deep enough.*

No normal grass fire could burn so hot as the plume of the flame that had been the War Song. Even in its death throes the thing was forcing him toward his doom.

He and Bax stood among the cattails near the thick, twisted oaks that formed the fatal forest. The small lake was a mirror of scarlet-yellow, twisting flame. The opposite edge was bubbling.

Bax whined softly. The water was warm. Arthur reached down with one battered hand and touched it. Not warm now. Hot.

The radiant heat was appalling. His face, chest, and arms burned. He and Bax turned, pushed their way through the thick stand of cattails and into the cool shadows of the forest.

There is a moment when desire rises so strongly in your body and that of your lover. And at that moment the only thought in both of your minds is, *Oh, God, where can we hide?*

In one leap, Uther reached that moment when her hand touched his. His body shivered with the force of his own need. How long had it been? He found he wasn't sure. After Igrane, there were only a few dim pictures of aging, lowborn women who were pathetically grateful for a king's attentions and the rich presents and increase in family status those attentions brought with them. And, indeed, he had been generous with the ladies and their families, if for no other reason than to salve his conscience about his uncaring use of their bodies.

But this girl . . .

Just then, the light faded from her eyes and she looked frightened. Aife returned.

'Yes,' Aife whispered, voicing his unspoken thought. 'Where can we hide?'

The dining hall was empty. He drew her toward him.

'Don't! Don't!' She spoke very softy. 'We will be on the floor. She has come! I see now the first time was only an imitation of what "She" meant for me. "She" sealed my womb for you. But tell me. Will it hurt? I was so afraid when I met the Horned One, afraid of the pain. But the drink wiped out my consciousness. Must I mix another?'

Uther's mouth was dry; he was only just barely able to speak. 'No.' But even as he answered, he found himself certain he was right and wondered how he could be so sure.

The vast hall was silent now. Sunbeams from the glazed windows high along the wall crisscrossed one another, a lattice of sunlight that formed a barrier to the monstrous forms, the knots of serpents, the fanged, clawed, winged, and scaled beings that populated the ceiling and the wall paintings that covered every flat surface in the room.

'This is an evil and unclean place.' As she spoke, he realized she was staring at the snake pit.

'No!' He unslung the harp from his back. 'No,' he repeated, opening the case and lifting the instrument from its scarlet brocade nest. 'Evil is a shadow, or so say the old ones, and that mad Greek Socrates. Evil is human folly, misunderstanding, misdirected good.'

'I wish I could believe you,' she said.

His fingers found the harp strings. 'This is my magic,' he said. 'A magic I abandoned for the sword so many years ago. I yielded to duty and forsook lore. But it returned to claim me. Hush and think only of the music.'

His hands caressed the strings. The great hall around them seemed to dissolve, leaving them standing alone in a sunlit meadow ringed by virgin forest.

'It is said,' she spoke, as if in a dream, 'that there is a place where lovers alone can go. A bright kingdom formed of air and light where none may intrude on their bliss.'

'Can we ask for more, beloved?' he asked. 'Tell me what you hear in the music.'

'The sounds of insects in the grass.' Her eyes closed. 'The sun on my face. It glows through my eyelids. The breeze on my skin. It cools and caresses me. The smell of air perfumed by meadow and deep, virgin forest. And from time to time, the sharp, distant tang from the sea. I hear also the forest sounds: a bird trill, the soft, whispered benediction as the trees answer the wind and the silence. When you have lived among others without respite, silence has a sound. A sound you long for, as I have longed for this. We're really here, aren't we? Somewhere else.'

He nodded and continued to play.

'Somewhere no one can touch us?'

'Yes.' And the music of the strings drifted into a simple melody, fair and ephemeral as a flower, fraught with the mystery of a beauty that changes forever and never stands still. The melody rose, arcing higher and higher, and finally vanished, glittering in the light.

He set the harp on the ground on top of its flat case.

'Keep watch,' he ordered the instrument as he

unwound his mantle and threw it on the ground. Severius had given him a fine one, and it was lined with red velvet. It formed a scarlet splotch in the grass.

'You have seen me naked,' he said. 'Now I want to see you.'

She turned, her eyes closed, and stood silent and compliant before him.

Overtunic, like a man's, off over her head. Blouse, like a woman's, easy – she hadn't bothered to lace it to the neck – also off over her head. No shift; she wore no dress. Only the tightly wound *strophium* concealed her upper body, her breasts. It floated away.

Her breasts were virginal, but she was not flat-chested, as she had seemed. He knelt before her, because the boots and leggings had to come off before the trousers and drawers. When he looked up, her body blocked the sun. Her hair was an aureole, a cloud of gold. Her blue eyes were open, and she was gazing down at his face, her hands rested on his shoulders.

When the leggings were gone and the boot laces undone, she stepped out of them. The drawstring that held up her knee britches simply snapped in his hand. A second later, they were down at her ankles. She wore only the loincloth, and it floated away the way the *strophium* had.

He touched her very carefully, touched the red-gold fur at the junction of her thighs, and found it moist.

'Afraid?' he asked.

'No.' She shook her head. 'Only wondering if I will feel your seed hot and thick spill against my womb.'

He wasn't sure where his own clothing went, but when he was naked, he put one arm around her shoulders, the other around her knees, lifted her very slight, light body, and placed it on his spread mantle. Red and gold, her body glowed against the velvet cloth.

'Possess me!' Her eyes were still wide. 'If the one-eyed stag in rut failed to do his work well, I would put the pain behind me.'

He took a deep breath, remembering her story about yielding herself to the ancient Horned One. As she said, the one-eyed Lord of the Wild had the tools to open a woman. But was such an experience a dream or reality?

He knelt and spread her legs open with one knee. They parted without resistance. He supported himself on his arms and entered her slowly, ready to withdraw if necessary. But except for a widening of her eyes, she seemed to have no reaction at all to his filling her.

She was warm inside, warm the way the sun is warm or porridge in the morning fills the body with its heat. Warm the way a fur mantle is during the winter. Her arms wrapped around his back, drawing him down on top of her. Her hips rose as she arched her back to pull him into her body as deeply as possible.

'Oh! What a delight,' she breathed.

The queen welcomes you, he thought, remembering the indifferent queen bee disemboweling and castrating the male to suck into her body every possible drop of his seed. If she did not feel some sadness at her consort's fate, he knew she would shrug and answer, *What would you have me do? He was born to die in just such a way. Of pleasure, of love.*

Her legs were wound around his hips; he could not escape their joining, even if he would. The pleasure seemed to spread from the center of his being, out and out, each wave claiming more and more of his body, until he was caught in a spasm of absolute lust and his seed almost seemed wrenched away to splash hot, silent, moist, against her womb.

But she was not the queen bee his instincts warned him about, and he found himself pleasantly relaxed, resting on her firm, young body when at last the fire faded to a scattering of coals. He eased off her breasts and cradling thighs and lay quiet beside her.

High above, clouds drifted past the sun, and the warm, golden light came and went. She cuddled against him and slept for a time. He knew he must have dozed also, because when he opened his eyes again, the shadow of the sentinel harp was longer, stretching far enough to touch their still-intertwined legs.

He sat up and ran his hand through his still-thick, graying hair and scratched the stubble on his cheek. *I must shave,* he thought idly, *or I will soon have a beard again.*

He glanced down at her and saw her eyes were open. They both rose and dressed, then walked hand in hand to the edge of the meadow, to the forest. When they reached it, Uther saw that the trees were very old and scattered in groves over an open parkland. They were all oaks, and rich producers of acorns. The ground under the trees cracked with each footstep. It was bright under the long, low-spreading oak branches, and there should have been more brush and undergrowth beneath the trees. But then he saw in the low damp places the multiple cloven tracks of deer and elk and knew they must find a rich grazing ground here.

Beyond this grove, he looked into another meadow and another grove, and beyond that, at the long, smooth-sloping fall of a riverbank. His eye caught the glint of sun on water.

His blood remembered places like this kindly – his blood, his soul remembered their richness, their beauty. In the spring the river was filled with salmon; through the summer, other kinds of fish. The winter acorn/ hazelnut crop was dried, and the acorns leached of their bitterness by flowing water were sufficient to make bread and porridge. In the autumn the boar fattened on acorns, feasted the people. Come winter, deer and elk and, to a lesser extent, her wild cattle, the aroches, were a year-round meat resource to be taken when needed.

'Look!' She pointed to the left, and he saw the barrow.

It was on high ground, near the river, and it looked out over the flowing freshets of living green land toward the more savage and ancient salt sea beyond. But the stars that rose over the river and the sea were the same.

The mouth of the barrow was pointed away from them, and they couldn't see if any of the dead lay at the entrance waiting for the dark of the moon, waiting for the wheeling stars to claim them.

'Time – outside of time,' he said softly. 'Does this still go on?'

They were standing hand in hand, gazing out over the golden countryside, breathing air so pure it seemed permeated by the light that sparkled from the flaxen grass, the shimmering tree leaves, and the glittering river, both of them filled brimming with absolute peace. He heard the whisper, the sound of scales sliding in the dry grass stems, and smelled the noxious reptile reek.

He spun around and saw it was already between him and the harp.

Aife turned when he did. She gasped and screamed. It was the biggest snake he'd ever seen and it was flowing in a diagonal, across the clearing to crowd him away from the musical instrument resting on its case near the mantle he had thrown down when they made love.

Very deliberately, he pushed Aife away and moved back, so as to direct the snake's head toward him and allow her to flee toward the harp.

'No!' she gasped, and stretched out her hand toward him.

'No!' he answered. 'No! There is a child!'

She looked down and touched her belly. By now the dreadful thing was between them. The stink was overpowering.

Thirty feet, Uther thought, *if it's an inch. And it's dead. God! It's dead!*

It was dead, a golem of a serpent, skin stretched over the long, curving spin with its bone arches, the same skin covering an empty-eyed skull with what looked like hundreds of long, sharp, recurved teeth.

'Take the harp.' He motioned her toward the instrument. 'It will protect you.'

Indeed, the sense of cold and dark was closing around him, but the graceful instrument stood in the now seemingly distant afternoon sun. She ran toward the instrument.

Then the meadow was gone, dissolving into a silver wave that darkened as it arced over him, white foam at the top, green glass slowly melting into a shiny obsidian black at the bottom. He threw his arm up against the sledgehammer blow of the breaking sea, but it slammed him down – not into choking black water, but against unyielding stone. The force of the blow drove the breath from his body and his vision shattered into shards of light.

He heard someone laughing and knew the voice: Igrane!

When his vision cleared, he found the meadow was gone and he lay on a stone floor, looking up at the wrath of a boiling sea as it pounded a crystal dome above his head. To one side of him, he saw light. It emanated from a source on the floor near him.

Igrane laughed again. He looked up at her. She stood three shallow steps above him. She was wrapped in a red velvet robe lined with silk. He could see the lining at the neck and sleeves, black against the bloodred.

He sat up, glad the serpent thing was gone. He was thinking, *Why? Why doesn't she just kill me?*

Above, the waves sucked and pounded at the transparent roof, and a swirl of green seawater would darken the glass and the room beneath. Then the stormy tide would ebb, and the sun would shine down into the domed chamber.

'He is a prime source of power,' someone said, 'could you but wring it out of his body.'

'And then I would be Merlin,' Igrane said.

'Yes,' was the answer.

It took Uther a moment to make out the speaker, black-robed as she was in the darkness of the vast hall. The first thing he saw was the twin sparks that formed her eyes. Then he found he could make out the face with the papery, mummified skin stretched tightly over the bones and the permanent, lipless grin of the teeth below.

'My lord husband,' Igrane said mockingly. 'Meet my friend, Ustane. It was her little pet who trapped you.'

'He can see me,' Ustane said. 'I'm surprised.'

'Yes, I see you only too well,' he said. 'You're dead, aren't you?'

'To all intents and purposes,' Ustane answered.

Igrane stamped her foot, a look of pique on her face. 'Enough of this jabbering. The less he knows, the better. I'm not looking forward to this either. Summon your servants, Ustane.'

The corpse in her black robe made neither sound nor gesture, but two figures appeared, one on either side of her. He could see enough of their faces to know they were as dead as she was.

'My lord,' Ustane said. 'Please remove your clothing.'

'Yes, get naked, darling,' Igrane said.

The king rolled over, then got to his feet. From a standing position, he could see the light source much better: an X, or rather two crossed lines glowing and flush with the floor. A Saint Andrew's cross.

The king knew the Romans sometimes crucified their victims that way as opposed to placing them on the upright Christian cross, as they had Christ. He'd heard once that there was some argument among the *carnifices* (professional slave drivers and executioners) about the two methods, the X as opposed to a simple crossbeam. Many of them felt that the X method allowed the victim to linger and suffer far longer than those suspended from a simple crossbeam, who usually perished from suffocation in a matter of hours. Whereas those on the X-shaped cross were pinned to the wood and must wait for hunger and thirst or extreme heat and cold to do their deadly work. Usually that took days, allowing for long survival periods, especially if the weather was good. A few hardy souls might last for a week or more.

The king suddenly found himself physically ill. He felt dizzy; his vision blurred as he fully grasped the implications of his predicament.

'If you please, my lord!' Ustane repeated. 'Undress, or my servants will strip you. And I promise, they won't be gentle.'

He glanced up at Ustane's servants and saw they seemed to be more sinewy and more greasy than Ustane was.

'They are capable of manhandling you, never doubt it, my lord,' Ustane warned him. 'They are constructed for strength. After I died, I was boiled and dried. But the sinew, muscle, and fat were stripped from their bones. Then the long, white fibers that make living things able to move were replaced, then packed in boiled muscle and corpse tallow before the skin was sewn back over their bones. They feel no pain, and are a wonder where strength is concerned.'

'I'm sure they are,' Uther agreed politely. He began to undress.

When he was finished, the two came down the steps and placed him on what he considered the Saint Andrew's cross. He adhered the same way Igrane had. He found he couldn't move. He closed his eyes and understood that he lay on the vortex of immense powers.

But what they were and how they were structured, he couldn't possibly imagine. He felt as he had when he first encountered a giant storm at sea.

He had been going to France to bring back his brother's bones and was on the channel when the blow began. The Veneti captain had no chance even to get the sail down; the wind carried it away moments after the storm began.

The Veneti lashed themselves to the ship. Because he was a prince, the captain tied him to the mast. The last thing the man screamed in his ear was, 'There is nothing else to do but hang on and pray!' He'd screamed the words over the shrieking of the wind.

The captain hadn't been fast enough about tying himself down, because the next breaking sea, a monster high as a mountain, dragged him fighting and clawing overboard into an ocean boiling with the fully unleashed fury of the wind.

Uther opened his eyes and saw Igrane standing at his feet. She was still wearing the robe. As he watched, she let it – or commanded it to – fall open, and her nude body glowed against the black silk.

'You see, my darling,' she purred. 'All you need do is make love to me. It's very easy. No chore at all. Consider how easily you pleasured that little sweetmeat sister of Lord Severius.'

She shrugged, and the robe dropped to the floor.

Lord! Lord! Yes! She was beautiful, more beautiful than when he had first possessed her on their wedding night. She had never met the standard of pale, blond beauty that seemed to be most admired by the present generation. She was tall, long-waisted, with a mass of straight, blue-black hair that hung down to her waist, a perfumed, silken curtain. Her long legs made other women's look short and stubby. The beautifully formed breasts and buttocks came as a surprise on her slender frame.

She smiled languorously at him, seductively, as though she were the one at his mercy, not he at hers. Her sex was shaved clean, a pale, plump mound between her thighs. She reached down and parted those ivory labia, exhibiting the scarlet, moist paradise within.

'I'm ready. My juices are a fountain. See how ready I am?'

She began to walk up between his spread legs. His body was responding; he felt it draw energy from the floor where he lay. Again he thought of the queen bee's marriage. Did the drone – soft, relaxed, lazy but always quiveringly ready to accommodate the (to him) immortal queen – did he know that his first union would be his last? Did he guess his pleasure would end in agony as he was castrated and disemboweled?

But perhaps it didn't matter. The urge was so massive, so powerful, so intense, it couldn't and wouldn't be denied – by the insect, by the man.

His buttocks were tightened, and he knew he was getting the erection of a lifetime. He closed his eyes. He was throbbing with desire now. Even with his eyes closed he could see the light emanating from the X-shaped cross. It shone through the thin skin of his eyelids and came up and went in time to the beating of his heart.

The touch of her hand on his thigh electrified him, and he realized she must be on her knees between his thighs. His eyes opened, and he found he was looking up, watching the waves breaking over the dome above. The effect was almost hypnotic. The water swirled deep green, frothed out at the edges, then withdrew, draining away and letting in the light.

He knew with a cold certainty that he would die here. But he didn't want to die handing Igrane something she obviously thought would gratify her intensely.

Both of her hands rested on his upper thighs now, and he knew in a few seconds she would slide his penis into her body. He kept his eyes fixed on the ceiling, knowing that if he looked at Igrane's impossibly beautiful body, whatever will he had left would be dissolved and he would yield to the burning need that seemed to control his body.

The dome above was a mosaic of triangles. In his youth, he'd studied the mathematical philosophies, and he saw, as he heard in music, the subtle workings of a mathematical order that could not be expressed in words, in the form of arching structure that seemed almost dynamically to leap over him, heading out to sea.

As he watched, it splintered into a thousand triangular windows, each with its own individual view of the green, lacy water sweeping over the top. And it was borne upon him that, though the picture in each triangle was the same, the view was slightly different in each, as though he gazed at one picture through thousands of different eyes and no two of those thousand eyes saw quite the same thing.

Then, as it had been for Igrane, the dome became a myriad of mirrors, each showing him her unearthly beauty as she knelt straddling his hips. Her fingers closed around his erect member, and she guided it toward the scarlet oval between her pale, nude labia.

He understood the trap was closing now. His eyes closed again, and the darkness behind his lids reminded him of the tomb. His eyes opened one last time in the tomb, and he studied the harp case in the light of the lamp. One lamp they left burning until the oil was exhausted and the spirit of the dead man departed, setting out over the sea of eternity to other shores. They hoped.

But did it? Or was this last, lonely essence that huddled beside the withered mortal flesh that had been its dwelling all that remained of what had been a complex individual human being, who, self-aware, thought, loved, hated, and with his fingers on the harp strings, cheated the magic of musical sound? Was this why they left the lamp, so that this scrap of soul could know his closest companions, the love of his life, accompanied him into eternal silence and darkness?

The shade penned in the tomb studied the flame of the lamp. As the shadow watched, for he was just that, but a shadow of what he'd been, the flame at length reached the last oil, elongated, rose up and up, until a narrow spire, it licked at the low stone roof of the tomb. Its final, smoky flare stained the rough rock-cut ceiling with soot, then died, leaving silence and darkness in its wake.

Now there was nothing left but the harp. The eyeless spirit could feel it. It was he and he it.

Igrane screamed.

Uther was jerked out of his trance.

'He's gone!!! He's gone! What happened? I had him. I was about to take . . .' She broke off. His eyes were open. They looked into hers.

'You son of a whore!' she screeched. And kicked him hard in the balls.

His body jerked and he sat up, clutching at his groin. She was barefoot, so the pain was limited, but it was bad enough. Even through his pain, he began laughing.

Igrane glanced at the two golems. 'Kill him!' she shrieked.

'No!' The voice rang harsh and metallic, and Uther realized it was Igrane's lady corpse-in-waiting, Ustane, who had shouted. 'Are you out of your mind, my lady? You might search for a hundred years and never be able to seize another opportunity like this one! He is ideal for your purposes.'

The vast domed hall was in shadow, the light faded from the symbol on the floor. Outside, above, the tide was rising, and the green seawater beginning to cover the dome. Whatever power the glowing symbol had to hold his flesh to it was completely broken, and Uther managed to wiggle to one side, out of its reach.

Igrane stood near the discarded scarlet robe. She snapped her fingers, and the robe rose. The sleeves slid over her arms, and it draped itself over her shoulders. She was pale with fury, her face perfectly white with it. Even her eyes seemed drained of color: gray crystals set in alabaster.

No, he thought. She was no longer quite human. She had deferred destiny too long. Slow the change was, but cumulative in its effect. Bit by bit, whatever was mortal in her was being replaced by something else that lived in this place. And which, in the end, would change her into something as alien to humanity as the foaming sea outside or the creatures imbedded in the floor with the shapes of shells, fish, worm, tubes, and even anemones that once inhabited a sea but now were caught crystalline shapes imbedded in the black rock that floored the room. Changeless, eternal, beautiful in their glittering decoration, but dead, all true life forever lost to them.

He laughed again. Even he was not sure why. Certainly, she would kill him. He had evaded her attentions. Even as he had triumphed over the spirit in the dog, so he had won a victory, a small one, and frustrated her desires. Maybe he shouldn't have bothered, but had she formed an alliance with Severius – and he was certain that was what she had in mind – together they might bring the High Kingship to complete destruction and their barbarian armies manage to extinguish his people's last foothold on the earth.

But for all his reasoned knowledge that he had taken the proper, moral course of action, he cringed with fear, knowing that he would be punished – probably horribly punished – for what he had done.

He was right.

Igrane screamed, 'Bring me a whip!'

He didn't believe a human could suffer so much without dying. Without even losing consciousness. After the first few minutes, he began to crawl, trying to escape the blows that opened his skin like the cut of a razor and raised weals as thick as his thumb. He found himself leaving a trail of blood that crisscrossed the gigantic, domed chamber.

When she grew too tired to swing the thing any longer, she transferred it to one of the sinewy golem corpses and the flogging continued until he had not the strength even to wiggle along on his belly in a vain attempt to escape. And he lay silent, wishing only for the end.

At this point, Ustane's remonstrances took effect. Ustane began screaming, 'Do you want to lose everything? Everything? You cannot tell what the effect will be if you kill him here.'

'Why shouldn't I?' Igrane was seated on one of the velvet couches, getting her breath and drinking a cup of wine. 'You said yourself, I am mistress.'

'Not – quite – yet!' Ustane's tone sounded like one rock being dropped on another one, a hard, dull thud. 'He has magic.'

'Magic!' Igrane forced a laugh. 'He is impotent! That is not magical in an old man.'

'That symbol would raise a corpse. Indeed it has. It is practically impossible to be impotent when lying on it, as well you know. The kind of magic that would stop the transfer of power through him to you is awesomely powerful.

'Faugh! You are like a child playing with fire. Neither knowing nor caring that the pretty flame can burn.'

Igrane's face twisted, and for a moment there was nothing beautiful about it. 'I want him to suffer.'

Lying on his belly, with his cheek against the icy black floor, Uther found his voice and whispered, 'And that wish to see suffering takes precedence over all other things, doesn't it, my queen?' he asked ironically.

Igrane leaped to her feet.

'Stop!' Ustane commanded. 'Think what you do! What "He" would have you do.'

'Very well. Then tell me, since you're so wise in the ways of this tomb, this empty mausoleum.' She gestured at the vast domed chamber that surrounded her. 'You tell me what to do now!'

Ustane moved across the floor. Uther wondered if she walked or did her ruined feet simply slide across the glassy surface, drawn alone by magic. In a few moments, she stood over him. *Odd,* he thought through his pain. He seemed to see through the thick, black robe she wore. Her body was that of a corpse buried for a long time. There was some roundness to her legs and arms where dried muscle and sinew had been placed over bone so that she was able to move. But her body was skeletal, with parchment skin stretched over bone except at her midsection, where she was empty as a basin between her leathery pudenda and the sternum that held her ribs in place. He could look into the hollow and see the dried, blackened muscle that sheathed her spine.

He closed his eyes and found he could still see her, and just as clearly as if she stood in the sun.

Magic! he thought. But what is magic? The horror that was Ustane had told Igrane he had magic. If this was what it was, it became simply another torment.

'He is not badly hurt,' Ustane muttered, surprised. 'Why is he not half-killed?'

'He's tough. He always was. He and that son of his. Twice he faced Merlin down, threatened to burn him. Merlin was always afraid of fire. Fire and cold iron. I don't know if he would have been able to do it, but Merlin was afraid he might. And I've seen enough of that old man to know if he decided on a course of action, nothing – and I mean nothing – would turn him from his path. I warned Merlin that he should kill Arthur and now I'm warning you, Ustane. The best thing to do would be to kill Uther now.'

Ustane's voice was a dry whisper, and Uther wondered how she made the sound, because the lipless, noseless face didn't move.

'No, in this strange place, he might be more dangerous dead than alive.'

'Very well. What? And be quick about it, because I want my supper and a bath. Then my maids can dress me. Severius will be expecting me at the banquet tonight.'

'He is trying to use you, that one,' Ustane said.

'Ustane, do you like lying imprisoned in your tomb?' Igrane asked.

'No, my lady.' Ustane managed to sound submissive.

'Then give me no further advice about a game I understand even better than you do. Sweet, cruel, stupid Severius will be bridled and led to slaughter just as easily as any of the cattle that graze in his meadows. He wants to be emperor, king, or whatever they're calling themselves now, and rule what's left of the empire from Ravenna. I've a good mind to let him. Then he might almost be worth sucking dry.'

Disaster, Uther thought. Disaster for his people. A combination of Severius and Igrane could – would – strip the kingdom down to its bare bones as thoroughly as a savage flock of sea eagles stripped the flesh from a corpse, leaving nothing. Not even a memory of a kingdom where justice, mercy, and truth prevailed would remain.

At least I will die. I will die and never know. Pray to fall as the warriors in Gaul who faced Caesar prayed to fall, before they saw their wives become the prey of a victorious army and their children's brains dashed out or those old enough to work sold as slaves.

But perhaps Ustane was right. Here in this horrible place, he could die.

'A tomb,' Ustane murmured. 'A tomb. Certainly, a tomb.' She raised a skeletal arm and beckoned the two golems. 'Fetch a litter,' she said.

Uther was loaded on the thing. It amounted to six straps stretched between two poles. They wrapped a sheet around him. Or at least, it looked like a sheet, white and flat. It did move of its own volition more or less, as Igrane's robe had.

'Why bother?' Igrane asked.

'We don't want him to drip,' Ustane said.

Yes, Uther thought. The weals that covered his body wept fluid and slowly oozed blood. *Yes!*

And with his mind, he ordered the sheet to form a funnel at one of the lower folds. It soon grew saturated, and he felt it dampen the cold stone floor under him. And when the two golems lifted his body, a mist of fine droplets scattered and fell with every step they took.

'There is a way to persuade him to cooperate,' Ustane said.

'How?' Igrane asked.

'Promise him a clean death.'

'No!' Igrane said. 'I will have him as a servant, waiting on me hand and foot for the rest of eternity. Because you're right, Ustane. Here he might be more dangerous dead than alive. So I shall make a present of his undying death to myself, regardless of whether we can torture him into compliance with my wishes or not.'

Ustanc shrugged.

Igrane walked over to the litter and spat down into Uther's face. He felt the wetness on his cheek and lips. He could see her as he saw Ustane; her body glowed through the robe. She was beautiful, sculpted the way a statue was. Her will, augmented by something else he couldn't clearly comprehend, gave her form and substance.

The sight of her almost undid his resolution not to react to her beauty. Almost, but not quite. The raw bodily pain he was in dragged him back from the brink.

'You are going to your tomb,' she told him with evident relish. 'There you will lie in silence and darkness at my beck and call forever.'

Then she turned away, saying, 'Take him, Ustane. And when you return, a light supper. I won't want to make a glutton of myself at the feast. I think quail glazed with honey. A salad of wild greens with a touch of citron and oil. And split, roasted capon stuffed with mushrooms. And prepare my bath. Scent the water with . . . I don't want anything too harsh.' She dithered. 'What do you think?'

'Oil of rosemary,' Ustane suggested.

'Perfect.' Igrane snapped her fingers.

'Wear rubies, topaz, and amber, but add heavy gold bracelets. You want to hint at wealth, not display it too openly,' Ustane said.

Igrane nodded and glided away into the shadows.

'When you reach the sea view room,' Ustane said, 'you will find your dinner waiting there.' But Igrane was gone.

Ustane signaled the two litter bearers. They lifted the stretcher. The king cried out in pain.

'You shouldn't have crossed her,' Ustane said. 'Had you done as she wished, by now you would be dead and beyond all suffering.'

'Dead as you are dead?' the king asked.

'Yes,' Ustane admitted as she led the way into the shadows. 'But dreadful an apparition as I am, death places me beyond suffering. As in time, it will place you.'

'Ah, then I can rot, as you have, but not die.'

'Yes. That is the way of it here.' Ustane whispered something, and a silver cup appeared in her hand. She whispered again and light appeared from the cup. Not in it; the light source was a star two or three inches above the cup. The light grew and Uther saw they were indeed carrying him through a crypt.

Was this place built? Uther asked himself. Or did it grow out of the ink-dark rock that formed the floor? Had it been built by human hands, the pillars and ribbed vaults that supported the roof would have been symmetrical and all close to the same size. Not so here; rather it seemed they traveled through a forest and the pillars were drawn up from the floor, the way glass is drawn into spirals to cover a cup. Then, when they reached the ceiling, they spread, arching out the way the branches did in an orderly disorder to create a stone ceiling decorated with a profusion of gems.

Gems. Yes, he saw their dull fire in the faint glow of the lamp.

Almost without thinking, he willed it to grow brighter, and it did – with a sudden flare that startled the corpse woman Ustane.

Abruptly, she cried out, and the litter bearers paused. Uther did see that the crypt resembled a forest in that it stretched away on all sides, many-pillared as the deep woods are. The ceiling was filigreed with amethyst, ruby, sapphire, cloudy and clear emerald, topaz – multiple shades – and gold-encrusted quartz.

Yes, there were tombs, and he could clearly see their contents: twisted, contorted things. All buried alive amidst the beauty, each mouth agape, eyes – where eyes remained – staring fixed on the absolute horror of their doom.

On each tomb an effigy rested, an effigy of the thing beneath. Odd. Though the corpses were wracked with anguish, arms up in many cases as though they had pounded the stone lids of their coffins, the statues reflected only peace.

At Ustane's cry, the lamp obediently dimmed again. She glanced around the vast, dark hall.

'That was you, wasn't it?' she asked.

'Yes.' No point in denying it.

'Now you know what you face. I will bury you. Tomorrow or the next day or the next, she will call you. Or maybe she will never want to be bothered with your tomb at all, and you, like they, will remain a shriveled, witless, frozen thing . . . for all time and all eternity.'

'Silence and darkness,' he said. 'It is all the best of us can expect. Silence and darkness. I will not be her "thing" then, as you are.'

He felt a cold anger mixed with a ghostly yearning and longing.

'I loved the night.'

He heard the words even though he knew it was not Ustane doing whatever she did to speak. The voice was a young girl's, and it seemed to come from a great distance, like a sound carried by the wind.

Ustane signaled the bearers again, and they started off. He found they were on a stair, a spiral stair with broad, shallow steps.

'We are going down to the very bottom,' Ustane said.

Down. The king closed his eyes and his senses said *up*.

He opened his eyes, and they still said up. The litter was tilted, his feet higher than his head. A stair. But a stair is between one level and another. All around him, the crypt, the forest with trees of stone and leaves of enduring fire at the roof stretched out. But perhaps it was a stair, because the floor of the crypt undulated, the pillars set like a forest on a hillside.

Then they broke into the light and the evening sun almost blinded him. The crypt was gone. Instead, they were carrying him through a forest. The trees were huge. Never had he seen such things. Their roots were as thick around as his body, and those were the small ones. The tombs . . . yes, the tombs were still there, but they were broken and misaligned as the massive roofs of the giant trees tore them up the way an old oak tips up a pavement. Some were canted so far up that they seemed to rest on their sides. Others were buried under the spreading mass of a tree's giant trunk as it grew over it. Others were buried in a litter composed of fibrous red bark, small needles, broken branches, and almost absurdly small cones.

What majesty, he thought. They were, those trees, majestic, towering so high the tops were lost in the cloud of high coastal fog. They grew on a slope that stretched down to the sea. The evening sun drove shafts of orange, golden light down among the giants and the whole hillside was dappled with its warm light.

'We are nearing the bottom,' Ustane said.

He was wondering where she was or thought she was when the litter bearers came to a stop beside an open tomb. It was half-filled by loam, the soft, thick bark, leaves, and cones of the giants above. It had a good smell.

They lifted him from the litter and again he cried out as they moved him to his bed. It stood directly in the shadow of one of the trees. Ustane gave another command and the two litter bearers lifted a broken stone lid.

He lay in a stone box, but the lid they placed over him was shattered and covered him only to the waist. But it shut with a satisfactory grind of stone on stone.

Then she and the golems departed and left the king lying there, still in pain, but at peace, listening intently and lovingly to the music of wind in the forest and the sea on the shore.

The very look of them jolted me. Mine, or if you like, the one that tried to kill me, had filed teeth and a face crosshatched with blue scars. But my father knew what he had been doing when he gave me my armor. Filed Teeth's first underhanded thrust skidded on my belly, and I slammed my sword hilt into his temple as hard as I could. He looked dazed, but wasn't knocked unconscious, and going down, his teeth fastened on the wrist of my sword arm.

They weren't ornamental, those teeth. He wore some sort of blades fitted to them; they slashed through my armor and a savage pain shot up my sword arm. I almost lost my grip on the hilt.

But someone – Albe – thrust a dagger into my left hand. I shoved the blade into his left eye. He let go of his grip on my wrist to scream and fell away.

I whipped around and Tuau was showing his worth. He was on the back of the most gigantic man I've ever seen, trying for a kill-bite. He was failing, because the giant's muscles were so massive, his fangs were caught in the blubber covering the neck and shoulder.

Cateyrin didn't hesitate, even though Meth hung back. She threw herself, rolling, at the huge man's legs. He fell, belly flopping, behind her. He fled.

Albe snatched back her dagger from my hand, but Cateyrin hissed frantically, 'No! No! No! Don't stay and try to finish them. We're very close to my home and the noise will draw more of them. They're everywhere and prowl all the corridors by night.'

Tuau gave a dreadful scream of fury that echoed all around us, bouncing off the black glass walls and the broken roof.

'That may help keep them off,' he said with some satisfaction as he licked his bloody chops.

I chose to believe Cateyrin. 'Go! Go! Go!' I shouted.

'I want some red meat,' Tuau yowled.

The filed-tooth one was dying in convulsions. The big man was up; he took a look at his companion, then, at the rest of us.

'Cateyrin, you lead. Now go! Move!' I commanded.

Tuau opened his mouth to protest. I think he wanted to eat the one with the filed teeth. Albe caught him a smack across the backside with the flat of her sword.

'You heard my lady! Move! Now!'

Tuau gave her a glare murderous enough to burn the bark off a tree, but did as he was told.

There were all sorts of noises from the fog around us, but we ran for about another hundred yards. Suddenly, the roof above us was intact again and the collectors of starlight filled the damp corridor with silver light.

'Here!' Cateyrin said, and dove for a dark spot in the corridor wall.

It was a hole – we had to duck to enter it. But once inside, we found we could stand upright, though the roof was only a few feet over my head. I could reach up and touch it.

The starlight collectors were here, also, and the narrow passage was filled by a blue haze.

'Cateyrin?' I asked. 'The passage we just followed is open to the sky, but this one isn't. How can the light get in here?'

'I don't know. No one knows. The people who built the city just did it that way.'

'I wonder if they were people?' Albe asked. 'It seems to me only gods could . . .'

'I am footsore and weary,' Meth snapped. 'Let's just see if your mother is really glad to have you back.'

The passage was so narrow we had to go single file. Cateyrin led, Meth followed, Tuau, Albe, and I brought up the rear. Tuau was pacing along beside Albe.

'Think she will let us in?' Tuau asked.

'Doesn't matter,' Albe said. 'We can overnight here. I'll bet you can kill something enough for your dinner at any rate. And my lady and I can hold this snake tube against all comers, if we must. I have enough loot in my pack to pay for food and some sort of lodging come daylight.'

Tuau hissed viciously. 'I had my supper all warm, twitching and leaking blood on the floor. But you and your nasty-tempered mistress made me abandon . . .'

This was as far as he, and we, got. We had come to an iron portcullis. The passage widened a bit at this gate, and we gathered in front of it. Tuau hissed, spat, and clawed at the iron grating.

'Oh, be quiet,' Albe said. 'Just relax and I'll scratch your neck and behind your ears.' She suited action to the words, and Tuau began doing shoulder dives against her legs, purring.

Cateyrin rattled the gate loudly. 'Mother! Mother! I'm home!' she shouted. 'I'm home. Let me in.'

At first, no one came. I noticed Albe glance apprehensively back down the narrow passage.

'I don't understand what's keeping her,' Cateyrin said.

Meth spoke up then. 'Yes. Well, I can. She probably thinks you're a ghost come calling . . . and even if you can convince her you're alive, she will probably repudiate you for disgracing her family and failing in your duty to—'

That was as far as he got, because we saw a light appear beyond the gate. When it drew closer, we saw a woman with a wax light in her hand.

'Oh, my God!' she breathed when she saw Cateyrin. 'Oh, my God! Daughter, sweet daughter mine. I knew she didn't predict your death, but I couldn't see how you could escape.

'Akeru!' she exclaimed, catching sight of the cat. 'How? . . . Fighting women!' She glanced at Albe and me.

'Mother, they're friends of mine. They helped me! Let us in. Please!' Cateyrin stretched her arms through the grating.

'Pull back, Cateyrin. I'm doing just that.'

The portcullis rose. We slipped through and it dropped behind us. We hurried into another corridor, this one dark but for the wax light Cateyrin's mother carried. The walls glittered oddly.

I stretched out my hand to touch them, and Cateyrin whispered, 'No! No! They're sharp.'

Indeed, my armor leaped out to protect my fingers.

'We can pull the walls together,' Cateyrin explained. 'And the crystals will slice any intruder to shreds.'

'How do you do that?' Albe asked.

'I don't know,' Cateyrin admitted. 'My mother is the ruler of this house. She does it. Before she dies, she will teach the secrets to me, now that I am past the danger of death among the mariglobes.'

The passage ended in a round, domed room. The shape and furnishings of the room were both familiar and unfamiliar to me. The central ceiling fixture concentrated the starlight as the ones in the corridor had, but the light was bright only near the domed eye itself.

Yes, I thought of them as eyes because that's what they looked like – a giant dragonfly's eye peering down at us. There were other lamps in the room, and the pale light from the dragonfly's eye was caught and reflected in them. They were of amber glass and so their light was warm.

Cateyrin's mother gestured with her hand and a warm, golden light spread through the room. It was very beautiful, round as my people's dwellings are, the walls hung with jeweled tapestries in silk, velvet, and cloth of gold and silver. Vibrant as the arts of the Painted People are and however wonderful their tapestries, they could not compare to these. Some were representational, and on them birds took flight forever. Fish leaped, flowers budded and bloomed, and trees textured in threads bent their heads before the wind.

Others were abstract, as are the ones the Painted People weave to represent the events of a lifetime. Each man or woman has his own and they can be read as the house posts can. Here is sunlit gold – a prosperous marriage. There, a splash of scarlet, a dangerous childbirth. Or for a man in battle, gray and white for sorrow and death. Bone is white, the winter sea gray-blue, the winter sky silver-gray.

I but illustrate an art that now is vanishing and being forgotten even among the Painted People. And families no longer care that once they sat and ate, made love, worked, and lived their lives surrounded by the woven records of those who brought them and their families into being, tilled the earth, fished the sea, fought, and loved down the ages until they created the times we live in.

But I could see from the tapestries in this room that however distantly related Cateyrin's people and mine were, we were kin. Hides that looked like those of the beasts we had seen coming into the city covered the floor, and cushions of damask, silk, linen, and fine, very fine, wool were scattered about the floor and around a black, round table surrounded by benches. Both table and benches resembled the low furniture found in chiefly houses among my own people.

Cateyrin was embracing her mother. Her mother was murmuring, 'Sweet, sweet baby. My little love. My honey bun. I was so afraid. God, I was so afraid.'

'Why?' Cateyrin asked. 'Didn't Nest say she didn't see death? I don't see what you were worried about.'

Albe chuckled. 'Young one, maybe your mother's faith isn't as strong as yours.'

Cateyrin managed to look prissy. 'Everyone knows Nest has a powerful geis and her predictions all come true.'

'Madame.' Albe bowed. 'We are sorry to intrude upon you unannounced, but circumstances prevented us from adopting a more formal course of action. I am Albe of the Out Isles. My lady here is Guinevere – affianced bride of Britain's King Arthur. Meth, I believe you know. And our friend is Tuau of the Akeru, who is an – Oath Cat.' She tried out the words. 'Yes, I think that best expresses it. Oath Cat of my lady, Guinevere. As I am an oath woman of hers and bound to take her head should she fall into disgrace or death.

'As you can see, we are no mean personages and can offer reciprocal hospitality should you visit among us. Though,' Albe added, thoughtfully, 'just how you would accomplish such a journey is not at present clear to me.'

'I am Ilona, member of the College of Seers.' Cateyrin's mother's answer was equally formal. 'And since you bring my beloved daughter home to me, you are honored and doubly welcome here as my guests.'

'Mother, we're rich!' Cateyrin said. And snatching the sack with the boxes of mariglobes in it away from Albe, she showed them to her mother.

Ilona didn't look pleased. She looked very disturbed.

'What's wrong, Mother?' Cateyrin asked.

Albe spoke up. 'Cateyrin, give your mother a chance to . . . understand what has happened. I think some food and rest might . . .'

'Yes, yes,' Ilona said. 'Please.' She indicated the table and low benches around it.

Meth began unarming himself. He was cursing under his breath. Cateyrin went to help him. Ilona left.

'Yes, you're rich,' Meth said bitterly. 'You and your mother. But what about me? I'm an outcast now. Cut off from my friends, companions, and kin.'

'What's wrong with you?' Cateyrin snapped back. 'We'll go equal shares with you and maybe you can use your part to found your own – '

'I liked my life!' He sounded furious. 'I was a trusted member of the *tuath*. Now where will I go? What—'

'Oh, stop! Just stop!' Cateyrin snapped. 'From the

367

very first, you've been acting stupidly, trying to give back the . . .'

Most of his armor was off now, but he was still wearing one of those ugly gauntlets, and he drew his hand up, readying himself to backhand Cateyrin across the face. Before he could act, Albe had his wrist twisted up between his shoulder blades.

'What?' she asked. 'You are a guest here. Would you insult the mistress of this house by abusing her daughter?'

Then she released him. Cateyrin drew back; her nose was still bruised and sore from Meth's earlier blow. Without saying anything further, she left, following her mother into what I surmised must be another room. Meth took one of the benches at the table. He didn't speak, but sat and looked sullen.

We sat down on another bench where we could watch Meth. He was making me uneasy. I didn't know if he could do anything to harm us, but my ignorance of this strange world was such that I didn't care to take any chances.

The table and bench distracted me. They seemed to be made of woven wood, polished on one side, left covered with bark on the other. Then I realized there were bands of green dipping in and out among the branches. The bands of green were tiny leaves. The table and benches were alive.

The table legs were roots that entered the stone floor through cracks in the glassy surface. The bench was the same. We sat on the smooth side of the richly patterned wood. Bark and clusters of leaves formed the other side. I could look down into the basket weave of both table and bench and see the tiny green clusters filled all the openings between the tamed withes. Table and benches glowed green-gold and brown in the amber light.

'How can it live?' Albe asked wonderingly.

Ilona entered with a platter of roast meat just then. Cateyrin followed with a mat and spread it to protect the living table from the platter's heat.

'To answer your question, it does very well for itself and has been growing here since before my great-grandmother formed this place into her dwelling,' she told Albe.

Cateyrin returned with a tray that held bowls of broth, vegetables, and platters of bread, three or four different kinds.

'*Wererooor!*' Tuau roared, demanding his share. He was behind Albe and me.

Ilona studied him. 'Raw or cooked?' she said.

'I don't care. I'm starving!'

'Mind your manners,' Albe said. 'Please! Thank you! And tear it asunder and crack the bones on the stone floor.' She pointed to the entry hall.

Tuau hissed and the hair on his neck stood up. His tail brushed out.

'Quiet, or I'll send you to play with what lurks outside in the darkness,' Albe said.

'Can't!' Tuau said.

'Can!' Albe gave him one of her slow grins. 'Can! And will. Behave yourself.'

Ilona returned with a haunch of something or other. Tuau glared at Albe, but took the meat politely enough, marched over to the stone-floored hall, and began to dine. Cateyrin brought wine and we followed Tuau's example and fell to.

Cateyrin and Meth began trying to fill Cateyrin's mother in on the doings of our day. Ilona stopped both Cateyrin and Meth when we got to the part where I collected the mariglobes without injury. I demonstrated my armor for Ilona. I thought she looked frightened when she saw what it would allow me to do.

I was puzzled by her fear, but by then, sheer

exhaustion was taking its toll. This day I had passed beyond the barriers of one world and entered another. Fought battles here and traveled many miles on foot. Except for the few days' mental and mortal fatigue I had suffered after burning the first fortress, I had never been so weary in my life.

The food and wine sank me into a stupor, and I had little energy to devote to questioning our hostess, and even less will for looking – as I saw it – a gift horse in the mouth. I was warm, ostensibly safe, and well fed. More than that, I could not ask. But that expression of sudden fear tugged at the edges of my consciousness, whispering a warning – her fear of what I could do, and the expression of dismay on Ilona's face when Cateyrin recounted our adventure with the Circe.

She and Meth fell to quarreling about it again. But I was simply beyond caring about what went on around me. I put one arm around Albe and rested my head on her shoulder.

'I must rest or die. I cannot think what has drained me so. But if my life depended on it, I could go no further.'

Albe helped me to a pile of cushions in the corner of the room.

'Mighty magic have I seen you do this day, my lady and queen. Such power as you exerted leaves no sorceress unscathed. Sleep now. I will watch.'

'Take care of those stones. We may need . . .' That was all I managed to say before darkness took me.

Down and down I went, drifting through dark waters from whence, both Maeniel and Dugald agreed, all life arose. Arose from the shadowed volcano-lit, lightning-limned storms of the first seas.

'It rained then,' Maeniel told me. 'Forever, the water cascading from the skies to boil away from the earth's fiery crust, become clouds, and rain down again. In time, the cycle slowed and the vast basins of the oceans filled.

Rivers ran, sometimes boiling hot but pouring through canyons of black lava, basalt churning the stones in their beds into the first soil and sand on earth.

'Then there is mystery,' Maeniel told me. 'God's spirit brooded on the face of the troubled new waters. The young moon drew them into tremendous tides that licked at the edges of the contents, wore away rock, and drew the building blocks of life from cold, dead stone and volcanic ash.'

'God?' I asked.

'God,' he'd replied. 'Or something else. I cannot say. But whatever it was, it set its hand to the task. Lightnings that lit the night like day were brighter than the distant sun seen through the eternal boiling storm clouds of midday, and between the anvil of raw new earth and the hammer of heaven, life flew up like a fountain of sparks from a forge or the flash of light when flint strikes steel. The sparks of life flew into the mother sea and the fire that we are – became us – began ever so slowly to burn.'

Because, as he said, we do burn. And the creatures of darkness I summoned to help me destroy the fortress taught me how hot we burn. They warm themselves at our fire and sometimes swarm around night-flying moths to our flame.

Once I asked Maeniel how he could remember these things that most humans, including Dugald, could not, or only do so under special circumstances. He told me that we gave up thinking with our whole brain long ago and buried these memories forever in order to become the smart animals we were. But he who enjoyed a dual nature, man and wolf, could still open these ancient passages to a past so distant it stretched beyond our crude measure of time and could only be traced back by changes in the seemingly eternal stars.

They, those stars, were the only measure of an almost infinite duration of life on earth. All animals shared in this capacity to remember life's beginnings and understand its meaning, as it was written into the very fabric of the universe. We humans were the only exiles from the garden of the world, the garden of the universe. Only we could not remember.

I drifted deeper into the well at the core of all being and for a few moments, I lamented my state. Sorceress, Albe had called me, and sorceress I had become. A mighty keeper of magics. And even now, in the depths of sleep, my consciousness would not leave me and I wondered if ever again I would truly rest. Or each night, would I wander open-eyed through all the endless layers of time.

Time, the tree, the world tree that year by year adds another ring of girth. Time, the maze, all duration measured from its entry to the center. Time, the maze.

Suddenly I was me and not me, and I entered a summer forest. I could sense a body, not my own but rather like the being I had killed in the guise of the fish eater. I had killed it to protect an ancient king, the father of my own ancestress, Treise, his child. This was the body I inhabited now, one very similar to the fish eater's.

I turned, looked back, and saw my own three-toed prints in the mud. Ah well. This is, after all, the point of memory: to know what is past, even if the past is not my own.

Such a forest I walked through. Never touched by human hands, it was filled by gigantic, ancient trees. I recognized an oak laden by ferns that had colonized the branches almost to the destruction of the tree. Under it, my toes bit into the thick mud of a sump crowded with low plants crowned by stiff, fan-shaped leaves.

Beyond the sump a stand of ash and linden so thick that I knew even with my great strength I could not force my way through them. So I turned, circled the tall, gray trunks, and found my way under a dark-barked, squat tree with shiny broad leaves that were such a deep green, they were almost black. It carried big, deep cream-colored flowers that drenched the air with fragrance.

An invitation freighted with regret entered my mind and directed me to a path through the grove of silver-barked trees. I followed the directions and picked my way among stately pillared trunks whose lowest branches began hundreds of feet above my head as I followed the meandering path through the damp, cool shadows.

At length I came to a small, sun-dappled pond thick with green waterweed. So like the sun-dappled stillness of the pond were the colors of the creature that even my eye didn't pick it out of its green-gold surroundings until it moved, raising its crested, sun-marked head to meet my eyes. It calmly continued chewing the waterweed in its mouth, swallowed, and hooted softly, musically, a greeting.

It had a build similar to the one I now wore: three-toed feet, strong haunches, arms and hands not fitted for fine tasks, as I knew mine were, but splayed and blunt-fingered so the creature could support itself when it bent down to feed. The fine, large eyes in the crested head met mine, and the being I was knew it need not ask.

They were long thinkers, these beings, and first who brought order out of chaos when my kind had been squabbling scavengers with only a rudimentary consciousness of the breadth, magnificent complexity, and sheer beauty of the citadel of truth these beings had constructed since time out of mind.

My people had grown to maturity, a happy maturity, under their tutelage and protection. But now . . . now, I had to know. And I, Guinevere, and the being whose body I inhabited, had to know . . . what?

And I remembered in my lifetime standing in the cave watching the massive heavenly body collide with the beautiful blue-green earth and the dark clouds boil up to hide its splendor.

I tried to draw away from the being I inhabited, but it was too late, long too late, for a river of pain-drenched loss tore through my mind; and the reason that belonged to my fierce comrade was swept away by its passage. I knew that all I loved or ever would love would be destroyed, and it and I were seized by madness, as I had been seized by madness when I invited the evil spirits into my mind.

Nightmares – humans have nightmares. *Not real,* I thought, and fled. *I'll die*, I thought, and I would die to escape the raging, endless, bitter sorrow.

Suddenly I stood with Mother beneath the falls where she drank from the pool filled with stars. From high above, the glowing falls flowed, sometimes forming a curtain of light when the wind wandering through the midnight forest blew the water out over the trees. Some of it dashed itself like a glowing mist across my face and eyes.

'Not you!' Mother said. 'Not you, and long ago.'

Then she was gone. Consciousness went out like a candle when the wick is pinched, and I truly slept.

Cateyrin woke me wailing. Ilona, her mother, was saying, 'Have done! Girl, have done! Didn't you know this would happen once the weak-minded young fool saw the Circe?'

'But he has taken all the mariglobes, too!' Cateyrin shouted.

My eyes opened. I was sleeping on the cushions between Albe and Tuau. The cat's head was resting on my outstretched arm, and Albe was curled up next to me, head on my shoulder.

'A curse on him!' Cateyrin was weeping now. 'I hope the jewels send her nightmares.'

Next to me I heard Albe chuckle. 'He has not got so many as he thinks,' she whispered in my ear.

'No?' I questioned softly.

'No,' she confirmed. 'I knew once that thing – she is not human, you know – got into his mind that he would betray us. Hell, he was ready before she paraded her charms. After he saw them, it was a certainty. He has one box, no more. I have the rest knotted into a strip of cloth around my waist. I'm sorry I had to give him the contents of the top box, but I was afraid the young fool might stick his knife into me to get them all.'

'We had been together so long,' Cateyrin sobbed.

Tuau lifted his head from my other arm. 'God, woman,' he snarled. 'You are loud as a crying queen in heat. Be still. It might be worth the price of those jewels to be rid of him. Your friend damned near killed us on the stair.' Tuau's spit and snarl temporarily silenced Cateyrin.

The room was bright, light pouring in from the multi-faceted eye in the ceiling. The leaves on the table and chairs in the center of the room had unfolded themselves and were drinking in the sun. Cateyrin and her mother were standing near it.

'It is to be hoped,' Ilona said, 'that it is to the Circe that he went. Because if he did not, we are all in grave danger.'

'Why?' I asked, sitting up.

'Because of your dangerous skills,' Ilona answered.

'Mother, they're fighting women,' Cateyrin said. 'The great families won't dare—'

'Merciful God!' Ilona snapped. 'She can – she alone can – give one of the great families hegemony. If they find out what she can do, they'll keep throwing opponents against her until she drops with exhaustion. God-born she may be, but incarnated in mortal flesh, and however strong, she, like all mortals, has her limit.'

'Woman, why didn't you tell me this last night?' Albe said. 'If I'd known, I'd have killed him.'

One of Cateyrin's hands was lifted to her lips. 'No!!!'

'Cateyrin,' Ilona snapped. 'Fetch curds and honey for our guests and make some bread.'

Then she turned to me. 'We must talk. But eat first. It will take some time for Meth to convince his own family to try to gain control of you. They will certainly not believe him at first, and with luck, may kill him before he has a chance to explain. However, if he goes to the Circe . . .' Her voice trailed off. 'Well, that depends on how smart she is.'

'He should know better,' Cateyrin said waspishly.

'Child! Child!' Ilona said, putting her arm around Cateyrin and pulling her against her breast. 'Face facts. Meth had a nice face and a pleasant disposition, but he was gullible to the point of folly and suicidally self-confident. One of the quickest ways to tell when a Circe has her claws in a man is when he tells you he is sure he will be able to free himself from her whenever he wants to. I'm sorry your first had to be such a fool, but it's as well the Circe captured him so quickly and you saw his true worth.'

Cateyrin began wiping her face with her hand. 'Any man can fall to a Circe, even the best.'

'Yes. Yes, dear, I know. Now go fetch honey and curd cheese for our guests.'

She sighed softly after Cateyrin left. 'Thank God she's alive. But no matter how many ways I cast the omens, I did not see her death. Neither did any of the others in the collegium, and when the lot fell on her, I consulted them all. I couldn't believe we were all wrong.'

'My lady,' I said. 'Tell me why these jewels are so important that for every few dozen you must sacrifice a human life.'

'We can't live without them. And the gods demand their due,' she said.

'But what do they, these jewels, do?'

'Cateyrin didn't tell you?' she asked.

'No. Nothing coherent.'

'Come with me.' She led us toward an alcove in the round room. There was a very narrow stair in the alcove; it spiraled down. She went first, I followed, Albe and Tuau trailed behind. The stair came to a halt looking down at a sunlit lake.

We are under the ground, I thought. How could this be?

There was a rope ladder on a ledge near the opening. Ilona dropped it and I saw the weighted end fall to a small promontory projecting out into the lake.

I climbed down.

The promontory proved to be the trunk of a gigantic, fallen tree that lay half-submerged in the lake. I stood on it and gasped at an abundance I could only dream of before.

The lake – actually it was more of a marsh – stretched out on all sides around me. It supported a vast variety of life. In the deep, clear brown center, I saw the darting movement of large fish as they hunted minnows, tadpoles, and surface-dwelling insects. Beyond that place the shallows began, and they were populated by the same broad-leaved plants I'd seen growing on the float- ing islands on our way into the city. They were very beautiful. The velvety-rose, black, red, and variegated arrowhead-shaped leaves shaded the still, brown water where small fish roamed, dragonflies hovered, frogs kicked, and water skaters danced.

I followed the log moving among the big, nodding leaves until I reached true marsh, a place thick with golden cress, blue-spiked pickerelweed, white-flowered waterweed, clumps of cattails where vividly colored birds nested among hummocks of reeds. The reeds were tall and short, some with red, fuzzy heads, others that bore plumes like papyrus, and yet others stately but with long greens, sharp, sword-shaped leaves that slid into an unwary human's hand and legs like so many knives.

I reached the end of the log and saw the magnificent lake was surrounded by a swamp composed of dense, drowned jungle, thick with enormous trees clothed in masses of vegetation so luxuriant it was practically impossible to know where the trees ended and the mass of guests and parasites they harbored began. The massive knot of twisted roots of the half-drowned trees towered over my head and I could walk no further. I stopped and saw a small, skin-covered boat tied to one of the tree roots. I turned and realized that Ilona had followed me down the ladder and was standing beside me on the log.

'What do you see?' she asked.

I told her and she nodded.

'This lake,' she said, 'supports my family. I and my daughter.' She reached out and lifted one of the broad-leafed plants from the water, and I saw the leaves sprang from a rhizome as thick around as my thigh.

'I harvest these and I have a food seller who will buy all I can take from the water. The bread you ate last evening was made of flour ground from these dried roots.'

'This place cannot be,' I said. 'We are deep under-ground and that sunlit sky above.' I stood looking up to the light even as I denied it. 'That sunlit sky is an illusion.'

Ilona laughed. 'Girl, you are blond as any woman I have ever seen and if you remain much longer, the illusion above will give you a terrible sunburn.'

'No,' I said.

'Yes,' was the reply.

I stretched out my hand toward one of the tree roots, but my fingers went through the apparently solid root as though it were mist and brushed stone. I jerked my hand back. The big, dark, velvet-leafed plant whose root she

378

had just shown me was near my legs. I grabbed at the thick stem; my hand closed around it and I was also able to lift the fat root out of the water.

I dropped it. It fell back with a splash. My mind was ready for the splatter of water on my leg and foot, but it didn't come. The water seemed to pass through my leg and foot as though it were not real, but a ghost.

'No!' I said again. Then I remembered Ure's last lesson. I reached for the root again. My fingers closed around it and I felt damp, soft, dirty wood.

Ilona was nodding. 'You are a sorceress,' she said. 'And you have just experienced the central paradox of this place.'

'A thing is either real or it is not,' I stated flatly.

'Not here it isn't,' Ilona said quietly.

Only a few yards way, I heard a harsh cry and a magnificent blue-crested waterbird took wing from a thicket of cattails. One wing passed through my body the way a wandering ghost goes through a door. I spun around, loosened my will, and stretched out my hand toward the wing. The tops of my fingers brushed sun-warmed feathers.

I stood there, heart hammering, almost too frightened to speak.

'The jewels do this,' Ilona said. 'They bring places like this within the reach of the women living here. You saw how barren the land around the city is.'

I nodded.

'Without the food provided by this place and others like it, how long do you think it would be before we starved? We cannot ráise more than a tenth of what we need around the lake in the valley. And food, my dear, is only the beginning. Every man, high or low, wise or stupid, strong or weak, noble or base, would kill as many as necessary to make a woman with talents like yours part of his family. You could have your pick among the first sons of all the great families, and the one who gets you would, in the end, achieve hegemony over all the rest.

'The gems are eaten only by women. Only women can wander among the many worlds to which the gems open the doors. Meth will tell the Circe about you and the Circe will sell the information to the seven great families.'

'Maybe Meth won't succumb to her,' I said.

Ilona gave me a mirthless laugh. 'Don't depend on it. Even now I'm sure they are welding a collar around his neck and he is sipping the waters of Lethe. To a Circe, men are just beasts of burden. They like their favorite Fir Blog better, far better, than most human males. Fir Blogs have big pricks and are almost never fractious slaves, whereas human men often turn vicious and sometimes have to be butchered for their meat when, after a few years, they develop a tolerance for the Lethe water used to stupefy them.'

'Butchered for meat,' I gasped.

'Yes, dear. I can see my daughter was not very . . . shall we say, informative . . . about the difficulties inherent in our society. But then, she's young yet and I have tried to shelter her from some of the more unpleasant facts about life in this city. See, she was very fond of Meth and if I'd filled her in on his probable eventual fate, it would only have upset her. But I feel I must be honest with you. You are in great danger and in desperate need of my services.'

My shoulders were burning and I could feel the heat in my face. I reflected that Ilona had been right about sunburn.

I heard Albe calling me. 'My lady! My lady! Where are you?'

I shouted back, 'I'm here! Not far from you! I'll return in a moment. I'm talking with Ilona!'

'Can't she see?' I asked Ilona, irritated.

'No,' Ilona replied. 'No, she can't. I told you, you are a sorceress. Remember? All she and Tuau see is fog or darkness.'

'I'm coming!' I shouted. 'I'll be right there.' And I started walking the log toward the rope ladder.

Ilona halted me with a touch on the arm. 'Do you comprehend what I have been telling you?' she asked.

'Yes,' I answered. 'Yes, I believe I do.'

How things work. How things really work. I had Maeniel's teachings to fall back on. He taught me to look beneath the surface and weigh deeds rather than words.

I followed Ilona back to her dwelling, where I sat at the table and ate curd cheese with honey and listened carefully to everything she had to say.

Women were at a premium here because they were the only ones who could use the crystal fruit to travel between the worlds. But not every woman was capable of the journey – only a favored few. The leaders of the seven great houses quarreled violently among themselves over such women, because by controlling them, they added to the power of the clan. The man married to a very talented woman became head of the family and wielded power over the rest.

'Cateyrin?' I asked.

'Has never shown any signs of talent,' Ilona answered. 'But you and your friend, Albe? The mere fact that you came to this world from another and demonstrated your skill when attacked by the party that accompanied my daughter . . . and add to that your magnificent armor, your abilities in my garden. All prove you are Women of the Wager.'

Women of the Wager. I knew what that meant. You see, among us there are many ways to marry.

You can sell yourself at the Beltane Fair as I once wanted to. It's not a bad deal, in spite of Dugald's fury.

381

The man who hires you hands your wages to the chief. If in a year you find you don't suit, why, you may take your money and go. Should you become pregnant, that's another thing. If the child is a girl, you may take it without penalty. If a boy, you may keep him only until he is five. Then his father or one of his kin must foster him and teach him to be a man.

Or most often, noblewomen or women of property are married off by their kin. That is to the family or tribe's advantage, financial or political.

Most women aren't rich enough or pretty enough or noble enough to be subject to these constraints. But among those who are, a woman who would not be sold like a cow or a horse may proclaim that she will not be possessed by any man who cannot defeat her in single combat. There are, as Dugald told me once, many more stories about such wagers than there are women who dare to demand them. But they happen often enough to be mentioned in the laws protecting women from abuse, and it would seem the women who were in demand as wives to the great families must prove themselves in magic and in battle both.

It is further said that the woman who makes such a wager draws her strength from the magic bestowed by virginity, and when she is deprived of her maidenhead, she becomes as all other women are – weak, biddable, and submissive.

Albe listened as intently as I did, and when Ilona was finished, she whispered, 'My lady, we're going to have to fight our way out of here. The law does not allow you to enter any man's bed save one.'

'I know,' I answered softly.

Suddenly she chuckled. 'I cannot think a maidenhead makes that much difference as far as strength is concerned. Mine's long gone and I am as vicious as any wild bull.'

'Why should those men want to bed only fighting women?' I asked.

'Those journeys the stones send them on are quite dangerous. Many don't come back. And of those who do, it seems the best fighters predominate. Your talents, your quite obvious talents, place the two of you among the best. But fear not,' she continued. 'You have come to the right place. I derive only part of my income from the lake you saw. I am a teacher of arms, an instructer in the martial arts.'

'The lake?' I asked. 'Where did the lake come from?'

'My great-grandmother was an undefeated fighting woman. She came . . . upon one of the gems, found the lake, and brought it here.'

'How is that possible?' I asked.

Ilona shrugged. 'I don't know. She left this freehold to her daughter, who left it to me. The lake is part of it. No one can take it from me, because no one can get to it without my help.'

'So the great families don't control everything,' I said.

'They like to think so, but no. No, they don't.'

Tuau came and rolled on his back and wallowed in front of Albe. She scratched his stomach. He moaned with pleasure.

'Oh, God, no wonder the little cats like you so much. *Mmmum, mum.* Oh, God.'

Then he whipped, landing on his feet, panting with pleasure.

'That's almost better than sex! Almost!'

Another cat moan, then he sat down on his haunches and began licking his balls. His penis popped out of the sheath, pink, curved, and rough-looking. He transferred his attentions from his balls to it. About six more fast licks, and it obligingly spurted seminal fluid.

Panting, he lay down on his stomach, paws curved around his white chest, and gave a sigh of contentment.

383

'Wonderful. Just wonderful,' he purred.

'God Almighty!' Albe rolled her eyes.

Ilona studied him and shook her head. 'Cats!' she said.

'Are you feeling strong?' she asked me.

'Strong as I ever am,' I answered.

'Good. In spite of all we have been through, I must earn my living. And it is time to harvest roots from the lake. I could use some help.'

I borrowed a smock, and Cateyrin took the stained silk I was wearing to wash it. This time both Ilona and I concentrated on helping Tuau, Albe, and Cateyrin ease through the veil that hung between this world and the one that held the lake.

The harvest went well. Albe, who was used to fishing with hook and line, went after fish at the lake's center, while Cateyrin hauled up loads of harvested roots and leaves. When Albe reached my side near the entry point, I asked her, 'How much are you here?'

'I'm not sure,' she said. 'I see most of the lake, but there is only fog at the edges.'

I placed my left hand on her shoulder and felt for the first time power gather in my body. I was afraid then of what it might do to her, but I began to let it ease into her.

She started suddenly. 'I can see it! The lake, the fish, the sun on the water, the drowned forest surrounding the lake.'

She looked down and said, 'I feel through the shoes the tree bark beneath my feet.' She looked at me. 'How wonderful to be able to do such things.'

I wasn't sure. I was afraid, afraid of what might happen if I made the lake so real, or our connection with it so strong, that the entrance closed and we couldn't get back. I eased back my concentration and let the lake fade slightly. Albe didn't seem to notice any difference.

My hand dropped and Albe strolled toward the narrow end of the fallen tree, fishing pole and line in hand. I watched her, troubled by what I had just done. I thought the thing was a fallen branch, black and water-logged, until it moved. It took me a few seconds to comprehend that it was the largest snake I had ever seen.

It was lying in wait among the submerged branches of the fallen tree, and it was exactly the color of the mottled sun on the brown water – black and gold with touches of red. The head lifted and the blunt nose slammed into Albe's chest. She went down, and in one ghastly instant, a coil as big around as a tree trunk was looped at her arm and chest. The rest of the snake was flowing over the log, preparing to take Albe into deep water.

I heard Ilona scream. My left hand shot out, and the snake became suddenly semitransparent. The whole world dimmed as I pulled Albe and myself back from the world where the snake was.

Albe slid out of the reptile's grip like smoke and began crawling toward me. The snake managed to look startled, baffled, and frightened at the same time. It had, after all, had a large prey animal in its coils only a second before. So he hurried his massive bulk over the log and into the lake beyond.

Albe stood staring after it. She seemed as surprised as the snake had been.

'Not so wonderful,' I said. 'Not wonderful at all.'

Magic! I remembered my visit to Ure. He'd warned me that every action has consequences, intended and un-intended. Beware.

I was shaking. By bringing Albe almost completely into the lake's strange world, I had inadvertently almost made her the serpent's dinner.

'I'm further away now,' Albe said calmly. 'Will I be able to touch anything here? I mean, how can I fish?'

'Give me the pole and line,' I said. I made them more real, but left her as she was, even though, later on, between chopping the gigantic roots into saleable lengths,

I had to visit Albe every time she hooked a fish, catch it behind the gills, and lift it out of the water. Her hands went right through them.

Tuau had no problem in this other world. Once introduced, he ran along the log and shocked me by jumping into the water, where he swam out into the drowned forest. He returned with a small, black pig. I was helping Ilona pull in a coiling, ten-foot root, and was smeared from head to toe with mud.

'How is it?' I asked.

He interrupted his meal, raised his bloody muzzle, and said, 'Lakes, swamp, marsh, more lakes, more marsh, more swamp. That's all I saw. And birds, all sort of birds I couldn't catch.' He looked annoyed. 'Nothing else.' Then he went back to gorging himself.

When we were finished and we had enough fish for supper, a whole roomful of what Ilona called broad root, we dipped up lake water and poured it over ourselves until we were clean. The sun was a distant scarlet smudge among the towering black silhouettes of the forest and Ilona had become uneasy.

'What's it like here at night?' Albe asked.

'I don't know. None of us, the keepers of this doorway to the lake, have ever cared to remain here after dark.'

Something screamed in the distance, a fierce, primal cry. Tuau, who had been sleeping off his earlier pig feast, lifted his head. His eyes glowed brilliant green in the last light of the dying sun.

'Cat,' he whispered. 'And a big one.'

'How can you tell?' Albe asked.

'*Werrrrrr!*' The sound conveyed annoyance. 'The distance, depth, the number of echoes. The throat is big. It couldn't carry this far across water if . . . I don't think I want to meet it. My kind get nasty if they catch you trespassing.'

Ilona had the rope ladder down. 'You go,' she said,

and Albe began the climb with Tuau draped over her shoulders like a scarf. I went last. I would like to have seen the stars, but I didn't dare to press my luck. And there were those snakes. . . .

The place where we bathed was a stone room with an insect eye – that's all I can think of to call it – that's what it looked like. At any rate, it warmed a tank of water all day. We soaped, then dipped buckets of water out of the tank and poured them over our bodies.

The tank was made of wood and had been hollowed out of a gigantic tree root. The walls were covered with the small leaves that decorated the table in the central room of the house. When I looked down into the tank, I saw the root was living and the water itself oozed out of the white, living tissue of the root.

I rested my fire hand on the wet, hard root and felt the tree. It didn't speak. Trees don't. I realized that later. But in its silent contemplation of necessities human and otherwise, I realized it was the city's life. It had – or I wasn't sure what my mind was touching upon – drawn the city out of the rocks. Someone had requested that it do so long ago.

Its systems – the tree's systems – made the city live. The water spilling around my hand from the root was pure, pure enough to drink even though the humans who lived in the city spilled waste, blood, garbage, dirt, and refuse into the river that bathed the trees' trunks and saturated their roots. The tree took up the water, purified it, and released it back through springs, wells, fountains, ponds, pools, and spigots, so that it could nourish crops, quench thirst, bathe flesh, cook food, evaporate, and pass into the wind to be drawn to polar caps where, as ice, it formed glaciers that melted and began the whole cycle again.

I pulled my hand away, afraid. Because I wasn't sure that the all-powerful being I had connected with couldn't swallow me up or create a seduction, a peace to which almost any living being might wish to yield.

There is so much to be said for a centered, silent consciousness, always vibrantly alive yet always at rest. But I lifted my hand from the tree's life, separated myself from its consciousness, and went to the practice room. Albe had proceeded me there. She was fencing with Ilona; they were using wooden swords. It was time for war.

Ilona said, 'You will not be left in peace. I'm sure that tomorrow the Fand will come.'

Ilona was right. She did.

Where must a forest end? Arthur asked himself. Not in a valley. There it might get thicker or become a swamp. But if he turned and followed the sloping ground on the mountainside, he might just be able to emerge above the tree line and find his way back down into the valley where his people lived.

The forest was as terrible a trap as he had ever been in. After his journey up the mountain and his destruction of the War Song, he'd been forced into it by the fire. Both he and the war dog, Bax, had been so exhausted when they escaped the flames that they both drank from a pool in the hollow formed by a twisted oak root, then slept until the woods filled with a pale, white light.

The fog was thick in the treetops, and he couldn't see where the sun was. He shivered because the air was damp and cold.

The trees were oaks that bore a very rough fissured bark, dark brown and shading to black. He knew it must be wet here most of the time, because their trunks and lower branches were colonized by thick swatches of very green moss and a sort of vining fern that grew in thick masses in spots where the gnarled and twisted branches were free of leaves.

In places high up, pearled by the drifting mist, he saw mistletoe with its white berries and light, ovoid green leaves. Except for the sloping ground, there was no indication where he and Bax had entered the forest. But he was sure they couldn't be far in, because when he'd knelt to drink and shared his water with the dog, he had seen the fire caused by the War Song's death glowing between the tree trunks.

But in which direction? Had he stumbled over the oak root as he came from the left side or the right? He couldn't tell. In fact, there were a half dozen similar twisted roots that formed small hollows filled with water. Bax was up and drinking from one now.

He turned and saw the nearest oak was a bit smaller than the rest and the bark offered good handholds. So he climbed as high as he could, up to the crown where the branches were too small to support his weight. He found himself almost drowning in fog. He could see nothing. In moments his face was wet, his hair drenched, and his shirt collar and sleeves sticking to his upper body.

He eased back down, knowing that he was indeed caught up in the ancient forest of dark enchantment. In some places there were warnings to wayfarers not to stray from the trails lest this lethal place claim them. It haunted his people's legends. Here heroes had pursued the boar and, trapped in this pathless waste, died of hunger and thirst.

The mesh of branches above guarded the sleep of goddesses, princesses, and Valkyries. Here the one-eyed slept by day and rose with the hounds of hell to lead the wild hunt across a stormy, midnight sky. Here rode the nightmare and her ninefold who troubled the sleep of heroes and lesser men.

And here the warrior's bane, the Morrigan ford, stamped the bloody linen into the stony streambed and scarlet stained the clear, mountain water.

His eyes met the dog's. Arthur wondered how long it would take the big mastiff to starve and turn on him. But right now, the yellow-brown eyes were clear and the fine, dark ears were pricked as he stared into Arthur's eyes.

Arthur looked left, but the dog looked right and pranced away over the corrugated surface of the ground. Indeed, the roots of the ancient oaks were so thick it was impossible to see the soil.

Uphill, Arthur thought. That would be better. He might stand some chance of emerging above the tree line. But Bax moved downhill as though he knew what he was doing, and Arthur followed.

The forest grew thicker and the trees bigger. Arthur had, when he hunted and fished as a young man, often moved through almost trackless wilderness. He had never seen a forest without game trails. This one had none. Walking amounted to clambering, sometimes slipping over the root system of one giant oak, later another, an exhausting task. But Bax led him on, seeming to know where he was going. So Arthur followed.

Sometimes he paused to drink at one pool or another formed by the tree roots. The water was tannic and left a bitter taste in his mouth, making him feel as though he hadn't drunk at all, since his thirst seemed unassuaged. Once he found a large acorn still in its cup. Its shell gleamed with a rich brown glow. But when he picked it up, the letters – or whatever sort of symbol they were – flared into the palms of his hands as they had when he cupped the water in the mountain meadow. The acorn vanished in a puff of smoke.

The dread forest tortured him with its sameness. The trees, all oaks, were alike and the same kind of oak. There was none of the individuality and variety of a normal forest. Above, the fog lingered, seeming sometimes too thin, and once he believed he saw the distant orb of the noon sun through the blowing swaths of vapor.

Bax seemed expert at picking a path, and since Arthur had only the dog's instinct (if instinct it were) to depend upon, he followed. At some time in the afternoon, he realized the wood through which he struggled was growing darker and darker.

Night, he thought. This was its only intimation here. No sunsets or sunrises, only damp, dripping trees, fog, and an encroaching blue twilight that slowly became thick, smothering, impenetrable darkness.

When he could no longer see, he found Bax had returned and lain down on a bed of tree roots. He knelt, and as animals will, Bax invited him to put his arm around his body and share its warmth. He did and found he was so tired that even the bumpy surface of tree roots seemed comfortable. His mouth had been dried by the bitter water and he was a bit frightened that even though his lips felt leathery, he felt neither hunger nor thirst.

This terrible forest couldn't continue forever, could it? But then his mind replied, *Why not? For some it had.* And they lost their way and wandered until they died or perhaps even didn't die but struggled forever, each day a perfect copy of the last, dull misery forevermore.

But Bax was warm and Arthur was lying against his back. The dog gave his hand a swipe with his moist tongue.

Why, if the only peace left is sleep, he thought, why let me sleep? And he did.

The first gray light woke him, and he found the hollows formed by the twisted roots around him filled with water. Again, both he and Bax drank. As he looked around at the fog curling in the treetops, the ancient trees that pressed in on him and the strange pale light that was all the omnipresent fog would let through, he thought, *I will lose my sense of time in this place.*

He hadn't been burned badly by the fire that drove him into the dark forest, but he did have a raw patch of skin on his right arm. It was healing now and itched. He scratched it idly and felt the sharpness of his nails.

Yes, he thought. Then he used his sharp right thumbnail to slice a mark into his skin on the inside of his left forearm. One today, one tomorrow – that keeps track of time.

Then, oddly, he felt stronger than he had yesterday. He felt no hunger and wondered if the massive dog Bax was also free of the need to eat. The dog stood quietly on the high roots of the tree before him. Then, when Arthur indicated he was ready to begin walking, Bax led him away into the dark-pillared, misty forest.

He decided he was stronger because he found it easier to deal with the trees. At first he had seen them as nightmare shapes in the gloom, hemming him in. But now, as he had grown to know them, he became expert at finding footholds among the multiple twisted roots that formed the valleys between each mountainous trunk.

Just as well, because the ground began to slope downward more and more steeply and the thick, tortured roots became a stair. Often he found himself stepping down the root system of one while looking into the crown of another. Sometimes the fog blew away for a second and he looked at the daunting view – a precipice clad in the living armor of the giant oaks that drove impossibly massive roots into the stony soil and held the iron-hard trunks and shiny, reflective green leaves to a foggy sky. Strong, they were strong in the way that the trees that composed the tower were. Burgeoning life-forms that ever renewed themselves, century after century, millennium after millennium, for all time.

He knew this was certainly so when he and Bax came to the occasional clearing formed by the death of one of the oaks and saw a sapling formed and rising from one of the dead oak's roots. Tall, slender, and fair, it reached upward for the light. Strength there; strength surrounded him when he came to sleep. And as he threw his arms around the dog's neck, he thought the moon must be out above the covering fog, because it glowed like chalcedony or sometimes a white opal sparkling prismatically with a thousand colors of blue, violet, gold, and rose.

The king, the Dark King Bade, must hope this forest would destroy him. This was Arthur's first thought between sleep and waking. It wasn't working. *No, not at all,* he thought as he sat up.

He studied the wet, dark-fissured bark of the nearest oak. Strength; he felt the strength of the tree in his body and he remembered the Flower Bride in her incarnation as the *creatrix* of the first trees. Those that bloom before the snow is melted or in milder climes, while the forest floor is still black with last year's fallen leaves. These trees bloom and blow: the willow, the tall, gray-barked ash, the oak. Their lovers are the cold spring rain, the late winter wind slashing the bare branches, and the boiling storm.

He closed his eyes and embraced her. She was soft as the downy red catkin of a willow and her breath was that of a mountain torrent, unbearably sharp and sweet at the same time. His pleasure was the frosted touch of winter's final rain, savage yet cleansing.

Then she was gone and he felt the strength of the trees; trees that endured forever, replacing themselves as they fell. It entered his flesh, the roaring blood in his veins, the dark, complex red marrow of his bones, as she prepared him . . . for what? He could not possibly imagine what such a transformation could presage in this life or another.

He had five marks on his arm when they came to the valley. It was no longer a struggle for him to find his way between the trees. In fact, sometimes Bax followed him as he made his way down the slope. He had noticed the wind was rising and from time to time it blew away the fog. He was able to glimpse the forest as a mass of shimmering green leaves clothing the slopes around him. That and the momentary sun on his face were an exquisite pleasure.

Yes, in the brief flourishes of wind he saw that he and Bax were walking into a V-shaped valley. A mountain torrent raced through the bottom of the fold of land between the steep slopes toward an unguessable destination. Above the vista of shimmering green, an eagle soared.

He remembered he had been an eagle once. A second after, he found he was again an eagle and he looked down through a magnificent bird's eyes and saw the river widen and spread as the forest ended and the water spread out to refresh a multifold garden that surrounded a soaring palace of light.

CHAPTER SEVEN

BLACK LEG RETREATED TO A GROTTO in the side of the mountain to lick his bruises. His body was pressed against the stone wall. Outside, the raven laughed.

'You weren't a great big lot of help,' Black Leg snarled.

'The wolf is a sacred animal to him,' the raven said. 'He did wrong in trying to kill you. He knows it now. You are linked.'

'Linked how?' Black Leg asked.

But the raven was gone and the helm rested in a patch of sun near the hollow tree where Black Leg's clothes were concealed. He dressed. His mood was somber. He'd come closer to dying in this engagement than he ever had before. He wasn't used to being afraid. The dream of being a great warrior had been an almost childish one, and he had been certain his natural advantages as man and wolf would grant him victory over lesser beings.

He saw this wasn't necessarily the case. Death had never been a real possibility to him. It was now, and he was surprised to find that he feared it.

When he was dressed, he clapped the raven helmet on his head, then stood looking out over the valley. He could go back to her. She didn't give a tinker's damn about courage or battle or even honor. But what would he be if he did? Her pet? A fool running from the one responsibility he'd been called upon to fulfill?

The morning breeze fanned his face and whispered in the brush and scrub oak that covered the hillside. No, there was too much man now in him to be a true wolf. And too much wolf in him ever to fully understand the men he had partnered with. But Cregan had ordered him to reconnoiter and, at least as far as Black Leg was able, he would obey his orders.

So it happened that a few hours later he was sitting cross-legged on a cowhide in Cregan's mews eating a pork loin and describing the party of Huns. The ashes of the drinking hall were smoldering across the courtyard. Cregan had burned it down as requested by the more fastidious members of the community. As many of Cregan's men as could fit into the mews among the very spoiled hawks were listening. The eagle behind Cregan was straightening her feathers with her beak.

'What I cannot understand,' Cregan said at length, 'is how you get so close.'

'I've hunted with my father and his brothers since I can remember,' Black Leg said. 'Often we lived by hunting and I'm good at moving about at night silently.'

'Yessss,' Cregan said slowly. 'I suppose that could explain it. There will be gold in that wagon.'

One of the other men said, 'The Huns have been victorious all along the coast.'

Cregan frowned. 'They are very close to being out of our territory and in more settled country. But they're probably too big a prize to let slip through my fingers. Many of the men in the village are up in the mountains with the herds. If word reaches the villa that I think they're making for it, the Roman lord there will send a detachment of Franks to burn us out. So . . .' He paused. 'Boys, all the men in the escort following that wagon will have to die. Because if word reaches the Franks that we've attacked one of Attila's parties, we haven't enough men in camp right now to beat off a revenge party. Hear me!'

Black Leg felt a sick horror as he looked around at the faces of the men surrounding him. No one appeared unhappy or dismayed. They were a hard-bitten crew, used to doing what was necessary to ensure their own survival.

Cregan read his dismay. 'Boy, if you cannot obey my orders to the letter, then remain behind and keep the women company. For if you let one of those sons of hell slip past you, I'll cut out your heart with my own hands.'

Black Leg felt a chill and the hackles rose on the back of his neck, as did the hair on his arms.

'No,' he said, then repeated, 'No! I'm in.'

Cregan grunted, then said, 'We'll try to reach the river at dusk.'

They did. No one was very heavily armed. No man carried a shield. Some, including Black Leg, had chain mail, but no one wore it. They carried swords and an assortment of ugly-looking pikes and spears, and the usual complement of knives, about three for each man. But no one wore anything that would clink, clatter, bang, or make any loud noise. They were armored in leather or simply wore padded shirts.

It was dark in the riverbed, and the only moon was a faint silver crescent, almost lost among a vast multitude of stars.

'Take point,' Cregan said to Black Leg, 'and let's see if you're as quick and quiet in the dark as you say you are.'

He was, even as a human, quiet as a wraith and he chose to lead the rest along in the shadow of the bank where they were almost invisible in the darkness. But it was Cregan who spotted the sentry. He hissed and his nails bit into the flesh of Black Leg's arm.

They both paused. Cregan's men needed no

instructions. They melted into the shadows as silently as ghosts.

'No fool, this Pict who you say leads them,' Cregan whispered. 'He expects trouble, if it comes, to come this way.'

The water was only a trickle between the high river-banks, and as long as Cregan remained where he was, no one could pick out either him or his men.

'Can you kill him quietly?' Cregan asked Black Leg.

'Wouldn't matter,' Black Leg said. 'There's someone up there with him that will give the alarm even if he dies. His horse. He's a Hun. They live with them, and some-one's got to cut the mare's throat first.'

'Hell!' Cregan whispered.

Black Leg and Cregan crouched in the hollow of the bank. Just ahead, a sandstone promontory jutted out.

'Come,' Black Leg said to Cregan, and went around the promontory. It brought them out of sight of the rest. Black Leg pulled off his shirt and his legs slipped out of his pants when he went wolf.

Cregan made a strangled sound, almost like a sob.

Black Leg turned human long enough to whisper, 'I'll take the horse. You – the man.'

'I should have known,' Cregan muttered under his breath. 'Her friends!'

Black Leg put the knife between his teeth, then he was a gray shape, then gone. It took him a few seconds to find a path to the top of the riverbank. He turned human when he reached it. He knew it would take Cregan even longer, so he crouched naked in the weeds until the sentry vanished.

He could smell the mare: horse manure, saddle leather, foam, and grain. The breeze was blowing toward him. He moved as predators know how, until the faint night breeze was directly on his face. Then he went in.

He cut the windpipe first, and when he heard the shrill

wheezing whistle, he drove the dagger deep into the jugular. She went down almost without a sound.

He met Cregan back where he'd left his clothing, became human, and began pulling his shirt on.

'You have a future at this, me boyo,' Cregan said.

Black Leg's hands reeked of blood and his stomach muscles were fluttering. He'd been terrified slicing through her windpipe; wouldn't have been enough, he'd been afraid she'd cry out. But she hadn't.

'Think he has only one sentry?' Black Leg asked.

'No! And you take your other shape and go find out.'

Black Leg blew out through his nose.

'Be still!' Cregan continued. 'I think I know where he is. Once there was a villa near here. It had a palisade that's mostly down now, but it had a stone building at the center. He will have forted up in there. He must have seen you.'

'Only as a wolf,' Black Leg said.

'You said he was a Pict,' Cregan whispered. 'And, like as not, he knew you were no natural wolf.'

Black Leg faded into his other shape. Cregan hadn't told him where the villa was, but then, he didn't have to. The wind was still blowing his way, and it told him a number of things about men, horses, cold, old stone, trampled grass, and the very faint tang of wood smoke.

Here again the Hun horses were the problem. He waited, crouched in the grass, until the wind was still. Then he moved forward at a skulking crouch until he saw the broken teeth of the palisade fence, darker shapes against the star-crowded sky. No, no wind. It was very still, and he slunk closer and closer.

The Huns didn't bathe often and Black Leg concluded later that's what saved him. His eyes were fixed on the ruined stone dwelling beyond the shattered walls when the overpowering stench of unwashed humanity flowed into his nostrils.

No, the Huns hadn't taken refuge in the house. They were waiting behind the palisade silently, probably taking shifts sleeping while they waited for what they hoped were deplorably careless brigands.

It took Black Leg an hour to extricate himself from the environs of the villa, all the while hoping frantically that Cregan wouldn't be so careless as to come looking for him. When at last he dashed into the riverbed, he found him where he'd left him.

He gave Cregan his report while pulling on his clothes and doing up his leggings. He concluded by saying, 'We could let them go.'

'Yes, and what will we do with the dead horse and man?' Cregan said. 'No, we've drawn first blood and now we must take the rest. The Frankish *dux bellorum* knows where the men in our village are. He won't think twice about a revenge raid to recover the spoils. No, boy, he must never know. Or find out much too late to be able to launch an attack. No!'

He and Black Leg crawled back to the rest.

'They think to ambush us from behind the palisade,' Cregan told them.

'So when do we hit them?' someone asked.

'First light,' Cregan said. 'We come out of the ground mist and it's as I said. Don't let a one of them get away. You!' He spoke to the big red-haired man. 'Keep an eye on what's left of the sentry. See if anyone checks up on him. If they do . . . kill them. You, Lancelot – whatever your name is – get some sleep.'

Black Leg curled up, wished he could turn wolf, and closed his eyes. The wagonload of loot. That's what made all this such a danger. The Frankish *dux bellorum* would never be able to get his irregulars to ride out against Cregan to avenge a simple raid. But a wagonload of gold – that was another matter. They would want some of that and now Cregan and his men were in too deep to back out. It was do or die now for both the men here and the women and children in the village.

Well, I wanted to be a warrior.

The sense of dawn woke him. He was a wolf and the end of night announced itself to his nose when the air grew so cold that thick mist hung over the barren fields around him. He scented the cold sweetness of the dew-drenched grass. His man's mind saw the stars and in their positions he marked the end of night.

Not night, not day, he thought when the sky began to brighten. He remembered Dugald's training. These were the most dangerous hours – the things not completely one thing or another. But more than knowledge, he remembered the garden the way his mind – not mortal, not wolf – had been able to read it.

He glanced away from the sky and out into the riverbed. A broken tree trunk was sunk in the gravel bottom. The raven was perched on it. It turned its head to one side and peered at him with one dark, red eye.

'You were no help at all yesterday,' Lancelot said, not knowing if he was speaking with lips or mind.

'No, but then you did not ask,' was the reply from the bird.

'Suppose I ask now?' he said. 'What is the price?'

He felt as though he stood on the edge of a cliff, ready to cast off into the wind and try to fly. And he wondered where birds found the courage to take wing for the first time. He felt a chill of fear.

'Death,' was the reply. 'Death is the price.'

'Whose death? Mine?'

This time he was sure the bird spoke only in his mind. 'Immortal or nearly immortal creature, born not human, not beast, able to call up an eternity of survival in and with your endless changes of form. Go from this place. Lie with your mistress, the ruler of living waters, springs and fountains. Dally with her and forget the dark ruin of our souls and mankind. Between the two of you, never and forever seal your conquest of the flesh. Death is our price. The death you will mete out to others. The death you will endure. The deaths you will see. So many you will see as those you love as both man and wolf fall away around you. And last, your death that waits at the end of the warrior's road.

'Go away, wolf, and when you and she suck the nectar of unending pleasure for ten ten thousand years, you will in the end weep and say, "Alas, I have never been alive." Hear me, wolf. Death alone gives meaning to life, and you will never fully live until you know you must die. And make your peace with the knowledge.'

Black Leg closed his eyes. He scented the morning and knew what the bird said was true. An everlasting evasion of responsibility was not life . . . however long it lasted. And the road he must tread was marked out for him.

He rose to one knee. Cregan was looking at him. The leader had passed the night wrapped in his mantle, sleepless and waiting for dawn. All around him Black Leg heard the others stirring. Then they were up. Someone passed around a flask of wine. When it reached him, Black Leg shook his head. Red, standing next to him, shrugged and drank.

Black Leg said 'yes' so softly the assent was almost inaudible. But the bird must have understood, because a second later there was a cup in his hand and, without hesitation, Black Leg lifted it and drank.

Wine? Mead? Something utterly unknown to mankind? It was sweet, sharp, and flowed through his veins like fire. In a second, he was fully alert, awake, energized, and ready to fight. He dropped the cup and it vanished before it hit the ground. He saw Cregan jump and realized he must have been watching.

'Ready?' Cregan whispered.

There was a murmur of assent, and they started out.

He followed, knowing that Cregan and the experienced warriors had certainly done this before.

Yes, the mist was thick and Lancelot could smell it. Every intake of breath moistened his nose. They were close to the villa and crawling uphill to the palisade when he realized he could see it lying like a faintly glowing shroud over the low fields, forest, and river around the ruined palisade. First light, not dawn yet. They would be able to see their enemies well enough to kill them.

One of the Huns – or at least that's what he looked like, with almond eyes, black hair, and yellowish skin – lifted his head, possibly alarmed by some sound. Cregan stood and cast the first spear. It took the man in the throat, sending him back, dying, behind the broken timbers.

Black Leg charged with the rest. There was enough of the palisade left to offer some cover. The man next to Black Leg took a spear in the eye and died. Black Leg tried to turn and bring his spear to bear on his attacker and found, to his astonishment, that instead of a spear, he had a sword in his hand – and a very good one.

He drove it into the man's throat. Then, spinning around, he beheaded another locked in close combat with one of Cregan's men. He leaped clear, looking for another opponent, and saw the Pict and the remaining living men bolting for the ruined house at the center. He was holding a spear now.

Black Leg needed no lessons in throwing a javelin. His third target died on the fallen stones of the once magnificent entryway.

Four horsemen exploded out of the ruined dwelling, riding hell for leather, all in different directions. Black Leg was holding a sling – one warrior was riding directly toward him, lance down, pointed at his chest. The lead sling stone connected with his opponent's forehead and tore most of the side of his skull off. Black Leg jumped away. The man he'd just killed was close enough to fall on him and spatter him with blood and brain.

As he landed, Black Leg saw the Pict try to jump a scattering of fallen stone from the foot of the broken palisade. His horse put its foot in a hole. The animal gave a blood-chilling scream of agony as its leg snapped and then it went down. Cregan's men swarmed him.

That left two, and Lancelot, as wolf, leaped away, flying through the tall grass and nodding weeds after them. He caught the first just as the horse reached the scrub forest at the foot of the hill. He leaped and sank his fangs into the powerful muscles of the animal's flank. The horse's rear legs gave way, and it went down on its haunches. The man on its back hadn't been able to saddle his mount, and he slid off over the tail.

But then the maddened animal got its legs back under it and Lancelot dropped away just in time to avoid a buck that might have broken his neck. He was in the air when he called his human shape and landed on his back at the shoulders, ready to leap up and fight again. He felt the handle of a weapon in his hand and the weight of its head as he salmon-leaped to his feet. He didn't even know what it was when he swung it at his opponent, who had also gotten his legs under him and was diving for Lancelot, a vicious, single-edged blade sax in his hand.

The mace head connected with his opponent's chest, crushing eight of the ribs on his left side and puncturing his lung in five places. The man went down, blood pouring from his mouth and nose.

Lancelot – for he was Lancelot now, terrible warrior, never bested in combat – spun around and saw the last escapee halfway across an open field, drawing closer to the forest. It had been many years since the fields near the villa had been plowed, but the ground was still soft and the horse's hooves were throwing dirt as it tried to make the best speed possible and reach the cover of the trees. Lancelot took out after the last man on the diagonal, trying to cut him off. He succeeded, but only just. The horseman was looming over him as he turned human. This man, one of the Huns, swerved his mount to make a direct hit on the powerful, naked warrior he saw appear before him, seemingly out of nowhere. In a second, he would ride him down.

But he didn't have that second, because Lancelot held a spear in his hand.

The birds give great weapons, Lancelot thought. The spearhead was narrow, pitted old iron, but the edges glittered razor sharp. It went into and through the Hun's body like a hot knife through butter.

The horse's shoulder caught Lancelot and sent him spinning, but he was wolf again and landed at a crouch when he hit the ground. The Huns were famous horsemen, and even dying, the Hun remained in the saddle as his mount gained the shelter of the trees. The wolf was in hot pursuit until he saw the dying man try to duck a low-hanging limb. He didn't make it, and his face smashed into the thick bark. It swept him over the horse's tail and down, smashing his nose and driving the bone up into his brain. He was dead before he hit the ground.

Lancelot stopped, his flanks heaving with exertion, surprised at the silence. The horse continued on for a few paces, then stumbled to a halt, her reins dragging in a sunlit clearing just beyond a big old yew tree. Black Leg sat, his tail waving gently. If he turned human, he would be naked, and naked wasn't comfortable in an early morning forest at a fairly high elevation. The temperature must be in the forties, he reflected as he began to consider how to retrieve his clothing.

In the distance he heard faint shouting and the

occasional scream. Cregan's men were probably mopping up. Then footsteps scrunched in the dead leaves at the edge of the woods. He was on his feet in an instant. He dropped into a crouch among the brush and long grass near the massive old yew.

Cregan stepped into view. He was carrying Lancelot's clothing. For a long moment, Lancelot remained where he was. The name she had given him was that of the warrior who had been placed among the stars. He was always a warrior in the stories told about him. And like the stars that formed him, he returned from the night sky to his people in the form of a mighty meteor, ablaze against the midnight darkness, to explode and burn out, leaving behind steel.

In fact, it was at the warrior's forge that steel had been invented and at last given mankind mastery over the earth. He was Lord of the Water and Light. Of course, that was why he had been drawn to the Queen of the Lakes and Fountains.

And for the last time, Black Leg was a boy. He felt the sunlight pass through his flesh, and around him the light woke the dew on the wet grass to a thousand rainbows. A wrenching, hopeless grief flooded his heart, and he knew the name Lancelot was his true one.

He stood to take his clothes from Cregan. The old man gave a start and stared at him in wonder.

'Boy, I believe for a moment I saw the sun shine right through you.' He sounded awed. 'So!' Cregan saluted Lancelot. 'So! Do the gods return from neverlasting to everlasting when we are in greatest need?'

The second raven exploded out of the yew tree and he went, as his brother had, for Lancelot's eye. But the wolf was too fast and the bird exploded into powder in the wolf's jaws. The powder was a stinging mist that burned and blinded the wolf, then coalesced into razor-sharp shards that turned his head into a bloody ruin.

Lancelot felt the quick, astonishing shock of a mortal wound. Slow, the transition was so slow – from wolf to man – in the journey from one to another, he understood at last that he inhabited another world, passed through it as he changed. He could stop . . . the brightness almost blinded him. Never in misty Britain had he seen such raw light; never breathed air so clear.

The ravine he stood in must once have run water, but long ago, because only rills were left in dry sand. The tree he was looking at bore clusters of vivid white and violet flowers and long, trailing green leaves. *Rather like a willow,* he thought.

But no willow ever had such flowers, glowing long, white, purple-spotted, throated flowers with deep, violet lips.

A man, naked, he dropped to one knee in the light-beige sand and drew, as he had when he called the storm wind, a word of command. Then the tree and the desert faded and he was standing in the clearing, dressed and wearing helmet and sword.

Cregan staggered back; his stomach lurched because he'd seen the wolf die in front of his eyes, then be reborn as a fully armed warrior. Both helmet and sword bore the raven appearance and both had eyes, red ones that gazed at him from the helmet and sword hilt – then slowly closed.

'It's never easy.' Ure spoke to me in my dreams. I know I must have moved restlessly in my bedding, because Albe said, 'Be still, my lady. The Akeru and I will watch. We take turns, even here.'

Then I sank into a deeper sleep. I stood on Ure's floor under the pines.

'You made me forget,' I said.

'Some of the most important things you will ever

know are things you have forgotten. That is where fear comes from. You forget pain, and in the same way the deepest tortures of sorrow. But part of you that cannot be admitted into our so narrow, rational consciousness – that part – remembers the agony of lost love, the searing, bodily pain of injury, and we feel that as fear.'

'Lesson one,' I replied.

'No,' the old man said. 'Lesson one was when you called Cymry to life out of compassion for Kyra's loss long ago, when you were a very small child.'

Then I was in the hut. The wind was shrieking outside and Kyra and I were huddled together for warmth. We had just rescued her and killed the pirates who had murdered her family. The head of their leader hung curing in the smoke above the central hearth. Kyra was sick – one eye gouged out by the criminal whose head hung above the fire. Her dress was stiff with blood, for she had been raped before she was fully recovered from childbirth, and milk dried at her breasts – dried because the child it was intended for was dead.

She went to rise and build up the fire, but I called Cymry, the head, from among the dead and showed her that he was trapped and that I could command him.

Kyra, I thought. *My mother in love.* My eyes filled with tears.

Ure answered my unspoken question. 'She is on the Isle of Women among the Picts. A great teacher, venerated by her people. And you will see her again.'

I felt the dawn breeze on my face, and the mist that hung among the giant trees in Ure's lair was tattered by even its slight movement. Big drops, condensation from the pines above, splattered on the wooden floor around us. In the distance, I could smell the sea.

'That was the first lesson,' Ure continued. 'And it set the pattern of your life.'

'Explain?' I asked.

'No,' he replied. 'And it is very important that I don't, because each practitioner of magic is an artist. Each brings something different to their art. You see, that is why I do not kill you, though you threaten the existence of all I love. None of my magics will tell me what you portend. And, for the first time in almost eight hundred years since I sailed from my Etruscan home and came here, I find myself afraid. None of them – earth, air, fire, and water – will speak your meaning to me.'

I glanced at Albe and Wic. They seemed frozen, cups in hand, both gazing at Ure in awe.

'We are alone here,' he said flatly. 'Let them be.'

'Such stillness for so long. How can it not harm them?' I asked.

'They are not still. It is we who have left them standing, talking together outside the flow of events you call time. For that is the core of my magic – the thing you call time.'

'What then will be the core of mine?' I asked.

'I cannot say, because your talent is so great that not even I can rule it.'

The very light breeze had dropped, the mist among Ure's pines had thickened again, and I looked out at the treetops all around us and felt very alone.

'Yes,' Ure said. 'Only I and those I bring can come here. Only I and those I keep belong here. Only I and those I keep can find refuge here.'

An incantation, I thought.

A second later, both Wic and Albe were stirring and I was a part of time again. I sat cross-legged on the cushions next to Wic and Albe. They were still drinking; my cup was empty.

'Oh, don't you need to question the head?' Albe asked.

'I have,' I answered.

I had done so while Ure and I were outside of time.

'Then I must have dozed over my beer.' She sounded

unconcerned. 'Old man,' she told Ure, 'you live in a devil of a place to reach, but once here, I believe it's worth the trip.'

'I am indeed a noble host,' he said. 'And my gifts are beyond compare.'

Suddenly he held a *kylix* in his hand. I don't know where it came from. One moment his hands were empty; the next, he was holding it.

The cup is a broad, flat Greek vessel, with two handles. It is glazed in black with pictures on the sides, painted in red. The flowing shapes of ancient Greek pottery are widely admired. No one makes such beautiful pottery any longer. Pottery – the pottery we make – is attractive enough, but utilitarian. No, this pottery dates from a place and time in the world when some genus of beauty inhabited the hearts of those living on the blue Aegean Sea and everything they touched became a hymn to the splendor of human creation. I think it was when we first saw ourselves as the heirs of divinity.

We are not so sure now of our place in the universe, and perhaps never will be again. But the cup was a lovely thing.

He proffered it to Wic. 'Fill it at the spring.' He pointed to the water flowing from the rocky prominence that lifted through his flooring. 'Then look into the water. If you see therein your heart's desire, drain the cup and it shall be yours.'

We rose and went to the spring. As instructed, she filled the cup and looked down into it. I saw the shock in her face and gazed into the cup, also. The image that looked back at her was unblemished and clean.

I shivered and glanced at her face, marred by the terrible purple birthmark that spread over one cheek, mouth, and chin. She simply stood silently and tears began pouring down her face.

'It's a trick,' she whispered at length, and stared at Ure. 'You can't do this. No one can.'

'Drain the cup and see,' he answered. 'The choice is yours and yours alone. But remember, if you refuse what the cup offers you, the magic that hangs about this place offers no second opportunity. Decide.'

Still weeping, she drained the cup. The terrible mark vanished from her face, and I realized how beautiful a girl nature had intended her to be. She was springtime, born of the last winter rains, clad in rags, walking barefoot through cold, dew-drenched grass to greet the dawn. Her shabby clothes (we were all a bit battered and worn) covered a body like a young virgin goddess. Her face was the living embodiment of sculpted perfection and her hair a riot of sunlit curls.

I felt as though someone had fisted me in the stomach, but Wic walked into Ure's embrace and Albe ended up holding the cup. I didn't see it leave Wic's hands, but Albe had it and she also walked to the spring and filled the vessel. She seemed to stand for an eternity gazing into the water. She shielded the surface from mine or any prying eyes, and I have never known what she saw. After a time, she looked out at the vast, silent pine forest waiting in the breathless hush before first light.

But then at length, she said, 'No! No! Old man, some roads run only one way. Sometimes you can't go back, even though the deepest desires of your heart would try to drag you.'

But she didn't throw out the water. Instead, she gently poured it back into the stream flowing over the boulder that led down to the river.

'Perhaps I will return,' she said.

'Perhaps I will allow you to return,' Ure said.

Then the cup was in my hand. 'Her' face was painted red on the black of the inner bowl. She held her distaff in one hand, serpent in the other. The owl looked out from behind her, its wings spread. A shaft of white light blotted out my vision and I woke with the sun in my eyes.

I found when I woke that I could feel the city around me. Perhaps when I spoke to the tree last night, I had established a connection that hadn't been completely broken. By day it was a hive of activity. Penned up at night, its citizens made up for their solitude by day. Day was in and of itself preparation for night. Marketing was done and dinner parties planned, food bought, much socializing went on. Gossip was exchanged about the ruling families' constantly shifting alliances: who was married, who murdered (a much more frequent occurrence), what new things had been brought in by the Women of Wager and when would this new clothing, drug, drink, furniture, weapon, food, or sometimes slave be put on sale by the fortunate woman's family. Quarrels were picked among men, duels were fought, assassinations planned by enemies, assignations were arranged by lovers – licit and illicit lovers. I was not sure of the difference, but cuckoldry and seduction were a sport to these people and there were lots of both kinds.

They worshiped also, praying and sometimes sacrificing to gods, dark and bright. I shivered at the touch of the tree's mind when it communicated the substance of some worship. Some of the objects of adoration reminded me of those beings huddled in the swamp to whose untender mercies the Saxons had devoted their captives. The tree was calmly indifferent to the vagaries of human nature. It was itself an eternal or nearly eternal thing, knowing humans as only savage, quarrelsome birds and small animals that took advantage of the shelter it offered and nested in its branches.

At best they were a source of nutrients and occasional entertainment; at worst, destructive pests whose more dangerous impulses had to be circumvented. Just how we were controlled wasn't clear to me, but there was a sense of vast power that lay just out of my reach. The tree might not exert its strength more than once in a thousand years, but when it did, I was very certain it was able to find a satisfactory solution to its problems. Satisfactory to the tree, that is. As far as the offending humans were concerned, I was not so sure.

'Awake, my lady?' Albe asked.

'Yes.'

We had been a long time at arms practice last night. Ilona knew a great many tricks that I, and I'm sure, my teacher, Maeniel, never heard of. They ranged from hand-to-hand combat tactics to maneuvers with sword, shield, or spear.

I was good – my armor helps a lot. It's a surprise to opponents when it covers my skin. But Albe was best. She learned, and quickly, everything Ilona had to teach, and she needed no second chances. Ilona might put her down the first time she demonstrated one of her special holds, but never the second.

And when a completely unarmed Albe took her sword and 'killed' her with a neck-breaking hold, Ilona owned Albe the best student she ever taught and told her that she could choose the man she wished to wed. Whoever that man was, Albe would probably gift him with the chance to become the total ruler of the city.

Albe smiled at that, and I saw in her eyes the same bleak sadness I had seen when she spoke about how she had scarred her face to prevent the pirate who captured her from selling her at a fat profit.

The sadness came – went – and her face showed the cold indifference of a killer.

My friend, I thought, *you do not care and the death of your enemies is only a way to keep score in the game that is all that is left of your life and your love.*

But now she was sitting up beside me, eating some

soft, yellow fruit the like of which I had never seen before and smacking her lips at its sweetness.

'I've been up for a time,' she said between juicy bites. 'But you were up so late, I thought I'd best let you sleep. Ilona and I put out the roots for the food seller. He left these for us to try. They are a novelty, newly found by a dreaming woman belonging to Meth's tribe and family. Here. Have a taste. Spit out the peel. It's tough.'

I did. 'Nice!' I said. 'Sort of like a custard. Very sweet.'

Albe was busy chewing. She nodded and indicated a bowl with more of the yellow fruit and other more conventional items, like grapes, apples, strawberries, and plums. I selected a bunch of grapes. They were red-brown and so plump they squirted juice into my mouth when I bit down.

Cateyrin brought us some bread, cold meat, and curd cheese.

'The longer I'm here, 'Albe said, 'the more I like this strange city. They have all manner of odd but new, pleasant things to enjoy.'

She cut a slice of meat with her knife. It was dense gray-brown and looked as though it might have been larded before it was cooked. I tried some. It tasted like slow-roasted, fire-cooked beef rubbed with spices and garlic.

'See? Have you ever tasted anything like that?' Albe asked.

'Yes, but only in the few chiefly houses I've visited.'

'We've nothing like it. Not on our islands. Whale, seal, fish, shellfish, and the occasional stringy old sheep and goat are all we get.'

'It's beef,' I said.

'Ha!' Albe replied. Her mouth was full. She was pairing the beef with bread and fruit and eating it. 'Cows are too valuable to eat. We get milk and cheese from them.'

'I don't imagine they eat them often here, either. Likely this is guest food.'

'Yes. We must earn our keep,' Albe said. 'Generosity requires generosity.'

When we were finished, we went to wash. I found myself speaking again to the tree while standing under a sun-warmed waterfall on rocks covered by soft moss. A mass of roots filled the room, growing all along the walls and down into deep pools in a tortuous passage that led away into the distance.

'Does this belong to your house?' I asked Cateyrin.

'No.' Cateyrin looked around in an uneasy manner. 'This passage extends the length of the city, from the top of the mountain until it drains into the vast caverns at the bottom of the valley. Many come here to bathe and relieve themselves. The water carries all pollutants away and the tree cleans the water when it runs through mats of roots growing all along the river bottom. But it is a place of truce and anyone who misbehaves here is punished by death. We . . . we don't . . . know how the tree does it, but they always die.'

I heard shouts and laughter from downstream. The voices were male and Cateyrin jumped out of the water and ran into the thick growth of cattails and water plants that bordered the stream.

'If they always die, why are you afraid?' Albe asked.

Cateyrin turned and blushed pink all over her creamy skin.

'I'm not afraid, but shy. The men and boys come here to look for pretty girls, and while they might honor the river here, that wouldn't stop them from waylaying me elsewhere. This is where I met Meth and . . . I don't want to form another connection so . . . soon. Besides, the game is to see them first and decide which ones you want to let catch sight of you. I like to know what I'm getting into.'

Albe laughed. 'Or what's getting into you!'

Cateyrin giggled, blushed furiously, and vanished into the tangled undergrowth.

415

I held up my arms, closed my eyes, and let the water flow over my face. One of the dragonfly's eyes shone down on me, concentrating the light. I didn't hear the voices any longer, only the sound of rushing water and snatches of a distant, wordless song that I knew originated with the tree.

I pondered my next more, not knowing that my path had already been chosen for me by forces I could neither understand nor control. I thought about 'Her,' seeing Her face in Ure's cup, and found I couldn't remember anything after that moment. I had come to myself when Albe and I fled Ure's strange steading. He had tampered with my mind after I spoke with the Faun's head, but I couldn't remember how or why.

Maybe he had tried to kill me. But I was sworn to Her service and just possibly he hadn't been able to accomplish my death. 'She' was a powerful protectress.

Or just possibly She had not wanted him to make a trial of my courage. After all, She had already done that.

But I could remember nothing more. No, that was wrong. There had been a flicker of memory in the last few seconds before Albe and I took the footpath down the mountain. I looked back. Looking back in some instances is a very bad idea. They say the great warrior heard some sound, looked back, and saw the dread hag washing his bloody winding sheet at the ford. And when you leave a loved one, you should not look back lest you see the mark of death – a bloody smear on their forehead.

I had looked back and seen that Wic, who believed herself healed, remained as disfigured as she ever had been, the purple birthmark swelling on her cheek and half covering her mouth, and I wondered if the powers Ure ruled were real or simply illusion.

Yes, but who can say if the illusion of great beauty is not as powerful as the reality.

Then Cateyrin came running back, shouting, 'Guinevere!!! Albe! The Fand! The Fand has come! Help!'

I called my armor and didn't bother to stop and dress. I did grab my sword when I reached the riverbank. The armor is in and of itself a form of clothing. It presents a hard, metallic surface at my breast tips and the junction of my thighs, and the rest of my body is covered by a woven filigree of twining, coiling motifs, beautiful in their own ways, as are the illuminations of the magnificent mass books the Irish make and dramatic as the carvings on the great, monastic crosses of the church. For we knew the cross of old before the Romans debased it into an instrument of torture, and it symbolized the earth's four directions and the divine center.

Let my flesh be bare to the earth and sky, and call the powers, I thought as I ran through the central room of the house toward the portcullis where Ilona stood alone, defying the Fand.

The Fand was just as beautiful as she had been last night, and she wasn't wearing much more: a gold, mesh dress dripping with what looked like diamonds. It draped her slender body, emphasizing her curvaceous form and concealing just enough to create a more intriguing invitation to seduction. She was accompanied by a glassy-eyed Meth and four of the massively powerful men Cateyrin called Fir Blog. These were dark with black eyes and a thick growth of downy, almost silken-looking, brown hair on their arms and thighs.

Humans don't have much of a hair pattern, not like a deer, a fox, or a wolf has, but these men did. The hair was thick on the outside of their arms and less thin, almost absent, on the inner aspect of their arms, legs, and chests. I couldn't see more than that, because they wore simple green tunics woven all of one piece with holes for the head and arms.

They wore chains around their necks, as did Meth, chains that seemed welded together, not clasped and much too small to be pulled off over their heads.

'Oh, Meth!' Cateyrin cried, and tried to push her arms through the grating to touch him.

I saw the Fand's eyes narrow slightly. That was all the warning we got. But Albe was fast, and she jerked Cateyrin back just in time to keep a three-foot gold scythe from cutting both her arms off. There was no hiding place in the corridor, and I felt a long, slow chill, because I could not see any possible way the Fand could have wielded it.

'Get back!' Albe ordered in so commanding a voice that everyone, including myself, retreated.

The Fand simply looked disappointed.

Tuau challenged her with a savage cat wail that lifted the hair on the back of my neck. The Fand glanced at him once, then dismissed him.

'Open the gate,' she commanded. 'I want the rest of the mariglobes and these two women.' She pointed at Albe and me.

'No!' Ilona said. Then she did an odd thing: she lifted a veil and gazed at the Fand through the meshes. 'I cast the omens last night. You will not enter here, Creature of Darkness. That much I saw.'

The Fand did not look impressed. 'You will do as I command. They all do . . . in the end. But I will give you one more chance.'

She stretched out one hand – her nails were an inch and a half long – and gently caressed Meth's cheek. 'Do you like this creature?'

Cateyrin started forward again. Albe and Ilona yanked her back. The edges of the Fand's nails glittered and threw back the light. Then she used the nail on her forefinger to cut an opening into the big vein on the side of his neck. The dark scarlet of blood was a shock against his pale throat. He didn't react or appear to know he'd been injured. One of the Fir Blog stepped forward with a cup and placed it where the stream of blood flowed into it.

Cateyrin made a terrible sound, but Ilona threw both arms around her and held her back. By then there must have been sufficient blood in the cup to interest the Fand, because she plucked it from her servant's hand and drank. When she was finished, she handed the cup back to her Fir Blog servant.

'Tonight this darling of mine' – she gestured toward Meth – 'will share an intimate little supper with me. But alas, only I will dine. Were he handsome, intelligent, witty, or even modestly amusing, I might allow him to continue to exist for a few weeks. But he is none of those things, so . . .'

She lifted Meth's hand and placed his smallest finger in her mouth. He reeled slightly, but had no other reaction when his hand fell away from her lips. Where his little finger had been, there remained only a raw, oozing stump.

'Get Cateyrin out of here,' Albe snarled.

'Not so fast,' the Fand said. 'Let me make my offer. I will return him to you. My larder is full and I have more slaves than I need. In return, you give me the two women.' She pointed to Albe and me. 'And let us say, half the jewels,' she continued. 'After all, you deserve a little something for your trouble. Fear not, the fighting women are a valuable commodity to me and will come to no harm at my hands. In return, I will leave my slaves here to protect you from those who might feel cheated by these women's theft of the mariglobes. Come, think of it. Five strong slaves. He' – she gestured at Meth again – 'is only slightly damaged. Half the jewels, a king's ransom. That many of the marvel stones, glittering wonder workers, all for you.'

'No!' Ilona snapped. 'Be gone, you evil thing!'

'Mistress Ilona, you didn't let me finish. When I show you that I have the means to take what I want, I believe you will have reason to reconsider my generous offer.'

Ilona, Albe, and I backed away, dragging Cateyrin with us. The dress the Fand wore shimmered with a fiery, white light. It grew brighter and brighter until it was almost blinding, and while we watched, the portcullis began to glow a dull red. Then it began seething, sending out the sort of vapor a new sword shows at the forge.

Yes, I thought. *She can make it red-hot. But even a red-hot bar won't give until it is stricken by hammer.*

But by then, the central bars were turning white and big drops of metal began to rain down from the melting gate to the floor. A hole began to appear in the center of the gate.

We backed deeper into the passage until we reached the central room of the house. The hole in the center of the dully glowing portcullis grew larger and larger.

'Close the wall, Mother,' Cateyrin wailed. 'Close the wall!'

She was speaking of the second level of defense, the wall whose dagger-sharp crystals met like a vicious set of teeth and could shred then crush anything between them.

'I can't!' Ilona screamed. 'I can't! It won't work!'

'No, it won't.' The Fand spoke, seemingly un-concerned. 'The machines that close the walls are metal, and they are melting also. As are your swords,' she added as an afterthought.

I tossed mine aside. Albe swore and followed my example. I imagine the hilt was heating in her hand, as mine was.

'Cateyrin, run!' Ilona screamed.

The actinic shimmer of the dress the Fand wore grew brighter. The white-hot bubbling of the metal in the door increased, and the hole grew wider.

I had only one idea, and I didn't think it was a very good one. But it was the only solution that presented itself.

I leaped toward the melting gate. It was only red-hot at the edges, and I knew my armor would protect me for a time. But even with the protection of my armor, I felt a flash of pain when my hand rested on the steel grating. I felt the surge in my chest as I moved the gate just a little from the reality of the city. Then I turned and ran back toward Albe and Ilona.

'Get me some water!' I shouted, and just then Cateyrin returned with a bucket.

I snatched it out of her hand, ran back toward the portcullis, and hurled the contents of the bucket directly at the steel grating. A second later, scalding steam filled the narrow corridor.

I threw the bucket back at Cateyrin. 'More water!' I shouted.

The air was clearing as the steam condensed into rivulets of water on the cold, stone walls. I found I could see the Fand again. She looked baffled, gazing at the cooling iron grating.

Then she said, 'I see. Here and not here.'

The portcullis thinned to the consistency of smoke and she stepped through the phantom steel. Dress glowing with light and heat, she walked toward me, saying in an oddly bland, conversational tone, 'Two can play at that game. You aren't the only one who knows that trick.'

Heat seared me as she approached, and the glitter of the stones in her dress was blinding. I cannot think now why I did not run. But in life I have always known it is better to close with the enemy.

She was only a foot or so away when my fire hand shot out toward the only part of her not protected by the glittering garment she wore – her face!

My arm and hand entered the maw of a monster. I felt

a half dozen rows of circular, saw-edged teeth spin and try to chew my hand and wrist to bits. A double row of a dozen suction-tipped tentacles rather like a squid's wrapped themselves around my forearm.

I hurled every ounce of my power into my fire hand and created something like a lightning bolt. The thunder-clap echoed deafeningly in the narrow corridor and what had been the Fand burst into flame. Only my armor saved me from the burst of raw, incandescent fury of the fire that consumed her. That and the fact that Cateyrin arrived with another bucket of water. I don't know if she hurled the contents at me, the gate, or the Fand, but I was the one who got drenched, and that may have saved my life. My armor was so hot, the corridor filled with steam again, and had it been a real metal ring mail, I would have been boiled alive in it like a lobster in its shell. But it was, thank God, a creation of the faery smiths, and it shunted heat, light, and flame away from my body.

Just as well. For a few seconds I stood transfixed in front of the pillar of flame that had been the Fand. Albe had been entirely correct. It was not human, probably not even female in any meaningful sense. If anything, it reminded me of fish we sometimes catch by night in deep drift nets. There is nothing to them but a mouth filled with daggerlike teeth and a lure that rises from the fish's back and dangles in front of that lethal mouth. On the lure, a light burns, and that lying light calls the prey into its teeth.

The thing I saw in flames before me was mostly mouth. It had, as I have said, a circular maw fitted with rings of teeth. Tentacles equipped with suction cups surrounded the mouth. The body was like a slug's, dark, wrinkled, and wet, but amazingly ropy, with fat, which fed the roaring blaze. Instead of one lure, as the angler-fish has, it had many, and the lure nodes scattered all over its body still sustained the shadow of a young human woman's delicate beauty, even amidst the flames. The devouring fire roared within the phantom of female beauty, illuminating and destroying it at the same time.

For perhaps a few seconds more, it continued to move toward me. Then it collapsed into a greasy, blackened but still flaming ball and I heard the golden rings and shimmering jewels of its gown clatter on the floor.

Death! It was smart enough to know death. Regret, not for its actions but for life itself. Then I saw a swamp at the bottom of a triple-canopy rain forest, a swamp created by rains of four or five inches a day. An endless green gloom shadowed by vast trees with trunks thirty to fifty feet thick, twined with vines growing so close together on the bark that the base of even the largest trees could not be seen. In between the trees, ferns ran riot and moss coated every rock and stone. A substrate so damp, so constantly wet that anything falling from above, animal or plant, rotted down to humus in a few weeks. It was filled by deep pools where these creatures took as prey any fallen or abandoned stray from above, and they fed long and well in the dark, stagnant water shaded by the tree ferns that carpeted the forest floor.

All that remained of the Fand by then was something that looked like a shrinking ball of tar with blue flames playing over the surface. With one foot I teased the ring-mail dress from under the small piece of still-simmering detritus. It was unmarked. I touched it with my foot. Not even hot. How? Why?

Knowledge flowed through me at the touch. Had I this power or was it somehow the dress?

The forest was the same one, but it was a bit more open here and the wandlike trees reaching up toward the sky looked far more primitive than the forest giants that surrounded the clearing. Or was it a clearing? The rocks that filled the open space looked like broken, jagged spires. The sky was gray and the omnipresent rain began sheeting down again, turning the moss that thickly coated the broken stone to a brilliant, vivid emerald-green.

Water came cascading down from above and poured into a hollow at my feet. I reached down to pluck something shiny from the mud and saw that the black stone seemed polished and was worked, the bottom recessed as though to form the lintel of a door. The golden rings were tangled with the broken stone and something else caught in the rings: the ribs and backbone of some animal, the brown bone so soft it crumbled at a touch.

The rings clattered then as they clattered now at the touch of my toes. *Use me!* The command was stark, clear, urgent in my brain. *Use me!*

I felt the repulsion generated by the fragmentary bones to the mind of the woman I was inhabiting. *No!* A reaction from her. *Folly!* A scream from the singing rings.

I/she pulled off my pack, ready to stuff the dress into it, when something broke the surface of the water beside her/me. I glanced to my right. Nothing, only a long-dead tree, twisted branches sticking up from a rain pool. My hands were shaking with both cold and terror. Though the air was thick as a blanket around me, the endless, driving rain was cold. I shoved harder, pushing the metallic, wildly jingling things down with the rest of my plunder.

Back! Back! I had to get back!

The suction cups on the tentacles pulled me upright. My back was seared by the most terrible pain I ever felt. Then . . . nothing.

I came to myself standing, holding the ring-mail dress in my hand. One of the women who ate the dreaming jewels must have gone to whatever lost world the Fand inhabited. That jumble of moss and broken stone had been a city once, probably so long ago it gave me chills to contemplate so vast a span of time. Its ruins lay under the endless monsoon, chewed by the burrowing tree roots, stone walls undermined by rain, splintered by choking humidity and suffocating heat by day and cold by night. Everything organic in the vast refuse pile long rotted away to feed the slender whiplike trees that crowned the mound and the thick moss that coated the few indestructible artifacts imbedded in the soaking soil.

She found it and failed. Despite the warning given her by the singing rings, she failed to put it on and was taken by the Fand.

The rings gave no warning. The Fand was dead.

Ilona drenched the smear of grease with some sort of cooking oil, and it flared anew. I looked up and saw Meth lying on his back near the portcullis. The chain had dropped off his neck and lay on the floor. The Fir Blog were huddled in a fearful group near the entrance to the passage. Their chains lay on the floor, also.

Meth moaned. 'No!' he shouted. 'No! You killed her!'

'Yes!' I told him. 'I got lucky.'

'No! No! No! No! She was the purest, most beautiful angel I've ever met. Oh ye Gods! How could you allow this?' He rolled over and buried his face in his crossed arms. Then he pounded his fist on the floor. 'She's dead! My only love is lost to me.'

Then he rose to his feet and I was glad he was on the other side of the portcullis. The fine wild light of madness was in his eyes. True, there was a rather large hole in the center of the iron grating where metal had melted and run, but I was fairly certain it wasn't big enough for him to crawl through.

He seized the iron gate and shook it violently. Then he turned to the four Fir Blog crowded near the entrance to the tunnel.

'You! You were her servants. Avenge her!'

The Fir Blog had lots better sense than that – they

stared at Meth, obviously completely convinced that he had gone insane.

Cateyrin screamed at him, 'Are you out of your mind? She was going to eat you! She did eat your finger. Look at your right hand!'

Albe strolled casually toward the portcullis. Meth shoved one arm through one of the square openings and clutched at her throat. She kicked him rather expertly in the balls. His eyes rolled back in his head until the whites showed. He slowly fell to his knees and then, more quickly, slid to the floor and curled up.

Tuau began making odd noises. I was about to ask Ilona to get him some water, then I realized the cat was laughing. He slapped one paw on the floor, then rolled over on his back and yielded to feline mirth.

Ilona said, apropos of nothing, 'I wonder if the portcullis will come up?'

Three of the Fir Blog fled, but the fourth stood his ground, frowning at us from under his heavy brow ridges. Then he spoke. His accent was so strong that even when I recognized the language, I couldn't understand the words. Later, Ilona told me he said, 'We are grateful. She was a . . . horror. Her kind are never very comfortable to serve, but this particular one . . . well, let me say only that many of us slit their own throats or hanged themselves rather than endure her . . . habits. Will we be pursued?'

'No,' Ilona said flatly.

He turned his gaze to me. I had garnered the gist of his remarks. I seconded Ilona. 'No,' I said.

He turned, ducked down, and vanished into the street.

'Mother!' Cateyrin said reprovingly. 'By rights they belong to you. Are you sure they can get along by themselves? After all, they're little better than animals.'

'Not everyone agrees with your low opinion of our brethren, my dear,' Ilona said. 'I believe they do well as free men.'

426

'They're not men, and without a master, they're feral. Meth says . . .'

'Meth is stupid as a flat rock,' Albe said. 'Raise the gate, so I can tie him up before he comes to. He has so little between his ears that if I hit him in the head again, it might ruin all he has left. He is only a bit smarter than a chicken, not so intelligent as a cow, and a pig could run rings around him in any contest I can think of.'

'He will be better when the Lethe water wears off, but tie him up tight until then,' Ilona said. 'When his head clears, he'll be so sick for a few days that nothing much will matter to him, and he won't be dangerous.'

The dress rang slightly as the meshes tinkled. I held it out, away from my body. I remembered Igrane's 'scarf.' Funny how your mind makes connections without any logic being involved. The scarf (or was it more of a mantle?) made the wearer invisible, and Igrane had asked me if I didn't think that my great ancestress Bodiccia had something similar to the 'scarf.' Something that reeked of raw power as the 'scarf' did. She had been on a fishing expedition; I could see that now. Trying to find out if any such artifact or even the memory of one was preserved among my mother's kin.

I'd answered with the truth, 'No.' But I knew such things existed and, further, I knew I might be holding one now. It didn't look like much, but then I had seen what it had done to bars of welded steel. It was blackened by fire and coated with the greasy ash deposit left by the Fand's burning.

I rubbed one dark ring with the ball of my thumb and found the filth wiped away. I gazed at the untouched metal glowing beneath. I threw the mass of dirty chain over my shoulder, and when someone strolled into the corridor leading into the house, I realized I was naked. Our visitor was a small, graceful, red-haired woman.

'Nest!' Ilona cried. 'What are you doing here?'

'Amazing you can ask that question. Dear, I feel I must break it to you gently. At least half the city is milling around in the corridors outside. And most of them saw one of the worst Circes enter with her armed guards and her newest doomed lover. Then something like an explosion occurred, and her fierce Fir Blog were seen running from the entrance to your little home. Without their chains, I might add.'

'They're free,' Ilona said. 'I hope the crowd didn't harm them. The Fand, the Circe, is dead.' She glanced at the puddle of still-blazing oil. It was clear now, and the dark material which I surmised was all that remained of the Fand seemed to have been consumed. Only a minor grease fire remained.

'Let me see if the portcullis will rise,' Ilona said.

It did, though with more creaking and rattling than I remembered.

'As I said, I hope the crowd didn't harm any of the Fir Blog.'

'No! No, love,' Nest said. 'They were running too fast to be caught. But one did stop for a few moments to tell us their wicked mistress was dead. He told my ladies, and I made so bold as to enter. Oh!' Nest exclaimed as she caught sight of Albe, Tuau, and me.

Albe was binding Meth hand and foot and didn't notice the horrified look Nest directed at her face. She turned her eyes to me and seemed pleased.

'My dear, how lovely. But aren't you a bit scorched?'

I suppose I was. My armor had turned most of the heat, but it, too, was blackened by smoke. I had no eyelashes and my hair, just growing back, was reduced to a frizz of curls. Then she glanced at Tuau.

Probably just for the fun of it, he gave a big cat yawn that showed every fang in his mouth. Nest bolted.

'God!' Ilona exclaimed. 'Now I'll have to talk her back in.' She let the portcullis fall with a crash.

'Tuau,' I said, 'can you find the lake by yourself?'

He glared at me. 'Is this the thanks I get for standing by you in time of trouble? You send me away to coddle some overexcitable female who – '

'Tuau,' Albe said. 'Go kill some lunch and shut up. I don't know how much help you were at this particular juncture. Seems to me my lady defended all of us, including you. We probably all owe her our lives.'

The glare he gave Albe could have boiled water. But he obeyed and started toward the stair, muttering imprecations under his breath in what sounded like three languages.

'Be back before dark,' Albe continued. 'Try to kill enough for the rest of us, not just yourself. And watch out for those snakes.'

'I am not – I repeat, not, a fool!' he spat as he entered the hole in the rock where the stair began.

Nest had come back and the portcullis was clattering its way up. Despite the noise, the two women were deep in conversation, with Cateyrin nearby, freely adding her comments.

'Let us finish our bath, my lady,' Albe said.

We returned to the river. It ran under the city, as well as through it, a rabbit warren of tunnels and passages, all filled with greenery and thick tree roots. They twisted in and out of holes in the rock and formed mats in the pools, which allowed visitors to the tree's domain to clamber up slopes and cross through flood fords to reach other beauty spots the tree nourished. Here and there, springs poured from the pure white inner part of the tree.

I pressed my lips to one, drank, and received a shock as I felt an increased awareness of the tree's living presence. I found out about the dress of chain mail hanging over my shoulder. There is a curious silence that enters the mind when we receive certain sorts of messages.

I left Albe and Cateyrin scrubbing each other's backs

and wandered upstream. Yes, the river was beautiful here. Torrents poured between big boulders and down chutes composed of broken rocks. Long falls tumbled over mossy tussocks and around islands thick with a kind of cypress bearing small cones and fine leaves. Between moss and the webwork of fine roots, a child could walk here safely.

The city was part of the river and the river part of the city. Savory cooking smells drifted to my nose from eating places that overlooked the water. Some were as informal as our arrangements on the floor in Ilona's house; others were glassed in with rich cloths on the tables and cushioned chairs, upholstered in silk, brocade, linen, and, sometimes, fur.

There were shops. I supposed they were shops. I have never been in any other city. These were glassed-in spaces filled with a staggering variety of goods, very much the sort I had seen when we made our entrance into the city. There were the usual: foods, wine, beer, mead, clothing. Furniture, an astonishing number of different kinds, some heavy, made of dark wood, others light, seemingly composed of strips of leather, cloth, and metal.

The array of both cloth and clothing was bewildering and so were some of the liberties taken with it. The women wore transparent gowns. Some wrapped themselves up or wore a tunic over them. Some didn't.

Among us, it's pretty clear what is worn at home or only in a sleeping place, and what is worn in public. Not so here. Beauty paraded itself near naked or covered in gossamer rainbow-hued silk. And jewels. God, what jewels. Collars of pearls, ropes of them, freshwater and saltwater, black, blue, brown, white, regular, and irregular. Gemstones, tourmaline, ruby-faceted, and cabochon. Sapphires, belts of them, twined with gold. Topaz, golden blue, aquamarine. Amethyst, amber garnet, brown, red, bright red, dark red. Opal. The opals were the most stunning among the jewels. Some were cut into thin plates and set in necklaces, belts, rings, bracelets, and headdresses. One woman I saw bending over a balcony rail wore only a loin-cloth wrapped in the usual way around the waist, up between the legs. The cloth was pale-blue silk. Her breasts were bare, and between them, set in gold and on a simple gold chain, was the most beautiful black opal I have ever seen. It was as long as the span between my wrist and the tip of my forefinger.

She leaned over the rail and called down to me. I was modest up to my shoulders, in cool but boiling foam from a dozen or so small cataracts rushing over jagged, rocky promontories that seemed to leap everywhere from the riverbed.

'How do you make those beautiful patterns on your face? By what art?' she asked.

I looked at my arms and hands and noticed my armor was still protecting me. She saw it glowing green against my fair skin. I didn't want to try to answer, so I moved away into a maze of staggered islands, each supporting a different ornamental tree. The one I paused under had deep-green leaves, beautifully patterned with white.

There was sand on the bottom of the pool next to the island. I dove down and rubbed the gold ring dress I had taken from the Fand in the sand. The flowing water and sand scoured the golden rings that composed the dress, returning it to its former splendor. Then I rubbed myself with the sand to clean my armor. The slight roughness of the sand made my armor leap out against my pink and white skin, but then, once clean, it vanished, leaving me looking much as usual.

I tried to drop the dress down at my feet. I thought it might need a bit more scrubbing. But it would not leave my hand, not even when I spread my fingers wide. The golden chain mail clung to my skin.

I lifted it out of the water and studied the way it was made. It was perfect: golden mail, the rings each one fastened to the one on either side and the one on top. Each ring with a small, faceted jewel dangling inside it. It was perfect, and that, in and of itself, was enough to strike fear into my heart.

All of the rings were the same size. All the jewels matched. Nothing we do is like this. Real mail is made by drawing iron wire, then cutting it into sections. Each section is then bent to form a ring connected to the layer above and the one beside it. The ring is riveted then, to hold it in place. I know. I have seen my friend Gray make mail and I have worn it.

These rings were connected, but perfect. No sign of rivets or the minor irregularities found in drawn wire. All the rings were the same size and the same shape, as were the gems. And I remembered with a chill that, though the roaring blaze that burned the Fand had blackened the metal, it was untouched and barely heated.

The mail dress was a simple one. It was a rectangle with a hole in the middle for the head. The hole was formed by two triangular openings, one in the front and one in the back. Again there was that strange sense of 'I told her so.' 'I gave warning.' Either one, it was wordless.

The Fand? 'No impression.' *No impression,* I thought. What? No impression? Animal? Predator? And again, I was standing in the rain, looking up at broken buildings. Moss. Mud.

And I really was there. I could smell the swamp, an odor of water, earth and green growing things, and the rain was streaming from my hair and wrapping my body in the peculiar coldness a driving rain brings to bare human skin, because I was naked in the rain. My fear snapped me back to the river.

Take me, something begged. *She won't mind. She is gone while she was wearing me. You need me now. The Fand . . . the Fand was an aberration. . . .*

I jerked my mind away with difficulty. *God*, I thought. *This thing is alive, and it can do amazing things.*

I glanced down and saw my feet were muddy. The last of the mud was just being washed away by the river.

And God! God! God! I was so afraid!

Lancelot saw when he returned to the ruined villa with Cregan that there were more of the ravens there, feasting on the dead. He waved one hand at them and said, 'Begone!'

They flew up with what sounded like a cry of raucous laughter and entered into some nearby trees.

'Never before have I seen ravens with red eyes,' one of Cregan's men said. He made the sign of the cross. Several others tended toward less Christian remedies, amulets or horns against the evil eye.

They had taken two of the combatants alive: the Pict and the Hun. Lancelot knew one thing with poisonous certainty: almost never did an adult male survive losing a battle in his world. The Romans took prisoners, but they survived only to go to their deaths in the arena or to a slower, more miserable death as forced labor in mines or road building. But here, no one had the time or the wealth to imprison a man, and in any case, a warrior capable of combat never would make a trustworthy slave.

Lancelot stared at the two bound prisoners and read the knowledge in their eyes. Three of Cregan's men had perished in the engagement, and their bodies had been returned to the river to be washed and shrouded for burial. The contents of the wagon were shared out among Cregan's warriors, both the living and the dead.

433

Lancelot had found that out when he returned to the river and he saw that the three shrouded bodies had gold and silver resting on their chests. Then he realized that one of the dead was Red, the one who had told him about his adventure with the lioness. No one knew him by any other name. He was only just recognizable, having taken a blow from a franca, a throwing ax, after which the Franks were named. His skull was split nearly to the teeth.

Cregan and the rest shared out the wealth and Lancelot found that after Cregan, he got first pick. He saw only two things he wanted. One was a necklace so old that he thought it might be the plunder of some ancient tomb. A thing of beauty, a simple chain of gold rosettes with rubies at the center of each rosette. Perfect tiny pitchers dangled from the chain. He knew what it was: a perfume chain. Fill the very tiny pitchers with unguents and the body warmth of her who wore it would release the perfume into the air, surrounding her with a cloud of fragrance.

'Ah, you do not forget your leman,' Cregan said when Lancelot chose that. 'You're right, son. She loves beauty and careful craftsmanship and has no need for more wealth.'

The other was a cloisonné bird of prey done in amber and garnet with a ruby eye. It was the fastener for a sword belt.

'Might have been made for you,' Cregan commented. 'And look, boys. He's not only modest and courageous, but frugal, too.'

Hearing the jeer in Cregan's remark, Lancelot blushed and looked uncomfortable.

'Actually,' he said stiffly. 'Did he' – he indicated Red with a gesture – 'have any heirs?'

A young man shouldered his way to the front of the crowd. He was dark, but his eyes were the same blue-green as Red's had been.

434

'He has three children by my mother,' the young man said. 'And while he was not the best father, gone most of the time, he was not the worst either. When he came to visit my mother, he was always kind and sober, and brought us all presents. A lot better than some of her other friends.'

How things work versus how they ostensibly work. Cregan's men weren't candidates for old age. Some might make it; most wouldn't. But they would have the best of everything while they lived, including women. A connection, it did not have to be marriage, with the men in the war band could be a profitable thing for a woman. Red had done what he was supposed to as far as his woman was concerned, given her and the children lots of presents. And tactfully, he hadn't hung around between bouts of lovemaking, leaving her well off and free to form other connections with more stable males, who would need her to do their dairying. Sheep and goats were herded for milk and wool as much as for meat. But every man needed a woman to make cheese, churn butter, and weave cloth. Here, as in his own land, women were wealth, and the possession of a skilled one was beyond price.

This was why Magda offered him her daughters. He was an investment.

'He was my friend,' Lancelot said. 'I haven't been here long, and even those I was friendly with I didn't know well. But he guided me on my first patrol, and I believe on longer acquaintance, we might have become close friends. So I would like you to take something from my share for your mother and the other children.'

The young man nodded and took a set of six chased-silver cups. The metal was very soft, a rich prize indeed.

'Almost pure silver. I should think the price of a good farm or a small herd of sheep,' Cregan said in a low voice as the others, each in the order of seniority, came to claim their share.

He sighed. 'In a way, I hate it. Some are born to sweet delight, others born to endless night. But you are generous as well as handsome and brave.'

'A winner in the lottery of war. At the moment. But have you ever considered the long-term odds?' Lancelot answered.

'All my life, me boyo. All my life. I can see even now that you will become a person of distinction. A well-respected man.' The jeering note was still in Cregan's voice.

The oxen were unhitched from the wagon; the contents of the cart were distributed among Cregan's men. The two prisoners were placed on the back of one of the animals.

Lancelot felt a terrible chill when he saw both men's legs had been broken ... after they were captured. Strong or not, they cried out when their captors placed them on the back of the big animal. The three corpses were placed on the other bullock's back.

Cregan thrust the lead rope tied to the ring in the first bullock's nose into Lancelot's hand.

'Boy or not,' Cregan said, 'it's time you were blooded.'

Then they marched away with their plunder back into the mountains.

This was a new road for Lancelot. It led past the high pasture where the village was located into forbidding country, up a steep slope thick with tall pines bearing cloudlike tops interspersed with thick growths of cedar. After they paused for the night, they watched the sun begin to set in a sea of purple clouds.

Most of the men were gone by then. They carried the other ox and their own dead with them. They turned off when the party reached the same elevation as the village, to return home. Only six, including Lancelot, remained. Six and the two prisoners.

The Pict was sitting hunched over the ox's neck; the

Hun looked semiconscious and was leaning against the Pict's back. When Lancelot pulled them off the ox, the Pict screamed and the Hun vomited and fainted. Both men stank. At some time during the day, they had fouled their clothing and their bodies were slick with oily perspiration.

She had given Lancelot some opium, among other things, when she left him at the pool. He washed his hands at a spring, whose water was so cold it numbed them, then mixed some of the opium with wine.

Cregan seized him by the wrist as he was walking back toward where he had placed the prisoners.

'Poison?' he asked.

'No. Opium,' Lancelot said.

Cregan shook his head. 'I want them alive tomorrow.'

'It's not that much,' he replied. 'If I could, I would. But I don't have enough.'

'It's a waste. The stuff is expensive. But it's your drug.' Then Cregan shrugged and released him.

The Pict swallowed the opium and wine quickly. The Hun threw up the first mouthful, but then took the rest and kept it down. When both men were quiet and seemed stupefied, Lancelot returned to the fire.

'What are you doing here, fool boy?' Cregan asked.

'Hell, I'm not sure myself,' Lancelot answered.

'You're young,' Cregan continued, staring into the flames without looking at him at all. 'Obviously, you're a powerful sorcerer. You have a beautiful immortal for a mistress.'

'She's not immortal,' Lancelot said.

'As far as someone like me is concerned – I probably won't live much past fifty – she might as well be immortal. And I suspect, so might you. Go back to her dwelling. Spend a few thousand years lying in each other's arms.'

'No!' He spoke in an impatient, angry tone. 'I . . . I

want to find out things about the world and life. The bad things as well as the good.'

Cregan snorted. 'Fool! You've made a good start today, and believe me, if you continue the way you're going, I guarantee you won't lack for occupation. Because, me boyo, there are far more bad things in the world than there are good. Likely, you'll get your craw full quickly enough.'

'She said you were the greatest warrior in the world. That's why I came to you,' Lancelot said.

'The greatest warrior in the world? Amazing. She thinks so, does she? Amazing. It's not an accomplishment I ever cared for. But ... tell me. Did Red ever confide in you about why he came here?'

'No.' The abrupt change of subject disconcerted Lancelot. 'And I hate to keep calling him Red. What was his name?'

'He didn't have one, not a real one. Slaves don't. They called him Red. Only in Latin, Rufus. He was a smart man, Rufus was. He could read and write. His parents were the administrators – business managers – for a Roman noble. You know what they are called. Honestores.'

Lancelot nodded. 'As opposed to the common people. Humilores.'

'Just so,' Cregan replied.

'I don't understand. If they managed the Roman's business affairs, if they were that high placed, why were they slaves?'

'Why indeed,' Cregan said. 'Think about it, boy. A free man might cheat his master and disappear, but a slave? Oh, a slave can always be caught and done to death slowly. And often as not, quite horribly, by the *carnifices* most Roman aristocrats employ to control their slaves.'

'*Carnifice?*' Lancelot asked.

Cregan gave a nasty chuckle. 'From the word *meat*,

boy. They cut a lot of it. Most of them are specialists at torture.'

'I see,' Lancelot said slowly.

'No, you don't. Not really,' Cregan said. 'But you comprehend enough for the purpose of this story. In any case, Rufus was doing most of the work the old couple had once done. His father was far too forgetful to be trusted, and his mother was crippled badly by an inflammation of the joints. The Roman lord was very tired of the aggravation and expense involved in caring for them. So he told the old couple that if they didn't drain the cup – a cup rather like the one you gave the prisoners, only with a lot more opium – he would sell the three of them to a nearby Frankish landlord. The Frank, not being a Christian, would have no compunction about putting the two of them to death and using their very strong son for the heavy work on his estate. The Frank, you see, had no big properties to manage as the Roman had. He didn't need an educated man to keep accounts. He needed beasts of burden. So, faced with this choice, which was no choice, the old couple drank laudanum and opened their veins.'

'Opened their veins?' Lancelot asked, the horror of the tale reverberating in his voice.

'You cut the arteries at the wrist and groin. You have to use a poniard, boy. Of course, the owner of the villa never told any of this to Rufus. To this day, I don't know who did. I think it may have been the Frank. The Roman would lend Rufus out from time to time. Who can say? But someone did.

'Rufus lay low. See, he found his parents in each other's arms, together in their blood-drenched marriage bed. And he was sick with hatred and sorrow. Besides, his master was guarded by a contingent of Hun mercenaries. He didn't trust either Latins or Gaels to protect him. But Rufus took some money and made a present of it to the captain of the Hun guard. They drank deep and that night, Rufus cut their throats – and his owner's. A kindness, cutting the Huns' throats. Had they survived, their master – his family – would have crucified every one of them.'

'So Rufus had to run,' Lancelot said.

'Oh, yes. And fast. Two nights later he joined my band.'

'He believed in what you are doing – in the Brotherhood of the Bagudae,' Lancelot said.

'Did he?' Cregan answered. 'I wish I did. He wanted a world where people couldn't control other people's lives. Where no one could become a means to another's end. Rufus was a true dreamer. Oddly enough, many of my men, many who come to me, are such dreamers. And, oh, I make cynical use of them to protect my land and my kin. I think such dreams are a lost cause, but who can deny the dreamers and the dispossessed? With every child who slides wet, bloody, and screaming from his mother's womb, the dreams of men like Rufus are born again. Bloody and dangerous the child is. Rufus's sons will likely not remember him, but they will be who and what they are because he dared and dreamed, hoping for justice for himself and those whom both man and God seem to shunt aside and whose misery is forgotten. Like his forgetful father and his crippled mother who were no more use to a Roman lord whose annual income came to five or six pounds of gold a year. A gold-plated asshole, who couldn't find the few coins necessary amid all that vast wealth to care for two slaves grown old in his service until they died of natural causes.'

'What are you doing with the prisoners then?' Lancelot asked. 'The Hun is slowly drowning in his own blood and the Pict's leg is mortified and turning black. He has gangrene.'

Cregan looked at Lancelot. 'Fool boy. You don't know

what I'm talking about, do you? I pay my debts, all of them, even to the dark Gods. Now go to bed. In the morning you will find out more than you want to know.'

Whatever drugs the ravens had given him before the attack had long since worn off and Lancelot was sodden with weariness. He wrapped himself in his mantle and fell into darkness. When he woke at dawn, he knew.

The wind had changed in the night, and it brought the stench to his wolf nose. The wolf whimpered, whined, and wanted to heave, though by rights the smell should have drawn him. It was the stink that hovers over every battlefield since the beginning of time. The stench of decay, human decay.

The Pict was awake, but the Hun was convulsing, obviously dying.

'Bring him,' Cregan said, pointing to the Hun.

They did, and entered a strange, twisted forest. They were above the tree line now. But once in a warmer past, it must have extended higher, and the hard, storm-polished wood still stood where living trees no longer grew. They reminded Lancelot of masses of driftwood on some long abandoned shore, silver-white and shining in the sun. For it was a very clear day and the sky above was as blue as some fine turquoise or a piece of lapis unmarked by cloud, fog, or even smoke.

Beyond the trees, they saw the fence – or at least, it looked like a fence. Posts and boards, bottom, middle, and top. And every few feet along the fence, a headless corpse was nailed.

The fence ended at a ridgeline and it had a few remaining spaces. The two men who had been helping Lancelot carry the Hun dropped back immediately to let him drag his burden alone. He was strong and the last few feet didn't trouble him much. Then he stood at the end of the fence. The Hun began to convulse again, body twisting back, arching violently.

Cregan took a deep breath. 'Look, boy,' he said, and pointed out over the ridge, at their feet, at the mountains in the distance.

Lancelot turned and the sight took his breath away. He found he was looking out at the heart of the Alps, snow-clad peaks that seemed to march on out into infinity, their lower slopes thick with pine, cedar, and fir. Blue lakes gleamed like so many scattered sapphires among fertile green valleys. A vista of almost unimaginable beauty, yet oddly fragile, did the white peaks seem as they floated above an unbelievable abundance of living gifts against the perfect blue sky.

The gouts of blood hit him like a blow. His head was half-turned as he gazed out at the glory beyond. The blood filled his eyes and splattered into his mouth. He had still been holding the Hun by the shoulders. He let go, staggered back, and crashed into the last post on the fence. One eye was blinded by blood, but the other saw only that Cregan had beheaded the Hun, and the resulting spray of blood from the headless trunk, driven by the last wild heartbeats, had drenched him.

'You are well and truly blooded now,' Cregan said.

Lancelot was glad his stomach was still empty. His gorge rose and he emptied what little was in it on the rocks at his feet.

'What's the matter, boy? Did you think it was a game?' Cregan asked.

Lancelot's sword cleared its sheath with a shriek. The eyes of the raven on the pommel were open, red and glaring. Cregan's men drew their weapons as one.

'No!' Cregan shouted, and jumped between the five men and Lancelot. 'We can't afford any more casualties, and he – is – just – too – good. Why heaven smiles on him and' – Cregan looked down at the Hun – 'abandons others is not known to me. But for the time, he lives. No one will ever defeat him. Now, leave it, all of you.' And he gave Lancelot one long, sour look. 'I believe his time with us is almost finished. Both he and I have done what was necessary to do.'

'The Pict,' Lancelot said.

Cregan nodded, then pointed to the Hun. 'Nail him to the fence. One is enough. If he will, we will give the Pict the choice between having his leg off at the knee and having his throat cut. If he chooses to let us cut off his leg, and if he recovers from the amputation, we will give him a horse and let him ride out. If he prefers to try another life and let us cut his throat, then we will bury him according to his people's rites. That is, let the carrion birds clean his bones, grind them, mix them in oil and spices, and send them into the heavens when we make the autumn bone-fire at Samhain. You have my word on it. And my word is good.'

'I know.' Lancelot sheathed his sword. He turned away and looked out over the splendor of the mountains, the thin, cold, almost cruel wind keening in his ears.

'I will not say good-bye,' Cregan said. 'I cannot think God is with you, but I think we will not see one another again.'

'Likely not,' Lancelot said.

Then they were gone and he was alone with the dead.

If there is death, Uther thought, *death isn't turning out to be a bad thing.*

He woke in the night and saw a full moon drifting among bright clouds high above the treetops. The tide was out; the sound of the sea on the rocks was splat-splash and whisper. The giant trees that sheltered him sighed very softly as the wind kissed them.

Am I supposed to hate this? he thought. *If I am, if this is what Igrane and her familiar Ustane think of as punishment, then they have chosen the wrong torture for me.*

True, it was a tomb, but he wasn't buried in it. The earth bed of composted twigs, leaves, and small branches was a soft nest, and the slab that should have sealed him in covered less than half his body. He felt a profound peace. Shadows moved among the trees, and he wondered if he was so weary after his ordeal at Igrane's hands that he thought, *come what may, I will doze and dream through whatever the night brings.*

Then from among the twisted strands and early spring criosers of bracken that floored the forest, the creature appeared and put its paws on the side of his sarcophagus. He saw it was a cat, not very big, with very short legs and a long tail. In the moonlight, he could see it was marked vaguely like a leopard with stripes and spots all over its body. It touched his nose with its nose, a standard cat greeting. He had been saluted by Morgana's farm cats in the same way when he was five years old. The greetings had ceased when he grew tall enough to overawe the cats. He had forgotten how comforting it was to be graced with cat politeness.

The cat dropped down and he found himself alone again. He could hear the creature's downhill progress through the undergrowth toward the sea. After a few moments, an apparition appeared that should have been terrifying. It was a massive creature that had aspects of both cat and dog about it. Paws like a dog's with a long, strong muzzle with a formidable array of fangs, shears, and grinders. It was marked a bit like a tiger, with a vivid array of stripes on the back, spots on the side all black set off by a coat that was almost burgundy even by moonlight.

For a second, he feared it might tear out his throat, but it made no hostile gesture. One hand was lying on his breast. It licked the hand gently and also touched noses with him.

Next, four women emerged from the shadowed gloom. They were tightly wrapped in dark mantles and their heads were hooded.

'Thank you for coming,' the first said as she lifted his hand and kissed it. 'Now! Now! We can rest.'

The other three followed suit, each kissing his hand and then vanishing into the forest.

Yes! he thought. *I had forgotten. Three times I was crowned, once with acorns and oak leaves, once with wheat. And last of all, with flowers. Once for the forest, once for the sown, and once for the meadows and the wide plains. Once for the living, once for the dead, and once for those flowers – the yet unborn.*

My blood. Igrane shed my blood here. Not a wise thing to do. It dripped on the floor, leaving a trail through the crypt, a trail the dead can follow to find freedom.

All through the night they came. He lost track, he lost count. Even the big, dead serpent who trapped him slithered out of the darkness to brush his hand with its forked tongue. He turned none away; he denied none the right to its nose touch, kiss, or caress.

Last of all, Ustane arrived. She crouched down, weeping bitterly.

'She is gone and is with the count, Severius. I don't want to die. Dire as my life is, I want it,' she said as she choked on tears. 'Who could know the power that is in you? Who could guess?'

'Power? Is this power?' he asked.

'Can't you tell? How long is it since you felt pain?'

This was true. The lash marks had covered his body; even the hand on his breast had dripped serum and blood. Now he lifted the hand. He tried to look at it, but the forest was dark now and the moon was low, near the horizon, strangely bared by the silhouettes of the massive trees.

'True,' he said. 'I feel no pain. In giving, we receive, and in receiving, we give. I had hopes my death would accomplish some good. If that is true, I have requited the universe for the gift of life and been favored above all other mortals.'

Ustane, kneeling, pounded her fists on the soft forest floor. 'She can give me life again if she would. Life. Life! I want it with all my heart and soul. The throb of blood in my veins, the breath in my lungs, the come and go of a heartbeat, the hours of light and dark, the soft beauty of sinking into sleep. The exquisite, exotic pleasure of food, the need for drink, the raw pleasure of quenching thirst. And sex, desire, the friction of flesh on flesh. The moment of raw transcendent beauty when fire pours through your loins, stiffens your nipples, and at last explodes through the flesh until you are drowning in sensation and satisfied, cunt hot, swollen, and wet, welcoming the hammer blows, stiff, deep, and hard, of his brutal and even cruel demanding desire.'

She quieted, panting. 'Life. I want it again. I want it forever. This was the hold the dark sorcerer had on me. This is the hold your sometime-wife has that puts her foot on my neck. If I kiss your hand like the rest, I also will become one with the dawn mist, the trees, the cool night air, the soft whisper and slap of the ocean. I, too, will sleep. And I don't want to. I was but a young woman when Merlin drained my life and energies for his own purposes. I had not lived enough. I was cheated of my due.'

He sat up. 'Come with me, Ustane. Bathe in the sea.'

'Sea? What sea? There is nothing but cold stone here and silence. The jewel crystals shine and glitter between the black pillars, spun from the earth when this place was made. The tombs are empty now, and my voice echoes from the stone of ceiling and floor.'

'Ustane, don't you see the trees or the moon setting on

the horizon? Smell the clean, spicy scent of the cold night air? Or hear the summer sea? The waves are growing louder now as the tide is beginning to turn.'

'What madness afflicts your brain? There is nothing here but emptiness and silence. All else is dust!' she wailed.

The sarcophagus lid covered him only to the waist. It was easy to climb out of the lower box.

'What are you doing?' Ustane cried. 'You can't leave me! You must obey my commands.'

Uther found when he stood, his head spun and he felt weak. The winding sheet he wore was stiff with lymph and blood, but oddly, his body seemed unharmed. Igrane had, with her whip, replicated the rite used to take a king's life in the unhappy event that he must be scarified. Only, if that rite had been performed, he would have been shot to death with arrows. But perhaps the weapon had not mattered so much as the pain and the spilling of blood. He was unworthy of this magic, but then, worth didn't enter into it. He had accepted the pain, blood, death, when he let his people place the three crowns on his head.

And however great the pain, the blood, and the conurbation visited on him by the fear of death, he had never in the slightest way rescinded his acceptance. The powers had taken him at his word.

Ustane knelt, beating her forehead against the loamy soil, whispering, 'No! No! No! It cannot be! There is nothing here!'

She can't constrain or rule me, he thought. *But then, nothing can. Not now.*

He turned his back on her crumpled form and looked out to sea. And saw in the distance, over the almost silken, smooth, quiet combers, the sky just beginning to brighten in those still, hazy moments before dawn. He made his way, albeit slowly, down to the ocean.

He found himself on a promontory stretching out into the water. To his left, he saw the crystal haven, its domes rising from among the rocks. To the right, the dark trees stretched away along the shore. In some places, they almost reached the ocean.

He stepped down very carefully and something shot away from under his foot, a small crab or fish. The water was cold and the boulder he stood on was soft with long growths of silken waterweed. It was, he thought, like treading on a woman's hair.

Below he saw more domes. They shone with the palest of light. He found he was standing at the top of a long flight of shallow steps that led into the black depths of the ocean. On either side of the stair, the crystal domes rose, shot with blue light. He was still wearing the winding sheet Ustane and her assistants had wrapped him in. It stank of blood, perspiration, fear, and his despair. It had wrapped his bleeding carcass all night long.

He shrugged it off and the white, stained wrapping fell into the sea. Just at that moment, he heard a sound like a vast sigh and the golden edge of the sun moved above the horizon's rim, tracing a river of fire across the water. A second later, Aife smothered a scream as he walked out of the sunrise toward her.

He staggered, dizzy with the sudden transition. Then, realizing he was stark naked, he began apologizing.

'Oh, God! Thank God!' she cried as she threw first her mantle, then her arms around him. 'I was mourning you and trying to think of how to save myself and the child.' She sobbed. 'Come inside before someone sees you. How did you get here? My garden is walled. The gate is barred. I saw you walk out of the sun as it rose by the cypress tree near the gate.'

Her room was very simple, almost spartan. The outside door had a heavy bar across it. The inner door opened on a shallow portico that looked out on a grassy

448

space with a fountain and a few leafless rose bushes. Inside, a narrow bed was against one wall, a chest pushed up against the other. The only other things in the room were weapons, lots of them: spears, swords, shields, clubs, maces, and halberds. They covered every inch of the walls, accompanied by chain mail, leather armor, and two or three different kinds of helmets, boots, shin protectors, and greaves.

'Good Lord!' he said.

But she pulled him toward the bed, climbed under the covers, and pulled the thick, woolen comforter up over both of them.

'I'm so cold my teeth are chattering. I thought you were dead. How can you be alive? You are covered by whip welts, just-healed welts. When did you have time to heal? You look as though you were beaten to death and then brought back. I'm so cold, so cold. I never want to sleep alone as long as I live. Never, never again.'

He held her until she stopped trembling and relaxed.

'How odd,' he remarked. 'Until I met you, I thought I was beyond passion. But now . . .'

When he kissed her, he found his lower lip was swollen on one side, and not all the welts on his body were completely healed. But the slight discomfort didn't trouble either one of them that much, and after a short time, they forgot about it.

'I'm warm now.' She burrowed in against him and sighed very happily. 'Did you mean that about the child? You think I could be breeding?'

'Yes,' he said. 'I think you are. I know you are. "She" looked at me, her eyes in your face. They glowed the way hers did when She wouldn't let me die.'

They were face-to-face, embracing. He lifted her chin with one hand and looked into her eyes. 'Listen to me. The pair of tumblers?'

She nodded. 'Alexia, Alex,' she answered.

'Yes.' He continued, 'If I fall, flee with them. They will bring you to my sister. We have invested the ring-forts at Cadbury, Maden Castle, and all the rest.'

She drew in her breath sharply and placed her fingers on his lips. 'No!' She hissed the word.

'Listen. I am the king, the Winter King. I must try to stop your brother. Do you understand me? I must. We . . . by now my sister – the Morrigan spirit is in her – holds all the ring-forts. She is a creature of the War Goddess and she will bring mighty war to the Saxons if I do not return.'

Her face was perfectly white, her lips quivered. 'He . . . Severius . . . my brother will kill you if he finds out.'

'Then let's not tell him,' Uther said quietly.

'How will you stop him? Then . . . how will you kill him? God, I wish you would!'

'Where is my harp?' he asked.

She glanced at the chest. 'I hid it,' she said. 'How . . . I'm cold again. This . . . a king . . . it's more than I bargained for. They hold the last horse fight today, but nobody, nothing, can vanquish that stallion my brother owns. Some evil lives inside of it. Some evil thing.'

'Yes, I know,' he said. 'And I will undertake to banish it.'

'Oh, I thought you only a singer. Why must you be a king? Had you been a bard, we might have run away together and been happy. Now . . . I don't believe I will ever be happy again.'

'Hush.' He cradled her in his arms until she finished weeping. Then he surprised himself and managed to dry her tears again.

By that time they could hear the household stirring about outside the door to her chamber. The slaves had fired the hypocaust that heated the villa and the room was warm. She still had the fine red and black velvet mantle her brother had given him. A shirt, drawers, and trousers were easy. She had plenty of men's clothing in her room.

She turned herself into a boy; shirt, trousers, boots, and mantle were the male dress of the time. But he was surprised when she wore a fine chain-mail shirt next to her skin and pulled the linen tunic down over it. She wore a long, nasty sax on one side, a dirk on the other. Both were covered by the tunic. She slid a long, slender knife into her boot. Boy or not, she was magnificent. The tunic was soft linen, the trousers blue silk, her boots gilded, and she wore a broad chain of gold set with rubies around her neck.

It was his turn to ask, 'Why?'

'If you are right about what you saw – that you saw "Her" in me – then the child is a gift that we – our people – have long dreamed of. She sealed my womb so I could bring a king to my people.'

'The son of a king isn't always a king,' he answered.

'No,' she said. 'But he can be. As for this' – she touched the necklace – 'I will not go to your sister undowered and a beggar. I can pay my way. And I will.'

Someone knocked at the door; they both started.

'My lady, will you need me? I'm anxious to get to the arena. The dancing has already begun.'

'No, Senta. I'm dressed,' she replied. 'You run along.'

Footsteps retreated into the distance.

'My maid. If the dancing has begun, the villa's probably almost deserted. So we won't have to worry about sneaking around.'

'The arena?' he asked.

'That's where they hold the horse fights.' She opened the door and looked both ways.

He opened the harp case and glanced at the instrument nested in its brocade. The strings thrummed softly without his ever touching them.

She was looking back at him from the door. 'Does it do that often?'

'Sometimes,' he said.

'There's no one around. No need to do any sneaking at all,' she said. 'We can go together.'

The arena was some distance from the house. On the way there, he saw Alex and Alexia doing a tumbling act for a crowd that had gathered at a roadside shrine. They had come to offer the gifts of the poor, some of the first spring flowers and a little watered wine. A man stationed at the shrine was selling wine, beer, and some truly wretched mead to passersby. But most of it wasn't going to the inhabitant of the shrine, who was variously described as Saint Anne or the Virgin Mary. The chipped limestone pylon that held the statue carven in low relief was badly worn and Uther was hard put to tell if the figure holding a horn was man or woman, naked or clothed. He suspected she had been ceremonially naked and had only recently, much to her surprise no doubt, been baptized a Christian. She had many names, he knew, and Anu or Anna was one of them.

Some of the beverages were being poured into a pipe at the foot of the slab, but most of them were being poured down the throats of the worshipers. Alex and Alexia were performing a rudimentary tumbling act for the crowd and being paid in beer and small coins. Someone pressed a piece of bread and a cup of beer into Uther's hand, and he recognized a few who had listened to his singing. They begged for some music.

He obliged with what could only be called a love song. It had been brisk, clear, and cold when he began to play. But as he caressed the harp strings and thought of the rising desire of springtime, the need of the elements, air, fire, and water, to make love to their consort the earth, the wind turned and a soft summer breeze began to blow from the south, bending the long grass and the winter wheat in the fields around and ruffling the petals that wildflowers were just beginning to open in the sun.

This is the origin of all song. The love of life, the love of its flow. Wind flows, rivers of air moving the trees as it passes; rivers of light flow from the sun by day, the moon by night. Water ripples and gurgles, spouting from the earth as wells and fountains, rivers and the long, slow-driving rain.

The people around him ceased talking, moving in closer around him, drinking in the beauty of his song. Feeling the ebb and flow of blood in their veins. Children in the womb ceased kicking. The old forgot to notice their aches and pains. The young were smitten by intense desire. For desire is like water or wind, an elemental thing knowing only the shape of its manifestations, and it has no words to describe itself. But he was lost in his own music and did not realize it until he heard the voices around him rise in song. He knew he had in his musical peregrinations stumbled upon one of the songs known by this motley people. He opened his eyes (he hadn't known they were closed) and saw she was singing along with them.

He reprised the music and another set of words emerged. Along the road, the now-stiff breeze brought the smell of roast meat. He smiled and, playing as he walked, began to lead them in the direction the smell was coming from.

Severius was feasting his people, and ahead at least a dozen large animals, cattle, deer, sheep, and goats, were roasting over open fires. It was obvious that most of this was to be eaten by the aristocrats who were gathered in large numbers at a pavilion near a corral and viewing stand. It was clear the seats in the viewing stands were also intended for the more aristocratic members of the audience, since most of them seemed to be taken. Cushions, throws, the occasional brightly colored mantle were draped over the wooden benches and in many instances servants were standing nearby to be sure none of the best seats were snatched away by casual passersby.

Igrane and Severius were walking arm in arm, nearly invisible among a crowd of brightly and expensively dressed courtiers. Uther stopped, because he spotted at least a half dozen he knew well and at least ten more with whom he was acquainted. All were rich; all were powerful. And all had sworn fealty to him.

The southern landowners were hedging their bets. They would follow the winner.

The outer circle around his straying wife and her new lover was warriors, several hundred of them. And he knew that if Severius received the support of most of the men and women around him, they could raise this many and possibly even more.

The stallion stood alone in the big corral where the horse fights were held. He'd obviously been bathed, his mane and tail braided, for the ceremony. He was beautiful with his black nose, legs, and tail setting off his shimmering silver body. He raced round and round just inside the high, barred fence, his dark silk tail bannered, held high, as he galloped the limits of his prison. So beautifully proportioned was the horse that he almost seemed small until he dropped from a gallop to a trot and it became clear that at the withers he was higher than any of the stablemen who watched him through the fence.

Big. The horse was huge, and no, nothing could defeat him. Uther shivered. He remembered what had been in the dog – Merlin – his ghost, his spirit? What inhabited the horse?

The horse ceased trotting, turned, and went and stood in the center of the corral. He looked bored and lordly at the same time.

'You see,' Aife said, 'how big he is? They have a black

. . . but no one expects him to be able to . . .'

Uther returned the harp to its case. The people who arrived with him scattered. The smell of roast pork drifted his way and he saw a dozen fire pits steaming at the outer edges of what he knew must be a ceremonial center. Beyond the corral and the viewing stands, a feasting hall loomed. It had a thatched rood and wattle-and-daub walls.

'For the soldiers,' Aife said, pointing to it.

'The amphitheater,' he said, and knew he was looking at it now around the hall, corral, and viewing stands. The sides sloped gradually upward, and he knew that with the roof of the hall occupied, the viewing stands full, and people gathered on the horseshoe-shaped mounding on the surrounding hillside, the ceremonial center would hold several thousand people.

'They used to, before the Romans came, choose a king here. Now they will again.' She pointed to a gibbet on the hill beyond the drinking hall. 'They have taken a man already. When the feast ends, they will take a woman.'

Yes, there was a figure hanging from the gibbet.

'A woman?' he asked.

'Yes. Do you know, that was why I was so afraid. I think it will be me.' She looked up at him. The pupils of her eyes were so dilated that he could barely see the blue edging that was the iris. It was a bright day, but her fear opened them like ink-dark wells.

She continued, 'I saw her with him last night. Even at the table, at the feast, she had her hand in his pants, playing with him. And while she was doing that, she was laughing and looking at me. Then he laughed, too, and studied me for a long time with a smile on his lips. They can't hang a virgin,' she whispered.

No! Uther thought. *No! Not even she would attempt* . . .

But then he knew with an absolute certainty how far

gone she was in evil now. And she would do anything that served her ends. He wondered if she would try to bring Severius to her crystal realm. Lay him on the same spot where she'd tried to take . . . what? What had she wanted from him?

Ustane said he would have died. Died of her love. Died like the drone bee in his final, savage mating with his immortal queen. Because that's what she was now – not human any longer, but a creature whose habits were dictated by her terrible thirst. As indeed Merlin had been before her. He trod the maze of Dis now, and he would be in the horse if he could.

They were close to the corral. Most of the wealthy were gathered at the pavilion filled with tables near where the meat was roasting. Severius was dining with Igrane and a crowd of well-wishers and accomplices. Everyone not dining or drinking was reclining in the shade of the pavilion, nibbling snacks passed out by pretty young girls who carried trays of food and wine among the guests.

The poor were gathering at a series of fire pits scattered at the other end of the amphitheater. As he watched, one pit was opened. The spectators gave a joyous shout, but jumped back because a cloud of steam redolent with the smell of roast pork erupted from the pit. Nearby, over a low fire, women were cooking up a sauce for the pork, caramelized onions, honey, and wine. Without thinking, he put his arm around Aife's shoulders. Then caught the death look Severius gave him from his couch in the pavilion.

Aife was looking in the same direction. 'He knows,' she said.

'Indeed,' the king said. 'He may well know.' Because Igrane was reclining beside Severius, the expression on her face one of raw terror.

Alex and Alexia moved up beside him. 'We didn't

expect to see you again. She' – Alex indicated Aife – 'told us what happened. How did you get away?'

'That's not important. Conduct my lady to the peasant feast and never again leave her side. Not until I give my permission.'

'What are you going to do?' Aife asked.

'Stop your brother! Move away, remember the child,' he whispered.

The three stood looking at him. 'Can I trust you to take care of her?' he asked Alex and Alexia.

They were both pale. They both answered, 'Yes.'

There was a shout from among the humble as two more pig pits were opened. The feast was in full swing now, and Uther was sure everyone for miles around must be gathered here, all feasting and drinking, especially drinking. That had started earlier, a lot earlier, than the eating.

Alex and Alexia led Aife toward the fire pit. He stood looking across the crowded square. Igrane was clutching Severius's shirt with one hand and whispering frantically in his ear. Severius was studying Uther with a look of icy calculation.

Will he shed my blood? Uther wondered. There are consequences to shedding a king's blood. Igrane knew that now.

He was standing to the right of the big corral that held the stallion. A whistling neigh pulled his attention away from Severius. A dog had somehow gotten into the enclosure. It was the sort of skinny cur that hung about the refuse dumps that appeared near any town or village. It had probably been drawn by the cooking odors and come hoping to beg some food. There were always some things the master race (human) wouldn't or couldn't eat, and the dog hoped to scavenge some of their leavings.

The stallion neighed when he spotted the dog. Then he reared, cried out again, and thundered toward the dog.

The little animal was no fool. She – Uther saw the dog was a bitch; her dugs were elongated, nipples engorged; she must have pups somewhere. She fled immediately toward the high fence surrounding the corral. She should have escaped the stallion, but one of the onlookers gathered at the fence wanted blood. The bitch gave a shrill *Yip!* as an expertly thrown rock blinded her. In pain, she slowed and, blood streaming from where her eye had been, turned and tried to run in another direction.

But the stallion was upon her. Uther watched, glad it was quick as the little bitch's head exploded into a hideous mist of blood and brain when one forehoof splattered her skull.

Then the entire crowd cheered the stallion on as the big horse trampled the dog's carcass first into a lump of bleeding carrion, then into dust-covered scraps of pulverized meat and bone. When Uther glanced back at Severius, he saw that he and Igrane were both smiling. They were looking at the children playing in the tent, near Severius's feet.

The world they lived in didn't understand or tolerate deformity. Dwarves, the hunchbacked, the lame, or those otherwise impaired in mind or body were dealt with in a summary fashion, usually abandoned in situations where they had little chance of survival. But there were those who dealt in such creatures, usually powerful landlords who had connections with the slave dealers who shipped their human cargo to Byzantium, where there was a demand for such creatures among the aristocracy. An effete aristocracy, corrupt enough to be amused by their antics.

Uther had heard that if they were not too mentally impaired, these twisted creatures could be taught no end of diverting tricks. There were about a dozen playing on a carpet close to Severius and Igrane. As Uther watched, Severius beckoned to one of his personal guards and pointed at a child playing among the rest.

The guardsman walked over and picked up the child by the scruff of the neck. He – it was a little boy – gave a loud screech, showing a big tongue and a mouthful of pointed teeth. The creature's face and body were hideously deformed. The right mouth and eye were twisted by a scar that created a hollow in his cheek. He was so completely hunchbacked that his head seemed to be in the middle of his chest, and so bowlegged that Uther was surprised the creature could walk at all.

The child still dangling in his grip, the guardsman began to carry him toward the corral where the stallion stood, snorting over the dog's remains. Realizing where he was being taken, the child screamed again, this time in terror.

A girl darted out of the pack of children and ran to the soldier's side. She was also deformed. Her face looked as though it had been made of wax and the wax had run. One eye was higher than the other, the mouth twisted and slack at the same time. The nose was really no nose, only two openings in the face. The hideous features were placed above a perfectly formed doll-woman's body. A dwarf, but exquisite body.

The girl witch – child or woman, Uther couldn't tell – cried out, a wordless sound filled with anguish. She reached up with one hand, trying to touch the fingers of the boy being carried by the soldier. The boy looked down at her face, answered, and tried to touch her fingers with his. The soldier pushed the tiny girl away and gave the boy's body a violent shake. But oddly enough, whatever brief communication the two shared seemed to quiet the boy, because he was silent and stared ahead with an expression of fatalistic acceptance on his face.

Uther could hear shouts of approval rising from the crowd around him. They were, he thought, enthusiastic about this new diversion.

He had a moment to decide what to do. No one would

consider a child this badly deformed as human. In fact, it would be possible to rationalize the boy's death as putting a merciful period to a life so filled with pain that it would seem more of a curse than a blessing to its possessor.

But this was folly and Uther knew it. What lives, with the occasional rare exception, wishes to live. Not should any living thing be deprived of life without good reason.

Alex appeared at his side just then. 'What do you plan?' he asked the king.

The harp was slung over his shoulder. 'Protect this,' he said, and handed it to Alex. 'Take care of Aife. Get her to my sister, if you can. And try to find and free the mare.'

Uther gave the corral that held the stallion a long look. The uprights were sunk deep into the earth, each resting in the skeleton of a sacrifice made to assure the sacred enclosure. Most of the sacrifices were probably human. But the cross-poles were lashed to the uprights with rawhide and were the enclosure's real weakness.

'You might also try to lower the fence, if possible.'

Alex nodded and vanished into the crowd. By then, the soldier holding the deformed child had reached Uther.

The king blocked his path. 'I will take his place,' he said.

'Have you taken leave of your senses?' the soldier asked. 'This thing's barely human.' He gestured at the child. 'Ten times a year king horse has faced a human in the corral. Ten times the man or woman died. And all are buried under the uprights. Next year the corral will be one post bigger, and you will have the post in your belly and be lying there, the dry sand turning you to dust.'

Uther reflected, *A high-prestige position Severius must be in. The effort to reach it must have been both his and his father's. Ten years of victories.*

Organizing an assault on the high king wouldn't be easy. The man who pulled it off would have to receive the support of every administrative district in southern England. The big Roman-British landowners would have to be willing to commit most of the barbarian troops who kept them in power; the power that had fallen into their hands when the Romans departed forever.

But nothing ventured, nothing gained. If they could capture the High Kingship, they would command the country up to Hadrian's Wall and sweep all before them the way the Franks had done in Gaul. In fact, Gaul was already losing its Roman name and becoming Franca, or France. The dark, violent barbarians had successfully come to terms with the Gallic-Roman landowners, intermarrying with them, recognizing Roman law and allowing it to exist alongside their own more rudimentary code. And together, the two peoples were struggling to keep the worst features of Roman rule intact: oppression, religious persecution, and exorbitant taxation of the independent farmers and craftsmen, those least able to bear the burden. Slowly, even this memory of freedom was flickering out.

I am one against the night, Uther thought.

He didn't say any of this to the soldier.

'No! Bring the child back to his keepers and tell Severius, if you dare, that there are reasons why men ride horses rather than horses, men.'

The soldier dropped the child. It scuttled away as rapidly as possible, and Uther heard a wild, loud cry of enthusiasm from the crowd. What Severius had tried to do was little better than murder, but a strong, grown man might give the horse an interesting fight.

As quickly as possible, everyone began running to the sloping sandstone sides of the arena. Uther saw they were slightly step-cut to allow seating in rows, about ten rows to the top, and the sacred enclosure was shaped like

461

a horseshoe, as was the corral. At the top were the best seats in the house, and many who had come brought chairs, cushions, and stools so they could watch in comfort. The other best seats were the viewing stands near the corral. These were already filled by the aristocracy from the pavilion. Severius and Igrane shared a comfortable couch at the top.

Uther turned and the wicked hatred in the horse burned from the beast's eyes into his own.

'Are you there?' Uther whispered.

And Merlin's voice answered, coming into his mind, *Yes, and I am going to kill you, old man. Your hour has come. When I was in the dog at the inn, the music your fingers called from the harp held me at bay. But now we meet face-to-face, hand to hand, and your magic is powerless against me.*

Uther nodded and began unwinding the velvet and brocade mantle he wore. He tossed it over one of the crossbars of the corral. He heard a shout rise from the crowd and a rustling all around him. At least two dozen of Severius's soldiers had stepped up and were pointing their spears into the corral.

In the sudden silence, he heard Severius's command. 'Once inside the corral, O singer of songs, there you stay. If you try to escape the stallion by crawling or jumping outside, my men have been ordered to run a spear through your body.'

Uther didn't trust himself to answer. In spite of his bravado when he spoke to the soldier, he was about as frightened as he had ever been in his whole life. He gave a curt nod to show he understood, then stooped over and dried his sweat-covered hands in the dust.

Then, as he accomplished this, he dropped down on his belly and rolled into the corral.

'Surprise, Merlin. Here I come,' he whispered as he cleared the bottom cross-beam.

The stallion thundered toward him, teeth bared. But Uther might as well have been born on a horse. His first ride was lost in the mists that surround early childhood, and he had known how to control any horse since he could remember. To him, riding was as natural an action as walking or running. There was nothing he didn't know about the tricks the brutes could pull on a frightened or inept rider. He'd seen, endured, and learned to counter all of them. Yes, there are indeed reasons men ride horses, not the other way around.

The stallion plunged in, charging right at him. He came to his feet in the hero's salmon leap, which takes a man to his feet in one movement rather than the two usually required. He dodged the stallion's charge as the man-beast raised his forehooves to dash out his brains, as he had the dog's.

When anything commits itself, brute or human, it's vulnerable. A second later, he was behind the rearing stallion and gleefully took the opportunity to land a savage, solid, paralyzing kick in the balls. The stallion screamed in much the same way as a man might have, as a raw agony whipped through his body. Uther felt Merlin lose his grip on the horse's mind. The tormented animal fled him, running to the other side of the corral and backing against the fence.

The horse backed so close to the poles that he ran one muscular buttock into the point of a spear held by the guardsmen who surrounded the corral. This time, the stallion shrieked with rage, spun around and snaked his head through the crosspieces and seized the shoulder of the guardsman who had inadvertently nicked him. The guardsman screamed and Uther winced as he heard the bones snap like rotten sticks between the horse's teeth.

But Merlin was frustrated, and Uther could feel it. He was trying to regain control of the horse. He wasn't interested in punishing or destroying anyone but Uther.

The depth and dedication of his hatred was so deep that it surprised the high king.

'Why?' he asked.

'Not even Vortigen ever dared defy me as you have. Almost . . . almost I managed to put my own candidate on the high king's seat. But you broke my hold over Arthur and I failed.'

By then Merlin was in control of the stallion, and he lunged toward Uther, thundering across the corral at him. This time, at the last minute the stallion pivoted and lashed out, aiming his iron-shod heels at Uther's head and body. Uther dropped and darted under the horse's belly, through the solidly planted forelegs, spun around, and delivered a powerful punch to the horse's tender nose.

The animal screamed again. The soft nose and upper lip are, next to the place where the king had landed his first kick, the most sensitive spots on a horse's body. Horses get nosebleeds; the nostrils are not only sensitive but large and filled with ropy blood vessels. Blood spurted from the horse's nose and pain nearly blinded him, again loosening Merlin's grip on the horse's mind. This time the horse trotted away shaken, blowing through his bleeding nostrils, and kept his distance from the man.

Rage, Uther thought, *is debilitating. Fear is invigorating. A horse will in any case tire more quickly than a strong man.*

Uther began to dream of victory. He reckoned without Severius.

The stone came out of nowhere, slicing open his upper cheek. He tasted blood on his lips. The second rock caught him just above the right eye, landing a glancing blow that tore open his forehead and blinded him in that eye as blood spurted from his forehead and poured down, blocking his vision.

The stallion chose that moment to charge again.

Uther tried to dodge, but the horse invented a new tactic. He swung his forehead at the man and, keeping his sensitive nose tucked under, slammed him into one of the uprights of the corral. Uther felt the wind go out of him in a whoosh, but his countermove was instinctive. He moved to one side, seized the horse's braided mane, and vaulted onto the horse's back.

The animal went insane. He reared almost straight up, screaming, enraged. For a second, Uther looked out over the heads of the crowd and a clear view of the screaming mass of people gathered around the uprights – spears at the ready, Igrane and Severius at the top of the viewing stands, fear and astonishment on their faces – all of this imprinted itself on his brain. Then another well-thrown rock smacked hard against his temple and his consciousness flew apart, shattering like a fine glass vessel when it hits the floor – into shards of dazzling light.

But even in the sudden darkness, he heard the howl rise as one from the throats of the spectators as the crowd became a mob. A second later, he was flying through the air, knowing he would land hard. But to learn the hero's salmon leap is to learn how to fall. His shoulders took the impact and he twisted as he landed, knees drawn up, heels driving downward, spine rigid, lifting him to his feet again.

A second later, he heard a scream as the first rock thrower died at the hands of the mob, and then another terrified shriek as the second rock thrower came flying headfirst through the crossbars and landed at the horse's feet. The maddened animal and Merlin were in full accord. The rage of one and despair and frustration of the other were ready to spend themselves on any target, and the prone man was the closest target. The horse reared and the iron-shod hooves came driving down. As with the dog, a spray of blood and splinters of bone flew into the air. Enraged and completely out of control, Merlin's control or any other's, the stallion reared again and again, trampling the shattered carcass before him into an almost unrecognizable lump of blood, meat, and scattered, brighter-red fragments of bone.

Uther had time to retreat to the other side of the corral, get his breath, and allow his head to clear. Victory was within his reach. For the first time in his dangerous journey, he sensed he'd won.

The stallion's fury was turning to exhaustion, and the sorcerer's grip on the animal's mind was slipping. The horse stood blowing like a bellows, his satiny coat covered with foam, legs trembling, staring down at the corpse in front of him.

'Merlin!' Uther commanded. 'Speak to me. You boasted you knew how to win this engagement between myself and the dread Lord of the Other World, King Bade of Anwin. You boasted you knew how to get him to release my son.'

'I lied!' the sorcerer sneered at his opponent.

Uther began walking toward the exhausted animal.

'Beware, sorcerer. I am the king, King of the Living, the yet unborn and the dead. I command you! Speak or I will banish you from the beast's mind to wander forever, to hang from the tree where dangle the heads of traitors and the foresworn rejected by both paradise and Gahanna, where Dis Pater rules. Leaving your soul caught between worlds in eternal misery, loneliness, and despair.'

The horse lifted his forefeet and let go a cry of sorrow so profound that Uther heard a gasp of amazement from the spectators surrounding the corral. They seemed surprised that an animal could make such a sound.

'Answer me, consular lost in darkness, lest you spend eternity fleeing to escape my curse!' Uther reached the horse, twined one hand in his mane, and vaulted up to his back. 'Answer me,' he whispered, 'and I will set you free.'

'Truly, I do not know. The answer is couched in the form of a riddle. But I will speak what wisdom I have garnered as I searched the omens. The madness that troubles my mind is a torment. I would give my life to be set free.' For the first time there was a plaintive note in the sorcerer's voice.

'A fair exchange. Tell me what you know,' Uther said. 'And you have my word, I will set you free.'

A strange sense of his own power shook him, and the crowd was silent as he urged the weary stallion into a cooling walk around the corral.

'The sword,' the sorcerer said, 'is in the stone, and she must bring Arthur the sword that is in the stone. He must lie with the Flower Bride of England and she must bring him to the sword that is in the stone. When he holds the sword in one hand and the cup in the other, he will be king in both worlds. That is all I know. All I have ever been able to learn.'

'And so, sorrowful spirit, be gone,' Uther cried aloud. 'Be – gone!'

The horse he was riding became only a horse, not a killing machine, and he recovered from the battle and seemed content to have the man on his back. Uther found he could guide the stallion with his posture and his knees. He was one of the finest horses Uther had even been on, and within a few moments of beginning his cool-off, the wild blowing ceased and the animal got his breath back. The crowd surrounded the corral three-deep, waving their hands through the bars or climbing the crosspieces, trying to touch the man or horse and cheering wildly. Entertainment was only rarely a part of their lives, and what they had seen today was the stuff of legends.

Even the Roman emperors had been afraid of the mob

at the arena, and most often had not dared to cross them. Severius and his glittering guests in the viewing stand looked intimidated. Severius was sitting upright on his couch, his arm around Igrane, her hand resting on his thigh. He was white with fury.

When the cheering died down and he could be heard, he bellowed, 'Loose the black!!!'

He was answered by wild cheers from the crowd. They tore away from the corral, back toward their positions on the sloping sides and top of the arena. Then Severius turned and spoke in an undertone to one of the Saxon mercenaries near him, a big, powerful man wearing a golden helmet and carrying the long shield of a true cavalryman.

The big mercenary began rounding up his compatriots and positioning them around the viewing stand to protect Severius and his guests. Uther reflected that Severius's people had no reason to love him, and his latest atrocity – murdering the young man who dared marry without his permission – had not endeared him to them. No, not at all. In fact, it might have been the final straw.

He turned the horse and brought him to the center of the corral. The horse stood quiet, breathing evenly. Even though his coat was still lathered, the perspiration was drying now, and since Uther was riding bareback, he could feel that the temperature of the big body between his legs was cooler. The horse's breathing had slowed dramatically. He was recovering from the exertions imposed on him by Merlin's turbulent spirit.

God! Uther thought at the stallion. *I love you and even if this struggle ends in my death, it has been an honor to bestride so magnificent a creature.*

From beyond the arena, Uther heard a wild challenge of another stallion. He backed the horse to the part of the corral facing the entrance to the horseshoe-shaped arena and they stood facing the opening. Uther glanced at the viewing stands from the corner of his eye. The Saxon mercenaries were gathered three-deep around them, but people were slipping away. The mercenaries might prevent anyone from entering, but those leaving were another matter. A lot of them, it seemed, didn't care for what they were seeing. They had seen one of Severius's servants murdered by the mob in less time than it took to blink an eye, then another shoved into the corral to be pounded to death by the horse.

There was obviously no love lost between Severius and his people. Some of them probably recognized Uther, and they told the rest. They suspected this day might not go well for all concerned, and they didn't want to be here when the riot started.

Then his attention was pulled away by the sound of another challenge from the gateway to the arena. The black horse reared against the sky. He was held by two grooms on each side. The ropes were attached to his headstall, but he reared, plunged, and fought his handlers every inch of the way.

Conversely, the gray, with Uther on his back, stood quiet. He only blew through his nostrils, stamped his forefeet, and arched his neck.

Uther knew how such fights went. They would lead the black to the fence and allow the two males to get their blood up. Then, since there was no gate and the crossbars were tied into position with only rawhide, they would drop enough of the crossbars on one side for the challenger to jump the remainder and pen the two stallions together in a fight to the death. This would never happen in nature. There, the loser could retreat or flee.

No, Uther decided. It was not going to happen that way . . . not today. The gray stallion had already fought a battle royal with him. The black was fresh and ferocious.

Uther leaped from the stallion's back. The corpse of the man who had thrown the rocks at Uther was still lying on its face . . . certainly he had a knife. Uther ran toward him, kicked the shattered corpse over on its back.

Sure enough! A sax crossways through the soldier's belt, blade bare, as some carried them, held by a stud at the belt line. Uther snatched it away from the corpse and ran toward the fence.

At the sight of the black stallion, the few remaining spectators had fled to better viewing points on the sides of the basin. The soldiers who had been around the corral were guarding Severius. Now he needed protection more than he needed Uther held captive.

A few knife slashes freed three of the cross-poles. Uther ran toward the stallion and gave him a terrific slap on the rump. The stallion galloped across the corral, gaining speed with every bound, leaped the two remaining cross-poles, and thundered toward the black.

The black's handlers pulled off his headstall and ran for their lives. A second later, the two stallions crashed together, breast to breast. A tremendous shout rose from the crowd and those still remaining in the viewing stands.

The black was no weakling. The gray bore him back on his haunches, but he did not fall. The gray was larger; his flying forehooves pounded the black's chest and neck. But the black could bite and did, sinking his teeth deep into the gray's shoulder until blood poured over the gray's chest and forelegs.

Both animals seemed glad to break and circle each other, tails high-bannered, looking for an opening. The black charged again, neck snaking down, trying for one of the gray's forelegs. But the gray spun around and lashed out with his heels. The black dodged a skull-crushing kick in the face, but took a thunderous blow to the ribs that staggered him for a second.

Then the two began circling each other again. Again they slammed together, chest to chest, rearing, slamming at each other with their forefeet. The gray lost his balance and went over backward, screaming, mane and tail flying. The black charged in, forehooves slamming down on the gray's face, neck, and chest.

But the gray was rolling as he landed, and a second later, he was on his feet. He looked dazed and was bleeding from a half dozen wounds inflicted by the black's hooves on his face and chest. Uther expected him to flee as the black pressed the attack. The gray's face and chest were sprayed with scarlet and blood was trickling from his nostrils. But he met the black's lunge and returned blow for blow with his forehooves.

The black backed, and both horses circled again. Both animals were bleeding seriously, big, scarlet drops splattering into the dust at their feet. To Uther's surprise, he saw that the black, fresh in the beginning, was now breathing harder than the gray. Less stamina, or had the gray's kick broken a rib? But Uther didn't know if the gray had another charge in him.

Then both animals backed away and stood stock-still. Aife appeared just outside the opening to the arena. She was leading the mare.

The gray reared, a magnificent sight even with his coat flocked with bloody lather and his mane and tail a wild tangle. He screamed, a cry of both possession and ferocity, and charged again.

The black turned tail and ran, thundering past Aife and the mare at the entrance and away, out across the fields springing green. Aife loosed the mare and Uther did the most dangerous thing he'd ever done in his life. He ran toward the stallion, seized the mane, and vaulted onto his back. He drove in his heels and the stallion, accompanied by the mare, began a circuit of the horseshoe-shaped arena.

Once – the stallion flew around the viewing stands, past the wildly cheering people on the sloping sides of the arena, around the empty drinking hall, over the ruins of the pavilion where Severius and his friends had gathered earlier in the day to feast and drink.

Twice – around the arena. Uther, from the stallion's back, saw most of the well-wishers Severius had gathered were gone, fled like the losing horse.

A third time and this time he bellowed above the shouts of the crowd, above the thunder of the stallion's hooves in the dust, 'The horse is a king horse, and only a king may ride him! I am a king. Thrice-crowned King Uther of the House of Pendragon! High King of Alba, my native land!'

Then the stallion stopped and the mare presented her tail to him. He mounted her, Uther still mounted on his back. The king had a moment's fear that his kick might have injured the stallion in an important place. But he felt giant loins beneath him bunch and relax as the stallion penetrated the mare, then bunch and relax again and yet again as his powerful thrusts sank deep into her body.

All around him the arena went insane. Severius's unhappy tenants charged the drinking hall and the viewing stands. Just before they collapsed, Uther saw the Saxon mercenaries surround Severius and Igrane and rush them away. The mob streamed out of the arena in pursuit.

The mare cried out, then the stallion, and Uther felt the stallion's spasms of completion shake the beast's powerful body like a minor earthquake. Then he dropped back and the mare pranced away. A second later, Aife had the mare and was pulling on her headstall. A second after that, she was on her back.

The two horses and the man and woman mounted on them ran from the arena enclosure, turned away from the villa and its surrounding fields and, breaking into a gallop, fled away into the golden afternoon.

CHAPTER EIGHT

S HE WAS SITTING IN A GROTTO FILLED with maidenhair fern. On one wall of the grotto, across from where she sat, a waterfall flowed down into a rock basin at her feet. The maidenhair ferns were lush drifts of deep green on wiry black stems. No human knew about this place, and she was more happy about that than not. Humans were destructive animals, and she wanted to hear the lost maidenhair sing for as long as they could survive.

The maidenhair, wild splotches of pale green on the black stems, sang of the fern world long before when conifers, cicadas, and flowering plants had not yet appeared and their cool, green, gentle darkness dominated the earth. They sang the balletic minuet of four cooperating stages that, perfectly realized in the dance with rain, gave rise to more gentle green life and they covered the rocky earth.

The ferns sang of a world even before her time, when tree ferns of types unimaginable to modern creatures formed vast forests where they and dozens of varieties of moss fruited and sent their spores into the winds and the whole earth was nourished by their touch. Lichens, those symbiotic algae of a dozen – no, a hundred – kinds, splashed every bare rock surface: red, gray, green-gray, orange, ruffled and flat pink, and black, their colors shining in the almost endless warm rain.

She closed her eyes to pick out the colorful threads of the ferns' music, then opened them to look into her mirror. She widened her eyes, making them larger. No. Might work in a painting, but not with real eyes. They took up too much of her face.

She studied the fingernails on her right hand. She wished them longer, and they grew. Stained with henna, they became talons a bird of prey might envy. She sighed. No, they would probably frighten him and, if not, he would laugh. She changed the colors to blue, then black. Corpselike. She studied the mirror and made her lips blue. God! No! She looked dead, a drowning victim.

Still, it might give him a perverse pleasure to couple with a corpse. She could lie very still. No, that was not her idea of fun. Nor his either, she suspected.

'Shit!' She put the mirror in her lap and spoke to the ferns. 'I'm bored. I just hope he's becoming the warrior he wants to be.'

She studied the mirror, its back gold, gracefully curved in a classic, very utilitarian design, an oval rimmed with leaves rather like a wreath, overlapping one another. The leaf pattern was so subtle they seemed less leaves than the suggestion of leaves. The face was highly polished silver. It had no handle, but was held between the thumb and second finger.

Where had she gotten it? She tried to remember. At a town. It considered itself a city, but it would be a small town to any city worthy of the name now. Near the Dardanelles. What was the name? Ah, yes, Troy.

She haunted a pool, an oracular pool at a temple near the house occupied by the chief priest of the city. The priest's house looked down across a low wall, on a beach where the traders pulled their shallow-draft vessels up on the sand and haggled with the chief's men and rulers of the city. They needed to come here, those traders. There was no other place along the coast where they could stop and take on food and water for the long journey across the blue Aegean to reach the cites and towns that were rising everywhere near rivers and springs. Growing wheat, not gathering it, and heady with their new riches, pastures filled with sheep, flocks of goats, and even the dangerous aroches, tamed wild cattle.

These people felt the wealth of the world; amber, gold, and loose nuggets of raw silver belonged to them, and they possessed the wealth in butter, new-made cheese, and, strangest and most visionary of all, beverages, wine – enough to buy what they wanted. The traders who provisioned themselves below the walls of Troy were ready and willing to sell them all they could gather on their voyages.

She closed her eyes and saw it as it had been then: the white, close-set houses spilling down the sandy slopes; the wall, whitewashed also. The traders and townspeople haggling on the beach. The priestesses stood on the walls, not bold enough to go among the traders. There were stories of girls carried off by merchantmen and never seen again. But the priestesses would cluster on the wall, and some of them would catch the eyes of bearded, dark, curly-haired men, and those men would make their way into the city by night to the temple.

The goddess stood as the lady, for she had no other name even then except The Lady. She stood at the end of a long – it seemed long – pillared hall. The image was of wood; her flounced skirts were decorated with ivory and she wore a mantle of Egyptian linen. She held a snake in one hand and a distaff in the other. All along the walls were cubicles where the priestesses waited. An offering was made at the high altar, then a priestess directed the man to one of the cubicles. In each, a girl lay. The bed was alder wood with a leather strap webbing and only a single linen sheet between the waiting girl and the night's cold. Whoever, whatever the man might be, the girl embraced him, opening her arms and legs.

She knew these humans were accomplishing remarkable things, but when the girls came to make offerings to the pool beyond 'Her' statue, their eyes were always so sad. But the high priest grew rich and the city grew rich, and even some of the girls were able to earn a dowry and marry. Not the one who devoted the mirror, though. It had belonged to a female lover, one of the other priestesses.

Disease didn't spare these women; they, most of them, died young, as this priestess's companion had. The girl was somber when she brought the mirror and a pair of filigree earrings to the pool. The earrings drifted away into darkness; the girl's eyes had widened in surprise when a hand reached out of the shadowed depths and grasped the mirror.

But it didn't do to let these humans know too much. They were so sad.

She looked into the mirror at her face again. It hadn't changed, but then, she didn't expect it to. Sentient beings were not her call, and the ones who would have understood, nurtured, and protected them were long gone. The last of them died when the world cracked. She had been only a child when the horrific destruction had been visited on the planet.

As she told Lancelot, her kind were tough, but not immortal, and many had died, swept away in the devastation. Others, seeing the beauty they had devoted their lives to preserving melting away in the crucible of heaven, had given up, yielded their lives to the chaos around them, and were destroyed.

The survivors fought back. Child or not, she had, joining the dragons and the few remaining Fauns in a battle to salvage what could be rescued from the ancient order now forever disrupted and lost. But then, who knows?

She closed her eyes and listened to the fern song. She ached to walk through those lost, silent forests that burgeoned when green growing things escaped the first seas and slowly began their spread across the barren continents. They filled the seacoast, then spread rapidly along the river systems. Tall thickets of horsetails, spreading water fern, growing on the surface of every pond and river. Vining creatures not fern nor water plant could cover rocks or grow across mud flats or sometimes rear up high as trees. Fern trees; how many kinds had there been? Some with long fronds that drooped like willows; others with tall trunks and fronds curled like fists. These rose on long, whiplike stems and managed to tower over the rest so high they were able to capture the sun on the darkest day, and when dry times came, recover the moisture of low-lying clouds.

These were forests of silence. There were no insects. The slow creatures of the seas, rivers, and pools had not yet learned to escape the water dominion, and birds were yet far in the future. The only sounds were wind strumming the forests as though they were some primordial musical instruments and water gurgling, rushing, drumming as rain, splattering and at last whispering on its way to the eternal sea.

Fern dreams. She had come to them during the centuries of struggle when she and her kind fought to keep life strong, complex, and resilient on this world, circling its tiny sun. She and her kind had won, and the fruits of her victory resonated in her blood and bone to this day. Yet when they had won and reached back, looking for the ancient knowledge that had created them . . . they found it was gone. All that was left to do was hope that when intelligent life emerged again from among their charges, it would begin again, the adventure of

478

thought and knowledge that had brought them into being at the beginning.

She wondered what Cregan would teach him, and was afraid her boy of water and light might find out from the embittered old warrior the folly and senselessness of it all. And that was too bad, if he did, because she herself, regardless of the immense amount of time she had lived, hadn't found life meaningless ever. In many ways, simply living was its own reason for existence. Each day brought some new surprise, some new beauty to be appreciated, some new piece of knowledge to be assimilated. Sometimes a new friend, as it had been the day he appeared at her lake; whatever happened, a red-letter day in her calendar forever.

She smiled into the mirror. Yes, her face was fine this way.

'I'm brooding,' she told the ferns.

'We noticed,' was the answer.

'We' was the proper term. They were all one organism and, like the water lily, were self-aware.

'I don't usually brood, and I can't think why I am now.'

A hummingbird, green and gold, a living jewel, dropped down into the grotto.

'There are no flowers here,' the ferns whispered to him.

'Water,' was the bird's reply. He flew in and out of the spray from the waterfall, then perched on a fern frond and rested. Hummingbirds do this more frequently than most humans realize. Their way of life is very strenuous.

'Love?' she asked the ferns.

'We think not,' was the reply. 'You have been in love often and never has it affected you this way. "Perturbation."'

'Perturbation?' she repeated.

'That's all we know, but we feel it everywhere, and it

is centered around your lover, born of water and light.'

'The sorcerer! The old sorcerer at the lake?' She gasped. 'I had forgotten, ladies. All I could think of was him, my need to capture him and begin a new affair of the heart. Besides, I despise these scavengers, each hell-bent on outdoing the other and grabbing hold of fragments of a past they don't even try to comprehend. Seeking only for the power they gain from controlling things that are shards of a transcendent whole, now lost. Lost forever.'

She became a swift cloud of mist, then rain, cascading into the basin at the foot of the falls. She barely heard the maidenhair fern's soft, 'My sister, good-bye.'

Lancelot slept through the day, or most of it. When he woke, he found the ravens covered the ground around him. In the afternoon, the clouds had moved in and now the sunset was a wash of vivid scarlet across gray cushions stretching out as far as the eye could see.

Night, he thought.

The Hun's body was nailed to the fence. His head was gone.

Lancelot stood. His mantle was hanging over a tree limb and the helmet and sword were hanging from a branch nearby. The ravens on the ground stared at him with red, unblinking eyes. Nothing of what he had seen in the morning was visible now when he looked down, only red-dappled clouds as far as the eye could see. Between the rolling fog and the overcast above and the covered stars above, he seemed caught between heaven and earth, isolated and alone.

The helm became a bird, took wing and perched on the top rail beside the Hun's headless body. Lancelot studied the bird. Something itched when he reached up and touched his face. He felt the dried blood on his cheeks and then when he ran his fingers through his hair, he found crusted blood there, too. The wolf nose smelled it.

'What would you do, O Lord of the Water and Light?' the bird asked.

The red orb of the sun was caught in the clouds and his eyes could look directly into it.

'Prepare myself for the responsibilities of battle,' he said. 'What have you to offer me?'

'Ourselves. Our souls,' the bird answered. 'Long ago, to achieve victory over our enemies, we yielded up our souls to eternal savagery and damnation in order to obtain victory. We achieved it. Our enemies were wiped out. But to destroy them, we doomed ourselves. So we haunted the valleys where you traveled and we had no peace. But you killed me, and now I am iron and carbon, and when I leave you, I shall sleep. So will my brother, who is your sword. The rest here ask the same gift of you.'

'Carbon and iron are steel,' Lancelot said. 'Or so my father, Maeniel, tells me.'

'And in the end, an inert thing that halts all enchantment, even one so wicked as ours,' the bird said.

The ravens studied him with their unblinking eyes. They were silent, crowded on the ground, the trees, the bushes, and even on the fence between the withering trophies of Cregan and his men. From where he stood, Lancelot could look down the fence and count fifteen corpses, all in various stages of decay. Then the fence, the trophy fence, disappeared into the dead forest.

'It won't work. Even if I had the strength to kill each one of you, you would still be trapped by the cold iron,' he said.

'No!' the bird answered. 'You read the garden. They – the ones who planted it – never returned to hear our case, so we are lost. What is the price of peace? You can read the garden. Tell us.'

481

Lancelot bowed his head and realized the ravens were like children. Nasty, vicious children to be sure, but children with a simplistic outlook on the massive evil involved in their actions. They had bargained with monstrous cruelty for victory and sold their souls.

He studied the sky. The sun was gone; only an opalescent band of greenish blue decorated the horizon where it had been.

I read the garden. And he had, but thinking about it was like trying to fly a dozen kites at one time and trying to keep them from tangling their cords together. He understood now what she meant when she told him the logic of the universe was beyond his powers. It was a maze that he could contemplate from time's beginning until its end and still not wholly understand.

He stood between two evil things: the birds and the trophy fence – the dead. On either side. But nothing is ever completely evil, and that was the most difficult paradox that the shapes of the garden taught him – and the one that most challenged his understanding. Compared with a discussion of good and evil, most other concepts were child's play.

He stretched out his hand and the sword flew into it. Then, as he had when he cheated death and raised a storm, he drew the logical path of love. The birds were frozen in their tracks, all but the one on the fence with the Hun.

'Tell me about him?' Lancelot asked.

'He . . . he was not a bad man,' the bird began, and the image of the Hun soldier appeared before the fence, eyes living, face grave.

'Very stoic, I suppose you would describe him,' the bird continued. 'He had an unhappy life. I think most men, most beings, do not have very happy lives. But he loved the vast plains where his family roamed. He lived in a hide-covered tent, and they wintered in narrow valleys where they planted a crop. But when summer came, they returned to the plain to pasture their sheep and goats.

'His people were very poor and the only way any family does any better than scratch a bare living is when they raid the villages that cluster in the river valleys near the water. His father went on such a raid and did not return. His mother went back to her family and when he was big enough to ride and fight, they pushed him to sell his services to the great Attila. They said he would get rich ... but ... now he dreams only of the endless grass and his little mare. She is long dead now, and so is he. Newly dead. And he wishes he had been a chieftain, so he could have been buried with her and ride out forever across his people's endless, rolling plains.

'There is such a sorrow in me, I can say no more.'

Lancelot said the incantation that was also a convenant. 'Each and both ride with me. A short term of service, and you are free to roam the stars. Each and both remember you were men.'

The raven that had been his sword said, 'Remember we were men. Is that the key? We sold our souls to escape mortality. Must we embrace it again?'

It was dark by then. There was no more light in the sky. But Lancelot had wolf's eyes and the dried, twisted body of the next was near him.

'It is inescapable,' he said. 'Speak!'

'You would not have liked this one, O sorcerer of battle.'

Then Lancelot saw a soldier, one who stood and gazed into his eyes with hatred.

'Long ago did I forget that I was ever human,' the bird said. 'But his memories sicken even me.'

Then Lancelot went on to the next. The birds followed.

483

The third raven said, 'We accept you, geis.' He flew to the fence.

The shape of the third warrior filled out in the gloom. He was very small; the face appeared beardless.

'Young,' the raven said. 'A Frank. There was sickness in his village. All his kin died. He was too young to work his father's land, too proud to go into another household and be treated like a servant. He joined the first party to cross the Rhine. He didn't think of death in battle. He didn't know that he could die.'

'It comes as a surprise to us all, I think,' Lancelot said.

'He is fleshless bones. Even the few rags of skin or cloth are gone. But there is a beautiful newness about his spirit,' the bird said. 'And a great peace.'

'A warrior's heart,' Lancelot said. 'A little time with me and you are free, bird. The boy is free now.'

It was dark and they were in the dead forest. The fourth raven flew and landed on the fence near something that consisted of only a few long bones and some scraps of leather and cloth.

'This geis is a thing of terror and pain,' the bird said, 'but it is mighty magic.'

'Speak!' Lancelot said.

'He was old,' the bird said, 'and felt his life a failure. His village was attacked and his people slaughtered, among them, his wife and child. He rode to avenge them, following his king, Clovis. He never could bear to return and try to take up his life where it left off. He followed his king, but rank and riches eluded him, though he was a fierce warrior.

'He took another woman, but his bitterness drove her away. Killing became a way of life. He is not certain when he died. His life was so like death already. She wasn't a bad woman, but he could never tell her how much she meant to him. This alone he regrets.'

Lancelot nodded. 'Will he come?'

'No,' the bird answered. 'He would sleep now.'

'Ride with me, bird,' Lancelot said.

'And I will spread my wings on the star road, O Warrior of Water and Light. It wrenches my heart that I remember now that I, too, would kiss one whose lips are dust. He never learned to feel or love. There is no hope where he is, but there is no pain. To live is to suffer. He denies you.'

'That's his choice, bird. Only once ride with me, then I yield you to the star road. Remember, you were a man.'

So the night passed. Sometimes there was anger, at others, spite. But most of the dead stepped forth and spoke through the birds, and all of the birds went consenting to their meeting with the dead. Lancelot began to know them, because they had come to him for final disposition and in hope of rest. Few spoke about battle, few about death. They knew, he thought, all they wished to know about that particular thing.

They spoke of women as mothers, wives, and lovers. They remembered meals and celebrations, friendships and always all sorts of love. Loyalties, sorrows, and many losses, cruelty, anger, and betrayal. They spoke with longing of the beauty of the world; how fair life had been and how they didn't appreciate it while they had it. And also, they longed, almost each and every one, to say 'I love you' to someone, somewhere, sometime – and suffered bitter regret for having left those words unspoken.

'I never was able to kiss her or him, father, mother, or child, good-bye.'

Lancelot felt as he walked on following the fence down the mountainside that the things he was hearing should blight his life forever. But somehow they did not, for only a few of the dead – the birds – questioned, turned away, and refused to speak about themselves and their lives. Most, almost all, had, however it ended, loved their time in the sun and were one with him in teaching the birds the value of humanity; the humanity the birds had forgotten. In all generosity he offered them back their souls.

'We accept your geis,' each bird said as it took its place beside one of the dead.

The only thing that bowed Lancelot down was the age and seeming endlessness of the struggle. They passed Franks to Romans. Men born under the warm Italian sun came here to die in what to them was a bleak wilderness. They were representatives of Caesar's legions, then men who enlisted under Marius. And yet other nameless Germanic warriors who rode into these mountains to raid and steal horses and sheep. Hannibal's men, Iberian Celts with fierce horses and elaborate jewelry. Greek mercenaries, Ionian cavalry, persons in trousers, tribesmen from across the Rhine, raiders from villages high in the mountains, villages set on piling driven into the water of mountain lakes. And last of all, Etruscan pirates to whom Rome was only a squalid village on the Tiber where pigs wallowed in the Valleys of the Seven Hills.

In the end the trophy fence was but a shadow among the trees, and it could be tracked only by calling the dead who moldered deep in the soil and were utterly forgotten. It ended at last when they reached the river. Lancelot stood on the high bank surrounded by his men. They were his men. Forty oath men, forty ghosts, forty ravens. He wore the raven helmet and sword, but the birds had added a breastplate over a chain-mail shirt, arm and shin guards.

The armor was heavy and he was very tired. He stood alone on the high riverbank watching the rest. A warrior with a bronze spear and wearing very worn clothing was walking along the river bottom, looking for deep spots where he might find fish. Others were scattered along the gravel beds on each side of the narrow stream. The light was gray and patches of thick mist lay in places along the

486

river. His men wandered in and out of them like ghosts – the ghosts they were.

A few lit fires and sat around them to warm themselves. One of them, a lean man in Roman dress, paused next to him. Lancelot remembered him, a surgeon with the Legions. But then he picked up extra work questioning prisoners under torture and that was why he'd ended nailed up as a trophy, his head swinging by the hair from a chieftain's saddle. He'd said after he was captured, they'd squared accounts before they killed him.

'There is no sun yet,' the Roman said. 'When it rises, we will be gone. We melt in its rays like the ground mist. We are dead and not dead, gone and yet not gone. You may summon us with a word. Simply say you need us. We will come. But I cannot think you will find us comfortable company. Yet I am not sorry I began this adventure.'

'What's it like?' Lancelot asked. 'To be . . . gone?'

'Like light everywhere and nowhere. We don't lose anything. We just aren't and then we are. And none of us know why any more than we knew why in the first place. I think that barbarian farmer has got a fish.' He pointed to the man with the bronze spear.

He pulled the limp fish off the spear and tossed it to a pair bringing along a small fire in a circle of rocks. One of them caught it, chopped off the head, and began to clean and scale it.

Just then Lancelot caught a flash of molten light as the first sun began to shine through the trees. When he looked around, they were all gone but the fire was still burning and the cleaned fish lay on the rocks nearby. He walked down into the riverbed, spitted the fish, and began to cook it.

A few minutes later, She rose from the deep pool downstream where the 'farmer,' so called by the Roman, speared the fish. It was like a glowing bowl filled by the new sun. One moment she wasn't there, the next moment she was. She was wearing a green and yellow dress that seemed made of autumn willow leaves. Like all her clothing, it left her breasts bare.

She walked toward him, her feet leaving no tracks in the sand and gravel riverbed. When she reached him, she touched her throat and glanced all around at the shining water, the fading mist, and the new day.

'What have you done? I have never felt so many in one place before.'

'The dead?' he asked.

'Yes.' There was dismay in her eyes.

'I don't know, and I'm not sure. The ravens came to me for redemption, and I tried to give it to them. I don't know if I succeeded or failed. But I'm afraid I might spend the rest of my life finding out.'

'I hope you found out about being a warrior, because I think that you have some problems that don't lend themselves to negotiated solutions.'

'That's a fancy way to say what?' He was eating the fish now and his mouth was full. He mumbled.

'You know that sorcerer that tried to get you to come with him the same day we met at my lake?'

'Yeah. I felt bad about leaving him there all alone.' He finished the fish, got up and walked to the slow trickle that represented the river and washed his hands.

'Don't feel lonely. I can't say I was all that interested in him either. Both our minds were on other things.'

He grinned nostalgically. 'We weren't thinking about much else. I wanted to lose my virginity and you were more than ready to help me get rid of it.'

'Brace yourself,' she said. 'You have some shocks coming and they are not good ones.'

He dried his hands on his leather trousers.

'Your little blond girlfriend is in a lot of trouble. She doesn't know it yet, but she is. She and her royal consort

488

are both the targets of a hunt by the King of the Summer Country, Bade.'

'King Bade is folklore,' Lancelot said in a lofty fashion.

She studied her fingernails. They changed to an orange color. It didn't go well with her white, rose petal skin. She sighed and her nails turned pink.

'You like that better on me?' she asked.

'Stop your distracting me,' he said. 'King Bade. He doesn't really exist, does he?'

'I wish,' she said. 'Next to "Her," he's the most powerful mortal being in the universe. Merlin found that out.'

'Merlin!' Lancelot said. 'What's he got to do with anything?'

'A lot. I just spent a very unpleasant ten hours with him. First, I had to capture him, then drug him to blow the cobwebs out of his brain and get him to thinking rationally. Then I had to pry the story out of him bit by bit. He's still pretty incoherent at times. Bade's curses are no joke, and when I did hear all he had to say, it scared the bejesus out of me. So I hope you learned what Cregan had to teach you, because unless I miss my guess, as Arthur's subject and the little blonde's foster brother . . .'

'Her name is Guinevere,' Lancelot snapped.

'I stand corrected. Guinevere's foster brother. I'd say you were involved in this whole nasty business up to your cute neck.'

'The old sorcerer is . . . ?'

'Right, bright boy,' she answered. 'He's Merlin.'

Neither Maeniel nor Mother were sympathetic about fear. I ducked my head underwater and let the current beat on my face for a moment. The water was icy cold here. When I came to the surface, my skin seemed to glow. The fear ebbed and I found I could think clearly again. The dress the Fand wore was still clutched in my right hand.

'Is communication absolutely forbidden?'

The question was a testy one. I transferred the mass of chain from my right hand to my left.

'What?'

Instant confusion dominated the thing's . . . mind? There were no more words, but a yearning took their place. It wanted to push me upstream.

Well, why not? I obeyed. The tree's connection with the city was complex. Here it served the people by breaking up into small freshets, alleyways of water between islands that, as I said, supported a large variety of ornamental trees. One held golden fruit similar to the type I had seen Albe eating this morning. A nude girl with a small basket was helping herself to the ripest ones.

'Do the islands belong to anyone?' I asked her. 'Or is the fruit free to all those who come here?'

She gave me an odd look. 'The fruit is part of the river truce. You may take what you like, provided you observe the geis and do not harm the tree. How could you live here and not know? Ohooooo!'

She gave a cry of horror. 'I know who you are!' She ducked around the island and peered at me past the tree's many low branches. 'You burned the Fand this morning!'

I held my position. 'Yes, I did,' I said quietly. 'She was trying to kill me,' I defended myself.

The youngster was a beautiful child, small breasts like buds, honey-colored skin, dark eyes and wild, curling dark hair that hung to her shoulders. She thought about my statement for a moment.

'Yesss . . . Aibell was a bad one, or so Mother says. Mother is a Circe. Have you something against Circes as a group?'

'No,' I said. 'We all live as best we can.'

She looked a bit less frightened, but still stayed well away from me.

'The Fir Blog say Aibell ate her lovers. Mother doesn't do that. She does make them work, if she can. It's not easy to get most men so besotted they will let you put a neck chain on them. But it can be done. Mother bags about four out of ten. It depends on the Lethe water, how susceptible they are, I mean.'

'Seems a lot of people here are pushed into serving others by force,' I said.

'It's hard to live here unless you belong to one of the more important families. And yes, if you slip below a certain level, yes, it's easy to be forced into slavery. Only the most resolute avoid becoming someone's dependent. There are all sorts of ways: debt, capture, drugs, poverty, or just carelessness. Mother says sometimes she thinks some of her men just want a quiet spot to recuperate after some failed venture. They get regular sex, medical care, and bizarre drugs. Mother's very good with drugs. She comes up with wonderful combinations.'

'Your mother accommodates all her men?' I asked carefully.

'Oh! No!' The child blushed. 'We have a dozen women in our household who take care of that. Mother pays them piecework – fees for each one. They count up the times and submit a bill. The men meet with Mother on a rotating basis. She tries to make it special for each one. The Lethe water has to be mixed properly in each individual case. But two ran away last week, so she must be recruiting again. That's why I'm here collecting this fruit. She uses it to flavor her potions and she's giving a banquet tonight in the Hall of the Tree.'

'The Hall of the Tree?' I repeated.

The yearning began again, and the chain dress tinkled. It was hanging over my left arm. I sensed irritation.

'Oh!' The child's eyes got very round. 'You have Aibell's *thing*! You did kill her. Tell me, did you kill her to get it?'

'No!' I said. I told the truth. I was defending myself.

'Caressa!' someone called. 'Caressa!'

The child looked around. 'Oh, it's my nurse. She will have a cat with a velvet tail if she sees me talking to you.'

The child began to move away into the maze of islands around us.

'Wait,' I said. 'What is the Hall of the Tree?'

'Oh, you *are* a stranger here, aren't you?' she said. 'I can't explain, but just keep going and you will come to it.' Then she vanished.

I didn't plan to keep going, though. I was tired and beginning to get wrinkled. Instead, I turned, looking for an open channel among the labyrinthine paths that wound among the trees, water plants, and rocks near the shore.

His arm was around my neck and my air was cut off before I knew what was happening. He pulled me under while trying to tear the garment away from my left arm. It clung to my skin. The pain was vicious, agonizing.

I reached up and grabbed the wrist on the arm around my neck. I poured heat into it, but because of the water, I couldn't make him burn. He shrieked and for a second let go. That was all it took.

I twisted free, turned, and slashed at him with the chain-mail dress. It was coiled around my left hand and arm.

It grew hooks. I swear I saw them appear as I swung the mass of chain at his face. The hooks tore through cheek, nose, neck, and upper chest. He went under and blood filled the water.

Suddenly, violently, the current increased, and it swept me downstream quickly. But I had time to see him surface again. The water around me was blood warm, but his eyes were open and his body was frozen, coated with ice. Then the cold lump of his ice-encased body brushed by me, propelled by a sudden strong current that seemed to affect only it. Then the frozen corpse went under and vanished.

I hurried out of the islands toward the banks, trying to get into the shallows and find the place where the river passed Ilona's lodgings. While I was wading, I transferred the dress to my right hand.

'You choose not to listen!! You fool!! How many in this city do you think would kill you for me? The river belongs to the tree. It defended you, otherwise you would have died. Now will you listen?'

I paused thigh-deep in the shallows near a pool I recognized as belonging to Ilona's house. The tree and other water plants had thickly overgrown the area. All around me I could hear furtive movements. I knew I was being watched. They had seen what happened to the one who had challenged the tree.

But as soon as I was out of the river, . . . they would close in.

'Throw it to us,' a voice called out of a thick stand of papyrus. 'Throw down the mail and we let you live.'

A second later, I realized I'd been drawn when a spear slammed into my back. I went down on my face. I rolled, trying for deeper water, and got there. I looked up into the shallows and saw at least four pairs of legs. The one who'd tried to drive the spear into my body wasn't one of them, though I heard him scream. The cry was loud enough to carry underwater.

He didn't freeze; he boiled. I saw the hairless, eyeless, scarlet corpse drift into a deep pool where the current seized him and pulled him away. Afraid or not, I had no choice. It was only a matter of time before one was able to seize me on dry ground.

I pulled the Fand's garment on over my head. In a

second, it had molded itself to my body. The neck expanded; the rings on the sides joined, then tightened. It grew sleeves that covered me to the wrists.

A second later, an eddy current pushed me back into the shallows and I stood up among a cluster of water hyacinths. I waded ashore, the spikes of blue flowers brushing my legs and ankles. I could see them – at least a half dozen big men watching me from the shadows among the long grass, tall reeds, papyrus, cattails, and cress growing along the shore.

One of them moved toward me.

'Let it be!' a rather authoritative voice called. 'She's wearing it and make no mistake, it will defend her. No one, however clever, could get it away from Aibell. And I don't think we will have any better luck with this one.'

It didn't take me long to find my way through the narrow passages into Ilona's house. Ilona and Cateyrin were bathing in the room where the open white root filled the hollowed basin with water and the dragonfly's eye in the ceiling warmed it.

'So you took the garment?' Ilona said, studying me.

'I had no choice. Too many were ready to kill me for it.'

'Nest talks too much,' Cateyrin said. 'I'll bet the whole city knows.'

'Probably,' Ilona said. 'I'd best lock the passage leading to the river.'

A second later I heard a gate rather like the portcullis at the front of the house drop in the passage behind me.

'Few care to defy the river and the tree, but I suppose if the stakes are high enough . . .' Ilona shook her head and sighed. 'Come with us. Nest is dressing Albe for dinner.'

'The Hall of the Tree?' I asked.

'Yes,' Ilona said. 'All the great families will be there

tonight. Nest says, and I agree, the more you try to hide yourselves, the more savagely you will be pursued.'

My armor seemed annoyed at the clatter of rings and flashed out to cover my skin. I could feel thought. Then, suddenly, the dress vanished.

My armor faded and I wrapped a thick, linen sheet around myself. And asked, 'Where did you go?'

'Nowhere!' was the tart reply. 'I know better than to make a nuisance of myself when I'm not wanted.' Then it gave an audible sniff of disgust.

'You annoyed it,' Ilona said. 'Best be careful it doesn't turn on you.'

'You tell that prissy bitch I never turn on anyone, least of all someone I've formed a bond with.' This statement was accompanied by an audible clatter of rings.

I was terrified of the damned thing, but if we were to be companions, I knew I must take a strong stand now.

'You stop!' I told it. 'And stop right now. I am this lady's guest, and courtesy is as incumbent upon a properly behaved guest as it is upon a generous host. No calling names, and no further insults, if you please.'

'Well!!! I!!! Never!!!' was the reply. 'I couldn't expect much from the Fand. After all, it was simply a means of composting dead, organic matter. It had only a little intelligence and no feelings. But I could tell the moment you touched me that you were a being, a mature being, enjoying the adventure of intelligent comprehension and contemplation of the universe.'

Then I got the strong sensation of something going off in a huff to sulk.

'Unhappy, is it?' Ilona said.

'It seems to be,' I said. 'But it made protestations of loyalty.'

'Let's hope it means them,' Ilona said. 'We all thought Aibell a very powerful being . . . but maybe we were wrong.'

The thing had to be listening, and I didn't want to say much. I was annoyed and angry. The intrusion and the lack of privacy the thing represented troubled me deeply. But part of Kyra's teachings had been about self-restraint and the perils of making important decisions when under the influence of any strong emotion.

'Albe?' I asked. 'You say Nest is dressing her?'

'Oh, yes,' Cateyrin said. 'Wait till you see.'

A few minutes later, I did see. Albe and Nest were together in what Ilona called her practice room, the place where she taught the martial arts. Every wall was covered by polished silver mirrors, and Albe was admiring herself. And there was much to admire.

Nest had repaired the ravages of Albe's face with a crystal mask. She filled each scar with tiny, sparkling crystals, and with the scars thus covered and repaired, Albe was a very lovely woman. Her beautiful eyes glowed like jewels among the fine chain and crystal that composed the mask. It was held in place by a snood of the same fine chain that held the crystal mask together. Thus fastened, the crystals seemed a part of Albe's face. When she smiled, frowned, spoke, the gems moved as though they were a second skin. Below the neck, she was clothed in armor.

The finest Roman armor was made by forming a model of the chest and stomach of the officer, then fitting the leather armor to the model. Thus had been done for Albe; from neck to groin the leather plates were solid. Filigree arm and leg guards protected her extremities. The armor was black and dusted with the same glittering crystals that covered her face. She was wearing Talorcan's shoes. They had adapted and simply looked like an extension of the intricately formed leg guards that protected her lower extremities.

'Well?' she said.

'Splendid.'

496

'When you are mated to a powerful man, don't forget the Diviners Guild,' Nest told her.

'With luck, I won't be mated to anyone,' Albe said.

I called my armor. In a breath, it covered me. I dropped the linen towel.

'This is inspirational!' I heard my invisible companion say. 'But you need no masks.'

Instead, the dress formed itself into the same sort of armor Albe was wearing, a formfitting cover from neck to groin. I felt conversation below the level of thought, and the golden bodysuit turned the same color as my skin armor, a shimmering green.

'Are we agreed?' came the question.

'I believe we are,' I answered.

'There will never be another night like this in Gorias,' Nest said, looking at me. 'But dear, do you always converse with yourself?'

'She's talking to that thing she's wearing,' Tuau said as he strolled into the room.

Nest backed away from me and got behind Ilona. Tuau sidled up to Albe and brushed against her armored legs, rubbing his cheeks and the fanged sides of his mouth against the filigree.

'Oh, that's soooo goooood. Oh, I just love you. Ohoooo.' He rolled over on his back, paws in the air, and wallowed, rubbing his face against the shoes Talorcan had given me. His purrs sounded like a hive of swarming bees.

Albe reached down and scratched his stomach. He batted at her arms with his forefeet, but when his claws began to slide out of their sheaths, Albe said, 'Watch it! Velvet paws, or Momma will spank.'

'*Eeeeeha!*' Half purr, half growl. He rolled over like lightning and began to lick his balls vigorously. His penis leaped from the sheath. '*Woooowoooo!*' he roared as it spurted.

497

Then he was up doing shoulder dives at her legs, yelling, 'Wooooo! You're sooooo beeeeeautiful! I juuuust love you!'

'Sit and calm down,' Albe said. 'Don't scare Nest.'

Sill ensconced behind Ilona, dear Nest asked, 'Why do you talk to your dress?'

'Because it talks to me,' I said.

Albe gave a crack of laughter. 'Serves you right for asking. He needs a collar,' she went on, pointing to Tuau.

'You stick out your hand to put a collar on me, you'll pull back a stump,' the cat said.

'Yes,' Nest said. 'Only slaves wear collars. By the way, speaking of collars, how is Meth?'

'I gave him something to help him sleep,' Ilona said. 'It will make the withdrawal from the Lethe water a bit easier.' She continued, 'Tuau, I can understand your feelings about collars, but let me put gold paint on your claws.'

Tuau lifted one paw and studied his six-inch razors. 'All right. If it doesn't take too long . . . fine.'

I resisted getting my nails painted the same gold color. Then I cleaned and examined my sword. It hadn't come to any harm during the battle with the Fand. My tinkly friend said, 'All I did was heat it. Don't blame me if anything's wrong with it.'

'Nothing's wrong,' I said. 'Heating it didn't hurt it.'

Ilona, Albe, Nest, and Cateyrin all looked at me.

'The dress again,' Tuau said.

'It's disturbing,' dear Nest said. 'We can't hear the other side of the conversation.'

'Speak for yourself,' Tuau said. 'I can. By the way, you being a Danae, I sort of expect strange events to surround you. But what *is* that thing? It gives me the creeps. My fur stands up every time I get near it.'

'Then keep your distance, you lecherous little weasel,' the dress snapped.

'Enough!' I said. 'Both of you.'

Nest, Ilona, and Cateyrin all laughed nervously. Albe studied me, a glint of amusement in her eyes.

'It must be dark by now,' Albe said. 'And considering the difficulties we had last night, how will we get to this Hall of the Tree? Last night we had to fight our way.'

'No, no,' dear Nest said. 'Tonight the Guild of Diviners will accompany us. We have guards with swords and torches to protect us.'

'I know about the seven great families, but I have heard nothing about your guild.'

'Well, we are a very important one, though there are a few others, such as the cloth workers and sellers and the grocers and butchers who are even more powerful and larger than we are. Most are smaller, though some few, even though small, are extremely wealthy, such as the jewelers and the perfumers. They don't number many in personnel, but can call on large reserves of wealth, if it becomes necessary for them to do so. Many belong to more than one guild. I belong to three, but my primary membership is with the diviners. I have auxiliary membership with the grocers and the preceptors.'

'Preceptors?' Albe asked.

'Teachers,' Ilona said. 'Knowledge is power and can be costly to acquire.'

I hadn't known about the guilds. I began to ask myself how many other things about this complex place hadn't yet come to my attention.

Albe looked uncomfortable. 'Should we have paid fees for the very valuable instructions we received last night?'

'Good God, no!' Ilona replied. 'You brought my daughter back to me and greatly increased the wealth of my house. The Fand had five of the mariglobes. Meth was carrying them. I think I will keep both the boy and the dreaming jewels, if it meets with your approval. I believe after a time, I can knock some sense into Meth's head. And the diviners serve many of the women belonging to the great families who use the jewels to venture forth in search of the novel and useful things that add to a powerful family's wealth. They come frequently to consult us about auspicious days and hours to begin their journeys and also to ward off bad luck that sometimes attends their efforts.'

'How many don't come back?' I asked Nest.

She gave me a shrewd look and answered softly, 'A lot, dear. A lot don't make it back. They're under a great deal of pressure from their families and their husbands to undertake these little excursions very frequently. Sometimes we can warn them off before the law of averages catches up with them and sometimes we can't. A mathematical philosopher once calculated the percentage chances of a talented diviner making a true prophecy and found our efforts were seventy-five percent effective. That's a great deal better than chance, at least enough to show that we are worth our fees. But there is that unpleasant twenty-five percent hanging out there, ready to eventually foil our best efforts. The more often the women hazard their lives . . . well, I could do the calculations for you, but I think you can see.'

'We can,' Albe said. 'Sooner or later the pitcher will go once too often to the well.'

Just then I heard the portcullis rattle loudly.

'They're here to escort us to the feast. Everyone ready?'

Ilona and Nest left first, followed by Cateyrin. I turned to Albe. 'Those jewels . . . ?'

'I have fifteen knotted together in a strip of cloth around my waist. There were twenty-five in all. I gave five more to Ilona, and she said she will hold them for safekeeping. And she has taken the five Meth carried for herself. She asked my permission . . . I said you wouldn't mind. I hope that—'

'Fine,' I said. 'It behooves us to be generous.'

I heard the portcullis rising and we hurried to join the rest. Yes, they were a considerable party. The ladies wore gray and carried lanterns, wax lights, and candles. The guards that accompanied them were Fir Blog men and women. The women wore the same simple green tunics as the men and were magnificent. They had voluptuous figures, large breasts, narrow waists and ample hips. Their arms were well shaped, but muscular and powerful. They had a very different hair pattern than the men. Their arms, legs, and faces were hairless.

It was getting dark outside and the tunnels and dwellings within the city were filled with powerful drafts. They flattened the Fir Blog women's tunics against their bodies and I saw the women were well furred at the groin. Some, like the men, wore chains around their necks, but many didn't.

'Are they free?' I asked Ilona.

'Yes. They are bound by oath to the Diviners Guild,' Ilona said.

The women wore swords, carried shields on one arm, and held up torches with the other hand. They completely surrounded the ladies of the guild. Albe and I crowded in among them and we swept along through the darkening corridors already beginning to fill with a starlit haze.

We moved fast. Nest led the way with a Fir Blog woman striding along beside her. I quickly lost track of where we were going, so convoluted and tortuous were the passages she followed. At times we stopped to let other large gray-garbed parties pass. Each of these parties was guarded by well-armed men or women, sometimes Fir Blog, sometimes human.

No party stopped to greet any other party. No member of any party stopped to acknowledge a single member of another party. The men and women both covered their faces with their mantles and ignored each other.

Occasionally I saw women garbed as Albe and I were, and though we weren't spoken to, we stared at each other and I got the feeling our looks were weapons and were being weighed and considered very carefully.

At length we reached the end of a narrow hall that rose like a ramp and opened into a broad thoroughfare. A Fir Blog stood at the end of the passage. He had an enormous halberd in his hand, and he blocked our way. I recognized him. Most of the Fir Blogs had dark eyes; none I had seen had the clear gray eyes this one had. He, like the rest, had a pelt. It was just as thick and luxurious on his arms, legs, and head, but it was lighter and glinted red-gold in the torchlight. He was a magnificent specimen of his kind.

I hadn't gotten a very good look at him on the road into the city, but there, standing upright in the yellow torchlight, I saw he was bigger than any of the others I had seen. Indeed, he would have to be to swing the weapon he was holding. It must have weighed as much as a full-grown man; war ax, war hammer, and broad-bladed spear in one. The metal was black and in places pitted with rust, but the edges were clean, shiny and sharp. They seemed to have received the recent attention of a file.

He and Albe studied each other. The crystal mask she wore filled in all her scars and her eyes glowed like emeralds set among diamonds. Both of their expressions were enigmatic, but I sensed that in some way, some place unknown to lesser mortals, they were alone together. He inclined his head briefly to Nest, then his gaze returned to Albe.

'The first families have not yet entered the Hall of the Tree. We must wait until they do. Goric cannot let us pass.'

'Goric? Is that his name?' Albe asked.

'Yes,' dear Nest said. 'He belongs to the Glastig family.

They wear black.' And indeed there was a chain around the magnificent man's neck.

Then we heard the tramp of many feet and the seven great families began to march past us. They were a glittering company. Those in black came first. Never have I seen so many jewels. Black sets off the fire gems, the glitter of gold, the starlike shine of silver. Also, bright colors, orange, red, green blaze brightly when set off by black. The armed and armored leading men were followed by the chief women of the house. Some wore arms and carried weapons, as the men did. Others, the young and beautiful, wore, as I had seen earlier in the day, a rainbow of transparent and semitransparent silks, satins, and brocades. Older women and those who were pregnant, while sometimes magnificently dressed, covered themselves with heavy, fur-trimmed mantles. Many of the women wore neck chains like the Fir Blog did. This chilled my blood.

'A woman belongs to her family,' Nest explained. 'Unless she runs away or another family captures her. Commoner women are free, and Women of the Wager. But aristocratic women – those who can't travel between the worlds – are only good for breeding and that is what they are used for.'

'They flaunt their charms,' I said.

'Oh, absolutely,' Ilona said as we watched the lower-ranking men and older women of the Glastig family pass.

The next group wore white, and they also ornamented themselves, using white as a base to display their wealth of gold and gems.

'There is no marriage, then?' I asked Nest.

'Oh, no, dear. The girls are only prime breeding age for a few years, and the heads of the great families will charge very high fees for the use of them. Once they have had a few girl children, they will be free to form connections of their own.'

'What about the boy children?' Albe asked.

Nest shrugged. 'Most are brought up as Meth was by the servants in the big households. Girls are more profitable. A girl can become a Woman of Wager, a breeder, or one of those who travels between worlds.'

Another gaggle of lightly clad women was passing. They were gazing at us and giggling.

'How do men rise?' I asked.

'Woman stealing,' Ilona said.

'Shush, dear. It isn't spoken of openly. But a man who can gain control of several women who can make journeys between worlds will become a power in his household. Women are abducted or run away constantly. And Women of the Wager are often defeated in combat.'

'That was why Meth became interested in Cateyrin,' Ilona said. 'My grandmother was a far traveler. You saw the lake. He and I both hoped that since such traits often skip a generation, she might show some talent. Her bloodlines are good, but so far she's shown about as much ability as the average rock.'

'She's young yet, dear,' Nest said. 'Give her some time.'

Black, white, now red was passing, and I didn't catch the name Nest murmured. The torchlight flashing on the ostentatious riches near blinded me. The dense scent of perfumes filled the air now that the evening winds were dying down.

Gold was next, and silver, then bronze, Meth's family. I got a dark look from the leading men, but no one cared to challenge me.

Then glass. Yes, the next group that passed seemed to be wearing glass.

'Won't it break?' I asked.

'No, dear,' Nest answered. 'It doesn't seem to be that kind of glass. One of the women in the black family brought it back many years ago. It's a wondrous material, but none know the secrets of working it outside of men in that family.'

They were a whole spectrum of wild colors, all transparent, all worn over very abbreviated, dark underwear. Though last, the men came slowly, showing off their bodies beautifully muscled under transparent armor, red, white shot with gold threads, green, the surface etched with patterns. I was dizzy with the splendor. Albe laughed aloud with delight.

Then they were gone, and the guilds and commoners began turning into the broad thoroughfare toward the Hall of the Tree.

I didn't know at the time, but a lot of this was in my honor. The struggle for primacy among the great families was so fierce, few of the ruling men could afford softer feelings. Albe and I had been talked of all over the city, and we were seen as an unparalleled opportunity for sole rule.

The guilds were frightened. They and their members lived independent lives, free of the influence of the great families. But there was always the risk of falling into poverty and being enslaved. So the guilds have turned out to be sure we were not deprived of our rights.

And there were others I didn't know about then, the multiple outlaw gangs that haunted the city streets by night. Men and women who preferred the uncertain life among the parts of the city ruined, abandoned, or perhaps empty from the first. They lived on what they could pick up, bravos who fought for pay, women who sold their bodies. This was considered an honest transaction as opposed to the Circes, who seduced men into permanent slavery with magic, drugs, or both. Dealers in philters, poisons, or weapons. Fulfill your wildest dreams for a time, until you wake up with a headache or perhaps never wake up at all.

The things Nest and Ilona told me only hinted at the

depth and complexity of the undercurrents here. All of these people had been drawn tonight to the Hall of the Tree.

We entered and began walking to the platform belonging to the Diviners Guild. I was speechless with amazement. Never in my life had I even imagined anything so large. This great hall stretched from the low, flooded forest that served as a bathing area up almost to the white towers that reared their spires against the purpling evening sky. Multiple cataracts dominated the river at the hall's center. They were quiet, none being high enough to create the rumble and thunder of a falls. The very biggest was only about ten feet. Most were under five. The water as it poured over the shallow falls was white with hints of green. Moss and waterweed of many kinds clung to the rocks.

Along the banks, the water was calm and clear, and it was very shallow. The bottom through the clear water formed a mosaic of symbols in many colors and odd shapes and sizes. They fit together like pieces of a puzzle with only thin, black lines delineating each one.

I felt the being I wore on my torso react: 'Sad! Beautiful! Power! Lost! Lost! Lost forever! Still speaks! But no one can read them!'

'You?' I asked.

'No! No!' was the answer. 'Like the Fand – the thing you call the Fand – I came into being to solve specific problems. But I can remember knowing things . . . once wonderful.'

Then it fell silent.

The tree's mighty branches divided the hall into platforms. The trunk grew along the shallows, and the enormous branches stretched themselves out over the river. Each platform of woven branches was a living thing, rimmed with a covering of green leaves. But the platforms were bare, as the tabletop in Ilona's house had been, only much larger. Each platform held chairs, tables, couches, and even beds. The largest were covered with carpets. The carpets were carefully spread so as not to prevent light from reaching the tree's leaves.

The light collectors, the insect eyes I had seen imbedded in the ceiling at Ilona's house and in the passageways, sprang out on long wands from the city's buildings and arched over the platforms and the river. The light from the star gatherers was very bright, like daylight on a clear morning.

The multicolored armor and jeweled trappings of the men glowed, glittered, and gleamed, as did the rainbow gowns of the women. I had thought the commoners would be drab in their gray gowns, but I was proved wrong. The gray robes were just that: coverings. They shed them as soon as they reached the guild platform, and I saw the women in Nest's guild were as, or even more, flamboyant than the women belonging to the great houses.

The young and beautiful advertised their wares. Transparent gowns of silk; jewels adorned them from head to foot. Nest wore a flame-colored gown. It was opaque, but slit up one side to above the hip. Through the slit I saw a woven gold band belonging to a pair of tights that covered her between the legs. The gown – pretty much opaque to the waist – became more transparent as it approached the neck. You could just see her breasts.

Cateyrin wore blue gauze with strategically placed onyx jewelry at breast and groin.

'I have to worry about finding another lover,' she told me. 'I don't know if Meth will be any good when he gets back on his feet. He may sicken and pine for the Fand.'

Ilona wore silver, pure, soft silver wands woven together. They covered her torso, but didn't hide much. She had the ripe, lush loveliness of a mature woman.

The first order of business was to eat and drink. The Fir Blog carried dinner in big hampers. I hadn't seen them because they followed the rest. In a few moments, they had the table spread and all manner of food on it: sliced roast, meats still warm; cold hams, big ones, thin and thick slices; soups, at least a dozen kinds, all in thick-walled, covered dishes that kept them warm.

Tuau arrived just as the food was being put out. He half swam, half walked to the branch that connected the platform to the tree trunk. He climbed up out of the shallows, stood on the narrow branch, and shook himself two or three times until his short, tawny coat was clear of water. Then he strolled out to the platform.

Albe was seated in a chair near me. He sat down next to her and rubbed his cheeks on her leg protectors.

'Where have you been?' she asked.

'I came a different way,' he said. 'Some of my kin are here, and I wanted to talk to them.' Then he began rubbing enthusiastically again.

'Don't make a spectacle of yourself,' Albe said.

'I? I? Make a spectacle of myself? How dare you! The cat is the most noble and dignified being. Each move we make is a miracle of grace and power, even sick, wounded, or dying. The tiniest cat's presence makes even the most flexible human look awkward.'

'Not when you're jacking off,' Albe said.

Tuau sniffed in pure outrage. 'Is this what I receive in return for my courage and fidelity? Insults from an underling? A mere courtier? We, the Felidae ... are perfect. And you, ugly monkey things, make much too much of the operation of those things between your legs. Why, good heavens, woman, they're not even properly covered with fur and the males have no hooks. Yea Gods, no wonder half of human females are dissatisfied with . . .'

'I stand corrected,' Albe said. 'But don't lick your nuts.'

'Tuau,' I broke in. 'How did you get here and what did your relatives have to say? I want to know. I'm very uneasy.'

'You have good reason, or at least, so Aunt Louise said,' he replied. He sounded haughty.

'Last I saw,' Albe said, 'Aunt Louise was threatening to eat you.'

'She was working. That psychic garden is very valuable. She wouldn't want to be in breach of contract. She's not as bad when she's off duty and in a good mood,' he added as an afterthought.

'What did Aunt Louise have to say?' I asked.

'She tells me that all the heads of families have been in close consultation since you arrived at the city. She says it's seldom the great families band together to do anything. Most of the time, they are bitter rivals. But someone . . . something made them sit up and take notice when you arrived. It's like they were warned.'

Yes, I thought. *No doubt they saw the primacy of one of their number as the worst fate they could envision. Albe or I might tip the balance of power.*

But what would they do about it?

'How did you get here?' I repeated.

'I have . . . claws. The reason you flat-footed creatures can't walk in the shallows is that the bottom is covered by tiny round beads, and it's impossible to stand on unless you can get a grip on the mesh the beads are attached to.'

'Hobnails! Spikes!' Albe said.

'Not allowed. Anyone seen wearing them is turned away by the first families. Besides, the tree rules the river, and if you try to defeat its intent, things can get nasty. Or so I'm told.'

Remembering my two assailants, one boiled to death, the other frozen, I found myself in full agreement with Tuau. Albe was her usual self. She always lived very much in the moment. At present she was eating beef wrapped in flat bread and drinking a fine red wine.

'I don't like it either,' Ilona said. 'I'm sure the cat is right. There are too many people here. But I cannot think what the first families might be planning.'

We were, it was true, the center of attention. The concentrated effect of all the stares we were receiving was unnerving. The chain-mail dress shifted and tightened.

'Why?' I asked. 'Do you perceive a threat?'

'Yes!'

'What?'

'I don't know. But I am readying myself to protect you.'

'If fights take place here,' I asked, 'where do they happen?'

'The platform is in the center of the rapids.'

'When does it appear?' I asked.

'When the challenge takes place,' Nest answered.

By now most of the various groups had finished eating. Our own Fir Blog women were dining on bread and soup left over from the magnificent spread at the center table. It was early, and the free aristocrats and commoners were still nibbling on the choicer morsels. But the slaves felt free to help themselves to the scraps left on the plates of the free and powerful.

Very near us a platform was filled with magnificently dressed men and women. The multiple gray robes lying around marked them as commoners. A young man stepped to the fore. He carried a wedge-shaped shield, had a mail shirt and leather armor and leg protectors. There was nothing fancy about his armor; it was highly utilitarian.

He jerked a knife from his belt and hurled it at one of the big platforms occupied by a great family, the one clad in black. A young warrior stepped forward and raised his shield. The knife thudded into it harmlessly.

The warrior pulled the knife from the shield and,

dropping to one knee, proffered it to what I took to be the head of the family, a powerful man wearing the same sort of helmet Amrun had worn when we met him on the way to the city; that is, it covered his whole face with only a T-shaped opening for the eyes and mouth. He accepted the knife and placed it on the table near his hand.

'He has accepted the challenge,' Nest said.

At least a half dozen armed women were sitting or reclining nearby on the black family's platform. The leader turned and spoke a name, and a slender blond girl stepped forward. She didn't look any match for the powerful commoner.

Then I saw roots rise out of the water from the midst of the rapids, and they began to weave themselves together until they formed a sloping, oval platform. More roots suddenly appeared, forming a set of stepping places out to the platform.

The little blonde was armored, wearing a fine, black filigree rather like Albe was wearing. An older woman, also in black, gave her the choice of several swords. She picked a light blade; the black hilt was set off by blue stones, as was her armor. Then she chose her helmet and shield. The helmet she chose was rather like the one worn by the family head. It covered most of her face. The shield was surprisingly small, oval black leather but with a spike in the center.

The crowd was watching avidly now, people standing on chairs and tables or crowded to the edge of the platforms. Another set of root steps ran from the commoners' platform to the arena. I can only call it that, because that's what it was. The woven roots formed a large, relatively flat arena, and I was surprised to see an almost dry area where the two could fight.

'What happens if one of them goes into the water?' Albe asked.

'The one remaining on the platform wins by default,' Nest said. 'But it's not a good idea to jump off. The current at the center is fierce and the loser often drowns as well. She is Maja. This is her first outing.'

'The child looks no match for that big man,' Ilona said.

Maja was making her way across the water on the roots. I was surprised to note that though they were not level, they were dry and she ran easily, leaping from one to another. The gray warrior waited until she reached the platform before he took his road to join her. When he reached the platform, he paused and saluted her, I thought in a mocking sort of way.

Then their blades clashed. She didn't seem strong, but she was quick. To my surprise, he didn't press her. He took his time, showing her his superior strength and skill by meeting and contemptuously casting aside all of her attempts to use her speed to get inside his guard.

But he turned each of her attacks easily. The spike on her shield was a problem for him at first, because she used it to push his blade further aside than was safe. Twice her blade skidded on his mail.

'That won't last,' Albe said.

It didn't. He slammed his shield into the spike on hers and jerked her toward him. But she got her sword up in time to drive a thrust at his midsection. Her blade bent, but the blow in the gut was hard enough and threatening enough to send him reeling back. She jerked her shield free.

He went after her as fast and hard as he could, forcing her back and around the platform until I could see it was taking all she had to beat him off.

'About now!' Albe said.

He dropped his shield, reached down, got her by the ankle, and jerked her feet from under her. She slashed at him, but hit only a glancing blow on one of his shin guards.

'A miss as good as a mile,' Albe said as he lashed out and kicked the blonde hard in the chin, snapping her head back against the floor.

He didn't stop there. He tore the sword from her right hand, then kicked the shield from her left. She lay motionless, disarmed, moving only weakly, a swelling bruise on her chin.

The cheers were long and loud. He flipped her over with his foot so that she lay on her face. He sheathed his sword, put down his shield, and reached down to pick her up.

She came alive with terrible speed and slashed upward. I remembered Cateyrin's ugly little knife with the hook. This one must have been even smaller, but it was long enough to cut his throat. For a second he seemed to be wearing a red bib. Then he toppled slowly into the white water rushing by. It foamed scarlet, then he was gone.

The cheers were thunderous this time as she struggled to her feet, collected her sword and shield, and made her way back to her own people. She received a hero's welcome.

'Good,' Albe said. 'She was good. I didn't see her palm the knife.'

'She did it when he kicked her over on her face. It was at her groin. He shouldn't have taken her so lightly,' Nest said. 'If he had searched her, he would have won.'

'No fair fights here,' Albe said.

Nest and Ilona both chuckled, a bit ruefully, I thought.

'The arms training in the great houses is magnificent,' Ilona told me. 'Whatever you have, their instructors will teach you to make the best of it.'

'Are such tricks common?' Albe asked.

'Yes, very common,' Ilona said.

I heard a thud and saw another challenge had been issued, this one from the reds. (Few, I found, bothered to remember the family names.) The challenge was directed

513

to one of the guilds, a rich one, I surmised, from the beautiful clothing of the men and women gathered on the platform and the number of Fir Blog slaves attending them.

There were no armed men on the platform. The knife thudded into the back of an empty chair. A modestly dressed older man nodded, but didn't assign a woman. Instead, the women gathered in a group sitting around a food-laden table and spoke among themselves. One rose. She was big, with dark hair but light skin. She wore a flame-colored shift. It was transparent. Under it were only some rubies clustered at the usual places, breasts and groin.

She stripped naked then and there and armed herself. The chain mail was silver-white and fit like a glove. It strapped up both sides. Big hinges held the webbing in place. Over it she wore fitted dark leather at breast and groin, along with the usual shin and thigh guards.

'She's much bigger than the average woman,' Albe said. 'She looks as though she might be the result of a mating between—'

'Hush, dear,' Nest whispered. 'And yes, she's certainly the result of some illicit coupling.'

'What is a licit coupling?' I asked.

Nest drew in a deep breath. 'Well . . . a young woman properly purchased for breeding may lie with any and all of her owners. A fighting woman who loses passes to the guild or family that defeated her. The head of the family may assign any or all males the right to her favors. Any two commoners unencumbered and free can join to form a household, or simply as a temporary arrangement for mutual pleasure.'

'It sounds as though highborn women have a bad time of it,' Albe said.

Cateyrin giggled. 'A lot of hard times.'

'Yes, they are sought after,' Nest said delicately. 'But

514

they are one and all very valuable property and any man in authority who ill-treated one would soon be assassinated by his own kin or poisoned by one of his wives. Our whole way of life depends on them. A woman talented herself or one who produces talented daughters will become a permanent member of the ruling council of the household or guild she belongs to.'

My stomach knotted as I watched the big woman make her way to the platform among the rapids. Some sort of etiquette seemed to demand the man wait until the woman reached the platform and was ready.

The red-armored warrior was also big and obviously a well-practiced swordsman. But the bout was inconclusive.

'I wonder if the reds have settled on a campaign to take Elise?' Nest said to Ilona as we watched a dazzling display of swordsmanship.

'The woman is called Elise?' I asked.

'Yes,' Nest said. 'She's famous, but there haven't been too many serious attempts to take her. There is a worry about her bloodlines.'

'How is this concerted attempt usually made?' Albe asked.

'They put constant pressure on her. Try to wound her. And when she is wounded, they give her no rest, until she is finally worn down and at last taken.'

'Couldn't she stay home?' Albe asked.

'No, dear,' Nest said. 'When a girl presents herself as a Woman of Wager, she has to show up. Otherwise her guild or family will find itself the target of bravos, the men forced to fight all the time.'

I drank some wine and knew what a rabbit with a wire around its neck feels like. Albe's eyes met mine, and for the first time, I saw fear in them. I drank again, deeply, and the wine was strong and made me a little dizzy.

The red warrior broke off the fight. Elise let him. Then

he retreated to his family's platform. She returned to her guild.

'By the way,' I asked Nest. 'What guild is that?'

'They sell prepared food.'

'Cooks?' I asked.

'No, more innkeepers, I would say.'

I glanced around. The Hall of the Tree was packed. All the platforms on the river were full, standing room only in some cases. There were buildings along the shore scattered among parklike open spaces. They were filled with spectators, faces at every window and roof. Families had gathered around picnic blankets in the open spaces among the trees, and beyond the respectable citizens there were shadowed areas where the green park trailed away slowly into the forbidden towers.

The night gangs were gathered there. They scarred their faces or, as the Painted People did, wore tattoos. Except that among the Painted People the idea is often some sort of beauty. These masks, skin paintings, and scars had only one purpose: to make the gang look as horrific as possible. Many of them were powerfully muscled, and I saw that free, or perhaps escaped, Fir Blog accounted for most of this murderous-looking crew. There were a lot of them; I couldn't see how many, because those crowded behind the first rank were in deep shadow.

I glanced at Albe. She nodded.

Ilona wasn't eating, though almost everyone else was. In fact, it seemed that the whole crowd on the platforms on the riverbank was fortifying itself with almost indecent haste.

Ilona looked very frightened. 'We should never have brought them here, Nest. We could have hidden them in the guild hall. We could have tried to smuggle them out.'

'We're going to have to fight,' Albe said, breaking in

on Ilona. 'And if we fight, it might as well be here as anywhere else.'

'If luck is with you,' Ilona said, 'and you can stave off defeat tonight, tomorrow I think I know a way to . . .'

I felt the dress tighten, then loosen on my body. 'Battle!'

'Yes,' I said.

I made myself relax. Even if I won tonight, I would be a hunted creature. I could feel the eyes of all the men and women on the great family platforms. The Faun had told me to pass through this world to the Summer Country. He didn't warn me that once I reached here, I might never escape.

Thud! The challenge knife pinned Ilona's sleeve to the chair. The knife came from the black platform.

I stood, watching octagonal stones rise from the water. The platform of roots also had vanished and the same stones rose from the riverbed to form a dueling ground for me. I glanced up at the tree. I'd almost forgotten it. I had been preoccupied with the people. But it arched overhead, green in the insect-eyed lights above. I drew my sword and saluted it.

Then I stepped from stone to stone until I reached the platform. It was broad and magnificent, three high steps above the roaring river. I stood on its surface and found I was looking out at the entire city.

My challenger was big, almost as big as one of the Fir Blog. But a man. He was quick; I saw that much as he leaped from stone to stone. He had the cold, self-confident look of a practiced warrior. The crowd murmured when they saw who he was. His arms and armor were practical and utilitarian rather than ornamental. When he reached the platform, he drew his sword. Mine was already drawn. He saluted me.

'Why, you're a lovely little virgin.' He sounded condescending.

517

'Thank you,' I said. 'I hope to remain one.'

He gave a pleasant laugh. 'No chance of that, my dear. You will be much better off if you make an accommodation with me right away. I'll tolerate a few harmless passes so that you may salvage your dignity. Then you slip. I put my sword at your throat and the deed is accomplished.'

'Suppose I don't agree?' I was surprised at my own pleasant tone.

Something ugly crept into his eyes.

'They say you are a stranger to our ways. So I had best explain what happens when a Woman of the Wager is captured. The men of the capturing family take possession of her body. All the men. Now, I can defend you tonight and say you are my own. Or I can yield you up to whomever I favor. That is the rule. The first night of a new woman can be ... shall we say, very painful.'

I got the picture, but it didn't matter to me much, because I was pledged to endure no second night. And I knew then that I would not. Perhaps Albe could reach me in time, but that didn't matter, though I was certain my head would be a powerful talisman to the Painted People. But if she didn't get there, I could do the deed myself.

Was the Hall of the Tree silent, or did the rush of the rapids drown out the sound and murmur of many voices? No. I glanced at the spectators and saw they were watching raptly.

'Well?' he asked.

'As you wish,' I answered. 'But a few passes, please, for the sake of my dignity.'

'Certainly.'

'And,' I said, 'I hope you're a man of your word.'

'You'll find I am, you little darling.'

Then he advanced.

I edged back as though nervous toward the edge of the platform.

'Now don't jump in the river,' he cautioned as he raised his sword.

I leaped forward, just a little out of his world. I hoped enough. I went right through him. There was darkness and a stench of muck.

A second later, I stood behind him. This was no time to hold back. Hero's salmon leap, both feet up. We were in the same world now. Both of my feet slammed into his back. I hit the ground rolling and saw my stratagem had worked. He pitched over the edge of the platform into the rapids.

The cheers made the lights on their long wands quiver. I raised my sword. More cheers thundered around me.

I was congratulated from another source, too.

'Why didn't you tell me what you were going to do?' The mass of mail on my torso shifted alarmingly.

'What?' I hissed. 'And give the game away?'

'True! True! What's wrong? You are still wound tight as dried sinew.'

'That was one. There are six more,' I snapped.

I gazed downstream and saw some helpful people were pulling my opponent out of the river. Just at that moment, I saw the second dagger fly at the platform where the Diviners Guild sat. Even from here I could see the handle was red.

The head of the red family rose. There was a loud murmur from the crowd.

'That trick won't work twice.' I spoke to my unseen companion.

'No, but then this time I don't think you will be facing a human.'

And I saw my friend was right. The pieces of armor in front of the leader of the red family had risen of their

519

own volition and formed themselves into the semblance of a warrior.

'I wonder where he got that? And, you know, it's very dangerous.'

'That's not helpful,' I said. 'What is it?'

My companion was uncharacteristically silent.

Helmet, cuirass, arm guards, leg guards, thigh protectors, greaves, and shoes. They hovered in the air, then turned in the exact way a living fighter would. One mailed glove stretched itself out for a sword. Someone placed the hilt of one in its hand.

'I don't know what it is,' my unseen companion said.

A shield rose from the table and took its position in front of the thing's arm. The stones began rising in the direction of the red platform. When they were in place, the thing leaped easily to the first and headed toward me.

'It's a construct,' my companion finally said. 'Something like a tool put together to solve a problem.'

'Not a lot of help,' I said. 'How do I defeat it?'

At that moment it leaped from the last of the stones onto the platform and was on me in a second. For a minute I was as busy as a fighter can be. Our swords rang together and struck sparks as I parried an attack as vicious as any that has ever happened to me. I danced in a circle, trying to get away from the flying sword and the empty helmet.

I could see the whole hall through the joints in my adversary. It was as though I faced an invisible opponent. I used a variant of the trick I had used on the first swordsman. It nearly got me killed.

I eased out of the world just a bit and let the sword pass through me. I felt it, but I was only a specter to the force of the blow. That gave me a clean swing at the space between helmet and breast plate. Or where the neck would have been on a human. My blade whistled through empty air and since I had to return completely to strike an effective blow, my foe's sword caught me at the waist.

It rang against the ring mail and threw me down. The next sight I saw was the thing's blade descending toward my face. I rolled clear and got far enough away to leap to my feet. The thing caught up to me in an instant and a second later, I was frantically parrying a rain of blows.

I fled to the only spot that offered respite, the world the ring mail came from. A second later, the rain was slashing at my face. My companion presented me with a view of the ruins. I found I was not in the same place I had been before. I was on the other side of the jumble of broken towers on a broad, shallow stair.

I'd been here before when I had fled the fish eater. The fish eater, King Bade, sent to steal 'Her' pool. He had tried to lay hands on immortal powers. 'She' used me to rebut him.

The immense shell of the rainbow chamber rose on my left. Even in the thick gloom of perpetual storm clouds it burned white, reflecting the giant curved steps I stood on. Green, gold, gray, churning like the turgid storm clouds above, lit by brilliant flashes of blue lightning and swirling patterns of silver rain. I'd taken the Faun's head in the chamber.

I called it, and the walls swirled into a symphony of green, then silver, followed by gold. My unseen companion gave a cry of shock.

'*Yiiiiiiee!* Warn me when you do things like that!'

I didn't have time to reply. The suit of red armor followed me into this world.

'You are measurably stronger. Try tripping it,' my companion shouted.

I slipped to the thing's left and brought my sword down hard on its shin guard. The shield slammed into me, but the ring mail protected my torso. I reeled back, but when I did, I saw my blow landed perfectly.

The thing had been pivoting on that leg to follow me. The other leg was in the air. I knocked it off its pins. It went down with a crash, flying into its component pieces.

'Get the helm! Get the helm! That's how it sees!' my companion shouted.

I threw down my shield. The helm was one of those Greek-style helmets, big cheek pieces with only a T-shaped slit for the eyes and mouth. It tried to roll away from me, but I got it by one of the cheek pieces, grabbed the nose guard, and turned the eyeholes to my body, trying to blind it.

The sword came after me by itself, slashing wildly, but apparently my stratagem worked. The sword didn't seem able to find me.

'Got to get back!' I shouted. I was afraid to make the leap. My movements in this world might have placed me over the river in the other one.

'Hush. I'm working on that. . . . Now!'

I made the leap. Actually, I was a little above the platform. I landed hard on my knees, near the edge. I hurled the helm into the river just as the sword slammed into my arm. My armor turned most of the force of the blow, but my right arm and hand were drenched in blood from an open slash wound just above my elbow.

But I went for the sword hilt with my left hand. I swung it once around my head, then out over the white-water rapids surrounding the platform. It vanished. The remaining bits and pieces fought me, but one by one, I ran them down and hurled them into the river.

The shield gave me the most trouble. It was triangular. It flew at me, point first. I slammed it aside with my sword, a blow that sent it flying out over the water. Once over the water, whatever motive power the thing had seemed to disappear, and it vanished into the river, joining the rest.

Then I stood on the platform, reeling.

'Two down,' I whispered. 'Five more to go. I don't know if I have the strength.'

The chain mail on my torso shifted and I felt strength flow back into me. My vision cleared; the perspiration dried on my body. My respiration slowed. Where I had been heated, I felt a cool breeze on my skin.

The audience in the Hall of the Tree was going wild. The cheers were causing the lights stretched out across the water to vibrate.

'How often can you do that?' I asked my friend.

'Not forever,' was the dark reply. 'Only two or three more times, and then it will kill you.'

'Why?'

'Limited concepts! Difficult!'

'Try!'

'I draw on you . . . your unused capacity. You are a smaller sentient than I am used to.'

'Sentient?'

'Intelligent being. The Fand wasn't – not intelligent. You are, but small. Your capacities are finite.'

'How soon is dawn?'

'Good! Soon! That might save you!'

'I hope.'

The cheers were dying down, but I saw something that boded ill for me. The heads of all the great houses were gathered together on one platform. I looked down at my right arm and saw the wound I had taken was crusted over and partially healed. I gripped the sword hilt near the guard and tried to relax my grip on it, but my fingers were a claw.

'Just as well you don't,' my companion told me. 'Flex your fingers a little. Try to relax, but don't let go.'

The hall was silent now. Every eye was on me or the platform where the family heads gathered. They were arguing violently among themselves. Five seemed agreed on something, but there were two holdouts.

At length the two – the gold and bronze – gave in and they formed a circle, arms over one another's shoulders, red, black, white, gold, silver, bronze, glass. I felt a wave of cold fly through my body. The sensation was rather like the one I felt when I jumped through the first warrior's body.

The lamps above dimmed, the light turned to shadow, and I saw light was beginning to brighten the white towers that were the pinnacle of the city. Then the lights came up again and the circle broke open. There was a warrior standing in a spot that had been empty before.

He wore motley; that is, the colors of all the seven families. One leg was black, the other red. One side of his torso gold, the other silver. One arm white, the other bronze. His helm was glass.

I heard a sort of sigh sweep over the crowd. The face covered by the glass helm was that of a skull. The voice was so loud I think everyone in the hall could hear every word clearly.

'Maiden! Prepare yourself! I am the one, the only, the never defeated bridegroom. Death!'

Lancelot and the Lady of the Lake found the sorcerer gone.

'Oh, fine!' he said. 'Now you've lost him.'

'I haven't lost anything, you twit,' she said.

He was biting into a ripe peach he'd just taken from the table on the porch of her dwelling and admiring the glass bowl he'd summoned to convince her of his new powers. As usual the beach was white, the sun was shining, and a cooling breeze was blowing off the water.

'Paradise,' he said. 'Maybe Cregan was right.'

'No,' she said. 'There's too much human in you. First you'd get bored, then you'd get crazy.'

'I didn't tell you what Cregan said,' he pointed out mildly.

'You didn't have to. I know what Cregan *would* say,' she snapped back as she was looking carefully up and down the beach in both directions. 'Shut up and help me look for him. He can't have gotten far.'

Lancelot sighed and was disturbed by a vague sense of something missing as he finished the peach. He took off his helmet and threw it up in the air. It became a raven and landed on the table with the food. It gazed at him with glowing red eyes.

'There's another human around here.' He turned to her. 'There aren't a lot of humans here. Am I right in that supposition?'

'Yes,' she answered, folding her arms. 'Far as I know, you, me, and Merlin are the only ones.'

'So one of us has gone missing. See if you can find him. And don't take all day about it.' He was annoyed at being called a twit.

'Haughty, high and mighty, aren't we?' the bird said.

'Please!' Lancelot added.

'That's better,' the bird said. It took wing. It circled wider and wider, higher and higher, then vanished into the blue.

Lancelot helped himself to some bread, butter, and curd cheese, saying, 'It probably won't take him long. And while we're waiting, why don't you put on some clothes. I mean, we're going to meet this sorcerer and surely you don't want him to see you the way you are now.'

She glanced down at the gold and green willow dress, then looked him directly in the eye.

'You keep a civil tongue in your head when you talk to me. Listen up! Whatever I may look like to you, I am not – I repeat – *not* a human woman. And what I wear or don't wear is none of your damn business. Is that clear?'

'I'm sorry, Your Majesty. Has your humble servant offended Your Ladyship? But I damn well don't see why you'd want to parade around half-naked in front of that corrupt, dirty old man. What? Does it give you a thrill when he gets all excited looking at your . . . amplitude?'

'My what?' She was laughing.

'Amplitude!' he repeated stiffly.

'Hell, I've heard them called lots of things, some of them very vulgar. But nobody ever referred to my "amplitude" before. No! Look, trust me. He doesn't think of me as a woman. At least, not since I burned all his clothes off, then his beard and most of his hair.'

'You can do things like that?'

'Oh, for heaven's sake. You saw a lot of what I can do when I want to extend myself. And he was dirty. He was lousy. He had things crawling in his hair, another set in his beard, and an even more exclusive group around his groin. His clothes were trying to crawl away by themselves when I caught up with them and perpetrated another massacre.

'By then,' she added thoughtfully, 'he was kicking and screaming like a two-year-old with a tantrum. I dunked him in the ocean four times. That quieted him down some. Then I held his nose and poured a potion down his throat. A potion that brought him back to his right senses. And when he sobered up, he was even more frightened than when he was out of his mind. I put some pressure on him to talk, and he sang like a happy bird. And speaking of birds . . .' Her voice trailed off as the raven circled and landed.

'About two miles down the beach, that way.' The bird jabbed its beak to the right, then became a bird-shaped helmet. The red eyes did as they usually did, glowed, gazed on the world for a long moment, then closed.

'He sounds disgusting,' Lancelot said.

'Humph! Speaking of disgusting, how long has it been since . . .'

Lancelot scratched his head. His short curly hair was stiff with dried perspiration, wood smoke, and grit.

'Too long,' he admitted, and entered her dwelling to use the pool.

After he'd scrubbed off most of the accumulated sludge, she joined him. They were washing each other when he said, 'If you're not a woman, I sure can't tell it. Everything seems to be here and arranged for maximum enjoyment.'

She kissed him. His hands wandered delightfully and expertly as she did so. Her breathing quickened.

'You're getting better,' she gasped.

'I should be. I'm getting a lot of practice.'

'Oh, hush!' she said, and made a gesture. A big, soft, fluffy cloth appeared at the side of the pool. He lifted her and carried her to it.

They both made quite a few sounds after that, but neither said anything more. Not for a long time. Not until the afternoon sun found his face and shone in his eyes.

'I suppose we had better go talk to him,' he said.

They both got up. He was surprised when she donned a rose silk tunic deeply embroidered at the neck and hem with gold and pearls. It covered her from neck to ankles. She found a steel-gray silk one for him. It was fastened at shoulders by wolf-head pins and belted with gold-braid rope, thick with fine granulation.

'Where . . . ?' He pointed to her dress.

'Poppia. Nero's wife,' she said. 'She was cremated in it. The bastard gave her a magnificent funeral. He ought to have. He kicked her to death while she was pregnant. Kept kicking and punching at her belly until she miscarried and lost the child. The Greek physicians and midwives couldn't stop the bleeding. She died that night. He was wild with grief.'

Lancelot looked down at his tunic in horror. 'This . . . ?'

'Was an offering on someone's funeral pyre. But the corpse wasn't wearing it. The pins and belt came from a central Italian tomb.'

'You go places like that?' he gasped.

'I had business there, and don't be a busybody. Besides, it would take hours to explain the circumstances of my visit. And yes, I go all sorts of places and don't owe you any explanation for my activities. Shit!' she muttered. 'You let them cop a feel, tumble around in the hay a few times, and they start acting like – '

'All right! All right! I get the picture,' he growled.

'No, you probably don't,' she said grimly. 'And you can feel free to disapprove all you want, but give it a rest. At least for right now.' She started down the beach in the direction the bird had indicated.

He followed. No matter how much she annoyed him sometimes, the afterglow of passionate lovemaking remained with him, and he found himself unable to stay angry with her. But the frequent reminders that she wasn't truly human and that their relationship depended on her making allowances for him inspired a deep fire of jealous rage in his soul.

He took her hand as they walked along together. They interlaced their fingers.

'I'm just jealous. I hate to think about losing you. But I've heard all the stories about mortals and beings like you. They never come to a very good end.'

'That's why you hear about them,' she said. 'Nobody tells stories about the ones that work.'

'Some of them work?'

'Most of them work. We're very stable individuals. We know what we like, what we don't, and none of us are shy about speaking our minds. I think ours is a very promising one.'

'That makes me feel better,' he said. 'I just hope when we find Merlin the sun won't have fried his brain.'

'No. There are structures all along the coast. One of them probably materialized for him.'

'What? There are other buildings around here?'

'Yes, but you can't see them easily.'

'Dead people's clothes. Invisible buildings. What else are you . . . ?'

'Settle down. They are not dead people's clothing. When they were devoured on the funeral pyre, they belong to me. And as for the structures, I'm not sure you would call them buildings. They aren't invisible. They just are a little bit somewhere else.'

'How did they do that?' he asked.

'It's like the tunnel between worlds. No one knows,' she said.

'Why?'

'We don't know. What we do know is that their ability to dematerialize preserves them. And when we studied the matter long ago, that was the best and only explanation we could come up with. When you want something to last a long time, you build it of sturdy materials. But if you want something to last forever, you arrange it so that it can widen the spaces between the little thingamajiggies that make up matter and avoid the deterioration caused by heat, cold, wind, rain that batters structures.'

'You sure that's the explanation?' he asked.

'No, but have you got a better one?' She pointed ahead. 'Look!'

He saw what appeared to be a small forest of white columns on a promontory overlooking the ocean.

'He will be there,' she said confidently.

'How do you make them come into being?' he asked.

'Sometimes you can't,' was her rueful answer. 'Once my house went away. I hadn't visited it in a long time, maybe a few hundred years, and I guess it got tired of waiting. I had to camp out in the spring that supplies the bathing pool and drinking water. Nothing wrong with that. There's a beautiful cave down there that is filled with sunlight from holes in the rock above. The walls and floors are lined with tiny quartz crystals. They shine like new snow on a bright day when the light filters in. But it does get cold there at night. You'd need your fur.'

'The house?' he prompted.

'Oh. After a while, it came back. I've been careful to check on it periodically every twenty-five years or so since.'

The ground was broken here. The beach changed to shingle and the dark rocks that looked like the remnants of an ancient lava flow formed a small peninsula that stretched out into the ocean. A broad, shallow stair led to the top of the promontory.

He was sitting in a stone chair in the middle of a slightly sunken garden, staring out to sea. He was, as she had said, clean-shaven with thick, salt-and-pepper gray hair. He was wearing a clean cotton robe the butternut color of homespun. When they reached the top of the stair, he turned to look at them. The expression of controlled horror in his eyes struck Lancelot like a blow.

'I thought I'd be seeing you again,' he said. 'And the bird. There are no birds here. I knew it had to be a messenger.'

The pavilion was to Lancelot like a scattering of mushrooms. Slender white, or were they white? Somehow they seemed to pick up the blue in the sky. Columns rose from fissures in the polished rock at his feet. Each column opened into a delicate stone parasol. They overlapped one another in a random pattern that created areas of both light and heavy shade. And like mushrooms, they were arranged in a ring around a sunlit garden.

The outer ring was small fig trees laden with fruit. The second ring held gooseberry bushes, again burdened with abundant red, translucent fruit. The innermost ring around a small pool held roses. They reminded Lancelot of dog roses, white with a pink blush at the edges and multiple golden stamens.

But no dog roses he'd ever seen were so large, each blossom wider across than the palm of his hand. Or so fragrant. Whenever the sea breeze dropped, the air was suddenly and seductively saturated with their fragrance.

The sorcerer shivered as with a chill. 'How long,' he asked in a tormented voice, 'will I stay sane?'

There were two more chairs and a bench around the garden. She pointed at one chair and a couple of pillows appeared in it.

'Here, have a cushion,' she said to Merlin as she handed him one. 'And,' she continued, 'you will stay sane as long as you stay here.'

'So I'm trapped,' he said.

'You could put it that way, if you want to. You could also say I rescued you. But whatever you say, there's not one damn thing I can do about King Bade's curse.'

'Nothing you can, or nothing you will?'

'Both,' she said, sitting down in the chair with the remaining cushion. Lancelot took the bench.

'Bade's not a god. But if there's such a thing as close with god, he's there. No, I don't want any part of a squabble between a cheap necromancer like you and the last remnant of beings who once aspired to comprehend the whole known universe.'

'He's half-mad,' Merlin snapped.

'Let me tell you something. At half-mad, Bade is still a hundred times smarter and more competent than you ever dreamed about being on the sharpest day of your life.'

He gave her a poisonous look.

'Don't even think about it,' she said.

The hot, dark eyes rested on Lancelot. 'Your paramour?' he asked.

'None of your business. I brought him here because he's Guinevere's foster brother and he needs to know what's happened to her and her intended, the young king. You were eager enough to tell me everything a day or so ago. What's the matter now? You trying to figure an angle? Some way to work out a quid pro quo? If that's what's in your devious skull, forget it. You start screwing with me, I'll drag you out in the ocean and hold your head under until you beg me to let you talk. You aren't the first slimy vulture, potted-up scrounger who wanted to exploit the remains of a magnificent civilization for your own personal profit. Types like you get on my last nerve, and it gripes me to have to share my personal getaway spot with a creep like you. But in the interest of limiting your suffering and in return for your help, I'll do it. But that's all I'll do. That's all you get. I will not help you make a nuisance of yourself to the rest of the long-suffering human race.'

'Everybody always knows where they stand with you, don't they?' Lancelot said.

'True,' Merlin said. 'You could not be clearer.' Then he continued, 'The truth is, I don't know as much as I wish. But what there is, I will share. The oracles began to speak of both of them before they were ever born. But I believe you, my lady, are well informed about divination.'

She nodded. 'A tricky and treacherous process.'

'Just so. I couldn't tell what they portended, only that it was something big. Very big. Unbelievably big. And the worst of it was, I couldn't tell what. I consulted other diviners. They seemed to know even less than I did. So . . .'

'You tried to kill us,' Lancelot said.

'Yes, I did that at first. I tried very hard. Then I used my credit with the Lord of the Dead to try to tie her to another man. He failed. I was surprised. Certainly the power of his hand exceeds the force of any mortal will. But she was not only able to defeat him, she acquired an ally in the Boar, servant of Dis, Talorcan. God help me, he liked her!'

'I do too,' Lancelot said.

Merlin sighed. 'I'm sure there is much that is likable about her. Arthur was certainly smitten. Together they might be an unbeatable combination.'

The Lady of the Lake seemed saddened. Lancelot kept his eyes on the restless movement of the sea. Merlin made as if to rise.

'What's wrong?' she asked.

'I'm dry. Talking is thirsty work.'

A second later a cup appeared in her hand. She held it out to him.

'What's in it?' he asked, accepting it gingerly.

'Whatever you want,' she said.

He took a swallow. 'Tolerably good wine,' he said, sounding surprised.

'Fine,' she said. 'Keep it. You don't have to worry about emptying it.'

'The cup remains full?' he said, looking down into the vessel.

'Yes. I have a whole set. These are ornamented with moonstones. Get on with the story.'

'You know whose side I'm on. Don't you?' he asked.

She snorted. 'Your own.'

'No!' He sounded angry. 'I'm on that of the civilized southern landowners. In the end, they will dominate the country. Arthur wasn't reliable. As high king I saw clear evidence that he would follow in his father's footsteps. And he would allow the barbarian tribesmen an equal voice in the government.'

'So you decided to imprison him also.'

Merlin looked almost sad. 'The High Kingship has endured so long. Even before the Romans came, groups from the Continent tried to bring it down. They failed. Most thought the Romans would succeed, but I think in a way, in the long run, resistance to their rule only strengthened those kings of legend. The Roman tide crashed against the mountains of Scotland. Then receded slowly, leaking away until they were gone. The only remnants of their greatness are a few very hard to heat villas and an abandoned wall.'

He sighed. 'Those oracles didn't warn me enough. He hasn't remained imprisoned by Bade. He's loose, and he's been successful in challenging Bade for power.'

'That part was not clear to me,' she said. 'How in the hell did you get Bade to act as Arthur's jailer?'

Merlin's face was stiff.

'Don't. Don't lie to me. Not if you value your life, don't.' She spoke quietly. 'I want the truth.'

'He . . . he was in my debt,' was the answer.

'For what?'

'I sent him a lot of slaves.'

She began laughing.

'Arthur is a king, and they have the right to ask for his help. But if this Bade is as powerful as you tell me he is, how could any human defeat him?' Lancelot asked.

'He doesn't have to defeat him, just limit him. And that can be done,' Merlin said.

She added, 'I think that may be where you come in.'

'Me?' Lancelot said. 'What can I do?'

She didn't answer, only looked into his eye. He met her stare for a moment, then turned away.

'Are you there?' he asked quietly. A half dozen ravens flew down, and his helm, belt, and sword appeared on the bench beside him.

'Yes, there are things I can do,' he said. 'But what about her?'

'She is at the City of Fire,' Merlin said. 'Her journey is her own, and you are not part of it.'

He sat silent for a moment, eyes closed. 'No, she has already won or lost. I cannot say which. I don't know. But there is no way for you to get there. If victorious, she will overtake you in the Summer Country. If not, I cannot name her fate. But this I say last.'

And he glanced at Lancelot. 'In this I speak truth and only truth. The three of you are treasured among the immortals and in many senses, you will never die. Part of the reason I pursued you so relentlessly is because my soul burned with envy of you. The king is a dream of power. She, Guinevere, is a dream of beauty and you are a dream of courage. And among the three of you, there is a dream of love. I cannot think she will lose. You and Arthur are her destiny. No lesser beings could destroy her.'

He turned to the Lady of the Lake. 'There. Are you satisfied?'

She nodded. 'Yes. You meet and exceed my expectations, sorcerer.'

The sun was still bright in the sky, but moving down close to the horizon. The shadows were long and the breeze was picking up. Merlin lifted the wine cup again and drank deeply.

'Any fish in that large body of water?' He nodded toward the sea.

'Some,' Lancelot said. 'But you sort of have to crack them like oysters. They have big plates all over their bodies, but the meat inside is really good.'

'Back there – ' The sorcerer indicated the strip of low-growing scrub beyond the beach. 'I found some sleep rooms and a hearth. I suppose I had best make myself at home. There's also a net.'

'We could run it through the surf,' she said. 'I've never been short of things to eat, and I've spent a lot of time here.'

'Any further advice?' Lancelot asked Merlin.

'I wouldn't presume,' he said. 'Besides, you and she and Arthur have handled things perfectly up until now. In this, I came off the loser.'

'I'll go get the net,' she said. Then she pointed to Merlin. 'You build a fire. And don't hit that cup too hard while you're at it. Wait until you get some food in your stomach.'

'What about these fancy getups?' Lancelot objected. 'You'll ruin that expensive gown. And what about my tunic?' he asked as he rose to follow her.

'The ravens can bring you some armor and I'll wear kelp.'

'Kelp? What the hell is kelp?' he asked.

'Seaweed,' she told him. 'It gets chilly around here at night, and it will keep me warm.'

'How in the hell is cold, clammy seaweed going to keep you warm?'

'Enough!' she said. 'I've been explaining things to you all day. Give it a rest and let's go find that net.'

CHAPTER NINE

ARTHUR VISITED THE EAGLE AGAIN. He studied the way the forest sloped down to the river and decided that there must be a game trail that paralleled the river and would take him without undue exertion down to the bottomlands that surrounded King Bade's fortress.

He sometimes stayed longer than necessary with the great bird. He liked her mind. It was clear and calm, utterly without fear or even anxiety. She knew what she was and what her people had been since time immemorial. When they had been without feathers and hunted in the shadowed glades of a primordial forest, thick with cycads and tree ferns. The insects were winged, but they were not. But clawed fingers and feet gave them command of the high canopies where they dashed from tree to tree with an agility only equaled now by monkeys.

At first the skies were filled with rain. The clouds were thick and the green of forests where tree was piled on tree burned against the racing gray cloud wreck that seemed to fly past without end. In time the skies cleared, cold came, and with it the feathers that made the miracle of flight possible.

He basked in her serenity, her assurance. It felt good to

slough off his complex humanity and join with her simple, clear vision.

Perhaps, he thought, riding the thermals of a morning and being carried higher and higher, *this was what happened to the wanderers lost in this dark forest. They yielded up their souls to an experience that brought their mortal torments to an end and filled them with peace.*

There was an absolute certainty about her life. There were no gray areas. She loved her mate and greeted him with a very pure passion as they clung together, spiraling down toward the treetops below. They made love over and over again, and they couldn't seem to get enough of each other.

Eggs and chicks. She was filled with youth and strength.

They honed their skills in the vast chasm of air between the clouds and the forest below, making sure their young were fed. Then the chicks were gone and he and she were alone together. Today was as yesterday, and tomorrow would change nothing, but be the same. World without end, not a prayer but a reality that glowed with absolute peace.

It came to him then that he knew who he was, also. He had no doubts, and his mind reached that point of rest, the vast stillness that is the knowledge of God. He watched the sunset with his arm over the dog's back. The sun painted the horizon gold, and a blue-green light blazed in the forest.

'Did you betray me?' he asked the dog. 'Take me to face the greatest enemy of my kind in this world?' Of course, he got no answer. But he was able to sleep very peacefully.

The next day he felt the first stirrings of hunger as he and Bax worked their way into a more conventional forest. There were game trails here and clearings where he could see the sun by day and the moon and stars by night. The first night out, he set rabbit snares and got three. He took the sinew and gut he needed to make a bow drill and fed the rest to Bax. Then he hunkered down near a small stream that was tributary to the river that bisected the valley.

He placed his hands in the water. He felt a coldness in the symbols that marked the palms of both hands. He'd made his first bow drill from a yew tree. The coolness penetrated his palms and ran up his arms and entered his heart.

The king had one other duty. He was priest, general-warrior, head of state, and it was his duty, as it had been that of the Roman and Etruscan kings, to consult the gods. Both pagan and Christian priesthoods had done the best they could to wrench the responsibility for the sacred trance from the ruler, but no one had ever been able to completely deny them.

No high king had ever been chosen who did not come from one of the great warrior societies, and simply in order to join one, both men and women had to be able to make the sacred journey. He made one himself, and 'She' had come to him. The memory made him shiver. He had the marks; the four claws of a bear scored his right shoulder from neck to waist. But he was glad he had them.

He had gone to his father the morning of his first awareness that he was no longer a child. He didn't know what or who came to him in the shadows between sleep and waking. Some boys and men told tales about what they met. Most kept their mouths shut, at least until they were much older and the memory was no longer raw. Or perhaps until they could make up something to their credit. But he remembered only the pleasure, and being naturally truthful, told his father so.

But Uther only nodded and brought him to Morgana, who made arrangements for him to use the mountain house. He wasn't happy. He was afraid. He didn't tell his father that. It wasn't in him to admit fear. He never had, he never would. But this passage was greatly feared by both boys and girls.

The rites girls faced weren't as painful or lonely as the boys' were, but she was sequestered in a small, lonely place and shunned for at least part of the time. For two weeks she was not allowed to speak, nor could she let her shadow fall on anyone's food or weapons, or any newborn child. And, as with the boys, they must partake of the cup.

The priestess mixed the drink and the visions it produced brought knowledge of the future to those engaged in the passage. Girls were – frankly – used by the older women during the rite. Used to foretell the future.

Each night the girl drank from the ceremonial vessel and then was left in isolation until the morning, when she was questioned about what she had seen. Two weeks of this could bring a woman near madness if the revelations were ugly or unpleasant.

The boys faced a shorter, but no less fearful, ordeal. They went to the mountain house where for six days they were not allowed to eat and drank only water. As the bolder girls did, they each night sought the trance and the knowledge it brought. They prayed for a true dream, a guide to their future status.

It was cold, and on the way up, Arthur passed the night with the shepherds just moving their flocks up for summer pasture. He took his last allowable meal with them, porridge with some sweet cow's milk. The ewes weren't lactating yet. The flat bread he ate with it was more barley than wheat, but the butter was rich and good. Then he took his leave of them and hiked up to the thatch-covered pavilion called the forest house.

There were no other trees so high up but pines, and a thick mist covered them. The forest house was only four stone posts, a low stone wall between them. The roof was thick with thatch. When he reached it, the low mist had dampened the walls and floor. Water was dripping down from the thatch and making plopping sounds on the brown needle-covered earth around the door. He was tired. The low clouds hovering over the mountaintop reduced visibility to only a few feet.

He made a bed with an extra blanket and slept through most of the day. When he woke, it was evening. The wind had blown the clouds away, and he sat wrapped in his mantle, watching the sun go down in the distant sea. From here he could tell he was on a mountaintop now. As he watched, the scarlet blaze of the dying light painted the trees on the hills that stretched out below him until they met the ocean. The air was clear and cold, and somewhere in his soul he mourned the departing light. He drank the first cup of the journey. Fire was forbidden, and the darkness thick around him until he saw the beauty of the stars.

His spirit soared. They had always been there, those stars, but somehow he had never really seen them. There was always a door to enter, or when sleeping outdoors when they were on the hunt, the fire flared. It needed to be tended and fed. When he was on watch or having the lessons, they taught him how to know them – tell time by their eternal consistency or find his way out on the open sea using them as beacons or do the same on a cross-country march: look for those patterns that would mark the houses and the direction he needed to follow to shelter, or at darker times, an ambush or a killing. The stars were among the tools he had been taught to master.

But now he needed nothing from them, and it was as though he had never seen them before. They cast the network of their splendor over him and greeted him as one of their own. He wrapped himself in his mantle and wandered through the dark, silent forest, watching them, keeping them company as they marked the long, slow passage of the night. Marveling at the beauty and imagination of what/whoever called them from the deeps of eternity and taught the mind of man to love their splendor.

He never remembered how or when he found his bed, but sometime before dawn, he did. He slept deeply and without dreams.

When he woke, the morning was well under way. He rose, washed. A bath in the cold water of a spring nearby caused such spasms in his muscles that he thought he might end in a permanent crouch. He didn't, but felt much better when his skin glowed with the flush of blood his heart sent to chase away the chill.

He took some time to make a rough broom from a fallen bough and some small pine branches so he could sweep the dusty floor and dispose of his used bedding. Then he remade his bed and sat outside, listening to the endless breeze that troubled his ears with its mild roaring, watching the sun cross the sky.

Near the spring where he bathed, a pair of birds was raising young. *Exhausting,* he thought. The adults ran themselves ragged trying to keep the four triangular yellow mouths full. The chicks rested between feedings, but as soon as Mother or Father – he couldn't tell which was which – came in for a landing at the edge of the nest, four heads were up, four mouths open, four sets of lungs screaming for nourishment.

Why did they go to all the trouble? Was it worth it? His mother hadn't seemed to think so. But there was that frantically working pair of birds.

Birds had no kings, no laws, and no families. What was there in a bird's world to keep them from dumping the worrisome chicks out of the nest and flying away to eat the tidbits they were so assiduously feeding to their chicks? The birds were hard at it.

He wondered what Igrane would have done with him if she'd been a bird. Probably fed him to the nearest snake. Remembering the years he'd spent with her, he thought perhaps he might have been better off.

When he looked up at the sky, he saw the clouds were moving in from the sea, drowning the golden light in gray shadow. That night, after he emptied the cup, he found himself haunted by the terror of memory. He slept and dreamed of her the way he always remembered her, bending over him (children are so small). The cold anger on her face reaching for him. He would wake himself up screaming, waiting for the pain to begin. Each time he slept, this same dream jolted him awake, shivering with fear, and oddly enough at the same time drenched with the sweat of fear.

He woke in the gray dawn glad the night was over to find the clouds had moved in, wrapping the world in silent gray vapor. He was lean, spare. He carried little or no extra fat. Hunger and the terror of the long night had taken its toll.

He didn't try to bathe in the spring today. He found that with the drug gone from his blood, he was able to sleep in peace, and he did for the most of the morning and afternoon. When he woke, it was still raining and the sky was lighter. He went down to the spring and bathed. But a look at the clouds flying past up high told him the night would be cold. Weather from the north was pushing them. So he didn't dare use his spare blanket to dry himself. He did have a clean change of clothing, so he dressed while still damp and then watched the cottony clouds dabbled in blood by the sunset.

He drank the cup, wrapped himself in his blanket and mantle, and tried to stay out of the icy wind while the forest moaned and cried out around him. Between the low clouds and the intermittent gusts of rain, he seemed wrapped in absolute darkness. The pines around him cried out in a thousand voices. A long, whispering rush as the tree limbs thrashed, loud cracks when something, tree or branch, gave way, a long, vast sigh that began as a whisper and gradually grew louder and louder, until its roar seemed to encompass the whole world.

As he looked up, he could see the tall pines bending, whipping in the blast, and the wild clouds, dim shapes above the darker trees, flying past, driven like shadows before the wind. In the dark, something roared. Once – his mind told him – there were no fires, and when the sun set by day or the moon by night, the world was an abyss of darkness. This must have been what it was like. To sit alone in the cold and the fireless dark and hear the creatures of fang, tusk, and claw – those born with all the armaments they needed to survive – yell a warning into the night that they were on the hunt. The roar came again, closer, and it sounded as though something moved among the brush and small trees growing along the narrow trail he had taken to come here. Something big.

He was trembling. Wild boar? No, not by night. Cat, or worse yet, bear? Either could be death in the night, in the cold, to an unarmed man. He had no weapon. They, like fire, were forbidden.

He heard the scream of a cat then. It came from near the pool where he bathed. The roars changed to snuffing and woofing. Dog. His disordered mind wished to believe it was a dog, but the sounds were too loud to belong even to a large dog, and the crashing and plunging in the undergrowth bespoke a massive creature.

Then, as if to confirm his worst fears, he heard the sound of claws ripping the bark as the bear reached up and left his mark high on a tree trunk. In the darkness, Arthur heard the cat scream again. The wind slashed at the high forest and moaned and seemed to cry out almost in pain.

Arthur wept. He cried hopelessly and despairingly, because he had not the courage to throw aside his mantle and bedding and walk into almost stygian darkness under the trees to meet his fate. Sometimes men did not return from these journeys, and he knew now he was never meant to return. The powers of the gods of wrath and circumstance. Things he could no more cease to believe in than he could stop breathing. These things had marked him as their own. And the bear had been sent for him.

But Morgana, mouth and tongue of the goddess, could summon the cat, and she paced the dark, sobbing forest, protecting him, even against the will of the cruel forces she commanded. Because in her guise as the cat, she was one of them.

Even in memory the despair and self-loathing he felt that night seemed to rest in his stomach like a stone. But it is the nature of the beast to hope to continue, no matter what. The deepest part of our minds doesn't believe in death. After a time, when his emotions exhausted him completely, he slept. And then he did dream.

Was it an arena or a dancing floor? The strange symbols on it fitted into each other and would have formed a solid but for the fact that there were black lines between them and each curving, graceful shape was a different color. In fact, they flowed through the spectrum, the colors seemingly formed of pure light, as though they partook somehow of the nature of the rainbow. He understood them to be kin to the symbols that flared in the palms of his hands, or on the bottom of the cauldron that ruled and protected the tower. He had seen inscriptions in languages he didn't understand, and he was sure that's what these were: the silent voice of a lost people.

He had a sword and shield. Poor stuff. The shield was the stiff hide of something dead, something that stank, ammonia, a sharp urine stench in his nostrils. The sword was old, the blade dark and pitted with rust, but crudely sharpened with a coarse whetstone to a dangerous edge.

All around him the garden bloomed, a riot of fruit and flowers. They mixed; ripe cherries covered one tree, peach blossoms pink and white on another. Flower beds were scattered everywhere, each holding a different set of blossoms. They were divided by gravel paths or sometimes only stepping-stones, a maze winding in and out between the trees and flowers. The men and women were gathered there, watching him. They were crudely dressed, clothes old and patched. Some of the women had children in their arms or clinging to their skirts. Only a few of them were together with the opposite sex. All . . . all, without exception, had terrible fear in their eyes.

He looked up. Towers loomed above him, towers in the sun. Or were they towers made of sunlight? The latticework of crystal that composed them caught the sun, transforming the warm light into multiple staircases. High-ceilinged rooms filled with art, representational and otherwise, tapestries and floating draperies moved in the wind. There was furniture there, but no piece stirred even the slightest recognition in his mind.

But he knew to move through those half-seen chambers was to experience a perfection of sheer formal beauty as close to the halls of paradise as any mortal being would ever get. To look at them in the distance made his throat ache with longing for a closer and more lasting vision than he would ever be allowed.

He didn't know how far the towers were until he saw what he knew must be his adversaries emerging from among the towers and racing across a long causeway that wound over the magnificent water garden surrounding the city. Shallow pools filled with water lilies in an unbelievable palate of colors, deeper areas reflecting the blue sky, and here and there and everywhere fountains played, coming and going, crystal water shining in the sunlight.

But 'They' were coming fast and They were as ugly as the garden lake and tower were beautiful. They were big and black and tan-colored, black bristles on the neck and shoulders, black face and snout. At the shoulders, bristles, not fur, began to grow lighter, until the back was a light brown, just the color of a lion's fur and much the same texture and length.

They ran on all fours and had cloven hooves. Each one carried a sword and shield slung over its shoulder. When They reached the end of the causeway ready to meet him on the dazzling arena floor, They paused. And he saw they were shape-strong.

They ceased to be animals but did not become men, though they stood upright. The legs and feet of the creatures changed and became more like those of a bear, covered with hair, long and so muscular they resembled tree trunks. The arms and hands seemed almost human but massive and covered by the same tawny hair that covered the legs, chest, back, and groin. The shoulders were two ax handles broad, the neck massive, but almost nonexistent, and it supported a head that resembled a wild boar more than anything else. The snout was a pig's, but no boar ever sported six tusks, each curving upward from the snout.

A pig's teeth are bad enough, yellow bone chisels, very sharp at the points. But these things had fangs, the upper ones fitting into the bone jaw between the upcurved tusks, the lowers short chisels with tips like razors. The whole face was covered by the black bristles, all but the black snout and big, dark eyes.

Studying them, Arthur decided the things could probably see better than he could. The things' foreheads were high and the eyes wide set. He wondered if they would all come at once. There were five of them, and he probably wouldn't stand a chance. But one at a time . . .

They looked at one another the way picked warriors will, as though they were saying, 'After you, gentlemen.' 'Oh, no, no, sir. After you. Please do the honors.'

Behind him Arthur heard the murmur of many voices and he could make out only one word: *tiaeloig*. This talk came from the humans behind him. Despite their interaction, he couldn't tell if they said anything or not.

Then one of them stepped forward. 'My kill!' the voice grated.

Arthur stepped back. The sword was well enough, but the shield? It was made of wicker and hide. It had only a hand grip. There was no place to put his arm. Such a shield, one that cannot be braced with the arm, is of only slight usefulness in a fight.

His opponent swung his sword in a mighty blow, a roundhouse arc that should have cut both Arthur and the shield in half. He didn't stay to meet it. He stepped to his opponent's right and slammed the shield into his sword arm. The blow was hard enough that it would have broken a human's forearm, probably in at least one place, and perhaps disarmed him.

But this was like hitting a tree – correction, a moving tree. The shield was forced back toward him, and the massive head dropped. Arthur saw the bone-white tusks rip through the shield, and when he felt the grip being torn from his fingers, Arthur let go.

He had his opponent where he wanted him: turning. Free of the shield, Arthur reached for his foe's left arm and spun him around. Normally he couldn't have moved so massive a being, but the thing was caught off balance. A second later, his back was to Arthur and he drove the sword in above the kidney, assuming the thing kept its kidneys there. The left side of the blade severed the spinal cord; the point tore through the pericardium, the left lung, and the abdominal aorta.

A second later the thing fell, dying, legs paralyzed, gushing blood from the massive torso wound, the snout, and mouth. As it fell, it ripped the sword from Arthur's hand and he found himself weaponless, facing four more of these horrors.

He woke rigid, heart hammering as though it wanted to leap from his chest, and sick with fear. A dream? He'd never had a dream so vivid, so real, before. Then he thought, *no, that wasn't true.* The ones he had about his mother were almost that sharp and clear.

Was that what he had been supposed to see? His tired mind could make no sense of it.

He rose and the icy water in the spring cleared his head. No, Morgana must not be allowed to protect him again, not tonight. No. There was another place up here. It was even more difficult to get to.

The forest house backed up to a ridgeline. At the end of the ridge was a high spur that overlooked a narrow fjord. Nothing lived on those windswept cliffs. No trees, not even seabirds nested on the shattered black rocks that overlooked the fjord. Wind and rain battered them, and extremes of heat and cold sometimes shattered the ancient Cambrian surfaces, sending sheets of stone peeling away from the cliff to shatter on the shingle by the sea below.

The chamber there was a hole hollowed out by wind and rain, but it was almost entirely open along one side, roofed only by a slab of rock with a rude bed chipped out of stone on the far wall. It took him the best part of the afternoon to reach it. No one went there now. The footing on the ridge was treacherous, and last year a young shepherd who braved the ridge trying to rob a falcon's nest was killed when the scree that covered the ridgeline collapsed and sent him tumbling down the steep slope into a pile of boulders.

In fact, the whole place had an uncanny reputation,

and it was reputed to claim at least one life a year. And sometimes more. He saw why when he got there, his nails worn away, his knees scraped and his hands painfully cut by the jagged flints on the ridge.

It was cold, silent, and utterly beautiful. The wind from the water blew constantly, and the opening in the rock looked directly out over the unchanging scene. The fjord below was the haunt of whales. From above he watched them spout and sport in the deep waters of the land, land split like a lightning-blasted tree in some cataclysm before the beginning of time.

Above the crack in the world, eagles hunted, and on the cliff below him, a pair of peregrines nested. From his own aerie, he looked down on them and the eagles as they circled above the fjord, where the water was a burnished mirror of the silver-blue afternoon sky. Light air and emptiness. If the powers wanted him, they could seize him here.

He sat and felt the sense of peace that comes to us when even a bad thing achieves its finality and we are free from doubt. He is gone. She is dead. I know, I have looked on the body. Our paths will never cross again. I am alone now, and the place in my soul he/she/it occupied will, whatever my fate, remain empty forevermore.

Or the absolute knowledge: soon I will die. It comes to us before death and presents itself as a fact. We feel little or nothing. We simply know and have journeyed beyond even the ability to mourn our own passing. This absolute assurance closes all doors.

Around the middle of the afternoon, he fell asleep. When he awakened, it was dusk. The setting sun was blotted out by a black squall line approaching the coast. The last light shone a lurid green. Wind was whistling and screaming among the rocks around him. He squeezed himself into a corner on the stone bed in the hopes of being able to escape a drenching. He was so tired, so hungry, he wondered if simply spending the night in this exposed place might kill him. But then, such fears were shameful and he discarded them.

The rain came with the darkness and so did She. To this day he could see her and concluded that She walked in her own light. Her hair was whipped by the wind, and her dress, a silver gown of spiderwebs, blew wildly. The moon was in her eyes.

He rose to greet his bride, stripped off his clothing, and, showing no fear, stepped toward her. The wild wind drove the icy rain, slashing at his face and then his body as though trying to cool the heat in his loins – heat so intense he felt as though he might be burned alive by it if he could not quench the flames in her body.

She smiled and he saw She was fanged. Raised her hands and he saw her claws. Mistress of the wild, mistress of the beasts She was, and She wanted him. And live or die, he would never deny her.

A second later, She was in his arms. They kissed and one of her fangs pierced his lower lip. He slammed his body into hers and understood what a sword, red and glowing, feels like when it is quenched at the forge.

He thought he screamed. He never knew.

She did scream, and sank her fangs into his shoulder. His male member went rigid again. He was still inside her. She threw her head back and he saw her open eyes had slit pupils like a cat or a serpent. Her bare breast tips were pressed against his chest, and they glowed so hot on his skin that he felt the fire pouring into his body.

Her eyes closed and her spasms shook him. 'Love me!' she said. 'Love me forever!'

Her love muscles caressed his staff. God, it was like being stroked by delicious warm velvet. He really thought he might die of sheer, raw, draining pleasure. It went on and on and on. Then he was quenched a second time. Darkness gathered at the edges of his consciousness.

'Again,' She said, and his whole body responded to her urgency and he was rigid once more.

The last passage was the most exquisite. He could never completely remember it. He felt as though he were only one thing. Desire roared through him as fire does through dry leaves.

'Love me forever?' She asked again.

One answers with the truth or one does not answer at all.

'No. No. Nothing forever.'

She roared and he felt the raking slash across his back as She dragged her claws through his flesh. But he was beyond pain, almost beyond thought, and certainly beyond fear. He had to have that coruscating, blinding pleasure again if he died for it. And it came, wrung from his whole body in an all-consuming roar of fire.

Then he was lying naked on the floor, too exhausted to move, and the rain mixed with hail was battering him. He might have died, but the landowner, afraid a king's son might harm his high pasture, sent the shepherds to search for him. When they found him, his body was so cold and he had lost so much blood they feared he might die. So they carried him down at once, and he woke in his bed warm, with his father bending over him.

Uther told him afterward that he had been shocked at the utter certainty he had seen in the eyes that looked up into his. And indeed, he had known since that day who and what he was. And whatever he might feel, he was always confident enough to proceed with any action as one who fears nothing.

The water in the stream seemed clean. He drank and went to find a yew. He found one on an outcropping, a jagged gray rock, and the ancient tree looked as though it had endured many cruelties. At some time in the past it had been split by lightning. The bolt charred and blackened most of the tree. But the part that survived had regrown and now the tree was almost as large as it had been before the lightning strike.

'At last.' He recognized the voice, Vareen's.

'You're here, too,' Arthur said.

'Yes. And no, the dog didn't betray you. Bax led you well. The forest is not in a place, and as you probably surmised, it indeed can go on forever. Had you tried to flee the king, it would have. But you didn't, and your magic was too strong for it. The tree before you endured Bade's wrath, not any fire from heaven. It survived and so will you.'

'Is the other one with you?' Arthur asked.

'Yes, I'm here,' She answered. 'Thank you for asking after me.'

He remembered them from when he had first come to the Summer Country. They told him how to escape the plateau where he had been imprisoned and got word to Morgana about where he was.

'Don't you find such a life . . .' Then he paused, because both of them were long dead. Their skulls were nailed to trees on the plateau.

She laughed and he remembered her graceful skull. She was young when she perished, and he thought She must have laughed frequently.

'Such a death, you mean?' She said.

'I suppose,' he said, spreading his hands.

'No, Lord Arthur. Death is not like life. This is why the dead say so little. The existence they have is impossible to explain to the living. But no, Lord Arthur, we are neither uncomfortable nor are we bored.'

'Come! Come!' Vareen said. 'We are using up his energy as we communicate with him.'

'Right now he has plenty. It's not like last time, when he had endured so much suffering,' She rebuked Vareen.

'Yes,' Arthur said. 'And it's pleasant to pass the time of day with you both.'

'*Humph,*' Vareen said. 'That's not why we came, though. And I think we should get down to business.'

'If you wish,' Arthur said, seating himself at the foot of the tree.

'As I said,' Vareen continued, 'when you chose to face the Dread King, your magic became too strong for him. He is very powerful, but not infinitely so.'

'Must I try to find a way to kill him?' Arthur asked.

'No!' She sounded alarmed.

'I agree,' Vareen said. 'And . . . I'm . . . not sure it's possible. And if possible, I'm not sure it's desirable. No! To do so would loose energies . . . that might . . . but, no. You probably couldn't in any event, but . . .'

'Stop dithering,' She said. 'He can't. You can't, Lord Arthur. But he loves to consider every contingency, even the impossible ones.'

'Did I kill her? The Queen of the Dead? The woman in the tower?' he asked.

'No,' She said. 'You didn't. And I don't know how to tell you what you did, except that she departed of her own free will.'

'It seemed so to me,' Arthur said.

'Yes, but what we came to warn you about is that now you must face Bade, and this tree is very important,' She said.

'How?' Arthur asked.

'That's just it. I don't know.' Vareen sounded frustrated. 'All I can tell you is that it is charged with magic.'

'I was going to make a longbow and a spear,' Arthur said.

'Yes. It will do for that. But I would be very careful what you do with them. In fact, perhaps it might be just as well if you picked another tree. The more I think about it, the more—'

'Vareen!' She said. 'I believe we have given him the agreed-upon message. Lord Arthur, on what you must do, you are your own best counselor. We can but warn. And remember, had you listened to Vareen, you might never have escaped your prison.'

Arthur grinned. 'True.'

'So,' She continued. 'Fare you well. The lady in the tower left you better armed than you know. May God go with you.'

Then they were gone. He knew and didn't know how he knew. The place was empty and silent.

There were flints around the boulder that the tree roots embraced. Arthur found some likely looking ones and set about making himself a knife. By dark he had the bow made. He found a hollow near the river and kindled a fire. He was careful to collect only perfectly dry wood, so that the fire generated little smoke.

Bax returned. It seemed he'd been foraging on his own. His belly was full and he was carrying a trout.

Having finished the bow, Arthur cleaned and spitted the fish, meaning to place it high over the fire and let it cook slowly in the smoke. By now it was dark, and he didn't think the small amount of smoke he needed to flavor the fish would be noticed by anyone. So he threw the scraps he had cut from the bow into the coals.

There was a strange silence. It was as though all normal night noises paused and he stood in a bubble away from the world. His eyes stung for a moment as the smoke from the green wood billowed up. He blinked to clear away the tears and she stood there.

His first thought was the shock of her beauty. Her hair was short and clustered in a riot of red-gold curls. She was wearing a simple covering of golden mail, a sort of sparkling dress that clung to her gently curved body almost lovingly. Her armor was not in evidence. Her fair skin glowed soft and dense as that of a newborn child.

Her beautiful eyes looked into his, wide and shocked, and he knew she saw him. A dripping sword was in her hand. He knew she had been in a fight and must have just made a kill.

Then as quickly as she had come, she was gone. Desire flashed through his body with the force of a lightning bolt. He had seen her only three times when, as she said, the dragons brought her to Tintigal. In the torchlight on the quay, he'd thought his eyes were deceiving him. In a pair of leather pants and a tunic very much the worse for wear, she shone like a diamond. Her speech was musical, her every move graceful as that of a young lioness.

The next day when they met in the afternoon, he had known he had not been deceived. But he had been tentative. He was young yet and knew his marriage was an important matter and that all three, his father, mother, and Merlin, would put pressure on him to seek the most politically advantageous match. This girl, however famous her name, was essentially a nobody.

Now . . . He stared into the fire, sunk again to red coals with a few blue flames flickering over them. *Now . . . I am not the man I was, . . . and she is not what Merlin and Igrane judged her to be.*

She had fought them to a standstill in the hall at Tintigal and summoned the servant of Dis to arrange her escape. Moreover, the man who acknowledged her as his daughter was manifestly not of this world. Her very strength would give his counselors pause and again they would advise against the match.

But then, he thought, *none of that matters. There are some things that simply are not decided by the rational part of the mind but by much darker and more powerful forces.*

He had known what his choice would be when he first saw her on the quay at Tintigal.

I want her, he had thought. *And I will not rest until she is mine. One way or another, she will belong to me.*

Sometimes the maiden's bridegroom is death. No people like to think of it, but the sacrifice is very powerful. Because she is the future of humanity? Because for a parent to bury his or her child is the very height of sadness? But it has happened, and I remembered Dugald telling me how the ancient heroes killed a maiden to wring from the gods a fair wind to Troy.

There was a vast silence around me and all I could hear was the rush and roar of the river and the falls.

Magic! Magic!

I remembered Ure's hall and the Faun's head hanging in the net bag from a pine branch. The sad, brown eyes looking into mine: 'You have danced the measure on the earthly labyrinth. Now look for the ballroom of the stars. She gave you power, for you took my head there.'

In a blinding flash it all came together, the odd script that marked the boundaries of the river, the swirling colors of the eternal dome. And I sensed it was eternal in some way, present in the beginning and then never-yielding even when the sun dies. In fact, I knew that it survived the death of a dozen suns.

I had forgotten. Forgotten the Faun's words. I saw Ure's plans. He had wanted to destroy me, but hadn't the strength. Or perhaps not the will. To take me out, he would have had to loose forces perhaps even he couldn't control. And this was probably true of Bade and Arthur.

Time is a maze; time is a weaving. Ure could play tricks with cups, but a human life is another matter. Both Arthur and I were now deeply set in the pattern of events, and day by day, it became more dangerous to try to be rid of us. Or perhaps a better analogy would be a house might stand if you destroyed one wall, but not two. The longer we were present, the more we changed things. That's why we had both been in danger since the day we were born. The longer we lived and fought, the more our enemies would draw back from the catastrophic consequences of our destruction.

Maeniel, the Gray Watcher, had known me since the day I was tested at the wolf den. He had given me the sword, his sword. Sheer time can make a thing magical. The blade had been forged in the high Alps when steel and the new world it brought were young.

I became aware that the vast chamber, the Hall of the Tree, was strangely silent; and I saw the crowd, my opponent, the whole world waited for my reply to the challenge. I gripped the sword hilt with two hands. Not difficult. It had been made for bigger, stronger hands than mine. I raised the blade toward the only dimly seen arch of stars beyond the lights.

And then I called the chamber. That's the only way I can describe it. I asked, not commanded, the mirror of infinity for help.

I was answered.

All light died around me. The Hall of the Tree became utterly dark, but the star road seemed to leap to brightness above. The Hall of the Tree went from silence to a deafening surge of sound as panic struck the spectators. I was inundated with the sound of their terror in much the same way a storm-driven wave covers the shore, sweeping away everything in its path. A howling darkness.

Then the sword blade went red. Scarlet light illuminated the whole chamber. In it, I could see clearly.

Albe and Ilona among the women of the Diviners Guild. The frozen expressions of terror on the faces of the crowds gathered along the shore as they turned and tried to run and realized that to do so would send them into the arms of the night-hunting gangs gathered between the buildings. Music drowned out the anguished cries of human despair as a deep chord rang out.

'I see!' I didn't know I was whispering until I was answered as the red grew brighter and brighter.

'Not all of it!' was the answer.

'No, but the music means something. The color . . . the emotion . . .' I did feel emotion: dull fury, rage, flaming anger, murderous intent were mine and not mine at the same time, and they seemed to sweep my soul along with them.

Then the blade was orange fire, warmth, reassurance, the skin of a fruit, velvet under my fingers. Taste, touch, and scent, not real but then unbearably real. Yellow. Time seemed to slow. Morning. Sunrise. Autumn sunflowers waving against a brown mowed hayfield and a dull gray sky. Sorrow, pain, loss, and, at last, a drenching of anguished despair.

To be capable of absolute commitment is to be vulnerable to absolute destruction. I understood that then as I had never understood it before. But nothing in me would consider turning back.

My arms quivered, my body was saturated with pain. Swept toward unnameable knowledge. I think the experience was then pushing me onward into those parts of the mind beyond rational consciousness, toward the experience of what we poor creatures of the dust might one day become.

A vision of how the wildflower blowing at roadside is connected to the drama of the sun's journey through time and space. The colors, the sound, the emotions came and went. They and much, much more. Think of a crystal sundial; each hour as the sun changes it, a new splendor is revealed. But all pass and it – as my mind did – remains the same.

Then it was over. The cheers were deafening. Fear had

given way to wild enthusiasm. I think people like to be frightened, shocked, confounded, and I had done all three. They loved me!

'You are immeasurably stronger,' my companion said.

'Yes,' I said, gritting my teeth. 'But here comes death.'

And he was coming, the motley figure with the skull's visage hopping from stone to stone toward the arena. I was all the more frightened, because he seemed unarmed. He carried a strange, shining object in his right hand. It glowed with rainbows just as my sword did now, the colors moving, changing as they danced up and down the blade.

He attacked just before he reached the arena. He let fly from the last stepping-stone. It came spinning toward me, whistling a high, thin cry of fury. I didn't get my sword up in time. I parried, but I couldn't completely deflect it. The winged disc slashed past my right leg and my armor didn't come up in time to protect me. It opened a narrow gash on the side of my right calf muscle. I felt the sting then, a wave of burning pain.

'You're hit!' my companion said.

'Stating the obvious,' I answered, watching the winged disc glide above the water and return to the hand of my adversary.

He laughed, and I saw the skull face behind the helm was a mask covering the visage of a living warrior. The pain in my leg subsided to a dull throb, but frighteningly, the leg felt weakened.

'Bad! Bad! Bad!' my companion said. 'The thing is poisoned. I think I can defeat it and . . .'

I had no more time to listen because the disc left the hand of my attacker in a twinkling and was slicing through the air toward my face. The sword came up – it seemed almost of its own volition – and sparks flew as the disc was deflected toward the shore.

The mob composed of the night robber gangs and the

ordinary citizens who were above the slaves but below the guildsmen took the brunt of the winged disc's fury. They had no swords to protect themselves. I saw a woman go down without a face, brains and blood spilling down her gown. A man's arm severed at the shoulder; his body spun wildly as he drenched the spectators with his blood. All this I glimpsed with my peripheral vision. Not to focus my attention on the warrior was death.

A second later I was aware that another winged disc spun toward me. I leaped to my left and the rising sword sent the disc up high over the falls behind me. I didn't dare hold my ground. The returning weapon might slice its way through my body.

As I darted past him, I saw the first disc was in his hand again, and then spinning toward my face. Again the sword seemed to parry automatically, but this time the disc slammed into the crowds on the other side of the river. Again the cries of terror and pain rang out. I knew if I fought a purely defensive battle, I was doomed.

For a few seconds, my adversary was disarmed. I drove forward and, going to one knee, drove a surprise thrust at a chink in his armor where a leg protector ended and his body armor began. At the same time, I tried to channel my fire from my hand through the blade and into his body. I didn't know if I could do this, but I thought it worth a try. I knew I had succeeded when he screamed and I smelled roasting flesh and saw dark, red blood begin dripping on the white stone at his feet.

But at that very moment, the first winged disc thudded into the gauntlet on his right hand. An instant later, it was flying toward my face. I had a second to know I was going to die. Then my unseen companion simply knocked me down on my face. The elbow of my sword arm cracked against the stone platform and I was almost paralyzed by pain.

'Help me!' I screamed at my companion. 'Help me! The pain!'

It vanished and I was levitated to my feet. Again time seemed to slow. I saw and heard the whistling disc and watched as his right hand rose to catch the blood-spattered thing.

He was to one side of me; I was almost behind him. Again I dove for another chink, this one behind the knee, a lovely place to go – for me, not him. The two big tendons that swing the lower leg are there, and the artery that supplies the foot and leg runs close to the surface.

He roared with pain, but he was fast, so fast. He pivoted, disc in his right hand, the left outstretched to catch the other.

Something screamed. It raged across my brain like a brushfire sweeping across a drought-stricken field. Pain slashed like a whip across my shoulders. Something warm and sticky was pouring down my back. I wondered if I was killed. I thought the second disc had sliced into my spine.

But no! I saw it curve in and be caught in the death-head warrior's left hand.

'Down! Down!' my companion screamed, and I knew why. There was no way I could parry both discs with one sword if they were loosed simultaneously.

Salmon leap. I rolled toward his feet. He leaped, trying to clear my body. But I had weakened one leg and his steel-shod toes caught in the golden mail. Hooks sprang out of it and pulled him down. As he fell, both discs left his hands, both swinging in an arc into the crowds on both riverbanks and any platforms that happened to be in the way. Wherever they struck, they decimated the crowds in front of them.

I felt as though I were riding a sound wave. Cries of pain, fury, sheer, blind rage thundered from both sides of the river. People near the river fled in all directions, trying to escape the savagery of those flying weapons.

A second later leaves, twigs, and small branches were pattering down around me. On the last pass before this one, a disc must have struck the tree. I reacted instinctively. I played hurt as he leaped to his feet. I rolled away, hoping to draw him after me. He crouched and stretched out both hands but the horrible execution the discs were doing among the crowd slowed them. As had the plants that bore the mariglobes at the roadside, the tree's sap was as I had hoped: venomous. It was bright red, the color of the foam that pours from a lung wound.

Plop! A clot of it landed in front of him. He glanced up, arms swung out wide to seize his weapons when they returned. The second red dribbling mass landed on his face.

I think the silver death mask protected him for a moment, but I doubt it was a good moment, because wherever the venom from the tree touched his skin, it seared him to the bone. His eyes sank in and became red hollows. The smiling grin, the ruthless bared-teeth grin behind the silver teeth, became a wet, scarlet hole. Then he went over backward and fell with a crash to the stones.

The two silver discs came slashing back. Whatever in his consciousness had controlled them seemed to be gone, because the first took his right hand off and then the second, his left. He was still alive then, because his stumps spurted blood. It jetted out in time to the last stuttering beats of his heart.

Then I realized that I and everyone else in the great hall was in danger, because those razor-edged discs were loose and they could no longer be controlled or aimed. There simply wasn't time for me to snatch up the gloves and pull them on. And even then, I didn't know if I could control the discs. Most of the humans they had brutalized on the first pass were dead or out of the way. The return was very fast. I got my sword in a two-handed grip.

Again it seemed to leap toward the disc of its own volition. The blade rang as the disc sheered off and down. A fountain of sparks leaped up as it sliced into the stone itself. The sword in my hand rose to catch the second disc and sent it in a wide arc, thankfully over the heads of the crowd. I caught it backhanded and sent it down again. An almost blinding shower of sparks rose. Many were hot enough and close enough to sting my legs and feet.

It took a second for my trembling body to realize it was over. I glanced up and saw the night ended and the stars fading. The midnight black above was gone and a blue cast was spreading.

'Dawn,' I whispered. 'Thank God! Dawn!'

Suddenly Albe was beside me, the big Fir Blog just behind, the one named Goric. My sword came up.

'No,' Albe said. 'He's a friend.' She caught my wrist.

'Yes,' he said. 'Right now my masters are preoccupied.'

I glanced around and saw fighting had broken out everywhere. The great families on their platforms were besieged. The long ramps leading out to them were filled with masses of struggling bodies. The gangs and the ordinary citizens seemed to have joined forces to take on the powerful. A few of the guilds were under attack, but for the most part, unless they were very rich, they were being left alone. Upstream the most dangerous-looking of the night gang men were jumping into the water and allowing it to sweep them downstream to the platforms occupied by the great families where they could attack from the rear.

'It's broken,' Goric said. He looked up at the shattered branches still dripping what looked only too much like blood. 'The great families broke it inadvertently perhaps, but until it heals itself, it will not think of us.'

Suddenly his body spasmed. He looked toward the shore. 'I'm being warned.' Then he gave a cry of pain.

My hand shot out and my fingers touched the chain. I felt it also, much the same sort of pain Igrane had lashed me with when she tried to force me to sign the marriage contract with Arthur. It jolted me. But then in an instant it was gone, vanished, as the chain dropped away from his neck.

He stared at me in stunned surprise, then his expression changed into something beautiful, an astonished joy.

'I didn't know you could do that,' Albe said.

'I didn't know I could either,' I said, staring down at my right hand.

Tuau screeched. It made us all jump. 'What are you three jawing about? Run! Your platform is disappearing.'

It was. The tall hexagonal stones were being pulled down row by row into the river. We fled out across the stepping-stones. The other three hung back and forced me to take the lead. I did.

When we reached the diviners platform, we found it empty, abandoned. The ladies ran, Albe told me, when the fight ended. Ilona didn't want to go, but she had to think first of Cateyrin.

'Follow me then,' Goric said. 'I can bring you to a place of refuge.'

The streets were almost deserted, empty. Those few we did meet were much more interested in securing their own safety than trying to hinder us. When we reached the entrance to the city – we had to pass through the plaza, the entry point that opened to the lake – I was astounded again by the myriad glowing shops filled with such a staggering abundance of beautiful and valuable things. I saw this time each tower had a lighted spiral stair that led up the center so that customers could climb up and up, looking and perhaps buying as they went.

'How beautiful,' I said. 'I would like to wander through here with gold in my hand. . . .'

And that's the last thing I remember.

Oh, I have a faint impression of Albe taking my sword. I was loath to let go of it, but I did. And I recall Goric picking me up like a child. When I awakened, I found I was lying on clean straw in what looked like a rocky cavern. It reminded me of a stall where you might put an ox or a big horse. There was a wooden partition next to me, not very high, only about five feet. To my left, Albe and Goric were lying against another partition in each other's arms. They were covered by something, a blanket or a woolen mantle, but Goric was bare to the waist. I knew without needing to lift the cloth covering them that they would be naked under it.

The sword lay by my right hand. The golden mail was simply a gown, mustard-colored, embroidered with gray at the neck, sleeves, and hem. It seemed made of a very soft deer hide.

'Where are you?' I asked.

'Here,' was the acerbic reply. 'But it's more comfortable for both you and me if I soften things while we both sleep.'

'You sleep?'

'What I do is enough like sleep so that I resent being disturbed for no reason.'

'Snappish,' I said.

'Tired,' was the answer.

I didn't think I would hear from it for some time. I sat up and looked into a woman's face. She was crawling around the partition. I could tell she was Fir Blog. Her hair was magnificent, long and black, but she'd obviously been beaten. She had a black eye and a swollen lip. She wore the usual green tunic. It was dirty and where I could see her skin, it was covered with weals. She had a chain around her neck.

She gazed at me silently for a long moment, then asked, 'Can you do for me what you did for him?'

'I don't know.' I was uncertain. The sword had been in my hand when I touched Goric's neck.

I reached toward her. She shied like a nervous horse. I could see why. The bruises on her body were evidence enough of her situation.

I said, 'I can't tell unless I touch it.'

She leaned forward, extending her head to me, but with her face turned away. I saw the lice crawling in her hair.

'They keep us chained up,' she said. 'We are not allowed to bathe.'

I stretched out my hand, praying to God: *I hope I can help this one.*

My hand touched the chain. This time there was no pain; it simply fell away. She remained where she was, looking down at it, her face averted. Then I saw that she was weeping silently, open-eyed.

I touched the bruised eye with my left hand. The smell of roses filled the narrow stall. My eyes closed, and I felt Mother's cold nose touch mine. But when I opened my eyes, she was gone.

I said, 'Mother,' and felt a warm paw in my hand. Nothing I could see, but I could feel it. When I glanced over at Goric, I saw he and Albe were saving their modesty with the blanket and watching the woman and me.

That's what I spent most of the rest of the day doing: taking chains off people's necks.

The word brought to us by the fugitives from above was that the city was in an uproar and the great families were having a difficult time gaining control. It might have been their preoccupation with their own troubles

567

that caused them to be so slow about realizing that their Fir Blog slaves had found a way to slip their collars. It was just as well, because I was so tired that about all I could do for most of the day was sleep – in between touching Fir Blog necks, that is. Goric would wake me and I would do my duty. There was nothing onerous about it, and it made me feel refreshed.

The gown was morose. It said, 'I hope these savages don't chop the human inhabitants of the city into stew meat.'

I remembered the sad, bruised, frightened woman I had seen that morning and answered, 'It would serve some of them right if they did.'

She told me I was a difficult sentient being. I said I thought I was just being bitchy. The gown's consciousness went off in a huff.

Tuau showed up in time for lunch. Like all cats, he has a great sense of timing. Somehow, no matter how preoccupied, cats manage to be punctual about food. While he dined, Tuau filled us in. No, the great families had not realized they were losing their Fir Blog servants. But someone had seen Goric go off with Albe and me, and there was talk of a raid on the slave quarters to 'rescue' us.

Albe laughed and cut her eyes at Goric. He smiled – actually it was more of a satisfied smirk. They both had that relaxed, satisfied look young lovers have. Old lovers, too, for that matter have much the same look. I envied them for a moment, wondering if I would one day have the same experience they were enjoying.

Tuau went on to say Ilona – no fool she – had given him a joint of meat to take to his Aunt Louise. Thus bribed, she promised to warn us about any raid the great families might be planning.

Goric surprised me by his questions. 'How good is her intelligence?' he asked.

'Mummm,' Tuau said. 'Pretty good. You know they give banquets for one another. Usually every family is represented at them. More than death by fire, they dread one family plotting treacherously against the others.'

'Odd,' Albe said. 'I would think that would take up most of their time.'

Goric laughed, and he and Albe exchanged a glance of perfect understanding. At that moment I knew they could rule this place, and I had no right to take her away from him.

Tuau went on to say that Aunt Louise was usually invited by one of the families to lounge around and look fierce. And since the ruling heads of the families had no high opinion of the cat's mind, she saw and heard everything; the proverbial fly on the wall.

'A useful acquaintance,' Goric said.

Tuau purred. 'Then I think we might come to an . . .'

'Leaving my service,' I said gently.

'*Wrrrouuuouo,*' Tuau said.

'Fess up,' I told him. 'What did Ilona say?'

He avoided my eyes. 'How did you know?'

'Good guess,' I said. It wasn't. Sometimes I just know things. But I saw I'd hit the mark.

'Ilona says you are leaving and in a way none of us can follow.'

I said, 'That may be true.'

A silence fell and they all looked at me in concern and, I think, a bit frightened.

'Let us speak of this later.' My voice rang with command. It surprised me that I should be so imperious, but apparently I had earned it, because I was obeyed. 'Better you should consider what you're going to do to maintain yourselves in freedom.'

Goric and Albe looked at each other, and he said, 'We spent last night talking about that.'

'Not all of last night.' Albe grinned.

'No,' he said. 'But a lot. What we would like to do is organize ourselves into a guild. We would be the Guild of Herdsmen. The animals you saw when we first met.'

'The deer with fangs?' I asked.

'Yes. They provide most of the meat for the city. Horrible animals, dangerous, difficult to control. But withal, very good eating.'

We were having some sort of dried sausage with greens and bread. My mouth was full. I held one up.

'Yes,' he said. 'We make it from the scraps on the carcasses and it's sun-dried.'

Probably use the innards, also, I thought. But then, no one ever wants to know what's in most sausage.

'However,' he said, 'we feel we might win the support of the other guilds. Their power counters the influence of the great families, and they are anxious to drum up as much support as they possibly can.'

Tuau scratched a flea carefully with his hind foot. 'The diviners will, I know,' he said. 'Nest told me. She said to pass the word along.'

'Yes,' I said. 'But what about when the herds go back to the stables in the city?'

He and Albe exchanged one of those speaking glances, then I saw his eyes focused over my shoulder. I turned and saw we'd drawn quite a crowd. At least a hundred of the herdsmen were waiting for us to finish eating. I rose right away and got to work.

Goric and I carried the chains to the river. Here it ran into narrow channels. The ground was very broken. By the side of the river, we stood under a falls that dropped in a dozen separate places from the lake above. It was impossible to see very far in any direction. The place was a jumble of pools, ponds, small lakes, all interspersed among broken boulders and scattered, gigantic slabs of rock, all overgrown with vines bearing vicious thorns and bright flowers; small trees and long marsh grasses with sharp edges that sliced into the skin of anyone incautious enough to handle them carelessly.

Goric and I waded into the river. It ran shallow here. I could see there were wild things in abundance: snakes, big lizards, rabbits, otters, frogs, large snails, and fish, large and small. Then I saw something that gave me a chill: paw marks, cat, like Tuau, but much, much bigger.

I looked back and was surprised to see we were already out of sight of the cave where the slaves were kept. We were alone. I wasn't alarmed, but wondered why he'd brought me here.

'You must go,' he said.

'Yes. And as soon as possible, before the great families regain their ambition to imprison me.'

'I thought of doing that myself,' he said bluntly.

I began to reply, but he held up his hand in a stop gesture.

'No. I gave up the idea when I saw what you could do. And when I spoke with Albe. I would say to you, remain here, become chieftain of our guild. Rule over us. But she tells me you are under a powerful geis.'

'I think my destiny was written before I was born,' I said. 'I dare not deny it.'

'Will you take her with you?' He looked as though his life hung on the answer to the question.

'No,' I answered. 'I must fly.'

'Ahaaaa. So that is the meaning of Ilona's prophecy.'

'Yes.'

'The sun capes. You will want one. Think you can use it? They are more difficult than they look.'

'I can try,' I said. 'I must reach the gates to the Summer Country. In my world they lie off the coast and are open only in the season of storms. And only birds can get to them now.'

His strange eyes gazed into mine. 'Over the mountain,'

he said. 'You must fly over the mountain. As to the sun cape, . . . we must steal one.'

'Goric!' I said. 'Slaves know . . .'

'Everything,' he filled in.

'Why?'

'We are so frightened of our masters, what they do affects us so much, we keep track and consider. What else have we to do but entertain ourselves with their intrigues? So I will put out the word among my people that a sun cape is needed. Someone will come forth with a suggestion, a workable idea. Have faith. The other question I would ask you is . . . do we allow the herds to be brought back into the city tonight? Do you think we can fool the great families one more day?'

'No. On balance I think you must take no chances. One night might make the difference between success and failure. If you are correct, the fanged antelope are the main meat supply for the city. Your ability to withhold them gives you the whip hand. The guilds would not easily forgive the great families for a disruption in the food supply. The great families may not understand justice, but they comprehend power. Most do. Demonstrate that you have it.'

He saluted me, raising his arm high.

'And,' I continued, 'arm your people and as quickly as possible. There is no time to be lost, because as soon as they realize their predicament, they will attack you.'

'You would have been a great chieftain,' he said.

'I must find Arthur!' I told him.

We walked quietly back to the rest. I found the advice I had given him about his people arming themselves was not needed. They were making spears at fires within the caverns. They were hardening the tips. Others were making knives and spearheads from flint. They were turning hides to make slings and melting bead for shot. When I paused to speak to them, I heard the words,

'We want our freedom and are willing to pay the price.'

'The price is sometimes rather high.'

I had a good many requests for my touch, and in the end a whole wheelbarrow of chain went to the river. A lot of these were upper servants from the great houses, but another large percentage looked as down-trodden as the first woman I had helped this morning. Many had bruises, some had recently been flogged. Seems these were the newly captured from their own world, men and women who were given the dirtiest and most dangerous tasks in the hope of beating them into submission.

I could see that in a number of instances it hadn't worked. Most were angry and rebellious, willing – in many instances more than willing – to die fighting for their freedom. The upper servants were less sure of themselves. They had loves and loyalties among their erstwhile masters. But most, however well treated, were filled with anger at the usurpation implied in their servitude, and I thought they would stand by their decision. Others were to some extent loyal to their masters but very much afraid that when the defection of so many of their kind became apparent, their masters would take out their rage on those few remaining slaves.

I spoke with the weapon makers and found my words respected far more than they would have been among any comparable group of human men. I acquainted them with the bolo, the spear thrower, and the bow, compound and simple. They in turn demonstrated the effectiveness of their stone tools and weapons. Flint takes a vicious edge, and obsidian is even more lethal.

At length I felt I had said and done all I could. By nightfall it was clear that no further slaves would be able to find their way here tonight. I drank a bit of wine and found myself drowsing over my food, so I curled up against the wooden partition and went to sleep. Albe and Goric joined me, and I was briefly aware of them.

Whatever they were doing, they were . . . hell, I knew what they were doing. But they were quiet about it. I didn't think Albe would be a screamer; and Goric, whatever he did, he was as quiet as a cat. So I enjoyed a good, long rest.

My dress – yes, I was still wearing it – woke me deep in the night. 'Someone comes,' it whispered.

The woman I had freed yesterday crept silently into the stall and crouched down near me. But she was careful not to get close enough to touch me.

'My lady,' she whispered. 'My lady!' she spoke a little louder.

I rolled over. It had been a smart move not to touch me. My sword was in my hand.

'What?' I asked, and added, 'Don't wake the rest.' I knew it was late. How did I know? I can't tell; I just knew. The stillness was profound. Almost everything, even the night hunters, slept.

'I am Micka,' she said.

'We are well met, Micka,' I replied. She blinked. I don't think she expected a courteous greeting. 'I am Guinevere.'

In addition, I noticed she was clean. Her hair was cut short and she was wearing a fresh linen tunic. She no longer stank but had the warm-bread smell of a woman who has recently bathed.

'Goric says you want a sun cape. Well, I know where one is. If you come with me, I will take you there.'

'Where?'

She looked baffled for a moment, then said, 'I'll show you.'

The dance, I thought.

You see, we use the dance not simply to convey inner meaning, but also to map the external world. Ure had danced the location of the Saxons on and along the coast. Both Maeniel and I understood him perfectly.

When the river left the lake, the water wandered away in many different streams into the badlands. Over the centuries when this world had an ocean, the stone was carven away by deep, fast currents as the ocean retreated and then tried to reclaim what it had abandoned in the wild jumble of rocky hollows, grottos, and caves that was left. Then at length when the ocean was gone, the river formed a chain of fens, swamps, ponds, and small lakes, all thickly overgrown with the desert plants I had seen on my way to the city.

Many of these were edible, and when the fanged antelope were penned up to be fattened for slaughter, she, Micka, and other foreigners were sent out to collect wild fruit and vegetation to keep them fed during the brief time it took for the meat to reach the desired level of tenderness. This was very dangerous work. The big cats prowled the badlands. More than one of her fellow slaves disappeared while foraging.

It was also possible in dry years to get lost in certain areas and die of thirst. The plants were not lilies, either. Most were venomous enough to cause anything from a rash or a scald to a deep ulceration on the skin of anyone forced to collect them.

All this she told me while we were on our way to what she called our helpers. I halted in surprise when I saw them: two of the big-fanged antelope. These two wore muzzles and had bits in their mouths. They were tethered. They try to gore you when they aren't. Yes, they had the long, spiral horns, muscular bay bodies, and sharp, cloven hooves. But both wore blanket pads on their backs, held in place by thick straps.

Mine tried to bite me when I grasped the reins. Micka slapped it on the nose and it quieted. But when I mounted, it threw me by rearing, and when I was down, it tried to kick and then step on me. Micka slapped it on the nose again, and again it quieted. But when I mounted the second time, it tried to scrape me off against a rock.

Micka slapped it cross-eyed this time, and I stayed on its back. I could see why they weren't tethered by the reins but rather with a chin strap attached to a stake. Micka turned it loose with some trepidation on her part.

It reared again and hopped three times on its hind legs. Then the forelegs dropped and it decided that since that didn't unseat me, I must be tough. Temporarily at least, it decided to behave. We took off at a gallop, a blistering pace.

'Won't we use them up?' I called out to Micka.

'No. It's the only way to stay on their backs. You have to tire them out. Even so, we must let them go at dawn, because there is no water for them beyond that point. We will be in the desert. Watch out! They are full of tricks.'

Indeed they were. Mine tried throwing its head back and braining me with its skull. I corrected that by slapping its face with the long end of the trailing reins. It gave up on that and tried to break my knees in the narrow passages between rock formations. I had control of the bit and made the beast sorry every time it did it.

By dawn the beast was lathered and tired, still running fast. Truth to tell, I was almost as tired as it was. I had to hold on with my thighs and knees, and my legs and buttocks were sore. I was sure from the slick feel that I had brush burns on my inner thighs and buttocks. I would have given anything for one of our four-horn saddles that held the rider in place and allowed him or her to pick the safest route.

The sun was well up when our mounts quit on us. Or rather, when they wouldn't respond to slaps and kicks or curses. Micka and I climbed down from their backs with a distinct feeling of relief, at least on my part. I was simply unbelievably sore. Once I was down, my mount tried to rear and crush my skull with a forehoof. I jerked its head down and gave it a truly terrible blow across the nose.

'You're getting the hang of it,' Micka said.

'I'd just as soon not,' I told her.

She unbuckled the girths and let the saddle pads fall to the ground. The halters were made of rope. She simply cut them loose with an obsidian knife. Our mounts still had enough energy to bolt. In that rocky, broken country, they vanished from sight in under a minute.

I wanted to rest, but knew it might quite literally be fatal if I allowed myself to get stiff. So we set out walking down the bottom of a narrow ravine that grew deeper and deeper. At first it was dark, but when the sun got higher, there was more light. Not that there was anything to see: layer on layer of eroded sandstone with outcroppings of darker rock, granite, and spongy lava. Where the wind had blown away the sand, it laid bare calcareous limestone packed with shells and the remains of other sea creatures, many the likes of which I had never seen before.

'Life is certainly more interesting with you than with the Fand,' my unseen companion said. 'Why are we doing this?'

'I want a sun cape.'

Micka was walking a little ahead of me. She turned and glanced suspiciously at me. 'You talk to yourself?'

'Mmmm, sometimes.'

She seemed satisfied:

'You will need instruction,' my companion said. 'All I can give you are the basics.'

'Go ahead.'

'Take off into the wind and in the sun. The sun gives the cape life, its motive, power. The air will buoy you up. Understand, this air is only another ocean. You cannot feel its force in the wind.'

I didn't understand, but I nodded as if I did.

'Hot air rises. The air in this desert gets very hot. The sun cape will allow you to ride the rising hot air higher and higher, but as you rise, you will feel the air cool.'

I remembered the fierce sea eagles hovering over the coast and I saw what my friend was trying to say. They seemed to fly without moving their wings.

Yes, I thought. *So that is the way of it.*

'When you feel the air catch another rising column of air, or if the day is hot, by then the cape will have absorbed enough of the virtue in the light to carry you forward. Turn in the direction in which you wish to go. If you go against the wind, expect a bumpy ride. If you go with the wind, take the best advantage you can of it and soar. You can't go too high, I think, but beware if you do, this ocean of air ends high above this world. Don't stop when you fly. If you do, it is much the same as in water. You will sink and the cape will drag you down. If you overshoot your objective, circle back. But I warn you, don't try to stop.'

'Here!' Micka said.

She paused beside a narrow overhang that cast a light shade into the ravine. I glanced up and saw the sun was nearly overhead. It isn't good to travel at noon.

'There are gourds a little further on.'

I sat down in the shade gratefully. She returned with what looked like a melon with a horny, segmented skin and spines, one spine to each segment.

'This is a big one. I don't know if I can get it with my knife.'

I drew my sword and sliced the thing in half lengthwise. It had pink pulp with a nasty taste.

'Don't eat it,' she said. 'Just tear out the pulp and squeeze it into your mouth.'

I followed her suggestion and quenched my thirst with the pulp while chewing jerky. It made enough of a meal that we were able to walk along the shadowed side of the ravine until dusk. As the sun was going down, the sides of the ravine began to grow lower and lower, until it played out, vanishing into a sea of low-growing plants that I recognized as the same kind that produced the dreaming jewels, Gorias Purples. These appeared stunted.

'Don't go near them,' Micka warned.

'No,' I said. 'I encountered them when I first came here. I know how dangerous they are.'

'Yes, well, these are worse,' Micka said. 'They used to send sacrifices here from the city, but the elders among my people tell me they died too fast. Only a few ever managed to get more than half a dozen.'

The evening breeze began and the mass of vegetation stirred oddly in the soft rush of air and seemed to whisper, sounding to my ears like the distant murmur of a curious crowd. Yes, they were stunted. While the first I had seen were over a foot tall and had leaves the size of a platter, these were only a few inches and the leaves no bigger than a cup, a small cup.

'He is out there with the sun cape. Nobody knows about him but me,' she said.

In an odd sort of way, the view was beautiful. The dying sun washed the leaves on the ocean of plants with deep orange and made the violet margins of the leaves near the stem seem to be black. The small white flowers glowed gold.

But there, out in the center of the lake of vegetation, I saw something flash and glitter. I shaded my eyes with my hand and saw the spread of the sun cape among the plants.

'So you can crash them?' I said.

'Oh, very easily,' my companion said.

'Think the one who piloted this one is still in it?' I asked.

'Very likely,' my companion said.

'Oh, yes,' Micka answered also. 'You can see his bones from the top.' She pointed to the low bluff above, where the ravine ended.

Micka had a small pack. She opened it while I made fire. As you know, this is not difficult for me. What I burned were last year's melon vines. Withered and dried, they lay in profusion along the sides of the ravine. Micka had a leather vessel, and she filled it with dried berries of some kind, a few wild onions, and more jerky. She had two stiff leather bowls that she filled with the resulting soup.

I ate and drank what tasted like the best soup I'd ever had. I was so tired that when I rose to walk back up the ravine to relieve myself, I found that I could barely stand. The few feet back to a bend in the ravine seemed like a mile, and the heat of my own urine scalded me. My body was so cold. I had barely enough strength to walk back. But I did.

'Cats?' I asked Micka. 'What about the cats?'

'They don't come here. No one, nothing, does. It is a very dangerous place.'

'What happened to the one riding the sun cape?' I asked.

Micka shook her head, but my companion said, 'It could have been any one of a number of things. Maybe he tried to push the cape too far and he was caught by the oncoming darkness. Maybe he tried to fly too high and perished when the air grew too thin for him to breathe. Or he grew so cold from trying to fly high up that he froze. Any number of things. See, the sun cape is like me. It tries to take care of its rider. It has a strong sense of duty, so if he perished high up, it would try to bring him down safely to where his friends could help him. But by then, it may have been too late.'

'Micka,' I said as she rose to go down the ravine herself. 'Stay close.' In the far distance I heard a cat scream. The last of day was only an iridescent blue line on the horizon. 'One of those cats might pick up our spoor and think she has herself an easy dinner.'

She nodded and returned quickly when she finished her necessary actions. I made her sleep on the inside between me and the ravine wall.

'I have,' I explained, 'weapons that don't show. You are more vulnerable.'

When we were settled, I asked, 'Micka, I think I can easily pluck a dozen or so of those dreaming jewels before I must fly away. Show them to Goric and Albe. They will help you sell them. You could become a wealthy woman and buy anything you want.'

Oddly, she began weeping quietly, but with deep, gulping sobs.

'What I want, I can never have,' she mourned. 'My own world back again.'

I thought of Albe. Albe, whose family had been killed and whose life had indeed been stolen by the pirates she licked.

'You can't give me that.' She sounded almost accusing.

'No,' I said. 'I can't.'

The simple admission seemed to quiet her. Her breathing grew more even.

'What was your world like?' I asked.

She spun me a marvelous fantasy of a green and white world of unending, open plains and magnificent forests where her people lived to follow the herds of elephant, wild cattle, horses, deer, and giant elk. In winter they subsisted on the gifts of the sea, hunting small game and gathering shellfish and finfish on the coast. Come summer, the herds moved north out of the forested lowlands and up high onto the steppes, rich plains teeming with burgeoning life.

Of necessity, the humans must follow them, and in the brief summer hunt, kill enough of them so that they could dry and store adequate meat to get them through the winter. Then when the herds turned south again, they had to follow. An arduous and often short life, but one she longed to live again, even in all its brevity and struggle.

I fell asleep listening to her tales of an elephant with long, shaggy hair and curled tusks so big he swallowed the sun. I didn't listen as well as I should have, but in my own defense, I will say I was very tired still from my many battles and I was sodden with weariness. So I walked all fat, happy, and stupid into the jaws of the trap.

They were eating trilobites and something that might as well have been a shrimp, except that where legs can be found on a shrimp, these things had gills. They were very small, but then you could eat the whole critter, crunching the head and shell up with the meat. So far as the trilobites were concerned, the edible part was the long set of muscles that formed the mound along the length of the back running from the carapace to the tail.

They curled up when caught, but uncurled when they were steamed. The head shield was cracked and removed, then the shell on the back was lifted, exposing the musculature of the tail. The meat was extracted rather the way a lobster's is pulled out, all in one piece, dipped in butter and then eaten. It was a bit better than lobster, because the stored roe near the carapace tended to drip down on the meat, giving it a light, mustard taste.

Lancelot was on his sixth. She was on her fifth, and Merlin had eaten three and could eat no more. The wine in his cup had undergone a subtle change to a white that tasted good with seafood. He was eyeing her speculatively. Being her prisoner wasn't going to be so bad. In fact, after the youngster was gone for a while, possibly, just possibly, she would let him comfort her.

She turned to him, the last morsels of buttered trilobite in her hand, and said, 'In your dreams, you louse. In your dreams.'

He turned scarlet at allowing himself to be so easily read. Lancelot looked baffled for a moment, then his expression changed to truculent. The boy would kill him in a second. In fact, sorcerer or not, probably could kill him if he succumbed to a fit of jealousy.

The birds that hung around him were always in evidence. When he had gone fishing, the youngster had stretched out his hand and received a helmet with a transparent face shield. Then he had pulled a jointed spear out of the air. The shield covered only his eyes, nose, and mouth, but it allowed him to walk on the bottom, breathe, and see whatever prey he wanted to take with the spear.

'It's been a rough last few months,' she said.

'Got any advice for me about King Bade?' Lancelot said.

'Try not to let him kill you,' she said.

'Thank you,' Lancelot said. 'Thank you oh so very much. Anything else helpful you can think of?'

'The sword is in the stone,' Merlin said. 'She has to give him the sword in the stone.'

'Where did you get that?' she asked.

'We were talking about the ins and outs of divination. One of the diviners told me that – told it to me several times for that matter,' Merlin said. 'She was most insistent. In fact, boring on the subject.'

'You don't get swords out of stones,' she said.

'Shows how much you know,' Lancelot said. 'Of course you do. Stones are where they start. Fire from heaven.'

Both Merlin and she stopped eating and glared at him. 'What do you mean?' Merlin said.

'Simple,' Lancelot answered.

There was a fire on the beach. Next to it was the bowl of cold boiled shrimp things. A pit near the fire, a mass of sea grass and three red, steamed trilobites. Lancelot tried

583

to pick up a trilobite, burned his fingers, and yelled, 'Ow!' He licked the tips of his fingers.

'Leave off worrying about your stomach for a moment and explain that statement,' she said.

'Swords are made from wire. Wire is steel, and it is drawn from iron ore that looks like a pile of rocks. I ought to know. When Gray ran out of scrap, which is better since some of the work is already done, we had to render iron ore and get bloom iron. That's something I never want to do again. It's dirty, hot, hard work. And we would be at it for two or three days at a time. Gray said that's why the smith was so keen to have him marry his daughter – so he had a son-in-law who would spend the rest of his life making bloom iron out of the ore he buys from Italy.'

'So,' Merlin said thoughtfully. 'So.'

'I'll tell Guinevere when I get there,' Lancelot said.

'That still doesn't fully explain the statement,' Merlin said.

'No,' the Lady of the Lake agreed.

Lancelot was juggling the last trilobite.

'Hell,' she said. 'You ate the other two already. You're going to burst.'

'He's a growing boy,' Merlin purred.

She gave him a long, slow look through her lashes.

'You do that again,' Lancelot said, 'and I'm going to cut his head off before I go.'

'God!' she whispered. 'Then hurry up and finish eating. We need to say good-bye. And I'll bet when we get finished, you won't have the energy to go slicing up anything.'

'If you're in love with him, why are you sending him off to help a woman he idolizes?'

She didn't answer, and Lancelot stood up. He leaned over and kissed her on the lips without touching her anywhere else.

'I'm salty, sticky, and greasy,' he said. 'I want a bath.' Then he walked away down the long beach toward her . . . home?

'Why?' Merlin repeated.

This time she answered. 'Something wonderful and terrible hangs about them. Some fate both dark and bright.'

Again the sorcerer said, 'That doesn't explain.'

'One,' she said, 'I'm not a goddess and I've learned that successful intervention in the lives of others is rare. It is best when humans work out their own destiny. Two, the fate that shimmers around those three is as gigantic as the aurora borealis. To interfere with such a powerful convocation of forces might be to do evil. In fact, I think it would. And I will not lend my very considerable powers to an immoral course of action. I won't knowingly do wrong. I don't own him. Young and mortal he may be, but the choices he makes are his own. I cannot . . . will not make them for him.'

With that, she rose and followed her lover along the beach and into the darkness.

When the birds came, Arthur knew they were no natural beings. Those eyes and their coal-like glow disturbed him profoundly.

'Are you from the king? Are you his emissaries?' he asked the first, a bird who flew out of the cool gray mist that hovered between first light and dawn.

Arthur was munching on a handful of berries. They stained the skin of his left hand dark purple. His right was occupied with digging a shallow pit to cover the ashes from his fire and such scraps left from the fish he had eaten the night before. He tossed a berry at the bird's feet. It looked at him with one eye, then the other, and last, in a most un-birdlike fashion, with both.

I wonder, he thought, *if they think different thoughts with one eye on the object of their interest than they do when they look at it with the other?*

'No! And Yes!'

He jumped slightly and drew in a quick breath at the sudden answer to both his queries.

'No and yes what?' This time he spoke aloud.

'No! I am not an emissary from King Bade. And yes, I am not sure how or why, but the use of one eye then the other does involve an awakening and an increase in comprehension. Which is why birds do it. As a man, I didn't need to, but as a bird, I can make use of the faculty, so I do.'

'You were a man?'

'Sort of. Maybe once. A long time ago there.' The creature's voice was frightened with a bleak, lonely sorrow. 'Now, you are right. I am an emissary, but not from the king. My lord is the Warrior of Water and Light. Not a man, but not a god, either. He holds my fealty until I die. He begs that you accept his help.'

'I need all the help I can get,' Arthur said. 'And anyone who in truth wishes to come to my assistance need not beg.'

'So be it,' the bird said and took wing.

'I have spoken with a bird,' Arthur said. 'He has promised me the help of the Warrior of Water and Light. I probably need to go soak my head in the snowmelt river. It might freeze the cobwebs in my brain. I could not but think I am caught in dreams or delusion, had not so many strange things happened to me.' Then he moved off with Bax leading him toward the distant towers of light.

Lancelot sat in a perilous seat, one made from the ancient enchanted oaks in the dark, endless forest. She

586

sent him there. The throne was hollowed from the trunk of one tree. It was ten feet across and crowned the last hill of the Forest of Forever and Nowhere. She called it that. When he said that was incomprehensible, she said fine, she sympathized with him. Then she pointed out to him the problem of it.

'This was well known to the ancients,' she said. 'The forest was like that.' And good luck to him if he ever became entangled with it.

He asked how Arthur got out and she said he hadn't. Bade had released him because Arthur had managed to defeat the forest in a trial of strength. Reluctantly, Bade had released him. She wasn't sure why. Bade's thinking was opaque to her. He was so much smarter and more powerful than anything that existed on earth now. But in the past, others had fought him to a standstill. He had never been defeated, only contained. It hadn't happened often, but it could be done. Just possibly Arthur was another such champion, and it was inconceivable that he would not champion his own people. That's what kings were created to do.

A king's life belonged to his people. They were entitled to sacrifice him, and if the conditions for such a sacrifice should be met, he was obligated to go to his death without complaint. The torque is a garrote and used to strangle its wearer. Damocles made them, and at one time that was why only noblemen and women wore them. It was a Damoclean reminder of the obligation of rank. Arthur would meet and exceed his obligations.

Lancelot, his back to the dark enchantment, looked out into the pillared walls of the more normal wood. It was spring and nature had decked herself in red-gold and green splendor. Near his feet, safely away from the vast, shadowed trap behind him, a spring burst out of the rock and gurgled away downhill across a bed of shiny cobbles toward the river. Lancelot sat on the polished wood seat and didn't know he looked impressive.

He wore leather pants and a woolen dalmatic tuniclike garment that was standard male dress of the time. It had long sleeves and he wore a linen shirt under it. It looked sewn on the hem, neck, and sleeves with rubies. But it wasn't. The things that looked like rubies were eyes, Argus eyes that saw everything around him.

The helm raven returned, perched on the rock above the spring, sipped some cool water, threw his head back and swallowed. Then he sharpened his beak on the rough rocks, honing it.

'My lord, mission accomplished,' he said.

'Thank you,' Lancelot said.

'Do not thank me,' the bird said.

'Why not?'

'She is right about Arthur. Keep away unless you absolutely have to go in close.'

'Why?'

'He is a stone killer.'

Lancelot nodded. 'So. But I don't think she had my welfare in mind when she cautioned me to stay as far out as possible. I believe she intended to limit the Dread King's knowledge of my presence. That was also why she told me never to mention his name.'

'To be sure,' the raven said. 'But he is still a stone killer.'

'I'm not lacking in courage myself.' Lancelot spoke a bit stiffly.

'No,' the bird said. 'You would go up against hopeless odds if you felt the situation demanded it. But he . . . he . . . Arthur would not even notice the odds.'

'Oh,' Lancelot said.

Arthur continued to move downhill toward the towers he remembered from his dream of manhood. He had been told he must fight supernatural beings and that's what the dream meant. This King Bade must be the one, and the terrible hog-featured warriors must be another.

Fat, confident, and stupid. That's what I still was when I awakened the next morning. The sun got up before I did, and its light was shining into the dry lake bed where the sun cape supposedly lay. Micka was gone, but I didn't have much time to wonder where, because in a few moments she returned with several of the melons we had gotten water from yesterday.

We refreshed ourselves with the cool melons and chewed some jerky. Then I went searching for a pile of rocks high enough to let me see down into the dry lake. I found a place where the ravine's sides looked climbable and went up. When I reached the top, I saw the sun cape lay spread in the very center of what had once been water.

Fine. Now all I had to do was figure out –

I heard a sound reminiscent of the distant *Heiiiii* of a hawk. It took at least a minute for my mind to consider the fact that there were no birds here, at least, none I had seen. The one exception was the lake that belonged to Ilona's family and strictly speaking, it wasn't here 'here.'

That was the only warning I got. The beak snapped shut.

I don't know if I screamed, didn't scream, fainted, or just had quiet hysterics. All I knew was that I was swept like a flying arrow over the lost lake. I passed over what seemed acres of those murderous plants.

There in the center, the scraps of the sun cape lay tangled with a few yellow bones. Even at the speed I was traveling, it was clear that I could make no use of it because it was ruined beyond repair.

'What! The! Hell! Just! Happened?' my unseen

companion screeched at the top of her lungs. Then she added unhelpfully, 'It's! Got! You!'

I could, I thought, start gibbering, but then my companion seemed to have captured that role. We were rising. The beak squeezing my midsection tightened as its owner reached the edge of the lake and caught the lifting air mass driven by the sun heating the rocks. We went up, flying in successively wider and wider circles as the thing used the thermal to propel itself into the sky.

The wings . . . I didn't believe the wings. No bird ever had wings like that. They were three times as long as my body, but more like a bat's than a bird's, webbed, furred with short, very, very short, down. White, the down made them shimmer like mother-of-pearl, and ever so slightly translucent at the edges that they glowed a bit, pink in the new sun.

Up, up, they swept, turning slightly to present the edge and escape the resistance of the air. At the top of the stroke, they flared into white, iridescent sails and caught the wind on their down surfaces, a magnificent down, driving the two of us higher and higher toward the golden blue of the morning sky.

'Your sword!' the dress screamed. 'You still have your sword! Kill! It!'

'I don't think so.'

We were high, so high that even fear was gone. At a certain point, I discovered, the ground below simply is not real. The dry lake was no bigger than a large platter, and we were rising yet, those magnificent wings pushing us. The flying thing had a long, narrow beak. It was not hard like a bird's beak is, but flexible and cartilaginous, or at least the edges were. I suspected that if I were not wearing that little mail shirt, the thing might have bitten me in half. As it was, the little ring mail was protecting me.

'Humph! I'm glad you know that. I am,' was the soft-voiced reply to my thought.

'Fine,' I said. 'Have you got yourself under control?'

There was a long silence; a long, chagrined silence. Then it snapped, 'Yes!'

'Fine!' I said. 'I hope you don't have any more bright ideas about me killing this thing, because if I do, or even if I swing and miss and upset it, it might drop me. And unless you can slow my fall . . .'

'I might. I'm not sure.'

'Not sure isn't good enough,' I warbled back.

'True! Only too true. We are very high, and if what I feel is correct, this . . . whatever . . . is unhappy. It's finding you a load to carry and if it weren't so important to get you to . . . to . . . I don't know the very high personage who commanded it to get you . . . it would set you down right now and forget the whole thing.'

I glanced to my right and saw the beak clasping my waist and beyond it, one troubled orange eye with a black pupil gazing at me. The head was covered with the same fine down as the wings were. It looked as soft as the fine fur on a newborn kitten. It was white on top and blue on the bottom. In fact, the whole belly of the creature was a pale blue. It extended out under the wings and even, I could see, to the downy legs that ended in long, smooth, narrow, folded claws. There was a slight crest on the head. The crest was striped with soft bands of blue, the same iridescent blue that covered the belly and underwings. All in all, a magnificent creature.

I was aware that I was clutching my sword.

'I can get that,' my companion said.

The thing vanished from my hand. I hung where I was, the creature's beak holding me. I saw the city, toy-sized, pass below me. The wings pulled us up and up, partway riding the thermals, partially by main force. As we passed above the tallest towers, I saw men and women of the city clad in furs standing on balconies and platforms amidst the white towers, the final pinnacle of the city's heights. They pointed up and watched the magnificent bird (was it a bird?) labor over them and clear the mountain peak.

The mountain that clasped the city was only one of a long chain of sparkling, snow-clad pinnacles beyond. I found myself sick with fear. It was cold already. I didn't know how high this thing could fly. Dugald hadn't been slow to tell me that there were reasons why mountains had snowcapped peaks. Maeniel had crossed the Alps many times, and also warned me about the weather high up. These pinnacles were taller than any I had ever seen, and I thought I might easily die of the cold.

But I didn't have long to worry. When we cleared the last towers of the city, I saw where the bird was going. It was like riding a falcon's stoop when the creature folds its wings in midflight and drops toward the earth to surprise its prey. This creature also folded its wings slightly and rode down the slope, sometimes only a dozen or so feet off the ground, into the largest canyon I have ever seen. The slope unrolled before me like one end of a dropped scroll, snow and ice, bitterly cold wind, then shattered marble, flint scree, black basalt.

Then the thing's beak tightened, squeezing me painfully. My companion acted to protect me.

'I don't think it means you harm. It said it just doesn't want to drop – *eeeyaaaa!*'

The wings snapped open and we soared over a massive gorge draped in a jungle at the lower elevations while at the bottom, a wild white-water river frothed and foamed. The bird floated lower, and even as frightened as I was, I gasped with delight. The jungle that clothed the lower slopes had, I think, no single flat spot. It existed on itself, feeding on itself, water and light. Massive trees with long, ropelike roots grew from pockets in the steep slopes. The thick, squat trunks were black with moisture. They supported an absolute riot of ferns that looked like cut lace: white, yellow, green, and red were mixed with moss on their branches. Vines that seemed to have no real rooting spot draped themselves over every place too steep for trees, and in between vines, trees, and ferns were flowers, single, glowing masterpieces of pink, purple, violet, gold, and soft combinations of pastels. Flowers in masses, black and yellow, orange, black and yellow, red, blooming along thick, succulent stems and protecting themselves with long, golden spines.

Even on the steepest slopes, sheer cliffs, the greenery colonized everything. On the more gentle grades (at best, most of them were very precipitous), there were scatters of what looked like eggshells, and they held quantities of food plants.

And oh, yes, I have forgotten about the birds. This gorge was a veritable paradise for birds. I saw iridescent ducks, geese with dark heads and gray bodies, deep blue with long, yellow beaks. Higher, the flocks flashed up out of the luxuriant greenery. Red and black, with loud voices and shining wings. Blue and gold, yellow and scarlet, burgundy and fire opal, they appeared for a second to delight the eye, then vanished again into the omnipresent green-velvet slopes.

I saw also that these magnificent lowlands were a gift of the knife-edged pinnacles above. They were crowned with glaciers, and the snow and ice that melted in the sun by day sent water cascading down into the river that roared and thundered below. You see, even in the bird's beak with the wind roaring in my ears, I could hear it tearing along in its rocky bed below. Waterfalls by the hundreds were scattered along the canyon walls. Some ran in shallow streams, dropping from rock basin to rock basin, water spewing out, sending a fine mist of droplets to drench the jungle slopes. Others dropped from above, hundreds of feet straight down, carving out whirlpool basins.

As we passed one of these towering falls, I fancied I saw a white city behind it glowing in green and gold trim from a seemingly endless spill of eggshell-white terraces decked with roses. I remember the beauty of it flashed before my eyes. The sun was shining through the flowers and leaves. They were translucent in scarlet, green, and golden light against the pure, white terraces.

Then the vision passed, and the bird dropped lower and lower as we entered a basin where the biggest waterfall I have ever seen created a giant lake, the water so clear that from where the bird flew, I could look down and see into the lake bottom. An awesome thing of beauty, it seemed an underwater forest and meadow. Low grass filled the center, thick as moss over dark splatters of rock. Fish of all sizes grazed over the meadow. Around it the long ribbon tendrils of some taller plants were wild splatters of bright green and transparent to the sun's rays as they flickered and danced gracefully in the current.

Past them and dominating the lake and the floodplain beyond were the trees. Never before or since have I seen anything like them. Each tree was very tall, and their tops extended above the walls of the basin, towering hundreds of feet into the air. They seemed to grow as well in water as they did on dry land. The roots extended out from the base of the trunk, forming a shield. The trunk grew up from the center of the shield very high into the air. For such giant trees, the leaves were oddly tiny and formed clusters of plumes that feathered red-barked, smooth branches. The tree trunks were a smooth jade-green, becoming almost green-black as they broadened and entered the shield at the base.

The trees allowed nothing else to grow where they grew. The base shield of each one butted up against the base shield of another, and they formed a perfect carpet of hexagonal, living tiles that blanketed the earth in the

594

shallows around the lake and extended out into the defiles of the floodplain where the lake emptied into a jumble of rocky, jungle-clad badlands.

Then I saw the city. Like the gazing bird, I saw it with one eye while the other looked into wilderness. It leaped up, a cluster of white and transparent towers held together by a matrix of those same, translucent green and red flowing vines.

And I understood something I had never known before, and never was clearly able to remember again. The universe unfolds into life. It arises from the stars, and flaring love-drenched emptiness into life, life unfolds into thought and will. A great experiment, but one that could have many outcomes, some sublime, some so destructive the mind turns from them.

But this glowing, glittering white city was sublime, as were the trees surrounding it and the flowers; those translucent ruby-petaled bursts of brightness sustained the city with the energy they accepted from the love of the ever-giving sun.

The bird circled the city's towers, rising, riding the reflected heat energy from the flowers and their spires, higher and higher. As it did, I looked into two worlds, because the city inhabited both. One world was the Summer Country, green, wet, fair, filled with seas, meadows, gardens, and forests. The other – a world barren in many places, without oceans dependent on the cruel mountain peaks to pull water from the air, freeze it, then send it driving down to endow the fruitful valleys below.

I don't know what the builders of the city called it. But for the Dread King, they were all long gone. But ever after, I always called it the City of Two Worlds.

About then the bird dumped me on a cold platform, a jutting balcony near the top of the tallest building in the city. Three-point landing, nose, knees, and the palms of my hands. I crouched, sick, dizzy, and in pain, with no protection from the icy wind, simply glad to be alive and on reasonably flat ground again. I wondered if I would be left here and if so, how would I survive the night?

One of the problems, Arthur thought, was that he didn't know what he was walking into. Could this Dread King Bade be defeated? From the accounts given by some of the escaped slaves, he was awesomely powerful. No one had ever even seen a dent made in his control over what they called his golden towers. Escape was possible. Many had escaped. Arthur had been accepted as king by the heads of the families of the escapees. A few held out, but even they were friendly to him. It was just that they were so afraid of the power that ruled the gardens and the golden towers.

Slave revolts had ended in death for all the participants. So in their view, resistance was out of the question. Yet if he went forward, he was committed to a head-to-head confrontation with the king.

He was moving now through flatter but more broken country. The trail – probably a game trail that ran along the river's rugged course – continued, but if he left the trail, the countryside around it was such a jumble of broken rock and thick brush that he doubted if he could have made more than two or three miles a day. This was landslide country.

The valley the river ran through was strewn with the remnants of rockfalls from the dark and endless forest from which he had come, and it was strewn between the massive boulders that composed the surface, with the corpses of the massive trees that formed the heart of its threatening immensity. Most were shattered, broken, and dead, trunks splintered, branches ripped away by their long fall. But sometimes the roots still clutched boulders and massive stone blocks.

The other side of the river was no better; worse, in fact, since there the ground sloped gently up for about four or five miles, then abruptly, sheer, massive, and very dark granite cliffs rose, seeming almost to crowd the sky. Fragments, some of them much larger than any house or church he had ever seen, lay piled on top of one another on those gentle slopes, and in places, rock slides had temporarily dammed the river and changed its course.

Why so many, he wondered. He found out that evening.

It was a nuisance trying to feed himself as he traveled, but there was no help for it. So he stopped early to set lines in a likely looking pool where the river widened, and also put out snares for rabbits and other small game. The broken ground was a paradise for rodents.

He'd just finished with the fishing lures when he was overtaken by what he thought was a sudden attack of dizziness. The whole world seemed to quiver around him. He dropped to one knee. A flock of finches feeding nearby burst into the air and several large water birds took wing, screeching.

Then the tremor came again, this time clearly not the result of anything he was experiencing. The earth shifted under his knee and he fell forward, catching himself on his hand and feeling the earth trembling under his fingers.

The crack was as loud as the crack of doom.

He leaped to his feet and turned in the direction of the sound. He reflected later, that was probably not the smartest thing to do during an earthquake, but battle training won out over caution. He saw, high up on the sheer cliffs above the river, a gigantic granite dagger break off and fall with what looked like – but couldn't have been – great deliberation into the churned-up mass of shattered rock below.

Then again he dropped flat, to escape fragments of the rockfall that exploded out from the center of the concussion below. He noted with some annoyance that when he felt brave enough to rise to his feet, his legs were shaking.

'That,' he whispered to himself with some awe, 'explains the condition of the valley.'

That evening he took five rabbits and three fish. He and Bax both ate well. A sense of warmth and comfortable repletion were new and refreshing things for him. So he sat quietly by the fire, dozing and puzzling over how to produce an attack plan against this King Bade. He had no allies that he knew of. The word of a bird . . . well, perhaps he was half-mad. Certainly his father had been sane enough, but some of the rest of the family walked with shadows most of their adult lives and no one ever knew if the specters that gathered round them were actually there or not. After all, a bird? What did a bird know?

He now had a wooden spear and a bow; in addition, a sufficient supply of sinew to string the bow. Arrows would take more doing.

His eyes drifted shut, and she appeared in his mind. He remembered her fragrance. She had her own. It had taken him a few minutes in her presence before he realized she wasn't wearing any of the scents his mother or her women wore. That fragrance belonged only to her. It was flowerlike, but very gentle, like something deep but very distant, carried along by a midnight breeze. A thing you never quite remembered, but then again, never quite forgot.

A fish jumped in the river, and he opened his eyes and realized he'd been dozing while he was sitting up. Without thinking about it, he picked up a small piece of the yew and tossed it into the heart of the coals. The green wood sent up a dismayingly large billow of smoke, and from the thick of the smoke, a face looked out at him.

But it was not hers. His instant fear jerked him fully awake. This was a thing out of a nightmare. The eyes were huge. Set in dominoes of black skin, they had big orange irises and small, deep-black pupils. He recognized it as the male version of the great queen who had given him the tower.

A very fine, dense growth of feathers covered the face. It was white, as the queen's had been, but with a deep red that began in a cluster of red feathers at the chin and continued up the face. The eyes looked out at him from the red V. Then the feathers continued up and up to a very high scarlet crest on the top of the head. A crest that, unlike the one that female wore, could not be entirely composed of feathers.

The rest of the face was flat, the nostrils almost non-existent but for the steady movement of the feathers that covered them as the thing breathed. The mouth was a slit – correction, a fanged slit – the fanged teeth projecting both up and down. The face had no expression he could read, but hate and disgust seemed to emanate from it like some foul vapor.

'Vermin! I cannot think why I did not exterminate your scavenger breed when you wandered no smarter than some vicious monkey across those African plains! I set the cats on you to thin your numbers. But breed you can and breed you will . . . like rats, like green snakes. Vermin. You were never more than a superior sort of vermin. I should have known that when you turned the tables on the big cats and perfected your thieving ways by taking their kills.'

'She was one greater than myself,' Arthur said. 'But she did not demean herself by insulting me. Indeed, she treated me with every courtesy.'

Arthur flinched as another blast of hatred and grief washed over him.

'Thanks to a thing like you, she is gone . . . gone

forever. And I am truly alone.' *Alone* was a wail of sorrow.

'She wanted her freedom,' Arthur said. 'Even if it were only freedom to sleep.'

'Why do I bandy words with such as you?'

'I think it's thoughts you bandy,' Arthur said. 'I hear no words.'

'Then hear this!'

The thing's small nostrils distended, then closed. The whistling shriek was high, thin, and at the edge of human hearing. Arthur fell to his knees. It felt as though nails were being driven into each ear as the mad cry lifted itself into sheer pain. Everything around Arthur – grass, brush, small trees, even his clothing – burst into flame.

The river! was the only coherent thought Arthur had, and he executed a low, flat dive into its icy water.

Whatever brought me to this city left me to spend an icy night on the small balcony. God, it was cold! It appeared there was no window or entrance to the soaring tower. I lay near the top, my back to one alabaster wall, looking out over the valley. I was in pain; my hands, knees, and elbows were skinned. It hurt to breathe. I think the bird's beak broke at least one, or possibly two, of my ribs.

'Can't you help me?' I asked my companion.

'I'm trying. I'm trying. But what are you up against?'

'The cold!' My teeth were chattering.

'Then go inside.'

'How?' I demanded.

'That panel. See it?' Yes, indeed there was a recessed panel on the back wall of the balcony. 'Push one side.'

'Which one?'

'Either!'

I got to my knees, cramping from the chill, and pushed

the right side. The panel pivoted at the center. Inside was a stone, windowless room. I stuck my head through and saw the room was empty, bare from wall to wall, made of what looked like fitted stone blocks. Windowless, doorless, and freezing cold.

'God, it's like a tomb,' I said.

'Yes. Well,' my companion snapped at me, 'at least it's out of the wind.'

'Suppose once I get in, I can't get out?'

'Wait!'

I had been on the balcony all afternoon while the air grew progressively colder and colder. I had explored the balcony from end to end looking for a place to climb down. There was none. The roses that grew in the hollow top rail of the balustrade had occupied me for a time. They were vining roses with long tendrils that curled around the railing and its supports. They bloomed profusely, but held no rose hips, seeds, or roots. They seemed to grow from the stones of the tower itself. Flowers and leaves were translucent to the light and blazed in the sun, green and scarlet.

'Don't touch them!' my companion told me, or rather, warned me loudly. 'I don't know what they are, but whatever they are, they're powerful.'

And indeed, whenever I drew near them, the armor leaped out all over my body.

For a time, I stood in the late afternoon sun to one side of the recessed panel and studied the tower. It reminded me of a bundle of rods of differing lengths. Some of the rods were covered with latticework, all bearing those same, glowing roses. Others, like this one, had multiple balconies. They were staggered and no balcony was directly over any other, but all had railings covered with the selfsame roses.

As the afternoon wore on, the wind grew colder and colder until by the time I confessed my fear that I would not last the night outdoors, the sun was a shimmering orange ball on the horizon.

'Well?' I asked.

'I can find no locks or bars,' my companion reported back to me.

'Did you check the center post?' I asked.

My companion gave an irritated little snort. 'I checked that first. No. And as I said, at least it's out of the wind. We're being watched, but I don't think the sentient watching us knows I'm here. So don't hold any loud conversations with me or get into any arguments. And you needn't roll your eyes like that. There's nobody nearby to comment on your forbearance.'

I sighed and stepped backward, out of the whipping, tearing wind, and closed the panel. It was pitch-dark in the room and achingly silent. I lay down near the wall.

'Can it . . . the thing that's watching us . . . hear or see me?'

'No, I don't think so. It's not very close or very smart. What the entity that captured you does is delegate his authority to this thing, whatever it is . . . snake, spider, roach, rat. Yes, it's a rat, and it's hungry.'

'Thanks. I needed to know that,' I said.

'Pish posh! For heaven's sake, the thing is a sentry. It's not going to eat you. In any case, it will soon be relieved by another sentry and it can go eat. From time to time the important entity drops by its servant's mind to take a look at you, then it leaves and goes on about its business.'

'Then become a dress and keep me warm.'

'No!!! The rat can see well enough in the dark to spot me.'

I was, to all intents and purposes, naked but for my armor. 'It won't matter if he spots you when I'm dead from the cold!' I snapped.

'Damn! Let me think. *Ummm* . . . the roots of those

roses pervade the whole building. Let me see if . . . *yeeeeee!!!* God damn!'

'Christ,' I whispered. 'You'll alert that rat yourself!'

'Stop fidgeting and harping and carping and crapping. You are the only one who can hear me. *Now shut up!*'

Bull's-eye! A wave of warm air wrapped around me.

My companion spoke in a lofty voice. 'Nothing to it. I just made a mistake and tried to be a root. Although I will say, those roses could fry both of us if we get it wrong.'

'If we get out of here, I would definitely stay away from them.'

The dress had some more things to say, but I fell asleep while she was talking. The early morning cold woke me. That, and a '*Hist! HIST!*' from the dress.

'What's wrong? And will you please! Please provide me with some warm air.'

The warm air arrived and my friend whispered, 'The sentry is gone. I hear movements. Something is going to happen.'

Two women opened a door I hadn't known was there and entered. At first I didn't realize they were women. Both were hooded and robed. The dogs were tightly held with choke chains.

I staggered to my feet. I managed a bow, but the room was icy cold and I began coughing. One of the dogs glared at me with cold, yellow eyes, laid his ears back and lunged at me. The woman was hard put to hold it.

'I don't like this,' the other woman said.

'Fine!' the one struggling with the dog said waspishly. 'You disobey *him*.'

The thing entered the door. It paused for a moment between the two dog women.

'She must be ruined and no use to him or anyone else,' one of the dog women said.

I didn't get a very good look at him, and I was just as

happy about that. He had cloven hooves and his massive body tapered up to a pair of shoulders that would have done credit to an ox. The face was that of a wild boar, actually a little worse than a wild boar. He had two sets of curved tusks and the usual set of teeth. I know, because they protruded from his jaw sort of like a chisel and a razor combined.

'Let's get it done,' one of the dog women said, and he advanced on me.

'You got my sword,' I whispered.

'Against that? You just think you're going to use a sword against that,' my companion said.

'Have you got any better ideas?' I spoke almost silently between gritted teeth.

'Tell me when you want it. A second later, it will be in your hand.'

He – and it was a he – was wearing trousers and a shirt. I could see the clear male bulge between his legs. He had an erection.

I backed away slowly toward the wall. I kicked back with one leg and opened that door. It didn't lead anywhere, but it gave me some running room.

I saw we had an audience. The corridor was crowded with people and the other balconies were filled. For a moment I was angry, but then I realized they didn't look happy and they weren't enjoying the spectacle. Instead, they seemed afraid. I knew I was being used as an object lesson.

So I shouted, 'I am a sacred queen! I must go only to one man and come to him a pure woman! All you accomplish here is my death!'

I got no visible reaction, but I knew I had been heard because the room vanished around me. I, the monster, the dog women, and the knot of spectators were all standing on a stone platform at the top of the world.

The thing's jaws opened. A pig's snout. A pig's

intelligent but cruel eyes, and a pig's chisel-and-razor teeth. He snarled out the grunting roar of an angry boar and charged me.

'Sword,' I said.

The thing's clawed fingers caught my arm. I felt his talons through my armor. But the sword was in my hand. I drove it through his body.

It let go of my arm and jumped back. Then, I think he laughed, if that sound was a laugh. With one hand he jerked the sword out of his midsection and hurled it spinning out over the city. I had given him a gut wound and I was sure he would die sometime soon, but not before it accomplished its objective.

No, I thought.

I stretched out my hand and called the sword. It came spinning toward me out of the sun and slapped down hard into the palm of my hand.

Yes! I had blessed it in the rainbow chamber, the labyrinth of light and color of the dancing floor of the stars. Now it knew me.

'Wonderful,' my companion said. 'Now cut off its legs.'

I crouched, sword in hand, and we circled each other, a stall for time. Then I noticed the wound I'd inflicted in his stomach was closed. The massive muscles that marched up the abdomen toward the gigantic chest were intact. There was only a little blood on his shirt. The click of those cloven hooves on the stone platform and the tearing noise of the endless wind at my ears were the only sounds I could hear.

Those roses surrounded the platform on which we danced this dance of death, and the flowers and leaves were translucent to and part of the light.

'I can't lose this battle,' I whispered.

'You won't!' the ring mail said. 'Next time he tries to close, cut off a hand, an arm, whatever you can reach. *Whoooeeee.* He stinks.'

He did. He stank enough almost to break my concentration. We were still crouched, circling each other. I shifted my position so the wind was blowing away from me.

'Thanks,' my companion said.

'Don't mention it,' I said as he leaped forward.

I swung the sword at an arm outstretched to seize me. But one-handed, the sword only bounced off his forearm. The wound healed in a few seconds.

I switched to a two-handed grip and we began circling again. I can't tell you how frightened I was. The thing – my opponent – represented a problem I couldn't seem to solve. I was tired already and hadn't eaten since yesterday. I was not unscathed by the battles I had been in. I had healing wounds in my right arm, my left leg, and now on the face where the thing's talons scratched me on our last pass. Blood from a cut on my cheek tasted salty on my lips. That bird had broken at least one rib, maybe two, and it hurt to breathe. Moreover, the dress kept herself hidden and I was naked but for my armor. The wind sucked the heat out of my body. My fingers, toes, nose, and ears were already numb.

'Warm me,' I whispered. 'Just a little.'

'Very well,' was the sour reply. 'But I'm using up what strength you have to do it.'

He got impatient and lunged again. This time I spoke to the sword. It blazed red and when I slashed his hand with it, I cut off three fingers.

The thing raised the injured hand and roared out what was obviously a demand. I didn't wait for him to be healed. I charged in and threw as much as I could into the sword blade. This time it glowed as though heated at a forge and it sliced off his right hand at the forearm. His blood spurted everywhere.

But he had a long reach, and by coming in so close, I had left myself open to a retaliatory strike. His fist slammed into the right side of my head. My right eye went blind and my left saw flashes of light. My head snapped back, and I went flying. So did my sword . . . in the opposite direction.

I called out to it again and felt it slap into my palm almost in the same second I felt the massive, taloned hand seize my right arm just below the shoulder. It was like being tossed by a bull, or being a mouse in the jaws of a cat. I was jerked toward him, and he hammered the stump of his right arm into my face.

One last try and I was finished. I ordered the sword to my left hand.

It went, my vision cleared for a second, and I saw the stump of his right hand drawn back to smash into my face again, the red, ugly, jagged edges of the bone protruding beyond the ragged skin.

'Give it everything I've got!' I shouted to my companion.

I felt the power pour into my left hand from my command of the blade, from my companion's control over my body. I know I swung. I didn't remember doing it, but with my left eye, I saw the sword shimmering white, cold as distant starlight, slice not into my opponent's neck but the savage boar's head. It sliced the skull in two below the eyes and above the snout.

Still the thing didn't die. But I was able to hack the thing's remaining hand free of my arm and jerk away.

I stood, both hands locked on my sword hilt, while the ruined monster circled me, blood spouting in gouts from what remained of the head and right arm until whatever reserves of savage energy kept him going . . . until at last he crashed to the ground and died.

All the human beings in sight fled except the two women with the big dogs. My blood was so chilled by a ringing cry of fury, despair, and suffering that I stood rooted to the spot until the two women reached me. They seized me, one on each arm, and said: 'Run!'

Arthur stayed hunkered down in the freezing water while the fire on the bank burned itself out. Then, as if to compound his problems, it began to rain, sheets and sheets of pale autumn rain, dreary as a swamp in winter, cold as a grave. To remain all night in the frigid water was probably death. Likely, he would die of exposure before morning. So he crawled out of the water in a very bad mood and found a wolf waiting for him on the bank.

He still had his boots and a lot of his trousers and leggings, but his mantle was completely gone and his shirt hung in rags. And it goes without saying that it wasn't helping him stay warm, because it was all soaking wet.

He was tough but freezing cold. It was late in the day and night was coming on. He was not overly impressed by wolves. He knew a lot about them. It was part of the job of any nobleman or chief to keep them under control and prevent them from becoming a danger, or – what was very much more likely – a nuisance to human beings.

They were rather better than human brigands because they had a sense of proportion about their depredations. In other words, they avoided going too far and provoking the wrath of farmers and stock keepers. That, and they helped to control the number of foxes and rodents resident in their pack territory. The fox was a much greater danger to domestic fowl, chickens and geese, than a wolf was, not to mention the young of sheep and goats. And rodents could be a massive danger to both field-grown and stored cereal crops if said rodents were allowed to multiply unchecked.

Besides, wolves were sacred, especially sacred to warriors and to the dead. And this quality of holiness was so ancient that it seemed only barely rooted in rational consciousness. He had been told as a boy by Morgana that from the time the world was created, wolves were there. Long before men entered into existence, the wolf had ruled the ancient forests.

When the Lady of the Beasts brought forth men from her womb, she appointed wolves to be human guardians. And indeed, it was true. As a hunter, he knew that in any unfamiliar territory, it behooved the hunter to find the resident wolf pack. They would lead him to game, showing him how he may survive.

As quickly as he could, Arthur began to search among the charred ruins of his camp for the bow and spear he had made from the yew tree. Meanwhile, the wolf sitting quietly in the rain near a large boulder lifted a hind leg and scratched vigorously behind one ear.

'Greetings,' Arthur said to the wolf. 'First I see birds, and they address me courteously. Now a wolf appears. Don't let me keep you. Say what you have to say and go back wherever it is you came from. For however much I respect your clan, I don't care to go to sleep in close proximity to a creature with such long, sharp teeth.'

The wolf stopped scratching and sat upright, ears forward. The world around Arthur vanished and he stood in a desert. He found himself in a dry creek bed looking at a tree that wore flowers as blue as the dusk around him. Power. Dusk and dawn represented power. Not day, not night were the doors to eternity, and he knew this doorway was the one the wolf came through.

The last sun was a dying fire on the horizon and the first stars pierced the black abyss above him.

'That's better,' the wolf said. And it was, because he was no longer a wolf but a fully armed warrior, the winged-helm bird beak resting down like a widow's peak on his forehead, wings sweeping down to cover his cheeks and the sides of his head, the tail a broad fan protecting his neck. A muscle cuirass, two birds, one looking right, the other left. Below the cuirass he wore the armor he had removed from the dead shape-strong being in the world where he first met the birds. More of the ravens formed his arm and leg protectors and his sword.

'I stand corrected,' Arthur said. 'I had no idea.'

'Even if you had no idea, you needn't have been so sarcastic,' the Raven Warrior said.

'If I failed in courtesy, consider my circumstances.'

For a second the rain ceased because the birds swept in overhead. The ravens circled, spinning almost like a wheel above both men. Then ceasing to hold their formation, they rose higher and higher against the cold, gray sky in a crowd, an amorphous, cawing crowd. Then, as if finding their direction, they swept down to cover the ground surrounding the Raven Warrior.

One stepped toward Arthur. The bird's head swept down in a bow and the wings opened.

'Greetings and homage, Golden King,' the bird said as it finished its salutation and stood upright once more.

'Golden King,' Arthur said. 'Well, the Golden King is standing here in the rain freezing his butt off.'

'Unnecessarily,' the warrior said. 'Spread your hands like this. The vessel in the tower belongs to you. It will come.'

'I want the vessel in the tower to protect the tower,' Arthur said.

The warrior nodded. 'Yes. She said you'd worry about that. But she said, Don't! Don't worry. It can be in two places at once.'

Arthur spread his hands and the beautiful bowl appeared between his palms. The birds shied away from its light. They scattered into the green, rain-drenched countryside.

The cauldron proffered luxury. Arthur refused, citing his need for the useful and indeed his preference for it.

610

And immediately he found himself clothed in leather trousers, leggings, and boots with dry stockings, a light wool and linen-blend dalmatic. A heavy woolen mantle was wrapped around his body.

He then asked the cauldron for weapons. He was met with simple incomprehension. He devoted his thanks to the silent beauty he saw suspended between his palms and basked for a moment in its warm light. Then, with a sigh of regret, he returned it to its everlasting vigil in the tower from whence it had come.

A few moments later, the two warriors were crouched over a small fire in the lee side of a massive boulder and out of the rain. More or less out of the rain; it depended on which way the wind was blowing. Lancelot had some provisions with him, and Arthur was dining on bread and some very strong curd cheese while the birds investigated the lines Arthur had set in the stream.

'I was sent here – I came of my own free will – because of my sister. I believe you may know her, she said.'

'She? Your sister?' Arthur asked.

'No. The Lady of the Lake. I haven't seen my sister in some time.'

'The Lady of the Lake have a name?'

'Well, certainly she has a name, but I can't tell you what it is, because I'm forbidden to reveal – '

'Do you have a name?' Arthur's mouth was full; the question was a bit muffled.

Lancelot found a small jug of wine and proffered it to Arthur. 'Of course I have a name.' He sounded offended.

'You are far from clear,' Arthur said.

'I can't see how I could be any more informative,' Lancelot said.

'I can,' Arthur told him. 'Try telling me who the hell you are. Who the hell your sister is. We can skip over the Lady of the Lake for now. Then you could explain just what the hell you're doing here and why, not to mention how the hell you came so far to find me.'

Bax arrived just then with a fish.

'I hope it's a trout,' Arthur said. 'I can't eat salmon.'

'Why?' Lancelot asked.

'Because I once was one.'

Lancelot digested this thoughtfully. 'I think,' he said slowly, 'we both have a lot of explaining to do.'

The Paradoxisus, that's what they called them; and the palace where they were located, the Paradox Garden. The two women told me to run, so I ran.

My unseen companion was not happy. 'You don't have the least idea what their intentions are,' she scolded.

I ignored her. I wasn't about to start talking to myself and convince ... whatever they were ... captors? Rescuers? They could well be either one. Convince them that I was insane.

'Hurry!' The one behind me urged me on when we reached the staircase. 'We don't dare tarry. He might reverse the steps and then we would never get out.'

'Reverse the steps?'

'Yes,' the one behind me said. 'Reverse the steps so we would have to run up to get down.'

I decided to let that one lie right there. I concentrated on going down the narrow spiral staircase as fast as I could. It was corkscrew, that stair, and almost entirely enclosed in a complex lattice overgrown with those blazing roses. But for the translucent green leaves, red flowers, and brown, thorny canes, everything else was white, the selfsame, alabaster white that composed the outside of the tower. But somehow between the sunlight, the sky colors rioted on in the alabaster jewel until it looked like the heart of a rainbow.

But I didn't regret it when the five of us, three women and two dogs, fled out through a high arched entryway and along a broad causeway over a beautiful, shallow blue lake. Flowers, water lilies of every imaginable color, clustered along with hyacinths, iris, pickerelweed, and lotus, scattered among the sprays of many diverse fountains.

On reaching the end of the causeway, the two women darted into a garden. Here I lost my way because this was not a very correct and well-laid-out Roman garden but a magnificent wilderness of groves containing ornamental trees; forest groves with oak, elder, beech, and even pine. Interspersed among the trees was greensward surrounded by flower beds, ponds, streams, and even waterfalls.

I was flagging now, but I think so were my companions.

'How large is this?'

'No one knows,' the woman said. 'It may continue forever. Some of the things pertaining to the king do go on forever. Or at least, so far that we poor humans cannot reach the end of them.'

Her hood had fallen back and I saw her face was lined and scarred as though she had once been beaten very badly. Her hair, once quite dark, had streaks of gray. As I watched, she unhooked the dog's lead and let him run ahead of us into a glade of young pines filled with dappled sunlight. The girl behind me followed suit. Her hood had also fallen back, and I saw she was much younger than the one ahead. She was a lightly built redhead with green eyes and fair skin.

'They won't go far,' the one ahead of me said.

'She hurt him. She really hurt him,' the young redhead exclaimed. 'I felt it. You know I can feel him.'

'Fine!' the dark one said. 'But let's get her under wraps before he recovers. And don't count any chickens, not only not before they hatch but not until they're ready to lay eggs or crow. I've been part of too many failed attempts at undermining his power that I begin by being pessimistic.'

'But, Annin, there is a king, another king, who is said to have been favored by the Queen of the Dead. I keep hoping . . .'

'That's it,' the older one, Annin, said. 'Keep hoping . . . and be careful.'

'You will be Annin,' I said. 'And may I ask your name?' I said to the redhead.

'Erika,' she said.

Then the clouds came down to earth. That's the only way I can describe it. We walked through mist so thick that we could see nothing for a few moments, and when we emerged, we gazed down into a tree-filled valley. Beyond the valley, a fortress of gray stone seemed to spring from a crag. It was overgrown with creeping vines from which hung drooping clusters of violet flowers.

Almost instinctively I turned toward it.

'No,' Erika said, tugging at my arm. 'That's why we say this garden may go on forever. We keep to a few well-beaten paths. No one who ever descended into that valley and tried to reach that fortress has ever returned.'

'The worst of it,' Annin said, 'is that we don't know if that's good or bad. But on balance, we think bad.'

I studied the fortress as well as I could from this distance and saw the windows were only black holes, half-covered by the crawling vines, and the towers were ruined, jagged, and roofless. I shivered a little, and we turned and entered an aisle of flowering shrubs that ended in a building that seemed to keep changing its shape as I tried to look at it.

'We live there,' Annin said, pointing.

I stopped. 'That doesn't look much better.'

'*Wheeeeee.* . . .' My unseen companion sounded delighted. 'You can control this. It's all in *how* you look at it.'

Annin paused. She picked up a stick and drew a diagram in a dusty spot under one of the bushes: two faces looking at each other on a chalice. I had seen such things before. Dugald's people were interested in them and he had acquainted me with them.

'Either or neither,' I said. 'The perception of the person looking at them makes the call. But they aren't real. Those are lines on the ground. An optical illusion, if you like.'

'Not here they aren't,' Annin said. 'That's what I meant when I said Bade might reverse the staircase. Among the towers, he controls perception. Here, we can. From time to time he fights us, trying to take control of our ... dwellings, but so far, we have beaten him off. When you killed the lust-driven Tailogue, I knew you must be a sorceress of great power.'

I looked back at the door to their ... dwelling and concentrated. From one point of view, it looked open; from another, closed.

'I see,' I said. I didn't completely, but enough of the idea behind the ... dwelling went home for me to function. In my mind, I closed the door.

'When we get there,' I said.

'Yes, that's safest,' Annin said.

'Has this thing a name?' I asked Annin.

'Paradoxisus,' she said.

Sometime, somewhere, during our wild flight I found I was wearing a dress again. This was a long, white dalmatic with golden embroidery at the neck and hem. It felt like silk. Heavy, raw silk.

'She wasn't wearing anything but her armor when we fled,' Erika said.

'Yes.' Annin spoke slowly. 'And where is your sword?'

'I have a sort of friend,' I explained lamely. 'Though I don't see why she chose' – I looked down at the silk dress – 'this particular style.'

'I'm not a *she*,' my companion said. 'Properly speaking, I'm an it. But I kind of like she. You could use that.'

'Thank you,' I said.

Annin and Erika gave me the same sort of odd look I was beginning to get used to.

'You talk to it?' Annin asked.

'From time to time,' I said.

Annin lifted her head suddenly, her eyes closed. A second later, they opened and she looked afraid.

'The Tailogue are out. Bade has recovered from the blow she dealt him. Run!'

Luckily, we didn't have far to go. I let Annin open the door. The dogs were waiting beside it and they plunged through it along with us. I never solved the internal geometry of the Paradoxisus, . . . the dwelling, as Annin put it. But then, I do not think its builders ever intended it to be solved. They generated the geometry to allow the inhabitants, or perhaps users of the Paradox, to go places they could not easily reach otherwise.

Inside, broad, shallow stairs converged on a stone circle with a star at the center; a star with many rays, each so constructed as to look three-dimensional. The rays moved as you looked at them, now seemingly constructed in high relief, but then they changed and appeared instead to be cut out of the rock and then somehow inlaid with silver.

'Whoosa,' my companion commented.

Staircase, staircases. Everywhere I looked I seemed to see another one. At first it seemed impossible to isolate one, but I got the trick of it. I counted ten, but then I found an eleventh.

'How many do you see?' Annin asked.

'I'm not sure,' I said. 'I count eleven, but I think I've spotted a twelfth.'

'You are indeed powerful,' Erika said. 'I've never seen more than seven, and Annin can isolate only about ten.

Sister mine, there is no telling what she could do with practice!'

'I think the star is a compass,' I said. 'How many rays has it?'

'Good luck with that. If you look at it another way, you will find it has dark and bright rays. No one has ever been able to correctly count them,' Annin told me.

'However did you master this place?' I asked.

'We haven't,' Erika said. 'Only some of it. But enough to use it as a refuge against the king.'

'We believe,' Annin said, 'that some of the places the stairs go may not exist any longer and that's why we can't reach them. Others, many others, are simply empty and dead, sort of like blind tunnels with a little something at the end. But they lead nowhere. Or rather, they touch places isolated even in their own worlds: the bottom of lakes, the tops of mountains, or deep caves in the earth. One goes to a river that never, as far as we know, sees the sun. The cave goes on and on, and it is very beautiful, but no exploration party has ever been able to find a way out.'

The shadows at the top of one of the stairs moved. I saw birds with black and silver wings, and then a woman, and the birds were a pattern on a black and silver dress. The woman appeared to be crowned with the white roses of faery, but as she drew closer, the roses vanished and her hair was gray. Her eyes were silvered by blindness and she felt her way down the steps with a blackthorn staff.

'Annin! Erika! She defeated the Tailogue. I felt it. Has she come? I can feel that someone is with you.'

'Yes,' Annin said.

'Very well. Bring her. She must attend her deliberations.'

Annin and Erika ran up the stair toward the blind woman and I followed.

Lancelot and Arthur reached the swamp the next day. They were still talking.

'Doesn't surprise me that Merlin lost control of the situation. He was always one to overreach himself,' Arthur said. 'My father hated him for . . .' He found himself not willing to explain his childhood to Lancelot. 'For various reasons. But Uther always said that he was the most astute political advisor he ever had. I don't think Father ever completely followed his advice, because Merlin was too much a partisan of the southern landowners. They want to rule the roost, and he's happy to aid and abet them in every way.'

'If you think he's smart, you should hang around her for a while.'

'Your Lady of the Lake?'

'Yes. And she thinks my sister, Guinevere, is the key to the whole thing . . your gaining the High Kingship.'

'Maybe I shouldn't try too hard to get back. These people here need me,' Arthur said.

'So do your father and the people of Alba. Do you love my sister?'

Arthur paused. The ground was getting soggy, and looking ahead, he saw that soon the two of them would be wading in water up to their knees.

'I hate to say love,' Arthur said. 'I hate the word. My mother used to say she loved me.'

'You don't like your mother?' Lancelot asked.

'I would cheerfully consign my mother to the devil. But judging by what Merlin told you about her probable fate, it is to be hoped she is there already. No, I won't use the word *love* about Guinevere. But I will say that I want her. I wanted her from the first moment I saw her on the quay at Tintigal. She was wearing dirty leather pants, a grimy shirt, and that magnificent red-gold hair was wild, blown by the sea wind. And yet somehow she managed without any of the artifice other women employ to be the loveliest creature I had ever seen. I wanted her then, I want her now. And I think I will always want her. In my bed, in my arms, seated next to me at the table and across from me at my councils of war. Riding beside me at the hunt and holding my hand when I die. I think that if I ever stop wanting her, I will be beyond wanting anything.'

'She is the Flower Bride of Alba,' Lancelot said.

'She will make me king in both worlds. I know that,' Arthur said. 'And the horror of it is that unless she is successful in her quests, I may never see her again.'

'Oh, I think she's been successful all right,' Lancelot said. 'Both Merlin and the Lady thought so, and whatever you may say about both of them, neither of them is a fool.'

Bax trotted from around behind them and into the water. The two men followed.

'He did say a funny thing, though. He said *we* were her destiny. *We,* not just you.'

Arthur threw him a dark look. 'Become her champion, if you like, but nothing more. So perhaps in some sort of way you are her destiny, but she is mine, and always will be while life lasts.'

The water between the trees was getting deeper, but Bax looked to be fairly good at finding shallow spots between the deeper pools.

'This swamp is supposed to be filled with traps and hazards,' Arthur said, looking around uneasily.

'Maybe that's if you're going out, escaping from the king. I bet he doesn't care much if you're going in. Yes, the entrance to a trap might be sort of easy,' Lancelot continued. 'In fact, I think you might expect it to be.'

Several of the ravens sailed in and settled on a branch near Arthur's face. 'You command them,' he said to Lancelot.

'No command about it,' Lancelot said. 'We have an agreement.'

'Oath birds?'

'Right,' Lancelot replied.

'Ask them to check the roads ahead.'

At his words, the birds took wing. They returned quickly.

One said, 'We see no hazards.'

The second said, 'By nightfall.'

The third cocked his head to one side, studied both men with one eye and then the other, and said, 'Be careful.'

I followed my two companions up the stair. It led to . . . I don't know. My first sight of it was sunlight on bleached marble. I did what I had done in the city: looked out on a landscape under a different sky. It didn't seem real, but rather like the wall paintings I had seen in ruined Roman dwellings where Black Leg and I played as children.

Maeniel brought us to see them, wishing to accommodate Dugald's desire that I learn about things Roman. It was not at all safe to poke around abandoned Roman ruins. They were the refuge of outlaws and brigands. But Dugald and Maeniel were tough enough to give pause to any who threatened us. And so we visited these places and he would sometimes reconstruct the life of Roman colonists for both Black Leg and myself.

Such a life seemed a great wonder to me. Remember, I was brought up in a one-room hut with a smoke hole in the roof, and the thought of having different rooms to eat, sleep, and bathe and even study was almost incomprehensible to me. Servants; no, we had no servants or slaves. Everyone pitched in and helped Kyra when she needed it. Outdoor plumbing was the norm. Black Leg and I used to fight over whose duty it was to dig the slit trench every week.

I remember looking at the wall paintings that depicted a life all but incomprehensible to me. I stretched out my hand and touched the picture of an ancient theater with stepwise seats leading down to a small stage. The image shimmered the way the reflection in a still pool does when something, a drop of water or a fallen leaf, troubles the surface.

I felt in my body, my mind, the appropriate displacement that would allow me to enter what to many others would simply be an image and no more.

How would I do it? I don't know. How do I walk or breathe, or eat or run or think, or even remember? I simply know how. And for the first time, I understood my gift as a sorceress. I had an instinct for the passage between worlds.

I stepped through and the dog women followed me.

The little amphitheater was old and long abandoned. It wasn't one of those massive arenas where gladiatorial matches or chariot races were held. This was a much smaller place where plays were performed, poetry recited, or musical entertainments went on. It was on a small island set in a deep, blue sea. I knew it must have been on an island because I could see the drowned remains of streets; temples, houses, and streets gleaming up through the blue-green water.

This amphitheater must have been on the highest point of the island, because it seemed to be all that remained of what must have been a fair-sized town. In the distance, to the east, on the horizon, I could see the outlines of a landmass.

But of what must have been here once, this was all that remained. There was a large number of people gathered here, both men and women. The blind woman – a priestess, I'm sure – stood on the stage. I walked down toward her, and I would have taken a seat among them, but Annin and Erika urged me toward the small stage where the blind woman stood.

I climbed the two steps up to the stage. All of the women were accompanied by dogs. They seemed decently dressed, but the men were a ragged, tough-looking bunch. They had few weapons. I saw only about a dozen knives, two swords; and though there were a lot of spears, most were the wooden variety.

Everyone, even the dogs, studied me curiously. The fear and curiosity that seemed to radiate from the audience called my armor, and I heard an audible gasp roll through the gathering as it flashed green against my fair skin.

'She is the one,' the blind woman said. 'I know. I feel it.'

'Libane!' one of the men addressed her.

I knew the name. She was clad in a green mantle and rules womanly gifts. There is nothing she cannot teach her adherents to do.

'Libane, why are you so sure this time? The Dread King so far has laughed at our revolts. Yet you are so sure that she' – he pointed at me – 'and the man . . . more than a man, less than a king, who comes . . . can free us.'

Another one of the men spoke up. 'No one ever spent the night in the queen's tower and emerged alive until he did. I was there when he cleansed their cattle and their bodies, setting his people free forever. He will speak law and knit up the division between men and women, between those the king allows some freedom and those who are treated like beasts.'

'Indeed she has shown herself to be mistress of the transit between worlds,' Annin said. 'Otherwise, she would not be here.'

'He,' Libane added, 'has withstood both the tower and the dark forest. How many others died in their toils?'

I had, I reflected, come to bring Arthur back home with me. My transit of worlds had been an accident, a simple necessity forced on me in my mission to rescue Arthur from his exile.

I sat on the Dragon Throne, one of the sacred queens of the first people to populate the White Isle. It was the duty of the queens to bring kings to the people. To lie with Arthur and make him high king was my duty. But I couldn't tell these people what was in my heart. We needed him, but I could see they did, too.

I turned to Libane and I saw the green mask of the Danae on her face even as it was part of the armor. It was very like the moment I met my father. From a distance, I saw only a fat, red-faced man who looked as though he might be a figure of fun. But as I drew closer, the mighty warrior of the Danae was revealed to me.

It was the same here. The face I had thought pale was simply impossibly fair. The eyes that looked shadowed by blindness were gray, the pale gray of summer clouds as they spread out over the mountains on a warm summer day. And she was wrapped in the green mantle and gown of the ever-living, ever-giving, ever-abiding earth.

'Libane,' I said, 'how can I keep my promises? To keep one is to break the other.'

'It is time,' she replied, 'for you to greet your much sought lord.'

We left the Paradoxisus at nightfall. Libane and Annin led the procession, and it was just that: a procession. King Bade's prisoners joined us. Many were worn down by labor while still young. I have never seen so many scars. And I know. I saw all of them bearing the marks of savage punishment. Some had been totally blinded so they could be used as draft animals. Many others were raked by whip scars. Eyes and hands were missing from many. The women, many of them designated comfort women, were a bold, cold lot. Most of their eyes burned with hatred.

In God's name, I thought, *how will we heal this?*

Libane and Annin stood one on either side of me, and the slaves waited along the path we traversed. As I passed, they greeted me and then fell in behind us, so I saw and knew all their suffering. Some families were intact, and they brought their children. Others knelt along the route and were taken in hand by adults that would accept them.

As we wound our way through King Bade's magnificent gardens, the procession grew longer and longer. I don't know how many people were there. Several thousand, I think, by the time we reached the swamp.

The dark water was bright with the reflections of the torches carried by the rebels with us. We stood and waited until Black Leg and Arthur waded out of the swamp. Before he reached dry land, our eyes met. I'm ashamed to say I didn't have more than a passing thought to spare for Black Leg.

Indeed, Arthur was the Golden King I had dreamed of. His clothing was shabby, but he filled the woolen dalmatic magnificently, shoulders broad as an ax handle. He was blond-bearded, and the shaggy hair on his head was spun red-gold.

I knew when our eyes met that long ago on the quay at Tintigal I had met a boy, but the person who stood before me in this hour was a man. A man and a king.

Read the third 'Tale of Guinevere'
THE WINTER KING
– coming soon from Bantam Press